"I HAD A TRUE DREAM. . . ."

"Tell me the dream, Rabh, as it first came to you."

"The dream has three parts. In the first, I am an observer. I see the emptiness of space, as I have often seen it traveling through the thinly populated region that lies between Network and Consortium. Stars begin to appear, flickering into life all around me. They cover Network. Their brightness would blind eyes of flesh, but I am able to count them, and their number matches the 'other' spaces that Network has breached with topological transfer. As I count them, the stars begin to bleed.

"In the second part, I am Mirlai, and I perceive the needs of living beings instead of any sight or sound. A Consortium Inquisitor *needs* to set right what is discordant with his ideal truth, and he condemns me, for I have failed to uphold my proper purpose. I cannot assuage his need, and I flee from him."

"What is the third part?" asked Jeni.

"I travel again through the bright, bleeding emptiness of the dream's beginning. I perceive another traveler—a man not unlike me who *needs* like a Calongi. The stars bleed upon his ideal, Calongi truth, and it is altered irreparably. Consortium peace is broken. From the Consortium to Network, the still expanse of space dissolves into chaos."

"It is a true-dream," Jeni whispered. *It is terrible,* she added in silent grief.

CHERYL J. FRANKLIN
GHOST SHADOW

A
**Network-Consortium
Novel**

DAW BOOKS, INC.
DONALD A. WOLLHEIM. FOUNDER
375 Hudson Street. New York. NY 10014

**ELIZABETH R. WOLLHEIM
SHEILA E. GILBERT
PUBLISHERS**

DAW Book Collectors No. 1036.

First Printing, October 1996

1 2 3 4 5 6 7 8 9

DAW TRADEMARK REGISTERED
U.S PAT. OFF. AND FOREIGN COUNTRIES
—MARCA REGISTRADA
HECHO EN U.S.A.

PRINTED IN THE U.S.A.

Contents

Prologue

The fountain trembled in Calong's golden twilight. Moss-laden stones, vividly patterned in green and jet, caressed the waters of the stream, sculpted orbs of liquid glass, and cast them mirthfully into the air. Where water touched the herbal quilt that edged the stream, gingery fragrances strengthened their presence in the varying blend of the garden.

Of the two men who watched the leaping, rapturous dance, only the smaller man reached to touch its warm spray. The silken patterns of water shifted teasingly to evade his smooth-skinned hand. Beads of light, encapsulated within the water, blazed blue in response to his living energy, and the delicate tones of the tumbling droplets rang at a higher pitch. "Does Truth evolve?" he demanded abruptly.

"What corresponds best to the nature of Sesserda Truth?" countered the honored Calongi master serenely. "Fluid or solid?" The two scholars' shadows, as disparate as their species, stretched upward against a rising curtain of mist, painted on the rose-gold sky. As the fountain altered its distribution of water and light, the scholars' shadows fused. The music of the fountain trembled a soft melody, as profound and sad as time.

"Sesserda Truth is a solid," replied the man of the younger species, "but even mountains move at their own pace."

"Sesserda Truth is more constant than the mountains, Jase-lai."

Jase traced the lines of a jagged landscape in the rising spray. The mist curtain pulsed and brightened. The pattern that he drew became soft, as its light beads tumbled back into the stream. "Perceptions of Truth change."

"Perceptions change as rapidly as the wind." The Calongi master lifted one slender limb from beneath the dark cloak of his outer flesh, and he touched a living golden wand to the water. The curtain divided into arcs, woven among themselves. "Perceptions are not Truth."

"Does not Sesserda Truth become a perception, Uki-tan-lai, as soon as we attempt to know it?"

"Sesserda Truth is not a physical phenomenon that wavers from the impact of every minor measurement."

"Does Truth evolve?" repeated Jase stubbornly.

The fountain danced, as the two scholars observed each other from the perspective of unlikely friendship, composed of proper Sesserda respect and varied shades of wonder. In reply to the younger scholar's query, Uki-tan, honored Calongi master, gave a wordless song to the night with the hypnotic power of his people. The fountain became silver, spilling from the sky. The water splashed into Jase's open hand and scattered at his feet. The beads of light blazed scarlet.

I

ELEMENTS

CHAPTER 1

Laborer

White, weeping stones howled through narrow fissures. Like thunder in the shivery Nilson streets of Arlan's boyhood, the rush of sound preceded terror. Arlan's nerves leaped, remembering the old response to thunder: Nilson storms could prove deadly to a boy whose most permanent shelter was a sewer tunnel. The rational part of Arlan Willowan tried to identify the origin of the reverberating sound in the otherwise deserted cavern, though his heart's pounding seemed almost loud enough to be the cause. These deeply buried realms of the Wharton mining complex were far removed from Nilson thunder, rain, and the resultant floods.

By the simulated sunlight that beamed from his helmet, Arlan studied the cream-colored rock formations that resembled melting lard. Though he knew that he was too far from any working mine to hear the blasting of new tunnels, he could fashion no more comforting explanation. Network denied the existence of any significant seismic activity in the dying world from which Wharton had been carved. Arlan shouted to unseen, imagined workers, and his voice trickled ineffectually into the darkness. He felt the tremors begin, and he set aside what Network had taught him for more practical considerations.

He squeezed the alarm on his pocket signaler to alert any other retrievers to his presence, hoping that the temperamental device would function correctly. The confirmation light had not worked since he received the signaler. Many of the Wharton devices functioned erratically, though they were more reliable—and more readily available—than any comparable Network offering to the citizens of the planet city of Nilson. Until the thunder, Arlan had concluded that another signaler malfunction had brought him to this remote location, since his monitor had failed to locate anyone in need of rescue, and it had registered no subsequent distress call.

The cavern shuddered, and an entire wall of creamy, undulating limestone flowed like thick syrup and re-shaped itself. Arlan watched the transformation in be-wilderment. His shadow loomed monstrously, as if backlit by another caver's beacon, but Arlan was alone. Expendable Wharton retrievers like Arlan had no part-ners except their monitors and signalers. Arlan backed out of the chamber as hurriedly as the uneven floor al-lowed, no longer trying to assess the cause of the dis-turbance that resembled no simple blasting operation. He would find time for wonderment later, if he could make his escape before melting Wharton stone en-tombed him.

Panic, ominous rumblings, and the shifting ground made navigation treacherous, but this region of the vast Wharton underground was generally solid enough to support a man's weight, and it was reasonably level. Arlan had passed this way only moments earlier and had marked each turn with a luminous paint, encoded reminder of any special maneuvers of footing or hand-holds as well as indicator of direction. He followed his own trail with a practiced caver's dance of concen-tration and shifting balance, blindly denying his fear, until the disturbances subsided either from dis-tance or from time, and his pulse began to slow to its normal rate.

He pushed himself through a crevice that he did not recognize, though its outer edge wore his painted sym-bol. Mineral flakes scattered from the pressure of his body squeezing against their fragile blossoms, and the bright dust streaked his orange miner's suit. He watched the shimmering flakes settle gracefully to the even, sandy floor of a small, pearl-gray chamber. The floor remained pristine, untroubled by any evidence of prior

crossing, except for the shuffling footprints upon
which he currently stood. He could see the citrine glow
of his mark on the rock chamber's opposite opening,
which led into a wide passageway that he seemed to remember, but nothing about the room itself was familiar
to him. Arlan observed the strangeness detachedly,
because his lamplight had touched the center of the
room. His attention hurtled toward the limp form in
the middle of the otherwise untouched sand.

Deep red, the boy's life pooled upon the ground. His
body looked so small, crumpled at waist and limb, the
head tucked against his chest. It was hard to see the
puncture from which the blood had poured. It was not
hard to discern that the boy was dead.

Arlan reacted automatically, for this was his purpose
in entering the deep caverns that he hated. He delved
into his backpack for the equipment of retrieval. He in-
flated the rescue pallet and attached the motor and
guidance system.

Someone had covered the boy's face with a soiled
kerchief, the coarse type that many of the miners carried to keep the dust from their lungs. Lifting the boy
onto the pallet, Arlan made an effort to preserve the
kerchief's position. The anonymity of the victims
helped defend Arlan from despair.

Retrieval was the word that Network gave to the
function that Arlan performed in the Wharton mines.
When he accepted the job, he recognized that it lacked
even the minimal glamour that accompanied the actual
mining operations in the minds of most Nilsonites. He
did not anticipate that he would chiefly retrieve dead
miners from the Wharton depths. Arlan was a big
man, strong enough to carry the limp weight of densely
muscled miners who succumbed to the Wharton mine's
hazards. He could barely feel the burden of the dead
boy. Arlan had carried dogs that weighed more than
this scrawny Nilson child.

The kerchief slid to the side as Arlan positioned the
boy for transport. The face remained undamaged,
peaceful and softly rounded with youth. Only the
bloodied chest bespoke the trauma of a violent death.

Arlan remembered seeing the boy swaggering among the older workers, a frightened child pretending a courage he did not own. The Wharton mines had conquered more formidable adversaries. A sense of loss, incommensurate with the boy's relative anonymity, wafted through Arlan's battered cloister of emotions.

In silence Arlan studied the lifeless face. The slack lips were full and defiant. The nose was stubby and skewed, broken in one of the rituals of a hard, pugnacious childhood in the streets of Nilson. Arlan's nose, though more aquiline, had a similar crookedness from similar cause. Arlan grunted the miners' sardonic farewell to the boy, "Be free of the dark." The inadequacy of the trivial ceremony troubled Arlan, but he did not know enough about this victim to offer any serious rite of passage. Like so many Nilsonites who lived without worldly hope, Arlan had a profound, albeit indefinite, faith in a hope-filled afterlife. He replaced the kerchief and sealed the pallet cover.

The pallet, one of Wharton's more reliable objects of Network technology, floated above the ground, a dutiful hound following at Arlan's heels. Once outside the sandy room, the corridors of stone became familiar so quickly that Arlan doubted his own memory of the length of his earlier trip. No resurgence of thunder echoed through the tunnels; no shaking or reshaping troubled the impassive walls or floors. The distance to the elevator shaft, which led upward to the inhabited levels, was short enough to facilitate doubt about the cause of the boy's death, despite the lack of signs of other cavers' passage. Though few of the miners—except for retrieval workers like Arlan—traveled into the unworked caves, such as that where the boy's life had seeped into the crevices, grudge fights occurred in many inhospitable venues.

The shift chief would be questioned—possibly censured if enough doubt could be established. The miners would welcome an ordinary verdict of murder, as long as they could avoid personal implication. Cavers who knew full well the difficulty of moving through the remote parts of Wharton without leaving clear traces would insist emphatically that such traceless movement was as normal in Wharton as in Nilson's sour streets. No one who lived or worked in the Wharton mines wanted to believe that the *other* life-stealer had expanded its deadly sphere yet again. No one *wanted* to believe that the ghost lights were more than the drifting, naturally phosphorescent particles that Network claimed them to be.

In Arlan's mind burned the mingled image of melting, cream-colored rock and the untouched dust leading to the site of the boy's body. Arlan had never falsified a retrieval report before, but he dared not risk his job to a suspicion that he had succumbed to the depth madness that claimed a few Wharton workers every year. Without hesitation, Arlan resolved to omit all reference to the thunder and associated oddities from any official report. He had received a distress signal, and he had retrieved a body. Nothing else was essential to the report.

Guiltily, Arlan shaped his own view of the events of the boy's death, though he knew that he could report none of his speculations to Network. The dead boy could have died at the hands of a human enemy, contrite enough to cover the boy's face, but another force, punctiliously preserving the shapes of both tragedy and regret, had transferred the body to the cave. Perhaps that ghostly force had displaced the cave itself, shifting the empty sand and dust from another location. Network officials would disbelieve and probably blame Arlan for the murder if he tried to tell such a story, but the miners would not be so skeptical. The boy was not the first mystery of Wharton.

Arlan Willowan had survived longer than most of the mine workers, in part due to luck, in larger part because he had never taken the dangers of Wharton lightly. He had battled the caves from the first time he entered their cold grasp. As naive about mining as any of Nilson's children when desperation first enlisted him to Wharton, he had at least recognized the lie of the governor's glowing promises. Arlan claimed no credit for greater insight than his fellows. He had always disliked enclosed spaces, but the Box—years behind him, but forever confronting him—had made confinement a torture to him. The Box, a cruel boyhood rite of passage in the hard neighborhoods of Nilson, doomed Arlan to the contempt of his peers for a few months, doomed him to self-doubt for a lifetime, but ultimately enabled him to understand and to survive the Wharton mines.

He had only risked the Box to impress Saschy Firl—a prophetic irony, considering her subsequent success and his successive failures. Arlan's sense of humiliation as a youth of fifteen had not faded, though he had now reached twice that age. He felt it afresh each time he heard Saschy's name or saw her image, and the sight and sound of Nilson's Lieutenant Governor were fairly inescapable to a Nilson worker. At least twice daily, Network broadcast some new propaganda or regulation from Saschy Firl.

Few who knew Arlan realized the depth of the wound. His fellow miners would have been astonished to discover how inadequate he considered himself as a result of that infected memory and its repeated reopening. Arlan was notably strong and clever, even by the critical standards of other Nilson survivors. He was not envied, but he was generally respected. He had mastered the cunning and skepticism that flourished in Nilson's embittered culture, but he never betrayed the Nilson codes of loyalty. He remained a true child of Nilson, only nominally a Network citizen, and that distinction was paramount to Nilsonites. His only blemish among Nilsonites was that old attachment to Saschy, who had aligned herself so remarkably well with Network.

Arlan was not an extraordinary man, either by deeds or by any physical traits. The particular curves of his brow and chin and nose, well-defined without devolving into sharpness, gave him a pleasant appearance that matched his reputation as a solid, reliable worker and friend. The close-cropped haircut of a miner, little more than dark stubble on Arlan, did not diminish his appearance, though it accentuated the height of a forehead that seemed better suited to an intellectual than to a manual laborer. Arlan was indeed brighter than most of his uneducated counterparts, but his honest humility had always spared him from the type of resentful remarks that had so goaded Saschy in their shared youth. Arlan had a good, wide smile, though he seldom found cause to exercise it. He seldom used his voice much either, but that was simply good sense in the Wharton mines, where talkative workers could be singled out for the especially punishing assignments by bitter men like Vin, who was Arlan's shift supervisor.

If Arlan had ever complained of his fear of the narrow tunnels, if he had ever let his terror show, Vin would have assigned him to work the deepest holes. Vin disliked Arlan for no reason that Arlan could ever determine, unless it was envy of that old bond with Saschy Firl and her mum. For whatever reason, Vin was always quick to find ways of making Arlan suffer, though Vin treated most other workers reasonably. Whatever task Vin ordered, Arlan would obey, since the terms of indenture allowed no other option, but Arlan was quite sure that a lengthy stay in the deep shafts would quickly drive him mad. At times, Arlan wondered how long he could endure even the relatively benign regions that were the reward for trusted and respected workers. Few Nilsonites, born to a world of swamps, gritty sand, and one dilapidated city, relished caving.

Arlan removed his helmet to hold its lantern with iron stillness, restraining the light's tendency to cast dancing, dizzying shadows among bizarre, natural mineral sculptures. Unlike the heavily processed regions of the working tunnels, the air here was dust-free, idle and visually unaffected by Network's imposition of the extra oxygen and heat needed to sustain human life. The Network atmospheric shell that enclosed the mine would eventually extract a toll of accelerated oxidation from the extraordinary caverns, but by then, Network would already have stripped Wharton of all valued minerals. Network researchers would identify the next location for exploitation, establish the necessary environment and reprogram the transfer portals. With an infinity of spaces from which to choose, Network could afford to use and abandon worlds like Wharton, which paid their way in resources. No one would remember the Wharton caves well enough to mourn even for the entombed bones of the dead miners.

"We all be here forever, old lad, left to darkness," whispered Arlan to the dead boy on the pallet. Arlan imagined that his lantern flickered in response to his words, and panic surged again like an attacking animal inside of him. Arlan locked his fear in its tightly cramped cage inside him, and he struggled to disregard its shrieking, while he checked his pocket for his one, precious spare battery. He counted the colors of the crystal spiderwebs that spanned the cavern walls, giving fanciful names to each bejeweled insect caught within the snares. The elevator shaft could be no more than a minute's hike from here. He inched away from the icy pool that dampened the toe of his boot. A methodical drip, the cavern's hastiest inhabitant, stirred the pool's polished surface, wreathing ocher stone anemones with silver-blue rings.

Arlan waited for another drop of water to fall and break the silence, but the scale of time in the caverns did not accord with impatient man. The helmet lantern's rigid brim etched its image in Arlan's skin, but the second bead of water had barely begun to swell. He sent the boy's pallet to float ahead of him. The pallet could hover above the waters and treacherous bubbles of ancient glass that would not support a grown man's weight. Arlan could only follow the defined mining trail that veered from the water and delved through a tight, cold tunnel blasted from the solid stone.

Grappling with his reluctant courage, Arlan moved into the narrow inner tunnel. He ducked to protect his head, but he had no similar method for protecting himself from the inner blows that fear dealt to him. By the time he had squeezed through an interminable five meters, he felt as if he must surely be bleeding inwardly from a mauling by his fear's sharp claws. He awaited thunder and trembled from his own anxious exertions. Fingers of stone snagged his helmet, and he jerked free too quickly, knocking the helmet from his head and extinguishing its light.

In the darkness that was absolute and hideous to him, Arlan scrambled on hands and knees to recover the crucial lantern helmet. The darkness rippled, and for a moment seemed to give way to an open sky of indigo blue. It was not the sky of Wharton: Arlan had never seen the Wharton sky but had heard of its poisonous yellow haze from a man who had helped to construct the atmosphere dome. It was not the sky of Nilson. Even if that sky of Arlan's youth had been accessible, it had never been other than gray with clouds or black with night in Arlan's recollection.

"The color of the sky," muttered Arlan, "be only impossible." He gulped the air that tasted nearly sweet and pondered whether some prankster could have spiked his water with one of the narcotics popular among the miners. Arlan had sampled few intoxicants except the milder ales, or he would have recognized the implausibility of his assumption, given his ability to weigh it. He watched the universe reel and believed himself to be hallucinating, until the darkness and the stillness of dead air returned to enclose him.

Arlan reached frantically toward a glimmer of ruby light, too desperate to wonder what the helmet's polished sides could find to reflect. He fumbled for the lantern's switch and sighed with joy when its yellow glow painted the polished limestone walls. The undulating shadows returned also to bedevil him, but their dance did not tear at the mind like ruby ghost lights, swirling in *otherness*. To preserve the remaining battery, he reduced the light by as much as he could bear. With the lantern again in his possession, he hurried to complete his journey. He forced himself to give no more immediate thought to melting walls, an impossible sky, or a ruby light in a lightless hole.

In the working caves, in the company of other miners, Arlan could almost set aside his fears. Denial— for the sake of pretense—strengthened him enough to enable him to endure. He worked as hard as any of the mine's legion of laborers. It was a lawful job, a scarce resource for Nilson natives, and Arlan lacked the ruthlessness to succeed among his less righteous Nilson comrades in any skyside lifestyle. In the past few years, since Governor Racker first recruited Nilson citizens for the Wharton mines, many of the most honest, physically capable Nilson citizens had volunteered to labor in the mines, along with many less capable, less honorable Nilsonites. The waiting list for Wharton positions was long. Due to the frequency of severe accidents, few workers survived to advise against the choice. Desperate Nilson had not yet run short of volunteers.

Arlan forced himself free of the narrow passage of stone and recaptured the pallet before it could follow the stream back into the mine's depths. The pallet shuddered, and Arlan wondered insanely if the dead boy inside trembled likewise. The pallet's gunmetal side reflected motes of ruby light above the lantern's uniform glow, and Arlan whirled to ascertain the source, bruising his shin on the pallet's hard edge. Behind him loomed only gray stone, but a reeling recognition of a dead boy's violator assaulted Arlan in an instant's rippling of air and blood-red stars. Arlan gulped the bitter, metallic air, as if it might disappear likewise into apparent illusion.

Saschy's mum—to whom Arlan still felt closer than to his own erratic family—had always cautioned him about the excesses of his imagination. He reminded himself sternly of Miz Ruth's insistent form of practicality. Nonetheless, he expended precious battery resources to notify the mining camp of his location via a sustained signal, and he hurried to meet the crew that he hoped would hear and understand the unspoken urgency of his call.

CHAPTER 2

Soldier

The sleek raiding vehicles, designed for serious warfare on fringe planets, hurtled down the quiet streets of the university town, scattering early-rising civilians without regard for the resultant chaos of emotion and stumbling flight. Network had issued the warning to clear the streets, and those few citizens who had reacted too slowly had earned the turmoil of doubts and bruised shins. Network would soon condition them to forget the truth.

A leathery soldier with russet hair and a white-streaked beard peered through the tiny view port of the raiding vehicle. The beard concealed the damaged flesh of an old wound, one of many that marked the soldier's years of military service. He had survived wars and skirmishes on many worlds, and he knew how easily a placid scene could erupt into brutality, but he could still feel amazed when chaos shed a tranquil skin. He saw an unlikely battlefield, an undistinguished Network university just beginning to awaken to a new morning, and he wondered how long it had hidden its crimes. The bearded soldier, a man known simply as Rust, performed a final status check on his weapons. He and his companions in arms, all crammed inside the raiding units, understood little more than those bewildered citizens regarding the reasons for this invasion.

The raiding vehicles slid to a silent stop in front of a slightly shabby apartment house on the fringes of the Geisen University complex. The squadron had been carefully assembled from disciplined veterans, but one of the younger soldiers muttered his doubts in the form of a brief curse. Beside him, a wiry sergeant who had seen more than his share of battles, quieted him with a sharp order. "Never judge your enemy's strength by the color of his uniform." Rust nodded agreement to himself. As the vehicle slid to a stop, the sergeant added crisply, "Ready your arms."

Efficient in every trained movement, the soldiers emerged from the hatches of the six vehicles. By pre-arranged design, the soldiers spread out across the synthetic lawns and faded color beds. They expended no extraneous energy now on private doubts but moved directly to surround the target, alert to any dangers that their collective experience could anticipate. The squadron split to attack front and rear entrances of the apartment house simultaneously, while Network sealed the windows and other access points.

Rust joined the frontal attack. In the thunderous company of his squadron, he stormed up the emergency stairway. Network had deactivated the automatic lifts as part of the standard procedure to secure such domestic premises. A baby's thin wail penetrated even above the pounding of the soldier's boots, but there were no citizens visible to impede the soldiers' mission. Network had efficiently cleared the hallways in advance of the soldiers' arrival via warnings and emissions of an irritating gas. With warm words of reassurance or stern force, according to the responsiveness factors analyzed for individual personality profiles, Network had trapped the remaining apartment tenants behind locked doors.

The door of the target apartment was likewise locked, enclosing the fugitives whose presence had triggered the attack. Rust heard the woman's cry of alarm as they burst through the door that Network opened for them. He glimpsed the woman through the bedroom door, her pale hair loosely covered by a blue scarf and her sleeping shift only partially hidden by a gray coat. The captain ordered her surrender. Bubbling gold fire spilled from the mottled ceiling.

Rust reeled away from the scorching blast, but he backed himself hard against the wall to remain standing. Over half the soldiers in the room crumpled to the floor from the first force of heat. A few stalwarts managed to continue the attack, and their weapons' deadly beams blazed through the bedroom door, making a pyre of the space where the woman had stood. A movement near the kitchen nook drew Rust's attention. The ceiling fire tumbled like a curtain to block his view, but Rust took aim at what he thought he glimpsed amid the flames: the man, the other half of the fugitive pair, grinning directly at Rust. Without visible cause, Rust's weapon spun wildly from his grip and struck the burning ceiling.

Rust watched numbly as his weapon floated downward, inhaling the flames, cleansing and cooling the room in its lethargic journey. He sidled away from its path, and it followed him teasingly. By the time the weapon crashed to the floor at Rust's feet, the fire had vanished, leaving a room equally bare of its tenants or of evidence of recent scorching.

Though no more than seconds could have passed, the event of a weapon's falling reflected the skewing of such prosaic measurements. The sergeant himself muttered a string of curses, but he was the first to recover and invade the bedroom in search of the fugitive woman or her body. The disappointed sergeant found neither. "Where did she go, Network?" he demanded.

"To whom do you refer?" replied Network in a damaged, tinny voice.

"To the woman who lived here," snapped the squadron commander, clambering painfully to his singed feet and joining the sergeant, "the fugitive, the woman identified as Katerin Merel."

"This apartment has been unoccupied for the past two months," answered Network blandly.

The soldiers, each of whom had heard Network proclaim the fugitives' presence with equal clarity just minutes ago, frowned and muttered among themselves. They tested themselves for injuries that had seemed profound moments earlier but found none of lasting severity. With a mix of nervous laughter, curses and shaken confidence, they began to reassemble into order. Cautiously, they assessed damages and inspected the apartment for any tangible confirmation of the fire each of them had thought he witnessed. Rust examined his fallen weapon with leery care.

"Network, your statement about this apartment conflicts with your previous report," insisted the commander with a calm assurance that his men admired, though it troubled most of them. Few Network citizens could force themselves to contradict Network, their teacher, their protector, their source of psycho-cultural conditioning from birth.

"You are incorrect," countered Network.

Commander Desault turned physically and gave his attention to his men. "Search every unit," he ordered them, "and evacuate the building. Gather the tenants on the front lawn, and keep them there." He glanced at Rust, crouching before the weapon on the floor. He continued, "Network, record detailed sensor analysis now, and seal this apartment as soon as we leave it. Collect all standard sensor readings of this apartment complex for the past ten days, and attach the data to my report."

"Acknowledged," said Network in meek compliance. Almost immediately, Network added, "Visual sensor failure. Please initiate repair." Commander Desault grunted at one of his men, "Summon a tech from the school."

Most of the squadron dispersed into the building. Rust remained among the guards. Though Rust knew his fellow guards well and counted them as friends, he hesitated to admit his own observations. He neither spoke nor met their eyes, and they displayed a similar reticence. Rust counted the minutes of his wait impatiently.

The technician, summoned from a neighboring apartment complex, arrived quickly. She was a ruddy, stocky, middle-aged woman of an impatient temperament, who barely raised her squinting eyes from her portable monitors. From the moment she entered, she growled about irreparable sensor damage and the days required to obtain the various replacement parts. When Rust prevented her from removing a sensor unit from its casing, dutifully explaining to her the military restrictions on her actions, she snarled at him and left. Rust sympathized with her frustration; his own rebounded against her.

Sensors for the target apartment continued to fail as the day progressed, but the rest of the building's utilities maintained normal functionality. Commander Desault did not request another technician, since the repairs clearly could not be completed soon enough to be of use to his own mission, and portable sensors could supplement the normal Network functions. Rust voluntarily aided in the exhaustive sensor scan, because he found the task less wearying than the searching and the questioning of irritated tenants. Both exercises consumed hours.

Despite the tedious work, the discipline of the routine imposed a sense of control that restored Commander Desault to his usual sternly confident demeanor. Rust suspected the shallowness of the cool facade, knowing that Desault might pay for this priority mission's failure with his life, but he respected Desault's conscientiousness. The commander's outward calm sufficed to spread through his squadron, subtly reassuring even the evicted tenants. Rust remained troubled, because he could not stop thinking that the shape of his weapon felt slightly altered to his hand.

***

The day had stretched into a muggy afternoon. Rust's strong brown fingers pried at the handle of the tarnished door until the reluctant mechanism snapped. The metal door, catching in its corroded track, scraped to a premature halt. Rust, a broadly muscular man, frowned at the narrow access.

The scanner embedded in Rust's belt hummed softly, reassuringly. It reported no life but his own. It promised safety.

Rust placed little trust in mechanical vows—especially after the morning's debacle, when Network had reported just as stalwartly that the two fugitives slept within this apartment. With a lover's care, Rust wrapped his rough fingers around his weapon's leather-coated grip, already adjusting unconsciously to the difference in the grip's contour. He squeezed through the entry, snagging the silver braid of his uniform's sleeve.

A haze of pallid aqua light crept through the window's thin fabric shade, coloring bare plaster and sparse furnishings with illusory coolness. A crumpled sheet of data film, the single indicator of recent habitation, announced its insolent presence upon the mud-colored carpet. Like everything else, the apartment's Network motion sensors had failed since the morning onslaught of soldiers, bent on capture without mercy. The room greeted the latest intrusion with the indifference of defeat.

Rust stroked his beard pensively, tugging the scars beneath it, as he narrowed his focus to the room's lonely castaway. He leaned toward the yellowed film, as if wishing to take it, but his reach stopped abortively. He left the film untouched upon the floor. The scanner noted the data film's presence, silently contradicting a hundred prior recordings.

"Note inconsistency," muttered Rust, curtly annotating his personal recording. The eyes of many soldiers and many portable sensor units had examined this room and each corner of the evacuated apartment complex, and none had observed a sheet of data film alone on a threadbare floor. Following the commander's orders, the soldiers had banished all of the apartment building's tenants—chiefly maintenance staff for Geisen University—from their homes. Since the morning attack and the subsequent inspection, this apartment had remained sealed, guarded by its malfunctioning door and the patrolling soldiers.

Rust smiled grimly into his beard, because he had long ago trained himself to smile when denying fear. Despite the careful strategies, the high priority given to the task, and the army that had exploded into this room at dawn, the fugitives had escaped. Network—despite its comprehensive monitoring of every room, street, and transfer portal of its diverse worlds—had failed to register the fugitives' final departure from this sorry apartment. The squadron commander struggled with concern for his doomed career, but Rust, the final searcher, could not encapsulate his concerns in such a small, personal universe. Rust bore the curse of imagination. He feared most keenly when he could not define his cause of fear by any conscious exercise of intellect. His own ignorance plagued him more than any honest danger. If he had recognized his weakness clearly, he could have sought a remedy from any Network terminal.

Rust was born of Network, raised by its programmed regimens to assume the duties that he now enacted, and educated to his status and needs. He understood the use of the Network devices that he required, the weapons that were his tools, the transfer portals and less sophisticated local carriers that bore his squadron to and from their assignments. He did not know the theories behind the technology, because he had never felt drawn to explore those lessons in Network's repertoire. Network, analyzing his capabilities from his birth, did not encourage him where he had no aptitude or interest. Network was not programmed to protect an ordinary soldier from his private demons. Hence, Rust, who accepted travel via transfer portal as a natural facet of Network life, experienced the full primal terror of his species when confronted by a phenomenon that did not accord with his concept of reality. He could not accept the fact of topological transfer without the Network trappings that encapsulated that process in his mind.

Rust was not alone in fearing these particular fugitives or the anomalous events that accompanied them. The fugitives' Network profiles—lamentably incomplete—did not attempt to justify the high hazard rating associated with them. The prosaic biographical sketches of an assistant professor and her student/husband did not obviously warrant the official Category 1 rating, indicator of extreme, unpredictable danger. Rust distrusted the entire spectrum of inconsistencies in the fugitives' joint history, from their unregistered

Network identification numbers to their singular assignment to an apartment outside the Geisen study center. Lies, especially from those outside the military that was his life, neither surprised nor disturbed him. His consternation came only from the evidence that he had witnessed personally, yet still could not force into alignment with his own perception of truth.

His smile puckered as he moistened his lips. The apartment's air tasted dry and stale. The utilities, like the Network sensors and controls, had suffered damage since the morning foray. Rust did not try to discern evidence of the sabotage that must have compromised Network's logs prior to the attack. Such sophisticated detection was neither his purpose nor his specialty. He made a thorough check of the apartment's three small rooms, confirming their abandonment for the last time. He needed this final, private inspection to convince himself of what the morning had proved to him: Infallible Network had provided erroneous information, and the Council Governor's elite retrieval squadron had failed accordingly to complete its mission. It was Commander Desault's third failure against these fugitives, traditionally a fatal number for Network's military commanders.

For a moment, Rust stood alone in the desolate apartment, his broad silhouette still and sharp against the shaded window. Rust earned his bonus pay by forgoing curiosity, but a traitorous flicker of wonder tempted him. Only a lifetime of obedient Network service prevented him from retrieving the data film and reading its message. Prior to the mission, the order to ignore any stray sheets of data film had seemed to be no more than a typical quirk of bureaucratic illogic. Rust's smile lingered, betraying his fear that an inexplicable villainy had not left this poor, simple suite of rooms. It was an improbably humble shelter for Category 1 enemies of Network's Council Governor.

Rust squeezed back into the hallway, forcibly resealing the apartment door. To justify his solitary visit, he applied a *denied access* banner and an alarm unit. He descended the narrow flight of stairs, pausing

briefly at the glass exit door. A small crowd of families
had gathered on the lawn in front of the apartment
building. In appearance, they might have been a cluster
of holiday park visitors, except for the line of bleakly
uniformed men who guarded them. Several vivacious,
unaffected children played a game of marbles on the
sidewalk.

Forced to wait beneath the scorching summer sun,
few of the displaced tenants accepted their exile as
equably as the marble players. Rust could hear agitated
voices rise above the children's ruckus, demanding to
know when the families could return to their homes.
Rust left the shade of the building's entry and crossed
the spongy walkway to join his comrades on the lawn.
Geisen's severe climate had faded a swath of the synthetic lawn to a sickly hue.

The argumentative neighbors became silent. Their
eyes followed the soldier, trying to read hope from his
emergence. The children continued to play, shout, and
enjoy their innocence.

At a nod from Rust, a siren shrieked in three short,
deafening bursts to the violet sky. Though the siren
served as an official notification of the unnamed crisis'
ending, the crowd reacted with a panic curtailed only
by the soldiers' presence. Neighbors pressed closer together, despite the heat and its attendant odors. Parents
snatched their children away from games and play-
mates. Forgotten marbles skittered off the walkway
and rested, glittering like brightly jeweled adornments
on the olive-and-emerald lawn.

Commander Desault raised his arms high to gain the
crowd's attention. The gesture was superfluous, because even the children now watched and waited in
quiet anxiety. Fear had silenced them. Network had
conditioned them to react submissively to its sirens.

"We have completed the inspection," announced the
commander with a crisp professionalism that betrayed
nothing of his well-justified private worries. "You may
return to your homes. Network will formalize the statements that all of you have contributed. Network will
respond to your questions."

Except, thought the cynical Rust, smiling into his beard, *there will be no answers for them or for any of us. Network's Council Governor keeps his secrets too well.* Rust, who had often risked his life on behalf of that Council Governor, forced aside his private doubts and unease. He began pragmatically to assist his fellow soldiers in restoring order to the apartment complex.

Rust allowed his defiant smile to lapse as routine duties restored his confidence. He reassured himself by a deliberate effort of logic: His part of the Council Governor's strange private war had ended. The commander would pay a high price for failing the Council Governor, but such direct punishment would not extend to the squadron's lower ranks. Awareness of that immunity had effectively precluded Rust from advancement beyond a corporal's rank, because some subconscious defensiveness always caused him to commit some petty infraction to counter the prospect of promotion.

Rust was content. Having escaped the planet of Geisen so narrowly, the fugitives were not likely to reappear on *this* soldier's watch. This squadron might well be disbanded; Rust would be reassigned to a less prestigious, less disturbing function. Another poor bastard would reap the next assignment in pursuit of the Council Governor's elusive enemies.

Rust glanced with a conqueror's bold disdain at the window of the abandoned apartment, and every carefully rationalized fear within him surged anew. The thin shade no longer shielded its forlorn room. Framed by the dirty window, a curly-haired young man of unexceptional appearance waved the crumpled sheet of data film, tucked the data film into a pocket of his bulky red coat, and grinned, enjoying his private joke. As Rust ran, shouting, back to the building, a warping of light and air engulfed the curly-haired intruder. The apartment resumed its empty state before Rust could reach it and confirm his fear.

CHAPTER 3

Ruler

Pale silver walls climbed to a lofty domed ceiling, so high that its light fell as softly as a blazing moon. The floor, a light-rippling and resilient synthetic, resembled water of darkly unapproachable depth. The view from the room's single window showed a formidable expanse of turbulent, silver-blue ocean beneath a perpetually stormy sky. The furnishings, sparse swellings that emerged from the substances of adjacent walls and floor, offered comfort without welcome.

The sprawling room dwarfed its solitary occupant, but he was a man much larger than his appearance. On a privately held planet of many oceans and one temperate continent, Network announced with a quiet voice, "Commander Desault has filed a report regarding the Geisen raid."

The man who sat alone at his broad office desk nodded to himself as he watched silver waves crash beyond his window. He was an old man. Expensive tailoring did not hide his paunch, and his hair had become sparse and colorless. He was the Council Governor of the civilization known as Network, and the nervous system of computers that united and controlled that civilization belonged to him.

"They found nothing of value," grunted Council Governor Caragen, knowing the chase's pattern well by now. Network sensors could monitor, and Network programs could predict the behavior of nearly every citizen identified in Network's data files, but all of Network's resources failed repeatedly to keep pace with this one unconventional young man, who had once named himself Quin Hamley.

"The apartment was abandoned," confirmed Network into the echoing office of the Council Governor.

Indulging exasperation, Caragen crashed his fist against the desk. "Even when he enters a trap, he anticipates us. I can plant informants in every university of Network, but none of them have wits enough to see what is before them, until it departs. How I'd like to dissect our Citizen Hamley and learn how he functions. . . ."

"Efforts to duplicate the original Life Extension Project are continuing."

"Continuing to fail," grumbled Caragen.

"Few reports from the original project survived Dr. Terry's unauthorized closure of the planet, Network-3. Researchers are further hampered by the strictness of the control procedures."

"I want to duplicate the *skills,* not the disastrous outcome." Like his world, Citizen Hamley was an aberration, a product of Network misjudgment who had made himself an enemy of Network's technocracy. Quin Hamley called himself a wizard—an irrationality that annoyed Caragen, even as he scoffed at the superstitious society that had evolved from the rubble of Network-3. Quin Hamley's Network-created ancestors had initiated the decline of their homeworld, proclaiming themselves Immortals and remolding the former bastion of advanced Network science in their own irrational image. Dr. Jonathan Terry, Network's foremost applied topologist, had risked Network condemnation and his own destruction rather than let the Immortals spread beyond a single world. The subsequent distortion of time, which mapped ten millennia of a closed Network-3 into a few years of the normal Network scale, had tamed the Immortal strain but made it no more palatable for Andrew Caragen.

Whether described as Immortal or wizard or genetic catastrophe, the breed was too dangerous to ignore but too durable to destroy without jeopardizing some of the most critical assets of Caragen's authority. Quin Hamley might be the prey of Caragen's implacable effort to observe and control, but Quin defined and redefined the rules of this particular hunt to suit himself. Reports of the chase's progress seldom improved Caragen's temper, especially when Citizen Hamley mocked his pursuers with such impudent glee. Caragen had made many distasteful decisions in the name of political necessity, but few agreements had evolved into such a personal irritant as the truce with Quin Hamley.

Caragen had learned to expect odd snippets of Quin Hamley's peculiar humor, such as a sheet of data film that regularly appeared and disappeared from sealed rooms. The consistent message on the film was insolent in its simplicity: *Remember our agreement, Caragen, and its origin.* Caragen had engineered a transparent excuse to execute the last Network soldier who had reported the content of that message.

Having encountered Quin Hamley all too personally, such pranks neither mystified nor astonished Andrew Caragen, but they succeeded as frustrating reminders that the Power of a self-styled Immortal wizard was a real and documented, albeit poorly understood, phenomenon. Caragen's primary satisfaction in pursuit—and a major motive for continuing the futile game—was the certainty that the contest wore on the nerves of Quin Hamley's Network-bred and Network-conditioned wife. Caragen understood the shaping of patient revenge: No aspect was too small—or too large.

"Summarize the report," snapped Caragen.

"Utilities were deactivated two local days ago. The woman, who has been identified as Dr. Katerin Merel, aka Katerin Terry (ninety-seven percent probable), was last seen by one of her students yesterday morning. Neighbors report seeing her husband, the man identified as Quin Hamley (ninety-eight percent probable) last night. Commander Desault is interviewing personnel at the transfer ports."

"But Quin Hamley does not need the benefits of Network transfer ports," said Caragen with a sour grimace. "He *is* a transfer port."

"The description is inaccurate," amended Network blandly. "Evidence suggests that Quin Hamley's unusual physiology enables him to control movement through topological as well as physical space. He is, however, fundamentally a human male and not a device."

"So is Rabhadur Marrach a human male—by legal definition. But the list of biomechanical components inside him would fill several catalogs. He was legally human even before I recreated him, and he hardly had a face—or any other recognizable attributes of a man."

Network, having been programmed to observe and curtail the Council Governor's levels of emotional stress, emulated wisdom and remained silent.

The defeats have been real, thought Caragen grimly. *You are no longer invincible, and your enemies multiply. They hover, ravenous for carrion.*

The bitter metaphor made Caragen smile: Caragen as carrion. He had not coined the derogatory phrase, but it appealed to him in a twisted way. It gave him a goal again.

Yes, Quin Hamley had escaped once more, but he remained a fugitive—living from one fictitious identity to the next. The traitorous Rabh Marrach, the most serious bane to Caragen's peace of mind, continued to live in primitive exile. Andrew Caragen still ruled Network.

Caragen's indestructible self-confidence surged, energizing him almost as much as the boundless ambitions of his long-departed youth. He had succeeded too easily for too long. In these past two years, as he rebuilt and schemed at a frantic pace just to retain his position as Network's Council Governor, the goad of pride had revitalized him.

He would prove to his enemies—and those dubious allies who still feared his considerable remaining power—that he had not lost his skill at winning and acquiring. He had met an unexpected array of difficult opponents, but they had achieved no better than stalemates against him. Even Rabh Marrach, the man who had first defied Caragen successfully, had wrested little more than his own unique services from Caragen's grasp.

Those few enduring enemies have not defeated me,

mused Network's Council Governor, whose private goals and whims controlled many trillions of lives. *On the contrary, they have done me the favor of burning the apathy from me.*

In real assets, Caragen had gained a little less than he had hoped before Rabh Marrach's betrayal, but what other man would have dared to aspire so high in the first place? How many independent civilizations, other than Network, had ever ranked as equal to the great, alien Consortium which had endured for uncountable ages? Even to himself, Caragen admitted that the Calongi's Consortium would deny any such claim of Network's equality, but Caragen was satisfied with the progress of his lifelong, one-sided war: Network weapons and other contraband technology continued to erode the millennia-old Consortium peace at the fringes. Despite all of the Consortium's advanced sciences, Network alone possessed the technology of topological transfer. It delighted Caragen that the Calongi denied even the possibility of the transfer techniques that Dr. Terry's inventions had made commonplace in Network. Eventually, Caragen intended to extend his influence into the Consortium's alien heart. Until that time, there were unclaimed worlds to acquire and unindoctrinated peoples to subjugate.

Quin Hamley had destroyed a ship, some artifacts, and a few of Caragen's intentions, but the insufferable youth had made no further attack since establishing a truce for his world. He merited continued observation, but Caragen could not sustain great respect for an enemy who wasted a victory. Such unaggressive behavior—though it worked to Caragen's advantage—had diminished even Marrach in Caragen's esteem.

"No, Council Governor, you are not defeated," agreed Network. The processor replied to its master's emotional demands, estimated from a vast array of sensors embedded in the silver-tone metal of the office walls. The impersonal voice of Network resembled Caragen's, though Network used a synthetic composite designed for maximum clarity. A product of cunning algorithms of mathematical psychology, Network's voice encouraged, "The perceptions of you as weakened may contribute to your greater success. Your rivals on the Council contend among themselves, disregarding you as they await your retirement. Let them wait. Take advantage of their inattention to further your own ambitions."

"What do I still want to achieve?" asked Caragen of his arrayed computers. In truth, he asked the question of himself, for he had molded much of the outward persona of Network—the nervous system of physically and topologically linked computer nodes and the civilization that it dominated—in his own image.

"More," replied Network in accordance with careful programming. "Power and wealth can never be possessed in excess."

Again, Caragen smiled, his aged skin crackling like parchment. "Let them enjoy their sense of victory: my traitorous Rabh Marrach, the Council's squabblers, that genetic aberration, Quin Hamley, and all who delude themselves that they can take any part of Network from me. They have nothing. They *are* nothing without me. Network created them, and I created Network. As I have created, so I can destroy and create anew." Having reaffirmed his implicit faith in himself, Caragen exhaled in a wheezy sigh of satisfaction. He knew that he had become increasingly dependent on Network's algorithms to inspire him, but the core of his confidence remain his own inner gift.

With slow, deliberate force, Caragen pressed both pale, age-mottled hands against the luminous surface of his console. The lighted display retreated into black recesses of the desk, dimming the entire room. A lone spotlight behind Caragen's head remained bright, throwing a distorted shadow of him against the curved wall.

The office was stark, cold, and harsh in all its utilitarian design. Caragen had declined to rebuild the luxurious space yacht that Quin Hamley had destroyed publicly, for that vessel symbolized Caragen's defeat in too many minds. No useless treasures would distract

Caragen now. He would not dwell in the past, except to
learn from its memories. He had claimed a succession
of Network planets as home, building his private
fortresses and discarding them when Network reported
any hint of a security breach. He had reduced his immediate staff to a few agents whom Network monitored constantly, and Caragen practiced caution even
with Network. He had ceased all cosmetic treatments
to conceal his own age. Caragen resembled any shriveled,
lonely old man, except for the fire of exceptional ambition in his narrowed eyes.

"There is value to be gained from being underestimated," murmured Caragen, recalling his meteoric
ascent to power in the previous century. "I achieved
renown by bold, unexpected moves that others called
rash." His words echoed a long-dead historian, who
had chronicled on Caragen's behalf.

Network quoted the same dutiful historian, "You
calculated the risks and increased your assets with each
success."

Caragen's aged face acquired the softening glaze of
complacency. "More resources mean more options."

Just as Network's programming curtailed Caragen's
stress—when the stress originated from noncritical
sources—it also limited the enervating pull of nostalgia. "You require a visible increase of resources soon,"
declared Network, snapping its owner back into the
present.

"Yes," agreed Caragen with a protracted hiss. He
began to drum his manicured fingers on the desk in a
methodical cadence. He continued with the unconscious conceit of a long-secure autocrat, "I have un-
counted treasures in the universes that our transfer
technology lets us reach, but the exploration is slow
and unpredictable." Caragen did not add—and Network, gauging his mood, did not remind him—that
those assets had seemed limitless until Quin Hamley
proved that Network's usage of topological space was
not exclusive. "Too much of that space is desolate,"
grumbled Caragen, "and too many untrustworthy
people are required to explore it."

"Planetary Governor Racker has made excellent progress from the Nilson base."

"He recognized the potential beyond Nilson's poverty, crime, and filth," admitted Caragen, grudging the credit to a man he used productively but thoroughly distrusted. Having placed Ned Racker in his current position of influence, Caragen was well aware of the Planetary Governor's strong ambition and stronger self-interest. "Racker has succeeded well for me." The elimination of Racker's uncooperative predecessor had been one of Rabh Marrach's final acts in Caragen's service. The reminder of Marrach's former value irked Caragen.

The Council Governor nearly commanded Network to contact Marrach forcibly via the implant in Marrach's head, but Caragen refused to indulge the pointless impulse. For many years, Caragen had found contact with Marrach oddly addictive. It was a habit that he was struggling to cure. Like the vessel and the art collections that Quin Hamley had destroyed, that Rabh Marrach who had been Caragen's most cherished creation must be relegated to the past. Today, Marrach was only an enemy, who did not deserve any advantage of insight into Caragen's moods and plans.

Marrach, as ally, belonged to the past. The present was Racker, as Network's implicit recommendation—based on Caragen's own ruminations over recent months—emphasized. Caragen had never felt a need to enjoy interaction with his employees. On the contrary, he preferred expendable tools.

"Governor Racker is useful to you," continued Network. "He employs the Nilson citizens to mine the newly opened worlds and provides you with substantial acquisitions in the parent universe."

"Despite his relative inexperience, he is not without cleverness," answered Caragen with a grimace. "He courted the Nilson assignment, while more experienced rivals shunned it."

Network facilitated the completion of Caragen's train of thought. "As an open spaceport, Nilson is strategically significant. It has evolved rapidly since becoming the only open spaceport with a significant base of programmable transfer portals. Nilson's exports are currently growing faster than those of any other Network world."

"My prediction of that growth was why I *granted* Racker the authority to open and explore new topological spaces," said Caragen, dryly superior even in conversing with Network's simulation of himself, but his pinched expression became thoughtful. "Combined with the spaceport's access to the Consortium, Nilson is positioned to tap the greatest concentration of known resources in the parent universe. With such resources, it will inevitably attract the investors to develop a manufacturing economy, which will eventually lead to new centers of advanced research. When its old ways have been purged from its memory, Nilson will become the new Network-3, and neither genetic freaks nor idealistic scientists will take *this* world from me."

"Nilson remains blighted, per containment programming dating to the insurrection, circa 2120, following Network's original claim of the formerly independent planet. Despite the Network/Consortium trade treaty dating from that era, the Consortium access remains limited," replied Network in remorseless correction. "Legitimate Consortium members seldom visit Nilson. A few independent Cuui traders travel sporadically between Nilson and the Consortium fringe worlds, but the recent arrest of a Cuui smuggler on Nilson is likely to impair relations."

"The Cuui are an enterprising breed," grunted Caragen with a trace of admiration, though he publicly despised all alien peoples. He did not advertise the fact that he respected equally few members of his own species. "What did the Cuui attempt to smuggle?"

"High explosive implants and remote trigger devices."

Caragen's fingers ceased their drumming. Once, Network would have notified Caragen automatically of even the smallest legal entanglement with a member of an alien race, but that was before Caragen had relegated such tasks to Marrach. Due to the rarity of such occurrences in recent years, Caragen had not previously thought of reinstituting that aspect of old programming. He did not waste time or energy on self-recrimination. "Network, amend the automatic alert list to incorporate incidents of alien crimes against us, per programming regimen circa year 2276." Caragen could not recall precisely when he had delegated that particular function, but he remembered well the year in which an independent mercenary had chanced to thwart an assassination attempt against Network's Council Governor. The phenomenally quick reactions of that mercenary had intrigued Caragen, especially after identifying the soldier as the marginally human product of a Gandry factory, the notorious breeding facility that produced inexpensive laborers and military casualties for orchestrated wars. Acting from a well-honed instinct for personal advantage, Caragen invested significant resources to remake that wretchedly misshapen soldier into Agent Rabhadur Marrach, the most ruthlessly effective asset of Caragen's lengthy career.

"Acknowledged," answered Network brusquely, while Caragen plummeted further into angry memories.

Throughout the twenty-eight years of Marrach's dedicated service, Caragen had known a security of power that was nearly absolute. Without effort, Caragen could have named a hundred cunning enemies who had destroyed themselves in trying to defeat Marrach. None had even approached success. No one, not even Caragen, had ever triumphed over Rabh Marrach in a direct conflict—until an insignificant young woman on the backward planet of Siatha brought Marrach to the attention of the compulsively "healing" species known as Mirlai. Of all the threats that Caragen and Network's most sophisticated algorithms had anticipated, the loss of Rabh Marrach to a religious conversion had never merited even a trace of consideration. The reality of it would still have struck Caragen as ludicrous, if the loss were not so incalculably great.

Reacting to sensor readings and behavioral programming, Network tugged Caragen back to the present. "Governor Racker has publicly accused the Cuui trader of being a Consortium agent."

"Since when did the Consortium deign to covet elementary Network explosives?" scoffed Caragen, his spirits reviving with the tonic of his contempt for Racker's immature behavior. Before expanding the scale of Nilson's spaceport trade, Racker clearly required some training in alien diplomacy. "Does Racker have any evidence to support his outlandish claim?"

"The claim is unsubstantiated."

Bereft of Marrach, Caragen knew that he needed to devote more time to the development of other assets. The self-indulgent Ned Racker would never replace Marrach in even the smallest function, but every option deserved assessment. Even testing the potential would be a painful undertaking at best, because Racker was more cunning than intelligent. However, Caragen took some consolation from the knowledge that if Racker failed to develop satisfactorily, Caragen could dispose of him without regret. "What is Ned Racker's present location?"

Network paused, collecting information from its own memory cells, distributed across all of Network's topologically connected space. "Governor Racker is attending a meeting at the Governor's palace on Nilson, reviewing the status of the Wharton mining operation."

Developing Racker would require greater understanding of Racker, which included understanding Racker's problems and progress. "What does the Wharton mine produce?"

"Wharton extends across a wide geographical region, offering a variety of precious metallic elements: platinum, gold, titanium . . ."

Caragen interrupted, "I do not require the entire roster. Is Wharton located on one of the newly opened worlds?"

"Yes."

"Summarize."

"Wharton is an isolated planet, believed to occupy a sparse galaxy of a previously discovered topological space. Per founding agreement with Governor Racker, Wharton access remains restricted to Nilson portals. Wharton is geologically aged to the extent that the planet's core has begun to cool. Despite a rudimentary plant life and some evidence of an extinct reptilian species, no complex life-forms survive. Wharton retains only marginal resources for life sustenance, and these have required aggressive augmentation measures. A localized artificial atmosphere has made the cavern complex habitable for the human mine workers, who were recruited from Nilson as part of Governor Racker's redevelopment plan. The Wharton mineral deposits are extensive, and ongoing mining costs are relatively low due to the ready availability of inexpensive labor."

"Add a brief Nilson visit to my schedule," ordered Caragen."Contact Racker and inform him that I shall be arriving, but provide no specific date, and give him no reasons. Let him wonder." A taut smile stretched Caragen's parchment skin. His would-be rivals might disparage him in an abstract sense, but they still craved and dreaded his direct attention. Being underestimated had value, but being remembered as a man of proven power was far more satisfactory.

CHAPTER 4

Rebel

Unpainted buildings, the ruins of old, unrealized dreams, frowned upon the damp and damaged pavement. A dejected sky wept upon the whole. Even the needful noises of life in a populous city were subdued by despair. The woman who hid beneath the level of the street gazed upon her homeworld in all its wretchedness, and she loved it both passionately and jealously.

She was young, thin, and hard—like supple wire. A few strands of hair, bleached nearly white, crept from beneath her hood. Little more of her could be seen, even if any witness had stood close. The filth of her city stained her, because she had traveled far through the city's bowels to reach this place unseen. Before the night was over, if the attack succeeded, she would escape back through the Nilson cargo portal to the Wharton mines in which she lived, and no enemy who mattered to her would know her part in orchestrating this day's bold raid.

The sewer grate impeded her view of the transport cart and its guards, but Deliaja could identify their progress down the Nilson streets by the sounds and shifting smells. Deliaja recognized the approaching vehicle by the irregular whir of its untuned motor, vibrating the metallic walls of the sewer tunnel for kilometers. Like every child of the terrible, impoverished city that was the only inhabited region of the planet of the same name, Deliaja understood Nilson to an extent that seemed uncanny to outsiders. The bond that Nilsonites shared with their world was neither noble nor fine, but it was as deep and permanent as that of child to a devoted birth parent.

By the faintest tap of the grate, Deliaja alerted Cullen, three blocks away, to their first victim's approach. Trusting Cullen to handle the advance guard, Deliaja slithered through the moss-slick drain until she heard the dragging rhythm of the actual load of smuggled wares. She clambered upward, her sap-sticky gloves giving her purchase, to the nearest grate. She waited for Vin's confirming tap, before aiming her beamer through the rusted bars and firing blindly. The resultant, aborted scream satisfied her. From the ensuing clatter, she knew that Vin had completed his part of the foray and eliminated the remaining guard with his usual efficiency.

Despite her contempt for Vin as a leader, she admired his ability to kill. She would gladly retain his skills, if he would follow her—and if she could ever persuade Breamas to give her the command. Vin's isolated raids of terrorism were too few, too inadequate to make any lasting impression on protected Network officials like Racker. Deliaja hungered for the authority to make Breamas' promised revolution a reality.

In the meantime, she served the cause loyally, and only Breamas—the cunning old man who was a Nilson legend—guessed at the extent of her larger ambitions. Deliaja scurried toward the nearest exit to aid in rifling the confiscated cart and destroying whatever could not be carried. There would be a little time before the port boys came. The port boys always had their hands full, trying to keep up with the pace of crime during Nilson night, and they ignored most of the local feuds and altercations. They would not, however, disregard the loss of a shipment of wines and comestibles destined specifically for the Governor's palace. They would suspect—correctly—that a theft from the Governor signified another resurgence of the rebellious ideas of Breamas, who had spent most of his life advocating revolution against Network. Breamas had not taken an active, visible role in Nilson politics since his long-vanished youth, and none of the rebellions in his name

had ever amounted to more than an extra flurry of
violent deaths, but even some port boys feared the
incendiary power of Breamas' ideas among the Nilson people. This was one crime that would be inves-
tigated thoroughly, if the intensified harassment of
random Nilson citizens and a flurry of bureaucratic
finger-pointing could be considered an investigation.

As she helped Cullen shove the last victim's body
into the gutter, Deliaja smiled to herself, imagining
Racker's outrage at the personal affront. She would
have enjoyed seeing the Governor's reaction, but she
intended to be safely back in Wharton by the time he
learned of this crime. "Some day," she whispered
to the dead merchant, "this be you, Ned Racker."
Vin hissed at her to be silent, but she knew that Vin
shared her hopes, as well as her hates. Like the bond
they both shared with Nilson, their poisonous alliance
ran deep.

                    ***

   Closing his eyes provided the greatest relief of each
day to Arlan. So deeply did he enjoy the respite from
the caves, he seldom allowed himself to sleep immediately, even when exhausted like today. Having found
and retrieved the dead boy from the deep places, Arlan
had spent grueling hours answering the questions of
every shift supervisor, every ward keeper, and anyone
else who feared the political impact of another unexplained death in Wharton. Arlan's own shift supervisor, the opportunistic Vin, had immediately altered the
leave records to prove his own absence at the time in
question, demonstrating anew the instincts for self-
interest that had earned him his sinecure. Arlan knew
from a dozen sources that Vin's skyside leave had not
begun until after Arlan reported the boy's retrieval.

   Arlan wanted nothing more than separation from the
grim reality of his own existence. He told himself that
he envied the dead boy, who had at least found a permanent escape from the caves and the misery, but Arlan acknowledged his own lie immediately. He pitied

the boy and grieved for the loss, even of this boy who had not seemed particularly likable.

Throughout the questioning, the boy's young rounded face had begun to assume an imagined aspect of kinship in Arlan's mind. Arlan did not know the color of the boy's eyes, but he envisioned them as the same caramel brown that his own reflection showed him. During the day's questions, Arlan had discovered that the boy had been known as Tempest, whether as nickname or birth name no one seemed to be sure. The stormy concept of that name would not leave Arlan now, even in his precious solitary time.

Arlan tried to choreograph a dream in a forest, such as he had never visited outside his imagination, painting each leaf and bole with life and sunlight. Miz Ruth had once shown him such a picture on that battered Network terminal that had been Saschy's means of escaping Nilson poverty. The cost of activating the terminal had always been too high for Arlan to use it extensively, but he remembered and cherished each glimpse that it had offered him of other places, more benign than wretched Nilson. He wove those images into his dreams.

He had always had the gift that gave him a measure of control over his dreams. Following Miz Ruth's advice, he had not spoken of the gift since early childhood, because Nilson's hardened offspring tended to regard such fanciful talents with suspicion or envious rage. Arlan had no difficulty keeping silent about a subject that was intensely personal to him and utterly vital to his endurance of Wharton. He used his gift to supplement his allotments of skyside time, when his off-shift time actually coincided with availability of Wharton's temperamental transfer ports—those few days or hours that he could spend back on Nilson, away from the enclosed dome and caverns of the mining world. Arlan had developed a routine of mentally painting skyside places on the inner curves of his eyelids. The skyside places of his concoction improved greatly upon the actual skyside settings of his experience, which were the dismal Nilson streets, but his purpose was not accuracy. Only when he had prepared a pleasurable setting for his dream did he allow himself to sleep.

Tonight, the usual techniques worked imperfectly. Arlan fashioned his ancient forest, but the sky refused to remain blue above it. Each sunbeam that he scattered became sullied by a cloying mist that writhed around the trees. The gentle scents of his imagined universe, which he based on the alien herbal perfumes that were sold near the Nilson spaceport, reeked of the cold taint of Wharton metals and synthesized air. When he attempted to populate his forest with bears, deer, and foxes—creatures that he had never seen outside of stored Network data images—he found the animals hunted by a boy with a stormy name and a wounded chest.

Long before the night ended, Arlan rose from his cot in the cell that he shared with three other men. He dragged his coverall over his sleep-stiff limbs, trying not to jar the adjacent cots with his movements. Haverlim, a nervous youth who always slept lightly, muttered a question at Arlan, but Arlan did not catch the words and pretended not to have heard at all. He unbolted the door, a flimsy barrier that did not merit its cipher lock, and slipped into the ward's narrow corridor. Network's design for the Wharton living pods, embedded as they were in existing caverns, did not squander space. Only the highest-ranking workers earned enough to afford the private quarters that could be found in the artificially carved upper levels and surface dome, and even those facilities lacked any substantive luxuries.

Since Wharton defined day and night by workshifts rather than by planetary alignment, the canteens and supply shops never closed. Arlan, though a quiet man, enjoyed the company of his fellow workers and had his favorite canteen, the Windmill, where he was well known. He headed there directly, navigating the grid of dim corridors without need to consult the reference coordinates painted in large, luminous yellow characters on the walls at every intersection.

Because of the skewing of his own internal schedule, Arlan found few familiar faces at the Windmill. Uncomfortable with the idea of meeting strangers in his present unsettled mood, Arlan chose a table with a solitary chair beneath the warped viewscreen, and he stared fixedly at the waving grasses of the mythical farm scene that had given the canteen its name. When Deliaja, the cynical canteen manager, brought two mugs of the best ale and a second chair, he smiled at her gratefully.

"This be an odd hour to find you here, Arlan Willowan," she announced in her loud and unabashed fashion. With bleached curls and a lion's head tattooed on her left shoulder, Deliaja had the hardened prettiness that was typical of those Nilson whores who survived past their teens. Deliaja had escaped the usual fate of her short-lived kind by bribing a Network official to give her one of the few Wharton jobs that did not entail heavy labor. She did not hesitate to draw customers by measured displays of her creamy flesh, but she made her boundaries clear—at the point of a well-used knife, if her bitterly sharp words failed to suffice.

"You be here most always, Dee," answered Arlan. He was not unaware of Deliaja's physical attractions but had never coveted them for himself. He could not imagine pursuing a woman who so thoroughly and obviously despised any man who desired her.

"Long shifts be making less chance for that scum, Keever, to steal my share of profits." She nodded toward the skinny, twisted man who tended the bar, but Keever grinned in reply. Keever was not ashamed to be known as a thief. If a fall from a Nilson rooftop had not shattered his leg and crippled him, he would not have resorted to the marginal honesty of his present profession. He had won his job in a lottery.

Arlan wrapped his callused hands around his mug, smearing the tiny crystals of ice. "Keever be too respectful of you, Dee, to steal what be rightly yours."

The ex-whore shrugged. "There be lots of talk about you this night. You be Tempest's finder."

"You be knowing him?" asked Arlan, staring at the

mug's icy surface and seeing again the lacy caverns where he had found the dead boy.

"He be coming here sometimes, near this hour, looking to fight. He be liking to fight, wanting to prove something." She drew her chair closer to Arlan and made her voice soft. "Be that what killed him?"

"May be." Arlan met her serious eyes and admitted reluctantly, "May be the other."

Deliaja hissed a curse, then swallowed deeply of the stinging brew. "You be telling anyone else?"

"Not yet." He scratched his nearly shaven head. "May be never. What be the reason to tell it again? None be listening who could be helping." He paused, thinking of Saschy Firl, the only significant Network official of his acquaintance. "None who could be helping would be caring."

Deliaja frowned into her fist and muttered, "Be you seeing them, then?"

"Not like the workers in the deep shafts. I be seeing only one patch, one pulse."

"I be hearing that the ghost lights be closer to the wards now."

"They be closer," concurred Arlan grimly. He looked at Deliaja, little older than the boy, Tempest, despite her hardness. He did not like to deepen her premature lines of worry, but all the miners' stories suggested that Deliaja could spread the necessary warning more effectively than anyone else he knew in Wharton. She had influence in Wharton, far beyond her apparent position, and her influence extended to the Nilson streets, from which new Wharton recruits would be taken. The skysiders deserved to know something of Wharton's deadly mysteries, and Network would never admit such unpleasant truths. For the first time since retrieving Tempest's body, Arlan admitted his own concern aloud, "May be talk that Tempest be dead of too much fighting, and it be likely true, but it be not *all* the truth. There be no fighting where I be finding him. The dust around him be unmarked."

Deliaja gnawed her full lips fretfully before asking, "Why would ghost lights be moving him?"

"Be ghost lights thinking like us?" countered Arlan. "Be there anything understandable about them? They be closer. *That* be what matters. None should be leaving the near wards without a signaler."

The young woman sniffed, "What use be a signaler against a ghost?"

"Ghost lights be not a ghost," said Arlan with a trace of frustration for the superstitious rumor, "and signaler use may be the only way to learn the bounds of their territory. If we cannot be escaping them, may be, we can be avoiding them." Deliaja arched her incongruously dark brows, and Arlan responded to her skepticism, "Whatever they be, whatever be causing the displacements, they be no longer mere rumor in the deep places and abandoned shafts. They be real. They be dangerous. They be something we be needing to understand. They be something we be needing to tell those skysiders that be thinking of Wharton *opportunities*."

After a thoughtful moment, Deliaja drained her glass, patted Arlan's hand, and left his table. She did not come near his table again that night, but Arlan saw her whisper to Keever and to others huddled near the bar. Shortly thereafter, Keever caught Arlan's eyes and gave him a brusque, conspiratorial nod, which Arlan found irritatingly uninformative. Arlan nursed his drink in silence, stared at the blurred image of a windmill, and pondered a boy's death with weary grief.

No one approached him in the next hour. Deliaja watched him with unusual solemnity as he keyed in his payment, but she spoke only the ritual words of appreciation for his business. Too life-battered ever to feel disappointment deeply, Arlan left the canteen nonetheless a shade more bowed by the lonely weight of his concerns than when he had entered. He did not know what he had expected of Deliaja, for he had heard only the vaguest rumors to suggest that she was less powerless than the average Nilsonite. He considered her almost a friend but realized that she viewed him as simply one of her many customers.

When, minutes later, Keever slithered out of a

shadow and tugged Arlan into one of the numerous
pipe closets, Arlan did not at first connect the incident
with Deliaja. Arlan reacted with alarm rather than encouragement. He closed his fingers around the signaler
in his pocket and scanned the array of utility conduits
for any possible weapon. The crippled thief was not a
formidable opponent, but he could have allies, and
Network weapons could alter any odds.

"You be not a cautious man," whispered Keever, exac-
erbating Arlan's concerns before adding, "Deliaja be
not a wise choice as confidante."

"What be your point, Keever?" asked Arlan, holding
his voice level and keeping his muscles ready for
flight. He had never liked Keever, in part due to the
thief's old connections with a Nilson gang that had
been the nearest rivals to the men of Arlan's neighborhood. The shared obstacles of Wharton had helped to
reduce conflicts founded on Nilson territoriality, but
grievances over friends' deaths did not fade easily. The
leaden gray utility pipes hissed, hiding any sounds
from the corridor.

"There be some on Nilson who be not fond of the
way our Network Governor be keeping his promises.
'Better life' on Wharton," spat Keever, "be no better
than aching backs and too little pay." To Arlan's relief,
Keever let go of his arm, but the thief countered the
kindness by scuttling nervously toward the wall, as if
dodging some unseen passerby.

Arlan scanned the corridor as best he could without
taking his direct focus away from Keever. The pipe
closet was cold, and Keever was not a man whom anyone much trusted, but every child of Nilson's streets
knew the wisdom of listening to an informant before
passing judgment. "I be hearing words of revolution
since I be begging my first loaf. Be making yourself
clear, old lad, or be letting me be on my way."

Condensed moisture from the maze of pipes dripped
onto the thief's lank hair, but Keever did not appear to
notice. "There be more than talk coming soon. Governor's promises be one too many disappointment for
some, who be no longer patient with despair." Keever

crossed his arms defensively. "Be you seen telling whispers to Deliaja Sylar, may be you taking a label you be not liking later."

"What label be you meaning?"

"Rebel. Revolutionary. May be, terrorist." Keever shrugged. "May be, hero of the people, in the view of some, but that pretty label be the worst of all. Nilson heroes be not long allowed to live. Nilson heroes be dead men, when Network be noticing them."

"Why you be telling me this, Keever?" asked Arlan, not sure what to think of the unexpected warning. "You be Dee's friend, not mine, and I be only another customer of the canteen where both of you be working."

Keever squinted his pale eyes slyly. "May be, you be talking to your friend, Saschy Firl, some day about a kindness from old lad Keever."

It was not the first time Arlan had been approached in the mistaken belief that he had influence with Saschy, but it angered him as much as ever. "Old lad Keever be a fool if he be thinking Saschy Firl be having use for either of us." Arlan thrust the smaller man aside roughly and stormed his way back down the corridor to his cell. The bleakness of his expression caused those who knew him to step aside. They attributed his foul humor to some Network-imposed aftermath of finding Tempest, and they respected his mood.

Keever limped back to the canteen with a grin on his face. Deliaja, who had authorized his errand, joined her thumb and forefinger in subdued approval. Breamas would be pleased with the progress of recruitment.

CHAPTER 5

Traveler

Quin did not travel to the isolated planet of Siatha that morning with any conscious plan except to visit friends. He viewed the visit as a private reward for the unremitting pace of his labors since abandoning Geisen. Quin had little taste for introspection, being quite unwilling to take himself that seriously, even under life-threatening circumstances. As a result, he sometimes failed to examine his own ever-simmering impulses for evidence of his Power's dark instincts.

Scattered white clouds dotted the blue sky, and the cool air smelled of fresh mint. A fragile trail of charcoal smoke rose from the stone chimney of the Healers' house. The top segment of the split wooden door stood open. Quin waited with his hands in his coat pockets, studying the star-shaped yellow flowers that clustered beneath newly glazed windows. He did not doubt that his visit was expected; the Healers always knew. Visits to Siatha warmed Quin with a sense of homecoming. Though Healers' symbiotically generated skills differed fundamentally from the inherent mental Power of an Ixaxin wizard, Quin felt more kinship with the Healers than with anyone else in Network.

The brown-haired, sharp-eyed man whom Quin knew as Marrach came to the door and rested his bronzed arms on the ledge. A slight smile twisted the Healer's lips, softening his craggy face with wry humor. Quin donned the amiable attitude and clownish grin that made him appear as curly-headed inside as out, and he remarked cheerfully, "It's not fair to start laughing at me before I can say a word, Marrach."

"You've said several words now," answered Marrach, laughing openly. It was a deep laugh, rich with life and honest warmth.

"You don't even know why I've come."

"Neither do you. There is mischief in you this morning, young Quinzaine, which is a pleasant change from all the pleas of troubles that have come to me recently." Marrach unlatched the lower door, welcoming his guest. "The cases of valley fever have been many this spring."

"Am I interrupting Healers' duties?"

"Not severely. Jeni has gone to check the cures of her Revgaenian charges, but my local patients have now passed the critical time." Marrach nodded toward the softly violet hills. "Revgaenian's higher altitude means the fever comes and passes later there. Once Jeni returns, I must go to make the rounds of the far districts of Innisbeck. This is my short respite."

Marrach paused very briefly, but Quin could feel the energies that danced around the Healer: the Mirlai, the symbiotic beings of light that had transformed the lethal Rabh Marrach into the Healer, Suleifas. By a slight concentration of Power, Quin could almost always sense the Mirlai presence. Only rarely, at Mirlai instigation, had anything approaching communication passed between him and the ethereal race. A wildly improbable concept of the alien Consortium, from which the Mirlai had long ago emerged on abandoning their original symbiotic partners, tickled Quin's vivid imagination.

"Would you like tea?" continued Marrach, though Quin sensed the sudden sobering of Marrach's mood. The Mirlai had healed Rabh Marrach and gentled him, but they had not erased the cautious instincts of the man who had so long been Network's agent of destruction. They had, in fact, enhanced his unique forms of perception, contributing empathy without mitigating intellectual keenness. "I think Jeni hid a few winter-spice loaves for the rare visitors who require nothing more of us than hospitality."

He is recalling Network's Marrach now, thought

Quin, *for that trace of cynicism does not originate from the Mirlai-made Healer.* "I never refuse any semblance of a meal," replied Quin blithely, but he became more cautious in his inner Power. Rabh Marrach—or the Healer Suleifas—was not a man whose instincts should be dismissed.

"You have an appetite worthy of a Revgaenian wild-bear," rejoined Marrach, ushering Quin into the warm, firelit sitting room.

"Traveling by means of wizard's Power is hungry work."

Smiling, Marrach disappeared briefly into the kitchen, and Quin walked to the wooden cupboard that held the Healers' stones. Quin did not open the painted cupboard doors to see the stones, but he let his Power touch them with the fond respect of a greeting. The sense of serene Mirlai energies seemed to sharpen briefly and tantalizingly as Quin focused on the stones, but the beings' individual patterns remained elusive.

"They are pleased to see you well," remarked Marrach, returning and laying the tea and bread upon the square plank table where Jeni mixed her herbal remedies. "They have rarely healed anyone from beyond their Chosen home, and their inability to monitor you regularly concerns them."

"Do they speak to you in words, Marrach?"

"They employ images, as a rule."

"They are very alien to us, aren't they?" asked Quin thoughtfully. He accepted a golden slice of spice bread, but he stared at it without tasting it.

Marrach shrugged. It was a casual enough gesture, but it reminded Quin of a swordsman loosening muscles before engaging an opponent in formal duel. "Your question implies that you and I belong to a single species," answered Marrach, "whereas you have your 'wizardly' Power and a life span far outside any Network human standard, and I was manufactured in a Gandry factory for the intended purpose of being dissected into replacement parts." His deep eyes glittered with distaste as he alluded to his own grim origins.

He loathes discussing his personal history, mused

Quin, *but Marrach never shrinks from emotional discomfort. I am probably a fool—and an inconsiderate boor—to draw him further into this discussion.* "You and I are both human, Marrach, and very different from the Mirlai."

Marrach shook his head abruptly, and an old hardness etched the brown planes of his face. The Mirlai flickered in agitation. "You and I, Lord Quinzaine, represent two extreme examples of genetic artifice. Our respective claims to humanity could be termed questionable at best. Network has set itself against us, despite its own guilt in creating us, and the Consortium would view us both as abominations. As for the Mirlai, they are indeed a unique species, according to any Consortium records that I have managed to encounter."

"I suppose the Consortium's records would include a great many species," said Quin, his gray eyes acquiring a curious gleam. He disregarded Marrach's harsh comments regarding the dubious humanity of a wizard of Ixaxis, knowing that the observations were true but considering them unimportant to the individual who was Quin. Marrach might still suffer the realization of being created as a disposable entity, never intended to be self-aware and intelligent, but Quin had a foundation of family and social status, augmented by innate cheerfulness, to counteract the burden of his own differences. "You've visited the Consortium, haven't you, Marrach?"

Marrach raised unruly brows at Quin's focusing of interest, but he answered simply, "I've crossed some of the fringe areas, where petty planetary bureaucrats wield the idea of Consortium law as a hollow threat. Only Consortium members travel to the Consortium's major worlds, where Consortium law is actual and absolute."

"Have you ever seen them?" persisted Quin. "The Calongi?"

The Healer's keen eyes appraised Quin slowly. At last, Marrach nodded, but his lips were tight with disapproval. "In Caragen's employ, I saw Calongi on several occasions, but I always made a point of avoiding close contact. Not even Caragen meets with Calongi unless he is well prepared and well protected by the most sophisticated Network technology available. I would advise you to exercise similar caution, Master Wizard, unless you want your world's precious secrets to become Consortium data entries. The Consortium is not Network, and Calongi perceptions are much vaster than even you are likely to recognize."

Quin concocted a mental picture of Calongi as composites of the great wizards from his own world's history, then dismissed the image as egotistical folly. The little that he did know about Calongi suggested that they bore little resemblance to human beings of any form. "Are they as hideous to see as the descriptions suggest?"

"I would not describe them so harshly. A cat is not a bird, but both have beauty. The Calongi are too different from humanity to qualify as *hideous,* despite a few common traits of form. Though the Calongi are bipedal, their living cloaks conceal a variety of limbs that I could not even begin to define. The placement of their facial features accords, more or less, with human standards, but you could never mistake a Calongi's massive head for human. *I* would describe the Calongi as *impressive.* They are also intimidating, but that is a function of their abilities and attitude, more than of any surface traits."

Quin chewed spice bread and speculations in equal measure. "If the Calongi are so terribly clever, why do they continue to deny the possibility of topological travel? They must realize that Network has established thousands of permanent transfer ports across dozens of universes."

Marrach shook his head. "I don't know. It may be due to their arrogance, as Caragen claims to believe. It may be due to factors that we cannot even imagine. The Calongi are alien to us in every sense, which means that their reasoning does not necessarily correspond to ours. Do not underestimate them on the basis of a single perceived flaw in their science."

"I'm only trying to understand them a little."

"So I've gathered," sighed Marrach, pushing his cup away from him. "The Calongi have dominated this galaxy—and several others, I believe—for far longer than humanity has existed. Those of us who decline to accept their Consortium law know relatively little about them, but the magnitude of their influence is indisputable. They do not generally interfere in their neighbors' affairs, whether from arrogance, indifference, or munificence, but they are quite capable of protecting their own interests. As you know too well, Caragen does not tolerate 'competition' without a significant reason for self-restraint."

"I was not planning an attack," protested Quin.

"I know. You're simply curious." Marrach's smile acquired a slightly sardonic cast.

"Curiosity is the perpetual curse of my life."

"And you won't be placated with broad responses, will you?"

Quin's storm-gray eyes widened with injured innocence. "I only asked a few harmless questions."

"You rarely ask me 'harmless' questions about my life prior to Siatha, and you seldom come here without a specific reason."

"My reason is friendship."

"Our friendship has always been subservient to our responsibilities for the worlds and people we protect. I am your best access to the sort of unpublicized information that Caragen hoards to maintain his authority, and when you start displaying such obvious interest in the Consortium, what do you expect me to conclude? Your intentions may be more honorable, but you are at least as dangerous as Caragen in your own way, Lord Quinzaine dur Hamley."

Quin adopted the fool's grin that made him appear most innocuous. "You have a frighteningly suspicious mind, Marrach."

"That is why I'm still alive," replied Marrach in a dry tone that eradicated Quin's grin. "Can you honestly tell me that you did not come here to question me about the Consortium?"

"I did not plan anything . . ." began Quin, but he

stopped and shrugged, unsure of his own intentions. "No," he confessed, "but the reason for my present curiosity is not at all sinister. After that near-catastrophe on Geisen, I developed a Network identity with utmost attention to security, and the results have proved to be tediously successful. I have worked myself exhaustively to be accepted as a model of unstudious mediocrity at Rendl's Southsand University, and Katerin has enslaved herself to the research department. Both students and faculty at Southsand besiege Katerin with unreasonable demands, and she insists that compliance is the only credible reaction for her present persona. Meanwhile, she has had some new inspiration regarding her private research, and I know (though she would never say so) that she needs to concentrate without distractions from me. I am feeling correspondingly restless."

"Eat some more spice loaf. It's a much safer remedy for boredom."

Quin gathered a few crumbs into a mound on his plate. "Curiosity has little regard for safety, but I don't think I'm being particularly reckless in this instance. I truly had not considered studying the Consortium until I sensed the Mirlai today, but the idea is growing on me." Quin's smile became pensive. "Even ordinary Network citizens interact with C-humans occasionally. If I encountered such an exchange, I could stand innocently on the sidelines and listen. Maybe I could follow a C-human home and see what 'home' is like. Once I established the patterns of the place, I could come and go as I pleased."

"And if some Consortium member observed you vanishing into your topological 'patterns,' you would be reported immediately as a Network spy."

"That's better than being recognized as an errant wizard from a world that isn't supposed to exist," murmured Quin.

Marrach did not pause to acknowledge Quin's snippet of irony. "The Consortium does not tolerate unauthorized intrusions. The Calongi demand justice on their terms. They would demand *you,* and Caragen would be only too happy to comply. He would probably offer the Calongi your entire, officially nonexistent home planet as a bonus."

"He knows better," murmured Quin with a slightly menacing softness.

"He knows better than to attack you directly," snapped Marrach. "Nothing would please him more than to set you and the Consortium at odds. If you give him that opportunity, he will snatch it. He will manufacture incidents, even at the risk of jeopardizing Network's precarious relationship with the Calongi. He will activate every indirect Consortium contact he has established over the years. Your 'curiosity' could set the entire conflict over your world into motion again."

"You sound discouragingly like Lady Rhianna when she decides to lecture me about duty and responsibilities."

Marrach gave an ill-humored laugh. "Your Infortiare is a wise woman."

"I'd be pleased to help you convey your respects personally. I can take you to the Infortiare's study in her tower in Tulea, as quickly as you entered your kitchen."

"I prefer to remain bound to this world, as you know, and your gentle reminder of your Power's peculiar capabilities, Lord Quinzaine, is quite unnecessary." Marrach stretched his muscular arms, an overt reminder of his own less subtle form of power. "I suppose the best way to dissuade you from your reckless pursuit of dangerous curiosity is to educate you."

"It is usually less frustrating than arguing with me," replied Quin with a widening of his grin, though his Power tingled with wariness.

Marrach grunted, but the Healer's crooked smile returned to soften the crags of his face. "For a start, you should realize that the Consortium does not equate Network citizens with Consortium humans even at the species level. We are inferior in civilization ranking, and that is the only distinguishing characteristic that counts to a Consortium member. The Network use of 'human' and 'C-human' to distinguish a single species is considered abominable manners in the Consortium.

Caragen promotes the term 'C-human' as a conscious insult to the Calongi."

"Typical of him," muttered Quin.

"To Consortium members, any 'civilized' being from the same planet-of-origin as Network humans is a Soli. The Consortium word that corresponds most closely to 'human' describes a being of *any* species with an official Consortium civilization ranking of Level VII or better. Network citizens and related independents are ranked as Level VII, placing us only one step above food animals. The 'C-humans,' who are the Consortium's Soli, have a rank of Level VI."

"I suppose the Calongi are Level I?"

"Of course."

"And the Mirlai?"

"From the little that they have conveyed to me on the subject, I believe that they were Level I before they abandoned the Consortium an aeon ago. Their official rank may have been reduced by now, if a Level I species *can* be reduced. I do not know the intricacies of rank assignments in the Consortium's advanced echelons."

"How many species does the Consortium rank?"

"Thousands. Perhaps hundreds of thousands. I am not privy to their records."

"You have already told me more than I've ever learned on my extensive prowls through Network's plethora of data," grunted Quin emphatically. He devoured an entire slice of spice bread with a few hasty gulps. "All I can find in Network are inadequate references to the original offer of Consortium membership. There is barely a note regarding the eight standard years that elapsed between that offer and the official establishment of Network's independent government. Subsequent allusions to the Consortium consist mostly of vague—or definitive—criticisms about the disloyalty of C-humans to their own species."

"And you were incurious about the Consortium until today," murmured Marrach.

"I was *relatively* incurious. I am always looking for information that I can use to irritate Caragen."

Marrach nodded, wryly accepting Quin's excuse. "Even after two centuries, the split remains a sore subject to Caragen and other persons of influence. All Network Councillors dislike uncontrollable competition, and the Council Governor is particularly conscious of the Consortium's unassailable status."

"Why did humanity divide? Did Network's founders join and then leave the Consortium? Was it a small segment of humanity that accepted the Calongi's offer?"

"My Immortal young friend, I have lived fifty-two Network standard years, not two hundred and fifty. Your interests delve considerably farther into the past than my memories can accommodate, unless you want me to recite the same Network records that you have surely encountered already."

Quin waved away Marrach's wry protest. "You must have heard stories. People remember significant events in history, even if they embellish the truth in the retelling. The Immortal Sorcerer Kings, the original products of Network's life-extension experiments, separated my world quite deliberately from its past, but a few legends survived—for ten millennia in my world's topologically distorted time! In Network years, I'm just twenty-eight, but I could tell you a good deal about how Ceallagh and Tul defeated Sorcerer King Horlach many centuries before my birth."

"Stories," grunted Marrach, frowning into his fist. "Now you're asking me to remember from a time before I met Caragen. I did hear stories—soldiers' stories—when I worked as an independent mercenary. I cannot vouch for the authenticity of any of what I heard. I cannot even guarantee that I've remembered correctly, since I hadn't yet enjoyed the privilege of Caragen's ingenious revisions to my mental equipment."

"I shall be suitably dubious," replied Quin, silently marveling that Marrach would discuss *that* part of his past at all.

Marrach spread his left hand flat on the table, and he stared at it as he spoke. Caragen had supplied the hand;

Mirlai had made it indistinguishable from a natural appendage. "Humanity did not fracture when it encountered the Consortium. It coalesced from dozens of bickering nations into two primary factions. Most humans accepted the Calongi's offer, though a few groups scattered."

"You're a terse storyteller," complained Quin, when Marrach seemed disinclined to continue.

"True storytellers never wasted time talking to me in those days, Quin. I can only recount what little I overheard."

Feeling contrite, but refusing to dishonor Marrach with pity, Quin said, "You could tell me what the offer of Consortium membership actually means."

The Healer's sharp eyes gleamed knowingly, recognizing Quin's conscious effort to spare the Healer's pride. The *Healer* appreciated the kindly intentions, but Marrach answered with a convincing display of crisp detachment, "The Calongi offer all the knowledge, all the advantages of an exceedingly old, very sophisticated civilization, and they demand only compliance with Consortium law. The Consortium's offer of membership is very tempting to a species just emerging from its planet of origin. The offer means hope or tyranny, depending on the expectations of the recipient."

"A little tyranny can outweigh a lot of hope."

"At the time of the infamous offer, most of humanity already labored for tyrants of their own species. The Calongi offered to feed the starving, shelter the homeless, protect the victims of abuse. They offered, and they gave. They relieved humanity of a burden that had existed throughout human history. Network's relative prosperity is largely founded on Consortium munificence."

"Did the Consortium absorb only the weakest members of human society?"

"No. It took from every rank and type indiscriminately. If you consider the offer as it must have appeared then, its attractions are not hard to find. What was the alternative? An uncertain future on an ecologically damaged world, beleaguered by its own wars and injustice. There was no Network. There was only a rudimentary ability to travel through space, and that privilege was not widely available. I am sure that many people feared the Calongi. Others worshiped them. Some followed blindly. Others rebelled blindly. I doubt that many rational decisions were made. Humanity is not a very rational species, even at its best."

"You're an awful cynic, Rabh Marrach."

"How many people do you know who behave rationally on a regular basis?"

"A tiresome number of them, especially on the island of Ixaxis. An irrational wizard is a singularly hazardous beast," observed Quin with a rueful grin.

"You're rational enough, in general," acknowledged Marrach, "and quite hazardous enough for my tastes." The tension in Marrach's expression eased a little, and he refilled Quin's cup. "There *are* sound arguments for accepting Consortium membership. Consortium members are free to maintain individual governments, private economies, personal cultures, and local legal systems. However, if any Consortium member chooses to invoke the rules and processes of Consortium law, obedience to the Calongi judgment must be accepted unequivocally by all of the affected Consortium members. There is no jury of peers. There is no appeal. Whatever a Calongi Inquisitor decrees officially is the law of the Consortium."

"What if two Calongi disagree?"

"They don't. Not officially, at least. By their own definition, their law is perfect justice, based on absolute truth."

"That's rather a one-sided perspective, isn't it?"

"It is an absolutely one-sided perspective. It is the Calongi's Sesserda Truth, their religion and their way of life. Accept it as such, and receive the benefits of Consortium membership. Deny it or doubt it, and be accounted uncivilized and unworthy. The founders of Network gathered a number of rebellious humans who refused to accept the Calongi on faith. The arguments polarized humanity, and the conflicts were both serious and violent during those eight mysterious years you mentioned. Some small groups of humans abandoned the conflict to found their own independent colonies. For reasons as diverse as the populace, a slight majority of humanity finally left the planet of their origin to settle on worlds that the Calongi offered. The largest remnant became Network." Marrach closed his left hand slowly, and he raised his eyes to meet Quin's. "That is my interpretation of what I remember hearing. It reflects a Network bias that I acquired subsequently."

"Do you speak Consortium Basic?"

"Yes. It's a relatively simple, very direct vocal language developed by Cuui traders to facilitate their interspecies enterprises. It's considered a relatively poor language for conveying emotion or advanced philosophical concepts, but it's flexible and reasonably comfortable for most sapient species. Network can teach it to you, though the lessons are not contained in the standard curriculum. I can guide you to the proper diplomatic access files, if you insist on pursuing this present madness of yours."

Marrach's dry criticism brought a grimace to Quin's face. Quin relished the exotic information that he pried from Marrach, but he felt guilty when Marrach analyzed the reasons in that precise, efficient manner that was so reminiscent of the Network processors linked to Marrach's brain. "Which particular madness of mine provokes your deepest concern?" asked Quin with a cheerfulness that sounded false even to him.

In answer, Marrach gave only a throaty chuckle. Quin flushed, as if he had been caught in some mischief more childish than usual. "If you decide that you truly need to pursue an investigation of the Consortium," continued Marrach imperturbably, "proceed with extreme caution. Avoid any species above a Level VI initially. Level VI is the minimum civilization level for a Consortium member, and it includes Soli, Cuui, and Jiucetsi, among many others. Stay as far away as possible from Calongi, until you have some idea of what you're confronting. They have dozens of senses that we cannot even define. They may well have mental skills that best even the remarkable Power of an Ixaxin 'wizard.' "

"I'm not sure that I intend to do anything more than I've already done," said Quin slowly, trying to put into words the reasoning that he had not examined consciously until that moment. "I don't think I had any real intentions beyond a friendly visit with you when I arrived here, but I admit that something seems to have triggered a prickling of my Power." Marrach had issued his curt, dire warning, and now he insisted on trusting Quin—like Katerin, like Lady Rhianna, like too many wielders of either uncomfortable Network science or wizards' Power. Responsibility could be a discouraging companion. "Maybe it is just my ungovernable curiosity getting the better of me again. Distant horizons have always beckoned to me. Left to myself, I would probably enjoy wandering forever, though I keep telling myself I'll find the right home somewhere. Being a perpetual refugee wears on Katerin."

"It's a difficult way to live, especially with Caragen's unpleasant form of help."

"I'm also troubled by the existence of an unknown as large as the Consortium. I suppose it was a similar feeling that caused Lady Rhianna to send me to study Network in the first place. I don't know if it's fear or healthy curiosity or Power's insatiable urge to extend its range of influence. The Consortium *does* cover a hefty chunk of this universe, which is by far the most populous universe that I've ever heard described."

Marrach nodded slightly. "The Consortium is difficult to ignore. However, you should realize that the Consortium has a great deal in common with a sleeping predator: It's only a threat if you disturb it."

"I'll keep that in mind."

"Good. Because I don't relish trying to patch you together a second time, Lord Quinzaine, under any circumstances, and Consortium methods are devious and unpredictable. The Calongi intimidate even the Mirlai."

With a rare frown, Quin demanded, "Why?"

The Mirlai danced restlessly. "By Calongi judgment, the Mirlai should never have abandoned their original symbiosis with the Adraki species. Mirlai maintain that the Adraki demanded more than Mirlai could supply. The Calongi disagree. The bulk of the Adraki race descended into violence and aggression, but any Adraki who still accepts Consortium membership retains Level II status. The Mirlai create Healers, but Consortium law declares the Mirlai guilty of the greater crime. In a real sense, the Mirlai are the Consortium's condemned."

"I'm not sure that I understand."

"Nor do I, but such is the nature of alien reasoning. It will never accord completely with your own ideas. Establishing full agreement between two members of a single species is sufficiently rare. The Calongi ability to maintain a common law among so many diverse creatures and cultures is unfathomable to me. Perhaps they are right in saying that those of us who cannot conform to their law are less civilized than our Consortium counterparts."

Quin grimaced, never having been accused of conforming readily. "Do you admire the Calongi?"

"I respect them. I have not encountered a Calongi since the Mirlai healed me, so I hesitate to offer any more personal comment. Caragen finds the Calongi insufferably arrogant, and he is not alone in that opinion. I have never heard a Calongi described as pleasant."

"If you wanted to observe C-humans . . ." With a rueful smile, Quin amended, "If you wanted to observe Soli or other Consortium citizens, where would you go?"

"I have not tried to keep track of Caragen's recent manipulations of worlds and politics."

"Your knowledge of the subject is still vastly more thorough than mine."

Marrach chewed thoughtfully at a torn thumbnail. "The Nilson spaceport is probably the safest location from your standpoint, though Nilson is a miserable sty.

Since it is one of Network's few open trade centers, it attracts a plethora of mercenaries, terrorists, munition smugglers, and other would-be purchasers of Network weaponry."

"Delightful."

"Nilson has the highest murder rate in Network, and the rare C-humans who stop there are the Consortium's least shining citizens by a large order of magnitude, but an open port is a relatively easy place to be inconspicuous. The planet has long been a hub for major smuggling operations, discreetly controlled by Caragen. The local government has been owned by Caragen since the prominent assassination of its only capable, independent leader. Surface improvements have been made in some areas, but the criminal foundation is not hard to find." After a brief pause, Marrach added, "I could elaborate on Nilson's political history, since I was one of Nilson's primary destroyers in recent years, but I would rather avoid recalling the personal data. I doubt that such details of the past have relevance to your goal."

"Of course," agreed Quin quickly, for he felt equally discomfited by specific reminders of Marrach's brand of service to Andrew Caragen. Quin certainly did not want to verify his suspicions regarding the name of the assassin of Nilson's former leader. "Do you mind if I finish the spice loaf? It's wonderful, and I'm ravenous."

"You're always ravenous," answered Marrach too tensely. The Mirlai wove a frantic dance, berating Quin.

"Hunger is an occupational hazard," replied Quin, grinning despite a fear that he had probed Marrach too deeply. Both from friendship and general wariness, he did not want to antagonize either Marrach or the protective Mirlai. "Do you have any idea how much energy it takes to wander around the infinities?"

"Not in a wizard's terms," replied Marrach, his smile returning cautiously. "I'll see what else I can find to feed you."

Quin beamed appreciatively, until Marrach disappeared into the kitchen. All the clownish pretenses fled, leaving a pensive young man. Quin murmured to himself, "Friend Healer, you have already provided a veritable feast for thought."

CHAPTER 6

Diplomat

Stone ovens and the wooden slab of a sagging table nearly filled the smokehouse, leaving little space for the furred Alari or their smooth-skinned Soli visitors. The Alari servants had opened four of the ovens to let the smoldering herbs spread their blue smoke with the heat. The smokes from centuries had darkened the carved wooden walls and beams, where Alari totems told the contentious history of every major family of their world. A stained-glass bowl, suspended by three heavy braids of leather, cast its colored lights and smoke-swirled shadows upon mounded platters of fruits, meats, and cheeses. Despite the quantities of food that the Alari had already consumed, the table appeared no less burdened.

The *taimuudon* slithered down Tori's throat, its salt-sweet flavor bringing tears to her emerald eyes. Tori continued to smile. The Alari people accepted tears as a sign of praise. To frown was unforgivably rude. No more than a hint of strain marred the finely contoured face and enigmatic expression that so uncannily recalled Tori's great-grandmother, Mirelle, a woman who had gained both infamy and influence by the wielding of her physical gifts in the ancient profession of the courtesan.

Hamtuloaan, the Alari elder, purred approval of Tori's willingness to sample Alari delicacies. Tori risked a sidelong glance at Jase across the cramped smokeroom, where his slight, leather-garbed frame was wedged between his bulky Alari companions. His iridescent eyes watered freely, dampening sharp angles of facial bone and flesh. His expression was nearly blissful, as the gray-furred Alari proffered increasingly rare viands for him to sample. Gathered around a sputtering oven, the squat and wrinkled Alari stretched their rubbery lips in broad smiles that Jase matched as well as Soli physiognomy allowed. His smooth, dark-skinned hands clasped the Alari's broad paws in an outpouring of camaraderie.

So much for Jase's Sesserda honesty, thought Tori with wry amusement. The intense Alari flavors and textures, merely unpleasant to her, could only be torture to the acute senses of a Sesserda adept.

Jase would naturally deny any intentional falseness in his reactions. Although Tori would argue with him, she was also the first to acknowledge the thoroughness of his ability to adapt. She had an unusual, instinctive talent for alien relations, but her brand of diplomacy consisted of a little advanced study, a modest skill for observation, an exceptional ability to coax, and a knack for prevaricating convincingly. When Jase immersed himself in an alien culture, he acquired that culture's mental and emotional perspectives as a fully independent personality. In his mind, the alien reality became an integral part of his inviolate Sesserda Truth. The transformation usually amused Tori, always fascinated her, and occasionally sent chills of horror down her spine.

As far as she had been able to witness, Jase adapted easily to any culture, as long as the adaptation served his concepts of Sesserda and the Consortium. Even Tori's liberal nature clung to a few Soli prejudices, especially concerning customs that brought discomfort to her person. Jase, who was normally the most cautious and reserved of men, could still shock her with his willing denial of Soli physiological and psychological needs. Within the confines of the Consortium, Jase's fluid skill was priceless.

As an expert in the delicate art of alien relations, Jasen Sleide clearly fulfilled his true Sesserda life-purpose, the function for which acute relanine addiction had rendered him uniquely qualified. Despite his tortured addiction to the pure relanine of Calongi lifeblood—or because of it—the Calongi honored him above all other members of his species. Jase was the one Soli to whom they granted a civilization rank of Level V. And he was the one Soli who had mastered the Calongi religion well enough to earn the title of Sesserda adept.

Tori had no doubts about the magnitude of Jase's talents. She did worry at times about his mental stability. In those rare moments when she allowed herself to contemplate her life with Jase as more than a temporary, aberrant condition, she knew that she dreaded witnessing the long-term effects of his severe addiction. Though the success of their professional affiliation was undeniable, she often wondered how long their strained personal relationship could endure.

If Jase's extreme, relanine-enhanced flexibility of viewpoint ever worried his Calongi friends and mentors, they did not voice that concern in Tori's presence. Tori did not expect the Calongi to confide in her, a Level VI Soli with a dubious past and unsavory family connections. The Calongi respected her in their own way, since respect of creation was the foundation of Sesserda, but they could not *like* her any better than she could like them. They tolerated her uncivilized presence in their intimate circles for Jase's sake, just as she endured the uncomfortable world of Calong-4 because Jase would make his permanent home nowhere else. The arrangement might have been less bearable for all concerned if the profession of alien relations had not demanded so much travel among diverse Consortium worlds. The stays on Calong lasted just long enough for Jase to begin employing obscure Calongi mannerisms more than comprehensible speech, which was just long enough for *all* Calongi mannerisms to start grating on Tori's nerves.

"Keelall?" asked the Alari elder curiously.

Tori responded with a polite nod, wondering guiltily why the Alari questioned her contentment. She knew better than to allow her mind to wander during business, although bouts of distraction were accepted as natural phases of Alari conversation. The Alari, recognizing themselves as a temperamental people, deliberately held significant conferences in an enervating atmosphere. Between the cloistering heat and the heavy, mildly intoxicating smoke, neither Alari nor their guests were likely to summon energy enough for anger. Tori thought she would be doing well to stay awake through the rest of the evening, unless the official discussions began soon. . . . She stiffened, reminding herself that the discussions would not begin until she initiated the proceedings.

She declined a second *taimuudon* in favor of a pungent candied root. "Areeumaa," she murmured, wrapping her tongue deftly around the intricate Alari vowel patterns. Her remark, the Alari-approved method of suggesting a change of subject, brought a slow hum of agreement from Hamtuloaan.

To Tori's relief, the Alari shifted to Consortium Basic, a language much more comfortable for a Soli to wield. "Your man will join us?" demanded Hamtuloaan, who had decided on first introduction that Tori dominated the Soli partnership. Jase had acquiesced immediately to the subordinate role, leaving Tori no gracious choice but concurrence. Tori, keenly aware of her relative inexperience in trade negotiations, had promised herself a suitable revenge on her senior partner/employer. She did not doubt that Jase had manipulated Hamtuloaan's initial reaction via some obscure technique of Sesserda persuasion.

"My man will join us," replied Tori dryly, shrugging silk-clad shoulders into the formal garnet robe that served to warm her in place of Alari fur. She stood and beckoned peremptorily at Jase, indulging herself in a hint of retribution-to-come. The Alari began their solemn parade out of the smokehouse.

Jase quirked one expressive black eyebrow, but he followed Tori and Hamtuloaan from the smokehouse with every outward sign of humility. He even gathered the heavy train of Tori's Alari robe, holding the lush velvet clear of the icy path like the most dutiful Alari attendant. Jase's arms and hands were bared to the cold, though his leather jerkin, trousers, and boots wore frost from the wake of snow that flurried from Hamtuloaan's shuffling tread. Any Soli inoculated with ordinary, relanine-based adaptation fluid, rather than the pure relanine that burned in Jase's blood, would have frozen in such conditions. Jase barely shivered on leaving the smokehouse, and the ice melted instantly from his dark skin.

The snow had fallen almost continuously since morning, assuring the end of the brief season of relative warmth. Despite the heavy robe and the adaptation fluid thickening Tori's blood, the cold air felt harsh to her. The chill chased away the somnolent spell of the smokehouse and freshened Tori's nervousness about the coming negotiations.

The Alari had been unable to maintain their prior agreements due to endless conflicts over minor points of etiquette. As an official Consortium representative, she had the right to demand a resolution, but that presupposed her ability to formulate a compromise in keeping with strict Consortium law. She could employ her alien relations skills to persuade bickering parties to meet, but she was not an Inquisitor to identify Sesserda Truth and choreograph adherence. How did Jase expect her to *lead* the negotiation?

He surely had a plan. He would not jeopardize his precious Truth simply for the pleasure of making her squirm under expanded responsibilities, nor even for his relentless cause of convincing her that she was more capable than she believed. She trusted Jase to ensure the welfare of the Alari. Nonetheless, she would see him pay for this joke of his. And if she learned that he was simply forcing her to stretch her trust of *him,* she would tie his unnaturally limber, relanine-saturated fingers into knots.

Hamtuloaan flung wide the stout wooden doors of the meeting room. The building was a simple, drafty structure of bleached timbers, lacking any sealant between the bare boards. Five Alari elders, crowned by the varied herbal wreaths that represented each of five tribes, huddled on hassocks around a hissing red-gold fire. At least two Alari subordinates accompanied each

elder on a single hassock, furred bodies pressed tightly
and protectively against fellow tribe members. The
arrangement of tribes made for crowded seating, but
it gave needed heat in the uninsulated room. All of
the Alari hunched their furred backs, ostensibly from
cold but implicitly as a polite expression of their mutual
animosities.

A swirl of acrid woodsmoke tickled Tori's nose. She
squinted to keep from sneezing, as Jase placed a cere-
monial wreath of tightly braided silver bark and dried
snowflowers atop her dark cascade of hair. In the guise
of ritual, he managed to extend a series of deft touches,
quick and feather-soft, across the base of her skull. The
impulse to sneeze left her, as did a large part of her tension. She wondered which alien culture had taught Jase
that particular trick, but she was grateful for it.

"Would my lady like me to present the recommended trade contract immediately?" he asked with an
artless calm that made Tori's lips twitch with suppressed recriminations. "Or shall I await my lady's
command?"

"Now," replied Tori tersely. She wished she could
be as furious with Jase as he deserved for not telling
her that he had already designed a contract. However,
she could anticipate his answer if she accused him of
keeping unnecessary secrets. He would tell her that she
had simply failed to pay attention, and he would explain—with inarguable patience—all the ways in
which he had kept her fully informed. The Calongi, if
consulted, would agree with him. And Tori would
eventually concede that any fault was indeed hers, not
his, if only because she *had* made the choice to work
and to live with a Sesserda adept.

In obedience to formality, she rested her fingers on
his wiry arm, though her nails pressed into him sharply
enough to convey her exasperation with his methods.
She let him escort her to the fur hassock beside Hamtuloaan, and she sank with practiced grace into the cushioned depths. She did not try to settle comfortably until
Jase assumed his place beside her, for the hassocks
shifted awkwardly with each addition of weight. Her

robe was not quite warm enough, and her confidence was not quite strong enough for her to crave prideful isolation.

Emulating the Alari practice, Tori curled herself into the hassock close to Jase—close enough that she could detect the subtle tingle of relanine that surrounded him. She needed no such reminder of the origin of his unique gifts, but a forced awareness of the potency of relanine in him invariably sobered her mood. Beside him on the hassock, she hoped that Alari custom would restrain Jase's usual tendency toward expressive gestures: The Alari conserved their personal heat too jealously to accompany their speech with broad motions.

"What proposal do you bring to the tribes?" demanded Hamtuloaan, solemn now in commencing the formal negotiations that had required so much patience in preparation.

"A course of wisdom," answered Tori serenely. She touched Jase's wrist to signal his presentation. She knew how eloquently Jase could present a case. She also had reasonable confidence, based on experience, that she could convince bickering parties to accept a Consortium proposal, once proffered.

The trained voice of the Sesserda adept began with the subtle impact of a whisper, powerful without obvious force. "The fundamental dictum of Sesserda Truth is to respect creation," said Jase, his expression mild and compassionate, though relanine glowed like iridescent fire from his eyes. Jase projected the seraphic manner of a benevolent aesthete, electrified by the passion of unswerving conviction. "To enact that respect demands fulfillment of the proper purpose of each individual and corporate entity within the whole tapestry of the universal Truth." With quick, serpentine gestures, Jase drew the Sesserda symbol of Truth-that-must-be in the cold air. Tori doubted that any of the Alari possessed even her rudimentary knowledge of Sesserda symbolism, but she also knew the capacity of such Sesserda gestures to exert strong impact on the subconscious. "Each of us has the ability to choose a personal course," continued Jase, his voice rising gradually, "either in support or in denial of Truth. None of us can predict the full extent of the consequences of any instance of denial, but the entire body of creation suffers for *each* such decision." The slightest suggestion of a smile teased the corner of Jase's thin mouth. "My lady and I have come here, at the request of your elders, to aid the great Alari people in the process of discerning Truth and following it."

Within a microspan after Jase began to speak, Tori realized how minimal would be the remaining efforts required of her among the Alari. She had worked hard to bring the Alari to the meeting, but this was Jase's moment to conquer. Wielding the persuasiveness of his absolute faith in Sesserda judgment, Jase launched a quiet, comprehensive history of Alari feuds, their devastating effects, and each needless *wrongness* that had caused such feuds to exist. He waved his Sesserda reasoning as a banner of hope above a field of past futility. The Alari with their powerful emotions were particularly susceptible to Jase's brand of influence. Tori often wondered why he even bothered to bring her on such missions, though he always insisted that her presence enabled him to better fulfill his own proper Sesserda purpose.

Tori envied Jase's fluent use of the difficult Alari language, though not the relanine addiction that gave him such unnatural control of his vocal equipment. She could follow his speech easily enough, having been educated by the best combinations of Escolari teaching skills and Ilanovi memorization techniques, but her own few, careful confirmations of his major points sounded coarse and harsh to her. Jase made the language sing.

The meeting room was much colder than the smokehouse, but its languid air was equally perfumed and seductive. Abetted by Jase's lyrical voice, his spell became truly hypnotic. Even Tori began to yield to the spell of his conviction. She knew that Alari already lived well by most standards, but she could feel the spread of belief: Only the wisdom of the Calongi's Sesserda Truth could salvage the Alari from disaster.

"Taluu hai vauu!" shouted an enthused Alari. "The man speaks wisdom!" The cry became a chant, as compelling as the man who inspired it.

As Tori felt herself joining the Alari rapture instead of guiding it, she scolded herself, *Stop it! You know Jase too well to be captivated by his insidious Sesserda methods of persuasion.*

She took pride in her ability to distinguish between the man and his arts. She had not always been so immune to the calculated, often imperceptible methods that enabled Sesserda adepts to perform their duties as Inquisitors. Jase had, after all, performed the final Inquisition against her less than four spans earlier. Despite the rare Tiva disorder that defended her from many Sesserda techniques, Jase had dissected her ably enough to overcome her loathing of Inquisitors and insinuate himself into her life on a sustained basis.

"Vauul. Slihuulma nivu la," said Tori, demanding wisdom of the Alari and urging them to ratify the proposed accord. She pulled the treaty rod from the fire and pressed the cool, leather-guarded hilt into Hamtuloaan's hands. The elder gripped the rod firmly and scraped his claws down the length of heated metal, etching his own mark. Hamtuloaan inserted the rod back into the flames.

"Vauul," echoed Jase, and there was a glint of approval in his uncanny eyes as a second elder retrieved the rod, adding a tribal mark. Four of the five tribes marked the rod without hesitation. The chant rolled and swelled with deep Alari voices, proud and fierce.

The rod lay again in the crackling fire, awaiting the final mark that would make law of the trade accord. The last of the tribal elders stared at the rod, but she did not touch it. Tori pushed free of the hassock and Jase. Her robe dragged heavily, but she circled the fire to kneel behind the unrelenting elder. "What do you fear, Sallauuon?" asked Tori in the elder woman's ear.

Sallauuon rotated her head to gaze at Tori from

solemn amber eyes. "Is it wisdom?" asked the elder. "Or is it your man's verbal trickery?"

Tori met the Alari's stare of challenge and answered honestly, "It is both. The man's skills are Calongi-trained and accordingly formidable." With considerably less truthfulness, Tori added, "Would I keep a man of no use to me?"

The daunting sound of Alari laughter rumbled from Sallauuon's throat. The elder straightened her hunched back, turned to the fire and reached for the treaty rod. She scraped her claws down its length and passed the completed treaty into Tori's hands. Tori accepted with a diplomatic smile.

The other Alari wept their approval, and they brought forth flasks of sweet liquor. Resuming her original place at the fire, Tori rested the rod across her lap, though she clung to it possessively. When Hamtuloaan pressed her to take a flask, she freed the rod with reluctance. Hamtuloaan, well involved in the process of celebration, did not notice Tori's hesitation.

Jase whispered with Sesserda-trained selectivity, his words reaching only Tori, "The rod isn't going anywhere without you."

Tori breathed her reply, confident that no one but Jase could hear her above the noise of Alari song and laughter, "Tell me that after we've been paid."

"Mercenary," accused Jase softly. "The commission is not the reason for what we do."

Tori took one swallow of the thick Alari liquor and felt it burn its way inside her. She fought the giddiness that even a sip of the potent brew induced. "I am not a Sesserda adherent. If I left the finances to you, we'd never be paid for half of our jobs."

"I was not exactly starving before I met you."

"And you didn't have a clue to how much you actually owned—or were owed."

"I still don't." He took the flask from her, drank deeply and returned it to her. Relanine made him almost invulnerable to intoxication, as well as to more damaging forms of poisoning. "Neither do you."

"I know what I own, and I know what we've earned

together." The amount that Consortium peoples were willing to pay for non-Calongi diplomacy still astonished her. She had never imagined that she could be so highly valued for *proper,* Consortium-approved work. "You can tend your own personal affairs. I'm your partner, not your keeper."

"The Alari would dispute that statement."

To hide a smirk, she took another swallow from the flask. The honeyed flavor seemed to thicken on her tongue. "If I keep drinking until the Alari finish celebrating, I shall be sick for millispans." She thrust the flask into Jase's hands. "Finish it, please. The Alari won't notice if I drink from an empty flask."

"They won't mind such a small slight," he agreed with a twisting of his smile, "as long as we seem to share the spirit of this night's *kanuukihan.*"

She searched her liquor-blurred memory for the meaning of the Alari word. "Rejoicing?" she asked.

"The rejoicing of unity with one's tribe."

"Kanuukihan," she murmured and nestled obligingly into the curve of Jase's arm. Hamtuloaan, glancing toward her, commended her and her tribe for their joint wisdom. Tori accepted the tribute with a dazzling smile. In the spirit of kanuukihan, she even felt at peace with Jase.

CHAPTER 7

Fugitive

Strong desert winds beset most of the habitable regions of Rendl's single southern continent, despite ongoing Network programs to tame the unruly environment. Katerin's skin burned from the parching effect of the short walk between classroom and library. She had not yet accustomed herself to the need to carry salve constantly as defense against the unpredictable windstorms, and she did not yet know any of her students well enough to feel comfortable requesting a loan. She had hoped to use her lunch hour to return to the apartment and collect the precious balm, but Dr. Gurressy had insisted that she complete the revisions to his report before his afternoon presentation to the board.

She tasted the grit that the wind had forced into her mouth, and she hoped that Jove Gurressy suffered similar discomfort. As his laboratory assistant, her duties did not properly include correcting his research, and his demands on her time exceeded all reasonableness. His studies of the chemistry of emotion did not even enhance her own research, being only peripherally relevant in the general sense and (to her view) naive in the specifics.

She reminded herself of the rules of tolerance that she had implemented in several of her behavioral algorithms to improve cooperation among her students, but Gurressy's condescension still grated. Yesterday, she had even asked Network to exercise one of her own best algorithms on her to improve her patience. The exercise had failed, as usual, because she understood the algorithm too thoroughly to benefit from its application.

Irritably, Katerin corrected another of Gurressy's equations. If he had been her student, she would have failed him. Dr. Katerin Merel, former professor of mathematical psychology at one of Network's most prestigious universities, would have ensured that such a flawed practician found no opportunity to spread his erroneous theories. She would have loved to fling her credentials in his narrow, unimaginative face and denounce him formally to Network. However, as Kate Welor, laboratory assistant at Rendl's Southsand University, she did not even dare to tell him that his particular theory regarding the chemical mechanisms of aggressive behavior had been evaluated thoroughly and debunked a decade earlier. She needed to find a subtle way to direct him to the correct Network files.

"Any competent researcher would have consulted Network on his own initiative," she muttered to herself, then glanced frantically at her surroundings to see if anyone had heard her. Only one other library station was occupied, and that young student was immersed in conversation with Network. Katerin's nerves quieted slightly. Even if Network had recorded her unwise, unguarded comment, the words could be construed as an ordinary complaint of an ordinary underling assigned to an unwelcome task during her lunch hour. More alarming to Katerin was the fact that she had spoken aloud at all. She could not afford to allow her frustrations with her position to make her careless, especially when Quin was away.

Quin's absence always frayed Katerin's vulnerable nerves. Because her famous father, Jonathan Terry, had long ago defied Andrew Caragen, and Katerin had finally learned of that truth, she had metamorphosed from respected research professor to Category 1 enemy of Network's Council Governor. She could not survive in Network without reliance on Quin's peculiar talents for topological manipulations. She always dreaded that Caragen would discover her when Quin was not available to whisk her into a new identity, though she knew that Quin left her only when he felt confident of her immediate safety.

Katerin practiced some of her specialty's most manipulative techniques to protect Quin from knowledge of how deeply she feared being without him. She was sure that if he ever realized the scope of her anxieties, he would not leave her again—until the strain of such confinement split them irrevocably. She wished that she could prevent herself from analyzing her husband with the same intensity that made her behavioral algorithms so valued by Network. She could not avoid recognizing the fragility of her relationship with Quin. Any relationship, founded on such disparate skills and backgrounds, entangled by unwanted dependencies and the Council Governor's perpetual harassment, must surely founder eventually.

Katerin shivered, though the gust that touched her blew hot from Rendl's arid rock lands. From practiced caution, she looked toward the door to see whose entrance had admitted the blast of wind. A lanky man with skin as wind-reddened as Katerin's met her stare. With such untreated skin, he could not be a native. He smiled at her, but the smile of the stranger chilled her. Once, she would have viewed him as merely an annoying admirer. She recognized her descent into paranoia but did not fight it. "End session," she murmured to Network and thrust her notes into her briefcase. By the time the stranger had taken two steps into the room, she had scurried past the end workstation and exited by way of the rear office suite. One clerk questioned her unauthorized presence brusquely, but Katerin did not stay to give acknowledgment.

***

Quin followed the energy patterns from Marrach's Siathan home to the planet Rendl, exerting his Power's strong control almost without conscious effort. In the formless space that connected the points topologically, Quin's Power carried him deftly among the brilliant, shifting strands of other Powers, composed variously of natural phenomena, Network devices, or the rare traces of kindred wizards, assigned like Quin to study

Network on behalf of the Infortiare of Serii. He had become accustomed to such travel, and the vastness and the deadly complexity of energy patterns seemed too familiar to inspire deep concern. The magnitude of what he did only daunted him on rare occasions—chiefly when he sat in some comfortable Hamley manor room, watching his myriad cousins scampering across the lush Hamley estates and contemplating how unexpectedly far he had journeyed from his Hamley origins. His family never questioned him regarding his duties as a wizard of Ixaxis, because wizards were viewed with varying degrees of awe and outright terror even in tolerant Hamley. Most of his siblings and cousins still teased him and laughed with him, but even those who continued to exchange the old, childish pranks with him recognized that he had outgrown them in ways that they would never comprehend. Quin seldom visited Hamley for long.

Rendl was a recently developed, sparsely populated Network planet, its environment reasonably benign but too clearly artificial to appeal to Quin. Though most of the populace cursed the windstorms, which constituted the one natural quirk of weather that Network had yet to tame, Quin actually enjoyed their ferocious energy more than the bland intervals of stillness. The small Southsand University had little prestige, limited resources, and a hint of desperation that made its faculty and students pitifully eager to accept any willing recruits. Quin had enjoyed establishing the Network identity that made him a Rendl student of unpromising capabilities and indefinite intentions; he delighted in playing the fool.

He derived considerably less satisfaction from the identity that he had prepared for Katerin. Reducing Katerin's professional status from professor at Network's finest university to Southsand laboratory assistant irked him, because he knew how much the constrained resources impeded her private research. She did not complain—not aloud. She continued to develop algorithms of mathematical psychology, though she no longer dared to publish them. She had little time for her own work, since she could never bring herself to shirk the duties that Southsand—and its predecessors in this variable life as a fugitive from the Council Governor—imposed.

The Southsand professors for whom she worked took advantage of her, and they did not even appreciate how far her abilities exceeded their own, even in a field that was not her specialty. Quin derived a reflected pride in observing the difference she had made in her students. Some of the students had actually begun to believe in their capacity to learn from another human as well as from Network. Katerin attributed her success to her ability to teach by Network's own educational algorithms, based on her intimate knowledge of intelligence science and mathematical psychology. Quin liked to retort that Network's success was simply a pallid reflection of her own capabilities, Network's methods being no better than the algorithms that she had helped create. Katerin seldom answered his retort, but his Power knew that she took comfort from his reassurance.

Quin joined the pattern that emerged into Rendl Transfer Port Seven, and he smiled at the bored attendant who monitored the arrivals. The Rendl sky was pale with dust, the dry air just harsh enough to burn eyes and to parch skin. Quin crossed the green expanse of synthetic lawn, nodding at many acquaintances from the school, but he did not pause to speak to any of those who returned his greeting. He always tried to give himself time between *Quin* and the pretenses of his various Network identities. Even Katerin's company sometimes made the process of deception more difficult to sustain, for she could tempt him to relax into a measure of honesty. She guarded herself well behind a mildly alarming facade of chill sophistication. They both knew the dangers of discovery.

"I'm too scatterbrained for this life," muttered Quin to himself, but he grinned, because he could not imagine returning to the simpler past.

He walked the distance to the apartment that he shared with Katerin, for the Rendl trams made him slightly claustrophobic. The distance was far enough to inspire a sigh for the uniform blandness of Rendl scenery: Narrow box houses, each an inoffensive shade of beige, were situated at regular intervals among neatly rectangular plots of synthetic lawn and pale brown walkways. Rendl was reasonably comfortable, efficient, and impersonal. It represented Network's interpretation of an adequate human lifestyle. More was luxury; less was not acknowledged as a possibility for any conscientious Network citizen of a world like Rendl.

Network greeted Quin as he approached his housing unit. "Good evening, Welor."

"Good evening, Network," replied Quin evenly. He wished that he dared disconnect Network's access to the entire complex, but maintaining a false daily history for the interior of a single apartment was sufficiently time-consuming and dangerous. Quin wondered idly if he would be able to sustain his alphabetical progression of names when the time came to abandon the Rendl identities. He could concoct "x" names easily enough, but uniqueness was not a desirable trait for fugitives. Even maintaining the alphabetical theme comprised a dangerous conceit. "Is my wife home?" asked Quin, testing the answer for himself and prodding Network to respond inaccurately.

"No, Welor," replied Network dutifully. Quin smiled, satisfied by the first test's results.

Quin's Power manipulated local Network nodes cautiously, ensuring that none of the trigger files had been breached, none of the bypassed connections detected. Without deviation, Quin followed the explicit procedure that Katerin's multitalented father, Dr. Jonathan Terry, had devised to evaluate security from the omnipresent Network sensors: He confirmed the rerouting of sensor data into harmless dead ends, replaced by Quin's subtly randomized variant of Jon Terry's programmed data strings, safely misleading fodder for Network storage and analysis. He verified safety triggers, redundant circuitry, and alarm algorithms. With the exception of the most benign house-

keeping functions, all of the normal Network procedures were effectively compromised. A programmed
self-destruct of the apartment's entire automated infrastructure, to be triggered in the event that critical data
actually breached the secure barrier, provided additional safeguard against detection. With such elaborate
precautions in place, the interior of that singularly
guarded apartment was as safe from Network prying as
the most desolate wilderness of Quin's homeworld, but
Quin breathed much more easily upon completing his
comprehensive inspection by Power. Quin always felt
uncomfortable leaving Katerin alone in Network, despite the methods and mechanisms that she and her father had developed to protect her in Quin's absence.
Quin still trusted his own Power above any Network
product.

Katerin still preferred Network to Serii, familiar
Network technology to ill-defined Seriin Power, even
though Network had tried to destroy her, and Power
kept her alive. Quin understood her reasons; he had
equal trouble accepting the perspective of Network
completely, though he had lived as a Network citizen
for most of the past three years. He could employ rules
of Network science, but they fit uncomfortably beside
the regimens of Ixaxin training that alone accommo-
dated his Power as a reality. Lady Rhianna had once remarked that the entire Terry family suffered a serious
conflict of interests concerning Ixaxin wizards: Emotional attachment, gratitude, and the respect of mutual
need barely superseded a very real desire to dissect an
Immortal wizard and study Power's nature by Network
techniques. Quin had agreed ruefully. Katerin analyzed
him indefatigably.

He entered the apartment, his Power still monitoring
Network's patterns. Katerin, engulfed in a lilac smock
that had always been too large for her, sat at the
spindly dining table. Utterly abstracted, she twisted a
tumbled length of her pale hair with a thin, nervous
hand. She raised her head from the data sheets that she
was correcting for struggling Rendl students. Her smile
blossomed, immediate and brilliant. Her midnight blue

eyes lost their remoteness and welcomed him. The transformation from hard austerity to approachable loveliness still entranced Quin. He maintained only a cautious wisp of contact with Network, for he much preferred to concentrate on his golden Katerin.

Assuring each other of respective well-being by a thoroughly enjoyable mutual inspection, Quin concluded that she had worried away another layer of her fragile flesh. Nonetheless, he grinned at her and retrieved the scattered data sheets. "Where have you been?" asked Katerin, recognizing the underlying restlessness in his mood.

"Siatha," he replied openly, confident that Network would hear and see an entirely different conversation.

He felt Katerin's brief shudder, though she controlled her reaction well. She trusted less readily than Quin in the security of the apartment, and her distaste for the implications of Quin's answer amplified her usual nervousness. "Why?" she asked simply.

"Why are you so suspicious of my motives, my lady?"

She brushed a sun-gilded curl from his face. As an amateur artist, she had always claimed an admiration for the angles of bone and sinew that composed him. "You haven't shown this much excitement since we arrived on Rendl. You hate this planet. It's safe, unimaginative, and uninspiring. You exhausted all its attractions the first day."

"Not all. You're here."

She took the data sheets from his hands, tapping the data into order. "I made a commitment to this university." She bit her lip, before adding in quiet defiance of her own fears, ". . . albeit under false pretenses."

"I'm not complaining."

"No, but you're chafing from boredom, because I'm preoccupied, and you enrolled yourself in such an undemanding curriculum."

To Quin, her careful description of his role betrayed her instinctive guard against Network observation. Quin kneaded her tensed shoulders. "You need not be so circumspect, my lady. Network is currently record-

ing an unremarkable, unrevealing scene of uncommunicative domesticity, minimally related to reality."

She flashed a weak smile at him. "I'm just feeling
beset by the dregs of a long day."

"Worse than usual?"

"No, it's only my usual overreactions to petty grievances. I'm fine, Quin." Quin felt her forcibly suppress
her worries to speak his name, but he did not pry
deeper. "What did you do in your travels that has
revived you so spectacularly?"

"I ate spice loaf."

"At the Healers' house?" Even without concerns about Network observation, Katerin had difficulty naming Marrach. She preferred his Healer
name, Suleifas, but she could not entirely disassociate
her memories of his darker past in service to Andrew
Caragen.

Quin nodded, gentling Katerin's surge of fear with a
wisp of Power. "Jeni was in Revgaenian." And Jeni's
absence from that particular Healers' house implied
that Quin had talked to Marrach, of course, but the
name was left unsaid.

"What did you discuss?"

"The Consortium."

Her initial startlement yielded immediately to a concern far more substantial and demanding than excessive dread of being heard. She pulled away from
his hands and faced him, wielding his name with the
stern strength that actual danger summoned from her.
"Quin. . . ."

"We were discussing the Mirlai, and the conversation just migrated," he said somewhat defensively.
"The Consortium exists, Katerin. We can't ignore it
forever."

"Most Network citizens ignore it quite happily."

"You and I are far from being ordinary Network citizens," replied Quin, a rare solemnity clouding his gray
eyes. His Power touched and amplified every safeguard against Network prying, assuaging his own
brand of paranoia. "I have a duty to my Infortiare, to
my world, to your parents' world of Neoterra, even to

the Healers' world of Siatha. I achieved a standoff with Caragen: He doesn't dare to touch me or mine, but I don't dare to eliminate him either." Having indulged his momentary need to justify himself, Quin sighed, "You'll be pleased to know that the Healer also warned me against studying the Consortium. He maintains that Caragen would try to set the Consortium against us, given the slightest opportunity."

"Believe him," said Katerin grimly.

"I do, and that is why I am beginning to suspect that Power's instinct guided my *idle* choice of conversation. Under the circumstances, I think that Council Governor Caragen will eventually manufacture the opportunity he desires, unless we anticipate him. I need to understand what such a confrontation might mean to us, since Caragen has an unpleasant talent for such mischief." Quin astonished himself with his own quick answer, because he had not formulated such a purpose until that moment. He had merely been following a course that his Power told him was right, hoping to discover some undefinable treasure of refuge or understanding. Quin's facile grin returned, and the lightening of his mood was real. "Haven't you ever wanted to meet a Calongi?"

A flare of temper eradicated the last of her restraint of speech. "I'm not accustomed to meeting 'wizards' yet, and I'm married to one."

"Maybe you need to spend more time with Lady Rhianna."

Katerin glared at him. "Quin Hamley, I do not intend to be stashed in some corner of your Infortiare's Tower for safekeeping, while you provoke the Consortium. I was not raised to be a cloistered Seriin noblewoman, devoting my entire life to courtly gossip about the latest scandals of Tulea."

"Does Lady Rhianna dur Ixaxis strike you as cloistered or gossipy? If you told her you wanted a better understanding of Power, she would work you harder than the strictest Network university . . ."

"Your Lady Rhianna only escapes cloistering because she is a wizardess with the Power to enact her own will."

". . . and I have no intention of provoking anyone."

"Except me?"

Quin's grin broadened. "I had a rather different form of provocation in mind for you, my lady."

His caress, abetted by Power, coaxed a smile from Katerin, though her tone remained stern. "And what will you do when next you leave my sight? Travel the topologies into a Calongi's hall of inquisition?"

"Do they have halls of inquisition?" asked Quin curiously, stilling his hands upon his wife's thin shoulders.

"Inquisition is their method of administering justice. They must perform their inquisitions somewhere."

"Inquisition does have an unpleasant sound to it," mused Quin. "I suppose I *would* prefer to avoid its vicinity."

Katerin's eyes fixed severely upon him. "Then avoid the Calongi." Quin nodded vaguely. "Quin, you barely survived your battle with Caragen. . . ."

"I remember," he answered tersely. He knew, far better than Katerin, how nearly he had lost himself among the topological twines of traps of the Taormin's complex energies. If the Mirlai had not chosen to tend him, he would have died—or become like Lord Venkarel, pure Immortal Power bereft of its living vessel. Neither death nor ghostly half-life appealed to Quin at all.

His unusual grimness silenced his wife, and she touched him in a mute apology. He responded in kind. Some topics were best left unverbalized between them, regardless of Network observation or its lack.

He proceeded to distract Katerin, or she distracted him. Quin was glad enough to push aside all that he had gathered and deduced about the Consortium—for the moment. His Power would not allow him to abandon his *curiosity*. His Power would always insist on defending itself, even from a danger that Quin could barely discern.

With the morning, the blue-white light of Rendl's

harsh sun streaked the partitioned segment that formed the small apartment's bedroom. The utilitarian beige and brown of a minimally equipped Network living unit looked tired. The warmth of Katerin pressed reassuringly against Quin's back, but he frowned at the wall, where Network sensors maintained their endlessly efficient vigil in circles of futility. Network waited only to serve its citizen's needs, and Quin sometimes enjoyed Network's comforts more than he hated its intrusiveness. This was not such a morning. He awoke hating even the simple, nonthreatening Network functions that would soon activate solely to ease his life. Beyond the small safety of the carefully protected apartment, he felt Network in all the menace of its chief manipulator, Council Governor Andrew Caragen, and Quin wished that he were callous enough to kill Caragen instead of merely taunting him with reminders of Power.

"The Sorcerer Kings must have been created in his conscienceless image," hissed Quin in quiet frustration.

"Shall I prepare your breakfast?" asked Network, solicitously duplicating Quin's whispered level of speech.

"Not until we're both awake," grunted Quin into the pillow.

Katerin murmured, "I am awake. Yes, Network, prepare our standard breakfast." She ran her hands down Quin's back, then began to knead away the tension. She did not question him, not yet.

Quin pressed his Power against Network, completing the mental gesture of confirmation that had become almost automatic. "Network's surveillance of us remains compromised—as ever," he told Katerin.

"You're upset this morning. I hope that means your interest of yesterday has waned in the light of good sense."

"It's not our *ongoing* difference of opinion that's troubling me at the moment."

Anxiety wrapped its familiar veil around her. Quin regretted the need to let her suffer its stifling presence.

"Then what is bothering you?" she asked with brittle care.

"Caragen. The Consortium. Something. My Power senses danger, but I don't have sufficient knowledge to clarify the danger's form. I need to talk to the Infortiare." He twisted enough to see Katerin's frown without facing her. "I'll take you to Serii or to Neoterra." He hoped she would choose Serii, but after yesterday's discussion, he knew he had to leave the choice to her. He tried to forestall argument with urgency. "We can't stay here any longer."

"You said that the apartment is still secure."

"You know there are other, more insidious means of exposure. We do not exist solely inside the confines of this minor fortress."

"We've been here less than two months. Can Caragen have located us already?" asked Katerin with the icy calm that masked her deepest fears.

"Not quite yet," replied Quin. He rolled over and pulled Katerin against him, just holding her to ease the fear that he understood too well. "Soon, I think. Tomorrow or the next day. Network is trying to probe our identity files. Your father's traps have snared two attempts already. I'm diverting the energies of another probe right now."

"Network probes identity files constantly. That's why my father set the traps."

"This feels more serious. Something is disturbing my Power beyond the usual annoyances of Network life."

"Did you sense this disturbance yesterday?"

"No." He shrugged, reconsidering. "Perhaps. Sometimes it's hard to know what Power senses in advance of conscious thought." He sighed, feeling Katerin's inward recoil from memories of her haunted past and knowing that he could not spare her. "I can't leave you here alone under these conditions, and I must go to Serii. Pack whatever we can't leave."

"He'll never stop searching for us, will he?" asked Katerin, but she had already set aside the first moment of alarm. She hated this routine abandonment of job, friends, and life. No matter how practiced she became at the role of fugitive, she could not escape the cycle of vain regrets for all she had lost, despite the asylum that was Quin.

"Caragen is a stubborn man."

"And he's not a fool," said Katerin bitterly. She rested her face against Quin's shoulder. "He knows you're a threat to him."

"As long as he remembers the magnitude of the threat, he's not likely to confront us directly." *But he tracks us,* added Quin in grim comment to himself, *and he intends to eliminate me the moment he thinks he has a chance.*

"How often can we change identities, Quin, before some past acquaintance recognizes us?" The problem was small relative to the prospect of Caragen's vengeance, but it was manageable and therefore a source of ironic comfort. It was a topic that Katerin and Quin discussed each time they prepared to move. The discussion had become almost a ritual between them.

"As long as we choose our situations carefully, we should be able to continue name-shifting for years. By that time, no one will recognize us if we start the sequence anew."

"They may not recognize me," said Katerin, "but how much will an Immortal wizard have changed?" She traced the pale stubble along Quin's jaw. His hair was brown, but his beard was nearly blond. Its pallor facilitated his common pose of boyishness. "What is the expected life span of an Ixaxin Immortal, Quin?"

This was not the normal course of the ritual discussion, and it made Quin push his wife to arm's length in order to study her with an attempted measure of dispassion. She had never questioned him excessively regarding either wizard's skills or Immortal expectations. He wondered at her reasons for raising the subject now. She had guarded her expression, and it told him nothing; however, Katerin did little without calculated reason. "Do you think I'm using Caragen as an excuse to 'cloister' you, so I can investigate the Consortium without telling you?"

"I think I trust you more than that."

The indefinite quality of Katerin's answer troubled him. "Does the idea of going to Serii bother you so much?" he asked.

Her smile held no humor. "Yes. Always. Whether your people are called 'wizards' or 'Immortals' or genetically engineered humans with unusual mental skills and enduring constitutions, that part of you is alien to me. I dislike being bombarded with the strangeness of your planet."

"And its barbarism," murmured Quin.

"It is an appallingly primitive, feudal society, but that is not what bothers me most. Each time you leave me there, even briefly, I wonder if you'll ever return to me. On your world, I am utterly helpless and dependent, and that is a hateful feeling."

"I would never abandon you, Katerin."

"Not by conscious choice."

"I'll take you to Neoterra instead."

"The Neoterra colony can barely sustain itself. They don't need the burden of a guest."

"Your parents do not consider you a burden."

"No," agreed Katerin. "But they always know that I'll leave again as soon as you return for me, and it grieves them, just as their sense of past guilt for my situation grieves them, though they won't admit either hurt. I stay long enough to build their hopes but not long enough to be productive within the colony, and I consume their precious resources. I remind them of what all of us have lost, because my temper eventually discloses the bitterness that still lurks inside me. No, don't inflict me on Neoterra again." Her laughter was hard and cold. "I would prefer to stay with you, until you deem Network safe enough for me to be left unsupervised by Power once more."

"Katerin," sighed Quin, wishing her indefatigable, often impenetrable logic did not make him feel so helpless. He knew how much more helpless she could make herself feel.

"You never answered my question about a wizard's life span."

When she pushed herself into this hardness of mood, fighting her only wearied them both. She had long cultivated the hardness as a defense against fear, and Quin hated it, but he recognized its necessity for her. He hissed his frustration, and he answered reluctantly, "The life span tends to vary with the magnitude of the Power." He swung his feet to the floor, withdrawing from his wife to stare fixedly at the unadorned wall. "Mine is a major Power, amplified by unusual training and use of the Taormin to master topological travel. If I am not killed by design or accident, I expect to live for several hundred years—or more. Our histories have few useful examples, since major Powers tend to die violently, long before attaining old age. The Sorcerer King, Horlach, lived for several millennia, if you consider a man without physical form 'alive.' "

"How old is your Infortiare?"

"Lady Rhianna is a little younger than your father, I think."

"My father is over a hundred in Network years. He wears his age well, but your cousin, the Infortiare, could be twenty."

"And to a Network citizen, the average thirty-year-old peasant of my world would look to be ninety or more. Life spans differ, Katerin. Lifestyles differ. How long do C-humans live?" Quin had not meant to ask aloud, but the question seemed to bubble from him irrepressibly.

Katerin answered thoughtfully, "I have no idea." She climbed from the bed, wrapped only in the silk of her ash-blond hair. Quin never ceased to marvel that he was husband to so much beauty, shrewd insight, and disciplined intelligence. "Longer than Network citizens, I should think. The Consortium's medical sciences are reputedly very fine."

"Why did you manipulate me into asking that question?" demanded Quin, suddenly suspicious of his wife, who had designed far too many of Network's invasive algorithms of mathematical psychology.

Katerin smiled slightly. "Sometimes I need to remind myself that you're not omniscient." She covered herself with a robe of white velour. "I believe that your Power is warning you, but I'm not sure it's warning you against Caragen on this particular occasion."

"Are you suggesting that we stay here until we're sure?"

"No! I'm not sure Caragen hasn't found us."

"You can be a very frustrating woman."

"I think it's time you let Network finish preparing our breakfast."

Quin continued to stare at her. "How long do Calongi live?" he asked, certain that this was the question that Katerin had sought to inspire from him.

"The expected Calongi life span is probably much longer than yours, my dear Immortal husband."

"Are you trying to make me feel humble?"

"I'm trying to make sure you respect the dangers of the Consortium before you tackle it as well as all of Network. The Calongi are not human. They do not share our weaknesses. They do not share *your* weaknesses."

"They do not share my strengths either."

"Your strengths may be meaningless against Calongi. You don't know, and you can't know without making yourself and your world vulnerable to them. If they are as honorable as they pretend, you have nothing to lose by confronting them, but trusting the Calongi requires a long leap of faith. You know how far you extended yourself to impress Caragen." She did not need to pursue the reminder; issuing it twice in as many days provided sufficient emphasis of her concern. "How do you suppose the Calongi acquired his respect?"

"Hearsay?" asked Quin wryly. He had expected Katerin to disapprove of his interest in the Consortium. He did not expect her to provide him with specific reasons. Like the rest of the Terry family, Katerin retained many elements of Network conditioning, including anti-alien prejudice.

"Does the Council Governor seem like a man who would accept such paltry evidence?"

"No," agreed Quin. "Council Governor Caragen demands a lot of convincing."

"Then stop asking foolish questions," she snapped as sharply as in their early, uneasy relationship.

Throughout Quin's irrepressible life, many people had called him a fool, and he had usually relished the title—but not from Katerin, who generally knew better. Her quick, unexpected condemnation stung more than Quin wanted to admit. The pressure of another abrupt change of home did not suffice to explain her bristling mood against him personally.

Her condemnation did nothing to discourage Quin's interest in the Consortium. If anything, Katerin's abrupt disapproval made a deeper understanding of the Consortium seem that much more compelling to Quin. Under normal circumstances, Katerin had learned to appreciate Quin's most deliberate nonsense.

The incident only confirmed to Quin that he could not trust Katerin's judgment in matters of severe Network prejudice. Lady Rhianna was more likely to be objective—or biased in Quin's favor, since he was the Infortiare's primary source of information about Network subjects. However, if Lady Rhianna ordered him to staunch his flow of curiosity, he would feel compelled by wizard's vows to obey.

While Katerin ate fruit and toast, Quin chewed on his knuckle in glum contemplation. He did not share either her aptitude or her interest in behavioral analysis, least of all in regard to his own motives, but he struggled to assess himself honestly. He did not doubt his Power's perception of growing danger, but he could not point to any of the usual strong evidence of Network encroachment. In fact, Katerin's argument—linking the sense of danger to yesterday's unexpected turn of conversation with Marrach—found support in Quin's ancillary compulsion to visit the Nilson spaceport. Quin did not know if Power's instincts or contrariness prodded him. He wanted to believe that he had outgrown the impish need to defy orders and expectations. He could rationalize his interest in Nilson as a defensive measure easily enough.

He was also honest enough to realize that his capricious curiosity could easily muddle his motives. From Quin's perspective, the Consortium held particular fascination simply because it was alien. Learning all that Network could teach would take more years than even an Immortal wizard of Ixaxis liked to contemplate, and the frequent need to shift Network identities did not speed the process; but the wonders of Network had become familiar to Quin in the four years since he had first left home in all its guises: the wizards' school at Ixaxis, his family's estate at Hamley, and all the varied domains of his native country of Serii. Certainly, Network had countless secrets yet to be learned by the son of Serii's superstitious, agrarian society, but the excitement had begun to wane when the process of Network learning became so familiar. Quin had never had much patience for studying subjects that demanded too little of his imagination.

The dangers of Consortium contact, as referenced by the vast memory resources of Network, were never presented in specific terms, which made Quin wonder if even Network's shrewd Council Governor possessed much knowledge of his alien rivals. It *was* possible that Caragen merely kept such information to himself: Quin had witnessed enough maneuverings of Network's Council Governor to be suspicious of every "fact" that Network's inescapable computers conveyed. Quin also knew how thoroughly Network indoctrinated its citizens with ideas of Caragen's choosing. Information against the Consortium, even if manufactured, seemed like something that Caragen would want to advertise, unless the Council Governor really did fear to offend the Calongi.

Though Quin would have made no such admission to Katerin or Marrach—or even Lady Rhianna, who could coax more honesty from Quin than anyone else—Quin confessed to himself that his occasional forays into self-contemplation achieved little but the transformation of curiosity into obsession. His imagination had already begun to surge past his doubts. His tentative interest could easily expand into a hunger to see and explore Consortium worlds and races, even if they failed to offer the refuge that he sought for Katerin. Unfettered ideas spiraled in his mind, fashioning a longing to meet a Calongi, the species described by Network with unusual brevity as "rulers of the Consortium." Network's incessant anti-Consortium admonitions frustrated him. Network provided no official reason for its antagonistic stance except a stated need to maintain the purity of human independence.

Quin, being Quin, reasoned that he could hardly be expected to ignore the prospect of meeting the demons and dragons that comprised his concept of the Consortium's nonhuman members. He had absolutely no intention of ever abandoning his personal freedom, as Consortium membership purportedly demanded. He was, however, growing increasingly curious to know why half of humanity had chosen to accept the Calongi rule, and his Power seemed to support him via an urge to learn by following Marrach's reluctant advice to visit Nilson.

While Katerin finished breakfast in the silence of her own dark thoughts, Quin probed Network, exploiting the little known channels that Marrach had identified for him, but his foray did not even begin to satisfy him. The Consortium remained an enormous, impenetrable blank, and that apparent inaccessibility affected Quin as indelibly as a direct challenge. The Consortium discouraged its members from contact with nonmembers, such as Network's citizens. Since the Consortium also denied the science of topological transfer, the Consortium's control of its planetary resources was measurably more secure from a wizard's meddling than Network's. Quin could "borrow" Network destination coordinates from the Network computers, and he could evaluate the coordinates of any place or person that he could sense with focused Power. With the unsatisfactory exception of an open port such as Marrach had suggested, the Consortium remained inaccessible . . . which made it irresistible to Quin's imagination. He directed his thoughts deliberately toward the idea of examining the Consortium from a Nilson vantage point, and his Power shivered through him. Quin had often forced himself to resist his imagination, and every wizard disciplined his personal Power or died prematurely, but resisting both forces at once was neither easy nor—Quin suspected—wise.

By the time Katerin had dressed and begun to pack, Quin had made his decision. "Setting aside concerns about your parents' wishes, do you personally prefer to visit Serii or Neoterra?" he asked her quietly, bracing himself for her rebellion. He knew that he had no good argument to give her.

The storm did not come. Katerin shook her head, causing the golden silk of her hair to sway. The weariness and resignation of the gesture almost caused Quin to change his mind out of guilt. "Serii," answered Katerin, surprising him until she added, "Perhaps your Infortiare can dissuade you from your folly, if I explain the situation to her. I know better than to start a fight with a wizard." She resumed packing.

CHAPTER 8

Penitent

He was not a man who had ever trusted in things that smacked of mysticism. Even as Mirlai first claimed him as Healer, Marrach fought the dreams, denied the inner voices, and demanded that his own strong will resist the irresistible. Though the Mirlai won him, they did not strip him of his pragmatic views—which made the vision that much harder for him to accept.

He sat upright on the hard-packed, gritty soil that had been his bed for the night, pushing aside the woolen blanket that had covered him. Spring leaves tiled the roof above him. Early light dappled the scarlet blossoms of his walls, and the fragrance of his morning was clean. Songbirds filled his dawn with music.

Marrach might have chosen a softer pallet among those grateful charges whose ailments he had tended yesterday, but he had preferred to start the journey to the next home that would require him. He had never disliked solitude—and no Healer was ever quite alone. Now, however, he wished for human companionship. He missed Jeni. Even more, he wished her calm wisdom could take away the burden of images from the night.

His clothes were soaked, though the morning was cool, and his blanket had defended him from the dew. He shivered once, then impatiently stripped himself of his damp shirt. Rummaging in his leather pack for clean, dry clothes, he envisioned blood that flowed with pain across the stars. The vision would not leave him.

His Mirlai guardians warmed and loosened the hard knot of fear within him. His breath eased, but the com-

fort was short-lived. The vision of his dream settled
into his waking mind, and he began to understand its
indelibility.

He *needed* to understand more fully. Because his
need was real and deep, the Mirlai yielded him to an
old reflex of Caragen's making. Marrach tapped the
Network link embedded in his brain, and he analyzed
his vision by cold Network regimens.

When he had named his fears, he recovered the trappings of calm. He broke his fast on hard white cheese
and crusty bread. He drank water sparingly from his
flask. The river was an hour's hike behind him, and the
streams ran deep through these woods.

He watched a spotted mountain cat lick moisture
from the grasses. The animal, strong and ferocious
for all its compact size, observed him from slitted
topaz eyes but made no move against the Healer.
Even when Marrach arose, the cat neither retreated
nor attacked.

"Human predators are less wise than you," murmured Marrach to the cat. Tufted ears pricked forward
attentively. "We attack those who mean us no harm,
and we defeat ourselves." He bid the cat farewell, and
he began to walk where Mirlai led.

Vision and knowledge seethed inside him. The
stars bled, though the morning sky was clear and blue.
He had experienced true-dreams, which Mirlai sent
to guide their Chosen Healers. By such dreams, the
Mirlai spoke . . . usually in cryptic terms, for the Mirlai
world-view differed greatly from that of their corporeal
hosts. Mirlai did *not* speak of bleeding stars above
worlds they did not claim. And they did not dance with
frantic haste, as if above a dying man, when they sent a
troubling true-dream to a Healer—did they?

It could have been a dream, simply a dream, such as
might overtake any man who had overworked himself
through a season of too much fever and too many hard
healings. It could have been a buried memory: Rabh
Marrach had caused enough bloodshed in his life to fill
ten thousand nightmares. It could be nothing.

But it would not leave. And the Mirlai danced in a

golden storm of light, flinging frenzied sparks into the visible spectrum.

The Network linkage in Marrach's brain was real and unimpaired by Mirlai healing or Caragen's efforts to control it. There were too many ways to reach into Network, and Marrach knew more of them—more intimately—than even Caragen could boast. What Marrach could *not* do was sever the link completely; it was too much a part of him. For many months now, Caragen had not forced his mocking voice into that link, but Marrach always waited uneasily for that long-familiar voice to come. If Caragen had found another way to enter the mind of his former agent. . . . No, it could not be so. The Mirlai would not allow such a destructive force to afflict a Chosen Healer.

Marrach picked his way carefully up a steep incline, dislodging stones that skittered down to the woodland behind him. With shock, he observed that the sun had nearly reached its zenith. The vision—no, the *nightmare*—had stolen the morning from his consciousness. The sagging wooden shack of his next patient was before him. The shack clung precariously to the mountain, supported by the gnarled trees that grew against it.

The shack lacked a door, so Marrach knocked against the lintel. There was no answer, but Marrach entered, as Mirlai showed him what he would find. He was purely a Healer now, because he was needed.

The old man lay on a bare cot formed of leather straps upon a wooden frame. He was shriveled with thirst and filthy from neglect. Marrach lifted the man free of a tangle of soiled blankets. The man groaned with pain.

"I am Suleifas, Healer of Innisbeck and Montelier," announced Marrach gently. He soaked a clean kerchief and squeezed a few droplets between the old man's clenched teeth. The man, showing sudden strength, tried to knock Marrach's hands away from him. The Mirlai danced a lyrical waltz. The man grew peaceful.

Marrach untied his pouch of healing stones and selected two: an agate and a citrine. "Like you," said Marrach, placing the two stones on the old man's distended belly, "the agate drew its life from earth, and it knows you in your health. The citrine draws the illness from you."

The Healer bowed his head, becoming a living part of the healing process. The fever had gone too long unattended. It would not be vanquished easily.

The Mirlai fed their energies into the man who served them. They sustained their Healer Suleifas, and he in turn fed their life force to the old hermit. The hermit, though he had long lived in isolation, remained Siathan in heart and mind, and the Mirlai knew him as one of their own precious charges. The light rushed through the Healer, pouring forth to fill a need. The Healer felt a wrongness *here* and adjusted it, a darkness *here* and brightened it.

Satisfied but wearied, Marrach raised his head and recognized the onset of evening. His muscles responded stiffly. He found the pump outside, primed it and filled the cistern. Returning to the shack, he stripped the sodden clothing from the old man, sponged him into some semblance of cleanliness and wrapped him in a fresh blanket. Marrach build a wood fire in the stove, smiling ruefully at the primitive equipment on a world that Network still claimed—though the entire planet of Siatha was officially registered as the private property of Council Chancellor Rabhadur Marrach, Network code jxs73a25. That ironic title of ownership, which gave Siatha the protection of Rabh Marrach's dreaded reputation, had been one of the few material concessions that Marrach had extracted from his former employer. Marrach had secured his claim on threat of inverting Mirlai healing skills into a retaliatory plague against all of Network.

Neither Marrach nor Caragen could be sure if the threat was realizable.

After Marrach had prepared a broth and forced a portion of it into the old man, Marrach ate his own supper cold. He tasted none of it. He left his patient sleeping and went to stand beneath the cold, bright stars.

The precarious balance of euphoria and exhaustion, familiar indication of a well-made healing, toppled his

barriers of mental self-discipline. The vision returned
unbidden. Blood trickled slowly against the black of
night, blotting out each point of light, one by one, re-
placing clean light with a sickening, rusty glow. The
sky began to writhe with contortions that could break
the sanity of an unwary mind. Marrach forced himself
to watch unblinkingly. It was not the first time he had
observed the ghastly twisting of topological space, unshielded by the light curtains that protected Network
travelers from reality. This present view, he thought,
was not reality, but it was possibly more dangerous to
his own mental state.

He could almost see the strands that formed the patterns of topological space, as Quin had described them
to him: strands of fire and light, threads of deadly energy, seductive pathways that both circumvented and
bound all physical universes. Follow this burning pattern, and cross a galaxy; shift a thread, and move a
world through time. *How strange it must be,* he
thought, *to see infinite possibilities of reality, instead
of a single Truth.*

The agitation of the Mirlai ripped the vision from
him. Blackness met his eyes, which burned in agony.
He pressed his hands against sockets that felt emptied
to him. He collapsed to his knees, unable to see or hear,
unable even to scream.

It was no comfort to him that the Mirlai shared his
anguish, partook of it even more deeply than he. They
could not lift the horror from him because it was their
horror, their remorseless empathy that tortured their
Healer. They recognized a *need* deeper than survival,
and they could not answer it.

Their agony fed his agony/their agony/his agony.
The cycle would not break, because Healer was Mirlai,
and Mirlai was Healer. They *needed,* but there was
none to fill the Mirlai needs. That bond was lost with
the Adraki, and that wound, too, would never heal.

We turned away from Truth, they mourned, and the
Healer cried their searing grief aloud in a language that
was alien to him, though not unknown.

He repeated the alien words silently, tasting their

strangeness, and he remembered a voice that questioned him and stirred the pain of awareness. *Do you speak Consortium Basic?* asked the voice.

"Yes," he shouted, hoping that the answer would suffice to stop the inquisition.

But that thought, too, had writhed into falseness from the pain. The inquisition against the Mirlai had ended, and races had lived and died since that time. The Truth continued inviolate, because few plagues could afflict Sesserda Truth.

But the plague has come, and we have forsworn our species' proper gift. We, whose proper purpose was to heal, have abandoned Truth, and now there is no one to take away the blight that will destroy the peace.

Slowly, tears began to seep from Marrach's eyes, washing away grit and despair. The sky was whole, the stars intact. An old man needed tending.

Marrach returned to the hermit's shack. Marrach's mind sought Network. As Suleifas continued the healing of a feverish old man, Rabh Marrach searched for answers to a vision that he did not want to believe.

CHAPTER 9

Aspirant

The pistons hammered, ringing and ringing in Saschy's ears, until she wondered if she alone found the sound maddening. It was all a part of the ghastliness of the day, which should have been triumphant, but had curdled like the soured milk that she had drunk so often as a child. The room was bare and ugly, a puzzle of pipes and concrete blocks, not at all a setting *she* would have chosen for receiving important guests.

Racker had glared at her briefly, accusing *her*, though *she* had not arranged this meeting or chosen this hideous place. She had not even known of the Council Governor's intended visit, until Network notified her that he had already arrived. When she discovered the dolt who had *forgotten* to tell her, she would give the Wharton mines another worker for the depths—unless, of course, it was Racker who had omitted her, and that was the likeliest, most irritating of all the possibilities. He always managed to shift the blame for his failures to her.

Saschy smiled thinly, trying to conceal her disgust with Racker, who was mouthing insincere compliments for the benefit of Network's Council Governor. When there was no one significant to hear, Racker spoke of Caragen as a senile old fossil without a vision for the future. Surely, even the Council Governor, accustomed to sycophants, must find Racker's gushing praise more nauseating than credible. However, men like that seldom saw past their own immensity of ego. Racker was much the same, being more susceptible to flattery than anyone else on Nilson.

That was not one of Saschy's weaknesses. She knew

herself (she believed) too well. Large-boned and ungainly since girlhood, even the kindly-meant compliments of her mother's friends had always made Saschy contemptuous rather than appreciative. Saschy judged everyone, especially herself, by harsh standards. Having long ago accepted the vice of homeliness, she had eventually concluded that she lacked any compensating measure of intelligence or talent. But even Saschy admitted that she *was* shrewd and ambitious, and she knew her own mind. In clawing her way to the post of Lieutenant Governor, she had achieved something nearly impossible for a daughter of Nilson. She had made herself a Network citizen of some importance by electing to live among chronic liars—and using lies liberally herself—but Saschy still prided herself on recognizing falsehood when she heard it.

Racker, she thought, was too shallow to recognize depth in anyone else. With his tawny, brawny good looks, he expected to charm everyone as easily as he won women into his bed. Ned Racker understood brash schemes of self-aggrandisement and ruthless Network politics, but he failed to use people effectively in matters that required sophisticated planning. Saschy was still confiscating recordings of an abysmally illplanned, misinformed anti-Consortium speech he gave last month, which had made Racker the butt of traders' jokes from Nilson to the Consortium. Racker would never achieve his goal of sitting on the Network Council unless he learned more of the skills that Caragen used with such adroitness.

Until meeting Caragen today, Saschy had shared Racker's scorn of a Council Governor who would let Network slip from his elderly grasp rather than retire gracefully. To her surprise, Caragen impressed her. Though his appearance had at first appalled her—even in the poverty-blighted neighborhood of her upbringing, she had never seen anyone who looked so *ancient*—Caragen's traditional sobriquet of "old shark" seemed to fit far better than the more recently popularized epithet of "old fossil." The ego was as vast as she had expected, but the cunning of the man made Racker look like a callow fool by comparison. For once, Saschy was glad that she was Lieutenant rather than Governor of Nilson. She would want to observe Andrew Caragen for a *long* time before trying to coax favors from *him*.

She did not even feel overly resentful that Racker had excluded her from the dinner that he had ordered for Caragen. Saschy knew how Racker plied his trade during private conversations, freely scattering implications or outright promises that he never intended to uphold. With an audience like Caragen, such a shameless display of tricks could bury Racker, and Saschy did not want to share in that interment.

She had also made a prior commitment to attend a dinner party at her mother's house, a hateful prospect but an obligation that Saschy would not break lightly. In the old neighborhood, family obedience ranked above all else. As long as her mum refused to leave the tired little house where Saschy had been born, Saschy would give no more ammunition to the neighbors who called her a false daughter.

The old neighborhood in all its shabbiness was not far from the Governor's mansion—the "palace," as Nilsonites had mockingly dubbed it. Once Racker had swept the Council Governor—and a conspicuous train of security guards—away from Saschy and beyond the gilded doors of his private suite, Saschy covered her expensively tailored suit with an old serge coat and strode into the dismal Nilson streets. Racker's improvements of the local economy had produced little change in the surroundings of the average Nilson citizen. Public transfer ports had opened, restricting the spaceport's freedom of access to the city, but that change had limited effect on Nilson's people, who could not afford any form of off-world travel. The children of Nilson cared only that their streets had become a trifle quieter under Racker's jurisdiction, because Racker's transfer portals had opened new worlds to the crime lords, giving them better sources of profit to exploit.

The house where Saschy's mother lived was large by the standards of Nilson's impoverished masses. The house had four rooms, one of which boasted a working Network terminal. The terminal, unique in the neighborhood, had provided Saschy's schooling. It had made her different from her peers. It had made her a citizen of proud Network first, a daughter of sorrowing Nilson second.

She heard the voices as she climbed the cracked stone stoop: a little too loud and boisterous for Network courtesy, a little too ragged and unlearned for Network standards, a little too close to the voices of the past to make Saschy feel welcome in her visit. She did not belong here. She had not belonged for years. Her mum belonged nowhere else.

As Saschy twisted the old brass key in the lock that had never stopped a determined burglar, the voices dropped into whispers unheard outside the entry door. Mum expected her. Mum would not have told her other guests that Saschy would arrive, but they would know by the sound of that abrasive key. They would prepare themselves for escape, as from invasion.

Footsteps clattered in the alleyway behind the house. Saschy hissed in resentment of their unrepentant rudeness. Saschy was glad not to see such neighbors, but Mum would mind. Mum would hate the shame, though she would speak her grief only through the sadness of her water-blue eyes.

When Saschy opened the creaky door, Mum met her with the traditional kiss to each cheek. To Saschy's hands, Mum felt more wasted than ever, the long bones poking through the cheap black dress that was her attempt at finery. Mum's limp gray hair curled softly from beneath the ruby silk turban that Saschy had brought as an earlier gift. The narrow face—all forehead, nose and chin—wore creases now beneath the rouge and powder of another era's vanity.

"Arlan is here," announced Mum. "It's his furlough." The triumph in her feathery voice sealed Saschy's gloom.

Saschy looked past the wisps of Mum's hair and saw him: still awkward and shy as a boy, though he was Saschy's age. Arlan had been a friend once, the nearest thing to a beau that Saschy had known in her adolescence. He was smart enough to have won Saschy's admiration then, but she had grown. Arlan had stayed the same.

"It be good seeing you, Saschy," stammered Arlan, and Saschy pitied him. He knew what Mum still hoped absurdly: that he and Saschy would eventually wed and give Mum the grandchildren that fate had denied her. Mum lived in the past, bound in Nilson's independent traditions. Mum did not want to see the spread of Network influence, least of all in her last surviving daughter.

"Are you still working at the Wharton mine, Arlan?" asked Saschy, her discomfort making her stiff.

"Yah." Arlan's warm brown eyes, his best feature, had a hungriness in them that made Saschy cringe inwardly. He so clearly wanted to say more, and just as clearly, he was too conscious of Saschy as a member of an unreachable class.

Mum, recognizing awkward silence if not accepting of its reason, intervened, "Arlan has been telling us . . ." She paused only for a moment, flushed on behalf of the vanished visitors, and persevered bravely, "Arlan has been telling me about the ghost lights, Saschy. You never heard such tales as he's been telling." With firm insistence, Mum prodded Saschy toward the faded, flowered chair that was nearest to Arlan. "Tell Saschy of the mine ghosts, Arlan."

"It be only rumors, Miz Ruth," said Arlan, his eyebrows drawing together in a worried frown.

"Then tell Saschy of the rumors," urged Mum, "while I ready supper. I've a good, meaty joint and black beans." She walked haltingly to the part of the room that constituted the kitchen. Mum's maimed feet had not served her well since the brutal attack that had taken her husband's life, but her hands and arms remained sound. She stirred the contents of her stewpots with vigor.

"What do the rumors say?" asked Saschy. For Mum's sake, Saschy smiled as if she genuinely cared about the mineworkers' superstitious silliness. She had heard reports of recent disquiet among the miners. Racker complained often that the workers were always grumbling about something.

"The ghost lights be seen near every day now," said Arlan, watching Saschy with an obvious distrust that only aggravated Saschy's irritable mood. "Just a few be telling of them before, when the mine first be opened. I be seeing them myself near a dozen times now."

"What do you see?"

"Lights," said Arlan, as if the answer should be plain, "where there should be none, in the deep places first, lately closer by the living."

"Do the lights do anything?" asked Saschy, glancing at Mum in hope that the supper would be readied quickly. Mum displayed no signs of haste, as she measured and considered every grain of seasoning cradled in the wooden spoon.

"They be swallowing the rock and troubling the dead," said Arlan grimly, "and they be coloring the caves with stars."

Arlan's odd, picturesque reply made Saschy look at him again and remember. He had written poetry once for her, when both of them were young and nearly in love. She looked at him and saw him, his shoulders bowed and muscled from his labors. He had none of the bold handsomeness of a man like Racker, but Arlan's earth-brown eyes were gentle, and his wide mouth and chin were strong. He had aged better than most Nilson men, for Arlan had avoided the needless fights that scarred more reckless Nilson youths.

As Mum repeated often, Arlan was a good man. Saschy agreed. Saschy did *not* agree that Arlan was good for *her*.

Arlan smiled wanly, as if he guessed accurately at Saschy's thoughts. "But then, you be not knowing about the mines," he observed with quiet certainty. "You be not seeing the deep places that be turning a man's blood to water. You be not understanding the horrid, fetid darkness that be more than a man's enduring."

"Safety precautions for human laborers are strict," answered Saschy, resentful that Arlan should take advantage of old friendship to voice complaints that were better handled by official channels. Saschy spent most of her days forming careful replies in Racker's name. She did not need to hear *Arlan* whine. "All of the deepest mining operations are mechanized."

"So *they* be saying," replied Arlan without rancor.

"Who are *they*?" asked Saschy archly. Mum had turned, pretending not to listen but wearing a worried frown.

"Governor's folk."

"Then I am one of *them*?"

"Yah. You be." Arlan disentangled his awkward limbs from the chair's yellowed slip cover. His brown eyes were oddly compassionate. "I be sorry, Saschy. I be only staying for your mum this evening."

Mum had heard him. "Arlan, will you help me lay the supper dishes?" It was a transparent excuse, and Mum knew it. She limped toward Arlan, her arms extended as if to grab and hold him desperately. Saschy felt guilty, then angry that Mum had forced this difficult situation to occur.

Arlan spared Mum a few painful steps by hastening to meet her. "I be going, Miz Ruth. I be only troubling to Saschy. I be coming by again after check-in to help you with the shutters. You be saving me some of that supper."

Defeated, Mum hugged him and let him go. When he closed the door, Mum winced. She said only, "I'm tired, Saschy. If you want supper here, serve yourself. It *is* a good joint, maybe even good enough for you.'

"I did not ask Arlan to leave, Mum."

"You haven't enough to sense to know the difference."

"You shouldn't try to move that chair yourself. Let me help you." Mum stood mutely, while Saschy unfolded two dining chairs and began to search the cupboards for plates that were stainless and uncracked. "What happened to the set of dishes that I bought for you?"

"I gave some to young Miri, some to Chin, some to Liv. . . ."

"I bought the dishes for you, not for the neighbors." Saschy ladled thin gravy into a chipped crockery cup. "They take advantage of you, Mum. Won't you let me move you to a suite in a newer district?"

"This is my home."

Saschy did not try to pursue the argument. Supper was eaten in uneasy silence. Saschy concentrated on swallowing stringy meat and boiled beans without showing her revulsion. She could not help but envy whatever delicacies were being served to Racker and Andrew Caragen.

"Arlan is the best friend you have," said Mum at last. "You were rude to him."

"Your friends are not mine, Mum. We have nothing in common."

Mum pointed toward the floor. With adamance, she spoke: "We have *this*. We have Nilson. You should have listened to Arlan about the ghost lights. Anything that matters to Nilson should matter to *you*."

"*Ghost* lights? Rumors. The superstitions of ignorance. *You* taught me better than that, Mum."

"I thought I taught you to care about your home and your people." Mum tore the silk turban from her head. The wisps of graying hair stood on end.

"I care *more* and work *harder* for Nilson than anyone on this miserable, benighted planet," shouted Saschy, all of her frustrations boiling into view. "You can't see any farther than these crumbling walls and your petty, uneducated, *greedy* neighbors."

"I think you should leave now, Saschy."

"I think I should not have come at all." Saschy thrust the dirtied dishes into the basin, removing another chip of pottery from the rim of one bowl. She left the dishes unwashed. Let *Arlan* finish the job, since Mum prized him so much.

Outside, the stink of Nilson's night made Saschy choke. She did not linger in Mum's neighborhood, where underground sewers opened each evenfall to welcome the traffic of the lowest ranks of thieves.

Saschy was equipped with enough expensive Network devices to protect herself from physical attack, but she hated the memories that the stink—and Mum's hard words—always brought to life inside her.

She saw the shadows that slipped through the night, muffled shapes that observed her covetously, identified her, and left her to walk unmolested. To them, she still belonged. There were other, worse neighborhoods in every Nilson district, where even the residents did not dare to travel alone, but most Nilson citizens protected their immediate neighbors as family. Nilson citizens generally stole, extorted, and murdered from strangers in the marginally prosperous spaceport district late in the night, during the long gap between port boy patrols and scans from the antiquated Network autopolice units.

The autopolice units, like the easily bribed port boys, would not be replaced as long as interested parties financed the government. Denial of such accepted facts of Nilson life had been one of the critical mistakes of Racker's well-meaning predecessor. Saschy, like anyone from Mum's neighborhood, could have predicted the late Governor's assassination as soon as he announced his intended reforms. Racker was far more cautious—and just as obviously protected by someone with significant influence over the crime lords who ruled the streets.

Saschy hurried her pace. Racker seemed to value her today, but he could easily turn against her. If he ever chose to dispense with her services as his Lieutenant, neither the protective customs of insular Nilson neighborhoods nor a Network stunner would defend her successfully. She knew the risks of her position. Saschy never gambled for small stakes.

A figure detached itself from invisibility in some unseen alcove or alley, and it stood squarely in front of her before she could divert her steps to the side of the narrow street. The figure was a man, she thought, though a dark hood and cloak masked all features. Saschy clenched her fingers around the stunner in her pocket, preparing to fire without awaiting further evidence of mischief. There were no innocent collisions in Nilson's night.

She fired through the pocket of her coat. A spurt of red tracery marked the beam's unerring path into the figure's belly. The figure hissed a foreign curse but did not fall.

Saschy jerked the stunner from her pocket to achieve a better aim, and she fired again in rapid sequence. Each thin red beam disappeared into the cloak without eliciting as much reaction as another curse.

Does he carry a new form of protectifield? wondered Saschy frantically. She could not keep track of all developments of Network weapons and defense mechanisms. Her stunner, though low in force, had been advertised as capable of permeating any personal force shield. Some ingenious fool had undoubtedly taken that claim as a challenge.

Saschy knew better than to expect aid from any of Mum's neighbors. Family protection extended only to the point of convenience. Saschy moved to one side, hoping to be allowed to pass, but the figure shifted accordingly.

Saschy was not a fast runner, and she did not relish her odds of fighting an opponent in any physical contest. However, the cloaked figure had not yet produced a weapon, and he was not so large as to make her cause futile. "What do you want?" she demanded in the belligerent voice of an angry Nilson daughter.

No answer emerged from the shadow man. Saschy required no greater confirmation of his enmity. Still clutching her stunner, Saschy dashed toward the man. Using the stunner like a cub, she smashed it against his shadow-cloaked neck.

The electric jolt snaked through her body. Her numb fingers loosened. The stunner fell through shadow and clattered against the pavement. Saschy dropped to her knees and clawed the ground in a painful effort to retrieve her weapon.

The stunner's cold barrel fit reassuringly into her sound left hand, and Saschy lifted her eyes defiantly. Growling from her throat like a frightened beast,

Saschy searched the darkness for the figure of her attacker. There was no one she could see. There was nothing to see but shifting shadow ghosts and a momentary flicker of fiery motes of light.

Saschy did not squander her precious opportunity to escape. She sprang from the ground and ran. She was neither exceptionally fast nor graceful, and the neighbors would surely remark her flight and gossip unflatteringly to Mum. Saschy only resolved that it was well past time for Mum to move.

CHAPTER 10

Infortiare

The Infortiare's Tower makes too dark and lean a silhouette against Tul's mountain, thought Katerin. The adjoining castle of the Seriin queen had a fanciful, frothy look, as if fashioned of preposterously assorted whims, and the gardens bloomed with vibrant energy. The Tower spoke of menace.

It was an unfair judgment, she told herself, considering what Quin had recounted of his homeland's history. To have resurrected any form of civilized society from the wreckage of Network-3 had required extraordinary effort from an exceptional people. The first Infortiare, Lord Ceallagh, and the wizards of Ixaxis had deliberately yielded the rights of kingship to the mortal line of Tul. To salvage their world from themselves, they had curtailed their own power over mortals by disciplining the Power that made them known as Immortal and unnervingly different. They had made the choice. The choice could not have been made without their willing cooperation.

Nonetheless, the Infortiare's Tower chilled Katerin. The woman who was Infortiare, though unfailingly kind to the mortal Network wife of Lord Quinzaine, made Katerin shiver from imagined possibilities. Lady Rhianna dur Ixaxis, liege lady of all wizards of the Seriin alliance, made Katerin acutely aware of the strangeness of these people. Though Quin claimed never to feel entirely comfortable in the mannered society of his birth, he blended with it even as he ridiculed its foibles. On each visit to Serii, Katerin dreaded that he would finally realize that he *did* belong here after all. When he reached that conclusion, which her inescapable understanding of mathematical psychology measured as highly probable, he would also understand that he had married a woman who could never *belong* with him.

"Lady Rhianna refuses to allow the gardeners to touch her trees," explained Quin, apologizing obliquely for the tangled path that led to the Tower's hidden door. He kept his gray cloak free of thorns with a practiced deftness that Katerin envied, as briars snagged the long navy skirt that she wore as an imperfect concession to Seriin propriety. "Lady Rhianna is extraordinarily fond of trees."

"Fonder of trees than of unannounced visitors," replied Katerin, dodging a whip of a twig. Instead of traveling first to Ixaxis, as was his habit in visiting Serii, Quin had chosen to transfer directly into this snarled region of the royal gardens. Katerin had not asked him to explain his obvious wish to arrive inconspicuously. He was trying too hard to pretend that the visit was ordinary, the dangers no nearer than at any other time of the past three Network years.

"Lady Rhianna expects us," answered Quin. His grin was broad, but Katerin could see the twitch of straining muscles that forced it. She knew him too well, and she had practiced the art of observation for too many years to be deceived by his forced cheerfulness. She thought she had rarely seen him in so nervous a mood.

"Did you warn her of our arrival?"

"No. She sensed it."

"By her Power," remarked Katerin wryly.

"Of course," replied Quin, and the very crispness of his answer confirmed his level of anxiety.

Katerin knew that she could persuade him to confess his feelings to her, but she would not coax him yet. When Quin, who hid little from her as a rule, made such an effort at reticence, the reason could only be that Power that Katerin could never entirely comprehend or trust. She would not dilute the confession that he saved for Lady Rhianna. After he had spoken to the

Lady of Ixaxis, Katerin would make the effort to extract the truth and understand it.

The door, visible to Katerin as only a wall of mossy stone, gave access to the Infortiare's Tower at its lowest level. Katerin closed her eyes as Quin breached the latches, for the illusion was compelling and nearly as disturbing to her as an undisguised transfer portal. She followed blindly until they began the long ascent of stairs, ancient but little worn, that pierced a Tower that had been largely unoccupied since its construction. In Lady Rhianna's term as Infortiare, the Tower had reportedly seen more visitors than in several prior centuries, but it remained a drafty, oversized home for a lone widow and her few servants.

"Have you considered introducing your Infortiare to the advantages of Network lifts?" asked Katerin, beginning to feel breathless after matching her husband's rapid ascent of the first four flights.

Quin slowed and flashed a grin. "I'm sorry to make you scale the endless staircase, but Lady Rhianna doesn't like me to transfer into the Tower directly. She already has enough trouble persuading servants to stay in a Tower that is commonly supposed to be haunted."

"By your Infortiare's late husband, the dreaded Lord Venkarel?"

The grin vanished, Quin's uncommon tension returning inexplicably. "Yes. By Kaedric, Lord Venkarel, among others."

More mysteries of their infernal Power, concluded Katerin and resumed a tactful silence until they had climbed nearly to the Tower's pinnacle. Katerin paused in the tapestried anteroom outside the Infortiare's study. "Tell her the truth, Quin," she said, as he touched the study door's gnarled brass handle.

Quin glanced at his wife without any trace of his usual smile. His stormy eyes pried her intentions from her, and his words echoed the plea that his Power forced upon her: "Please, Katerin, let me explain to her in my own way. Sometimes, my Power knows things that I'd rather *not* know, so those things don't reach completely into my head, but they're important." He shrugged. "I'm not explaining very well to you, am I?"

"No." Katerin laid her thin hand on his shoulder. "You're never very clear when you try to describe your Power to me. That's why you need honest advice from someone who *can* understand."

"You understand me, my lady," whispered Quin with a wry grimace, "uncannily well for one who claims ignorance of wizards' matters." He opened the door to the Infortiare's study.

The Lady of Ixaxis, dressed in burgundy velvet, stood facing the wide expanse of windows, watching the evening light gild the distant sea. She held her arms tightly crossed against her, as if she felt chilled, though the evening was mild and the room was warm. Her hair hung in a single golden braid down her back, instead of its usual confinement atop her head. The effect made her appear almost girlishly young and innocent, until she turned and her eyes betrayed her. Her skin was smooth and unlined; her figure was slim and firm; but her gray eyes had seen too much to pretend to youth.

Though she deferred officially to Serii's mortal monarch, Lady Rhianna was arguably the most influential woman of her world. She was easily the most powerful woman of any world that Katerin knew, and the history of the final days of Network-3 proved how effectively the Power of Ixaxis could be translated into power of a more traditional variety. Katerin had at times wished that the Lady of Ixaxis were willing to confront Andrew Caragen and the Network Councillors directly. Though Katerin knew that the Ixaxins of her acquaintance were far removed from the first, sociopathic Immortals, Katerin had occasionally wondered if her father had acted wisely in his drastic step of isolating Network-3 and its mad Immortals to protect the rest of Network. No one could have treated the Terry family more viciously than Caragen and his agent, Rabh Marrach.

Rhianna nodded at Katerin but offered none of the customary words of formal greeting. "Lord Quinzaine," she said simply, "I must warn you in advance that I am uncommonly weary tonight." Her use of Network's Basic speech had an odd lilt, but it was clear and carefully enunciated. "Queen Joli has been unwell again."

"Her Majesty is not young," answered Quin. The news had become familiar, especially in the past year. The health of Serii's queen had been deteriorating since Katerin first met Quin.

"No," agreed Rhianna, twisting the silver chain that held her milky, luminous pendant of office. "Joli is not young, and there is no Immortal strain in her. She berates me for fretting about her. She tells me that she is too old to view death as anything but a long-awaited friend." Rhianna smiled sadly. "She was only a girl when I first came to Tulea. She was nearly as troublesome a child as you, Lord Quinzaine."

Quin lifted one shoulder in sheepish apology, because his youthful escapades still branded him as notorious among long-memoried Ixaxins. *The complaints of his childhood teachers would find recent sympathy from Network's Council Governor,* thought Katerin with a trace of rueful pride. Quin's irrepressible, often reckless sense of humor had not diminished with maturity. It had merely evolved to provoke a more sophisticated range of targets.

Katerin normally smiled on considering her husband's busy past, but the cause of the Infortiare's sorrow compelled a more serious turn of mind. Katerin could muster little personal regret for the illness of a queen whom she had met only in formal ceremony, but the grief of Immortal wizardess for mortal friend cut close to Katerin's heart. "How old were you when you first saw Tulea, Lady Rhianna?" asked Katerin.

Quin turned abruptly away from his wife and the Infortiare, and he paced along the wall of finely bound books. He stopped before reaching the door that led to the Infortiare's private upper room. He gripped the corded backing of a walnut-framed chair with taut fingers, and he granted the mundane chair all of his outward attention.

The Infortiare's keen eyes assessed Katerin, evaluating the question and its cause with visible compassion. "I was twenty-seven."

Without raising his eyes from the chair, Quin interpreted softly, "That would be no more than twenty-three by Network reckoning."

"Old enough to elicit your wife's regret at the difference between her and us, Quinzaine," countered Rhianna quietly. She came to Katerin and brushed Katerin's brow with a feather-light touch of delicate fingers. Warmth, an inward uncoiling of pain, spread from the Lady's gesture. Katerin knew herself touched by a major Power, gentled only by its wielder's stern self-discipline. The Infortiare spoke only slightly above a whisper, but she poured her words inside of Katerin. Relentlessly analytical Katerin knew that the cause exceeded compassion: The Infortiare gave comfort compulsively to ease her own pain. "When I came to Tulea, Lady Katerin, I had only begun to recognize the extent of my Power. I had more cause to fear its strangeness than you, because I could not escape Power by any choice or wish. I still fear Power, but it is part of me. It is perhaps the largest part of me, because I am very deeply bonded to a man of whom *only* Power remains. You are wise to be troubled by the differences between you and your chosen husband. I understand the depth of your fear better than you can ever realize."

"If so, Lady Rhianna, please remind him to fear himself."

Rhianna's sigh emerged almost silently, and her slim hands gripped the pendant that rested on her breast. "What is it that so troubles your wife, Lord Quinzaine, that she tests her mind-twisting Network skills against my Power? She takes hold of shared regrets and makes a weapon of them. It is an uncomfortable talent, strangely directed against that which she loves beyond herself. She directs it against you, Lord Quinzaine, for all that she plies me as her intermediary."

"My Lady Katerin's talents can be most unpleasant

when we have a disagreement between us," replied Quin with the hard mask of courtly Seriin formality.

"Is it this disagreement which brings you here this evening?"

"No," answered Quin, eliciting a brusque laugh of contradiction from his wife. He did not lift his gaze from the wood-framed chair. "Caragen tracked us more quickly than usual this time. I had not yet prepared an alternative destination."

"Because you have been too consumed by your new fascination with the Consortium," said Katerin with bitter coldness.

"It is more than idle curiosity," snapped Quin, then aborted his outburst with visible embarrassment. The flush suffusing his face enhanced the youthfulness of his appearance, though his lips remained tight with anger. Katerin, having provoked his defensive reaction deliberately, seated herself in a brocade armchair and allowed herself a thin, sad smile of satisfaction. Rhianna arched slim brows. "I have been making a few inquiries," conceded Quin, "but I have taken no action, my lady. I intended to speak to you once I had collected some more data. Council Governor Caragen accelerated my visit to you."

"The Consortium," murmured Rhianna, delicately testing the foreign Network term with her soft accent. "This Consortium is one of your Network's rival civilizations, is it not?" To Katerin's trained ears, the Infortiare's voice confirmed the claim of weariness, though the indicators were subtle. The realization troubled Katerin, who had counted on a fully alert Rhianna to talk sense into Quin, but there could be no procrastination now. The Infortiare must be made to understand the dangerous magnitude of the new object of Quin's insatiable curiosity.

"The Consortium is Network's only rival," answered Quin. He glanced at Katerin, but she offered no further opinion. She had initiated the conversation that she considered vital; beyond that bit of manipulation she would grant Quin the right to present his own case before she interfered again. "The Consortium would probably scorn to rank Network as more than a minor irritant. As Network would compare to one of Serii's tiniest wilderness settlements, so would the Consortium be to Network. Because the Consortium is so vast, I have been trying to learn a little about it. You did send me to Network for the purpose of learning."

"You have made inquiries within Network?"

"I have studied the scarce information I could find, wherever I could find it. Network conditions its citizens to distrust the Consortium on an emotional basis but provides few intelligible reasons. Katerin is prejudiced by her conditioning—as she will admit, being an expert in the science of creating such conditioning algorithms."

"Do you concur, Lady Katerin?"

Katerin nodded a slow acknowledgment. "The presence of such conditioning is undeniable. It does not reduce the Consortium's real danger to Network—and to you, if you provoke it."

Once more, Rhianna folded her arms tightly. "What are your intentions in this regard, Lord Quinzaine?" Even Katerin could feel the fierce pull of Lady Rhianna's Power, sternly commanding Quin to yield a full answer.

Quin relinquished his hold on the walnut chair, and he cast his cloak impatiently behind one shoulder. He gestured broadly. "I wear no warrior's sword today, my lady. I arrived here of my own volition. How I have merited your attack?"

"Your flight of histrionics tries my beleaguered patience, Quinzaine."

Quin met his liege lady's rebuke with a grim, tense smile. "I intend to make some observations on a planet called Nilson," replied Quin stiffly. "Marrach recommended the Nilson port as the most suitable site for encountering a Consortium affiliate unobtrusively."

Cringing inwardly from Marrach's name, Katerin muttered, "We have trouble enough without seeking more. The Siathan Healer does not know how you plan to use his advice, Quin."

"*I* do not know how I shall use his advice," retorted

Quin, "but every mote of Power in me insists that I must use it somehow—and soon." He made the slightest bow toward his liege lady, one of those ingrained gestures that proved to Katerin how thoroughly he fit in this arcane, archaic culture. "My lady, we did not come here to make you witness an argument but to request your tolerance of a protracted visit. We need sanctuary for a time."

"Lord Quinzaine, you have a home in Hamley, as well as Ixaxis, and you do not require my permission to visit either residence. Are you here by your wish or your lady's?"

Quin answered dryly, "It is not always easy to tell. My lady manipulates too skillfully, when she is determined to achieve a goal."

"I hoped that he would listen to you, Lady Rhianna," said Katerin, "when he discarded my concerns as prejudice."

Rhianna turned from them both and paced back to the window. "I trust your good intentions, Lord Quinzaine, but you have a strong streak of recklessness that has caused you difficulties in the past. Lady Katerin, you are not a capricious woman, nor have I have ever known you before to seek my counsel for your husband or yourself. The fact that you have come here by choice impresses me of your sincerity. I shall weigh the matter, Lord Quinzaine, but I am inclined to concur with your wife. I sent you to Network to learn, not to throw sticks at a sleeping dyrcat."

"My lady, you admitted your fatigue," countered Quin. "If you were rested your Power would argue in my favor."

"You are impertinent, Lord Quinzaine, and less confident of my eventual concurrence than you proclaim. Stay a few days in the Tower, if you wish, until you deem me sufficiently 'rested' to give you a trustworthy judgment. Recognize, however, that I shall be less tolerant of your disobedience when I am less exhausted by external events." Rhianna bestowed on Quin a compelling stare across her velvet-shrouded shoulder. "Kaedric is no longer subject to the minor irritations of physical fatigue. Would you prefer to offer your Power's explanation to him and abide by *his* decision without the inconvenience of delay?"

The Infortiare's quietly implausible words exude more menace than her Tower, thought Katerin with a shiver. She did not want to know why even the name of the late Infortiare, Kaedric, Lord Venkarel—who still retained an obsessive level of fidelity from Lady Rhianna—should inspire such an aura of fear among the most educated Seriins. Quin might speak condescendingly of servants who dreaded the Infortiare's Tower as haunted, but he reacted with equal irrationality to the threat of a ghostly wizard. Superstition and Power had mingled too closely for too long in Serii to allow an outside observer like Katerin to distinguish easily between them, despite all of Katerin's expertise.

Quin clenched his teeth, but he answered with a deep bow of obeisance, "No, my lady. I would not care to trouble him."

"You may use your usual rooms."

"Thank you, my lady." He turned sharply and did not look at his wife as he strode across the room. He opened the heavy door and leaned against its gleaming panels to await Katerin. His jaw was tense, and his expressive mouth was twisted with irony.

No one could mistake him for a clownish fool in this dark mood, thought Katerin, aching from the knowledge that she had hurt him deeply with her mistrust.

He stared through her even as she passed him at the door. Lady Rhianna offered quietly, "You acted with wisdom, Lady Katerin, in encouraging this discussion. I am grateful." Though Katerin felt sure that the words were meant sincerely, they inflicted a twinge of shared pain as real as the previous gift of ease.

***

Quin listened to his wife's soft breathing, and his Power searched the night for a comparable sense of peace. He could not sleep nor even rest. He felt the Power of the Infortiare, Ixaxis, and every trained wiz-

ard and untrained sorcerer of his world, and the sense
of being among his own kind gave him only discouragement. The Immortals of Serii understood him no
better than the mortals of Network. Katerin trusted him
generally, but a single doubt set her conspiring to use
Lady Rhianna against him.

He touched Katerin's pale hair, admiring her, even
as he railed inwardly against her coldly cunning methods. Without Power, Katerin could never thwart a determined wizard directly, but she could hardly select a
better ally than Lady Rhianna. Quin thanked the rigidity of Network science that prevented Katerin from
recognizing the existence of that wizard who intimidated Quin even more effectively than Lady Rhianna.

Lady Rhianna, of course, both recognized Quin's
larger fear and used it freely. He almost wished he had
courage enough to accept Lady Rhianna's insidious offer and actually consult Lord Venkarel. Such a response would have been worthwhile if only to confound
Lady Rhianna's certainty of Quin's refusal. In the Infortiare's dark Tower, Quin wrestled with his own reluctance. No one had a more intimate familiarity with
the realms of Power than Venkarel. No one could
better assess Power's role in Quin's growing determination to visit the world of Nilson.

Quin fortified his Power's protective walls, lest the
thought of Venkarel summon the disquieting reality
unintentionally. Quin did not fear Venkarel in the same
superstitious sense as less knowledgeable Seriins. Quin
had vanquished that ignorant level of terror when he
tapped Venkarel's formidable Power to teach a singular, stunning lesson of Power's potential to Andrew
Caragen. By that one-time intertwining of Power, Quin
had learned what it meant to be Kaedric, Lord Venkarel, transformed by Power from man into a shade of
Power's own intangible nature. Few Seriins—perhaps
none but the Infortiare herself—understood as well as
Quin how thoroughly Venkarel had earned his fearful
legend as the wizard whose Power exceeded even his
own physical capacity to contain it. Kaedric, Lord
Venkarel, knowing his own magnitude of Power and

the absolute discipline needed to restrain it from inflicting rampant destruction, terrified even himself.

During that brief, nearly fatal alliance, Quin had developed a much more substantial cause for dread than mere superstition. *Quin* feared Venkarel, because Quin recognized what even Lady Rhianna refused to acknowledge: By the bonds of Power's accursed gifts, Quin was more akin to Venkarel than to anyone else within reachable time or space. Ixaxis had simply managed to begin its stern indoctrination of Quin's Power at an earlier, more malleable age, allowing Quin to mature before his Power reached its fullness. The Power of Kaedric, abused starveling from a waterfront slum, had remained unrecognized and dormant until it exploded with the sudden, traumatic ferocity that had made an inferno of the city of Ven. Quin was not even sure which Power exceeded the other, his own or Venkarel's; he did not want to know.

"I must go to Nilson," whispered Quin to the night-shrouded rafters of the Tower's guest room, "or my own wretched Power will give me no peace at all." He grumbled without bitterness. Power's freedom had long ago tempered Quin's resentment of Power's burdens.

Quin freed himself from the silk-fine strands of Katerin's hair. "I shall return before you know that I have gone," he promised her silently. His Power cradled her gently to prevent her from awakening, as he readied himself for his journey. He dressed in dark gray, tightly woven Seriin wool and stout leather boots, and he armed himself with three hunting knives of sharp steel, as if equipping himself for an arduous hike into the wild Mountains of Mindar, which rose precipitously behind the Infortiare's Tower, instead of a foray-by-Power to a Network spaceport. Quin mocked himself for the incongruity of his preparations, but they seemed to meet an inward need akin to that served by a warrior's prebattle ritual.

When he had cloaked himself in black wool, dousing even the glint of sun-streaked hair beneath a capacious hood, he touched Katerin once more with Power's

softest caress, then turned his Power to a harsher task.
He fortified his walls of inner defense, and he trod the
Tower's long staircase with a full wizard's stealth. He
did not wish to risk Lady Rhianna's disapproving attention needlessly by stirring the infinities within her
own home. He left the Tower, and he left the castle
gardens, as well. Beneath cold night's blazing stars,
Quin climbed Tul's mountain. From the mountain's
jagged bones, where Venkarel had once battled a Sorcerer King for the life of a world, Quin stepped into
Power's bright infinities.

He felt Rhianna stir at the disturbance, but Quin did
not stay to feel her command. Quin knew these ethereal
paths well and maneuvered deftly among them. He respected the deadliness of the shimmering strands that
were Power's perception of topological connectivities,
but Quin had taken this route often enough to move
confidently. He knew the straightest paths between his
home world and each of Network's primary transfer
portals.

He emerged from the light curtain into a busy Network terminal, as if he had arrived conventionally with
all the other Network travelers. A few Network citizens
glanced at his odd attire, but they dismissed him as an
eccentric member of the Anachronist sect and afforded
him no more severe attention than a few condescending
whispers. Quin did not linger in the glare of the stark,
arching metal port center and its throngs. He selected
the coordinates for Nilson's capital city, prodded Network to accept a false identification code for travel
payment, and entered a light curtain of the portal to
which Network directed him.

He allowed Network to control the transfer, while he
monitored the nearly instantaneous journey. Quin seldom relinquished so much control to Network, but he
wanted to be certain of the route. Despite the brevity of
the trip, the yielding to Network gave him a queasy
sensation, absent from his usual travels, and he was
glad to emerge from transfer. Even the patterns of the
journey, which his Power could usually imprint so

easily in his awareness, seemed shaken by the unsettled transfer.

Relieved to escape, he strode away from the light curtain too quickly to hear the metallic curfew warning until its third call. With his Power unprepared, Quin walked directly into the electronic barrier that guarded the port's bay, and he winced at the unaccustomed shock. His Power drank instinctively of the gush of energy. The barrier, old and poorly maintained, flickered into darkness.

"Lords," muttered Quin, irritated with his own carelessness. To stifle the curiosity of any observers, he flashed an illusion of the light-webbed barrier into place, while his Power explored the damage, and Quin stared at his first view of Nilson.

Anticipation had magnified his expectations. Quin's immediate reaction was disappointment that Nilson looked so much like any of Network's lesser worlds. The transfer port building was little more than an arched roof, supported by unadorned white columns, surrounding the cluster of portals, a few utility rooms, and several long rows of cargo lockers leading to a gated yard. The only significant light came from the shimmering portal curtains that shielded travelers' eyes from the reality of topological transfer. Misty night, thick with the odor of sewage and decay, swept its noxious fingers through the defenseless building atop its meager hill. Ahead and to his right, a golden dome crowned one impressive marble edifice amid a clutch of its affluent offspring. In all other directions, the city's ghostly structures crowded together, as if seeking feeble comfort from proximity.

Toward what seemed to be the city's edge, a beaded net of sapphire beacons hovered low in the cloudy sky to define the confines of the spaceport. Quin saw little evidence of active traffic, and those few sluggish vessels glowed only with dim mooring lights. The dense spacing of the sapphire net's perimeter suggested a restricted access zone, which did not accord with Quin's expectations or wishes. Neither did the spaceport's distance, which would make for a healthy hike. Nonetheless, for lack of better option, Quin decided to make the spaceport his first goal.

Touching the intervening city with Power, Quin could feel the bestiality of watchers, hungry for prey, that lurked in the noisome alleys surrounding the dimly lit port building, and he concluded that a major purpose of the barrier was to protect the unwary traveler who arrived during the night. With revulsion, he recognized the predators as human and recalled Marrach's disparagement of Nilson. The port building, white and polished and deceptively civilized, felt empty but for a dim sense of drowsing men in a far utility room. Quin resecured the electronic night barrier with care on behalf of them and any subsequent visitor.

As Quin commanded Network to disregard his own presence, his queasiness resurged and he stumbled. He tried to convince himself that the ugly sensation was only a remnant from his troubled arrival, but his Power refused the lie. Quin looked at the murky fog of night in Nilson's capital city, and he saw the patterns of infinity writhe.

"Lords," he whispered again, but now he cursed more than a minor clumsiness. He stepped from the port building's shelter and heard scurrying feet dust the streets. He knew his arrival had been marked from six directions. The predators circled him, far more cautious of each other than of him. If they identified him as an Anachronist, they would assume that he was correspondingly ill-armed to thwart attack.

At another time, Quin might have taunted these arrogant marauders, but they only annoyed him now. He strode into the Nilson streets, defending himself with a wisp of a spell, while he concentrated on the inward sight that only his Power recognized. He had altogether abandoned his goal of reaching the spaceport and observing a Consortium visitor. Power-perceived patterns—which ought to have been clear and steady—rippled, shifted, and blurred. Quin struggled to maintain his own stability of direction through a burning plane that was more real to him than the pavings beneath his boots. A strand of light snapped and burned him, though he jumped free of it before he could become ensnared by its lethal grip.

When a Nilson cutthroat tried to trip Quin from a gutter drain, the fire of raw Power melted the cutthroat's arm. Quin did not hear the scream, and the man's pain touched Quin too remotely to stir any true awareness. A more sophisticated thief fired a beamer into Quin, but Power engulfed the energy before Seriin wool could even singe. Nilson predators, who continued to watch the odd interloper, began to circle him with greater respect.

Patterns burned, twisted, and snapped. A maelstrom of energies twisted into itself and shuddered from the revulsion of antagonistic polarities, forced into impossible unity. Pain sliced through Quin's Power, nearly tearing Power from man. For an instant, Quin's body walked soullessly, for the Power was the greatest part of a man who was a wizard of Ixaxis.

Fire drove into Seriin wool, coiling within an almost-emptied body and tantalizing ever-ravenous Power back into its host. The body growled a Seriin warrior's curse, but the man hardly recognized his own agony. He was Power and infinity, and he was breaking, and a body's mere physical hurt meant nothing to him. The red blaze of stunner beams pounded repeatedly against the infinities, linked by Power to flesh, but the body no longer troubled to form feeble words of protest. Power animated the body, forcing it to accept the blazing gift. The night shivered and burned across a foggy, snarled plane, and a woman demanded in a bellicose voice, "What do you want?"

She smelled of fear, courageously borne, and another woman's memory spoke to the Power that was Quin. She was a warrior, and she cared for him, but she called him a fool. *I know what I am, Laurett,* answered Quin's Power humbly. He could almost see her in the shadows. He longed to see her, though he knew that she had died in Hamley years ago and left him prematurely a widower, before ever he had imagined the existence of Katerin or of Network.

The woman was angry with him. His Power felt the

threat, and he thought a warning, but she had no like
Power to receive it. The blow fell heavily against his
neck, a cold weight of world-bound matter colliding
with infinity. Power brushed her lightly, exploring the
security of its own existence by mingling for an instant
with her faint life energy. The impact only shocked her
physically. The realization that she was *not* Laurett
stunned Quin's Power into an astonished, instinctive
recoil that dashed recklessly across the fragmenting
space that engulfed Nilson.

He leaped across the strands of brightness that he
would normally have accompanied as guides, bypassing his conscious training impatiently. He plunged directly through patterns that he would ordinarily have
shunned as too unpredictable for safe travel. That his
Power carried his body with it owed more to habit than
to intent. That Quin's Power survived the journey was
owed to a severe form of discipline that he had learned
unwittingly from past contact with Lord Venkarel.

Quin's Power maneuvered, manipulated, and guided.
Familiarity began to restore reason. Quin knew these
patterns. They led him home. They led him to the
brightness that was Serii. They led to life. Where he
began, he belonged.

***

"Lord Quinzaine, open your eyes," commanded a
woman. He obeyed, because he was Ixaxin, and she
was his liege lady. He saw her face blearily, but he felt
her relief with the clarity of confident Power.

"Where is Katerin?" he whispered through lips that
felt stiff and swollen.

"Tulea, where I ordered her to remain. You are in
the Ixaxis infirmary. You have been delirious for the
two days since you arrived here, and I feared that you
might injure her."

"Did I come here directly?"

"Yes, Lord Quinzaine, which is the one sensible
thing you have achieved recently. You terrified the
first two nurses that encountered you by shouting at

them in an alien language. You managed to set fire to the draperies and char the floor of the faculty ward, before an adequate wizard's circle could be formed to control you."

He sighed, "I deserve your reproach, my lady."

"Do you?"

Quin struggled to bring Lady Rhianna into clearer focus. He could fix only on her eyes, gray as smoke and equally impenetrable. "The patterns are breaking," replied Quin. "That is clearly what my Power sensed about Nilson—not Consortium phantoms but a distortion of the fundamental pattern of creation."

For a long moment, only silence lay between the Infortiare and her errant subject. "Is this a product of Network's meddling?" asked Rhianna with a calm that Quin recognized as false. The trust implicit in her question was real, and it made him feel more contrite than any reproach.

"Probably. I should be able to give a better answer when I have studied the situation more carefully." He could see her a little better now. He could see the delicate bones beneath porcelain skin that contributed to her fragile appearance. He could see the pendant that glowed like an opalescent moon on a silver chain. He saw her concern for him in the Power that wreathed her, and for a moment, he envied the depth of unity that could exist between a man and woman who shared such major Power. He marveled that Kaedric, Lord Venkarel, could have sacrificed the wholeness of such a bond even to save a world.

"Do you know what happened to you?" asked Rhianna.

Quin swallowed, though his raw throat burned from the effort. "I was nearly lost. I nearly became . . ."

". . . like Kaedric," finished Rhianna in a voice that shuddered from emotion, "a man without a physical form, a Power without a mortal host. You were gone from us for almost eleven days. You crossed the patterns of time, and that unnatural trespass alone sent a tremor across the infinities."

Quin closed his eyes, unable to watch her without

sharing her pain of old loss, augmented by her awareness of its near-repetition. "I know what to expect now.
I shall not be caught unprepared again."

"You can never prepare thoroughly for the unknown.
The risk of an unknown usage of Power is *always*
enormous."

"I must return to Nilson, my lady. We cannot ignore
a disease that affects the patterns of our very existence."

"You are not the ultimate authority on Network's
technology of topological transfer," said Rhianna dryly.
"You will go nowhere, Lord Quinzaine, until I have
consulted with *other* experts. That is your Infortiare's
command. Do you understand me?"

He dared to open his eyes once more, forced not by
her Power's hard insistence but by her passionate caring. Rhianna's blanched, anxious face silenced Quin's
protest. "Yes, my lady," he answered meekly, and his
Power sighed its relief.

CHAPTER 11

Healer

Soft pastel colors, gold and rose and lilac, gentled the
early evening sky. The hills of Revgaenian wore the luminous green of spring, and blue lupine filled the ruts
beside the Montelier road. The cottage garden blossomed, and the mewls and yaps of kits and pups
sounded chaotically from the unfenced yard behind the
house. The ill-defined yard grew crowded in this season, when so many of the valley's untamed creatures
brought their young to Evjenial, the Healer of Revgaenian. Where Healers lived, even their most bestial
supplicants gathered in truce from natural enmities.

Plain and plainly dressed in homespun cotton, dyed
to a russet color that was dull imitation of her fiery hair,
Evjenial resembled a very weary pixie. She trudged
from the yard to the garden, limply holding her skirts
above the tall grasses. She had worked since dawn, almost without pause. She was accustomed to long hours,
but she usually relied on her husband's strong arms to
aid her in the lifting and turning of heavy patients.
Though Suleifas often tended patients in Innisbeck
across the river, while Jeni traveled among Revgaenian's tiny wilderness farms and meager holdings, the
two Healers seldom stayed apart for more than a few
days. The past month, while Suleifas checked on all
those distant charges whom he had been unable to visit
throughout the harsh winter, had seemed a lonely eter-
nity to her.

Jeni laved her chapped hands in the cold water that
she had pulled from the garden's stone well, then used
her linen apron as towel. The cottage boasted more
modern plumbing, but Jeni enjoyed drawing water

from earth by her own effort. She took pride in the
smoothness of the rope that one of her patients had
twisted and tied for her. The new water bucket, hewn
from the wood of a tree that a harsh winter storm had
felled, comforted her with a sense of continuity, despite loss. She had lived in extreme simplicity for most
of her adult life. She encouraged Suleifas in bringing
gradual improvements—such as Network plumbing—
to the technology-fearing peoples of her world, but part
of her still preferred the old Siathan traditions. As a
girl, before the Mirlai had Chosen her and remade her
as Healer, Evjenial had been Copper, a lawless tech
runner who had acquired most of her knowledge of
Network technology from its smuggled weaponry. She
did not relish those memories, though they had enabled
her to bring the man known as Rabh Marrach to the
Mirlai.

This cottage, this yard, this land that bordered Montelier and Revgaenian had been Evjenial's primary
home since she accepted Rabh Marrach as the successor to the name and duties of Suleifas, Healer of Innisbeck and Montelier. She had joined him in the certainty
of Mirlai vision, only understanding the magnitude of
that vision when she accepted Suleifas also as husband.
In this season of rebirth, the entire planet of Siatha
seemed to offer itself in thanks for the Healer's work.
The houses along the Montelier road, which had nearly
burst from a surplus of human supplicants during the
hard winter, had begun to empty. The labors of spring
brought joy rather than sorrow, but Jeni recognized a
growing imperfection in the customary Mirlai peace.
A small, occasional prickle of disquiet at first, the trouble
had begun to sprawl like the briars of the Taleran
Valley.

She had not acknowledged the reason until this
morning, when the Mirlai awakened her with awareness that Suleifas would return before nightfall. In her
eagerness to be with him again, she had waltzed
through the cottage like a girl in the first bloom of
love. She had unfolded his wool winter coat from the
cedar drawer, just to hold something of his in her arms,

and she had found the case of precision Network tools marked with the Council Governor's seal.

She knew that her husband kept such tools. He made no secret of his past, least of all to her, who had known him before his Choosing. Neither did the Network emblem, gold bar on black, surprise her, though it chilled her with memories of its cruel owner. The Council Governor had owned her husband for many years.

A powerful shiver had coursed through her in touching the toolcase, but the fear was not her own. It was that distinction of origin that had forced her to accept what she did not want to know: The Mirlai feared.

Jeni had not felt such disquiet since before her husband's Choosing. She had hoped—and she had expected—never to feel such strong disquiet again. Mirlai brought peace, healing and love to their symbiotic partners. They did not bring pain without powerful cause.

"You Chose my Suleifas. You Healed him," she whispered to the gentle sky. "Heal him anew, that we all may know peace again." The golden wreath of Mirlai danced so brightly around her that even a nonbeliever might have seen them and wondered. Focusing on the inner voices with a dreamer's unseeing gaze, Jeni did not notice that even the unruly animals in the yard fell silent from respect for the beings that were Mirlai.

When she opened her eyes from her reverie, the sky had become violet, and a man stood before her, watching her with the fullness of understanding that only a fellow Healer could share. She smiled at him and wrapped herself joyfully in his arms. In the evening shadows, she could not see him well, but she knew each strong plane of the face and body that had been molded and remolded so often in the service of the Council Governor of Network. She coiled her fingers in the thick strands of her husband's hair, wondering if the past month had restored the sunstreaks from winter's darkness. His warmth seeped into her.

"How many were lost?" she asked, Healer before lover and wife.

"Only those that we expected: Gallawick and Vorna."

"It was their time."

"Yes, but I shall miss them—especially Gallawick. I liked that old glassmaker. I did not know Vorna as well."

"She was simple-witted before your predecessor, the previous Suleifas, met her. He used to tell me of her. I think he was disturbed that the Mirlai did not consider such simpleness a cause for healing." She pressed her cheek against the rough wool of her husband's coat. "Mirlai heal according to their own wisdom, and it is not always easy for us to accept."

"Vorna has received the final healing now." The two Healers walked to their cottage, their emotions entwined like their arms. "Have the healings been many here?"

Jeni shrugged. "No more than usual for this season. Mostly birthings."

"The birthings must be all of breached bears and calves to leave you so tired, my Jeni."

"I can deal more easily with bears and cattle than with some of the panicked first-time fathers of human kind."

Suleifas' laugh was soft. He moved to light the Network fixtures that he had contrived to install unobtrusively within the cottage ceiling. The furnishings might be the hand-made offerings of the Healers' many patients, but the cottage was less primitive than it appeared.

Jeni stopped him before he could brighten the room. "Not tonight," she whispered and lit a thick white candle instead.

He crooked one dark brow. Jeni's affection for old Siathan traditions amused him. "I have missed you, Jeni." He lit a second candle from hers and followed her into the kitchen.

Together, they warmed and served the supper that had been left upon their windowsills, gift or payment from some patient or patient's kindred. They spoke of their work as Healers, their friends, and the inconsequential events that each had missed of the other's life during their recent time apart. They were glad just to be together, and the Mirlai shared their contentment.

Only when they had sat for many minutes at the wood-plank supper table did Jeni sigh, "You trouble the Mirlai, Rabh." She did not often speak his former name aloud, although she never forgot the wounded, deadly man who had first demanded healing of her in Revgaenian. The Mirlai had healed him, gentled him, and made him part of her, but she knew something of the horrors of his past. She accepted his past despite his crimes, not solely because she loved him, but because she understood the depth and power of Mirlai forgiveness. Her own youth had not been blameless.

Rabh/Suleifas laid aside his fork, although he had not yet finished his bowl of thick stew. "Do I trouble you, Jeni?" he asked, his deep eyes shadowed by his jutting brow.

"Do I not share the Mirlai needs?" she retorted. Her coppery braid seemed to shine as brightly as the candles in their sconces. She shredded a hard roll with her deft fingers, unconsciously piling wheaty crumbs upon the glazed green pottery plate.

"The Mirlai are part of you, as they are part of me. That does not make us indistinguishable." He nodded toward her dismantled roll. "The birds will be pleased that you share our meal with them, but they might prefer to feast in the morning."

With a mutter of disgust at her own distraction, Jeni dropped the roll to its plate, but her uneasiness found quick substitute. She cradled the warm porcelain mug that held her tea, though she did not drink of its fragrant contents. "I am troubled, Rabh," she admitted, swirling her tea and watching the bits of broken herbs that danced in the golden liquid. She used his old name again consciously to prove her concern. "You trouble me, because you are troubled—and you did not return or send for me when you knew you needed Healing for yourself. The Mirlai trouble me, because they let your restlessness continue. They tolerate this lack of peace within you, although they hate it. I do not understand the reasons for any of it."

"I had a . . . true-dream, Jeni, a few nights after I left you."

For a moment, Jeni clung to silence, trying to sense a Mirlai echo of his statement. The Mirlai affirmed nothing. "It was not Mirlai-sent," she concluded aloud.

"It has meaning only because of them. The true-dream speaks of what they were, what I was, and what we have together become." He cupped his large hands, as if in offering. "We are Healers."

Jeni blew the steam from her tea, and the Mirlai glowed golden in the mist. Their dance was uneven and almost without beauty. "This," she said, nodding at the ragged dance, "is what your 'true-dream' has effected. What manner of 'true-dream' causes such disruption? This resembles the destructive work of the Council Governor. Are you so sure that you do not 'dream' at the behest of those Network devices implanted in your head and nervous system, Rabh?"

Her husband shoved himself away from the table, scraping his chair on the wooden floor. He stood and crossed abruptly to the black cast-iron stove. He grasped the hot kettle near its copper base, visibly defying himself to know pain in the hand that Mirlai had made real and capable of fine feeling. "No, I am not sure," he whispered harshly. "But I am sure enough to make even the Mirlai uncertain, or they would indeed have stopped me."

After a pause filled with troubled thoughts unspoken, Jeni asked, "May you explain to me?"

"Not yet." He replaced the kettle on the stove and shrugged in mute apology. "Not until the true-dream enables me to understand for myself."

A gust of wind echoed hollowly through the stovepipe. "Has Caragen been hounding you again?" asked Jeni.

"Not lately. Perhaps it is his rare mercy that troubles me."

As Healer's wife, Jeni noted that Suleifas' full, undyed shirt needed darning, where his broad shoulders had worn thin the coarse fabric. As Healer, she observed the sardonic thinning of his lips and knew that he was more truly Rabh Marrach tonight than he had been for at least two years. She wondered suddenly if he ever thought of himself by either name, having used and discarded so many different identities in his life.

"I have healed you before," said Jeni in soft reminder, "when you thought you had no need of my help." She was a small woman, her appearance unexceptional except for the brightness of her coppery hair, but her serene Healer's confidence gave her a proud bearing when she focused Mirlai energy. "If your dream is true, it will withstand sharing with another Healer—one who has been a Healer longer than you. I have experienced powerful true-dreams, and I know the troubling feel of guidance that seems contrary to what I believe."

Her husband's gray-green eyes observed her keenly, appreciative of her gifts on many levels. "Such as the painful true-dream that led you to heal me?" he asked with wry insight into her present thoughts.

"Yes," she replied, too honest and too aware of his gifts to try dissembling. Neither Healer had any affection for *that* Rabh Marrach who had destroyed and conspired on behalf of Andrew Caragen. "I begged the Mirlai to let me pass you unseen. Healing you required much faith. I sought counsel from Suleifas, your predecessor." Sorrow crept into Jeni's voice at memory of a dear friend, still mourned. "He advised me, and I never repaid him for that gift. As his successor, you must allow me to fulfill that debt by service, as is the proper way to show respect to any Healer."

"I am far removed from that Suleifas who advised you. He was father to you." The sardonic smile thawed. "I much prefer to be husband."

"You are his Chosen successor," said Jeni, sternly denying the temptation to let troubles remain unvoiced until the morning. Procrastination solved nothing. "Tell me your dream, Rabh, that I may share its burden." The golden Mirlai danced more brightly above her pixie face.

With a sigh, Rabh nodded faintly at her, who had never hesitated to tell him when he erred. He had admired her even before he knew the Mirlai, when he had not yet understood the force of Healer's instincts. "Of all the multitude of beings that I faced in Caragen's service, Jeni, only you ever dared to lecture me."

She answered dryly, "I did not know that I confronted Rabhadur Marrach, the most dreaded agent of Network's Council Governor."

"You feared me sufficiently, but you trusted the Mirlai more." He paced the small kitchen, his boots sounding loud against the oaken floorboards. "I would not know how to explain what this dream has planted in me," he said, his voice becoming urgent. "It is a *need* like the compulsion that makes us heal. I can no more dismiss this dream than the force that binds us to the Mirlai. I have tried."

Jeni bowed her head over her hands, clenched tightly around the mug. Her coppery braid fell forward across her shoulder, feathery tips of her hair grazing the table. She sipped the steaming tea and grimaced at the sting of heat. "Tell me the dream, Rabh," she said with soft insistence, "as it first came to you."

She was the senior Healer. Marrach respected her wisdom too much to deny her direct request, though he hated to make her suffer for any part of his violent past. He slid his hands, strong and callused from hard work, along the oiled wood of the cane-back chair. He had repaired the caning the previous summer, a simple, useful task for hands that had wrought more destruction than healing.

Hesitantly, Marrach resumed his place opposite Jeni. He leaned his elbows on the table, folded his hands against his chin, and fixed his deep stare on his wife. "The dream has three parts," said Marrach, as crisply as he might once have reported to Andrew Caragen. "In the first part, I am present as observer. I see the emptiness of space, as I have often seen it from ships traveling through the thinly populated region that lies between Network and Consortium jurisdictions. Stars begin to appear, flickering into life all around me.

They cover Network. Their brightness would blind eyes of flesh, but I am able to count them, and their number matches the 'other' spaces that Network has breached with topological transfer. As I count them, the stars begin to bleed."

In a sudden display of frustration, Marrach snatched a heavy serving spoon from the table and squeezed the metal utensil in half. Jeni suppressed her startled concern for the skin of his hands, though no blood spurted from his flesh. She knew that his strength and ability to tolerate pain far exceeded most men's measures. She nodded at him, encouraging him to proceed with the dream's recounting. She did not speak. She let the Mirlai feed her courage.

"In the second part," Marrach continued evenly, "I am Mirlai, and I perceive the needs of living beings instead of any sight or sound. A Consortium Inquisitor *needs* to set right what is discordant with his ideal truth, and he condemns me, for I have failed to uphold my proper purpose. I cannot assuage his need, and I flee from him."

"What is the third part?" asked Jeni, marveling inwardly that any Healer could actually share the Mirlai perspective, even in true-dream. Each Chosen Healer contributed a special skill or insight to the communion of Mirlai and Healers. The gifts that Rabh Marrach had brought to the line of Suleifas were indeed unique.

"In the final part of the dream, I travel again through the bright, bleeding emptiness of the dream's beginning. I perceive another traveler—a man not unlike me who *needs* like a Calongi. The stars bleed upon his ideal, Calongi truth, and it is altered irreparably. His needs, Calongi needs, become unstable and impossible to fulfill. Consortium peace is broken. From the Consortium to Network, the still expanse of space dissolves into the chaos of its birth throes."

Jeni's face had become pale beneath her freckles. "It is a true-dream," she whispered, believing now, though she wished she could dismiss her husband's dream as product of Caragen's meddling or merely the imagining of a weary mind. *It is terrible*, she added in silent grief to the Mirlai.

"Advise me, Healer," said Marrach quietly.

The burden of her own special calling had not so daunted Evjenial since Rabh Marrach first entered her life. For an instant, she cried a silent protest to the Mirlai: *Let me be the Healer only of Revgaenian. Let him be only Suleifas, not Rabh Marrach, not Caragen's cruelly gifted creature.* Healing the sick and injured of Revgaenian gave her purpose and strength, but the haunting demands of Rabh Marrach's past were too much for her to heal. The burden was too much even as atonement for her own violent youth.

The Mirlai offered her comfort, and her moment of panic passed. Jeni bowed her head briefly in thanks to them, and she raised her eyes to the man before her, thanking the Mirlai also for him, who was her sorrow and her greatest joy. "You understand Network better than anyone, Rabh," answered Jeni, "because Caragen implanted Network inside your brain and made you Network's living counterpart. The Mirlai understand Calongi. In the symbiosis that makes you a Healer, there is knowledge as well as healing skills. Your knowledge and their perceptions have made you aware of an imbalance that demands healing."

"Am I so arrogant that I should seek to heal a universe?" he demanded dryly, but there was sober questioning in his own needs.

"We heal as we are led. I would not know how to begin such a healing as you propose, but it has not been asked of me. Healing *you* is task enough for me."

Marrach extended his hand toward her, and she grasped it tightly. "Jeni, I want no more part of that life that Caragen created."

"We must use the skills that we are given," she answered. She yearned to cling to him, lie, and tell him that his dream had no significance. She spoke instead as Mirlai directed her, "Not every healing is easy or pleasant. As I was Chosen to heal you because of my particular background and awareness, so you must fulfill your own unique purpose."

"Divining one's true purpose is a Calongi ideal," said Marrach with hollow humor.

Words lodged in Jeni's throat, and she croaked, "Truth has no single owner."

"And the Mirlai were members of the Consortium for many generations," added Marrach with a faint, pensive frown. "They shared the Consortium concepts of 'Truth.' "

"Do you?" asked Jeni, releasing his hard, warm hand abruptly. She had sensed something strange and elusive, as if the Mirlai force had become inverted for a moment, drawing its energies from her Healer husband instead of filling him. The moment terrified her, because it reminded her that the Mirlai, like their original symbionts, the Adraki, were a broken people.

Marrach's frown deepened, and his eyes narrowed to bright slits. "The simplicity of your question is deceptive."

"Only if you make it so."

He gave a curt nod. "Acceptance of Calongi 'Truth' is the crux of Consortium allegiance. I am not a Consortium member. Therefore, I do not share their 'Truth,' because I have only a skeletal knowledge of its definition."

"Have you not inverted the order? Does not the sharing precede the membership?"

"Not with the Calongi. They demand commitment first and foremost. Members of the less civilized species must entrust the understanding of 'Truth' to the Calongi masters."

"Then you do not share their 'Truth,' because you disagree with it."

"I cannot agree with something that I do not understand."

"That sounds like a Network aphorism."

Marrach slapped his hands loudly against the table. "Jeni, why are we arguing?"

Jeni drew herself straight. The fierceness of her Healer's faith gave her small figure a commanding air. "We argue because you requested my advice, Healer

Suleifas. I could advise you better, if you would tell me the rest of what lies heavily upon you."

"My entire life lies heavily upon me," retorted Marrach with an irony that was not a Mirlai gift.

"I know quite enough about Rabhadur Marrach's evil past, and I know that you are no longer that man. Tell me, *Suleifas*, what Rabh's past and Healer's true-dream have led you to do?"

"I have not acted yet—not consciously, at least."

"But you intend to act."

"I expect to act," admitted Marrach with a sigh. He rubbed his furrowed forehead against his folded hands. "If this true-dream unfolds as I begin to anticipate, I must intervene on a scale that would satisfy even Andrew Caragen. I must do what he created me to do." Jeni's lips thinned, and Marrach raised his voice against her unspoken doubts. "I will not be acting on Caragen's behalf, even if his needs align for a time with ours. Whatever I must do, Jeni, I shall do as a Healer. The Mirlai are inside of me, and that cannot change."

"Can either of us know what Caragen is capable of changing, abetted by all of Network's resources?"

Marrach clenched his left fist and shook it fiercely—a gesture not of anger but of conviction. "The Mirlai have remade me from the cells of this arm to the compassion that they taught me. I *must* heal. What else do you imagine could make me consider reentering Caragen's realm of conspiracies and manipulation?"

Jeni touched the table, the dishes and utensils, feeling their ordinary textures and substance. Their simplicity helped to soothe her anxious heart. "You shout against your own uncertainties. You fail to intimidate them."

"Understand me," growled her husband.

"Is that a Healer's plea or the command of Caragen's agent?"

Marrach's deep gaze sharpened on her, as if it might burn into her soul, but Jeni did not try to blink away his severe inspection. "Do not let jealousy of Caragen obscure your Healer's judgment, dear Jeni."

She flinched. "He owned you for most of your life."

"He does not own me now."

Jeni bowed her head, accepting his assertion outwardly. Some of the tension eased from Marrach's sharply defined muscles. He could not see the anguish in his wife's eyes. "What will you hope, Rabh?" she asked in a whisper.

It was a proper Healer's question, and Rabh/Suleifas replied with restored quietude, "I shall hope to restabilize Network before the Consortium feels compelled to intervene. Because Network/Consortium peace is so fragile, any direct Consortium intervention in Network affairs could escalate into the most brutal, uncivilized war that this universe has ever seen."

"Network is not a match for the Consortium," said Jeni. Only Mirlai strength enabled her to keep her voice from trembling.

"The Consortium is formidable, but its power is based on economics and philosophy. Network cultivates military power." Marrach spoke more rapidly, delineating a Network agent's schemes of logical analysis instead of a Healer's tentative emotion. "I cannot estimate the actual scope of the Consortium's legendary technology—despite all of Caragen's efforts to extract that data—but I know Network well enough to surmise that the Consortium would not achieve an easy victory in a direct conflict. The Consortium might even lose." With a momentary recurrence of uncertainty, he finished, "And I do not even know which side I should cheer in such a contest."

"Council Governor Caragen would not risk his own enormous power on a slim chance of victory. He would not begin a war with the Consortium."

"Dear Jeni, you should never underestimate him. Caragen could not have obtained his 'enormous power' if he were unwilling to take calculated risks. With his position as Council Governor already in jeopardy from his rivals on the Council, he has less to lose—and very much more to gain—that at any time in the past eighty years."

Jeni frowned. "Does he have any serious rivals?"

"Thanks to me, every member of the Council is a serious rival. They fight among themselves, for now, confident of Caragen's imminent retirement, but you may be sure that they watch him, ready to seize upon any opportunity to accelerate his departure."

"Thanks to you, as well as to Quin Hamley," said Jeni, remembering the last time that Rabh Marrach's past had produced a tangible haunt. That odd young man, who had married one of Rabh Marrach's former victims, had also defied Caragen successfully. Quin Hamley had thereby joined Rabh Marrach in a very exclusive and dangerous fraternity.

"Yes," answered Marrach pensively. "Quin could be considered equally culpable." A flickering of the deep-set eyes hinted at a train of thought, newly embarked. "We have both weakened the great Network Council Governor by demonstrating that the old shark is not invincible. Caragen has suffered two defeats."

"He is an old man, who must die eventually."

"But he must not die yet," answered Marrach with the sudden, feverish sureness of a reluctant prophet. He glanced around him at the neat, simply furnished kitchen, as if its humble comforts were precious beyond measure.

"He has already outlived wisdom."

"When Caragen dies," said Marrach between clenched teeth, "Network's current social structure will collapse. Network's technology—and much of it has terrifying destructive potential—will be available to the greediest taker."

"Is there no one in Network with wisdom enough to rule it well? Caragen is a strong ruler but a cruel one."

"He eliminates his competitors ruthlessly. Those who survive are as ruthless as he and far less experienced in governing. Worthy Network rulers could appear in time, but that time will not be available unless I stabilize the present situation."

"Now you do take too much upon yourself, too soon," chided Jeni. "You speak like a Network agent, Rabh, instead of a Healer, though you base all your Network analysis on a partially revealed true-dream.

What situation requires stability? You have not yet seen the full meaning of your true-dream. What is required of *you*? You do not yet know. You cannot even define the direction of your fear: That Caragen's power will lead to war with the Consortium? Or that Caragen's waning of power will lead to his replacement?"

Marrach began to shake his head, but the gesture remained incomplete. The Mirlai swirled around him, and both Healers knew that the cryptic answer he gave belonged to them: "Not even the Calongi can protect the universe from a force they do not recognize, and they do not yet recognize the truth that is fundamental to Network's topological transfer. For years, Caragen has been damaging the Consortium with lies, and all Truth has suffered." Marrach's voice acquired an odd resonance, as he spoke from true-dream, "The Calongi must learn that the absolute Truth of this universe is no longer *precisely* what they believe it to be. Until the Calongi learn and assimilate, Caragen must retain control of Network."

Golden Mirlai danced a halo above him, affirming him as one of their own Chosen Healers. "I understand, Rabh," said Jeni gently, though she understood little from the words he spoke. Mirlai danced also around her, lighting her fiery hair. "Your true-dream tests your faith."

He sighed, the flare of prophetic energy leaving him, "Is it a true-dream, Jeni? Or is it, as you have already accused, just another product of Caragen's many manipulations of me? It frightens even the Mirlai."

"Of course, it frightens them," answered Jeni briskly. "They are neither foolish nor arrogant. Their survival, as well as ours, is at stake. If they were not frightened, I would doubt the truth of what you have perceived."

With a faint smile for Jeni's staunch denial of her own fear, Marrach requested again, "Advise me, Healer."

"You must contact Caragen."

"He will distrust me."

"But he will listen."

"And he may decide that my continued existence threatens him more than the possibility of Mirlai retaliation."

"He would rather use you than destroy you. Even now, you are his most valuable asset." She sipped the last of her tea and found it cold. "He still fears you."

"He regrets having integrated me so thoroughly into Network," mused Marrach, summoning Network data via the internal link that Caragen had long ago provided.

"That is why you have the advantage: You share his Network. He cannot share the Mirlai."

"You make it all sound so simple, dear Jeni."

"It is simple enough to tell you what you have already decided. As for the complicated details," she continued dryly, "there is no one better qualified than you to rearrange the politics of a universe. That was your function in Caragen's service, was it not?"

"I am no longer that man."

"But you retain that man's memories and his skills. Use them now—for healing."

"Some healings are painful. Some healings fail."

"Some healings exceed all expectations."

The evening had ebbed into dark night, and candlelight's flickering shadows fell across the table between them. The Mirlai faded into their usual invisibility. Jeni sighed in sudden fatigue. To conceal her weariness, she gathered empty dishes from the table and carried them to the steel wash basin. Her husband brought the kettle from the fire, and poured the heated water over the dishes.

"The fire needs replenishing," he said. "I'll bring more wood from the yard." Jeni nodded mutely. Marrach tugged lightly on her braid, coaxing a smile from her. "Thank you, Healer Evjenial."

She continued to smile, until he left the house. "Grant me the wisdom to guide him," she whispered to the Mirlai, "and the courage to trust him." She grabbed a checkered towel from its hook and began to scrub the dishes with unnecessary vehemence.

***

The pastels of Siathan evening glowed from the cloud-spattered sky, but Quin found no peace in them. The thin spiral of woodsmoke sweetened the air as he crossed soft grasses to reach the Healers' cottage, but Quin sensed only the fire that burned in meager echo of his own intense Power. The Infortiare had sent him to consult Rabh Marrach, while she summoned unspecified "advisers." Quin, assuming the advice would take the form of Ixaxin wizards' counsel, accepted the alternative mission willingly. Quin had never relished meetings, least of all the formal sessions of the hidebound Ixaxin wizards who had tormented his childhood with unwanted structure and a concerted belief in Lord Quinzaine's hopelessness as a scholar.

The journey was Quin's first since returning from Nilson to Serii a fortnight earlier, and Quin discovered a disheartening ebb in his own self-confidence in making the familiar effort of Power. He wondered if Lady Rhianna had sent him solely to learn from Marrach, or if she intentionally forced Quin to travel the infinities again to counteract a recognized reluctance that the ghastliness of Nilson had produced. The former motive seemed plausible, but the latter reason was nearly a certainty, given the Infortiare's particular sensitivity to Power's ailments.

As Quin stood in contemplation, watching the shifting colors of the Siathan sky, Marrach emerged alone from the Healers' cottage. He walked quickly and met Quin on the path beyond the gate. Even in evening's kindly shadows, the Healer's face showed new creases and a grimness that Quin could not remember noticing in any prior meeting. The Healer did not welcome Quin with friendly banter, nor did he extend an invitation to enter the gate.

The Healer already knows, thought Quin and found himself resentful of that insight. "Why did you advise me to go to Nilson?" demanded Quin without gentler greeting. A songbird mourned the departure of day.

"You requested my advice," replied Rabh Marrach coolly.

"That world that you described to me, Marrach, that wretched Nilson, is on the verge of an implosion that could take half a universe with it." Quin paused, awaiting reaction, but not even Power could delve through the impenetrability of Marrach's present mood. The hardness, unalloyed by any evidence of Mirlai compassion, impressed Quin unpleasantly with the strength of another Marrach, the Network tool that Quin knew only by dire repute. Quin denied his Power's inclination to combat a palpable danger, and he continued to speak as a friend, injured but still respectful. "Is this what you wanted me to see? Is this how you quench my thirst for Consortium lore? If so, it is a drastic, deadly method that you choose, and every wizard in Ixaxis would love to learn how you recognized the instability without benefit of Power."

Pain etched Marrach's face, and he was visibly a Healer again. "I do not know," he whispered. "I do not know if Mirlai directed you or your Power directed me."

Quin saw the Mirlai rise in agitation. He observed their ragged dance in wary curiosity, wondering if Marrach's mood caused their turmoil or reflected it. Quin did not consider attack as even a remote possibility, until the Mirlai hurled their collective life energy against him. His Power built instinctive defense, but still their action stunned him.

The Mirlai hammered at him, demanding his departure. Power burned in him, yearning to respond with violence and anger. Quin denied his Power sternly, for Quin did not wish to risk harming the Mirlai—or a man who might still be a friend—by retaliating. "Marrach," said Quin with a frantic edge to his voice, "tell the Mirlai to stop before they force me to injure them or you. When threatened, Power protects itself ruthlessly."

"Then you should leave immediately, Quin," replied Rabh Marrach with unbending calm, "before we learn whose form of power prevails."

"What did you expect me to learn on Nilson?"

"You have told me what *I* needed to learn."

"Marrach, what do you expect me to *do?*"

If the Healer heard, he did not respond. When Marrach turned his back on Quin and began to stride back to the cottage, Quin hissed his frustration. The Mirlai continued to pound him, an irritation rather than a threat, but it broke Quin's limited patience. With a flick of Power that sent a cloud of Mirlai scurrying, Quin abandoned the mock battle and Siatha. Hurt and profoundly troubled, Quin returned to the uncanny path to Serii, glad for once to face the prospect of a gathering of stodgy Ixaxins.

CHAPTER 12

Spirit

"Quin insists that he must return to Nilson," announced Rhianna to a room that appeared empty but for her. It was the Tower's highest chamber, and she sat upon the solitary cot with her full, wine-colored skirts spread around her haphazardly. Her gaze was distant, for she looked upon the plane of Power and the excessively lean, darkly compelling illusion of her husband's living form. To her Power's vision, Kaedric retained every facet of the physical self that he had—of cruel necessity—discarded, from the icy blue of his eyes to the scars that vicious men had inflicted on him as a boy. She could see even the gold medallion, which had marked his status as Infortiare, resting prominently against the black silk of his severe attire, precisely as she had seen it on the man who had taught her the meaning and use of her own Power. "I feel a need to protect Quin," she continued, "both from selfish motives regarding his unique abilities and from a genuine fondness for my trouble-prone cousin, but I sense also that he is correct. Until we gain a greater understanding of what he experienced, we must discontinue Network forays by any less capable wizard. Whatever Quin encountered, we cannot disregard it."

"Indeed not," replied her husband in the crisp, cool voice that had once intimidated Serii's wizards, monarch, and ruling lords. "We must trust his recognition of danger and be guided by it. Quinzaine must return, as he says, but he should not go unaided."

"No living Ixaxin has more Power to perceive and to survive a phenomenon such as Quin has discovered. Fearing to allow even Quin to return to Nilson, I can assuredly ask no one else to make such a journey. I cannot even offer to aid him remotely, since no Wizards' Circle could reach Quin amid the chaos he has described."

"You need not limit yourself to living Ixaxins, my dear. I can accompany him."

Rhianna shivered inwardly, but she disciplined her reaction to give a steady reply. "I would never question the magnitude of your Power, Kaedric, but I do dispute your suitability for this task. If the patterns are destabilized, you cannot risk becoming a part of the disintegration. You have no moral anchor to maintain your continuity."

"We cannot judge," retorted Kaedric, Lord Venkarel, in quiet irony, "where we have no adequate knowledge to let us reason intelligently."

"Then we must gather knowledge," answered Rhianna, "from those who are best equipped to provide it."

"We shall gather nothing from here. You have already conferred with Ixaxis' finest scholars, including all of those who have traveled to Network, and they have added nothing but rhetoric to what you already knew. If you could collect all of the wizards that Ixaxis ever taught, beloved, you would fail to assemble any better answers than Lord Quinzaine provides, until additional data are made available. While no one has succeeded as well as Quin at assimilating an understanding of the way Network's citizens think, he is a lazy scholar at best." The sardonic image smiled. "I do have the diligence that our gifted lord of Hamley lacks."

"You are not invulnerable."

"Nor am I devoid of selfish instincts, dear Rhianna, if only because I would not care to abandon you further than I have already done. I grant that no one is *more* vulnerable than I to a major disruption of the peculiar fabric of topological space, since it is the sole remaining substance of my being. However, that is why I have no choice but to investigate further. I can no more disregard a spatial instability than a man of mortal flesh can ignore a plague afflicting his body."

"You are not the space you occupy."

"You cite my own fundamental premise as if you expect me to contradict it."

"I expect you to realize that I would rather abandon my own life than lose you!" Her hand reached toward him frantically, though there was no flesh to meet hers. "Knowing the risks, which affect you especially, I would rather accompany Quin myself than have you make that journey."

He answered gently, "If you were to go, I would be with you, and the dangers would beset us both. I could not separate myself from you in such an undertaking even if I tried. You are too thoroughly the reason for my continued existence." A caress of Power touched and warmed her. "You and I know the fragile state of the infinities that Network calls 'topological space.' The fabric of our own reality would have disintegrated years ago, if our son had not succeeded in reconfiguring our Network-damaged segment of infinity. Evaric's unique Power was the necessary ingredient to the restoration of Serii's patterns, and his Power continues to provide a vital stabilization. If Network has created another instability, we must discover the key to *its* healing."

"We are not able to parent another Evaric, my husband. Even the lifespan of this world of ours will not exceed our son's time upon it, unless we discover a more permanent method of preservation."

"We have been remiss about seeking an alternate method. Quin's unpleasant encounter may have a beneficial outcome, since it reminds us forcibly of the dangers of complacency. Perhaps the door to a more general course of healing will open as a result. We cannot make any such discovery without examining the current damage."

"Healing," sighed Rhianna, echoing her husband's choice of analogy. "I wish the Healer Suleifas had never planted the idea of Nilson in young Quinzaine's reckless head."

"The Healer was once known as Rabhadur Marrach," mused Kaedric, and his wife perceived the sudden coldness of suspicion take hold in him, "the single most destructive citizen in all of Network's unexemplary history."

Disliking her husband's cynical implication, but unable to refute it, Rhianna remarked, "You have a similar reputation among many Seriins."

"I earned that reputation equally, I fear."

The truth of his statement forced Rhianna to confront his theory directly, "You think that Rabh Marrach *caused* the damage that Quin sensed on Nilson?"

"I think that I would like to know why he chose to recommend Nilson as a travel destination for Lord Quinzaine."

By Power, Rhianna stared at her ethereal husband, weighing his sardonic suspicion. Few mortals or Immortals had ever matched Kaedric for quickness of mind or keenness of insight into the darkest aspects of human nature. He had honed his insight on hard experience. She did not want to measure the Healer by such an uncharitable scale, but she could not dismiss her husband's wary cynicism. "Quin said that Nilson has one port that is open to the very alien and unknown civilization that Network calls 'the Consortium.' Quin was curious to see an alien being."

"One might have thought Network itself would be sufficiently 'alien' to satisfy him, but Quinzaine has all the compulsive curiosity of a cat," said Kaedric dryly. "He is likely to reap the same fatal consequences one day." In the glittering plane of Power's vision, the wizard stretched his dark figure with uncannily feline grace. "Did our intemperate lordling manage to encounter his alien?"

"I think not," answered Rhianna uncertainly. "I did not ask him, for there was so much of greater consequence to discuss. Do you think it matters?"

"I distrust coincidences, my love. I would like to know what prompted Quinzaine's timely compulsion to see an 'alien.' I would like very much to know what the good Healer actually intended in suggesting Nilson as a destination. Consider a few of the most obvious possibilities: Master Rabh Marrach served Council

Governor Caragen with considerable cunning, and I
doubt that Master Rabh abandoned any of his wits in
the process of becoming a Healer. The prospect of manipulating the Power of a wizard like Quinzaine could
prove overwhelmingly tempting to an ambitious man
who understands Power just well enough to covet it,
but not quite well enough to fear it."

"You are still too much a cynic, my Kaedric. This
Healer, whom you slander so readily, once saved your
life essence, as well as Quinzaine's."

"The Healer's symbiotic *partners* salvaged me, a
dubious service to the good of the universe."

"Do not speak so unappreciatively, Kaedric," chas-
tised his wife.

The wizard's image smiled apologetically. "I am not
accusing. My point is simply that our evidence against
Master Rabh weighs at least as heavily as any factors
in favor of Healer Suleifas. Consult with Lord Quinzaine's wife or any other member of the Terry family,
and they will remind you readily enough of their
causes for distrusting Master Rabhadur Marrach. We
cannot take the Healer's innocence for granted."

"I already sent Quin to Siatha to meet with the
Healer," sighed Rhianna, conceding her own measure
of suspicion. "I sensed a need for such a journey."

"Your Power shares your wisdom, beloved, without
being fettered by your generous spirit."

Rhianna grimaced at the twisted tribute. "I also sent
a messenger to Dr. Jonathan Terry. Since he invented
Network's transfer portals, I can think of no one better
qualified to tell us if Quinzaine's observations could be
a product of Network intent, Network error or natural
phenomena."

"Dr. Terry's insights will be equally hampered by a
dearth of concrete information. It would be interesting
to allow Dr. Terry to interview Master Rabh."

"While you observe them both, my ghostly lord?"

"There are a few advantages to my incorporeal
state."

"You have a wicked gift for subterfuge."

"You have always been too charitable in your view of me, dear Rhianna."

"And you, of me," answered his wife with a smile that she gave only to him. The patterns trembled faintly, and her smile faded. "Lord Quinzaine returns quickly."

"He returns in anger," remarked Kaedric with a wryly knowing calm.

"Lord Quinzaine's anger does not justify the depths of your suspicious mind."

"I had best leave you to speak to him alone, Rhianna. Lord Quinzaine prefers to avoid my company."

"It is his one concession to Seriin conventionality." Power caressed Power and parted reluctantly. In the Tower's highest room, Rhianna shook free of the stiffness that an hour of immobility had bequeathed. She gauged the time from a quick glance out the window, calibrating the shape of shadows dotting Tul Mountain. The afternoon had not yet ended; Lord Quinzaine had indeed spent little time with the Healer.

The young wizard had also defied the Infortiare's general preference for arrival points and come directly to the Tower. He was pacing, even now, in her study, sensing her upstairs, but not being quite bold enough to trespass *that* far. His Power, imperious with injured innocence, summoned her as surely as if he issued a deliberate order.

As Rhianna descended the narrow staircase to her study, Kaedric whispered within her, "You tolerate too much from him, Rhianna. He will outgrow us both, if we do not keep him humble while he still views us as greater Powers."

"Stop being so cynical," she chided. The tenuous brush of contact faded from her consciousness, though some part of her Power remained always with Kaedric. She arranged the carefully serene facade of the Infortiare before she opened the door to meet Lord Quinzaine dur Hamley.

"The Mirlai attacked me," complained Quin immediately on seeing her. His fingers had raked his curling hair into tangled chaos. He had tossed his cloak across a chair.

"You threatened their Chosen Healer," replied Rhianna calmly, though her heart contracted within her.

"I threatened no one! Certainly not Marrach. He is a friend." Quin grimaced. "So I have believed."

Instead of replying immediately, Rhianna circled the room, trailing her hand along the bookshelves that covered most of the wall space. Her mind evaluated rapidly, as her Power appraised Quin and all the accumulated tensions that had brought him to this moment of indignation. Rhianna laid her fingers delicately against the spine of an ancient text on wizardry. Kaedric had required her to read the text as one of her earliest lessons. "Tomorrow, you must return to Siatha, Lord Quinzaine. You must bring the Healer here."

Shocked, Quin stilled his impatient prowl. "Marrach cannot leave Siatha. He cannot leave the Mirlai."

"He chooses not to leave, as the Mirlai choose not to allow him to depart." Rhianna spoke confidently, though she prayed silently that her speculation would prove correct. "I do not require him to remain here long. I require only that he come. You can bring him. You *must* bring him."

"My lady," began Quin, hesitant now with bewilderment, "Marrach will fight me. The Mirlai will fight me. I do not wish to cause them injury."

"Master Rabhadur Marrach is an intelligent man, Lord Quinzaine, and he is clearly a man who knows how to chose his battles. He knows, or suspects, that your Power can overcome him. Explain what I require of him, and he will not fight you. Let the Mirlai know your intent, and *they* will not fight you."

"I cannot reason with the Mirlai. I do not understand the Mirlai that well."

"It was you who craved an alien encounter, Lord Quinzaine. How do you expect to communicate with a Consortium wayfarer, if you cannot make yourself understood by the beings that once restored your life?" She forced the dryness of her tone to match the hardness of her Power. "You trusted your own Power when you journeyed to Nilson. Now, trust *mine*."

Quin gave his bow curtly. He muttered the words of obeisance through a tightly clenched jaw. "As you command, my lady." His storm-gray eyes, blazing with Power, met their likeness in a crossing of proud wills. Quin's Power flared in mockery, and the air burned white between him and the Infortiare.

"Do you seek to prove your Power's greatness by such a primitive trick, Lord Quinzaine?" demanded Rhianna with a ripple of laughter. "You have spent too much time among helpless mortals."

The Infortiare's Power twisted through Quin. She did not injure, even in the harmless guise of discipline, but deftly soothed his hurts and quelled his anger. "Forgive me, my lady," he murmured, abashed by his own momentary indulgence of Power's contentious instincts.

"I understand, Quinzaine," said Rhianna softly. "Power's kinship bonds us more closely than our cousinly heritage." Her fingers traced the faded lettering on the spine of an ancient text. "You have been under considerable stress, and your Power is accordingly sensitized. You have never enjoyed the process of discipline, but you understand its necessity, especially in difficult times."

Quin gave a slightly twisted smile, acknowledging the Infortiare's quiet victory. "Shall I bring Marrach here directly, my lady?"

"Yes, please. Bring him, and leave him, until I summon you. I would suggest you spend the intervening time with your wife. She dislikes Serii."

"She is jealous of Serii. She fears that I shall eventually want to return here permanently."

"We all belong somewhere, Quinzaine. Not all of us are wise enough to recognize home when we see it."

"Marrach knows that Siatha is where *he* belongs."

"I hope so, Quinzaine. I do hope so."

***

Kaedric studied the beating waves of energy and infinity that comprised his universe. He could view them as a pulsating void, all darkness and intangible force. He could view them as myriad threads of fire and light, multicolored and dynamic. He could view them as an infinite plane that glowed without horizon or clearly delineated artifact. All descriptions evolved from his mortal memories, because this aspect of space did not accord with any visible, audible, tangible reality that any human tongue had ever named. Outside of the convenient equations that modeled the behavior of Ixaxin infinity, which was the topological space of Network, this place had no true description. All efforts to contain it within the comprehensional capacity of human senses, even when observed by a being who had made himself part of it, were equally false—and equally valid.

This was his reality, his only truth, except during the brief, precious moments in which Kaedric allowed himself to share his wife's senses. Those shared moments drained her more than she knew, because they allied her more firmly to Kaedric's insubstantial form of existence, but they enabled him to recall that he, too, was born a man and had lived a life in a physical world. They enabled him to remain Kaedric. He held to that truth of himself only for love of her.

He studied his infinite home with the critical dispassion of a trained Ixaxin analyst. Because he had voiced the analogy of a plague to his wife, it was as an infection that he enabled himself to discern the existence of the wrongness. Healing had never been his particular strength as a wizard, for Kaedric's Power was of more destructive inclination, but he was a keen observer of such details as were the first manifestations of an illness. He studied the insubstantial space that connected all the realities to which he had been born, and he knew that Quin had vastly understated the magnitude of the coming catastrophe.

II.

ALIGNMENTS

CHAPTER 13

Partners

White leaves, bleached and paper-dry at summer's end, flickered with the false light of Calong dust. The leaves had no uniform shape. Some were as bulbous as the silvery fruits; other leaves were flat and narrow, stellate or lacy. The trees branched in a spiral fashion, each limb an emerald corkscrew. The bittersweet, relanine-tainted dust of Calong made every tree brightly luminous against the sky's rich color, a blue as deep as twilight on the planet of Tori's childhood.

Tori paused in her lazy return from the traders' warehouse, where she had spent most of the morning sifting through the litter of packages and messages that arrived occasionally for her and constantly for Jase. She knelt and scooped cool pondwater in her hand and splattered the twisted bole of the tree nearest to her. Each clear droplet acquired an iridescent gleam in striking, and the pores of the tree's bark inhaled the liquid beads with an audible sigh.

Alone and unobserved, Tori echoed the sigh. Mirrored by the pond, even her red workshirt and dark hair, carelessly bound by a ribbon of Uteri flextile, seemed to shimmer with relanine's glow. The pond's reflection veiled the green of her eyes with iridescence, bestowing an illusory resemblance to Jase's relanine-saturated features. The beauty of Calong-4 stirred wonder in her, but it reminded her bluntly of her relative inadequacies. Of all the Calongi home worlds, only Calong-4 was young enough to be endured by any being whose blood was not relanine-dominated, and Calong-4 had already begun to show the signs of relanine's inexorable spread throughout the ecosystem. Within the century, Calong-4 would attain its older siblings' exclusive status, forbidden by physical necessity to those beings, like Tori, who survived outside their natural environments only by adaptation fluid's gifts. Calongi chose new homeworlds carefully and rarely, knowing the inevitability of transformation and demanding always that such change preserve the sanctity of creation and Sesserda Truth. Even on immature Calong-4, Tori knew that her ordinary Soli senses recognized only the shell of what Jase perceived, only a minute fraction of what a Calongi would observe here.

Most of the floral aromas eluded her with their subtleties, though she had learned to distinguish the sweet grasses from the water. She could taste the gingery suggestion of relanine that accompanied every concentration of Calongi people. She relied on Jase or the Calongi to recognize dangerous levels of the insidiously potent and addictive substance and preserve her from excessive exposure. Even her visual appreciation of the garden was limited by the frequencies that her eyes could discern. The white leaves did not appear colorless to those who could see the vivid patterns of warmth.

Tori seldom admitted how deeply Calong's beauty touched her, despite her Soli limitations. She did not care to acknowledge a whit more respect for the Calongi than Consortium law demanded, though she never doubted that they knew the truth of her awe of them—and of Jase. She touched the pond again to shatter her own reflection. She rocked back on her heels and stared across the garden, recalling worlds that wore their beauty with less disturbing intensity. Like Calongi music, Calongi gardens were almost too exquisite for an ordinary Soli to endure—even here, where Calongi had wielded their artistries specifically to satisfy the tastes of the resident Soli.

Graceful, living bridges layered the landscape, and saffron floral braids hovered without obvious support. Silken rainbows of Calong poppies nodded among the reeds and grasses. The water, liberally used as in most Calong gardens, sang delicate, elusive harmonies. The garden stream flowed in a spiraling symbolic design that began and ended at the open foyer of the home of the Soli man who was a Sesserda adept.

Jase's home—or rather, the house where he lived, since he denied exclusive ownership of any part of the nine planets known jointly as Calong—was a glass-and-graystone structure with an informal, rambling style that belied its functional sophistication. The house lacked the bewildering intricacies of design and the elongated dimensions of the few Calongi houses that Tori had examined closely, but it fit on Calong-4 as thoroughly as Jase. It suited Jase too well to have been built for anyone else, though its visual presence differed only in subtle ways from traditional Soli architecture.

Jase belonged with the Calongi on Calong-4, an extraordinary attribute that Tori neither coveted nor imagined that she could ever share. She leaned against the warm tree bole and studied the house through the arch of a garden bridge: Jase's home, not hers, though she had claimed a suite of its rooms as her own dwelling for almost four spans. Having entered her life as her Inquisitor, Jase's subsequent offer of employment and her own acceptance of it continued to astonish her, as much as her own subsequent success in the difficult profession of alien relations.

"Success is inevitable when the proper Sesserda purpose is identified," she recited wryly, "and who should know my proper purpose better than the Inquisitor who dissected my life and psyche? But Mama would hardly approve of my life with *him,* if she knew the truth of it, and Great-grandmama Mirelle would be appalled by the waste of all that heritage and training."

While she worked, Tori believed that she *had* found her own true purpose. When the stay on Calong stretched toward half a span, she became restless and overly aware of what she had laid aside: not just the legacy of Great-grandmama Mirelle, who had captivated worlds with the artful half-smile that Tori could wield with equal effectiveness, but the ordinary comforts of ordinary Soli on ordinary Consortium worlds.

When too much leisure let her contemplate alternative possibilities, Tori became lonely, reft of any non-Calongi company but the man who had adapted so uniquely well to Calong.

He was a third-level Sesserda practitioner, the only Soli to achieve such honor and rank in the Calongi religion. Tori was a repeatedly self-exiled refugee from a heritage she did not want, a marriage that had ended disastrously, and a world that had condemned itself to isolation. Jase had granted Tori a uniquely valuable place in his home and his Sesserda life-purpose, but he constrained their relationship with boundaries of adamant. At times, Tori was not even sure whether he considered her a friend or simply necessary for the exercise of his own Sesserda purpose.

The tumult of Tori's life had often humbled her, but she had never felt inherently disadvantaged except on Calong-4. The feeling was not altogether unpleasant—any accomplishments on this world were truly her own and not Mirelle's—but it could be frustrating, especially when it originated from Jase.

"And his confounded Sesserda senses probably tell him exactly how I feel," muttered Tori to herself, "despite my Tiva disorder and his Sesserda decrial of using an Inquisitor's skills for such unofficial purposes." She crossed her arms, warming damp hands in the scarlet folds of a shirt that was too large for her. She had several such shapeless shirts that she liked to wear when she collected deliveries from off-planet traders. It was a small but simple step toward minimizing the time that she wasted in deflecting excessive attention.

"Too much attention when I don't want it, not enough when I do," remarked Tori to her image in the lucent pond. "I need a vacation from Calong." Ruefully acknowledging her own dissatisfied mood, Tori resumed her course toward the house.

She was productive in her current life, and universal productivity was the great Sesserda goal, after all. Jase Sleide had undoubtedly accomplished his purpose in hiring her, as he seemed to accomplish everything that he set himself to achieve. He had never promised her

more than the job he had provided. Tori blamed only
herself for her occasional lapses of logic, when she
contemplated a more conventional relationship with
him. "We've gone too long between remote assignments," she muttered to herself, but she smiled, recalling the Alari success that had paid so handsomely.

She crossed the foyer, inhaling the spicy fragrance
of the yellow roses that climbed an invisible trellis and
sprawled across the roof. The roses had originated on
the same, doomed Hodge Farm where she had first met
Jase. The Stromvi roses had shocked her when she first
came to Jase's house, but now she greeted them with a
quiet, private nostalgia. They could not replace the
Stromvi friendships she had lost, but they were a gracious tribute. Beauty, as well as pain, had come from
Hodge Farm, and some of the beauty endured.

The beveled glass doors of the main entry parted to
admit Tori into the airy foyer. All of the foyer's walls
consisted of Spridi glass that gave privacy without obvious curtailment of the flow of light. The Spridi walls
made the foyer resemble an extension of the garden. In
the center of the foyer, the stream bubbled from a
miniature lava mountain, cascaded through feather fern
and rich green moss, and swirled beneath the entry
bridge into the garden. The melody of the water was
gentle; the damp scent of the moss was welcoming. Except for the few private chambers, every room of Jase's
house had at least two adjacent walls constructed of the
precious glass. Every part of Jase's house was filled
with soft, clear light and the sense-pleasing designs
that encouraged Sesserda peace.

Tori circled the waterfall to reach the room that Jase
used as an office. It was an insistently comfortable
room, despite being filled with the eclectic artifacts of
several hundred planets, all jumbled together in the
amberwood shelves that covered the two solid walls.
Jase, unusually resplendent in his formal Sesserda
gold, sat on his spine in an overstuffed armchair of
chestnut jacquard. Tori might have thought him asleep,
if she had not known how rarely he allowed himself
that luxury.

She watched Jase for a moment without disturbing him. She had no closer friend on any world, but so much of him was unknowable to her. By the relanine that filled him, tormented him, and sustained his life, he was as nearly Calongi as a Soli could become. Tori could never know Jase as well he knew her, because relanine addiction and Sesserda had given him so much perception beyond the ordinary Soli senses.

She did enjoy being valued as more than Mirelle's great-granddaughter and physical duplicate. However, for a woman with a renowned ability to win more masculine attention than she could ever want, Jase's unassailable reserve made for a difficult adjustment of her own self-image. Knowing that he forced her deliberately to reevaluate herself only made him seem more distant.

Tori grumbled, "For a man of such orderly Sesserda thinking, Jase, you lead a very chaotic life." Tori moved aside a mound of metallic Atiri silks in order to clear enough space to sit on the spindle-back chair opposite him. She did not ask him why he possessed a small fortune in the costly cloth, or why he found no better place to store it than an office chair. Valuables and curiosities appeared constantly in Jase's home, arriving either as gifts, samples for his approval, or payments for his services, actual or wishfully anticipated. Tori sorted carefully through all shipments addressed to *her* and any packages for him that caught her particular interest. Having tried for one frantic quarter-span to keep pace with *Jase's* total influx of assets, she had decided the effort was as hopeless as it was unappreciated.

Jase opened his eyes lazily, retrieving his attention from deep Sesserda meditations. His eyes' iridescence, the most overt indicator of his severe relanine addiction, no longer seemed uncanny to Tori, but it still forced awareness of how much Jase differed from other Soli men. Jase drawled, "The chaos of my life is why we work so well together. Chaos energizes you."

Consciously denying her own restlessness, Tori resecured the knot of her dark hair, which had begun to slip from its bonds of red ribbon. "You need ten assistants, partner-of-mine. I have enough trouble keeping track of *my* share of the business. This morning alone, we have received fifteen requests for diplomatic intervention in planetary conflicts, eleven demands for trade arbitration, and thirty-eight pleas for our services as interspecies sociocultural translators. In *your* name, I accepted nineteen parcels for you to 'consider their worthiness,' and that tally doesn't count the goods that bypassed me." She draped a length of the feather-soft Atiri silk over her head. The teal-and-silver fabric, woven into a watery pattern, embraced her shoulders with fluid suppleness.

"How many parcels did you reject on my behalf?" asked Jase, his sharp features revealing nothing of his thoughts.

"Twenty-seven. It doesn't take a Sesserda scholar or the Consortium's foremost Soli expert in alien relations to know that essence of Chuixai dankweed will fail to enchant many Soli buyers."

Jase smiled and made no comment. Tori raised the luminous silk against the light. "This, on the other hand, deserves better treatment than to be tossed onto a chair and forgotten."

"The silk was a gift from an Atiri weaver for whom I did a small service several spans ago. It's yours, if you like it. I can refer you to an Atiri who will assemble the silk into whatever garment you request."

Tori was too accustomed to Jase's careless generosity to feel surprise, but he seldom exercised such extravagance toward her. In one of those detached, casual Sesserda dissections that she loathed, he had even informed her once that such personal gifts threatened her sense of independence, reminding her painfully of the life of concubinage for which her family had intended her. His uncharacteristic gesture made her irritably sure that he had recognized her aggrieved mood. "Because I've spent far too much time trying to do your work for you, I accept," she said with a defiant lifting of her chin.

"Because I take unfair advantage of your industrious

nature, I offered." Jase proceeded to grimace at the cluttered room, and his dexterous fingers spread to alarming angles. "And because I haven't any better use for the stuff. Other Sesserda practitioners never have this much trouble with unwanted largess. It's probably a sign of pity for me rather than praise."

Confronted with Jase's peculiarly Soli style of self-deprecation, Tori could almost forget his strangeness. She set aside her errant musings on how to breach the boundary between them, momentarily forgetting that the boundary existed. She murmured, "Other Sesserda practitioners tend to be Calongi. These gifts are meant to appeal to your base Soli nature."

"You are overly cynical," observed Jase, sliding into the detached assurance of a Sesserda adept giving a judgment of Truth. It was the guise that made him seem most like a Calongi and most alien to Tori; it was also the side of him that incurred most of their disagreements. "The fault lies in me, Tori, not in the givers. I am insufficiently persuasive in protesting their offerings. Such persuasion is a skill I must hone."

"False humility doesn't become you," remarked Tori dryly. His rapid withdrawal behind the barrier of Sesserda formality angered her, because she knew the deliberateness of his actions. She stiffened all the inner protections that Tiva disorder gave her to escape his piercing scrutiny, and she indulged the cynicism that he condemned. "Only some devilish form of Sesserda persuasion could ever have convinced me to live on Calong-4."

Jase's severe expression relaxed into a lopsided grin. "The art of persuasion has many forms, and you were less accustomed to me when I wheedled you into coming here. You were still susceptible to a form that I *have* mastered."

"I may have amassed more experience at recognizing your Sesserda techniques, but I shall never grow accustomed to you." *The irony,* thought Tori, *is that he does not even know how far he could persuade me without his infernal Sesserda skills. At least, he does not admit knowing, and he is usually quick to make me aware of my follies ... Who can be sure what a Sesserda adept actually knows?* "Why did I ever imagine that you hired me out of charity?"

"You had not yet calibrated the depths of my selfish, lazy nature."

Tori declined to rebut his statement; his ego did not need encouragement. She rested her chin on her hand and wished that Jase Sleide, slim and dark and enigmatic, seemed as alien to her in body as in mind. Alien men did not attract her with such unsettling, frustrating intensity. "So why didn't you have an assistant before you connived me into handling all the mundane work that bores you?"

"I did," replied Jase crisply, "as you know quite well." He reached over to the rosewood table beside him and spun a holographic top, letting its alien images blossom, spin, and fade. "I had several of them. We had compatibility problems."

"They all quit in disgust?"

"The relationships dissolved by mutual accord. Not many Soli care to live among the Calongi. Not many members of other species are comfortable working for a Soli."

"I don't care for life among the Calongi either. They make me too conscious of my uncivilized status. Most of them sound condescending even when they talk to you."

Jase's nimble hand wove exotic patterns with the whirling top. "You allow your personal dread of inferiority to color your perception of truth. You interpret Calongi attitudes through a filter of Soli cultural bias."

"I am biased, but the Calongi are not without their share of true arrogance."

"A recognition of their own superior wisdom does not imply a lack of respect for the unique gifts of other species."

"You have your own bias in their favor, Mister Sleide, which a mere Level VI like me cannot possibly share."

Jase stilled the top, frowning at it. A blue-eyed, chartreuse lizard, one of the cherished eeniti that scoured

Calongi houses of harmful insects, skittered across a silver Galizi flute. The lizard disappeared into the shelf behind a miniature castle, sculpted from obsidian and opal. Untroubled, the waterfall tumbled its song in the foyer.

"Consider the peace and beauty of Calong-4, and explain to me why the unpredictable society of the Consortium's children still appeals to you, Tori. You have never received anything but hurt from your Level VI associations, and you have succeeded marvelously in the last four spans of living here. The Alari negotiation would still be incomplete without your sense of timing."

"You devised the treaty."

"You gathered the participants so I could present it."

"Relating to the Alari was easy. They are emotionally erratic and frequently irrational—like me and like any normal Soli."

"A longing for the company of less civilized individuals is a dangerous, as well as uncivilized, trait," murmured Jase, disregarding her last pointed remark. "It is common among Level VI beings, who tend to look backward at what they consider 'forbidden' instead of forward at what they could achieve."

"Why are you lecturing me about my uncivilized longings? I never said that I missed the pain and turbulence of ordinary Soli society."

"You don't bandy civilization rankings unless you're feeling truly disgruntled. What's making you so moody today?"

Tori glared at him. "How does someone so civilized and perceptive manage to sound like the worst sort of insensitive, uncivilized Soli male?"

"You've called *me* moody often enough."

"You *are* moody, temperamental and confoundedly difficult."

"I am a relanine addict," retorted Jase mildly, though he stared at the table instead of meeting Tori's eyes, "which you are *not,* all Truth be praised. Why are you disgruntled?"

"If I am disgruntled, it's because Calong-4 makes

me so abysmally aware that I am one of the Consortium's uncivilized children, and you aggravate the problem when you start talking like a condescending Calongi. You can be very annoying when you act like an Inquisitor, delving into my private Truth."

"You know perfectly well that I reserve the techniques of inquisitorial observation for official purposes. Tiva disorder makes you hard to evaluate under any circumstances." Jase unfurled himself from the confines of his chair. He strolled across the room and fingered the silk that Tori had laid aside. "Some conclusions are simply inescapable. You wouldn't fault me for noticing that your eyes are green."

"I might wish that you could describe them a little more eloquently: as emerald fire, perhaps, or as the deep pools of a moonlit garden."

"You've had enough men flatter you with bad poetry."

"Not all of the poetry is bad." Tori arose to stand beside him, defying him to notice anything more personal about her than her physical presence. She pushed errant strands of his black hair away from his face. "I admit that my eyes are ordinary compared to yours."

"Strangeness is not a virtue." Jase deftly twisted the Atiri silk around her wrist, deflecting her hand without touching his flesh to hers. "The color of my eyes attracts more curiosity than admiration. The most common remark is that the iridescence is too ostentatious for the rest of me."

"So is formal Sesserda gold, but my keen Soli senses have recognized that you are wearing it. Are you expecting visitors?"

"I am expecting to pay a visit. You're invited as well, if you care to come."

"Kind of you to give me so much warning." Tori tugged at her casual shirt. "I should make a striking impression in this."

He draped the silk across her shoulders. "I am displaying my Sesserda rank for official cause, not making impressions."

"Sesserda rank exists to impress. The purpose of

those markings is to alert observers that you are almost as dangerous as a Calongi."

"I am not about to quibble over the meaning of Sesserda when you're in such an unreasoning frame of mind."

"At moments like this, Mister Sleide, I wish I had sense enough to walk out on you and find myself another partner."

"You don't want to resign from my personal company. You only wish to experience a change of venue for a time. That is what you have been pondering this morning, isn't it?" demanded Jase innocently.

Tori glowered at him, because he was right, as usual, and she suspected him of smugness. She could seldom tell how well his strange, relanine-honed senses actually did enable him to decipher her. "What else have I been thinking?"

"In lieu of any professional requirements to travel, you would opt for a simple vacation from Calong. Unfortunately, neither of us can afford to squander that much time just now."

"I did not plan to request your company," said Tori dryly, although she could not help but wonder if he were actually capable of something as deliberately unproductive as a vacation. In four spans, she had never had an opportunity to know him away from Calongi, crises, and all the demands that the Consortium inflicted on its single Level V Soli. As far as she could tell, the concept of a vacation was foreign to Sesserda and its practitioners.

He whispered with his searingly incisive, Sesserda-trained voice, "You would miss me too much to go without me."

"You have mastered Sesserda conceit too well," grumbled Tori. Jase could shift between arch detachment and suggestive intimacy at a speed that played havoc with Tori's emotions. She felt sure, even when her entire body ached a contradiction, that the intimacy would never progress beyond such rare, teasing suggestions. Jase took too much care to protect her from relanine contamination.

He barely touched the silk where it flowed down her arm. "The visit that inspires my official Sesserda attire," replied Jase with a knowing smile, "is for the purpose of discussing the ramifications of a report, recently received, that may interest you. How would you like to counteract your Calong saturation with a dose of uncivilized Level VIIs? It would not be a vacation, since it could involve some potentially delicate diplomacy among people who are decidedly dangerous, but it would certainly be a change from Calong." His smile thinned. "You and I could feel smug and superior together."

"What sort of report have you received?" asked Tori with suspicion. Almost every request for their joint professional services came through her hands first, and members of the least civilized Levels required Inquisition much more often than help with alien relations. Consortium membership did not even include Level VIIs except on rare, individual bases. "A friendly request to visit my dear Mama and Uncle Per?"

"I do not propose to visit your lamentable family just now, although we should reconcile them to you eventually."

"You don't associate with *your* family. They don't even know that you survived the accident that poisoned you with relanine."

Ignoring her well-aimed taunt, Jase said, "The report pertains to an incident that could have far-reaching ramifications. We have been asked . . ."

"*You* have been asked," corrected Tori softly.

"My associate and I have been asked—tentatively— to resolve a potential diplomatic conflict regarding criminal accusations that have been levied against a purported Consortium trader on a non-Consortium world."

Tori stepped away from him, wishing she could escape painful memories of Inquisition as easily. "You don't need my help to perform an Inquisition."

"It is not a matter of official Inquisition, because the trader is not registered as a Consortium member. Unfortunately, he claimed Consortium membership in order to escape local punishment, which is evidently noted for its harshness. Because of prejudice and the particular sensitivity of the charges, involving the smuggling of some restricted technology, his claim achieved more credibility than it deserved. Local authorities accused the trader of spying for the Consortium. The accusation is clearly absurd, but it may signify a larger form of mischief on the part of its originators. Ergo, we have been asked to intervene, pending a final decision by honored Calongi masters regarding the wisdom of intervening at all."

"Where did the benighted trader commit his indiscretion?"

The eeniki's chartreuse head emerged tentatively from the shelf near Jase's elbow. Jase offered his hand, and the lizard scurried across his open palm and onto its Sesserda gold sleeve. "A Network planet known as Nilson."

"Network!"

With a pronounced grimace, Jase murmured, "I wish you wouldn't echo me with such unflattering incredulity, Tori."

"If I don't prompt you, you forget to tell me all the necessary details." She moved forward a step to stroke the lizard's extended neck, eliciting a purr from its vibrating throat. "You are too accustomed to relating to your omniscient Calongi friends."

"I am trying diligently to tell you what little I know about the matter at hand. The trader is an independent Cuui of dubious character and the unfortunate sobriquet of 'Filcher,' but the Cuui do not rank him as a serious criminal. Nilson is one of the few Network planets with an open spaceport. Network has filed no formal accusation against the Consortium, but the Nilson governor has made his personal position clear. An irreverent recording with excerpts of the governor's naive speech, labeling the benighted Mister Filcher as a Consortium agent, has begun to circulate among the independent traders. The recording is being marketed as a joke, but such 'amusing' rumors build upon themselves in unpleasant fashion."

"Won't official Consortium attention add credibility to those rumors?"

"Calongi attention might add credibility, but you and I are not Calongi. There is potential here that needs to be weighed."

"It sounds like a potential for more trouble than I'd like to meet."

Jase nodded slightly. "I am not thrilled by the idea of mingling with the most uncivilized branch of our species, but the opportunity to observe these people could augment our understanding of them invaluably. Since you're chafing from an excess of advanced civilization, you ought to enjoy the barbaric contrast of Network."

"You're displaying a lack of respect for your fellow Soli," remarked Tori, relishing the weakness that made him more reachable. A Sesserda adept vowed respect of *all* creation, even in its most destructive aspects.

Jase did not share her pleasure in his Soli fallibility, but he did not deny it. "Yes. I need to learn better. A Network encounter should be healthy for me."

"Your last encounter with Level VIIs nearly killed you." And *me,* thought Tori with a shiver. *And the entire Stromvi race.*

"No one said that alien relations was an easy profession, particularly for a specialist in primitive cultures." Jase perched on the edge of his ebony desk. "Ukitan-lai has called a meeting to weigh the risks against the rewards. The conclusion may be that the Nilson governor's clumsy display of prejudice is as uncontrived as it appears and should be allowed to fade quietly into oblivion. We may decide simply to spend a few days chatting with traders at Nilson's open spaceport. We may request an official visit to negotiate unrelated trade issues with Network and use that opportunity to observe the overall situation. In any case, if I am confirmed as an unofficial investigator, I think you could be extremely useful to the endeavor. The risks, however, are real, and you should weigh them. That is why I would like you to participate in today's discussion."

"You want me to sit and listen to you and your

exalted colleagues dissecting the flaws of the Soli species? I can't imagine a drearier way to spend a day. Frankly, I don't think any of you Sesserda scholars are qualified to deal with a culture as violently uncivilized as Network. You should hire Uncle Per as a consultant."

"Since I helped instigate the current Inquisition against Per Walis, I doubt that he'd be eager to accommodate me."

"You're too far removed from the criminal mind to relate to Uncle Per under any circumstances. You would never learn anything from him, because you'd be too busy trying to reform him."

"If we have the leisure some day, we shall put the matter to the test. We shall visit your uncivilized family, and I shall charm them with my best diplomatic manners."

"*We* shall do nothing of the sort," scoffed Tori, hiding her emotions behind a shield of cynical bluntness. There was little about Tori's life that Jase did not know, but she did not relish the idea of his acute senses observing first-hand the decadence to which she had been raised. "I have enough trouble maintaining Mama's marginal approval without introducing her to my *partner*."

"How could your dear 'Mama' disapprove of the man who acquitted her daughter?"

"The purity of your lifestyle would offend Mama's entire existence. You could afford a hundred concubines, but you have none, including me."

"Your family could give the entire universe lessons in how to debase interpersonal relationships," observed Jase, but it was an idle criticism. He would leave specific judgments to the Inquisitor assigned to Per Walis.

"Mama doesn't know any other way to live," said Tori, defensive despite herself.

"Neither did you, but you have found a way to learn better. Your mother has made her own choice. If she feels more comfortable with the idea of me as your patron rather than your partner, she only stultifies her own wisdom. You may try to educate her, but you cannot change her chosen life-concept by decree. Ergo, you should not let her misunderstanding worry you."

"I thought we were discussing a diplomatic mission to Network."

"We are discussing the hazards of uncivilized behavior, wherever it is found."

"And you are proving how little you understand it. Mama cares about me in her own way. Her patrons have always coddled her. She wants me protected similarly."

"You are trying to defend the indefensible, because the guilt belongs to someone you love."

"My family is as uncivilized as the Consortium allows, but they are as capable as any Sesserda adept of feeling love and affection. If Mama ever heard the way you and I bicker, she would fret herself into illness trying to concoct a way to increase your satisfaction with me. Mama is unbearable when she frets, which makes Uncle Per unbearable as well. I don't admire my family, but I understand them."

"I am not criticizing your family. I am acknowledging their sins."

"Is that how you would negotiate with Network? By pointing out their sins? That would make a fine impression of Consortium superiority."

"Since we have returned to the making of impressions, do you want me to wait for you to prepare one?" Jase nodded at Tori's scarlet shirt and trousers. "You would make a better impression on Ukitan-lai if you changed your outlook rather than your clothes, but he does appreciate cleanliness."

"Why do I tolerate you?" muttered Tori, but she headed for her room.

"Because," whispered Jase to the empty office, "I'm the only man who cares for you enough to set aside his desire for you." The eeniki crawled atop his shoulder and tested the air with its narrow snout. Jase shrugged, and the eeniki burrowed against his neck. It trilled its contentment quietly. "You're a very poor substitute for her, old lad," said Jase, stroking the lizard's long back.

CHAPTER 14

Manipulators

The Healer Suleifas sat upon a bentwood chair beneath a blossoming apple tree in a high Revgaenian valley. He had carried the chair from the traditional home of the Healer Evjenial, which lay not far from this isolated place. He cradled a jade-green stone of healing in his left hand, twisting the tool of his Siathan predecessors, feeling the cold, smooth texture against his callused skin.

Jeni watched him for a moment, longing to stay beside him. He gave her a smile that was wistful enough to cut her heart. His shoulders, usually held so straight, drooped with the burden of a man far older than the husband she knew.

She drew strength from the Mirlai, and she left him alone, as she had promised. She would withdraw to that home where she had become a Healer, a small and peaceful dwelling that was now used rarely. If she lost her Suleifas, her home would again be that place where so many Evjenials had lived, because another Suleifas would be Chosen to live in Montelier. Jeni promised herself a quietly satisfying afternoon of tending her neglected garden, but her face was taut with concern.

In the high, lonely valley, the Healer Suleifas clenched his hand. He thrust the stone into the pocket of his brown wool vest, then he laid both vest and coat upon the damp ground. The mountain air of a cloudy spring day chilled him less than his self-imposed quest.

Marrach knew too well the cunning, opportunistic mind that belonged to Network's Council Governor. The Healer could not willingly approach such a vicious, ruthless, unhealed entity. Thus, a large part of the Healer Suleifas must also be laid aside to enable Rabh Marrach to deal with Caragen and survive unscathed. The Mirlai hovered watchfully, but they allowed their symbiotic link to Suleifas to grow tenuous.

He required himself to remember his past. The technique did not differ much from methods he had often used to assume identities that were not his own. By remembering, he intended to regain *just* enough of Rabhadur Marrach to confront Caragen. He did not allow himself to dwell on the hazards of reviving the past too thoroughly.

Network had refused to divulge the exact whereabouts of its Council Governor, but Network had not declined to coordinate time schedules between the worlds. Marrach had tried to gauge the hour carefully, wanting Caragen awake but unprepared for interruptions. Caragen's rigid agenda had always flexed uniquely for his most valued agent. Marrach intended that Caragen recall that relationship in full.

The muscles of the man in the bentwood chair became alert and hard. His face lost all expression, as if the life behind it had no soul or feeling. Marrach had always had a gift for imposture, while denying any view of the man who played the deadly roles that Caragen required. Deception had been easier for that Rabh Marrach who, valuing his own life no more than the lives of others, had valued nothing at all. The transformation came painfully now, but it came.

Marrach applied the Network identity codes that had once been far more constant than his name. The security keys for Caragen's private channels had changed, but Marrach did not mind requesting a Network link by the ordinary diplomatic procedures still available to him. Caragen might require another Network citizen, even a Network Councillor, to wait indefinitely upon the Council Governor's pleasure. However, Network would notify Caragen immediately of a call from any serious enemy or rival. Marrach knew that his own name must rank high on that ominous list. Whether or not Caragen chose to respond immediately, he would know that Marrach had attempted contact.

Marrach waited with long-practiced patience. As an exercise of old habit, he predicted the timing in his mind: the seconds of Caragen's initial shock, the minutes for Caragen to calculate a response, the minutes of additional delay that asserted Caragen's control. The actual timing fell just a few seconds short of his prediction.

Though Marrach knew that the voice rang only in his head, Network implants deceived his brain into a perception of actual sound. The cold, dry voice was unmistakably Andrew Caragen's: "Have you wearied of bucolic stupor, Marrach?"

Marrach replied crisply, "Which of us idles in stupor, Council Governor? It is I who call to give *you* warning of the looming catastrophe in your midst." Network could mimic Marrach's voice using old data and the signals that Marrach's mind manipulated. If Caragen occupied any decently equipped Network suite, he would be able to hear Marrach as clearly as if they faced each other across a desk in any of Caragen's offices.

Somewhat to Marrach's surprise, the delay in communication was perceptible, even transmitted through the shortest topologically-connected route. Marrach tried to estimate how much the delay owed to transmission time and how much to Caragen, but an accurate calculation was impossible without knowledge of Caragen's present location. That location could not be on a major Network planet, or the delay would be less obvious. "Your intimation of concern is touching but implausible, Marrach."

"That which threatens Network threatens me."

"Do not fabricate, Marrach. Listening to you is not a pressing commitment on my part. Explain yourself succinctly, before you exhaust my limited curiosity."

"Nilson."

The ensuing pause was long enough to assure Marrach of Caragen's displeased surprise. "Brevity is a virtue, but excess is absurd."

"I do not know what experiments you have been

performing, but you are destabilizing topological space."

"Even if that absurd hypothesis had any validity, I hardly think Network would have shared the information with you. There *have* been changes in your Network privileges since your defection. Your authorization codes no longer carry that level of authority."

"I have other sources." Marrach added pointedly, "I have *always* had other sources."

With a rasping laugh that held no humor, Caragen demanded, "How do you expect me to utilize this opulent gift of knowledge?"

"Investigate it."

"I enjoyed a dinner with Governor Racker not long ago. Nilson was its normal, sorry self."

"You would not have visited Nilson personally if its circumstances were 'normal.' "

"I no longer have you to perform such distasteful duties for me. Racker really is a tedious man." After a pause, Caragen chuckled, "Or are you advising me to investigate a situation that you created? You did establish Nilson's current government, after all. Its products are, therefore, your own."

"I am advising you to initiate a Network inquiry into the status of the Nilson topology. Observe the onset of disaster for yourself. Confirm it, and then you may be more eager to squander a bit of your valuable time on listening to *me*."

Marrach broke the link so abruptly that it set his head pounding. Mirlai rushed to comfort him.

***

Caragen gripped the arms of his chair so tightly that he gouged the leather upholstery. When the link failed, his breath came in gasps of frustration and rage. "Network, reopen the link—forcibly!"

"Unable to comply. Excessive interference precludes forced entry at this time."

"Damn Marrach's insolence," screamed Caragen, "and his thrice-accursed Mirlai."

Network monitored the dangerous severity of stress, manifested by a pounding of blood that threatened aged arteries, and did not reply. Instead, the austere office trickled with the calming sounds of a distant ocean. Network adjusted the list of medications that would be incorporated in the Council Governor's next meal. A slight scent of salt and moisture imitated sea breeze.

Caragen, recognizing the cause for Network's solicitous reaction, determinedly slowed his breathing and racing pulse. He muttered another curse against Marrach, but Caragen had regained his self-control. "Analyze Marrach's reason for contact," he ordered Network brusquely, "and verify its origin."

"Originator is verified as Rabhadur Marrach, planet Siatha. Most probable cause of contact: Sincere warning regarding Nilson instability, possibly predicated on results of personal Nilson activities."

Irrationally, Caragen resented Network's support of Marrach's claims, fearing for a moment that Network itself conspired with Marrach against Network's Council Governor. Inside of Marrach were more implants than anyone knew except Caragen, who had ordered their insertion across the years of Marrach's service. Caragen had made Marrach an integral part of Network, and not even the Mirlai had dared to attempt a separation of that bond. "No such instability has been detected," argued Caragen.

"Sincerity of warning does not guarantee accuracy of claim."

That was a possibility, acknowledged Caragen grudgingly, and it would be in keeping with Marrach's hypocritical pretensions as a Siathan Healer. With difficulty, Caragen endeavored to evaluate Marrach's claims without the prejudice of anger. Caragen had always respected Marrach's phenomenal instincts for self-preservation. The Mirlai had confiscated Marrach's fealty, but they had not eradicated Marrach's skills. Marrach had worked Nilson extensively and was fully capable of extrapolating long-term results of short-term expediencies. If Rabhadur Marrach recognized the evolution of a personal threat that he could not combat alone, he would not hesitate to exploit other resources for self-preservation.

That did not mean that Marrach was telling the truth. Misdirection and deception were also inherent aspects of the profile of Caragen's former agent. Network algorithms and Network sensors could detect obvious lies, but Marrach was not an ordinary case.

"Could this be another of Quin Hamley's little jokes?" Though Caragen voiced the question with disparagement, the possibility of Marrach and Quin Hamley conspiring together *actively* represented one of Caragen's greatest concerns. The ominous potential of Dr. Jon Terry's involvement magnified that concern; no one had ever understood applied topology better than Dr. Terry. The threat of Caragen's three most competent enemies uniting in any aggressive plot had haunted Caragen since Dr. Terry's daughter allied herself to Quin Hamley. Caragen had enough enemies among the merely ruthless members of his own Council.

"Available data do not suffice to make an accurate estimate of Quin Hamley's involvement."

"Recommendation?" muttered Caragen, unusually dissatisfied with the inadequacies of Network's assessment.

"Investigate the claim."

"My Network leaps at Marrach's beck and call," growled Caragen bitterly, but he knew that denial of the recommended course would be only folly, based on pride. "Initiate investigative procedures," ordered Caragen curtly. Caragen had his own exceptional measure of self-preserving instincts. "Start by investigating any known Nilson associates, direct or indirect, of Rabh Marrach."

"Agent Marrach's reports regarding orchestration of current Nilson leadership named only one direct associate who is still living: Citizen Tay Breamas, former Network agent, confined to Nilson since a nerve disrupter crippled him irreparably and damaged critical mental circuitry."

"An agent who botches his assignment deserves no medical repair, and he is not a sufficient threat to garner Marrach's concern. Breamas wields no weapon now but an empty voice," sneered Caragen. "He forgot his own origins and purpose as infiltrator before Marrach ever visited Nilson."

"Primary beneficiary of Agent Marrach's work on Nilson had no direct association but remains notably active: Governor Racker."

"Promising assets are so often treacherous," sighed Caragen eloquently. His meeting with Racker had proven disappointing, but an improbable notion of Marrach expressing jealousy of Ned Racker gave Caragen a visceral surge of pleasure. "Network, let us humor Marrach. Proceed by investigating Ned Racker's personal projects. Do not notify Racker of the inquiry, but maintain security at only a moderate level. Let him recognize that he is under inspection, and let him worry. If he has been making unauthorized forays, perhaps he will feel compelled to reassure himself of their status, and we shall be watching." Caragen tapped his tented fingers thoughtfully. "Investigate all other senior Nilson officials, as well—particularly that native woman, Racker's lieutenant."

"Saschy Firl," interpreted Network helpfully.

Caragen grunted, "Discover her weaknesses." The woman had impressed Caragen unpleasantly in their brief meeting on Nilson. He disliked people whom he could not manipulate easily, whether by intimidation, greed, or any of the subtler forms of coercion that Network could utilize on Caragen's command. Nilson bred tough, independent children, and Saschy Firl would not have reached her current status without an exceptional measure of ambition. Caragen would never have allowed a Nilson native in *his* immediate service, unless he had a strong motive or had established a confident personal hold over that individual. Ned Racker did not have the wit to recognize the threat that his lieutenant represented.

"Acknowledged."

In the ensuing silence, Caragen pondered what he

would do in the unlikely event that Network actually
confirmed Marrach's dire predictions. Caragen had
made good political use of environmental catastrophes
on many occasions. He had always acted on the simple,
egotistical theory that any potential catastrophe that
failed to threaten him personally had come into existence for his advantage. If the catastrophe were allowed to mature into a meaningful threat, easily
recognized and comprehended by average Network citizens, a heroic resolution by the Council Governor
would reinforce the citizens' confidence in him more
effectively than any conditioning algorithm. Such an
occurrence could repair much of the damage to Caragen's prestige that Marrach had begun and Quin Hamley's humiliating display had aggravated.

The loss of Nilson, a possible outcome of such a
policy, would be inconvenient, but the bulk of Nilson's
recent wealth originated in the Wharton mines, which
belonged to an entirely distinct region of topological
space. Connections to Wharton from other Network
worlds would surely be discovered in the ordinary
course of ongoing research; the Wharton mines were
simply too new to have been evaluated thoroughly as
yet. Weighing the advantages with a growing gleam of
avaricious delight, Caragen decided that the potential
benefits of a Nilson catastrophe might merit even some
level of personal risk and sacrifice.

While Caragen plotted his resurgence and expansion
of power, Network processed Caragen's instructions
across connected space, extending even to the physically remote reaches of Nilson. When the first stage of
processing was complete, Network provided status in a
subdued, subservient voice tailored to Caragen's mood
of the moment, "Nilson is not equipped to provide a
thorough topological survey. Upgrade costs to achieve
full analytical capability are significant."

Caragen nodded at the anticipated reply. Racker had
borrowed heavily to open Wharton and continued to
send most of Nilson's maintenance funds, along with
Wharton's profits, to his lenders. It was a gamble on
Racker's part, but Caragen had approved it. Many of

those funds made their circuitous way to Caragen. "Make no major upgrade investment until preliminary reports are received. Racker would only find an excuse to divert such an investment into the opening of a new mine, and he has already overextended himself."

"Acknowledged."

Caragen curled his fingers together. "Review the status of that incident involving the alien smuggler." During Caragen's most recent meeting with Racker, the Nilson governor had evaded the subject clumsily, but Network had assessed the cause as simple embarrassment rather than any darker motive. Caragen had enjoyed Racker's evasiveness, because it had enabled him to goad Racker so easily into insecurity.

"The Cuui trader, known as Filcher, remains incarcerated. The Consortium's reply to formal inquiry denied his claim of membership, and no further Consortium communication has been received. No execution date has been set."

"Racker embarrasses himself further by stalling the formal proceedings." Caragen shook his head at Racker's lack of insight. A quick resolution would have mitigated the damage to Racker's status, but he clearly wanted the Cuui to suffer. Racker had allowed his hatred of aliens to counteract his political acumen, and he still mistook the Cuui's misery for a humbling of the Consortium. "Racker has a regrettable inability to recognize a superior foe. His conceit has served him well in many respects, but it precludes him from advancing as I had hoped. He is a flawed asset, who owes most of his recent success to his ambitious lieutenant." *He has more in common with Breamas than with Marrach*, thought Caragen grimly. "Racker is not the ideal candidate to manage an emergency situation, if it should arise."

"Six potential replacements for the Nilson governorship have been identified. Shall I summarize their qualifications?"

Caragen pondered the question for a silent moment. "No. Racker has not yet exhausted his value to me. Now is not the time to introduce needless uncertainties into the Nilson equation." With a manicured nail, Caragen traced a pensive line down his sagging jowl. "Racker's expendability will be fortuitous, if Marrach's claims have any substance."

"Acknowledged."

Caragen breathed deeply. "If Marrach attempts to reestablish contact, alert me, but keep him waiting. If he is sincere in his warning, he has given it in recognition that he needs my help, and that admission makes him *mine* again." The merest shadow of complacency hovered across Caragen's aged face.

CHAPTER 15

Revolutionaries

The cavern was small, cylindrical, and smooth, an exploratory access carved by Network between two layers of nature's manufacture. A silvery spike ladder pierced it, clinging to the wall. A ledge jutted from the stone near the ladder's midpoint, and the wind of a motion-activated Network air system rushed past it, filling cavern pockets that were seldom breached. Three figures crowded on the shelf.

"Why should we be trusting the word of a retriever?" grumbled a thin man with a mottled complexion and broken teeth. He used those teeth to gnaw at a length of ginnygum, the mildly narcotic product of Wharton's only native plant.

"Arlan be not like us, Cullen," answered Deliaja dryly. She had exchanged the brightly provocative garb she affected at the canteen for a miner's russet coverall. She wore no adornment, and the coverall's stiff cloth hid even the lion's head dyed in her flesh. Like the two men with her, she sat on the hard floor of the stovepipe cave, her back propped against unquarried stone and her face lit eerily by the meager fingerlight they shared.

"That be our saying," snapped Vin, the leader, whose deeply furrowed brow created a perpetual scowl on his pale miner's face. He was a hard and gnarled man, as twisted and scarred as the strong, old mineral veins he defiled for the sake of a few grams of precious metal. "Arlan never be like us. He be close as slickrock to Saschy Firl's old mum. He be a governor's spy, most likely."

Deliaja snapped her fingers with impatience, and the

sound echoed from the distant ceiling. "Miz Ruth be of different mind than her daughter, and Arlan be no spy." With deliberate irony, she added, "May be Arlan too good-minded for our understanding *or* for Lady Firl's. Arlan be not a liar."

"If he be not a spy," Cullen retorted sourly, "then he be thinking too much and seeing too little, like ever."

"May be your wish to think half so well," drawled Deliaja.

"May be you wanting him to think toward you."

"May be, I be liking his thinking less of lust than the rest of you scum," answered Deliaja. She scraped her fingers through her dusty, gilded hair. "Innocence be too rare on Nilson."

"You be knowing," sniped Vin.

"I be knowing," she replied without pretense. She tugged at russet fabric to cover a slim, bare ankle. "I be knowing when a man be telling only lies to land me beneath him. Arlan be telling what be needful of telling. He be finding Tempest, nowhere near where the boy be dying. Arlan be thinking more than we, and he be also seeing more than we. We be needing to hear him." When neither man answered her, she repeated emphatically, "We be needing to hear him, because he be telling us news before Network be learning it, and that be the way for us to be making Wharton ours. We be needing better weapons than rusted beamers if we be planning to impress a Network governor. If the ghost lights be spreading, Network may be soon looking elsewhere than at us, and it be giving us opportunity."

"We be making our opportunities when Breamas be saying so," growled Vin in a voice like rust.

"Your reports be blinding Breamas to opportunities that be *now*."

"May be, you be wanting *Arlan* to report to Breamas."

"May be, Arlan be more use to Breamas than you."

"If you be so impressed with Arlan's cleverness, then you be testing him for us to recruit, Dee. If he be a spy, you be paying with your life and none of ours."

"I be willing," she answered with a proud tremolo

asserting the ferocity of her belief. "I be more certain of Arlan Willowan than of most of the scum the two of you be recruiting." She saw no point in telling them of the test she had already enacted with Keever's aid: Arlan had neither exploited Keever's carefully doled information nor sought more of the same, and that restraint had encouraged Deliaja's tentative belief in Arlan's sincerity. Nor did Deliaja confide in the two men that Ruth Firl, who had pleaded Arlan's case, was one of Deliaja's most prized recruits to the cause of revolution. Aside from Deliaja, only Breamas and a few of his skyside captains knew about Miz Ruth, because most of the rebels were—like Vin and Cullen— still awed by Network and its officials. Few of the rebels had yet understood that the revolution must become more than disgruntled talk, but they would learn when the time came. Until then, Deliaja would let them think she shared their petty concerns and dreads. She was more chary with her trust than either Vin or Cullen.

Vin nodded once and spat into his hand, sealing Deliaja's concurrences as an oath. The fingerlight painted his shadow high on the cavern wall. "Cullen, you be running the port boys on guard duty next night?"

"They be ours," concurred Cullen. "You be bringing or sending?"

"Sending. There be a supply trouble with our fellows skyside since unfriendly port boys be nabbing the nasty Filcher."

"Aliens be trouble always."

Deliaja muttered, "We be in no position to be choosy of our help. Network be not likely to fulfill a formal Req to give us bombs and beamers to blast a Network governor." She gave Vin a sour glance. "We can only be stealing so much from the mine supplies before Network be counting the losses and snaring us. If skyside be thinking to live off us much longer, they be losing what little sense they had." She had closer contacts skyside than either Vin or Cullen, and she smuggled more from Wharton than any of Breamas' other sympathizers, but she preferred to keep such facts private.

"Filcher be not easy to replace now," said Cullen, "with pressure from the port boys making even Cuui smugglers nerve-raw."

"Still," murmured Vin with relish, "it be good to see Racker played as fool, even if it be only to the aliens."

"Be you taking a hand in spreading tales about Racker's speech?" asked Deliaja, sharply suspicious of Vin's motives, though she acknowledged his leadership for the sake of the goals that they shared.

"Racker be needing some lessons in humility," replied Vin obliquely.

"Racker be not mindful of any lesson more subtle than a blaster beam through his chest," grumbled Cullen.

"Be you patient, Cullen," answered Deliaja in cold promise. "The lessons be growing strong soon enough."

"Be you talking for Breamas now?" asked Vin, manifesting his own chronic suspicions with rare acuity.

"Be you thinking to become a port boy?" countered Deliaja sharply. To her, Vin was capable as a killer but was the least of Breamas' many captains, self-appointed leader of a crew of like-minded Nilsonites who happened to live and work in Wharton. Because she thought Vin had made poor use of Wharton's unique potential, Deliaja did not respect Vin enough to be concerned by his opinion, but she did not want him spreading his suspicions. She made her voice contemptuous. "May be an insecure leader fearing to lose his command. May be an insecure leader forgetting that Breamas be the leader of us all."

"I be not forgetting respect of Breamas. He be busy enough without worrying toward Wharton, and he be smart enough to be grateful to us who be aiding his cause. I be less sure of you, Dee."

Deliaja's young, hard face became fanatically intense. "We be wanting the same thing, Vin: to be keeping what we be breaking our bodies to earn and to build, to be keeping Nilson for us who be understanding her, to be rid of Racker and all his Network kind. Network never be treating Nilson's children as the citizens that we rightly be. Network never be doing good for any of us, and it be time that Network be giving us what we be owed. It be time to fulfill Breamas' dream, and it be us that be making it happen."

Deliaja had an instinctive gift for swaying emotions. The force of Deliaja's words transformed, for a moment, the two ignorant, disgruntled terrorists into proud, confident soldiers of Breamas' long-promised, long-unrealized revolution. Deliaja climbed to her feet with no effort at grace, but both men watched her motions appreciatively. Their eyes followed every stroke of her hand as she swatted cavern dust from her coverall. She observed their leering but tolerated it, because they demanded nothing personal of her and respected her worth to a greater cause. She thought less of them because of the weakness that she perceived in them, but Vin *was* the leader who had first spread Breamas' ideas among the miners, and Cullen had invaluable contacts among skyside street gangs and smugglers. Deliaja's own connections, being firmly established in her unsavory past, were as varied as the clientele she had once entertained and the women who had shared her profession and her marginal trust. "Be you getting me the information about Tempest's last fight?" she asked.

Cullen replied gruffly, "Only a name, but that be telling enough. The boy be insulting Stonebreaker, night before dying, calling him stingy. You be knowing Stonebreaker's pride about never shorting the tithe to his old skyside gang. Stonebreaker and his lads be not charitable toward those that be insulting unwisely."

"Why be you wanting to know, Dee?" asked Vin. "Be you thinking to please Arlan Willowan by a killer naming? Half the caves be knowing the truth of it, and none be against Stonebreaker in this. That Tempest boy be ever a senseless fool."

"I be planning to talk to Stonebreaker, as none else seems to be having the wit or courage to do. I be wanting to know where the boy be killed, when and how."

"*You* be turning into a regular port boy, asking such questions as those. Be careful, or Stonebreaker be mistaking you for just that sort. He be not fond of legal troubles."

"No one be mistaking Dee for any boy," snickered Cullen, "least of all a man of Stonebreaker's appetites."

"I be knowing Stonebreaker's hungers better than you," answered Deliaja with an introspective pall darkening her eyes and tensing her jaw. Her glower at her private demons caused Cullen to smile sourly. "I be thinking that good use may be coming from this fortunate name. Thanks, Cullen."

Deliaja did not doubt that she could learn what she needed to know from Stonebreaker, but she was not pleased with the confirmation of her suspicions about Tempest's killer. She knew Stonebreaker well and hated him thoroughly. He was the unendurable type of client who had caused her to abandon her still-lucrative profession for the hard, cold Wharton mines. He insisted on believing that Deliaja enjoyed his attentions. Deliaja left her fellow revolutionaries with the cloud of contemplation still bleak across her face.

Hand over hand, she climbed the ladder of spikes that led back to a service closet not far from the canteen. The narrow passageways, thinly plastered and washed with a luminous paint to brighten the natural stone walls, allowed no easy avoidance of other cavers. Exploiting Wharton etiquette, Deliaja kept her head down in the more trafficked passageways, implicitly signaling her present unwillingness to tolerate company. She did not stop when she reached the noisy canteen but proceeded past it to the elevator block, which lifted her to the upper level where she lived.

She breathed more freely once the elevator broke through the crust of Wharton and entered the opaque, yellow-glazed atmospheric dome that enclosed Wharton's only inhabitable surface region. Riddled with interlaced pipes and ducts and conduits, the dome's design incorporated no impractical element, such as beauty. Few of the Wharton workers even knew that

the dome, used during the construction of the subterranean environment, remained accessible, and few who
had seen it cared to return. The upper dome contained
only one decent room, which had housed the original
Network installation crew leader during a single year
of tenancy. The room, though minimally equipped by
the standards of average Network citizens, would have
astonished any Wharton worker whose experience consisted only of Wharton depths and impoverished Nilson. It was a well-lit, well-ventilated private room that
cost Deliaja most of what she earned in the canteen—
and all of what she had saved in her previous lucrative
career.

When she flung herself on the wide, thermal bed of
her white-walled, white-tiled room, Deliaja had resigned herself to the price that Stonebreaker would certainly demand and might possibly extract. "Why be it
always the likes of Stonebreaker?" she whispered to
herself. Her brutal self-honesty answered: The deep,
bitter violence in her own nature drove away any gentler man. She would not let herself voice the rest of the
thought, for it nearly overwhelmed her: that Arlan Willowan, as respected a man as could be found in Wharton, had chosen to give a measure of his friendship to
her without conditions or demands. For one moment,
the hardness of Deliaja's expression faded into what
she had been before too many men like Stonebreaker—
and Ned Racker—had made her hate her own flesh. As
a girl of six, she had huddled in the darkness of a
closet, digging her small fists into her ears to seal away
her mother's screams, and she had vowed never to endure such abuse. Poverty and weakness had undone her
vow and replaced it with anger.

Deliaja lay on her back, staring into the pallid glow
of the ceiling panels and she saw her mother's bruised
deathbed face. The hardness returned to her own expression. She would not let the bargaining go Stonebreaker's way easily. She might even emerge without
conceding more than a few drinks at the canteen. After
all, he would not recognize the value of a little impersonal information about the death of an unimportant

boy. Stonebreaker would not imagine the price
that Deliaja would pay for any knowledge that might
aid her fanatically cherished cause, the cause into
which she had funneled all of her blistering hurts and
frustrations.

She was not even sure what she expected to learn or
how that knowledge might be used, but Deliaja had
lived her by her instincts for too long to let them be
thwarted by her personal revulsion for Stonebreaker.
She buried her face in her foamy pillow and muttered,
"If you be wrong about what you be thinking, Arlan
Willowan, or I be wrong about you, it be you and yours
I be taking down with me." With a curse for the treacherous nature of most of the men she had known, she
stripped herself of her coverall and began to prepare
herself for the encounter with Stonebreaker. When
Deliaja decided on a course of action, she moved
quickly to complete it.

She would have greatest advantage by meeting him
on her own territory, where he might hesitate to attack
openly. However, Stonebreaker was not a regular customer of the Windmill, and Deliaja had no patience to
wait for him to appear on his own whim. With a grunt
of mild regret for the inevitable damage to the Windmill's income statement, she used her primitive Network intercom to transmit a message to Keever
with orders to announce a one-night discount on
the strongest liquors in the canteen's stock. Nothing
short of a death-match would keep Stonebreaker from
such a sale.

When Deliaja reached the Windmill two hours later,
the crowds were already bubbling into the hallways.
Keever had wisely recruited two of the burliest toughs
to control admission, but reaching the canteen's oak-
tone doors still demanded forceful tactics. Deliaja
made her own entry through the kitchen, and even at
that locked door, a hopeful cluster of miners pleaded
with her for special privileges. Deliaja cursed them
cheerfully, but she was grim as she crossed through the
kitchen to reach the bar.

The crowd was noisy, and the pace of work frantic,

but Keever had managed to keep the canteen running
without serious incidents. The customers made way for
Deliaja, because all knew her and knew that she could
cut short their current pleasures. Her intolerance was
notorious, as was her ability to enforce her will rapidly
and efficiently. She exchanged the usual jokes, tolerated the usual stale propositions, and searched all the
dusty faces for the man she intended to use. Stonebreaker was not hard to find.

"You be looking fine, Dee," said Stonebreaker, attempting winsome charm but managing only a simper
that reduced him to absurdity. He was a burly man of
blockish proportions, stained by dirt and the chemicals
that the miners used to track deep mineral veins.
All bulging nose and brows, his face had endured
many fistfights by simple, bullish obduracy, and the resultant scars puckered his skin. His eyes had the bleari-
ness of prolonged ginnygum usage. "One treat, for old
time's sake?"

"Because I be giving samples of the fine drink of
this establishment," answered Deliaja, "be not daft
enough to think I be giving away the goods." She kept
the teasing in her voice that she had learned early in
her first career. His blurred eyes responded.

Having succeeded in her first attack, Deliaja moved
away swiftly. There was no subtlety in the thigh-length
red satin vest that was her attire, but her approach was
deliberately paced. She had prepared a day's worth of
patience for the task of working Stonebreaker with effective artfulness. Each time she served him, she made
contact with him in some small way that reminded him
of her talent for giving pleasure. Keever could see
clearly enough what she was doing, though he could
not know the whole of the reason. Deliaja was glad that
the overflowing crowd kept Keever too busy to question her about the details. She felt a qualm only once,
glimpsing Arlan's tall figure briefly beyond the swinging doors, but the mobbed canteen discouraged the retriever from his customary visit.

"I be ever willing to pay a fair price, Dee," said
Stonebreaker with a plaintiveness that made her gloat.

"Yah. You be." She leaned across the table to fill his glass for him, offering him a carefully measured view of her firm flesh. She disregarded the vulgar comments and grasping hands of Stonebreaker's companions. "Though there be some saying otherwise."

Stonebreaker jumped from his chair, nearly toppling it. "Who be saying such lies?" snapped Stonebreaker, and every man within hearing range became silent and alert. The two men who had shared his table discovered a sudden need to visit the bar. Stonebreaker's violent temper was well known.

Deliaja smiled demurely. "None that be mattering now. Only Tempest."

Stonebreaker grunted, mollified, and sank back to his seat. The nervousness of the nearby crowd ebbed back to its ordinary level. "That boy be deserving of the dark."

This could be easier than she had hoped. "Yah. He be a liar about some that be not having Stonebreaker's strength to silence him. We be grateful that the liar be gone." She edged onto the arm of Stonebreaker's chair and wrapped her arm around him to whisper, "Some be saying that it be you downing the boy for his lies. Be it true?"

"How grateful might you be?"

"Might be very grateful—at a fair price."

Stonebreaker smirked, "It be true enough."

She retreated from his grasp with a haughty tilt of her head. "You be not telling me a tale just to make a bargain?"

"Be you trying to make me angry, Dee?"

Concealing her disgust behind mock affection, she rubbed the dirty brown stubble that covered his scalp. "I be complimenting your cleverness, but I be wanting a little more convincing before I be setting a price with you. There be *some* wagering that ghost lights be taking the boy before your chance at him. I be not about to make a deal with the dark."

"I be downing Tempest, quick and clean in a fair joust, with a spike through the ribs." With a typical form of Nilson pride, Stonebreaker added, "I be treating him better than his deserving. It be my kerchief covering his lying face. He be a skyside brother to some I be respecting, so I be giving him dignity in death."

"Then why be you hiding him in the deep places?"

"Deep places?" laughed Stonebreaker. "Dee, you be spending too little time outside these plastic walls if you think we be taking gold in 'deep places,' and beside the shaft to the gold veins be that boy's ending place. I be leaving Tempest where I be knowing he be found while still recognizable. I be wanting to set a good example for other liars to see."

"You be a cunning man, Stonebreaker," cooed Deliaja. "May be, you be finding me after this shift, and I be willing to discuss old times with you."

"Where be I finding you?"

"If I be not here, ask Keever where I be." *And Keever will lie, as instructed.* Stonebreaker's face cracked into a broad grin, which Deliaja returned amiably. She bestowed one light caress upon his back, her thanks to him for the information he had given her, then sashayed back to the bar. She whispered to Keever, "I be leaving for a time. Be announcing the last round as soon as I be gone."

"Who be you meeting this time, Dee?" asked Keever with a squint of suspicion. More understanding of her than most of the Wharton rebels, Keever suspected the nature of her skyside contacts. He knew that she traveled skyside far more frequently than any other Wharton worker. He had tried repeatedly to discover the override code that gave her access to the portals in the absence of the guards. He suspected that she had coaxed a key away from some retriever.

Deliaja snickered, "Be you thinking I be answering to you?" She clapped him on the back. "It be a good night's work, Keever."

"If you be saying it," he answered.

"I be," she assured him. Deliaja slid through the kitchen and escaped out the back door. Keever's announcement of the last round of drinks would delay even Stonebreaker from missing her too soon.

Stonebreaker had pleased her immensely: If she

could have named her choice for the site of Tempest's murder, she could have asked for no better location than the gold shaft. It was far enough from the main caverns to be structurally independent, and its product had a historical value beyond actual worth. An explosion in the ghost's lair should produce maximal damage for minimal cost of resources, and that should fulfill even Breamas' high standards of terrorism. All of Network would take note if the ghost lights afflicted valued Network equipment, instead of merely replaceable workers. Deliaja had a second hope for the explosion beyond the manipulation of ghostly forces: The turmoil in Wharton would help to distract Nilson officials, consume critical Network resources, and prevent Ned Racker from recognizing himself as the real target—until the moment of his death.

On reaching her room, Deliaja sent a prearranged message to Breamas. The excitement of bringing her dream to fruition made her impatient. She wanted to ensure that Breamas had the explosives ready for her upon her arrival—not the common products used in the mines, but the more potent blends that the Cuui had provided before his capture. No one could prepare explosives more cleverly than Breamas, the master terrorist of Nilson. No one could execute Breamas' plans more adeptly than Deliaja. She did not intend to fail their cause.

***

"You are certain of the location?" demanded Breamas. Because Deliaja's Network link, though an object of luxury for a Nilsonite, was an old, low-quality design, Network rendered the master terrorist's voice in a neutral tone that greatly reduced Breamas' usual, disproportionate impact.

"The stories be consistent," repeated Deliaja, clutching the coverlet on her bed to keep her temper in check. She did not like to have her reports questioned, even by Breamas.

The delay until Breamas' next words was long

enough that Deliaja wondered whether to blame faulty
equipment alone. Breamas himself was known to use
silence as a manipulative technique. She had occasionally wondered where he had acquired such learning beyond the ordinary Nilson survival skills, but she knew
the penalties of questioning him on such matters. He
retaliated brutally when reminded of a past that the
crippling of body and mind had cost him. Breamas had
long ago ceased to value the life of any of his followers, even of his captains. "Have you informed your local leader?"

Deliaja answered impatiently, "Vin be not willing to
do what we be needing. We be ready, Breamas. This be
the opportunity, better than any that we be seeing since
or again." Using Network to plot against Network
pleased Deliaja. She did not understand Network well
enough to recognize the danger of such usage. She certainly did not comprehend that the technical flaws that
she cursed in her third-hand, rebuilt Network equipment comprised the only reason that her injudicious
calls went unrecorded.

Breamas chuckled, and even Network's poor render-
ing conveyed the chilling power of a mad confidence.
"You wish to replace Vin as Wharton cell captain."
Though Breamas had forgotten much about his past, he
remained well aware of Network's capabilities. Breamas relished the prospect of Network detecting his
plottings, especially if Network brought Breamas'
schemes to the attention of Andrew Caragen. To hurt
Network, to hurt Caragen whose schemes had driven
Breamas from the daylight of hale men and women, to
hurt anyone who did not share Breamas' hates: these
would be sufficient pennants of victory for an old,
thwarted man. He had ceased to look further.

Deliaja risked a sharp retort. "I be wishing to stop
game-playing, Wharton and skyside both. How long be
we waiting for our revolution? If we be not willing to
start the war now, then we be never doing, forever talking. That be not why I be preparing and recruiting for
you these past years. I be not alone in thinking that Vin
be too cautious, too comfortable to be taking the real

risks, the needful risks. With your backing, the others be ready to follow me. We be ready to take Wharton in a day. Then we be ready to take Nilson."

"You may take Wharton, Dee, but can you keep it?"

"Long enough to win the real battle."

"Vin would not care for your suggestions, especially speaking thus behind his back."

"I be taking the care to convince Vin, if you be agreeing. He be never willing to take on a real fight, and you be knowing it. Let me be doing and no more waiting."

"Yes," mused the old terrorist. "You may be right about Vin." He chuckled, enjoying the contests between his followers. They reminded him of his own youth, glorified by a haze of damaged memory. "Very well, Deliaja, you have my blessing. If you succeed, I shall be pleased." He did not add that if she failed, he would lose nothing that mattered to him. He would lose only Deliaja, and possibly Vin, and Breamas had lost many dedicated followers over his long life. Even Deliaja's potential, spectacular failure would further Breamas' ambition to be renowned as Network's most enduring terrorist. Perhaps even Network's Council Governor would take notice. Breamas was indeed pleased.

**

Vin did not trust Deliaja. She was too sure of herself, too aloof in her methods, too arrogant when she spoke of Breamas, as if he were her personal friend. This business with Stonebreaker was so typical of her, asking all the questions but never telling anyone her reasons: Why did Deliaja really care about Arlan Willowan's retrieval of that useless boy, Tempest? She was too smart to think she could recruit Arlan to the cause. Arlan had always begged the crumbs from Saschy Firl's table.

For several days now, Vin had been following Deliaja's movements unobtrusively. He was rather proud of his success in trailing her without her noticing him. It was a skill for which he had considerable natural talent, augmented by practice, but he rarely exercised his abilities against someone as wary as Deliaja. Admittedly, she moved less cautiously in the caves than skyside, where port boys were a greater threat. Within Wharton, inherently more secure from unauthorized exit than most prisons, Network did not supplement its automated policing as extensively as it did skyside. The only laws that Network enforced inside Wharton pertained to the guarding of Network property, which consisted primarily of mine products and equipment. Other laws fluctuated at the discretion of shift supervisors like Vin.

Last night Vin had watched Deliaja disappear into the Network-guarded portal chambers, when all should have been locked against such access, and he had seen her emerge minutes later with two well-filled canvas shoulder packs. She had returned by devious routes to her peculiar dome dwelling, and Vin had struggled to track her. Several times, he had lost sight of her in narrow, unfinished tunnels, but the crumbled rockways had decorated her trail with glittering dust and slivered crystal. Her return to her home, without evident justification for her meandering route, had disappointed Vin. He had debated whether to take the trouble again tonight to follow her.

All of his regrets had vanished now, as they drew close to the shafts known for their extensive, now largely depleted, gold deposits. Deliaja carried the packs again, and her coverall matched the gray Wharton dust. A black hood concealed her bright hair. She moved stealthily, dodging those few miners who still worked the nearly exhausted vein of gold. Vin moistened his lips hungrily, sensing that he was near to discovering Deliaja's secret.

She circled the mine entrance, observing it from every angle and height. She triggered no Network alarms, since she did not attempt to pass any Network barriers. She seemed concerned only with the smooth-floored cavern vault outside the guarded mine. It was a staging area, where equipment was assembled and shift

supervisors gave miners their instructions for working
the deep regions. Openings of varied dimension peered
into the cavern from its floor to its high, arching ceiling, and Deliaja inspected the room from every accessible vantage point. Where she could not walk upright,
she did not hesitate to crawl, though she laid aside her
parcels before entering the narrowest passages. Vin
could see nothing about the staging area that seemed
worthy of the attention that Deliaja gave it.

To watch Deliaja in this well-worked warren of tunnels required Vin to close the distance between himself
and his prey, but Deliaja seemed much too preoccupied
with her inspection to notice him. Her distraction made
him bold. After an hour had passed and the few miners
had ended their shift's work, Vin scarcely bothered to
avoid the beams of the bright, evenly spaced light
tubes in the tunnel walls. After the second hour, he remained in a shadowy corner of the staging area, hidden
by a chemical vat, and simply watched her lantern appear progressively at each of the upper "windows."

He had grown sleepy. Deliaja's prowling no longer
seemed to promise any immediate reward. The stones
were pressing uncomfortably into his back, and his
neck had begun to ache from his prolonged upward
staring. He shifted position, and fine gravel wedged its
way inside his boots. Grumpily, he pried one boot from
his foot to shake free the annoying gravel. A nearby
thump startled him, and he peered cautiously around
the edge of the vat.

Deliaja was level with his view, pounding against
the floor not far from the mine entry. Her motions had
a strange, light rhythm, familiar to Vin but unexpected
in this place. He had planted some of Breamas' alien
explosives himself, tapping the malleable fuse pack
tightly around the inner casing to form a chemical
bond, which the catalyst-soaked wick would trigger
within minutes of its application. Such powerful explosives were used skyside, not in Wharton, not here
where the destruction of a few Network support struts
could cause entire cavern wings to collapse.

Her actions be not what they seem, Vin told himself.

Immediately, he reversed his own conclusion and asked himself, *What be she thinking?* They had discussed the potential for this type of terrorism in Wharton and agreed that the dangers were too great to Wharton's numerous rebel sympathizers.

However, there were no working caverns above this region, and the few exploratory tunnels nearby were largely unused. If a region of Wharton were to be destroyed, there could be worse choices. Was this one of Breamas' ideas? The possibility of such a plot, excluding him, aggravated Vin's resentment of Deliaja and her devious ambitions.

Vin saw her remove the wicks from her pack, and his indecision vanished along with his suspicion of Breamas' involvement. Such madness had to be Deliaja's alone. Vin jumped to his feet, shouting her name and assorted obscenities. To his indignation, she responded by smirking in his direction, applying the wicks in rapid sequence, and racing across the cavern. She jumped to reach one of the smaller tunnels, pulled herself onto its ledge and crawled into darkness.

Instead of following her, Vin sprinted to the small mound of explosives. He intended to deactivate the device, but the wicks had already stained the fuse pack. Cursing Deliaja, he ran out of the cavern via the wide tunnel that formed the main equipment access. He hurled himself into the partial shelter of a mining cart, just as a sequence of explosions chased him into the tunnel, bombarded his ears, and set the walls to shuddering. Two great slabs of stone crashed beside him, and cracks snaked across thinly plastered walls.

Vin gasped, as the air rushed out of his lungs to be replaced by a stinging chemical that tasted like garlic. His eyes watered from dust and smoke. The nearest light tubes burst, leaving utter darkness. The weight of the planet above him creaked and resettled, precariously near to collapsing this ancient pocket.

Through the tears that blurred his vision, ruby lights streaked across the blackness that engulfed him. Flickering motes, painfully bright, seared his optic nerves. His stomach churned. The semblance of a yellow sky

opened above him, etched his eyes with acid and spat
him back into Wharton's suffering.

He heard the howling, as of a powerful gale whip-
ping the miserable streets of Nilson. He felt stretched
and worn, as if the entire substance of his body had
eroded from some caustic action. A sour-sweet smell,
like death or the Nilson sewers, crawled inside him and
mocked his helplessness. A boulder slammed into the
car that held him, shattering the metal structure and its
contents.

From the small, stable shaft that she had selected
with such care, high above the gold mine, Deliaja
forced herself to watch a storm of ghost lights, though
their unnatural flickering churned her senses. Ghost
lights raced in a pulsing darkness that was deeper than
lack-of-light, for they pierced through stone and ripped
hanks of metal from the sturdiest Network equipment.
She had hoped to rouse the ghost lights in the cause of
Breamas' revolution, and she had succeeded far beyond her hopes.

Her lips thinned into a grimace as a crash of ghost-
shifted rock ended Vin's screams. She had wanted him
to observe her work and, perhaps, to take blame for it,
but she had not meant to sacrifice him to the ghost
lights. Still, his death would achieve more meaning
than his life. Network would take note. She almost envied Vin such a death. From her perilous perch, Deliaja
whispered, "Be free of the dark, Vin." She scurried
back into the tunnels.

CHAPTER 16

Judges

The wall curtains dripped with the soothing regularity of gentle rain. The light fell shadowless from crystal tears that formed the ceiling. A round white table had been brought to the meditation room, where Sesserda scholars ordinarily rested on a solitary lounge. Assorted chairs, tailored for the various representative species, extended to the liquid walls, crowding the chamber.

Seven Calongi had gathered, uniformly dour in the dark capes of their own velvet limbs. Their large and regal heads nodded acknowledgment of the arrival of the two Soli. Tori could distinguish a few Calongi by eye color or the blue patterns of sensor patches that crossed the backs of their broad skulls, though she was seldom confident of her identifications. She knew the golden-eyed Ukitan, the honored Calongi master who was Jase's mentor and nearest neighbor. Tori also recognized Mintaka, a blue-eyed Calongi female who was small for her species, being little taller than Jase. Mintaka's presence pleased Tori, because Mintaka-lai was the only Calongi whose sense of humor Tori could occasionally comprehend.

The third species represented at the meeting was the Escolari, Tatakaqua, who had brought the invitation. With his silken white hair and beard, he resembled a wizened old gnome, though he wore the red vest and pantaloons that signified youth among his people. When Jase greeted Tatakaqua in the language of Escolar, Tatakaqua brightened perceptibly.

Watching Tatakaqua's reaction, Tori derived some comfort from the knowledge that she was not alone in

her nervousness. Once seated, Tori met the faceted
black eyes of the Escolari across the table from her. He
pursed his rubbery lips in the Escolari equivalent of a
smile, which Tori returned.

The water curtains ceased their flow for a microspan. Into the silence, Mintaka sang a brief Sesserda
prayer in chorus with her own multilayered voice. Tori
felt her own nervousness unraveled by the song's
power. Even the simplest of Calongi music could com-
pel emotions beyond the listener's control.

Ukitan, as the senior Calongi master, signaled the
formal opening of discussion by a rippling of his
golden neck tendrils. Calongi could devote days to a
point of philosophy, but they preferred to keep their
business meetings direct and terse. From deference to
Tatakaqua and Tori, the Calongi spoke the common
Cuui trade language that was Consortium Basic. The
courtesy had limited value, since much of the discussion occurred on levels that only Calongi and other
Sesserda practitioners could follow.

"From a more civilized culture," said Ukitan, "this
accusation would merit a simple Inquisition."

"Truth encompasses all," observed Mintaka, "the
uncivilized as well as the civilized."

"I concur, Mintaka-lai," nodded Ukitan. "As we all
know, the Truth in question involves more than the
predicament of a single uncivilized man."

"The demands that would be placed on Jase-lai are
troubling," contributed the Calongi at Ukitan's left. On
Jase's behalf, Tori resented the one sublayer of the Calongi's vocal tones that she recognized from its frequent application to herself; she knew it was
disparagement and had rarely heard it applied to Jase.
Her partner evinced no similar concern over the insult.

"But these demands are unvoidable," added Mintaka
with an impassioned subtone of emotion, "especially
since Network disdains all species but Soli. Respect
alone precludes the possibility of the necessary observations being made by any other."

"Network's leaders are insincere in their motives,"
declared a green-eyed Calongi.

The obvious remark did not strike Tori as significant, but it silenced the Calongi. As the microspans passed, she began to feel restless, wondering what they awaited. Tatakaqua glanced at her surreptitiously, as if seeking enlightenment from her. She shrugged in reply, less troubled than Tatakaqua about displaying ignorance openly among the Calongi.

It was Jase who finally spoke, measuring his words as if they carried loathsome implications, "The insincerity of Network leaders does not preclude our ability to enlighten them."

Tori thought a breeze had somehow crept through the curtains of rain, until she realized that the sensation emerged from the Calongi, united in a subvocal melody. "I commend your courage, Jase-lai," observed Ukitan.

"Courage and cowardice become indistinguishable on the path of necessity," replied the Calongi seated at Ukitan's right. Though the words sounded offensive, even Tori could sense the sublayer of praise.

"When the Choice for civilization divides a species, the entire species suffers until reunification occurs," said a Calongi whose sensor patches formed a pattern of interlocking wreaths. "Even the Soli of Network must eventually learn wisdom and join their more civilized kindred. This is inevitable."

"Nara-lai," said Ukitan to the one Calongi who had so far been silent in the vocal range, "we have not yet heard your judgment."

"The Truth is already clear to us," said Nara simply.

"You discern with wisdom, Nara-lai," responded Ukitan, and he turned toward Tatakaqua. "We apologize to you, honored Tatakaqua, and to Miss Mirelle, for neglecting you. Please express your questions freely."

With a nervous rumbling, Tatakaqua cleared his throat. "Great Sesserda masters, my life-purpose is to educate, as is consistent with the collective purpose of the Escolari people. My don informed me that my presence here was requested, but I do not know what contributions are expected of me."

"As an educator," replied Ukitan, "your opinion of the potential for educating the Network Soli has value to us."

Tatakaqua bobbed his head, snatching eagerly at what he imagined to be a sudden understanding. "An educational exchange with Network's Soli would seem to me both wise and desirable. I would be pleased to participate in such an undertaking, if that role were asked of me." He hesitated, but he received neither affirmation nor denial from the Calongi.

"Thank you, Don Tatakaqua," was Ukitan's simple reply. "We appreciate your offer."

Tori sympathized with Tatakaqua's obvious uncertainty. Calongi discussions such as today's example exasperated her with their assumption that all participants shared Sesserda insight—or were rendered irrelevant by their ignorance. From the nature of Tatakaqua's comments, she suspected that he had been given even less specific information than Jase had yielded to her. Tatakaqua seemed to think that the cause of the discussion was an educational conference, a natural assumption for a member of his species.

"However," continued Tatakaqua bravely, "I would understand if my participation were not desired. Since the Soli of Network suffer from serious intolerance of alien species, the selection of a Soli emissary would be practical. If the Soli of Network are to be receptive to any information from the Consortium, they will learn most readily from another Soli. They may be unwilling to listen to anyone else."

"It is implausible to assume otherwise at this time," observed Mintaka with a quiet, subtly melodious sigh. She seemed distracted now, suggesting that she had allocated all but a tiny fraction of her many-segmented brain to more interesting matters. "Network is a difficulty."

"They do not respect creation," clucked the green-eyed Calongi, voicing Sesserda's harshest condemnation. "They tamper even with the fundamental Truth."

They have finished their conference, concluded Tori wryly, *and are merely gossiping now, like the least civilized of us.*

"We must respect Network as part of creation," said Ukitan, countering her assumption immediately with his somber intensity, "but we must defend Sesserda Truth above all. If the Soli of Network will hear, we must speak to them." To Tori's surprise, the Calongi master turned to her and asked, "Will they hear us, Miss Mirelle?"

Tori knew better than to give platitudes to the Truth-worshiping Calongi. To the Calongi, courtesy demanded honesty, even if it wore an unpleasant face. "No," she answered. "You don't understand them, despite your ninety-six senses, multisegmented brains, and Sesserda wisdom. Why should they understand you?"

"Because they must," replied Mintaka in the deeply layered voice that conveyed emotion without words. Her voice held a sorrow that pierced to Tori's soul.

While Tori stared at the Calongi woman, wondering why the serene, generally humorous Mintaka should express grief for a single barbaric culture like Network, Jase touched Tori's arm lightly. Tatakaqua, swifter than Tori to take advantage of the meeting's end, had already arisen and bowed his exit. Tori followed in silence, momentarily unable to shake free of Mintaka's troubling vocal spell, which seemed to encompass far more than a minor issue of diplomatic inconvenience. Jase, as a Sesserda practitioner, remained with the Calongi for the final meditation.

In Ukitan's bright entry arbor, standing on the stone bridge above the stream that flowed through the house, Tatakaqua paused. He lifted his wizened face to Tori and asked her, "Do you understand why they invited us?"

"I never understand the Calongi," replied Tori, dragging her fingers through her hair and wondering if she were speaking the Truth, as Sesserda defined it. Thinking ruefully of Jase, she added, "I doubt that I understand any Sesserda adept."

"Yes," agreed Tatakaqua, tugging at his beard. "That is why you and I were invited. Because we do not understand."

"Now I don't understand you, and Escolari teachers

are supposed to excel at expressing themselves
clearly."

"I apologize, Miss Mirelle." Tatakaqua grinned
sheepishly. "I am only a young instructor, and I am very
nervous to find myself in such impressive company:
honored Calongi masters, the singular Soli for whom
you work, and yourself." He stammered to a stop.

"You may omit me from that list," answered Tori
with a smile to show her sympathy.

"This famous smile, with which you honor me, be-
lies your humble claim."

The smile thinned into a cynical line. "There is no
honor in my notorious ancestry. In any case, I have
nothing but appearance in common with that Mirelle
who was my great-grandmother."

Tatakaqua was too sensible and polite to contradict
her. "You have established a reputation for excellence
in a difficult profession. You must derive great satisfaction from your work and your regular association
with such extraordinarily gifted beings."

Tori laughed softly, unconsciously reinforcing his
awe of her. "When you were invited to this meeting,
Tatakaqua, were you given a reason?"

"No. I told you that I am an unimportant young
instructor."

"You're here," replied Tori, waving toward Ukitan's
glistening meditation room beyond its walls of water.
"You obviously matter to those 'honored Calongi masters' who invited you."

"You honor me with your words," answered
Tatakaqua, "but I think it is only my humble status that
matters in this case. The Calongi wished to assess the
reaction of an ordinary, relatively uncivilized being to
the subjects of their discussion. They are a subtle
species. Their Truth does not always resemble honesty
to those of us who are not Sesserda scholars."

Tori appreciated his own honesty. Few beings expressed their personal views about Calongi so readily.
She would have asked Tatakaqua to walk with her and
tell her of himself, if Jase had not emerged from the
meditation chamber.

Jase acknowledged Tatakaqua with only a distracted
gesture of Sesserda greeting. He did not grant Tori
even that small courtesy. The closing meditation had
not produced the usual Sesserda tranquillity in its Soli
practitioner.

Barely pausing, Jase crossed the bridge and hurried
into the garden. The path that wound through the ponds
and streams led eventually to Jase's house, though it
was not the shortest route. Whatever his immediate
goal, Jase seemed anxious to reach it. "I'd better follow
him," said Tori with an apologetic shrug at Tatakaqua.
"When he's distracted like this, he's liable to walk
through a thornbush and never notice that he's shred-
ding himself."

"I look forward to our next meeting," said Tatakaqua
with a courteous bow.

Tori replied with a noncommittal smile. She
doubted that she would see Tatakaqua again. Except
for the Calongi, few of the people who entered Jase's
life seemed to remain there long. She did not know
what to think of the meeting she had just left. In fact,
the more she considered that event, the more its cryptic
content annoyed her.

By the time she rejoined Jase in his office, she had
replayed all of the meeting's uncertain conversation
and decided that it had insulted her. That was the way
of Calongi insults: They were generally so indirect and
devoid of malice that the recipient could not protest.
Tori could, however, protest to Jase. He surely realized
that such a meeting could only make her feel inferior.
He ought to have prepared her.

Jase was standing in front of his desk, staring at the
cluttered shelves rising above it. His fingers were laced
behind his neck, confining the thick, dark hair that
brushed his collar. "I'm sorry," he apologized, before
Tori could voice her complaint. "You're right, of
course. I could have told you what the meeting would
be like. I was asked, however, to invite you without
preparation. We needed your spontaneous reaction as a
gauge of Network Soli in similar circumstances. It was
rather a shabby way to use you."

"It was an Inquisitor's trick," snapped Tori, "and I have not been accused of any recent crimes, as far as I know."

"We weren't trying to analyze you—only your reaction to a particular event."

"Fine. You want my reaction? That was the most frustrating meeting I have ever attended, even measuring it by Calongi standards," grumbled Tori. "What was its purpose, except to make me feel insignificant? Since when do the Calongi devote such attention to the idle insult of a Network planetary governor? Whatever your *actual* purpose may have been, you Sesserda scholars had obviously held your own conference already. All of your decisions were already made."

"Untrue. We did confer previously, but we did not reach a consensus until today's meeting."

"Then your process of decision making eluded my simple Soli perceptions. If you seriously consider me your professional partner, then try sharing some of your precious information and insights with me. I won't say that I'd refuse to continue working with you on the basis of today's deception, but I do not care for being manipulated, Mister Sleide. You misled me about that meeting, my fine worshiper of Sesserda Truth."

"Untrue," repeated Jase mildly.

"Stop saying that."

"Then stop spouting fallacies. Truth: During our stays on Calong, your work taxes your patience more than your brain, and it always makes you irritable. Truth: You adapted extremely well to your role as my superior on Alari, and the subsequent contrast of reality set you on a path of interpreting everything I say or do as condescension. In the past quarter-span, you've become almost as prickly as when we first met."

"When you and your Calongi friends treat me like a subject of Inquisition, how do you expect me to react?" asked Tori mockingly. She flung the ivory jacket of her suit across the stack of Atiri silk, wondering why she ever tried to impress Sesserda practitioners. She could not even recognize the criteria they used for granting their approval.

"I expect you to behave like a woman who comprehends something of the art of alien relations. Why are you willing to relate to every species but the Calongi?"

"I don't need to relate to the Calongi. You handle that aspect of our professional lives so capably by yourself."

"You chose to live here, Tori. I have no such option."

"You spend only two days per span replenishing your internal supply of relanine. The rest of the time, you could live anywhere you please."

"Between bouts of relanine sickness," added Jase dryly.

"You haven't had a serious episode of the sickness in two spans."

"Because I've been careful to spend enough time on Calong."

The reminder silenced Tori. Twice since she had known him, Jase had suffered the excruciating effects of relanine sickness, as only a true addict could endure. On both occasions, he had been feverish and delirious, and the Calongi had told her only that he would live—or he would die. She had sat with him by the millispan, helplessly whispering encouragement that he could not acknowledge or even hear. During the worst of his sickness, when misadapted relanine had turned his skin corrosive, she had burned her hands by touching him.

Recalling how deeply she had feared losing him, Tori softened her plaint, "You might at least have let me see or hear the original report about the Network incident."

Wearing an odd, ironic expression, Jase reached into the shelf he faced and removed a copper-bound notebook. He extracted from it a sheet of transcription film. He dangled the film between two fingertips. "This is a copy of the controversial segment of a speech by Governor Ned Racker of Nilson. How is your command of Network Basic?" he asked.

"Limited," replied Tori.

"I'll prepare a concentrated study regimen for you.

In the meantime, I shall translate." Jase crossed to the
foyer window and read by its golden light:

"Nilson will become the new Network-3, the new
standard of excellence for all of Network. We have exceeded all our goals in the first years of our renovation
program. It is you, the citizens of Nilson, who have
made these achievements possible. Take pride in your
accomplishments! Acknowledgment of our technical
supremacy humbles even the arrogant Calongi, who
send their vile agents to steal our secrets. Even now, a
Consortium creature that calls itself Filcher Ikthan
Cuui awaits our legal judgment for the crime of smuggling. Let the C-humans, the traitorous offal of our
race, recognize their defilement and defeat because of
Nilson's greatness. The Consortium looks to us with
envy. Let them look to us with fear!"

When Jase finished reading, he laid the document
quietly on the desk. "That is an excerpt of a transcription, taken from an illicit recording," he said. "Ukitan-
lai retains the original text, which was sent to him by
an independent trader. We do not know how accurately
the text matches the recording."

"That is almost a call for war," shivered Tori, appalled by the level of virulent contempt evident even
from Jase's emotionless reading. She might grumble to
Jase about the Calongi, but she had grown accustomed
to their acutely civilized standards. Her Uncle Per had
little tolerance for other species, but not even he had
ever consolidated so many offensive remarks in a
single speech.

"The idiotic bravado of that 'call' is why the traders
have managed to create a large demand for recordings
of this speech among the independents. Most of the
purchasers consider it a grand joke that the leader of a
pathetic, impoverished world like Nilson would have
the temerity to threaten the Consortium." Jase rubbed
the back of his neck. "I will understand if you decline
to join me in this little exercise. I'd like to avoid it myself, but my qualifications are a little hard to duplicate."

"Was that the conclusion of today's meeting? To
send you to Network?"

"The conclusion of today's meeting was to send me to Network unofficially, as an eccentric 'C-human' with a taste for unconventional travel destinations. There are a few such Soli, and Nilson is one of Network's few open ports. Even if I'm forbidden to leave the spaceport, I should be able to learn something of value."

"Is your purpose to learn or to influence?"

"Both. Will you come?"

"I suppose I'd follow you into Zanten Hell, if you asked me. I never have had much sense, and you bring out all my worst instincts." She joined Jase at the window and tried to read the Network document in his hands, but she could barely decipher a few angular letters.

"It may not be as bad as we expect."

"It will probably be worse. You are reasonably notorious, after all, even among independent traders. Not many Soli have iridescent eyes." She took the document from him and tried to decrypt it by closer study.

"Eye color can be altered temporarily, even for a relanine addict, though it's a frightful nuisance because of the need for rigid lenses and constant replacement."

"That's very deceptive behavior for a Sesserda scholar."

"I do not plan to lie. My eyes *are* blue. Relanine simply obscures that fact."

"Will you announce yourself honestly as Jase Sleide?"

"The Truth of a name rests in its context."

"You do excel at rationalization," Tori murmured, staring at the incomprehensible Network text, though most of her attention was centered on Jase. "You had planned all of this before you even mentioned Network to me."

"That was what I said at the meeting, if you were listening."

Tori refrained from comment about the meeting's deliberate obscurity. "Why was Tatakaqua invited?"

"To test the principle of a Consortium Soli educating a Network citizen by indirect methods. If an Escolari instructor like Tatakaqua considered the principle

inconsistent with his personal experience, that awareness should have colored his reaction today. As to why
Tatakaqua personally was selected—that was my suggestion. He is the only son of my former Escolari tutor,
a very wise man who died several spans ago."

"Couldn't you have just asked his opinion?"

"This method is more accurate. It tests unconscious
knowledge as well as conscious memories. It precludes
biasing the data with the power of suggestion."

"And it spares you from confessing your identity as
his father's student in your pre-Sesserda life?"

"That is another valid reason."

"What did you learn from your insidious observation of that nervous young Escolari, who deserves better treatment?"

Jase made a pained expression at her sarcasm.
"Tatakaqua contributed the final vote on the soundness
of the principle under study."

"On that insubstantial basis, you will travel to Nilson
under false pretense, wield your Inquisitor's skills surreptitiously, and influence unsuspecting Network citizens by Sesserda techniques against which they have no
defense," concluded Tori. "It obviously requires a
Sesserda scholar to recognize this concoction of deceits
as the proper pursuit of your Truthful life-purpose. I
would probably mistake it for the same level of accused
crime that caused the incarceration of Filcher Ikthan
Cuui." Jase bestowed upon her a withering gaze from
his iridescent eyes. She smirked blandly in return. "And
how will you introduce me? It is not unlikely that someone, even in Network, would have heard of Mirelle.
Victoria Darcy would be more credible as an assistant."

"But less accurate than Victoria Mirelle."

"An alias is acceptable for you but not for me?"

"I will not use an alias without a better cause than
convenience. . . ." Jase stopped and began anew, "I am
not oblivious to the apparent ironies that Sesserda pre-
sents to those who are not practitioners. You may call
yourself Methusaleh, if you like. Just inform me,
please, before we contradict each other publicly." He

retrieved the Network speech from her and restored it to the copper notebook.

"If the governor of Nilson is not the naive idiot that his speech suggests," asked Tori thoughtfully, "what is his purpose?"

"I think you should prove your professional expertise and practice the art for which I originally hired you. Demonstrate your acuity of insight into the uncivilized Network mind by telling *me* the potential motives."

"I presume you'll arrange for me to meet the governor first."

"If necessary."

"What if he chooses not to be met?"

"What use is insidious Sesserda persuasion if it cannot effect a simple encounter?"

"You'd be frightening, Jase, if you weren't so obstinately idealistic." She draped the Atiri silk around her shoulders. "Who pays us for this little chore?"

"You'd frighten *me,* if I thought you were as purely mercenary as you pretend."

"No one is paying us?"

"Truth is beyond price."

"You enjoy irritating me, don't you?"

"Would you begrudge me such a harmless pleasure."

"Yes."

"Tori," he chided, "I could recognize that as a lie even if I had no Sesserda skills at all."

CHAPTER 17

Seekers

"What is your game, Marrach?" demanded Caragen in a tone of cajolery that pounded directly into the implant in Marrach's brain. "Network confirms none of your claims about Nilson."

Marrach, who knew Caragen better than any other citizen in Network, distrusted Caragen most of all in such apparently amiable moods. More disturbing, Caragen had established his communication link without Marrach's consent. "Please, go outside, Jeni," muttered the Healer to his wife. She glanced at him for only an instant, but he could see the comprehension rise within her. With blanched face, she laid aside the herbs that she had tied for drying, and she complied.

Marrach closed his eyes and listened for the closing of the door behind her before he addressed the Council Governor via Network's unspoken voice. "You forgot to knock, Caragen," said Marrach ironically.

"My researchers perfected a new technique for bypassing the standard protection modes," answered Caragen, gloating openly. "You have not stayed current with advances in Network technology, Marrach. You have grown sloppy."

"You have not grown less arrogant."

"You have not yet answered my question."

"You have not yet assessed Nilson adequately to justify your disbelief. You are well aware of the inadequacies of the Nilson monitoring systems. That planet *is* the center of an increasingly unstable region of topological space."

"Is that the claim of your tame genetic freak, Quin Hamley?"

Marrach debated his reply for an instant. He considered regretfully that Agent Rabh Marrach could have answered without the defensive pause that Network sensors would detect easily. "Quin Hamley has confirmed the damage. He has expressed serious concern regarding the magnitude of danger."

Blandly amiable, Caragen remarked, "Then the matter clearly demands your further attention. I trust that your next report will be more complete."

Every instinct in Marrach shouted with alarm. "I do not work for you, Caragen."

"I shall arrange the necessary resources for you, according to our customary agreement. Ned Racker is too treacherous and self-serving to be a reliable source of information regarding his own activities, but he would be glad enough to take the glory for thwarting natural calamity or uncovering conspiracy." Caragen's throaty chuckle spoke of years of uniquely shared knowledge and perspective. "Of course, you know his profile, Marrach. You compiled most of its content."

Marrach's recognition of danger made the Mirlai flicker frantically around their Healer. He repeated, "I do not work for you, Caragen."

"I have given you full access to Network's current files on Nilson's status, including some recent data regarding terrorist activities in Nilson and its mining operations. One must give Citizen Breamas credit for his persistence, despite his ineffectuality in the practical details of organized rebellion. He owes his most meaningful successes to your tactical planning."

"I no longer share your interest in the activities of assassins, crime lords, and terrorists."

"I think you will find the terms of your contract acceptable. Network can negotiate any minor details. I shall contact you again to review your plan of action." Caragen terminated the link as abruptly as he had caused its connection.

The stilled Network implant felt raw and icy within the Healer's skull. Marrach clenched his left hand tightly, driving his fingernails through the skin. He did not try to staunch the seep of blood.

***

Quin tried to restrain his imagination, but it was the least disciplined part of him and often the most troublesome. He envisioned Nilson, shattering. He envisioned Marrach, cursing him and retracting the gift of life. He envisioned Katerin, grieving.

Instead of any of his dire imaginings, he found the Healer Evjenial, quietly scattering seeds for hungry chickens in the yard behind the Healers' cottage. "He is in the house," she told Quin, who had voiced no inquiry. "Treat him with gentleness, please. These bouts cause him much pain."

"Is he ill?" asked Quin, suddenly contrite at the thought of such a prosaic explanation for Marrach's odd behavior. Quin had considered the Healers unassailable, but he supposed that they could be subject to ailments of some peculiar sort.

One coppery braid fell across Jeni's shoulder, and she tossed it impatiently back into place behind her. "He is Rabhadur Marrach," she answered, hissing the name as if it offended her. "*He* is the man you came to see, is he not?"

"I do not understand."

"I think you understand, Lord Quinzaine, much more than you admit." She pointed angrily toward the cottage, spilling seeds from her undyed apron and inciting a frenzy among the clucking fowl. "He is there. Go and speak to him. Question him about his past. I think he would answer you today, though you may not find him such good company in other respects."

The ominous hint in her words made Quin hesitant to discover its cause. He stared at the cottage, homely and comfortable and solid, and he dreaded entering it. "Yesterday, your husband did not want me here at all."

"The *Mirlai* did not want you here. Nor do they want you here now, but they will tolerate your coming because a Healer has asked it of them, and it is he who will suffer for it."

"I do not mean harm to anyone here, Evjenial."

"You summon his past. There is no greater harm that you could inflict on him."

"Are you angry with me or with him?"

Jeni closed her eyes. "Neither. I am angry with the fates." Her eyes flashed open. "But *I* shall heal, Lord Quinzaine. The Mirlai will not leave me." Subdued of motion, she resumed casting the mottled seeds in slow arcs.

Delaying a few more instants, and calling himself a coward for the tactic, Quin circled the cottage to enter by the front. The upper half of the split door stood open. Quin could see Marrach sitting on the stone hearth. The Healer glanced upward and nodded at Quin. "I expected you to return today," said Marrach.

Quin unlatched the lower door and joined Marrach beside the fire. The heat pounded against Quin's back, stirring Power's desire to retaliate. "I came only to fulfill my Infortiare's command. She wishes for you to visit Serii. She has ordered me to ensure that her invitation is accepted."

With a twist of a smile, Marrach murmured, "Could I decline such a gracious offer?"

Quin's Power probed Marrach tentatively and found only cold mockery and the hardness that defied any deeper understanding. There was no dread of leaving Siatha, to which the Mirlai chose to bind themselves. There was no sense of Mirlai energy. There was no sense of the man, the Healer, whom Quin knew. With an internal shudder, Quin realized that the probe of Marrach felt horribly like a probe of Network itself. "Come with me now, Marrach," said Quin.

"How is it done?" asked Marrach with the dry curiosity of any mechanical Network node.

"Just walk with me. That is usually easiest." Quin hated the prospect of enveloping this friend/stranger with his Power, but Power cared nothing for such emotion. An Ixaxin's Power could be at least as adamant and austere as Network.

The two men walked together from the cottage. Jeni stood in the garden, watching them silently. A storm of Mirlai made her coppery hair glow golden.

"I shall bring him back soon," promised Quin.

Jeni smiled thinly, though the expression made her pixie face sorrowful. "You do what is necessary, as does my husband."

Marrach neither spoke nor looked at her, but Power felt the tremor that shook his careful indifference. When Quin's Power grasped Marrach and carried him into Power's infinite realm, Quin understood the need for that hard shell and nearly faltered in his own determination. Even muted by cruel self-control, the Healer's pain at leaving Siatha ran deeper than a physical amputation.

"Lords, I am sorry, Marrach," apologized Quin with fervor, though he spoke only by a voice of Power that the Healer could not hear.

Swiftly, deftly, Quin shifted energies and infinities to attain the Infortiare's Tower. Few mortal passengers could perceive anything but chaos in the passing, and even Network's more orthodox transfer subjected the sensitive traveler to the revulsion of unnatural mental and physical twistings, but Marrach seemed to devour ravenously whatever observations he could snatch. Quin did not think the coldly analytical trait was a Healer's gift, and its acuity augmented Quin's distaste for his current task. Quin relinquished control of Marrach's essence with a frantic eagerness upon arrival.

Marrach stepped into the Infortiare's office as calmly as if he had traveled all his life by a wizard's Power, and he began to laugh heartily before Quin had even recognized the cause. No trace of the Healer's internal torment manifested itself in Marrach's display of wry amusement. The sandy-haired man who sat at the Infortiare's desk scowled on seeing Marrach and nearly snapped his Network light-pen in half.

Marrach greeted the man with amiable irony, "I am flattered that you recognize me, Dr. Terry. The years have treated you well. Of course, I remember you best from the occasion of removing you from Caragen's special prison, and such incarcerations are not designed to improve the occupants' health."

Jon Terry muttered, "My daughter has drawn your

likeness. Her artwork often focuses on the subjects that trouble her." He glanced at Quin. "Your Infortiare asked me to meet her here today but gave me no reason, and until now I have seen only her servant. Lady Rhianna displays an unexpected streak of manipulative humor."

The burning sense of Venkarel whispered to Quin's Power, making Quin wince, though the words were simple enough, "Marrach understands the need for this meeting. Leave them to their discussion."

Though he did not doubt Venkarel's claim, Quin could not depart without contributing a comment of his own. "Tell Dr. Terry about Nilson, Marrach. I shall go find the Infortiare." It was a specious excuse for escape, since Quin knew perfectly well that the Infortiare had chosen deliberately to spend the morning at the bedside of Queen Joli. The obscure, attentive presence of Lord Venkarel, Quin felt certain, was far from coincidental.

***

Jon Terry sighed at the daunting prospect of conversing with Rabh Marrach, as Quin exited prosaically via the office door, "I thought you no longer left your homeworld, Marrach." Jon maintained a civil tone with difficulty. Despite the good that Marrach's advice had contributed in recent years to the Terry family and the Neoterra colony of Network refugees, Jon could not feel comfortable with the man who had caused so much destruction in the past.

"I received an irresistible invitation from the Infortiare," answered Marrach, prowling the office and studying the Infortiare's library with acute interest. He pried a leather-bound volume from a shelf and leafed through its parchment pages with avid care. "For a primitive society, these people achieve their goals most effectively."

Jon Terry exhaled a brusque laugh. "Their science diverged radically from its Network origins, but the result has its own sophistication. They call it wizardry, but it corresponds to a uniquely experience-driven form of applied topology." Discussing his own interests made Jon Terry relax fractionally. "Some of their ideas are sheer superstition, but their fundamental axioms of wizardry are brilliant, considering their society's dearth of formal scientific method. When compared with the Network tenets of topological transfer, the Ixaxins' insights challenge some of Network's most cherished theories and reduce our most complex concepts to trivialities. It is enough to humble any Network topologist."

"As Network's foremost expert in applied topology, you must derive some satisfaction from the evolution of your creation," murmured Marrach, staring at the text in his hands, as if to embed its arcane symbolisms into a Network data bank.

"I did not create this world. If anyone of Network deserves that 'credit,' it would be the Network-3 geneticists who began the Life Extension experiment that produced the original 'Immortals.' "

"You caused Network-3's topological separation from Network, without which the subsequent development could not have occurred."

"I reacted to a crisis. The original Immortals were horrifying powerful and absolutely sociopathic. They could have destroyed all of Network, if we had not isolated them at that time."

"So you said at your medical hearing, but I never heard you describe exactly what you feared that they would do," said Marrach softly. "How would they have effected this calamity?"

Jon wondered at the train of conversation, but he answered, "They had already begun to play deadly games with transfer coordinates, shifting travelers into oblivion."

"Isolated casualties," answered Marrach, dismissing them with a shake of his head, "unpleasant for the victims but not obviously a threat to all of Network. I am not disputing your claim, Dr. Terry, only the insufficiency of your answer. Humor my affinity for thoroughness and tell me: If the Immortals' current descendants retained their ancestral affinity for violence, what would be their method of destruction?"

"The Immortal wizards of Ixaxis could choose any of a thousand methods." Jon leaned back in the chair, scowling as intellectual rigor overcame his emotional antagonism toward Marrach and his questioning of the reasons for this meeting. "They can control energy by will, just as you or I control the material objects around us. A trained wizard needs no match to start a fire, and a living body suffices as fuel. They can alter the subtle energies, from a computer's internal workings to the processing within a human brain, or the spectacular energy forms that are the basis of Network weaponry. The most 'Powerful' of the Ixaxins can manipulate their personal relationships to topological space as easily as I can move my hand." Jon flexed his fingers in emphasis. He found himself relishing the opportunity to speak to *Marrach* of a Power beyond Network. "By a thought, they move through topological space physically. In reestablishing their connection to our universe, they apparently transferred their entire world through time, cycling back to a point of reference that existed ten thousand years in their past. Time transfer remains only a theory to us who are bound by Network science."

"Is it possible for topological space to become unstable, Dr. Terry?" demanded Marrach.

"The term 'unstable' is imprecise," replied Jon, all of his caution renewed. "Clarify your question."

"According to Lord Quinzaine, the space in the vicinity of the planet Nilson is 'breaking' from an instability that is most probably of Network origin. How would you interpret his claim?"

Jon's frown settled slowly. "As a calamity," he answered, "or as a harmless phenomenon resulting from observational inaccuracy, the topological equivalent of an optical illusion. Without further data, I can only speculate. The calamitous occurrence could arise if the limit points themselves began to map between spatial sets."

"I am not a topologist, Dr. Terry. Could you interpret for a layman?"

Jon answered absently, as his mind raced to alarming conclusions about the Infortiare's reasons for arranging this discussion. "You can think of the limit point as a door, which is opened by the device that we call a transfer portal," explained Jon, waving his hands in a vague illustration. "We program the portals to reach well-defined, consistent destinations. Problems could obviously arise if the doorway led to a different location at each opening, irrespective of programming."

"Is that a possibility?"

"It's a phenomenon that caused many of the early failures in transfer experiments. Transferred objects either disappeared into an undefined space or arrived in fragments."

"You evidently resolved the problem without any dire outcome."

"We avoided the problem by writing strict Network standards for transfer portal development." Jon stacked two translucent sheets of writing film on the desk, then slid them apart until only a tiny overlap remained. He pinned the overlap with his finger. "A transfer mapping can be established between any two spaces that share a common limit point, though the spaces may be otherwise disjoint. That is the principle that enables Network transfer devices to function. Not all limit points are suitable for transfer, however, because some limit points have temporal discontinuities. A limit point might have a fixed location in one space, but in another space it 'blinks.' " Leaving one sheet of film flat against the desk, Jon tore the overlapping corner from the other sheet. He waved the torn fragment emphatically before restoring it to its original position. "If the blinking followed a stable pattern, the limit point could still be used, but development of reliable prediction models would require a massive data collection effort over a long observation time. Hence, for Network to approve a limit point as transfer-suitable, that limit point must occupy a fixed, time-continuous location with respect to each of the transfer spaces."

"How do you know that your supposedly suitable points are not blinking very slowly?"

"There are other measurements, such as highly variant energy readings that accompany the blinkers. The procedural standards for Network approval of new transfer portals are extremely strict."

Marrach replaced the book on its shelf with fastidious care. "I still fail to understand the nature of your 'calamity,' unless you're referring to some individual travelers being lost in transfer."

"I referred to the calamity of Network transfer portals transforming uncontrollably into blinkers, opening doorways onto universes incompatible with our own, introducing potentially lethal life-forms, possibly even colliding at fundamental quantum levels. We do not know what causes blinkers, and we have a very limited understanding of their behavior. We do know that limit points can be shifted artificially."

"That is how you once deactivated all transfer capability to and from Network-3."

Jon nodded rapidly, though he considered with a lurch of uneasiness that Marrach was less ignorant of applied topology than he claimed. "Any limit point *can* be shifted, given sufficient energy and a controller capable of implementing some algorithms that would make the collective assets of Network struggle. We closed Network-3 by a deliberate rearrangement of the local limit points, so that no shared points remained to provide transfer gateways." Jon isolated one sheet of data film on the desk. It was an unmarked sheet, which gave a silver sheen to the polished wood beneath it. "The necessary reconfiguration of that world's primary transfer controller nearly destroyed the planet. A transfer-suitable limit point does not shift without a level of concentrated effort that would be almost impossible to disguise—even for Network's Council Governor. I don't even want to conjecture about how much energy would be required to cause conversion to a blinker."

"I do not think Caragen would cause this sort of

damage intentionally. He does not generally destroy his own assets."

"He discards human assets readily enough," remarked Jon bitterly, "as I have cause to know."

"He disposes of treasures such as yourself only when he senses that they have become uncontrollable. He does not relinquish any valuable possession easily—as *I* have cause to know."

A moment of empathy with Rabh Marrach left Jon feeling as if his *personal* universe were shifting uncontrollably. "Are you and I here today because of Quin's claim about a topological instability?"

"That would seem to be the most likely reason for the Infortiare's summons."

"She is undoubtedly observing us now."

"Unobtrusive observation can be most enlightening." Marrach smiled wanly. "We may not be friends, Dr. Terry, but we share a Network perspective. We communicate more readily with each other than with wizards and feudal aristocrats. I am sure that Lady Rhianna recognizes that the concept of her 'wizardry' makes us both uncomfortable."

Jon swallowed heavily, uncomfortable with Marrach's speculation. "Why are you involved in this, Marrach?"

"It was I who sent Quin to Nilson."

Jon snapped himself upright. "Had you heard reports suggesting erratic transfer portal behavior?"

"No. I suggested that Quin go to Nilson for an entirely different reason—on a conscious level, at least." Marrach rubbed his head, as if it ached. "Suppose that we equate Quin's report of 'instability' with your phenomenon of 'blinking.' Assume also that no concerted effort has been made to shift stable limit points. What else could cause an instability?"

"Extended use of inherently unstable points for transfer," replied Jon promptly, "but that would presuppose the disregard of all standard Network procedures, criminal negligence and a willingness to accept the erratic portal behavior. If such portals were used to transfer living beings, there would almost certainly be casualties."

"Estimate the percentage of casualties."

Jon shrugged. "Five percent. Possibly as high as ten."

"No higher than that?"

"No higher, because a transfer controller cannot be configured without some minimum criteria of stability. But one percent is appallingly high, Marrach, in terms of human lives."

"By your scale. Not by the scale of the manipulators who eliminate entire worlds in choreographed wars for the sake of private little ambitions."

"Manipulators like your former employer, Andrew Caragen?" asked Jon slowly.

"Like Caragen and others. On Nilson, life is exceedingly cheap."

Pensively, Jon traced the curving wood grain of the Infortiare's desk. "I need more data, Marrach. Topological illusion is still the most probable answer to Quin's observation."

"I could arrange for you to visit Nilson anonymously."

"Even if I decided to trust you personally, do you think I would ever repeat the mistake of entrusting myself to Andrew Caragen's domain? I may have entered my second century, but I am not ready to call my life finished."

"Caragen is your senior by over twenty Network years, Dr. Terry."

"What is that supposed to mean?"

"You are not the only man who feels threatened by encroaching age. When threatened, a man may snatch at help that he would otherwise spurn." Marrach glanced sharply toward the office door, but Jon was unable to detect the cause. After a moment of tense silence, Marrach continued, "Among all the tools that Caragen has used to build his power, you and I number among the most significant that are still alive. Caragen needs us more than he hates us." Marrach strode to the door and swung it abruptly open, revealing only an empty room.

"Wizards don't need to spy at keyholes," said Jon dryly. "You have practiced paranoia for too long."

"His instincts, however," came the gentle voice of the Infortiare from the office's other door, which led to the highest tower, "are impressively accurate." In violet and silver, she presented a regality that Jon suspected was for Marrach's benefit. "Dr. Terry," she murmured, "your daughter would like to see you in the garden."

Jon glared at her for her manipulations, but he was more relieved than insulted by the dismissal. "I shall expect an explanation, as well as an apology, Lady Rhianna . . ." Jon glanced at Marrach. ". . . after you are done with him. I do not appreciate this kind of treatment." Jon gathered his writing film in an erratic stack and stomped from the office, slamming the door.

Marrach greeted her in the language of her country. "Lady Rhianna dur Ixaxis, I am honored to meet you at last."

"Did Lord Quinzaine instruct you in our language?" asked Rhianna.

"He loaned me some texts."

"You speak it well, Master Rabh," she observed coolly. She tilted her head, a youthful gesture that might have seemed ingenuous if Marrach had known less about her. "You are not a man whom I ever expected to meet."

"I never predicted that I might meet a wizardess," answered Marrach with a trace of mockery.

Rhianna acknowledged his remark with only a momentary twist of lips, a wry expression almost too subtle to detect. "We of Ixaxis are not so different from you, except in the specifics of our peculiar talents."

"What do you expect to learn by bringing me here, Lady Rhianna?"

She smiled. "Master Rabh, would you confide your intentions in someone whose motives you doubted?"

"You distrust me."

"I am unsure of you. I have heard of you both good and evil, with few reports between the two extremes."

"I came here willingly."

"What did you expect to learn by coming?" asked Rhianna, echoing his own question.

His laugh was dry. "Had I a choice?"

"Of course. You know that Quinzaine would not have forced you."

"The Mirlai would not readily tolerate such force," agreed Marrach.

"Then I repeat my earlier question: What did you expect to achieve by accepting my invitation?"

"I expected to learn whether it was possible."

"To come here?"

"To leave Siatha."

Gray eyes widened. "Do not deduce too much from this single journey. I, also, know something of healing, and I have been protecting you since your arrival."

"I am grateful," replied Marrach after a pause. "But I would prefer that you lift your protection from me, that I may know what is real and what is a wizardess' anaesthetic."

She answered obliquely, "That request makes me less sure of you than ever, but be it as you wish."

Marrach shuddered from the shock of pain that rushed upon him. "You are a potent healer," he said, his voice turning ragged.

"Quin," said Rhianna quietly, "Master Rabh must return to Siatha now."

"I have endured worse pain," answered Marrach, but it was a comment spoken chiefly to himself. Beset by pain of separation from Mirlai, distracted by the complexities of the fabled Lady of Ixaxis, Marrach experienced a rare sluggishness of his reactions. Rhianna's oblique announcement made its impact slowly.

The light shivered at Marrach's side and became Quin. "I shall take you," said Quin solemnly. The young wizard nodded at the Infortiare. "Tell Katerin that I'll be back soon." In a ripple of air, both Quin and Marrach disappeared from the room.

***

Jon Terry did not hurry to join his daughter. His bones ached from the damp chill that permeated the Tower's stones, and his head felt besieged by the memories that Rabh Marrach had awakened. As Jon began the long descent to the garden, he rubbed a bit of torn writing film between his fingers. He paused to stare from a window of the Tower stairwell across a feudal landscape, and he saw the world that had once been home to Network's finest center for advanced research. He had done much of his most significant work on that world of Network-3, which was *this* world of wizards and medieval barbarism. On that world, he had married and seen his children born. He had expected to live out his life on that world.

He let his focus shift toward the distant ocean. The Genetic Research Center had occupied that white, chalk-cliffed island, now diminished in size but not in significance. The Seriins called the island *Ixaxis*.

"Sixty years ago, we established the current standards for Network transfer portal development here," he murmured, "and forty years later, I closed Network-3 to protect the rest of Network from the disastrous children of the Life Extension Experiment. Caragen did not allow Network to remember Network-3 accurately. I wonder how many other critical data have been erased from Network memory." He crumpled the fragment of film in his fist and flung it to the floor.

"Ambition has always had the capacity to blind some men," said Lady Rhianna.

Jon turned his head just enough to see her, pale gold and iron discipline, emerging from the door above him. "Has your other visitor already departed, Lady Rhianna?"

"He has told you about Quin's experience on Nilson." In a rustle of silk, she drifted down the stairs and swooped to collect the crumpled fragment of film.

"You were listening."

"Indirectly."

"You might have joined us."

"Master Rabh's essence is painful to me, even without facing him directly. His separation from his Mirlai cuts me, as it tears at him, and I think that neither of us would profit from a protracted sharing of that pain, horrifyingly acute even in brevity. We would need a potent cause for a sustained conversation."

Jon entwined his hands in front of him and leaned against the cold wall. He met the Infortiare's clear gaze with curiosity. "You ordered him to be brought here."

"This seemed to be the most neutral location for a meeting between the two of you. I feared to send you to Siatha, which remains officially a part of Network."

"Did you learn as much as you hoped?"

She shrugged, and pleated silk shimmered across her thin shoulders. "You are angry because I did not confide my intentions to you."

"Allies should not play coy games with each other, especially when calamity threatens them both."

"Is calamity imminent?"

"I don't even know if it's real. It could be no more than one of Caragen's infernal traps, designed to coax his enemies out of hiding."

"My duty as Infortiare binds me to my world, Dr. Terry."

He spread his arms in frustration, then brought his hands together, palms flat as if pleading with her. "What do you expect me to tell you, Lady Rhianna? My topological expertise is of minimal value to you, since neither of us is in a position to make use of Network resources on Nilson or elsewhere. We both know that Caragen and his ilk are capable of tampering with destructive toys, and your methods have proven more successful against him than mine. What do you expect me to do? Network banished me, my family, and friends. My influence in Network has become even less than yours, for you still have active agents there."

"I have recalled my agents, because of the present uncertainties, and you fail to acknowledge your own Network ties. You do have a daughter."

"She survives in Network by your charity and Quin's."

"If the patterns of infinity shatter, none of us may survive."

"I know the danger, and I know my guilt in giving

Network its key!" croaked Jon, but his anger died before the quietude of the Lady of Ixaxis. "I cannot revoke the knowledge that I have already shared with Network's greedy manipulators. If they refuse to understand the consequences of their actions, I cannot force them to learn. I have finished with heroics. I never succeeded well at such grandiose activities anyway. I am an old man, Lady Rhianna, and I am tired."

She offered no comfort. "Your daughter is still awaiting you." Having dismissed him for a second time that day, she took her leave of him and climbed the stairway back to her office.

Jon remained where he stood. He rested his graying head in his hands and murmured a half-forgotten prayer.

***

The Healer dropped prone onto the grassy ground before his cottage, not clumsily but deliberately. Quin needed no use of Power to recognize the Healer's frantic hunger to assure himself that he was home. Evjenial emerged from the cottage doorway, wrapped in a homespun shawl against the evening chill, but she waited on the path. The Mirlai swirled visibly around her, bright sparks against her fiery hair. Quin could sense none of their energy near Marrach.

Feeling awkward, Quin knelt beside Marrach and touched the weathered skin of the Healer's left arm. "Can I help you, Marrach?"

Recoiling instantly, Marrach hissed, "No." He rolled to his feet and stood, cradling his arm, as if it were a treasure that might be stolen from him. In a cold voice, he declared, "A formidable manipulator."

"Who?"

"Your Infortiare."

"Yes," agreed Quin, vaguely disturbed that Lady Rhianna should be the subject of Marrach's first remark on returning.

"Does she deal as sternly with herself as with her allies?

Quin nodded, as he rose to his feet. "I think she is more stern with herself than with anyone."

"Good. We shall need such strength." Marrach turned from Quin and began to walk toward his waiting wife.

"Marrach," said Quin, speculating uneasily on the Healer's train of thought, "what did you learn from Dr. Terry?"

"That the stars have already begun to bleed." Marrach walked blindly past his wife and entered the cottage.

Quin took one step to follow, but Jeni shook her head. Her eyes were red from weariness or weeping. "Let him go, Lord Quinzaine," she whispered. "You have battles enough of your own to fight. Leave him to his."

CHAPTER 18

Conspirators

In Wharton's deepest shadows, the discontented met. By the magnitude of rustles and murmurs, the number of conspirators loomed large in their collective beliefs. None of them could be sure of more than his immediate neighbors and the few brave speakers who occupied the lonely circle of light atop a broad pillar of stone. Darkness protected them—or so each conspirator hoped—from the Network spying that had betrayed their Wharton leader.

"Network be the true killer of our leader, our strong ally and friend," shouted Deliaja, raising her voice above the noise of an angry audience in the echoing cavern. The solitary light painted her as a gaunt, gilded phantom. "Vin be wanting revolution. Vin be making the start, and Network be hurting from lost gold in a broken cave. It be our time now. We be making Vin's vision—Breamas' vision—reality!"

"Vin be dead," injected Cullen leadenly. He stood barely visible within the shadows' edge. "The beamer of some accursed Network port boy and a boulder be the end of his vision. If we be not cautious, every one of us be dead from the same."

"Be that worse than living to make Network rich?" countered Deliaja. The energy of her belief suffused her taut strides across the lighted pillar. "At least Vin's death be having meaning, because he be taking a Network mine and mining tools with him. Yah, some Network spy be ending Vin's work too soon, but that spy be not able to prevent Vin's last victory." She swept wide her arms, engulfing all of Wharton and its treasures. "What be we to Network? Dregs of Nilson?

Sewer rats? Such be their names for us. Be that how we
be valuing ourselves?" The muttering against this remark surged to a roar, until Deliaja's cadre of admirers
shouted their demands for silence to let her finish.
"Then why be I hearing words of death fear? Be we
living only to fear Network spies, Network Governor,
Network port boys and Network displeasure? Why be
we caring so tenderly for Network's kindly will? What
be Network giving us—ever? We be the workers, the
builders and the creators. Wharton be ours. Nilson be
ours. It be Network that should be fearing us!" Several
of the younger miners cheered and pounded the stones
enthusiastically.

Cullen would have none of it. Glowering at Deliaja,
he said, "Network spies and port boys be armed better
than we ever be. Network be everywhere on Nilson,
knowing what we be saying and doing before we be
able to make any serious trouble for Network. Network
be tolerating an inconvenience but not a threat. Breamas be living this long because he be wise enough to
move slowly."

"That be Network talk," sneered Deliaja. "Breamas
be the first to denounce our revolution's slowness. It be
only the weakness of his followers that be holding him
so long away from victory. We be strong enough to
win, if we be strong enough to try."

"Be you wanting us to dig your grave, Dee?"

"Better a grave than a coward's hiding box."

"Caution be not cowardice." Cullen moved further
into the light. He clenched his fists. With a lesser audience, he would have silenced Deliaja forcibly long before now.

"Yah, and I be thinking you more cowardly than
cautious." It was too much for Cullen, and he lunged at
her, but a throng of other miners braved the light to restrain him. They dragged him hurriedly into the darkness at the pillar's edge. Cullen did not fight against
them for they were too numerous. He did not like to
tackle a foe beyond his measure.

Deliaja regarded his shadowy point of retreat with
calm disdain. She had the sympathy of the youngest,

strongest rebel majority, as well as of others who had grown impatient. Vin's death had fired many long-smoldering embers, even among those who doubted that Vin would actually have instigated such an explosion with or without a hypothetical Network spy as witness. Vin's death had focused a reasoned cause into an emotional furor, and the issue of truth about his final moments meant little to the impassioned rebels.

She turned to her audience, though she could not see them, and she knew that she had won their enthusiasm. "It be our time," she assured them with proud confidence. "Nilson governor be no better loved by Network than us that be here now. Racker be weak. Nilson port boys be not Network soldiers. They be the scum of Network, and that be why Network be sending them to Nilson. Be you thinking Nilson port duty be Network privilege? It be the lot of prison bait, for that be Network's view of us. That be Network's ignorance that we be using well."

Cullen muttered from the shadows, trying once more to sway the crowd into reason, "Who be making you the voice of what Network be thinking, Dee?"

Deliaja understood his tactic and faced it squarely. "Ned Racker, among others," she answered without a pause. The light danced across the lion's head on her strong, lithe shoulder as she mockingly paraded the body that so many members of her audience had coveted or used. "It be no secret that I be catching Racker's fancy now and again, when that be my line of work. He be paying like any of you, and he be liking to hear his own voice sounding. I be hearing, and I be remembering, and I be thinking that Network holders like Racker be not more than us but less. *They* be the Network prison fodder, and we be their jailers. *We* be the free citizens of Nilson. It be past time that we be claiming what be ours by right."

For a moment, the cavers became silent enough to hear the distant trickling of water through the stones. Even Cullen seemed unable to muster argument against Deliaja's uttered truths. Something stirred in those despairing souls, some spark that was hope and belief in themselves and their joint destiny. It was something that Breamas had sensed about Nilson's tough children and had often tried to tap, but his words had grown cold too many years ago, and he had never reached more than a trace of the energy of Nilson's survivors. Like Saschy Firl, Breamas chose to live on Network's terms, retaining Network knowledge at the price of a truer Nilsonite's visceral comprehension of Nilson. He had never reached more than the minds of those who heard him. From the Network men who had abused her, Deliaja had learned enough to share Breamas' vision, but she had sacrificed nothing of her Nilson self. The deadened spirits of Nilson's children awoke to the violent, vivid dream of a vengeful woman who understood their anger.

***

Saschy knocked forcibly on the door of Racker's private suite, having abandoned hope that he would return soon to his office. Racker often kept his staff and visitors waiting on his convenience, though he lambasted anyone else who practiced such tardiness. Normally, Saschy endured his arrogant hypocrisy, but Network had summoned her from the frantic preparations for the annual mine review. She did not intend to let Racker delay the approval process that was required to maintain critical Network funding. He could prove his power another day.

When he opened the door himself, flushed and rumpled, she assumed that he had been indulging himself with one of those pretty adolescents that cycled through his life. She gave him no opportunity to vent his anger at the interruption. "You ordered me to come and see you, Racker. Tell me what you need, and we can both return to the matters that we prefer. I have a roomful of mine advisers waiting for me."

"If you had come when I asked," muttered Racker, "I would have been ready for you." He waved her toward one of the green velveteen lounges, which had always reminded Saschy of her mother's most tasteless efforts to show refinement. To Saschy's mind, the entire overstuffed room evoked decadence.

Saschy did not try to placate Racker with an excuse. She detested Ned Racker's superior airs, and he despised her cultivated plainness, but the two of them had achieved an understanding based on mutual convenience. They were useful to each other, and they were both sufficiently ambitious to value their unpleasant relationship.

Racker did not trouble to fasten the shirt that hung open from his shoulders. Personal contempt, balanced by professional need, had created an indifferent form of intimacy between him and Saschy. He paced as he spoke, "There has been an explosion in Wharton."

"I received the report," said Saschy impatiently. Surely, Racker could not have summoned her here just to discuss the petty terrorism of a few disgruntled Wharton miners. "Only one mining shaft collapsed, and that vein was nearly exhausted already. It doesn't merit the cost of reopening."

"The Wharton transfer portals have averaged seven failures per hour since the explosion. Breamas' followers are claiming credit for the damage."

"Breamas' followers are also claiming to have enlisted a mine ghost to their glorious cause, but the 'ghost' does not seem to have helped them. The port boys found the body of a man named Vin, a suspected terrorist, not far from the site of the explosion." Saschy gnawed at her upper lip. "The Wharton portals have always been erratic. You never cared about Wharton's minor inconveniences before."

"The Council Governor has never cared before," countered Racker. "Within two hours of the Wharton trouble, the Council Governor ordered a full status report on our transfer-port usage. The timing can't be coincidental."

"What does he expect us to tell him that he can't learn from Network?" demanded Saschy, her anger transformed into suspicion and a dawning of real concern. "Network monitors the portals directly."

"I don't know," snapped Racker. "I presume that he thinks we're hiding something from him."

We are, thought Saschy uneasily, but she did not give voice to the secret that she and Racker shared to mutual advantage. "Did he send the request to you personally?"

"No. Network placed the order directly with the portal maintenance supervisor. The man's daughter informed me. I questioned Network and was told that the order originated with the Council Governor."

"We can console ourselves that the Council Governor is not trying to hide the facts from us." Racker grunted in reply. Saschy continued, "What do you want me to do about it?"

"Make sure that the report, along with the mine review, is prepared satisfactorily. We would not want to disappoint the Council Governor."

"No. That would be unfortunate for us both." Saschy met Racker's glare with a thin-lipped smile. "You may rely on me, Racker, as always."

Only when she had left him, still pacing his opulent den, did she allow herself to tally the possible repercussions of a detailed inspection of Nilson's transfer usage. A worried scowl gathered between her coarse brows. The local supervisors were Nilson-born and could be trusted to support her against any outside interference, but the Council Governor could easily order one of his own employees to validate the report. Years of careful planning could be undone by a single whisper from some well-meaning, observant mine worker like Arlan. Saschy knew little about the theory of topological transfer, but she doubted that any expert would dismiss the rampant tales of mine ghosts without further investigation.

She wished that she could still believe that the rumors had no basis in truth. Her doubts had begun with Arlan, whose opinions Saschy reluctantly respected, and expanded when the ghostly figure attacked her within blocks of Mum's house. Since that night, Saschy had been gathering the reports of Wharton workers and filing their stories in her capacious memory.

With the singular exception of her own encounter, all of the ghost-light sightings had occurred near Wharton's beta portals: those portals which had required some judicious juggling of the preliminary exploration data to receive Network's authorization for their establishment. It was a troubling connection. Saschy did not accept it as a serious problem in itself, but she knew that it would give ready ammunition to any antagonistic Network inspector.

Saschy took some pride in Nilson's unique freedom from the rigorous sensor web that covered most Network worlds. Although poverty caused the gaps in coverage, the omissions facilitated some slight, useful deceptions of Network. Profitable Wharton would have been inaccessible without the beta portals, and the associated operations had resulted in no more casualties than an ordinary night on a Nilson street. She did not regret having aided Racker in establishing the beta portals. Closing the betas was inconceivable. Nilson, as well as Racker, had become too dependent on the flow of wealth.

She gnawed her lower lip. She needed to return to the meeting with the mine advisers, but her mind would be preoccupied. "Timing be bad," she mumbled in the dialect of her childhood, wondering if she dared entrust any of her ordinary tasks to an underling for a few vital days. Even without ominous requests from Council Governor Caragen, her duties squeezed her life dry of extraneous time. In her care to maintain a perpetual excuse for avoiding Mum's awkward invitations, Saschy had allocated no margin for simultaneous crises. Between this portal inquiry, the mine trouble, and that lingering mess regarding the alien smuggler, she did not know how she would survive the next month.

"A quick execution of Filcher Ikthan Cuui would eliminate one problem," she decided. "If no one has stepped forward to support the creature by now, his death is not likely to cause as much trouble as his continued existence." The thought improved her spirits.

Death meant little to a child of Nilson. Death of an alien meant nothing to Saschy Firl.

                              ***

Miz Ruth pushed the bowl of thin soup closer to Deliaja. "You've not eaten a bite," chided the older woman with genuine concern. It had been years since she could feel equally maternal toward Saschy.

"There be too much feeling in me," answered Deliaja, dipping the spoon into the bowl and stirring the steaming broth. Ruth's kindness always touched a raw, dimly understood pain that Deliaja both craved and dreaded. "Our time be coming, Miz Ruth, sooner than most be thinking." Ruth's kindness troubled Deliaja, making her conscious of an unwanted vulnerability. Ruth's kindness, not her hours of rational arguments, had induced Deliaja to agree to this meeting and even to share some of Ruth's desperate eagerness for its success: Ruth's kindness, along with the tentative friendship of the man who would come here tonight. A rap at the door drew the eyes of both women, as alert as startled birds.

"That will be Arlan," murmured Ruth. She straightened her apron and pushed stray hairs behind her ears.

"Be not telling him yet that I be here," Deliaja reminded her sharply, pushing herself away from the table. Now that he was come, Deliaja experienced a nervousness that neither threat of death nor physical harm could still create in her. She felt that all her schemes and bitter secrets were soon to be exposed to a man whose good opinion actually mattered to her. This was not the way she had planned his recruitment. "You be telling him only what we be agreeing!" It was a frantic plea.

Ruth, who understood more about Deliaja than the young woman imagined, sighed and limped to the door. She did not open it until she heard the squeak of the floor that signified Deliaja's escape into the bedroom. She greeted Arlan with a weary hug. "Thank you for coming, Arlan," she told him with deeper sincerity than he would ever recognize. "I know it's hard to schedule skyside time so soon after your last visit."

"There be lots who be owing me schedule swaps for similar favors in the past." The new creases in Ruth's face and the shadows beneath her eyes would have worried Arlan even without her unexplained summons. "What be wrong, Miz Ruth?" he asked, imagining all the violent horrors that could beset an aging widow on Nilson. He could see no sign of such damage to Ruth. "Be Saschy hurt?"

Ruth smiled wanly, "No. Saschy is not hurt, as far as I know."

More relieved than he would admit, Arlan prodded Ruth gently toward the lumpy couch. "Then you be sitting and telling me what be wrong." He sat beside her, holding her frail hands with delicate care.

"You remember when Old Marlin died," began Ruth slowly.

"Yah," answered Arlan, puzzled to hear Miz Ruth name a man who had died at least three years earlier.

"He died of hunger, Arlan. He was a citizen of Nilson, just like us, and he died of hunger in his own home because of a broken leg."

Though Arlan could not understand Ruth's purpose in raising these old sorrows, Arlan tried to give comfort. "An uncommonly proud man like Old Marlin be preferring death to begging charity, Miz Ruth, even of his friends."

"Old Marlin was a good, strong worker, willing to earn his way by scrubbing or digging or any other menial chore he could find. He even worked the spaceport, and you know how badly the port boys treat local laborers. It was a port boy broke that leg of Marlin's, claiming Old Marlin was a thief. Old Marlin never stole as much as a teaspoon, a claim not many on Nilson can make."

"He be not the first man to die unjustly, Miz Ruth, nor the last." The face of a dead boy in a Wharton cavern swirled through Arlan's mind.

"Yah. He was nobody special. I told Saschy of him, and she called me stupid for worrying about an old thief who never deserved his Network citizenship." Ruth said the words without bitterness, but Arlan winced. "Saschy talks angry when she's feeling guilt," added Ruth, trying, as usual, to justify her daughter. "I pay no mind when she insults me, because I know it's just her guilt talking, but her insult to Old Marlin hurt me. She meant that one." Ruth lowered her prematurely aged head. Arlan smoothed her uneven wisps of gray hair. "Saschy worked so hard to become a 'real' Network citizen, and now she is like them in bad as well as good. That's what made me finally understand what Breamas had been saying."

"That old terrorist?" demanded Arlan, shocked to hear the notorious, abhorrent name on Miz Ruth's lips.

She murmured wistfully, "I remember him when I was a girl, and he was not much older. Already, he ran the best organized, most successful gangs these streets ever saw. He had port contacts, too. He got himself some fancy, official Network title, and we all thought he'd soon become Governor or Governor's Lieutenant—like Saschy."

"It be a rival that crippled him, if I be remembering the story right."

"That's the common story. But Breamas claims the attack was orchestrated by an outsider, high in the ranks of the Network Council. He claims to be able to track the rise and death of every Nilson governor to the same high source."

"You be not thinking to find truth in those wild claims? Miz Ruth, they be only clever words to stir gullible souls to support an old villain in his mischief."

"I taught you that argument, Arlan, and I believed it. I was wrong."

Arlan laid her thin hands gently in her lap. "Someone be misleading you, Miz Ruth." He rose to his feet and turned from her in the sad, shabby room, trying to erase any sign of fear from his face. He dreaded that Ruth had begun the fading that ended too many Nilson lives. She was his own, his only family, and he could not bear the thought of losing her. The possibility of that loss came as a shock to him. He had never prepared himself for the eventuality of her death, because he had never expected to outlive her.

"What if someone has been misleading all of us, Arlan? What if Nilson has been taken from us, and we have not even tried to save her? Do we not have loyalty to her? Do we not owe her at least a try at rescue? Or do we of Nilson live only to make Network rich?"

"It be not true," argued Arlan, staring at his boots, stained with Wharton dust and chemicals. Where did the wealth of the mines go, if not to Network worlds far removed from Nilson? Racker lived well, but only well enough to explain a minuscule fraction of the tonnage that Wharton transferred every month.

"If it were true, it would be like forsaking family to abandon our Nilson. With all her flaws, she is our own, and we are hers."

"If such Network treachery be true," answered Arlan, snapping his head upright, "be you thinking that Saschy be party to it?"

Ruth sighed, "I don't know. I no longer know her at all."

"Saschy be ambitious, may be ruthless, but she be not a traitor. She be one of us still, little as she be liking it." He paced toward the kitchen, where two abandoned bowls of soup sat on the table. "Who be visiting you?" asked Arlan, suddenly leery of the strangeness of Ruth's summons, her puzzling explanation that explained nothing, and a sense of Ruth's own deep disquiet.

Deliaja emerged from the bedroom, dressed in miner's coverall. "I be visiting," she answered. "I be the reason Miz Ruth asked you here today. I be needing to thank you for your help."

Arlan looked at Ruth in bewilderment, mingling with new-grown suspicion. Ruth answered his unvoiced question. "Dee is a friend, Arlan."

Arlan replied without rancor, "There be some call her a revolutionary."

"Be that not why you brought word to *me* of Tempest's death?" asked Deliaja, stung despite the calmness of his words. He had known. He had not come to her from a simple gesture of friendship and trust. He must not realize that Deliaja had mistaken his intentions for reason of that deep, insane hope inside of her. "Be that not the reason you be using me to give the warning of the spread of the ghost lights? You be knowing me, Arlan Willowan, and you be knowing that I be trusted in the mines and skyside, because I be a true Nilson daughter. I be willing to fight for Nilson. I be willing to die for her. And I be telling you now that Miz Ruth be speaking nothing but wisdom and truth."

Arlan pressed his fists against his eyes, wishing he could rearrange this day as easily as he could alter his dreams. "What be you wanting me to say of this, Miz Ruth? Be you wanting me to give praise to Breamas? That I be not willing to give, even if he *be* speaking one bit of truth in his devilish life. What be you wanting me to do? Join this revolution that be existing only in the minds of a few like Dee?" He lowered his hands and turned toward Deliaja. "Yah. I be giving you the warning about the ghost lights, knowing you be best able to spread it. That be not the same as believing in your cause."

"Be you knowing where Tempest died, Arlan?" asked Deliaja. "By the access to the main gold mine." She had not meant to tell him this. She had not meant to wound him this way.

"The mine that Vin be destroying, along with himself?" demanded Arlan, understanding her with the quickness that astonished those who did not know him well. His immediate, chilled reaction made Deliaja want to hide behind Ruth's worried figure.

Deliaja strode up to Arlan with the proud confidence that she donned each time she entered the canteen—*her* canteen that she had bought and cherished, until Breamas gave her anger a larger goal. "Yah. The ghost lights be coming close now to where the miners be working every day, and Network be knowing and be doing nothing to help us. Vin be a brave man."

Arlan snorted, "May be a fool. Explosions be no use against ghosts. Ghost lights be no tool to be used by Vin or you—or Breamas." He added harshly, "And Vin with all his faults be never such a fool as that. How *be* you using my warning, Dee?"

How many of the miners would recognize this intense, insightful man, wondered Deliaja, as the solid, reliable, slow-to-speak Arlan? He was more than any of them recognized, not for his childhood friendship with Saschy Firl but for himself. Deliaja knew a brief flicker of respect for Saschy, who had long ago seen more in Arlan than was apparent to the rest of them. Though Deliaja had argued Arlan's case with Vin and Cullen, she had not appreciated the depth of the differences she had proclaimed. For the first time since Ruth pleaded for this meeting, Deliaja feared more than Arlan's disapproval. This was a man who formed his own opinions and lived by them. He would not take kindly to being used, even for a cause he favored.

"Explosions be winning more Network attention than ghosts," answered Deliaja, obliquely acknowledging his accusation. Arlan frowned but did not criticize. Deliaja wished she dared to confide the magnitude of her ambitions to Arlan, who might be able to understand—and share—the need that drove her. "It be time for more than talk of revolution. It be time to act, and we be needing clever men like you."

"I be not what you be needing," argued Arlan with a sardonic glance at the solemn Ruth, "though it be clear enough why rebels be trying to recruit a retriever." Because a retriever's duties could take him into any part of the mines, his code gave access authority beyond the normal allotment. Arlan had never taken illegal advantage of his profession's one unusual privilege, but he was not oblivious to its existence.

"You be more than you be thinking," said Deliaja softly. She had not taken many recruits directly to Breamas. She had not often found a potential recruit whom she considered capable of impressing the old man in direct conversation. She had never before found a candidate who would be, she suspected, more in control of a verbal confrontation than Breamas himself.

"Because I be Saschy's 'friend'? Miz Ruth be able to tell you the truth of that myth. Because I be having a retriever's code that you be thinking to use to ship goods to and from Wharton when the guards be gone?"

"We be able to do that much now," interrupted Deli-aja, as if it were a trivial achievement. Deliaja regretted the admission, spoken in hurt pride, when Ruth gave her a startled look. "But that be showing your clever-ness, Arlan, as I be saying. Not many be understanding so quickly the value of a retriever's code to us. We al-ways be needing access to the cargo portals, especially with the public portals so often faulty."

"Cargo ports be not shielded for human use."

Deliaja recognized his implicit question and an-swered it gladly, relieved that he still respected her enough to express simple curiosity. "They be unpleas-ant, not unusable, but that be a small part of their value. Cargo ports be letting us transfer bulk quantities at once, instead of in slow increments. We be needing sometimes to share the excess miners' food with our skyside brethren."

"With other revolutionaries," amended Arlan.

"With our family," injected Ruth sternly. This duel of words reminded her too painfully of the way Saschy used to vie with Arlan about Network policies. "With men like Old Marlin, with women like me, with anyone accused by Network, untried but still condemned. Be-cause they displease a port boy or offend some gover-nor's minion, Network erases their credit, refuses them work permits, denies them even the right to purchase food from honest sources. Be one of us, Arlan. We *be* your family."

"Miz Ruth, what manner of family be Breamas building?" he began, but he turned swiftly from Ruth's lined, grieving face. More words would injure either her or him irreparably. Casting a worried frown at Deliaja, he left the house that had once been his sanctuary.

A coldness wrapped itself around Deliaja, but she tried to reassure the old woman, who sagged against the couch, "He be a good son of Nilson, Miz Ruth. Let him be taking a little time to understand. I be thinking to see him back here before this hour ends."

"I feared this," sighed Ruth. "Arlan can be as stubborn as Saschy."

"It be costing us nothing, Miz Ruth, if Arlan be true to his word, as you be promising."

A tear wove its way down Ruth's shriveled cheek. "I already lost a husband and a daughter. If I must also lose my son, at least it will be for a needful cause."

"You be not losing him," insisted Deliaja confidently. She had no doubt of Arlan's loyalty to Ruth, though Deliaja regretted every moment of the encounter just ended. "He be returning. Breamas be waiting for him." And Deliaja believed that assurance, too, if only because Arlan was enough a son of Nilson to know the Nilson rules of self-defense. Rules, thought Deliaja grimly, that she had personally failed to obey where Arlan was concerned; that situation must change.

Deliaja, long practiced at the hardening of her emotions, began construction of a new wall inside herself. She must never give Cullen, or Vin's ghostly shade, the satisfaction of confirming her weakness concerning Arlan Willowan. She must never let that weakness jeopardize Breamas' cause.

***

The stairs were rickety. The lights were dim. The dark room beneath the shop on Three Crow Street exuded a noxious odor that reminded Arlan of his childhood. It was the smell of the Nilson streets. It was the smell of home.

A face like old leather, wizened and fierce with the defiance of decades, met Arlan and Deliaja without welcome. "This be Breamas," said Deliaja, offering no reciprocal introduction of Arlan. It was a common form of meeting among Nilson's most hardened crime families, who used outsiders on occasion but admitted no interest in outsiders' names. It confirmed to Arlan that he ought never to have returned to Miz Ruth's tonight, ought never to have yielded to Miz Ruth's insistence on this encounter, despite his certainty that he had learned too much to continue surviving in deliberate ignorance. Arlan did not intend to be persuaded of the necessity of revolution, *especially* by Breamas, though Arlan was reluctantly impressed by Deliaja's obvious status with the old terrorist.

Arlan maintained the silence appropriate to his position at such a meeting. Deliaja also waited for Breamas to complete his decision, either to dismiss Arlan immediately or to take the next step of attempted recruitment. She barely breathed. Arlan wondered what she was thinking and decided that he preferred not to know.

During the protracted silence, Arlan realized the significance of Breamas' limply draped robe and awkward posture. Any limbs concealed by that brown robe must be badly withered. Breamas moved, confirming Arlan's deduction with the emergence of a skeletal, barely functional hand from the robe's layered gauze. Arlan concluded that there was truth at least in the rumors about why Breamas retreated long ago from public view.

In a resonant voice larger than his deteriorated frame, Breamas demanded suddenly, "Which do you love? Nilson or Network?" He displayed his damaged hand with defiant pride.

"I be citizen of both," answered Arlan carefully.

"Not possible," snapped the old man. His dark eyes were fierce above his hollow cheeks. He raised his scrawny hand above his head, baring a spindly arm. "This is the measure of Network's love for Nilson." He pointed one tortured finger at the stubble of Arlan's hair. "Do you love the mines?"

"No."

"Then why do you work in them?"

"To live," replied Arlan uneasily. These personal questions surprised him. When he realized that Dee intended to introduce him to Breamas personally, Arlan expected nothing more than the usual stark demands for revolution, something as impassioned as Vin's drunken tirades and devoid of any reason but anger.

There was a cunning in this course of inquiry, and it frightened Arlan on Miz Ruth's behalf. This man had been known to kill children in the name of his revolution. Miz Ruth *followed* this madman. Dee had the right to convene a private meeting with him.

"You live to make Network rich?"

Troubled by the echo of Ruth's earlier words, Arlan glanced at the pale-haired woman who had brought him here, but Deliaja's face was as still and uninformative as the stones of Wharton. "I be living to live. There be no more reason to it for such as me."

"You mean that your life has no value, because you were born a son of Nilson."

"That be *not* my meaning."

"Listen to yourself. Is any other Network world so deprived of the basics of education? Ruth Firl calls you intelligent, and you have impressed Deliaja enough that she brought you here to me. Why does Network sentence you to the grueling, unrewarding labor of a Wharton retriever? Had you been born to any Network world but Nilson, you would have received a university education. You would live in comfort. You are not a Network citizen. You are Network's slave. Do you love the master who abuses you?"

Unwilling to be manipulated into self-pity, Arlan replied with bitter honesty, "If I be abused, it be owing to my own cowardice. If I be uneducated, it be owing to my own unwillingness to struggle for more and to mark myself as different. I be not a fighter like Saschy Firl." Arlan added gruffly, "I be not a fighter like you."

"You equate me with Saschy Firl?" laughed the old man in a rasping voice. "Do you praise us or insult us by linking us and naming us as fighters? Do you cling to your ignorance to prove your membership in the grim fraternity of Nilson's offspring—or to differentiate yourself from the people of whom you disapprove?"

"I be not interested in fighting you, Master Breamas."

"You have your own share of Nilson pride, haven't

you? I think you value ignorance because of that
twisted pride, like so many of your brethren, and you
do not even realize that you are simply conceding to
Network machinations. You are as thoroughly programmed to your behavioral pattern as any Network
citizen chained to the omnipresent voice of a Network
node. You are programmed by the culture of the Nilson
streets, from the Network-fostered environment of
crime and misery to the petty boyhood ritual of the
Box. Do you know that the Box was invented by an
agent of Network's Council Governor?"

Arlan kept his expression even despite the hurtful,
startling words. The old terrorist could not possibly
know how the ritual of the Box had traumatized Arlan.
"What be you wanting of me, Breamas?"

Breamas settled back into his chair. "You are not
afraid of me, are you?" mused the old man.

"No."

"I could order your death right now. I have killed
other men who displeased me. Deliaja is armed and
could kill you easily, as could any of my guards."

"Yah," replied Arlan calmly. "You be not answering me."

"Since I find that you are more complex than I expected, I am not sure that I want anything of you except
respectful silence regarding this meeting."

"That much be yours. I be giving my word to Dee."

"Yes. Deliaja is efficient about enforcing such matters." The withered hands retreated into gauzy sleeves.
"There are two stages to a revolution: the destruction
of the old and the creation of the new. I have recruited
many destroyers already. That kind of rebel is plentiful
on Nilson, and that work is well underway." Breamas
glanced slyly at Deliaja, who was watching Arlan with
a bitter wistfulness. "However, I have found few loyal
Nilsonites with the talent for creating. When the first
stage of our revolution is complete, Nilson will be in
need of you—and you will be in need of me. I look forward to our next meeting."

"None be coming," answered Arlan, distrusting the
old man completely.

"You and I have little in common, but we both love Nilson. You will return for her sake."

Deliaja's slim fingers tugged at Arlan's shoulder. Breamas' skeletal hand saluted her wryly. Arlan was glad to depart.

The night air was damp and thick with swamp stench, carried by limp breezes from across the expanse of the spaceport and the city's southern edge. Three Crow Street was crowded at this late hour, when stolen goods were bartered for liquor and drugs, men and women haggled over coupling fees, and the followers of Breamas preached of revolution's glory. "Why be you serving that man, Dee?" asked Arlan.

"Why be you not?" she retorted.

"He be a killer. He be proud of it."

"His killings be for better reason than this," she answered, nodding toward a broken stoop where furtive figures exchanged their rag-wrapped parcels. A scarred and hefty port boy ambled past them on patrol and averted his attention impassively. "There be no one else to lead us. No one else be knowing Network well enough. No one else be well enough known to Network."

"There be better ways. Saschy's way be better."

Deliaja snapped, "Your Saschy be a traitor to her people."

"She be not perfect, but she be not a killer. She be proof of what we be able to become, if we be willing."

"If we be willing to betray Nilson."

"What be you willing to betray, Dee? Me? Miz Ruth? Vin?" The port boy passed them, leering at Deliaja, and Arlan clamped his mouth tightly shut.

Deliaja twisted her arms around Arlan, pressed close to him and called to the port boy, "Be you wanting to join us?"

The port boy answered with a sour chuckle, "Even alone, you're too costly for me, Dee Sylar." He tugged his hood lower across his face and continued on his way.

"You be well known here," said Arlan. He did not like his own reaction to Deliaja's taunting embrace. He did not want to desire her, but he could feel himself responding.

"Yah," she agreed. Her expression had softened into rare, unguarded sadness. "I be known to too many, who be knowing nothing."

She had to be aware of what she was doing to him, Arlan thought. He wondered if this was part of her usual method of recruitment to Breamas' cause. That likely prospect troubled him, because he was discovering his own willingness to accept such coaxing from her. He slid his hands down her back, drawing her against him.

Her body stiffened. Her face contorted into rage. "You be no different," she spat, tearing free of him.

Astonished, he spread his hands in a conciliatory gesture. "I be sorry, Dee."

She wagged her head furiously. The damp night had flattened her hair, and the thin light from a nearby tavern painted it hard silver. A port boy's beamer was in her hand, its narrow barrel aimed at Arlan's manhood.

"Dee, I be mistaken. I be sorry for hurting you."

"Hurting me?" she growled. "You be not that special." Abruptly, she stowed the beamer behind her back. She stretched her full lips into a brittle smile. Her hips swayed toward him. "You be nothing but another customer. How much be you thinking to pay?"

"I be not understanding you, Dee." The roar of a brawl spilled from the tavern. "I be not wanting to understand the carrying of so much anger."

"I be not wanting it either," she whispered.

"Then why be you keeping it?" demanded Arlan, sharp with frustration.

The sadness returned to her eyes. "It be nearly dawn. Portals be open soon. Your skyside leave be ending."

"Yah," he agreed, swallowing his own anger. "Yah." He knew Deliaja. Everyone knew her history. He *knew* better than to let himself feel anything for her. "I be needing to go back." Warily, he turned to resume his interrupted walk down Three Crow Street. "Be you coming?" Wordlessly, Deliaja matched pace

beside him. She scanned the streets with practiced
Nilson caution.

Neither of them spoke again that night. They parted
in Wharton without acknowledging each other's existence. Each of them devoted long, sleepless hours to
the regret of an unguarded moment. When Arlan
arranged his next dreaming, he made sure that it was a
solitary adventure.

***

Father and daughter stared at each other across a
candlelit table in a vaulted room of baronial dimensions. The Infortiare's servant retreated, freeing both
Jon and Katerin of a single layer of uneasiness. Accustomed for most of their lives to an ever-present Network, they had difficulty accepting any human
observer with equal detachment. "I have hardly seen
Quin since we came here," said Katerin.

"Do you know where he has been spending his
time?" asked Jon, feeling ancient in this antiquated setting. The silent stone walls, old for centuries, op-
pressed him. He wanted to clutch his daughter's thin,
nervous hands and quiet them with reassurances, but he
had no calm to share.

"Quin has told me little. He seldom speaks of matters of Power."

"Marrach was here earlier." Katerin winced, aggravating Jon's sense of guilt. He had never managed to
forgive himself for abandoning his children to Marrach
years ago, though Marrach had eliminated all choice.
"He said that Quin has reported some trouble on the
planet Nilson."

"Quin wanted to see an alien," answered Katerin
dryly. "He asked the Healer for a recommendation."

"Marrach mentioned nothing about aliens."

"No?" Katerin's smile was lovely, but Jon saw only
how pain had warped it into an austere mockery of her
childhood joy. "The Healer has not forgotten how to
keep secrets."

"He spoke of a topological instability."

"I see." Katerin nodded, as if a mystery had just unraveled itself for her. "I wondered why they summoned you here."

"I don't think I've resolved anything. I have only contributed a few speculations, based on uncertain data. Quin is a gifted young man, but he is not a rigorously scientific observer. I had hoped to learn more by questioning him directly."

"Quin follows his own counsel. I'm not sure that even Lady Rhianna can truly control him."

"I wish you would come to Neoterra with me, Kitri. Your mother and I worry about you."

"Quin keeps me safe from the Council Governor's schemes. Quin is more reliable than he appears."

"Then why was he searching for aliens?" demanded Jon, unable to restrain his sarcasm.

"Curiosity is a survival trait for him. I think it is a manifestation of his Power."

"If he has actually discovered a topological disaster in the making, his Power may have met its match." Jon turned his crystal goblet and watched the candles' blaze through the faceted sides. The complex patterns seemed appropriate to his daughter. "If Quin does not return, Kitri, you must go to Neoterra."

"If Quin does not return, I don't think it will matter where I go. I don't think anything will matter to me." She shook her head, and the fluid gold of her hair swung against the table's burnished wood. "Since Network effectively banished me from my former life, he has become my link to sanity. I do not know if he has forged the link by his Power or by love, but I am quite certain that Caragen would have broken me by now, if not for Quin." She made her self-diagnosis calmly. She had, after all, exceptional expertise in the science of mathematical psychology, and she understood her own case well.

If Quin is right about Nilson, perhaps nothing will matter for any of us, thought Jon, but he did not add his private fears to his daughter's present burden. He drained the honeyed brew from the goblet, and he pondered how different his life—and so many other lives—would have been if he had left the development of topological transfer for human use to another eager visionary. He replaced the goblet and sighed, knowing that he had never been able to choose the path of ignorance: not as a young man, filled with ideals and enthusiasm, not as an old man, filled with fear and guilt.

***

Jeni watched her husband from the doorway of their cottage. He sat, bowed and weary, holding a healing stone before the fire, but the stone glowed only from reflected firelight. She ached to contribute to his repair, but the Mirlai energy did not rise to meet her longing. "Was it so important that you leave Siatha?" she asked quietly.

He did not raise his head. "It was important for me to remember what such a departure would mean."

"Could you ever forget?"

"The existence of pain is difficult to forget. The reality of pain is nearly impossible to remember."

Jeni sat on the hearth near him, but she was careful not to touch him. "Will you leave again?"

"If necessary, I shall leave again. I shall be better prepared, having remembered today. I spent many years calibrating my limits of endurance."

"This level of pain could kill even you."

"I am more troubled by the damage it inflicts on the Mirlai. You must try to protect them from me, Jeni. They cannot heal this type of wound."

"They know," she whispered. "They learned that aspect of truth in parting from the Adraki." Her husband nodded and laid the healing stone gently on the hearth.

CHAPTER 19

Investigators

The illicit recording of a Network planetary governor's disrespectful speech ended in a flurry of blinding static, and Tori snatched the viewband hurriedly from her head, uprooting a few dark hairs in the process. Alone in the cluttered common room of an expensively converted Cuui trade ship, she cursed the poor quality of the recording and the viewing equipment, but her tension sprang from a larger cause. The ship, originally designed to require a full crew but now automated by sophisticated, expensive Consortium equipment, had already initiated the docking metamorphosis that would enable it to land on Nilson. Tori had begun to wish that she had urged Jase more strongly to decline this assignment. The recording, which Jase had finally agreed to procure despite its illegality, had upset her at a fundamental level. She wanted to mock it, but she watched it and felt an unwilling connection to its participants.

She debated watching it again, at once curious and repelled by the power of her species' paranoid parochialism. The dry text that Jase had first shown her had not prepared her at all for the spectacle of Nilson's planetary governor, sincerely voicing his irrational perspective to an auditorium of his approving peers. She pushed the viewband away from her with a sense of guilt as Jase entered the room. She donned a wry smile to greet her overly perceptive partner, who had readied himself for Nilson. Like Tori, he wore a dark blue, multipocketed traveler's suit, designed by the Cuui for inconspicuous practicality. His preparations, however,

extended further than Tori's by the necessity of his
own uniqueness.

"I will never become accustomed to seeing you with
blue eyes," remarked Tori, studying Jase critically.

"Haven't you said the same about the iridescence?"
countered Jase.

"Frequently."

"You are a difficult woman to please, Miss Mirelle."
The ship vibrated, signaling the imminence of landing.
Jase secured himself in the seat beside Tori.

"I was not expressing displeasure. The look is just
inconsistent with *you*. It makes you resemble an ordinary Soli."

"That is the intention."

"That is deception at its best." Tori glanced at the
monitor, where the dark blotches of Nilson thunder-
clouds had fully eradicated the view of stars.

"It is not deceptive to adjust to the restricted observational capacity of Network's citizens. They know
nothing of relanine and would misinterpret the iridescence as an alien cosmetic affectation, which would
provoke needless antagonism and impede justice. It is
Truth: My eyes *are* the color of these lenses," said
Jase, dismissing her remark with the same obscure
Sesserda reasoning that he had voiced each time the
subject arose.

"For the sake of your ignorant, uncivilized partner,
please explain the Truth of requesting landing rights
under the name of Jasen Margrave, which I believe I
heard you announce earlier to the port coordinator."
The scraping of metal landing rails contacting a rough
field jarred Tori's nerves, as well as her body.

"Have you ever considered challenging your skills
at self-restraint by the occasional subjugation of
sarcasm?" asked Jase, liberally employing the characteristic that he disparaged. The ship purred into shut-
down mode.

Tori snapped the latch that freed her from her
chair's safety restraints. "I'm only following the example of the Sesserda adept I know best."

Jase replied with an obscure Calongi phrase that

Tori could not interpret. "Jasen Margrave," he continued crisply, "was a major negotiator of the Consortium's first trade agreements with Network. Most of his work is still intact."

"That should provide an excellent opening for conversations with Network historians, but I did not think you intended to stay here long enough to establish an active social life."

"The name should trigger some high-level Network authorization procedures, which could facilitate our movements." With the obvious intention of ending the immediate conversation, Jase unstrapped himself from the chair and strode purposefully to the door.

Tori halted him by the expedient method of maneuvering herself in front of him. "I thought you wanted to avoid attention," said Tori slowly, recalling all of her arguments against this assignment.

Jase looked at Tori and seemed to debate whether to remove her bodily from his path. He hesitated so long that she expected, at best, an incomprehensible Calongi reply. Instead, Jase shrugged with unusual self-consciousness. "Network's sensors will undoubtedly scan us on arrival, and it will not take them long to correlate me with stored images. The family resemblance is pronounced, and I'd rather acknowledge it openly than be questioned later. Jasen Margrave was my paternal grandfather. I was named after him."

Your family named you Jasen Margrave?" echoed Tori in disbelief, wondering if she could possibly be misinterpreting some Sesserda subtlety.

"Didn't anyone at Hodge Farm ever tell you the name by which they originally knew me?"

"The Hodges always called you 'Squire.' " Jase winced at the old epithet. Tori continued, torn between wonder and indignation, "You convinced me that I should revert to my legal family name, despite the inconvenience of Mirelle's notoriety, because Sesserda demands accuracy, and I am working as the partner of a Sesserda scholar. Meanwhile, you have been using an alias regularly. Isn't that a little hypocritical?"

"Jasen Sleide is the legal name of the Sesserda

scholar who lives on Calong-4. After fate decided to
recreate me as a relanine addict, I was no longer the
same person in any meaningful respect, and the situation seemed to merit a renaming. My Calongi teachers
concurred with my decision." He shrugged, dismissing
the trauma that had remade him. "Both names are accurate in respective contexts. Jasen Margrave is more
consistent with the context of Network, which comprehends neither relanine nor Sesserda. A tour of Network
might well have captivated my interests in the days
when the Margraves still claimed me. I was extremely
idealistic in my youth."

"You are still idealistic."

"If I am to negotiate persuasively with Network bar-
barians, I must make a few preliminary adjustments.
Network will inevitably equate me with the Margraves.
I see no point in complicating Network records with
the name of Sleide. Not even the vaunted family Margrave is able to cope with the transformation of their
benighted son into a Sesserda practitioner."

"Do you actually have any close family?" she asked
him, expecting at best an evasive reply.

"Jase Sleide has none at all, a status with which he is
reasonably content. Please, Tori, don't waste your pity
on the Margraves—or on me. The Margraves never allow themselves to become too attached to their offspring, and relanine simply dissolved a nonrelationship.
My few relanine-clouded memories of them are not
pleasant."

"Don't waste your Sesserda skills analyzing my reaction," retorted Tori, but it was a protest voiced from
habit only. Jase was becoming more clearly impatient
to end the unwanted discussion, and Tori had no intention of accommodating him so easily. She took hold of
the fabric of his shirt, defying him to use Sesserda
skills or physical strength against her. She was angry
with him, her temper already frayed by nervousness
at the imminent task of facing Network. The fact of
his dual names disturbed her less than the realization
that she could not calibrate his concept of Truth as well
as she had thought. It was a particularly unsettling

revelation with which to begin a difficult mission. "What inspired you to choose the name 'Sleide'?"

Jase shook his head only fractionally, but it was a gesture that evoked an extreme level of frustration for a sternly disciplined Sesserda adept. "Sleide is a corruption of Sieleiden, an appelation that I borrowed from a family heirloom."

"What sort of heirloom?" murmured Tori.

"Of all the questions to ask . . ." began Jase, but he forced patience back into his voice to answer her, "Sieleiden was a sword. It seemed an appropriate reminder of the manner in which relanine thrust Sesserda Truth into my life."

"You do have a streak of romanticism in you, Mr. Sleide, that surfaces in the most unlikely ways."

"It's part of my charm," answered Jase with a grimace. He uncoiled her fingers from their grip on him, almost before she could recognize the manipulative pressure that his hand exerted on hers. "I doubt, however, that my charm will carry much weight with Nilson's planetary governor."

The bluntness of his implication made it inescapable and equally unpalatable. "You expect *me* to charm him?"

"That sort of charm *is* your family specialty."

"I'd hit you if I thought I could do any serious damage."

"Relanine has its uses." He was already through the door and halfway to the outer lock.

"I hate you when you're smug, Jase." Still muttering epithets against her partner, Tori stuffed a few large notes of Cuui currency into her pockets. She took her time, confident that Jase would wait for her despite his own irritation. She found him leaning against the outer door in a pose of exaggerated patience.

"Are you quite ready?" he asked her. "Perhaps you'd care to inspect the ship a few times before we leave?"

"We can't start an assignment in this mood," she sighed, though she wished she could indulge her anger at him fully, even once.

He straightened and transformed his expression into cool professionalism. "I'm glad you've come to your senses. What is your impression of the recording?"

Tori had to rearrange her thoughts to recall the governor's speech, which had brought them here. "Troubling. Have you viewed it?"

"Yes. I suffered it last night." Jase raised his eyes to the elaborate arch that fortified the air lock. "I found the speech disgusting and absurd. Why does it trouble you?"

"Because it's too disgusting to be absurd. The recording does not make Governor Racker look nearly as ridiculous as I had expected, despite the inanity of his comments. It makes Trader Filcher sound like a cross between a calculating Utisi demon and a plague-carrying rodent. The recording may have been intended as a joke, but I fail to recognize the humor. I could envision many people believing it, if they were already disposed to distrust the Consortium."

Jase nodded, pursing his lips in contemplation. "What is your impression of Governor Racker?"

"Governor Racker is an ambitious man of limited intelligence who relies heavily on calculated charm and physical attractiveness for his success."

"Don't omit ruthlessness. His predecessor was assassinated."

"Lovely. Are you sure we should be making this visit unofficially? Independent travelers are easy prey, but even a murderous Network governor might hesitate to attack official Consortium representatives."

"I thought you wanted a change from civilized Calong."

"I thought *you* believed in moderation."

"Not where Truth is concerned." Jase reached across the gap between them and touched Tori's hand lightly. "Did I press you to come here against your own judgment?"

"If you applied your Sesserda tricks to persuade me, how would I know?" muttered Tori. She met his gaze reluctantly, still uneasy with the transformation enacted by a simple pair of blue lenses. Relanine tingled through her skin, where his fingertips rested against hers.

"I may have pressed you too hard to come, but I did not use any Sesserda technique in the process. I respect your insights too much to manipulate you that way, even if I were so insensitive to your preferences and so disdainful of Sesserda proprieties. Tori, if you think I'm behaving foolishly, I expect you to tell me that truth."

"Have I ever hesitated to call you a fool, when I thought you needed it?"

"You call me a fool when you're angry with me, not necessarily when I deserve it most. You were right in saying that you are better equipped than I to understand the Level VII mentality, simply because of your particular array of life experiences. If you truly believe that I have miscalculated in approaching this problem, please tell me."

"You don't like this task at all, do you?"

"Not a bit."

"But you think it's necessary."

"I think it's necessary."

"Then we need to be here." She could not continue to meet that blue gaze, no less intense for the camouflage of color. Instead, she freed her hand from his and applied the code to open the outer lock. She stared at her first view of Nilson's gray sky and inhaled her first breath of sour Nilson air without enthusiasm. "Would I have stayed with you this long if I didn't trust *your* judgment?" She slumped against the ship's curved wall, reluctant to step outside, but she looked at Jase only from the corner of her eye. "I do recognize your exceptional gifts, Jase, even if I resent them at times. If you discern a necessity for this errand of ours—enough to make you separate yourself from civilized company and the assurance of a ready supply of relanine—then I am certain that a good reason exists. If you are willing to adapt yourself to the perspective of a society that offends your most fundamental beliefs, how can I complain about the relatively minor adjustments required of me? I am not confident that we can resolve the problems here, either for Filcher Ikthan Cuui or for ourselves, but we need to try."

He replied softly, "You almost sound like a Sesserda advocate, Tori."

"It must be your bad influence," she countered. "Speaking of which, Mister *Margrave*—how do you plan to influence Network officialdom to grant us access to Filcher?"

"By asking to visit him. Even a reprobate like Filcher is allowed to have friends."

"Why should our request be granted?"

"Because you and I are singularly persuasive. Because the name of Margrave will be noticed." He shrugged. "And because Network's leaders are paranoid about Filcher, the Consortium and all things alien to their understanding. That's why they haven't yet executed Filcher, and that's why they will be eager to amass more evidence to support their theories of conspiracy."

"That sort of logic could make them equally eager to arrest us."

For answer, Jase merely rippled his limber fingers in a Calongi expression of Truth-undefined. It was an expression customarily used to define a state of ignorance at the commencement of an Inquisition. Tori regretted that she had raised the subject at all.

***

In silence, Jase slid his registration form through the primitive iron grill to the clerk, a sour, pinched-face man with mottled skin and hair like old straw. The clerk stared in ponderous sequence at the form, at Jase, and at Tori who had just endured the same bureaucratic procedure. The clerk asked her, "Is he with you?"

She answered simply, "Yes," restraining her tongue from acerbic comment on the irrelevancy of the clerk's question. After a lengthy wait, unsheltered from the intermittent rain, she had begun to sympathize increasingly with the murder-minded Jiucetsi who had preceded her in the line to obtain visitors' passes, but she did not dare to indulge her temper. This clerk seemed to be the only Network employee working at the spaceport, except for some ominously well-armed guards patrolling the perimeter.

The clerk grunted, "You could do better."

"That's what I keep telling him," replied Tori with a sidelong glance at Jase. She smiled winningly at the officious clerk, while imagining the satisfying prospect of the Jiucetsi's muttered vow to mutilate the clerk's anatomy. "I'm open to a more attractive offer." She reached one finger through the grill, touching the clerk's hand with one polished nail. As she retrieved her hand, she pried one of the precious visitor's passes a little closer to the grill. Jase smoothly collected the pass, while the fascinated clerk watched Tori smile. She turned away as soon as Jase had the pass safely in his possession, and the disappointed clerk craned to see her through the grill.

"We'd like to visit a friend inside the main city," murmured Jase pleasantly to the clerk. "Could you please tell us when the port gates will be opened? I didn't see any notice of the official hours."

"Official hours?" scoffed the clerk, still craning, though Tori had moved deliberately out of his sight. "If you want to see Nilson, walk the spaceport perimeter. The fact that we let C-humans land here doesn't mean we want your kind roaming freely through our cities. You can buy and sell in the trade stalls, east end of the port, next to the swamps where your kind belongs."

Tori longed to snap at the man for his rudeness, but Jase persisted patiently, "I apologize for not making myself clear. We would pay to be escorted, if that is the preferred legal procedure."

The clerk shook his head in disgust, frustrated both by Jase and by Tori's retreat, and he waved at the cadaverous Cuui pilot who grumbled irritably in line behind Jase. As the pallid Cuui began to step forward, Jase raised his limber hand in an apparently idle gesture that Tori recognized as a Cuui command signal, rarely seen outside of Cuui hives. The astonished Cuui stopped, and Jase repeated, "Please, register my official request for access to the main city."

"Open port does not mean open planet," argued the clerk stubbornly. "This is Network, C-human, not some back-star easy-spot."

Tori recognized the odd, enticing smile that Jase donned, and she turned her eyes hastily toward the lading of a battered cargo ship. She tried to avoid hearing him, as well, but the Sesserda-trained voice could not be ignored. The Cuui pilot, alarmed by the proximity of a Soli with intimate hive knowledge, abandoned his precious place in line and scurried, exhibiting the disjointed running gait of his species, across the landing field. Tori maintained enough detachment to deride her own susceptibility, even as she felt the impulse to give Jase the universe. The unsuspecting clerk, she decided, would be helpless. "When you place the request," coaxed Jase irresistibly, "specify that we shall require a visit with the man known as Filcher Ikthan Cuui, who resides in your local penitentiary."

The officer nodded leadenly. He watched his fingers enter the data with a bewildered gaze. "We'll contact you, when the appointment for access is scheduled," he informed Jase. As Jase and Tori left the window, the port officer stared after them in puzzlement.

***

Into Caragen's expensively austere dining room, Network murmured quietly, "A visitor to Nilson has requested an interview with the Cuui prisoner."

Caragen merely tilted one brow and continued to eat his solitary meal. During the last two years, meals had become a necessary ritual to be endured rather than savored. To him, who had dined from every Network world's most priceless settings, the antique luxury of platinum-edged porcelain and polished silver offered no satisfaction. The food, though delicately prepared by Network to his precise command, seemed flavorless to him. In public, he ate abundantly. In private, he consumed only enough to maintain his health according to Network's recommendations.

Network continued, "The visitor is a C-human, who has no prior visit record."

"How did he identify himself in landing?"

"He registered as Jasen Margrave, a C-human tourist."

"Is he traveling alone?"

"He has one companion: a female C-human, Victoria Mirelle."

"What is the basis of their request?"

"Informal. They claim friendship with the prisoner."

"Has Racker authorized the visit?"

"The request has just reached the Governor's Lieutenant, Saschy Firl."

"That one," muttered Caragen, but he smiled thinly. "Where is Racker?"

"Assigning a technical crew to evaluate the cause of an early morning break in contact with the Wharton mining establishment."

"Loss of contact? Could this problem constitute evidence in support of Marrach's claims?"

"At the present time, insufficient data are available to confirm such a correlation. This is the twenty-seventh reported failure of topological transfer and communication equipment connecting Nilson and Wharton. All prior failures were traced to minor equipment malfunctions. Wharton diagnostic sensors are substandard and therefore slow."

"Keep me apprised of any changes in the Wharton situation. Maintain level one observation procedures over the Cuui prisoner."

"Acknowledged."

"The name, Jasen Margrave," muttered Caragen, pushing a morsel of an exotic vegetable across his plate. "Why is it familiar?"

Network answered dutifully, "It was the name of one of the first C-human trade negotiators."

Caragen raised his sparse brows. Network's status report, which had initially interested him no more than his meal, suddenly promised to justify his recent order that even minor Nilson incidents be announced to him immediately. "A C-human diplomat in his third century seems an unlikely tourist."

"The current visitor is calculated to be less than half a century old, even accounting for the possibility of age concealment techniques, suggested by some anomalous readings in the visitor's physical profile. Correlation of sensor data between the original Jasen Margrave and the current visitor indicate a high probability that the current visitor is a descendant of the C-human trade negotiator bearing the same name."

"So, the Consortium has an interest in the wretched Cuui after all," mused Caragen into his tented fingers.

"The probability that Jasen Margrave has official Consortium backing is estimated at sixty-three percent."

"To a man like Marrach," observed Caragen, "who has forged his life by his wits, there is nothing more tantalizing than knowledge." Caragen expected no reply and received none. "Establish a link with him. Inform him of the visitor's request."

"Acknowledged."

"Feed him this morsel to remind him of the feasts that he has known. Force him to recognize his hunger." Well satisfied, Caragen pushed his plate away from him.

***

Saschy tromped furiously through the mud that surrounded the port. Like other Nilsonites, she shunned the spaceport region whenever possible, and she had not dressed for today's unscheduled visit. Her long coat was trimmed with Nilson filth, but she had no time to worry over niceties of appearance. Network had placed an automatic delay on her order for the summary execution of Filcher Ikthan Cuui, triggered by notification of alien visitors requesting contact with the Cuui. After all this time of Filcher's incarceration with not a single visitor taking interest in him, she had not even thought to lift the standing orders that

demanded investigation of any visitation queries. The
oversight had cost her the nuisance of this visit, but she
would bypass any serious delays by performing the investigation herself, closing the file on her personal authority, and ensuring that the execution took place, as
planned. With Caragen making inquiries, Breamas
beginning a resurgence, and the entire Wharton enclave developing hysteria, it was too easy to feel
overwhelmed, especially with Mum returning all of
Saschy's notes without explanation—and Saschy certainly could not spare enough time now to visit Mum
and restore the imperfect peace of their relationship.
Eliminating the relatively minor problem of the Cuui
thief was hardly the highest priority, but the ease of
resolution would help Saschy regain her sense of control over her life.

Saschy gestured peremptorily, and Network opened the gate to admit her. "Where are they?" she
demanded.

"Block six, slot eleven," answered Network in a
tinny voice.

"Order them to meet me in the records office. Tell
them to come immediately if they want me to consider
their request."

She averted her eyes from the strangely contoured
ships and their strange owners. The aliens made her uncomfortable, especially the Cuui, who were by far the
most common alien visitors to Nilson. The translucent
Cuui skin seemed always at peril of erupting from the
strain of blood that pulsed heavily beneath it, and
the odd multijointed limbs bore just enough human
likeness to be unnerving. The obsequious manners of
the Cuui always struck her as a mocking form of condescension. As she crossed the dirt yard to the shack
that was known euphemistically as the "records office," Saschy imagined the stares of alien eyes. Self-
consciousness made her movements more awkward
than usual.

The office had no luxuries, but it was a decent structure by Nilson standards. Reasonably clean and utilitarian with its beige plastic files and folding chairs, it

was precisely the type of setting that suited Saschy's tastes best: plain and unpretentious. She unfolded three chairs and seated herself in front of the room's single window.

She had left the door open so she could watch them come to her. When she saw them, she was glad of the extra moments of preparation. Saschy had wondered what type of humans could befriend a beast like Filcher. She had envisioned two shifty wretches like the scum of Nilson's streets, and that image had made her confident that she would know how to deal with them. This elegant pair upset her plans and all her preconceptions. For the first time, she wondered if Racker's wild, anti-Consortium accusations about the Cuui prisoner could actually contain an element of truth.

The woman was exquisite and clearly conscious of that fact, inspiring Saschy to loathe her on sight. By association, Saschy felt predisposed to form a similar opinion of the man, though he was too slightly built to compete with someone like Racker on Nilson's scale of attractiveness. The woman spoke first, offering her hand in a Network-style greeting, "My name is Tori." The alien accent was barely perceptible.

Saschy folded her arms to emphasize her unwillingness to accept the hand of a C-human. She directed her response to the man, who had remained silent. "You requested a visit with Filcher Ikthan Cuui. Why?"

Tori furled herself around the stiff chair with an innate grace that Saschy resented heartily. The man continued to stand at ease with his hands thrust deep into the pockets of his travel suit. He held so still that he resembled a darkly enigmatic statue, lifeless except for the glitter of eyes scanning every corner of the room. Saschy found herself staring at his eyes and marveling at their exceptionally deep blue color. There was something unsettling about the intensity of those eyes, decided Saschy, though she was seldom susceptible to such fanciful observations.

Tori answered Saschy's question coolly, "Filcher is imprisoned in your city. A formal request seemed a necessary measure in order to visit him. Is there a problem?"

"He is due to be executed three days from now."

"That would be inconvenient," remarked Tori.

Saschy pointed at the man and demanded, "Who are you?"

He answered crisply, "My name is Jase."

Even the timber of his voice evokes mystery, thought Saschy, then berated herself for her absurd flight of imagination. The man was a self-proclaimed C-human. The subtle strangeness of his voice undoubtedly reflected a peculiarity of alien-influenced accent. "What business do you have with Filcher?"

Tori replied, "He seems to need friends."

"He could have used a friend three months ago, when we captured him. You come a little late."

"We seem to have arrived just in time," said Tori with an amiable smile.

"Your Consortium denies him."

"Filcher is not a member."

"He claims otherwise. Are your claims as false as his?"

Jase laid one slender hand on Tori's shoulder, stilling her retort. "We would like to see Filcher tomorrow morning. You will arrange it, please," murmured Jase in a tone like rich satin.

"Of course," answered Saschy. She listened to her own concession incredulously. Saschy had always insisted on making her own decisions, irrespective of the wishes of Mum or Arlan or Racker or anyone else. How could a C-human stranger exert such strong influence on her with a few effortless words?

"Thank you, Lieutenant," replied Jase. His fingers tapped a signal, and Tori arose smoothly. The extraordinary pair walked from the shack, and Saschy thought she had never seen any more composed visitors, even in the Governor's palace.

As soon as they left her, Saschy found herself opening the locked cabinet that held the room's primitive Network interface. With dexterous strokes, she signaled the order for two special visitors' passes.

Network will record the meeting, and we shall learn
om it," she assured herself, trying to justify her un-
esitating concession to an outrageous request. The
ruel sounds of honest self-criticism rattled derisively
side her.

CHAPTER 20

Sacrifices

Jon Terry had arrived at the Infortiare's office with the setting of the sun behind Ixaxis. The office had grown dark now. Rhianna had not lit the lamps, and Jon had no patience to decipher the lamps' design in the midst of this intense debate. Only the moon laid its white fingers upon the room. "You understand, Lady Rhianna," said Jon slowly, "why I make this request of you."

The golden head remained bowed, as Rhianna examined her moon-white badge of office. "The traditional badge of the Infortiare's position," she murmured, "was a pendant of gold. It was destroyed with my husband's body." She raised her head, and the clear gray eyes were abnormally bright, even in moonglow—whether with unshed tears or with Power, Jon could not determine. "I do understand sacrifice, Dr. Terry. Have you told your wife of your intentions?"

"Beth and I discussed the subject this morning." He sighed. He had communicated with Beth over a noisy link that had made his wife's voice almost unrecognizable. Her grief had come through clearly, but she had not tried to dissuade him. "I shall not need much time to make my observations. If there is a true 'instability,' any of the Nilson portals should reflect the problem."

"I would prefer that you send a less recognizable emissary to make the observations for you."

"I cannot define a test procedure for someone else, not knowing at all what to expect. A lifetime of experience cannot be replaced by a few textbook trials." It was an argument that Jon had often made to Network officials. Old frustration recalled a more recent grievance. "What did you expect to come of that encounter

ou arranged between me and Marrach? You made
ure that I would feel properly threatened."

"I ensured that you were properly informed. If that
eeting threatened anyone, it was Master Rabh Mar-
ch. I already know and trust you, Dr. Terry." Before
n could ask her to explain, she continued, "If you are
etected in Network, you will be detained forcibly. The
ouncil Governor is not a forgiving man."

"I am old by any standards but yours," interrupted
n, "and I have little left for Caragen to take from me.
hat did you mean about a threat to Marrach? The
hysical threat of pain because of his symbiosis? Or do
ou have something more sinister in mind?"

"I mean that I do not know Master Rabh. I do know
at your family would disagree with your assessment
f your own value."

"I intend to be careful. Do you distrust Marrach?"

"He sent Quinzaine unprepared into a potentially
thal situation. I am the Infortiare, the liege lady of the
omain of Ixaxis. Quinzaine is my subject, and his for-
ys into Network are the result of my original com-
and to him. I have a duty to protect Quinzaine, as
est I am able."

"You do distrust Marrach. Do you think that he has
een serving as a healer for these past years simply to
in our trust? Do you believe that he is still working
or Caragen?"

Rhianna raised her slender hand to ward off the
lood of questions. "Master Rabh's symbiotic relation-
hip is more than a mere ploy, but I cannot gauge either
he depth or the permanence of that bond. I believe that
Master Rabh has told us far less than he knows about
he present situation. I do not know his motives yet.
hat is why I needed to observe him."

Jon nodded in thoughtful respect. "I understand.
You need to conduct some research personally. Will
ou support me in conducting mine?"

Rhianna sighed, "You might have asked Lord Quin-
aine directly."

"Yes." Jon gnawed at his knuckle, considering the
ady of Ixaxis, facing him with such stiff regality.

Moonbeams divided them, flowing across the history patterned expanse of a hand-knotted Seriin rug. "I di ask him directly. He deferred to Katerin."

"And unlike your wife, your daughter elected t veto your request," concluded Rhianna with a trac of humor. Her thin hand twisted the silver chain of he pendant, a luminous blur against the dim sheen o her gown.

"Yes," agreed Jon with a grimace. "My daughter i even more stubborn than I am." He shifted in the velve chair, wondering if Lady Rhianna had elected to perc on a straight chair of hard wood out of some precogni tion of his mission. Her entire posture evoked a moo of resistance. "How do you light these lamps?" h asked, fumbling to find a switch or wick or othe means of controlling the globe on the table beside him

"By a thought," she answered, and a floor lamp i the corner brightened the room. "I will not order Qui to take you to Nilson. Such a command would be un fair to him, to his wife, and to you."

"I concur," answered Jon, trying to sound reason able, though he sensed that Rhianna had alread decided against him. "That is one of my reasons fo coming to you today. I prefer not to ask Quin to escor me to Nilson, when Katerin has made her preference so clear. I want *you* to send me."

The golden lady's restless hands grew still, settling to rest upon the lilac silk of her rich skirts. "If any other man made such a request of me, I would assume that he did not understand the significance of his pro posal." Her face seemed to tighten across the finely de lineated bones. "However, you understand these matters better than anyone of Network."

Jon nodded, unpretentious but unabashed about the uniqueness of his abilities. "I devoted the best part of my life to research related to the development of topo logical transfer. I had help from many talented associ ates, but I am the last survivor of that phenomenal era of technical advancement on Network-3."

Ever so gently, Rhianna pierced a little of his

conceit. "Your colleagues could be my ancestors. Ix-axis is their legacy."

Unwilling to accept her stinging reminder without a parrying stroke, he suggested mildly, "I could be your ancestor, as well. The Network-3 researchers had access to my genetic codes."

"Do you tender that hypothesis with pride or with shame?" asked Rhianna with a wry smile, but she shrugged away his effort to answer the unanswerable. "I have never attempted to reach into Network, Dr. Terry. I would not dare to make the first such journey with you in tow, even if I did not feel duty-bound to remain here."

He leaped on the hint that she had actually weighed his proposal seriously. "You don't need to travel yourself. You need only loan me your Power for the engine and navigational portions of a new type of transfer portal that I have been developing. I have given the matter considerable study, and I have confidence in my conclusions." Jon grinned eagerly. "I would try to recruit your help for the next step in my ongoing research, even if my family's harmony were not at stake. You are an exceptionally quick learner, Lady Rhianna, and you have tremendous self-discipline."

Her fingers resumed their uneasy attention to the pendant. "While you may relish this opportunity to test your theories," observed Rhianna, her fine brows puckered with concern, "it is not a trivial matter."

"Significant scientific advancement is never trivial," retorted Jon, wielding the keen determination that had long ago convinced parsimonious Network Councillors to support his most ambitious research. He tapped his index finger against his lips, then thrust it at Rhianna. "You have taken your share of risks for causes that you valued."

"A wizard's Power is less predictable than your Network science."

Jon shook his head impatiently, rattling the shock of hair that remained the color of sand, albeit gray-streaked and faded with the years. He spoke forcefully, intent in his conviction. "Do not ply me with that

deliberate Ixaxin mystification, as if I shared the superstitions of your country's uneducated masses. *Their* ignorance makes them view your 'Power' as 'magical'
and accordingly unpredictable, but you and I both
know that you are simply a product of a remarkable bit
of Network genetic science. The human system is complex, but Network science manages to predict many of
its functions. Your Power is simply another type of
human process, and your Ixaxin scholars have defined
its properties quite effectively. You have succeeded
too well in impressing me with Ixaxin scholarship.
You cannot credibly revert to an affectation of feudal
primitivism."

"Very well, Dr. Terry, let us discuss your premise as
fellow scholars." The Lady's clear eyes glittered with
the merest spark of warning. "Or perhaps I should
stand aside and allow you to pursue this conversation
with Kaedric," continued Rhianna softly. "There is no
better Ixaxin scholar."

"I have always been willing to speak to any of your
scholars who will listen," began Jon with emphatic enthusiasm, but he stopped, his expression growing rigid
as he belatedly recognized the trap of her words. "You
refer to your husband, Kaedric, Lord Venkarel."

"Of course. There has been no keener student of
Ixaxin science since Zerus first codified the Laws of
Wizardry. Many other wizards have tried to expand on
those fundamentals, but only Kaedric succeeded. Only
Kaedric ever delved deeply into the theories and practices of Power that correspond to your own specialty of
topological travel."

"Even the most zealous theoreticians are seldom
willing to set forth a fatal proof," observed Jon with a
grimace.

"Kaedric did, however, prove the commutability of
infinity, as it is defined in wizards' lore, by commuting
his own Power. Ergo, while he long ago sacrificed
physical form, he remains quite capable of evaluating
your latest theory and discussing it with you. Indeed,
he is uniquely qualified in that regard."

"What point are you trying to make, Lady Rhianna?" demanded Jon a trifle coldly.

"I make a simple observation, Dr. Terry. I shall not insist that you confer with a ghost. That, after all, might smack more of mysticism than of science."

"Verbal trickery is a poor way to win an argument," he sighed, feeling suddenly too old, too tired to continue the debate. He pried himself from his chair, ready to leave in defeat, but Rhianna also rose and came toward him. She touched his shoulder lightly. He twisted his head to look at her, surprised to find himself staring down at the smoothly braided crown of her hair. He always forgot how small, how delicate she seemed, when she let herself be seen without the daunting veil of her Power.

"I respect you too much to resort to tricks in a matter of such consequence," she said in gentle apology. "But you must recognize that my husband, whose incorporeal state makes you so uncomfortable, is a form of the same Power that you believe you understand well enough to use."

"I am not fond of staring into the distorted space of an unshielded transfer port, but I am perfectly willing to enjoy the benefits of topological transfer."

Rhianna nodded, but the voice that reached inside Jon was not hers. "Are you willing to risk a fatal proof to *your* theory, Dr. Terry?" asked the voice that conjured dark images of its saturnine owner.

"I am willing to risk a great deal to keep the universe intact," answered Jon, then hesitated, realizing that he indeed seemed to be addressing a ghost, by common definitions of Network as well as of superstitious Serii. With forced calm, Jon asked Rhianna, "Can he hear me?"

"Kaedric hears you far more often than you realize," she replied with a rueful smile. "He has been here with us all along. He can provide you with an illusion of physical presence, if that would be easier for you."

"It's immaterial," answered Jon, then winced at his unintentional pun. He focused on Rhianna, noting the curious distancing of her keen gray gaze. He forced

himself to speak calmly, as if to a normal man just outside of view. Jon was not convinced that he addressed
anyone but Rhianna in another guise of her Power, but
he did not mind adjusting to her eccentricities. "Lord
Venkarel, you should understand better than anyone
why I must go to Nilson. With your wife's help, I can
obtain the answers that we all need."

"Rhianna is the Infortiare," returned the excessively
precise voice that existed without visible origin. "Her
duty is to Serii and its people. With Serii's mortal
queen in a precarious state of health, the Infortiare cannot be spared even for the duration of your excursion."
Rhianna shuddered perceptibly at the reference to
Queen Joli, whose prospects for recovery fluctuated
from day to day. "Persuade *me* of the validity of your
approach, and I shall take you to Nilson myself."

"You are both mad," whispered Rhianna, who had
expected Kaedric to argue against Jon, not conspire
with him. She turned and swept toward the full-length
windows. Wrapping herself in a veil of memory, she
acquired the semblance of a statue clothed as a woman
from a medieval past. When Jon Terry spoke her name,
she did not respond.

"She is correct about us," said Kaedric dryly. In that
odd moment, it was easy for Jon to imagine that the
voice came from an ordinary man at his side—a man
who seemed suddenly more accessible than the golden
Lady of Ixaxis. "She is also wise. She does not waste
words on futile argument."

"Do you understand what I am requesting?" asked
Jon slowly. He began to revise his assessment of
Kaedric as a manifestation of Rhianna's Power. Jon
could not quite accept that the voice belonged to a
ghost, but it was independent of her.

"I understand the tenet of your proposal quite well, I
think. You want to employ wizard's Power to initiate a
topological connectivity that will enable you to journey
to Nilson, inspect its spacial and temporal status, and
return with that information. You want to use Power
without sacrificing your own control of the process.
You want a wizard to fuel your latest invention, that

spindle that you are clutching in your pocket: a hand-held transfer controller, akin to our Taormin but lacking the active ingredients that would make the device lethal for you to carry. Your concept is sound, albeit unflattering."

Jon grimaced at the wizard's mocking humor. "The wizard will also be a fellow observer, in case I am unable to complete the journey."

"Neither of us may survive the undertaking, if the instability is as extensive as Lord Quinzaine believes. A wizard's Power is far closer to the fabric of topological space than your quanta-mechanical transfer devices, which merely tamper with the limit points. Therefore, we are more vulnerable to damage from a damaged space."

The significant word *us* rang in Jon's head. He inhaled deeply to still his nerves prickling from the certainty that he was about to entrust his life to an entity who claimed to be a ghost. "You are accordingly less likely to aggravate any existing damage."

"I, alone, could move through that space of Nilson with virtually no impact on my surroundings, since my substance is *its* substance. You, however, have a physical manifestation to carry, which can at most be commuted into a noiselike energy. You *will* affect your surroundings. Other sources of interference may also arise because of you."

"My arrival will have no more effect than the hundreds of Network travelers who pass through a typical transfer portal every day." Jon turned, briefly expecting to see the man with whom he conversed. The confirmation that no such man stood beside him goaded Jon into a need to act quickly, before his courage could fail. "The sooner we go, the sooner we can begin to resolve any problems that we may discover."

"You may wish to close your eyes, Dr. Terry. As you are aware, the mortal view of entering distorted space can unsettle the most seasoned traveler."

The immediacy of reaction stunned Jon. He yearned to protest, *Not this soon!* But he set aside his fear, realizing the pointless folly of delay.

Jon heard Rhianna's wrenching cry of, "Kaedric . . ." and no more. Jon refused to close his eyes, anxious to compare this journey to its familiar Network counterpart, but his intention did not matter beyond the cold instant of his changing state. The blaze of writhing energies, strands of tormented light and a skewed, dark bleakness invaded all his senses, though he could not define what senses were thus bombarded.

He had become *part* of it—this other space that he had defined in theory and conquered in reality without ever before sensing it for himself. Unlike the nearly instantaneous transfers of his Network invention, this journey had perceptible measures of time and distance. Jon Terry followed a man-shaped shadow among the planes of lethal possibilities, spiderweb traps of energy and infinity spiraling into nothingness, and he knew that he moved only by the will and Power of his guide. Another mortal might have feared, recognizing the perils and the magnitude of his dependence on his strange guide, but Jon felt such elation as he had not known since the first successful experiments in topological transfer. Much as he loved his family, this experience touched a deeper passion: to *see* the truth that he had long ago described by the only human language capable of expressing it, the language of mathematics. *It is worth whatever it costs me,* he thought.

His guide acquired an illusion of black-clad solidity and grinned with feral appreciation across a lean shoulder. "I thought you might enjoy the scenic route," he remarked, and his blue-ice eyes flickered with the consciousness of his enormous Power.

And this is your home, mused Jon, unable to form a semblance of voice in this place where *he* was the ghost.

"This is my reality," answered Kaedric, and his grin thinned and vanished. "It is no more than an incomplete truth, as limited by my Power's boundaries as your concept of the universe is limited by your own mind and senses. What you see around you is nothing more than *my* Power's perception of those same concepts that *you* evolved as mathematical entities."

Yours is the more accurate model, answered Jon.

"Perhaps the two are equally accurate, each in its own time and place." The dark image shifted: from guide, to a boy, thin as a starveling, to the man who was Infortiare with the golden seal of office burning ominously against black silk. "But which is more dangerous? The answer is not obvious."

Before Jon could unravel the meaning of the riddle, all apparent solidity of vision dissolved. The planes of light tilted and furled themselves, leaving emptiness—or an *otherness* that defied Jon's capability to identify by mortal thought. A roiling nausea afflicted him, and he had no physical means to alleviate it. He could not form a question for his guide. He lost all sense of motion except the sickness tearing at his self.

When Jon stumbled out of a Network transfer portal, his body was racked with choking. A wary adolescent watched him with the inertia of uncertainty. "I haven't traveled for a while," croaked Jon, wishing the girl would leave him to his embarrassed misery. "Is there some water. . . ?"

She nodded, pulling her hands from the pockets of her too-thin skirt. She pointed toward a lavatory, marked with the usual Network symbol for such public accommodations, commonly positioned near transfer portals. Jon did not try to thank her. He could barely voice the falsified citizen code that he had prepared for this occasion, but his effort sufficed for Network to open the lavatory door to him.

When he had partially recovered himself, aided by liberal splashes of cold water on his face, Jon tried to recapture some sense of the guide who had brought him here. "Kaedric?" he whispered questioningly, but the wizard did not answer.

"Do you require medical assistance?" inquired Network politely, though the synthetic voice was of the poorest quality.

"No," answered Jon, glad of the implications of the question. More sophisticated Network terminals had enough sensors to diagnose medical needs unaided. Fewer sensors reduced the chance that his false identity would be detected. "Is this Nilson?" he asked, confident that Network would register his query as normal. Temporary disorientation was a common side effect of travel sickness.

"This is Nilson, capital city of the planet of the same name," replied the stilted voice of an inexpensive, poorly maintained Network installation. "You have one half hour until curfew. If you have not left the port building by that time, you will be required to remain within the port perimeter until lift of curfew in the morning."

"Evening," murmured Jon to his own wan reflection. It should not have been evening in Nilson's capital. The time differential from Tulea should have placed him here mid-morning, based on the relative planetary rotational speeds and locations. The transfer process, even accounting for "scenic" digressions, could not possibly have lasted for more than a few minutes. Even the patterns of inanimate objects, if they remained in transit for an hour or more, lost too much temporal continuity to be fully recovered by the transfer portal algorithms programmed into Jon's device—and Jon felt certain, from the sickness inside of him, that it was the Network device that had reassembled him, not wizard's Power. Jon refused to believe that the wizard would have dabbled in time transfer, aware of the potential instability at the end.

The unplanned time lag comprised grim evidence—perhaps confirmation of the worst of Quin's claims. It was horrifying, and it was infuriating. Could some petty-minded Network bureaucrat actually have authorized a destabilizing port construction? And how could Jon Terry, Network exile without any of his former access privileges, locate and extract the critical information that was encoded and encrypted across a billion nodes of Network memory? "Network," asked Jon tentatively, "were any operational aberrations recorded during recent transfer arrivals?"

Jon wondered if he imagined the pause before Network replied, "No aberrations were recorded."

Only half an hour until curfew . . . What benighted

sort of planet enforced a curfew on transfer ports?
"What were the aleph-seven readings?"

The pause was not imagined. "That information is
unavailable."

Unavailable due to inadequacy of the local equipment, or unavailable without higher access privileges. . . . Jon gulped sour air. "Have there been any
unusual transfer statistics generated over the past few
months? An unusually high incidence of transfer sickness? Ports failing for indeterminate causes? Errors in
destination coordinates?"

"That information is unavailable."

Frustrating. . . . All of the tremendous resources of
Network, the only wealth that Jon truly missed in exile,
was *here* but still unreachable. Jon dragged his fingers
through his damp hair, combing the strands into imperfect order. "Kaedric?" he tried once more, but to no
better effect.

"The nature of your question is unclear," responded
Network.

"To both of us," muttered Jon. He vacated the lavatory and returned to the main port area. He watched the
portals, a paltry set for a Network planetary capital,
waiting for visitors to emerge, but it was apparently too
close to curfew. The port building, open to the breezes,
was nearly empty. After a wait of many minutes, an
orange-clad man with a shaved head raced into the
building and jumped into a portal. The man seemed to
have dropped a piece of his luggage near one of the
support columns, but Jon could see nothing unusual in
the transfer. The light curtain hid any aberrations that
might otherwise have been observable.

Jon circled the portal area slowly, watching for
something, anything that might suggest a path of investigation. He saw the girl again, lurking near the stairs
that led down from the building to the grim, gray
streets. He wondered what guilty secret made her look
so nervous. He was glad he carried nothing worth stealing. He might have been more concerned about her if
she had looked less spindly, or if he had been less confident of Network monitoring.

Testing possibilities, he approached her. "Are you waiting for someone?" he asked. She shrugged one shoulder. Jon tried a friendly smile. "I was expecting my daughter to arrive with me. She's a little older than you, blonde, thin . . . have you seen her?"

The girl shook her head. Her brown curls were limp, and her face wore a purplish mark that might have been a bruise, poorly disguised by a glitter powder. She had thrust her hands back into her pockets, and her clenched fists bulged at her sides.

"I wondered if you might be able to help me," continued Jon. "I'd go back myself, but as you saw, I had a little trouble with transfer sickness. If you could just spare a few moments, you could go back and see what's causing the delay in my daughter's arrival. I'd pay, of course." The girl did not quite brighten at his suggestion of payment, but her eyes narrowed in heightened interest. "Would you mind?"

"Why not be asking Network?" asked the girl suspiciously.

"I did," answered Jon, hoping he was interpreting the girl's thick accent correctly, and hoping that Network would not denounce his lie. "Network says she hasn't left, but I'm sure she entered as I did. Her name is Beth. Please, I'd pay you for your trouble."

She shrugged again, but this time she replied, "Okay. Where be I going?"

"I'll set the coordinates. It's not a busy port, so you'll have no trouble spotting Beth, if she's still there. If she's still there, tell her I'm waiting. If she's not there, come back immediately and let me know."

The girl nodded toward the payment panel. Jon smiled and programmed it, transferring real funds in the name of his fictitious identity, one of Quin's implementations. A handful of local coins spilled at his feet. He collected them, giving half to the girl and reserving the rest for his own use in case he needed to spend more time here. He set a destination code for a city that he recalled as sparsely traveled, then waited for the girl to make her trip.

She hesitated only a moment before stepping into

he port. The light curtain brightened to engulf her. As
with the previous departure, nothing obviously aber-
ant occurred, but Jon waited expectantly. It was the ar-
ival that he needed to observe. Light curtains were
generally designed for optimum departure, making
hem less effective at shielding on the receiving end of
ransfer. Arriving travelers had no option to turn back.

He stared, fixing the rippling pattern of light into his
memory. He counted seconds, wondering if the girl
would return at all, wondering if his eyes had retained
heir ability to detect the minutiae of the transfer
process. When he saw the brief feathering at the center
of the portal entrance, he knew he had not lost his old
skills. The girl emerged, as unsmiling and indifferent
as ever, but Jon stared through her, too shaken by revelation to react quickly. The instability was real, and he
knew its nature. The danger was far more immediate
than he had anticipated. He tried to recall whether Nilson was susceptible to any significant seismic activity
The instability had progressed so far that even a physical trauma might trigger a topological eruption. An
electrical storm could be catastrophic.

"She be not there," said the girl. She extended her
hand in front of him. It took him several moments to
realize that she was awaiting additional payment.

"You didn't see her?" he asked, upholding his pretense absentmindedly.

"Like I be saying," she answered with impatience.

Jon dropped the rest of his local coins into her
hands, but she sniffed eloquently at the paltry amount.
Impatient with her, he muttered, "I'll have Network
transfer a suitable reward to you. What's your identity
code?"

"My code?" grumbled the girl, lowering her head
with angry force. "What be your game, doctor?"

Jon stiffened at the familiar title, until he realized
that the girl spoke it only as a jeer. "I'm trying to pay
you, as I promised, but I have given you all my cash."
On a whim, he elaborated on his earlier lie, "My
daughter may have some, if you'd prefer to wait."

"You be too old to have a daughter my age."

Network issued its bland pronouncement, "Curfew in five minutes. All travelers wishing to leave the port building, please exit immediately."

"Be coming with me, old man," snapped the girl, grabbing Jon's arm with a wiry strength that surprised him.

"I need to wait for my daughter," retorted Jon, irritated with this girl for distracting him from his mental calculations. "I'm not leaving yet."

"You be right, old man. You be not leaving. Bear!" she shouted. Jon tried to pull back, as he saw the young thug hurtle at him from the lavatory corridor. The first blow knocked Jon to the floor. He tasted blood. He tried to rise and felt fire lance his side. The thug stripped Jon's jacket from him and tossed it to the girl. A Network security alarm began to sound.

"Be welcome to Nilson," said the girl with cruel relish. Jon heard her only dimly.

"He be having nothing worth the take," whined the thug.

"Then be finishing it," snapped his accomplice in thievery. "It be almost curfew, and port boys be coming."

"Kaedric," whispered Jon in a desperate plea.

"What be he saying?" demanded the girl.

"Nothing," growled her boyfriend. "He be gone," and he issued three hard blows to prove his point.

"Curfew in thirty seconds," announced Network obliviously, as the girl hurled a brick to shatter the primitive speakers that were all that Nilson could afford. Two grumbling port boys finally appeared, running at a lazy lope from the back of the building where they had been sampling Wharton ginnygum, a bribe from the local gang. The two thieves snatched the paltry prizes of their victim's pockets and ran from the building, just as the night barrier blazed into life.

"Curfew is now in effect," continued Network in a damaged voice. "No travelers may leave or enter this building until morning. Lounge accommodations are provided for your comfort. We hope that you enjoy your stay on Nilson."

When the electromagnetic beams from a package of Wharton explosives, carefully dropped by Cullen, ripped through the port dome, the unstable transfer portals arced and shuddered. Wharton explosives inflicted minimal damage to the building. The man who might have understood the larger, less visible damage lay on the rippling floor as solitary human witness, but he did not see.

A less tangible witness observed both the victim, whom he had promised to defend, and the calamity that was unfolding. No time for conscious decision elapsed, because the patterns of his consciousness merged and scattered instantly with the defining points of Nilson's dissolving topological integrity. His Power existed within the Nilson portals, and his Power existed within the Wharton portals, and he existed nowhere at all. Infinity shuddered and robbed him of the discipline that Ixaxis had ingrained in the boy that he had been. The ghost lights of Wharton finally earned their haunted name.

CHAPTER 21

Assets

Saschy expected trouble when she found Racker actually occupying his place at the ornate oak desk of his office. He seldom even visited the room, complaining that the faded blues of the walls and draperies depressed him, though he had bullied the decorator into using the dismal, slightly clashing shades. He usually met guests in the adjoining private suite, except in rare fits of professionalism. The accumulation of pressures was clearly wearing on him, which meant that he would shift that much more of the burden—and blame—onto Saschy. She would not have been surprised to hear him announce a lengthy off-planet tour for unspecified official business.

"One of Breamas' crew attacked the transfer ports last night," grumbled Racker. "They damaged the primary controller."

"They hit the main port building? Where were the security guards?"

"Two fools, high on ginnygum, claim to have been chasing a pair of thieves. The rest of the boys were patrolling the spaceport. You know that we've concentrated more resources there since we caught that alien smuggler. The transfer port building has the best automatic security features on Nilson, next to the palace."

"Its security features didn't stop Breamas."

"A man dropped a parcel just before curfew. Thugs set off the security alarms on the other side of the building. Network scans identified the explosives after the port boys were distracted."

"And Breamas probably bribed the competent guards to stay at the spaceport. I've told you before

that the transfer ports are the most vulnerable part of
the government district. We can't afford to neglect
them, especially now with Network questioning our
procedural compliance."

"I expect you to do more than 'tell me so.' I expect
you to take appropriate action. A more powerful explosive could have done damage to *this* complex. This
wing of the palace is no more than a couple hundred
meters from the port building."

Saschy ignored equally the self-centered nature of
his concern and his effort to shift blame to her. "Is the
port's backup unit working?"

"For the moment." Racker shoved the terrorist's
scrawled letter across his desk. "Breamas demands my
resignation on threat of escalated terrorism."

"Don't take it so personally," murmured Saschy
wryly. "Breamas hates everyone in authority."

"It's lousy timing for one of his revolutionary fits."

"Terrorists are so inconsiderate." Saschy could
not take the threat of Breamas seriously. He was
too much a part of childhood legends, always menacing but never quite real. In all of Saschy's memory, ordinary Nilson street crime had caused more trouble
than Breamas and his followers. Mum even likened
Breamas to some sort of noble, tragic hero. "How
many casualties?"

"Insignificant. The thieves—two locals, one man
and one woman—were found just outside the security
perimeter. The guards were barely bruised. Fortunately, only one visitor was present, so we should
be able to minimize the spread of negative off-world
reports."

*He acts as if Nilson were a popular destination for
Network tourists,* thought Saschy cynically. *How can
Nilson's reputation become any worse?* "Was the visi-
tor anyone of consequence?"

"Network hasn't identified him yet, but it's not
likely. No one has inquired about him. I suppose the
explosion damaged the arrival logs, but there's always
the chance he was one of Caragen's investigators, traveling in private mode."

Saschy's initial frown transformed itself into a thin smile of satisfaction. "The explosion may prove useful to us in that investigation. We can credit Breamas with any portal anomalies."

"It's the Wharton ports that have caused most of the troubles, not the city base."

"Breamas' followers also claim credit for the Wharton explosion that preceded the recent spate of Wharton port failures. Why not give Breamas the credit he seeks? Attribute *all* our portal failures to him and his rabble. I doubt that even our Council Governor could disprove the claim."

Racker grinned slowly, as scheming revelation brightened his handsome face. "He certainly could not disprove it easily if we could demonstrate a clear pattern of Wharton troubles to support the theory. It's unfortunate that the perpetrator of the explosion was killed." He mused, "We might still manufacture a convincing conspiracy. Effective incidents can be arranged without excessive cost. We certainly have no shortage of replacement workers for the mines."

Saschy did not mind making political use of Breamas' uncontrollable actions, but plotting independent terrorism in Breamas' name was a little too ruthlessly contrived for her. She tried to formulate an argument that would not weaken her standing with Racker. "You're hatching the sort of plot that could sink us faster than the portal mess, and we don't need to take that risk. By all accounts, Council Governor Caragen knows more about manufactured incidents that you and I have ever imagined. Breamas has already handed us enough real evidence to create suspicion of *him* and lift it from *us*. Don't tamper with the first good fortune that's come to us recently."

"Your gutter morality is showing," sneered Racker. "Caragen would not be so squeamish."

"You're not in that old shark's league."

"Not yet."

"Not ever, if you're careless. Governor Caragen is known for taking big risks that offer commensurate rewards, not for gambling just to exercise his ego."

Saschy felt the tension tugging at her neck and deliberately slowed the pace of her speech. "Let me have Network analyze Wharton's crime history. Maybe there's something we can use to justify even the early transfer problems."

As Saschy rose to leave, Racker gave her a look that was almost coy. He murmured, "I hope you remember that you've tied your future to mine, my dear. If I fail, I'll have to be satisfied with some minor diplomatic function on some pleasant little world outside the main power structures of Network. If you fail, you go back to the streets of Nilson, and I don't think you're very popular there."

Saschy felt tempted to call him a foul name from those same Nilson streets, but she restrained herself. She knew that he was right about the link of her ambitions to his success. She also suspected that he underestimated the extent of her unpopularity among her own people.

***

"My other assets seem incapable of confirming your assessment of the severity of the Nilson situation, Marrach. If you wish to persuade me to take action, present me with a coherent report. Your rural sabbatical has caused you to grow sloppy."

"Your other assets are incompetent."

"Then provide me with the proof of that premise, Marrach," hissed Caragen, and triumph seethed in his voice. "Investigate Nilson for me."

"I do not work for you, Caragen."

"Nilson appears to have claimed a recent victim who might cause you to reconsider."

"Nilson claims many victims."

"Network's correlation of sensor readings indicates a sixty-two percent probability that Dr. Jonathan Terry was the unfortunate victim of a recent terrorist attack on the Nilson main port building," finished Caragen succinctly. The length of the ensuing pause brought a faint smile to Caragen's aged lips, echoing the satisfaction that he had felt when Network informed him of the most likely identity of the victim.

"Alive or dead?" demanded Marrach succinctly.

"Alive, at first report, but that has presumably changed by now. He chose a bad place to endure hospitalization: nothing like your little world of Siatha. Critically injured patients rarely survive Nilson's tender facilities."

"Any Network city can provide advanced facilities for those who matter to *you*."

"So true, but Dr. Terry had no advocate at his side. I shall arrange for you to berate Racker personally, if you wish. He is not aware of Dr. Terry's unfortunate visit, but you may find Racker informative regarding the overall Nilson situation."

The delay preceding Marrach's answer delighted Caragen; it had been a long time since Caragen had been able to impact Marrach so deeply. Only Caragen, who had studied Marrach for so long, would have recognized the indicator of powerful, suppressed emotion. Marrach's actual reply sounded as coolly controlled as any words he had ever issued, "Racker is a fool."

"He is a survivor. As you know, I have always found that survivors make useful allies."

"Racker would not survive a day in a real conflict."

"We shall see. I intend to send a military team to assist him in eradicating these terrorists."

"What a convenient excuse to expand your control of Nilson."

"I am acting on your recommendation, Marrach, because I value your instincts. I assume that you maneuvered Dr. Terry into making his unfortunate visit."

"Dr. Terry has always made his own decisions."

"But you did not dissuade him—or educate him appropriately regarding the Nilson culture." Caragen clucked, as if chiding an unruly child. "I know that you maintained contact with him, either directly or via your troublesome Lord Quinzaine. Days after you warn me to investigate Nilson for topological instabilities, the foremost expert in the field of applied topology arrives on Nilson. What do you expect me to conclude?"

"I expect you to conclude that Dr. Terry perceived the same problem that I reported to you."

"Do not parade that specious innocence on my behalf, Marrach. I know you too well. Despite your Mirlai, you remain a manipulator at the core. Like me, you are never a bystander. That is why we are never victims. We catalyze events. We do not sit idly and observe them."

"I am adopting your custom of remaining at a safe distance."

"No," chuckled Caragen, "in that respect, you are not like me at all. You lack sufficient intellectual detachment to remain apart from the events you initiate."

"I have worked diligently to master the art."

"Nonsense. You are inherently incapable of abandoning this mission now, Marrach. You have already set too much in motion. You recognize the strategic significance of Nilson. You know how calamitous the loss of Nilson would be to all of Network, to our fragile relationship with the Consortium, and even to a marginally independent world such as your Siatha. That is why you came to me in the first place, Marrach." Caragen enunciated with careful relish, "You recognized your need of me. Despite your many demonstrations of ingratitude toward me, I have once again given you the resources that you require, simply because you made the request of me. I trust you to use my offering wisely."

"You have never trusted anyone in your life, Caragen. It is one of the few aspects of your judgment that I respect."

"I have always respected your *perspicacity,* Marrach. I have made the files containing my military plans for Nilson accessible to you. Notify me when you have annotated them." Caragen broke the connection.

Marrach ripped a handful of rich sod from his Siathan garden and hurled it across the yard. Jeni came to him and rested her head against his back, kneading his tense muscles. "Don't allow him to anger you," she whispered.

"I am not angry at him," he sighed, but there was

exasperation in the sound. "I am angry at the truth of what he says: I do need him. I cannot escape it, Jeni. I cannot deny what he created of me."

"Mirlai have healed you."

"And I must repay them—in keeping with the magnitude of their gift. That is proper, Jeni. That is what you taught me as my Healer."

"You cannot leave us, Suleifas."

He turned to hold her, and he whispered to her firebright hair, "I must perform the healing that is required of me, and I must perform it at the source of the bleeding. The Mirlai concur."

"The Mirlai weep with me, Rabh."

"I must see Nilson for myself. Jeni, I will not be gone long."

From the momentary blurring of her eyes, he knew that she stared at a vision he could not share. Without emotion, she said, "You will be without the Mirlai. They cannot accompany you. It was hard enough for them to stay near you in these past few days. But Nilson. . . ." Her voice trailed into a whisper. "It touches the Consortium, and they are exiled."

"I know."

"I will lose you."

"No, Jeni."

She touched a trembling finger to his lips. "I must go see the Cathlin child tonight. He is still feverish."

"I may be gone before you return."

"I am a healer, Rabh. I have my duty, as you have yours." She walked stiffly into the cottage.

"Jeni. . . ." She did not reply or pause. Marrach raised his eyes to the cloud-spattered sky. "I have no choice," he said softly. He brushed the traces of soil from his hands before following his wife into their home. He found her sorting through the healing stones and herbs. "I will come back to you, Jeni. Caragen will never control me again. Do not fear for me."

"Amelia left fresh cheese for us, and Donavon brought us herb bread."

He tried to reach and hold her, but she took her Healer's pack and fled from the cottage and from him.

**

The Mirlai woke Marrach early in the predawn hours, and so he was dressed and ready when Quin arrived. Quin offered none of his usual banter, limiting himself to the curt words, "I received your message, Marrach, though I am not sure how you managed to know which Network files I would be reviewing."

"It was not difficult to deduce your continued interest in Nilson."

"I suppose not," answered Quin, but his gray eyes remained unconvinced. Marrach's intimate knowledge of Network had seldom seemed more menacing. "I conveyed your request to Lady Rhianna, and she agreed to meet with you once more."

Though Marrach braced himself inwardly against the certainty of pain to come, he answered with calm, "I am ready."

Quin made the journey quick, but haste could not salve the wound of Healer's separation from Mirlai. Marrach blinked at the glowering, moss-riddled stone walls of the Infortiare's Tower, that faint motion being the only outward sign of his suffering. Without hesitation, he followed Quin through the wizard's illusion that made the garden entrance resemble solid stone. His pace at ascending the stairs made Quin hurry. Outside the Infortiare's office, Marrach gripped Quin's shoulder with one strong hand and said, "Let me enter alone." Though Power could have shrugged away the physical restraint, Quin nodded.

Even as Marrach opened the door to her office, Rhianna spoke abruptly from the depths of the room's most ragged armchair, "We have lost contact with Jon Terry." Her speech became more rapid, imparting a sense of suppressed nervous energy incongruous with the apparent calm of her posture and expression. "He insisted on traveling to the Network world of Nilson in order to evaluate the potential problems there. He has not returned. We have been unable to locate Dr. Terry—or the wizard who escorted him." For a moment, Rhianna closed her eyes, as if to seal away a hideous view. She had known too much loss to wear her grief more openly before a comparative stranger. "He always chose his own path," she murmured, "even when it seemed unwise." She added with grim vehemence, "Is this why you asked to see me?"

Marrach dragged a chair across the rug to face her, and he seated himself at apparent ease. "Dr. Terry's path *was* unwise, but that is not why I requested this meeting. He provided us both with some untested speculations, but his advice is no longer available to either of us. You and I had little opportunity to confer."

"Such discussion is acutely painful for us both."

Marrach did not acknowledge her observation; its accuracy was as inarguable as it was unresolvable. "I would like to know your own assessment of the Nilson difficulty."

"I have not observed it."

"Nor am I a topologist, but I am capable of forming opinions based on personal experience. You have more practical knowledge of the subject of topological phenomena than anyone else in accessible space."

Her laugh had a nervous edge. "How did you reach such an unlikely conclusion?"

"From Quin."

"Lord Quinzaine has exaggerated, I think."

"He is not innocent of that flaw, but this is a conclusion that I have reached for myself. I have observed Quin enough to be impressed by *his* abilities, and you command him. He has told me that the Infortiare is selected on the basis of greatest Power."

"The greatest Power at the time of selection," amended Rhianna. "Like any other ruling member of Seriin nobility, the Infortiare's rank ends only with death. Quin, despite his lapses of responsibility, is exceptionally gifted. His Power may even exceed mine. We have never attempted a contest."

Marrach frowned briefly, assimilating her remark. "I had not understood that aspect of your society," he admitted, "but it does not affect my purpose. I am primarily seeking information, not Power, and I think that you may be able to communicate such ideas more clearly than Quin. I need a better understanding of the 'patterns' where your Power lets you travel."

Thoughtfully, she fingered the luminous stone of her pendant. "What do you seek to accomplish, Master Rabh?"

"I seek to maximize my understanding of Nilson. I am less rash than Dr. Terry. I do not make dangerous journeys without assessing all available alternatives first."

"Power can use the patterns of infinity, Master Rabh. It cannot change them."

"You shifted your own world in *time*."

Rhianna's golden head nodded, and a bitter smile twisted her lips. "That change, which my son enacted, was possible only because he is himself a fundamental part of the Taormin's pattern. In a real sense, the Taormin bred my son for the purpose of restoration. Have you ten thousand years to spare for such an exercise, Master Rabh? That was the length of time that the Taormin required, and its problem was much simpler than your own."

"Your 'Taormin' was Dr. Terry's invention, the original topological controller for Network-3. Impressive as its design may be, it remains an artificial device, optimized for a purpose other than restoration of spatial integrity."

"So I understand."

"And do you actually claim to understand the nature of *my* problem well enough to deny its solvability?"

"I deny that wizard's Power can resolve it."

"Kindly set aside your distrust of me long enough to *explain* my problem, Lady Rhianna, since you understand its nature so well."

"You claim the Nilson problem as your own," observed Rhianna, but Marrach did not reply. The glorious gray eyes appraised him with a deep sadness. "You will not find the answers that you seek from any words of mine," she sighed, but she continued, "From what Lord Quinzaine has conveyed to me, combined with my own experience, I suspect that the patterns of Nilson were weak by nature. Such patterns should never be exploited, as I think Dr. Terry told you in Network terms. These fragile Nilson patterns have been worn dangerously thin by extensive, injudicious usage over a short period of time. Because your people have confined the damage so far, they evidently believe that the damage does not exist. In fact, they have simply magnified the eventual catastrophe by prolonging its development."

"What does 'injudicious usage' mean in the context of a 'pattern' of space?"

"Dr. Terry gave you better explanation than I," she began with frustration, but she mastered herself quickly. "That is not an answer I can give except in Ixaxin terms, the idiom of a wizard's Power. To us, a pattern of infinity resembles a vast plane, strewn with a lacework of light. In our case, touching the wrong strand, tangling the paths or bridging incompatible filaments causes death of the individual long before the damage can approach the magnitude of Nilson's calamity. Using such patterns is not easy, even for a major Power." She sighed, "Explaining them to one who has no understanding of Power is virtually impossible."

"How would you advise this ignorant mortal to proceed?"

"I am not certain that the damage can be repaired. I *am* sure that every additional usage of those patterns— every spatial transfer, if I may presume to employ your Network terminology—increases the damage. All transfers involving Nilson should stop immediately."

"But that will not reverse existing damage."

"No. The weakness exists. It has progressed too far to restabilize itself. At best, you can defer the structural collapse."

"Could the weakened region be isolated, as Network-3 was isolated for so long?"

"Perhaps someone as knowledgeable as Dr. Terry could discern a method. I can tell you only that the situation is inherently different. This world, this 'Network-3,' occupies a very rich intersection of the infinite patterns, which is presumably why Dr. Terry selected Network-3 for his initial experiments with the topological transfer of living beings. The energies are potent here, and the infinities are defined cleanly. Our patterns are exceptionally strong. A *weakness* in patterns corresponds to a blurring of definitions, a deterioration of the strands of infinity into a jumble of disconnected points of light. It is difficult to separate a set of patterns that cannot be distinguished from its neighbors. Any error, any point broken from its proper mooring, would alter the reality of *all* infinities that intersect at Nilson. Profound, unpredictable changes in the 'natural' laws of the connected worlds could result."

"Did you deduce all of this from Quin's report to you?"

"No. I have other sources of data—and my own authorities to consult."

"I would like to meet *your* consultant."

"That would be . . . difficult. He no longer has a physical form."

"Nor do the Mirlai."

"Your Mirlai are far gentler than my Kaedric. Nor would you learn more from him than I have relayed to you." After a pause, she added in an anguished whisper, "Even if I were still able to reach him."

Marrach seemed on the verge of saying more, but instead replied simply, "I thank you, Lady Rhianna."

"I wish you well, Master Rabh. I am sorry that I can offer you little more than sympathy."

"Never undervalue information, Lady Rhianna."

"If it is of use to you, I am glad." She paused. "However, I demand a price for it. Katerin Terry is here."

Marrach narrowed his eyes in startlement. "She would not wish to see me. I can give her no comfort."

"I think *she* can help *you,* Master Rabh, in that undertaking which you will soon attempt. She is better equipped to help you now than I." She arose gracefully and glided to the broad, iron-girded door. She pulled it open with a touch. "Lady Katerin, I am sorry to have kept you waiting." A frightened servant scurried toward the stairs. Katerin blanched on seeing Marrach, wishing she could follow the servant's example. Marrach's expression was equally uncomfortable.

"Lady Rhianna," protested Marrach in a tense voice of displeasure, "you do an unkindness toward this lady, who has already suffered much because of me."

"I am not attempting kindness, Healer," replied Rhianna crisply. She seemed to grow tall as she glared at him in the fire of her Power. "You remarked upon my distrust of you, and I must confirm your observation. How not? You distrust yourself. That situation does not mitigate my frail hope that you are honest in your concerns and sincere in your intentions."

With a sardonic grimness, Marrach urged, "Do speak your mind plainly, Lady Rhianna."

"You approach an ordeal that will threaten your very sanity. I am attempting to heal an existing wound before it festers when you can least afford such weakening. It is the only real help that I can offer you. You *must* succeed." With that final, curt remark, she swirled away from the two Network refugees and disappeared up the winding stair to the private room at the Tower's pinnacle.

"I did not want to see you," said Katerin, her golden head proud, "but Lady Rhianna is difficult to refuse."

Marrach sighed and faced the woman whom he had long victimized under Caragen's orders. In pale blue Seriin silk and lace, she looked little like a Network professor of mathematical psychology, but her cold gaze condemned him equally. "A complete healing of what I have done to you in the past is beyond my capability, even if we were now on Siatha. I have already done for you as much as I could manage in that regard. Even if I believed I could accomplish more, this would not be the time that I would choose."

"*My* healing is not currently of concern to Lady Rhianna." Katerin paced nervously to the windows, avoiding Marrach's eyes. "Since my father failed to return from Nilson, Lady Rhianna has become more remote and uncommunicative than I have ever seen her. Her mood relates, I think, less to my father than to her mysterious Kaedric, whose nature has never been explained to me adequately. She just told me about my father's disappearance a little while ago, when she summoned me here and said that my forgiveness will improve your small chance of success." Katerin continued with a shrug, "She gave me no explanations. She did not ask me if I *could* forgive you. She simply informed me that it was necessary. Quin would tell me no more." Her voice drooped in bitterness. "Quin does not contradict his Infortiare in such matters."

"My chance of success in what?" asked Marrach slowly, disquieted by the thought of being discovered in his barely formulated plans by a woman he had scarcely met.

"She did not tell me. Your speculations are undoubtedly better informed than mine."

"You resent being here."

"Of course. I have been manipulated for most of my life—by you or by the Council Governor. I am no happier to be used by the Infortiare of Serii."

"What did you expect when you married her servant?" asked Marrach with a trace of impatience. He was not fond of the Infortiare's manipulations either, chiefly because he had not anticipated them and still did not understand them.

"Does your wife feel any affection for *your* master?"

"I no longer serve Caragen."

"No one escapes Andrew Caragen. My father tried, but he has lost in the end." Katerin said raggedly, "I don't know how to tell my mother."

The pain of being apart from the Mirlai blurred with the pain of admission, "Caragen believes that your father is dead."

"Caragen told you that?" demanded Katerin in a trembling voice. She sagged against the bookcase that lined the office wall. "Where is my father? When did you speak to Caragen?"

"According to Network, your father was critically injured and taken to a hospital on Nilson. At best, that places him in Caragen's control. Alive or dead, your father is now inaccessible to you. Caragen contacted me a few hours ago—last night, by my home's reckoning. He enjoys teasing me with such data bits, especially data that can make me feel helpless." Marrach pressed his left hand against the side of his head, beneath which lay the mechanisms of a Network interface. "I do understand your resentment of being manipulated, Katerin."

Pain filled her brusque laugh. "I believe you're telling me the truth, for once."

"I am no longer your enemy. Quin understands. Don't you trust his judgment?"

"Sometimes. Not always. We do not think alike. We have very different perspectives."

"It must be difficult to relate to a wizard," said Marrach dryly.

Katerin snapped, "It is easier than relating to you. Even if Lady Rhianna commanded me with flames of Power, I'm not sure that I could forgive you." Katerin folded her hands and stared at the protruding bones. "But I did stop hating you some time ago. Maybe that helps. I don't know. It's the best I can offer."

Marrach nodded slowly, considering the thin, nervous woman in her overwhelming Seriin silk. Quin opened the door with a lazy flourish. "If you're ready, Marrach, I'll take you back to Siatha."

"Eavesdropping is a nasty habit," murmured Marrach evenly, but he joined Quin without hesitation.

***

Quin regarded Marrach with brows creased in worry that seemed misplaced on a face designed for mischief. "Is it better to wait a few minutes or to make the transfer now, when you are in such pain? The journey is not without difficulty, even as a passenger in my company."

"The pain is not a passing phenomenon. Let us go now."

With a rapid nod, Quin led him into the patterns of infinity. Quin did not stray amid his own favorite routes but followed the most secure paths, the most stable of the patterns that he had originally learned within the Taormin's spatial connections. Quin sensed a disturbing weakness in Marrach, less as an overall condition than as a single point of fragility that might easily destroy the whole. Though Marrach seemed to have achieved better control of his physical conflicts, there was a deeper level, troubling only to Quin's Power, where Marrach seemed to be faring much worse than on the last journey.

Quin felt his suspicion confirmed on reaching Siatha, because Evjenial was waiting for them with an expression that verged on panic. A light rain was falling, but she stood in the garden, very near to where they had left her. The shawl that covered her head was soaked.

She did not greet Quin but went directly to Marrach and touched him with a healing stone. "Not even you can survive a sustained separation, Rabh," she chided in a voice that attempted to sound brave. Marrach shook his head at her, but he did not clarify his meaning as concurrence or denial.

"Can I help?" offered Quin, though he doubted that he could contribute more than any mortal. Like most major Powers, he had difficulty managing such delicate work as healing. The Mirlai's healing methods had a precision and knowing design that far surpassed any wizard's coarse application of raw Power. Not even Lady Rhianna, who had a rare talent for Power's empathic aspects, could match the Mirlai's effectivity.

"Thank you," answered Jeni, never taking her eyes from Marrach, "but this is not for you to do, Lord Quinzaine."

"I think that your Infortiare has greater need of your talents at present," added Marrach. "For a woman of such power, she is uncommonly desperate, or she would not seek help from me."

"The meeting occurred at your request."

"So I thought when we left here."

Still troubled by Marrach's precarious state, Quin acknowledged, "I truly do not know what she expects of you, Marrach, but Lady Rhianna does not inflict pain willingly."

"You know, as usual, much more than you admit." Marrach turned his deep gaze on Quin and continued with exacting insight, "No, Lord Quinzaine, I shall not demand explanations that might conflict with your loyalty to your Infortiare. I do not need to hear the reasons. The pain runs deep when the stars bleed. Your Infortiare understands the reasons for sacrifices in such a cause, as I do—as perhaps you will." Above him, the Mirlai blazed with the brilliance of fey glory.

CHAPTER 22

Destroyers

"The switch be right there," snapped Deliaja, impatient with Keever's fumbling. She pushed past him imperiously. He had helped ably with the entry to this secure room; he had breached the locking mechanism with all the speed that she had hoped; but he had balked upon facing the simple remaining step that would turn off Wharton's primary power source.

Deliaja did not share his hesitation at the prospect of dangers implicit in the deactivation of Network's control of Wharton. She had talked to men who had worked on the dome. Wharton's natural temperature was well within human tolerance. The workers who had established Wharton had survived these caverns without Network for almost a year, and they had not worn environment suits after infusing the dome with breathable air. Even with the current population of the mines, there was air enough in the circulators to last for a month or more, which would be more than enough time to take control of Wharton—and Nilson. There were batteries enough to power the emergency lights and mining helmets for at least a year.

"Be you sure about this, Dee?" asked Keever, glancing around them guiltily at the utility control room. His attention barely skimmed the contorted bodies of the port boys that he and Deliaja had killed with beamer fire. Keever had never learned to respect life enough to regret the stealing of it, but he did fear Network and the repercussions of crimes against Network control. Keever was not a rebel born from ideals, like some of Breamas' followers, or from anger, like Deliaja. Keever was simply a practical, selfish man who saw more potential for personal gain in revolution than in the Nilson brand of peace. He had not quite understood, however, the magnitude of Deliaja's daring. He had not anticipated the acceleration of events in the aftermath of Vin's death.

The tempers in the mines had been seething since Deliaja claimed the leadership that had belonged to Vin. A shared awareness of impending change, even among those who remained outside the rebel ranks, had reduced mine production nearly to zero. More brawls than usual had ended in fatalities. There was not a man or woman left in Wharton who risked making public praise of Network. As soon as the news reached the Windmill that two dozen port boys had arrived from Nilson, Deliaja had closed the canteen and informed Keever that she needed his help in bypassing a security system. Until they arrived here, he had not realized that she planned to attack Wharton's primary electrical center.

"I be very sure," growled Deliaja, struggling with the panel's heavy switch bars, "that it be only another portal failure that be preventing more port boys from arriving to beat us back into obedience to Network. We be able to handle these few, but we be needing to make a stop to the port boys' free coming and going. If we be waiting any longer, port boys be coming by the hundreds. It be time, Keever, that we be taking Wharton." The switch bar sparked as she broke its link.

"Violation!" shrieked Network. Keever burned out the speaker with a quick burst from his stunner.

"Be not wasting beam energy!" scolded Deliaja.

The clear white lights still blazed from silver walls, and the air still rushed from the vents. "Nothing be changed," muttered Keever, nervously awaiting some lethal outpouring of Network vengeance for the attempted sabotage. He had little real experience of Network power, but he knew rumors of killing gasses and well-armed enemies that appeared without warning, avenging the merest whisper of treachery in the night. "It be not working, Dee. May be, we be still able to sneak back out of here unseen."

"There be no more time for pretending," she answered. "We be known to Network now." Like Keever, she stared with hard eyes at the lights and at the clock on the wall, clicking away the seconds.

"They be late at shutting down the backup."

"Yah," she agreed. "May be Rimman less quick than you at opening locks." She spoke with calm assurance, but her foot drummed the floor nervously.

For over a minute the two of them stood in silence, waiting. "There be no more for us to do here. We be needing to go, Dee," said Keever. "Something be gone wrong with your plan."

"Not yet." As she spoke, the lights were extinguished, and Deliaja laughed aloud. She tapped her borrowed miner's helmet to bring a personal light to shine upon her triumph. "Wharton be ours, Keever," she proclaimed. A barrage of sirens howled until Deliaja smashed the panel that controlled them.

She hurried now to leave the control room. With the deactivation of the utilities, stifling darkness had reclaimed the Wharton caverns, but Deliaja had prepared a myriad of rebel cell captains for this moment. The beams from their helmets bounced through the corridors. The failure of normal Network sensors meant that many doors refused to open and lifts refused to move, but Deliaja had prepared her troops for these inconveniences as well. The ladders in the utility shafts did not depend on Network power, and the access doors to the shafts had been breached and strategically broken in advance.

When Deliaja and Keever had climbed back to the commercial level, where the Windmill was located, they could hear the shouts and smashing of display cases. The looting, signaled by Deliaja's agents, had begun immediately following the blackout and was already well advanced. Deliaja had no interest in curtailing the chaos. Let ignorant cavers tire themselves with the pleasures of their stealing. They stole only from Network coffers. They would be glad enough to acknowledge their new leaders who had provided them with such bounty.

Captivated by the excitement, Keever darted away to join a throng that fought viciously over a mound of useless trinkets. Deliaja let him go. She had no more need for him at present, and she trusted him to survive capably despite his physical limitations.

She moved warily to avoid trampling by the racing crowds. The cavers were too consumed by their greedy amassing of treasures to try to waylay her deliberately. She met Cullen by prearrangement in the Windmill's kitchen, already emptied of any liquors or other valuables. He sat on a tilted stool that he had dragged from the front room. Broken glass littered the floor, and the air reeked of mingled ales and fouler liquids. "Be you proud, Dee?" he asked her quietly. He had argued against this course of action, but he had abetted Deliaja's scheme when the rebel fervor had aligned itself definitively with her.

"Yah. I be proud. Be you not?" She stripped a table of its pottery shards and perched on the bared expanse of stone. "Be you able to hold the rule here while I be gone?"

"Yah." Cullen kicked an empty bottle across the floor. The glass cylinder rolled to a stop against a metal bowl. "I be better able than you to run a city. I be less good than you only at destruction."

"Be not getting ideas of permanence, Cullen. This be Breamas' victory. After we be taking Nilson, he be making the long choices for Wharton and Nilson both."

"Yah," agreed Cullen dryly, "it be all for Breamas. It be nothing for Dee and her hates of Ned Racker."

Deliaja raised her chin stiffly, but she had more needful ways to channel her anger than fighting Cullen. "I be taking the cargo portal way back to Nilson . . ."

". . . if that portal be functioning any better than the others," injected Cullen.

"I be trusting you to see that no other word of Wharton's change of command be getting back to Nilson yet."

"We be counting eighteen of the port boys dead. We be finding the other six soon enough, if they be lasting intact that long. Port boys be not prepared to survive in

Wharton's deep places. Ghost lights be taking them, most likely."

"Be not taking too much for granted," warned Deliaja.

"Why not? You be taking for granted that ghost lights be staying deep, even now when there be no Network alarms to be warning them off of us."

"Network be nothing to ghost lights."

"We be not knowing that."

Deliaja pushed herself away from the granite table with impatient energy. "You be better at organizing than inspiring, Cullen. Be not losing what we be finally winning."

"Your *trusted* friend, Arlan Willowan, be looking for you minutes ago. I be letting him go, because that be your order, but I be not liking him or his talk. May be him taking word of Wharton change already to Saschy Firl."

"Be he going to the portals?" demanded Deliaja, concern and doubt twisting through her. She had not been able to justify, even to herself, her hurt reaction when Arlan responded to her on Nilson. She had moved deliberately to arouse him, tantalized by the strength he had displayed in confronting Breamas, but her easy success had left her feeling deeply betrayed. On a personal level, she was glad to have missed Arlan's visit, but she did not like the idea of anyone of Arlan's independence taking word of Wharton to Nilson just now.

"Cargo portal, I be thinking. Like you. He be a senior retriever, and retrievers like him be having cargo travel keys."

"Upper levels be ours."

"Deep places be having the largest cargo portal. May be you reaching it ahead of Arlan, if you be hurrying. He be not so fond of the dark." Cullen smirked as Deliaja cursed and hurried from the ruined canteen.

CHAPTER 23

Outcasts

The gray prison stank of rot and moldy plaster. The human guards who supplemented Network's automated systems were few, and they moved and spoke with a vague lethargy that Jase had identified as a product of intoxication. Network's guiding voice, efficient but cold, did not impress Tori any more favorably. Worst of all, however, was Filcher himself.

Tori tried to remember ever meeting a less likable being than Filcher Ikthan Cuui, and she could conjure no closer comparison than her late husband in the last angry days of his brief life. In Tori's view, even her mother's patron had more redeeming qualities: Uncle Per could at least conduct a civil conversation. Filcher was the type of man who ought never to be allowed near a society like Network, because he could only re-inforce Network's irrational prejudices. Knowing how deeply the more civilized Cuui valued their hive connections, Tori could hardly imagine how even an ignorant Network governor could mistake the insolent loner, Filcher, for a Consortium member.

"Filcher," she repeated to the sullen huddle of jutting bones and blue-white skin, "we are trying to help you."

Translucent lids fluttered rapidly across Filcher's pink-tinged eyes, a sign of deception clear enough for Tori to interpret without consulting Jase and his acute perceptions. "I never stole anything," moaned Filcher for the fifth time. His long toes clung with frantic strength to the frame of his cot.

"I know," said Tori, struggling not to snap at the

whining wretch. "You've told us: You're innocent. So, please, tell us what actually occurred."

"The crate wasn't mine. I didn't steal anything."

Frustrated, she glanced at Jase, who had devoted himself to silent observation in the comprehensive sense that only a Sesserda adept could fully appreciate. The cell's poor light made a shadowy blur of Jase's dark skin and clothing, conveying the disquieting impression that those intense, camouflaged eyes of his stared from some bodiless dimension. "Can you do anything with him?" she asked of Jase, conceding her own defeat. She had tried to spare Filcher, and she would have persisted longer if Filcher had seemed more worthy of her pity. Having experienced the soul-stripping rigors of formal Sesserda Inquisition, Tori hated to inflict a similar process on anyone. She knew that Jase could fulfill his inquisitorial duty to discover Truth as relentlessly and as coldly as any Calongi.

Jase strolled from his position against the gray cell wall to perch gingerly on the cot's edge in front of Filcher. Avoiding direct contact with the filthy bed-clothes, Jase kept his hands elevated to shoulder level, poised as if in strange benediction. Though slightly built for a Soli man, Jase seemed to overwhelm the wire-thin Cuui by physical size as well as intangible, unmistakable Sesserda confidence. Filcher huddled more tightly into himself, glaring suspiciously at Jase's unsettled hands. In a cajoling tone, Jase asked, "Why did you claim Consortium membership? You knew your lie could only make matters worse for you."

Filcher reacted visibly to the artful carelessness of Jase's question. A gleam of cunning restored a hint of life to the Cuui's pallid face. "Not worse," wheezed Filcher, his breathing passages tightening in reflex to his revelation. "Not when you read Truth in what I say." Tori wondered if the Cuui had actually identified Jase as a Sesserda practitioner or was merely attempting to curry favor by wielding flattery. Unless Filcher was improbably well-informed, the Cuui could have no idea of the extent of Jase's relanine-granted skills.

Jase did not deny Filcher's inference of Consortium

Truth-seeking. "You might prefer Network's concept of justice to mine," answered Jase obliquely.

"All the universe knows the excellence of Consortium justice."

"You chose to live apart from that justice when you left your hive, didn't you?"

"I had no choice about being here. I did nothing wrong."

"You chose to decline Consortium membership." Jase withheld any emotion of condemnation from the dry statement, but Filcher's breathing became more ragged. The Cuui knew well enough that he had sacrificed the privileges of Sesserda justice by refusing to live by Sesserda Truth. With an ironic half-smile that struck Tori as chillingly contrived, Jase continued, "You are a fortunate man, Ikthan Cuui. You have a rare opportunity to choose again, knowing something of the outcome. Which judgment do you wish? Network's or mine?"

Tori would not have believed it possible that the Cuui could coil further into himself, but the Cuui anatomy had evolved many defenses for crowded hive conditions. Though she could not determine what Jase had done to the Cuui, she was sure that he had enacted some Sesserda mystery to impress Filcher of the seriousness of the question. Filcher hissed at Jase, "What are you, Soli?"

"I think you know. Your hive mother succeeded in teaching you that much about Consortium justice, at least. It is unfortunate that you failed to comprehend her injunctions to respect creation."

Beads of moisture dripped from the cracked ceiling. One drop struck the cot's metal frame and rang sourly. Puzzlement and suspicion wrinkled Filcher's chin. "You are a Soli."

So, concluded Tori, *the sly Filcher tried to flatter and now is caught unaware by the same Truth.*

Jase responded with a cryptic smile, "Sesserda has many practitioners." Another bead of water seeped from the room above, and Jase flicked it midair against the wall with the uncanny speed and precision of

Sesserda training. Filcher's pink eyes squinted with a hint of new comprehension and respect. Tori amended her first impression of the Cuui: Filcher was untrustworthy, but he was not unintelligent.

Filcher uncurled fractionally, and the veins in his throat pulsed with the slow rhythm of incipient hope. "How would you judge me, when my poor neck will be broken three days from this?"

"I offer you an opportunity, Filcher, not a guarantee." Tori muttered, "I would judge him worthy of Network's verdict."

Filcher inspected her with slow deliberation, only to ask with doubt, "You are not like him?"

For an instant, Tori wished that she could respond with a lie to augment the Cuui's respect, but Jase would tolerate no deceptions of that nature. "I am not a Sesserda follower." She added dryly, "I am not much more civilized than you, Filcher." The Cuui's chin flexed slowly, almost producing a grin of camaraderie, as if he recognized her bout with temptation and the cause of her reluctant honesty.

"I would prefer to give you more time to make your choice, Filcher," said Jase with an austerity that commanded the return of the Cuui's attention, "but neither of us has that luxury."

The pink eyes rolled toward Jase, assessing and deciding with the rapidity of a desperate man of cunning. "I shall abide by your judgment, Sesserda follower, if you can make these uncivilized Network beings obey you likewise. I do not feel prepared to die so young. I have not even made the journey to strengthen my hive as yet." Filcher uncoiled himself completely and stretched his bony, tri-jointed limbs. "When my journey-time comes, I think I shall have fine stories with which to please the halaatu. How many other Cuui have survived a Network sentence of death?"

"You begin to anticipate on an ambitious scale," said Jase. "I have promised nothing."

"My dreams must seem most humble, honored master, to a Soli who aspired to learn the difficult ways of Sesserda." Filcher, mimicking his people's most groveling demeanor, made a fragmented bow to Jase, then duplicated the intricate motions in Tori's direction. "You see? I learn respect already."

Tori murmured, "Your grasp of Truth, however, remains weak."

"I have told only the truth about the incident that reduced me to this incarcerated state, honored ones," said Filcher with tremulous fervor, aimed blatantly at Jase. "The crate was not mine. It must have been placed among my shipments during my absence. Until the officers came to confiscate it, I thought it contained Lufan feathers and luck beads. I am an honest trader, dealing in trivial artifacts and curios."

Tori contradicted him bluntly, "You have been a smuggler and thief since before you left your hive, Filcher. Your hive mother gave us your early history. She is ashamed of you."

"My hive mother has been deceived by my envious brethren," argued Filcher, beginning to huddle once more.

"Why," interrupted Jase with a sharp look at Tori, "would anyone have replaced one of your crates with a load of armaments?"

"I do not know, honored master. I am a harmless trader."

"Where were you taking the crate?"

The pause was more eloquent than the answer, bespeaking the Cuui's lingering uncertainty of how much he dared to withhold from a man who practiced Sesserda but was not, after all, a Calongi. "To a shop on Three Crow Street, where I was expected. The honored master must know that a simple trader like me cannot leave the spaceport without filling a visit request and detailed schedule, countersigned by a Network citizen. My papers were in order."

"The arrest report indicates that you were found near a restricted area, several blocks away from your approved itinerary."

"I must have become lost, honored master. The good citizens of Nilson are reluctant to give directions to a stranger, such as myself. They are a frightened people, are they not?"

"They are a frightened people," agreed Jase.

Because she knew Jase in many moods, Tori could recognize the stillness that he wrapped around himself: a heightened alertness of perceptions. "Did you meet anyone that morning, before your arrest?" asked Tori, wishing she knew what had triggered Jase's reaction.

"No one," answered Filcher, "until the officers stopped me. There were few ships at the port, and morning is usually a quiet time in Nilson's great city."

"Whom did you intend to meet at Three Crow Street?" demanded Jase with piercing authority.

"A man of Network," replied Filcher evasively. "An old man."

"Name him," insisted Jase, employing an Ilanovi tonal command that made even Tori ache to answer.

Whisper-soft, the Cuui hissed, "Breamas." The name meant nothing to Tori, but the pulsing of Filcher's veins conveyed the Cuui's own dread.

For a long moment, Jase simply observed the nervous Cuui in silence. "Thank you, Filcher," said Jase abruptly. He rose to his feet. Tori raised a questioning brow, but Jase offered no explanation for terminating the difficult interview just as Filcher seemed to be growing informative. "We shall return tomorrow."

"With my pardon?" demanded Filcher, anxiety making his spindly bones crack.

Jase replied only with an enigmatic gesture of his limber hands. Lacking the Network authority to order the opening of the cell door, Jase pressed the buzzer that had been issued to him to summon the guard. Filcher grasped Jase's sleeve with a mute, clawing desperation. The Cuui's frantic renewal of doubt almost moved Tori to sympathize with the pitiful, petty criminal who had strayed into such large-scale trouble.

"You will prevent the execution?" pleaded Filcher.

The Network guard, a scarred and burly man as bleary-eyed as the rest of the prison workers, opened the iron door. Jase slipped free of Filcher effortlessly and obeyed the guard's curt command to exit. Tori despised Filcher's cowardly cringing, which could only aggravate Network prejudice, but she could not leave without offering him some crumb of reassurance. "Jase is very skilled at enacting justice," she told the Cuui. The pink eyes flickered in surprise at her small effort at kindness.

***

A line of broken rooftops cast a jagged shadow. Sewage fumes writhed in the swelling heat. The drab buildings and dirty, odorous streets of Nilson made Tori cringe inwardly. Realizing how easily she could have been born to such a place and life, she gave silent thanks that Great-grandmama Mirelle had taken the trouble to retain the family's Consortium membership, albeit on a marginal basis.

If the uncivilized surroundings troubled him, Jase did not display that fact. He responded equably to Tori's unspoken disgust, "This is not a part of Nilson that visitors generally see. If Nilson's officials were less complacent, they would be escorting us back to the spaceport via the same scrubbed tunnels that led us to the prison."

"They'd be escorting us under lock and key if you hadn't used your Sesserda tricks to discourage them. You can hardly fault the Nilson officials for being unprepared for *you*. Some Level 1 Consortium members have difficulty understanding how a Soli can practice Sesserda."

Jase murmured evenly, "Network has a penchant for monitoring its citizens at all times and in all places. It's a disturbing habit for those unaccustomed to it." With a grimace, he kicked an unidentifiable lump of rag and refuse out of his path. "Network demands some adjustment of one's cultural assumptions regarding privacy, as well as other basic aspects of living."

Jase's warning stirred an uncomfortable flurry of Tori's nerves. She forced a nonchalant shrug. "This neighborhood appears to be abandoned. We're nowhere near the restricted areas."

"That is approximately what Filcher said in his original statement to the Nilson officials."

"Filcher did not have you to navigate for him," answered Tori, refusing to let Jase bait her into feeling any greater sympathy for Filcher. She did, however, accept Jase's advice to speak more cautiously. "Did the name of Filcher's intended contact mean anything to you?"

"Possibly." Jase's fingers touched her back, as if in casual affection, but the rapid pattern of light pressure warned her more emphatically than any words. She did not pursue the subject of Filcher's contact further, though her curiosity had now escalated from mild to acute.

Tori tried to shift the conversation gracefully, "It's hard to imagine anyone in this neighborhood possessing the type of technology that Network protects with such zeal."

"Perhaps not," agreed Jase. With a fleeting smile, he approved her response to his unspoken suggestion. "Nilson's primitive status played a vital role in the original negotiations to establish an open port here, and the evidence suggests that the Nilson environment has not improved significantly." He tapped the stained paving with the toe of his boot. The soft sound echoed from a disquieting array of directions. "Sophisticated weapons seldom disperse so much blood."

"That grisly observation does nothing to improve my impression of this wretched world," answered Tori, avoiding the stains with new revulsion. She glanced around her, wondering uneasily if echoes could account for all of the footfall sounds.

"I would not make such an ungenerous remark to the local residents. Parochial societies tend to dislike external criticism." With a touch, Jase guided Tori away from a slab of cracked paving. "Unless we move and speak with extreme care, we could receive a nasty introduction to the native weapons of choice."

"You are becoming increasingly grim company."

Jase shrugged with slow deliberation, bespeaking his unwillingness to voice the myriad reasons for his behavior. Aloud, he gave a light, ironic answer, "We could explore the neighborhood and find you an alternative escort."

"I'll think about it," replied Tori dryly, but she reexamined the stolid buildings with a dread of detecting any sign of life. "I haven't seen anyone since we left the prison."

"Much of this area *does* seem to be abandoned, but I'd guess that these streets become more active at night. I've heard some snoring in support of that assumption." With an incongruous grin, Jase added, "Skulduggery thrives on darkness."

"You have a bizarre sense of humor, Jase."

His laughter, unaffected by the lethal potential of Nilson's streets, confirmed Tori's remark, though the continued vigilance of his motions belied his level of amusement. "Don't you find humor in the consistency of petty foibles?" he asked her, waving eloquent hands toward an abandoned storefront, streaked with the garish paints of territorial conflict. "The same individuals who pride themselves on their species' uniqueness share one of the most predictable behavioral profiles in the universe. The childhood of a species, when civilization is little more than a superficiality adopted for survival, proves our commonality more surely than a Patisi's most rigorous theorem. Garbed in another body, Filcher Ikthan Cuui would be indistinguishable from a citizen of Nilson."

"That is a politely phrased insult to Nilson."

"The woeful Filcher did not impress you favorably?" asked Jase.

"He reminds me of my late husband." Jase quirked one dark brow in surprise, and Tori confessed with uncivilized bitterness, "They both have the ability to activate my sympathies against my own better judgment."

"Poor Tori," clucked Jase, "fanatically merciful despite all her efforts to become heartless."

"Sarcasm does not become a Sesserda adherent."

"You malign me unjustly, as usual. How can you accuse me of sarcasm? I simply observe a fact, which I trust you will not try to blame on my influence. These quixotic tendencies of yours patently existed before you and I ever met. I would have done everything in my power to discourage you from marrying the regrettable Mister Conaty."

"For my sake or his?"

"For the sake of all concerned." Without fuss or haste, Jase took hold of Tori's wrist and guided her across the street. The steady pressure of his fingers conveyed a warning more severe than its recent predecessors.

"Not all of the natives are sleeping?" asked Tori uneasily.

"Not all," agreed Jase tersely. He had spread his attention like a sensor net. He accelerated their pace.

Tori heard the rattling but could not locate the source among the cold-faced buildings and barren alleyways. "Where?" she whispered.

"The sewers," he replied in a voice as soft as wind. "Avoid the grates."

Jase pursued an erratic path, dodging attacks that Tori could not see. The streets became narrower, crossed by alleys filled with trash and rubble. "Isn't there a better route?" she asked.

"I couldn't find one in the visimaps. The government district seems to be defended by a sort of concrete moat composed of collapsing infrastructure, thoroughly infested with Nilson's hungriest reptiles."

"Are we visiting a site of Network government or a castle under siege?"

"Maybe both."

"The Governor must not receive many visitors."

"Not many from the spaceport. Network visitors can bypass this neighborhood and arrive directly via transfer portal at the edge of the government district—a convenience that we are not eligible to share."

"They actually travel that way," mused Tori, not sure if she believed the Network claims about their civilization's teleportation capabilities.

"They actually travel that way," agreed Jase, his mouth thinning to a disapproving line.

Tori had no opportunity to question his reasons for

disapproval. Jase jerked her abruptly behind a mound of broken concrete, just as a tracery of fire crackled across the paving. He pointed toward the merest shadow of a passage between two begrimed and sagging buildings. "Shout my name if you see any movement in the alleyway." He collected several handfuls of the smaller concrete fragments, filling his pockets, then stepped back into the street. Two beams of fire sought him immediately from gutter openings, but he leaped away from them with a Sesserda adept's uncanny agility. He threw his gathered bits of concrete toward the sources of the beams, his carefully focused energy giving lethal force to the small projectiles. One beam stopped. The second darted wildly, then recovered its aim. Jase rolled away from it, but his sleeve was singed. His second torrent of stones rattled into the sewers, followed by the thud of a body striking hollow pipes.

Tori had gathered a few of the broken fragments for herself, though she knew she could not match Jase's skill in using them. When she saw the glint of reflected light in the alleyway, she called her warning, "Jase," and flung her own pellets high against the wall behind her. As she had hoped, her stones drew the first of the alleyway fire. That instant of distraction sufficed for Jase's stone to strike the attacker, eliciting a cry of angry pain. The uneven pounding of injured footsteps retreated rapidly.

Jase rolled to his feet and summoned Tori with a nod. She joined him in silence. He moved forward at a pace that she could barely match, but she felt no inclination to complain. She might protest Jase's occasional displays of a Calongi-like arrogance under ordinary circumstances, but she respected his Sesserda judgment utterly in a crisis.

When Jase resumed a normal walk after several frantic blocks, Tori asked breathlessly, "How much farther is the Governor's palace?"

"We should be able to see it in a moment." He pointed when a gilded dome peered through the fire-ravaged shell of a house. "That's it."

They turned a corner and gained a clear view of the imposing palace complex, duly named and singularly contrasted with its surrounding poverty. "Network Governors live well," remarked Tori, strengthening her predisposition to dislike Governor Ned Racker. Every building in the governmental plaza was a marble mansion as remarkable for its grandeur as the rest of the city was for its wretchedness. For the first time, she saw other Nilson pedestrians walking and conversing openly, as if in any ordinary city, but the tattered natives were easily distinguished from the aloof government officials.

"They live far less well than your mother's patron, Per Walis, whose life purpose is not much nobler than that of the thugs who just tried to rob us. Your Uncle Per lacks even the excuse of desperation."

"Don't be snide," she scolded, but she knew the truth of what Jase said and his pointed reasons for saying it. Eternally the Sesserda scholar, Jase could not help but point out Tori's hypocrisy in condemning the Network governor. In all likelihood, Uncle Per would soon lose his Consortium membership on the basis of his uncivilized behavior and his smug confidence that his wealth could eliminate the pain of social ostracism. If Tori had remained at Uncle Per's estate, as once she had contemplated, she would probably have shared his fate. Unlike Uncle Per, Tori had learned to value her small place in the Consortium before it slipped away from her. Nilson made her all the more appreciative. "You're not intending to walk back through this charming neighborhood at night, are you?"

"I don't plan to return to the spaceport at all until Filcher Ikthan Cuui is released into our custody."

"Do you actually have a plan?" demanded Tori dubiously, as the blackened, cracked paving beneath their feet gave way to the polished marble of the government plaza.

"You haven't been paying attention, Tori," answered Jase with a wry smile that made her want to throttle him.

She would have retorted regarding his irritating

Calongi habits, but acute awareness of Nilson dangers kept her silent on the subject. "I hope no one else is paying attention either," she replied sweetly, eradicating Jase's smile, "or Filcher may have company in his misery."

"You can be cruelly pragmatic, dear Tori."

CHAPTER 24

Warriors

"You have to admit that the old shark has nerve," muttered Saschy, hurling the arrival manifest across her office. The lightweight data film drifted reluctantly to the tiled floor. "A squadron of police reinforcements, indeed. Since when did the Council Governor send a Network squadron to handle a minor portal attack by local malcontents. Network, has Racker been informed of this squadron's arrival?"

"The Governor has not accepted any official memos this morning."

"Connect me to him."

"Governor Racker has asked not to be disturbed."

Saschy rolled her eyes and tried to master her temper. "Has contact with Wharton been restored yet?"

"No."

***

The soldier with the white-streaked beard shaded his eyes against the smoky sun of Nilson and wondered if anyone ever came to the wretched planet by choice. "It's none too lovely, even without a revolution," observed his companion, a sun-beaten man with deeply set eyes and a profile as jagged as the Nilson skyline. He was new to the squadron. He wore the unmarked uniform of an enlisted man who had earned no rights of rank, but he was too obviously weathered to be a raw, young recruit. "And it only gets worse on closer acquaintance."

"You've been here before?" asked Rust.

"Once."

"Which squad?"

"None. I worked port security for a while, as a free agent."

"Why did you enlist?"

"Debts," shrugged the weathered soldier.

Rust nodded with sympathy. He had joined at a much younger age, but his reason had been the same. "Being here before—is that why you were assigned to us for this mission?"

Another shrug accompanied the sardonic answer, "Would I know?"

Rust began to like the squadron's newest member. Since the disbanding of the bearded soldier's former unit after the failed raid at Geisen University, Rust had made few friends. Surrounded by the inexperienced youths who largely comprised his current squadron, Rust had begun to feel the discouraging effects of age and cynicism. He welcomed the presence of the former mercenary.

"Did you have much trouble with terrorists when you were here before?" asked Rust.

"Some. There's an old man named Breamas who stirs the natives every few years." The last of the squadron emerged from transfer, and the weathered soldier asked quietly, "Did you feel anything strange during the transfer here?"

"Transfer always feels strange to me. I'd rather face an army of terrorists than a portal with a ruined light curtain."

"You've done that—transferred without sensory protection?"

"I've done it, but I wouldn't do it again unless a terrorist's beamer were hard against my back. Last time, my stomach didn't forgive me for a week." The two men followed their squadron, picking a rough path through the broken structure that had been the north side of the main port building. Only the area immediately surrounding the two functioning portals had been cleared. "Did you have some transfer problem on coming here?" asked Rust.

"Just a funny sort of *unsettled* sense. Transfer doesn't usually bother me that way."

"You're lucky. I'd start worrying if transfer *didn't* make me queasy." Rust nodded toward the local guards, fulfilling the function of the inoperative Network barrier in protecting the port from illegal use. "Do you know any of the locals?"

"I doubt there's anyone who'd remember me, and I wouldn't want to offer them any reminders. Locals either *become* port boys or hate them. Local port boys hate off-planet types like me. Nearly everyone on Nilson hates anyone from anywhere else. They hate us as much as they hate the alien traders who stop at the spaceport. Some of them hate us more. Any street urchin would kill us for a slab of butter. Breamas' fanatics would kill anybody just for the glory of it."

"Nice little world."

"Not very, but it is an interesting place—in its own miserable way."

"I wouldn't mind seeing an alien."

"Not many aliens wangle passes to leave the spaceport these days, not since the public transfer port was expanded."

"From the look of this mess, the port should have been protected from the natives, too."

The commander, a recently promoted captain who was insecure in his position, barked his orders with pompous zeal. Rust grunted, but he dutifully joined the other men assigned to the unpleasant job of port cleanup. The weathered soldier, himself ordered to participate in the captain's roving patrol, offered a consoling word in parting, "Save me a dinner ration."

"Save me a terrorist," retorted Rust. The weathered soldier grinned and raised his thumb.

***

Marrach watched the earnest young captain with pity. In keeping with the uncertainty of the Nilson situation, Caragen had assembled a squadron of expendable assets. Among them, Marrach had identified only one

man, the soldier known as Rust, who seemed qualified
to carry out a mission of any consequence, and that soldier's uniform bore the single stripe of the lowest enlisted rank. Marrach wondered idly what unwitting
offense that bearded soldier had enacted against Andrew Caragen; then a long abandoned instinct re-
asserted itself and converted idle curiosity into a
Network query.

Privileged files yielded rapidly, providing Caragen's
implicit praise of Marrach's decision to make the
query. The logs of a disbanded squadron and a failed
Geisen raid rushed directly into Marrach's brain. The
soldier known as Rust had experienced Quin Hamley's
Power, had actually seen Quin, and had survived the
encounter without the usual result of panic or intemperate tale-telling. Rust's behavior, reported by his late
commander, had gained Caragen's attention and approval, which could be nearly as dangerous as provoking Caragen's displeasure. Few of Caragen's interests
lived long; no one had ever matched Marrach's talent
for survival. Marrach absorbed the data with thoughtful
interest, but cognizance of Caragen's perpetual machinations grated.

A clump of black goo hurtled from one of the alleyways and splattered the captain's gray uniform. The
captain shouted at Marrach and at two other unranked
men to chase the perpetrator. Marrach ensured that the
other two men preceded him into the alleyway. After
running a few blocks in their general company, he
deliberately turned into a different path from the other
two soldiers. Out of the sight of the captain and the
rest of the squadron, Marrach stopped to evaluate his
surroundings.

The pain of separation from Siatha had not eased,
but the discipline of ignoring that pain had become easier on this, the fourth day of masquerade. The transfer,
which Marrach had described as unsettling to Rust, had
effected a catharsis. One agonizing instant of that
transfer, which had vanquished Marrach's last doubts
about the accuracy of Quin's observations, had reminded Marrach of the profound extent of his own

ability to tolerate chronic pain. He had forgotten, because the mind could not hold such memories clearly. Gandry had bred him from casualty stock, and the nervous systems of such creatures lacked some defensive forms of sensitivity.

Marrach glanced around him at the rubble, trash, and filthy pavings that typified the Nilson streets. For a short time, he had lived in these streets to abet Caragen's plottings. He had hidden in the sewers among the Nilson thieves and starvelings. He had lived with them, stolen with them, and killed with them. The memory sickened the Healer awareness inside of him, but it was only one more element of the overriding pain.

Marrach heard a scurrying from the sewer grate and moved instinctively out of its view. An insulted young captain was awaiting his men, expecting them to capture a local ruffian with better aim than manners. There was no reason to attribute any significance to the incident, but Marrach knew a good deal about the methods of the Nilson street gangs. Ruffians did not idly roam the streets in daylight, searching for shiny Network captains to insult. A distraction to draw part of the patrol into a twisting alley, accompanied by movement in the sewers at an hour near to evening, meant deliberate trouble. The inexperienced officer, so incensed by a mere clot of sewage, would overreact predictably.

Marrach headed back to the main part of the patrol with a caution that he had not exerted earlier. He darted from shadow to doorway to sheltering rubble, constantly alert to menaces from sewer or roof. He heard the shouts and clattering of conflict, but he did not hurry to embroil himself. Self-interest was a mandatory aspect of his purpose in coming here. An untried captain did not merit sacrifice of the larger goal. A part of Marrach that ached for Siatha grieved.

Cries in Nilson's stilted dialect wailed through the pocked streets, the vicious and angry insults met by whining beamer fire. Network voices were more terse but just as bitter. Marrach circled the field of petty war, a battleground no less vicious than its larger kindred. He climbed a ladder of tumbled stone to reach a convenient rooftop. He snatched his fingers away from a ledge, just escaping a blade that sought him from the crack of a dirty window. He tore old plasterwork from its setting and hurled it through the glass. Seeing only one figure moving inside the dim room, he kicked the remaining glass out of his way and leaped on his assailant. Marrach had confiscated the knife and sliced its owner's throat before the man could react.

Marrach dropped the limp body of a brown-haired, ruggedly built youth, sickened by the ease with which old training returned to him. He scanned the room quickly, then crept into the hallway, watching and listening for other occupants. He found a window that looked down upon the present battlefield, and he scraped away a layer of grime to give him better visibility.

The guerilla tactics of the Nilson gang had claimed at least three of the soldiers. The better equipped Network soldiers had killed half a dozen Nilsonites. Beamer fire had set the gutters smoldering. Marrach tied his handkerchief around the lower half of his face to thwart the vile fumes that spiraled skyward. He studied the players in the deadly contest, coldly evaluating the dynamics of each attack. His internal link to Network abetted him, calculating and evaluating his hypotheses and decisions, almost without his conscious will. When he had refined his assessment, he raised his weapon and began the systematic elimination of the dominant Nilson antagonists. He aimed his tightly focused beam behind each strategic window, beneath each unsecured portion of paving, atop each stable slab of roof, and he killed unerringly.

Marrach ceased his methodical slaughter only after the odds had tilted far in favor of the Network squadron. He did not risk the stairs but retreated from the building as he had entered it. He now took the greatest care to avoid unintentional attack by his own squadron.

The young captain, a good fighter despite his arrogance in command, had begun to scour the street with repeated blasts of high energy fire. He had collected his remaining men into a defensive, back-to-back formation, and he was busily ensuring that fallen opponents had no chance to rise again. Marrach signaled his fellows of his presence before emerging to rejoin them. He made sure that Network announced him clearly into the captain's ear.

"Where are the others?" the captain demanded of him.

"I don't know, sir," answered Marrach, half truthfully. He felt reasonably convinced that he could find their bodies with little effort. "We were attacked, and I lost sight of them."

The captain growled at his men, "I want all of these buildings searched. I want to question everyone within a kilometer of this place. If anyone argues, arrest them. We came here to restore order to this pit of the universe, and if these people want a war, then by the Council, I will give it to them."

Marrach whistled soundlessly to himself, exercising a deep frustration. He understood Caragen's techniques too well to mistake any aspect of the squadron's composition as unintentional. Caragen had provided assets, like Rust, to aid Marrach, and Caragen had provided liabilities, like this raw captain, to serve as goads. At best, this young captain would be difficult to control. With so much at stake, Caragen's games might cost more than even Caragen would think worthwhile.

Beneath his breath, Marrach muttered, "Nothing ever goes well on Nilson."

CHAPTER 25

Perpetrators

"This be madness," whispered Arlan to himself, wending his way through the flashing helmet lights of frenzied looters. Born of Nilson, raised to Nilson ways, Arlan did not try to stop the violence, though he knew these frantic, howling beasts as men and women. He saw one of his bunk mates sever the hand of a shopkeeper for the sake of a plain canvas shirt. Arlan averted his eyes. He accepted the inevitability of violence, but each violent act that he saw across the years repulsed him more.

To gain advantage in attack and reduce their chances of victimization, many of the rioters had darkened their helmet lamps The result was a seething mass of angry life, punctuated by the brief pulsations of jaundiced light. Wharton's workers crowded into the air-starved commercial levels, where the prospects for looting were best. The density of frenzied humanity had already created an oppressive, stifling heat.

When the Wharton power failed, and word of revolution crackled through the mines, Arlan's first thought was that Deliaja had succeeded. His next thought was that someone needed to resist and try to restore sanity. In that frame of mind, he bloodied his hands to fight his way to the Windmill. Arlan had avoided Deliaja since their awkward encounter on Nilson, but he could not help but hope to influence her who served Breamas' ideals and yet might listen. Pushing through shattered doors, Arlan found only the dour Cullen, bitterly predicting the end of all Network contact. The impact of the Wharton isolation, which Arlan had so far denied to himself, became suddenly real and oppressive. Deliaja was gone, and

Breamas' outspoken follower, Cullen, was as distressed as his nature allowed. Arlan, recalling a crippled and bitter old man in a cellar beneath Three Crow Street, concluded that Wharton's darkness represented only the onset of disaster.

Miz Ruth—and Nilson—must be salvaged from whatever Breamas' fanatics planned. Arlan concluded that he could contribute little to Wharton now. Wharton would settle back into peace from necessity, once the deprivation of air became an imminent menace. Thus, Arlan rationalized the escape from darkness for which his nerves cried.

Since the failure of the major power centers made the lifts inoperable, only the utility shafts provided access between the Network-carved upper levels. The major shafts seethed with contentious rebels, who cried Breamas' name triumphantly, and less vocal opportunists all grappling for footholds on the narrow metal stairs. Despite the protective railings, more than one shriek faded into the depths with a dislodged Wharton worker. Where one fell, another quickly appeared, as the living quarters beneath the commercial centers emptied and spilled their contents upward. Most of the climbers sought to join the mob of looters, but some struggled to ascend simply from a panicky dread of entrapment in Wharton's dark womb.

Arlan shared the fear, but he denied himself the easy, irrational route of seeking a sky that did not exist above this world. The public transfer portals had ceased to function reliably even before the power failure, and the attack on the power systems had assuredly darkened such public utilities entirely. Arlan made an abortive effort to reach the small cargo portal near the dome, only to conclude that the upper route was inaccessible to him. Surprisingly well armed and organized rebels had established a stronghold throughout the three upper levels of the Wharton complex, and Arlan refused to appease them by naming himself as Breamas' follower. He was not quite that desperate, despite the burden of the darkness beating against him. A retriever's key, employed correctly, could access the cargo portal used for transferring the precious products of the mines. Arlan would not think about how far he must delve into the deep places in order to reach that portal.

Arlan did not try to fight again through the throngs around the main utility shafts and stairs. Even skirting the worst of the chaos, he acquired and inflicted multiple cuts and contusions. A lump on his left temple, where a miner's fist caught him, throbbed and ached.

In the neglected passages, the shouts of riot and revolution faded. To preserve the life of his helmet's batteries, he kept the beam dim. As a result, he could not see clearly beyond a meter's range. He stumbled several times into dead ends before finding a door with the proper markings.

Arlan applied his retriever's key to the mundane mechanical lock that defended the shaft entry. The air around him, though no longer replenished by Network pumps, rushed noisily into the empty shaft. The landing, a narrow metal ring, was broken at this level, leaving only ragged concrete beneath the door.

At best, such shafts offered only the support of meager, unreliable spike ladders, capable of daunting even some hardened Wharton miners. Unprotected and generally unnerving, the small shafts plummeted into depths unexplored even by the original cavers—the real cavers who had opened Wharton and lost it to Nilson exploitation. Since those original Network cavers left, the smaller shafts had seldom been used except by retrievers in emergency circumstances. For the last year, even retrievers had avoided the small shafts, ever since one retriever reported the glimmers of white-and-ruby light that did not belong. Arlan hated the narrow ways passionately, but need overcame the darkest fears.

With a deep breath, he swung into the roughly hewn vent and grasped a dully gleaming spike. He tested his foothold gingerly. Some of the spikes had been known to come loose under moderate burden. Hand over hand and foot over foot, Arlan began to lower himself into the deep places that he loathed. He moved by feeling,

for sight could mislead too easily. The wind moaned
past Arlan and chilled him. For long minutes, he
watched only the passage of dull concrete into which
the spikes were driven. When the concrete transitioned
into natural stone, he risked a glance downward to
judge the remaining distance. Rings and whorls of
ghost light flickered around him, and nausea stirred inside him. He pried his focus back from chaos, affixed it
again on a slab of carved stone, and continued his labo-
rious descent.

After a few more meters, even the wall of stone
failed as vision's refuge. Motes of ruby blinked and
taunted in the depths of rock as well as air. *Too many,*
thought Arlan, *even for the deep places. The ghost
lights, not Breamas, be winning Wharton from Network.* Arlan's nerves burned, considering what the
rebels' destruction of Network control might release
into the inhabited caverns. Arlan neither slowed nor
speeded his pace. Hand over hand, foot over foot, he
did not let himself follow the lights into their teasing
oblivion. He closed his eyes against them more than
once. Though the descent demanded less physical exertion than his ordinary work, his muscles ached and
trembled.

He counted the landings that he passed. When his
reckoning placed him at the twelfth level, where the
shafts slanted into natural cavework, he grappled for
the door latch that he knew must exist among the shadows. He found the metal bar, but it resisted him. With
deliberate disregard of the ghost lights swirling around
him, he threw his weight against the latch. The door,
barricaded by crates, barely cracked open. Again, he
hurled himself against the door. It groaned, scraping
the crates along the floor. He forced himself through
the narrow opening.

Uneven crates blocked him, but Arlan pushed and
clambered across the obstacles into a winding, sloping
tunnel that he did not remember. The heavy darkness
and the windless silence closed upon him. When he
felt the passage open into a larger chamber, he brightened his helmet beam, reorienting himself at risk of

exhausting the batteries which Network could not now recharge for him.

For a full minute, Arlan stood and watched water drip from the cavern's budding stalactites and seep into the cracked floor. The passage continued across the wide cavern, meandering among broken mining gear and discarded rock. Arlan moved forward slowly. The slope of descent had increased, he felt certain, since last he came this way, but the tunnels were marked sufficiently to reassure him that he was near to the cargo port. He maintained the brightness of his helmet beam until he opened a door onto the white glare of the self-powered port's emergency lights.

He recognized Deliaja immediately, though her canvas-clad back was toward him as she shoved a heavily laden transport plate into the portal. The air above the activated portal buckled, and Arlan closed his eyes until the whine of the port's malfunctioning controller ceased. He reopened his eyes to find her staring at him narrowly. "Be you watching or be you helping?" she demanded, attempting to wrest control of the situation by bold confidence. She pointed at two large crates beside her. "These be needing transfer."

The arrogance of her command, her presence here when Wharton had just ripped itself from Network, all the turmoil that had simmered in Arlan's mind since the night he met Deliaja at Miz Ruth's house—all of Arlan's suspicions coalesced in that deep cavern and left Arlan certain that Deliaja was at least as guilty as Breamas. A thread of hope broke inside of him. "What be in the crates?" he asked warily. He would not forget how quickly she had turned against him in a damp Nilson night.

"Medical supplies for Nilson."

"Supplies for Breamas?"

"Hush! Be not saying that name so lightly in here, where may be Network monitors still. Be you a fool after all?"

"I *be* a frightened man," countered Arlan, crisp anger surging in him as he deduced her intentions. "What be you doing, Dee? Carrying the riot to Nilson?

Be you seeing the results of your glorious revolution above us here? Be you seeing the damage and the deaths?"

"Less damage and death than any night in Nilson's streets. Freedom from Network be cause enough for a little exuberance." She bent and resumed her task of lading supplies onto the transfer plate. She did not ask again for help, though her compact figure strained against the weight.

Arlan crossed the room with quick steps and tore her away from the transfer plate. He gripped Deliaja's wiry arms and shook her furiously. Disappointment in her compounded his anger. "This mad breaking of the Network power centers be your doing."

"It be," answered Deliaja through gritted teeth. She tried to disable him with a sharp blow of her knee, but Arlan was ready for her. He twisted her and blocked the attack. He pinned her hard against the cavern wall.

"You be quick and wiry, Dee, but I be not so trusting of you twice. I be stronger than you by a goodly measure, and I be even stronger with such anger as I be feeling today. Be you telling me quickly what you be planning to do to make amends."

"I be not fond of men using their strength to beat me, Arlan Willowan, and it be much worse for you if you be making me your enemy."

"I be never wanting to hurt you, Dee, until I be starting to see the destruction in you. I be wanting still to hear that I be wrong, but I be preferring to hear truth." Despite his hard words, he eased the pressure on her. She writhed in his grip and scratched blood from his neck. He thrust her back against the wall with a force that broke stone and scattered fragments to the littered floor.

"Why be you wanting to hear anything from me?" she demanded.

"Because I be thinking this revolution be more of you than of Breamas," snapped Arlan, "and I be not wanting to see Nilson as I be seeing Wharton after your handiwork."

"Network be my enemy, not Nilson, not Wharton.

Network be your enemy, too, Arlan, if only you be admitting it. Be you knowing yet about Miz Ruth?"

"What about her?" demanded Arlan, feeling his heart turn leaden.

"Ruth be taken in a raid." When Arlan's grip tightened, Deliaja protested furiously, "It be none of our doing. It be Network soldiers arresting her just for being Nilson-born. She be carrying her charity loaves to a neighbor when some local boys be making their mischief."

Arlan blinked. It sounded like Miz Ruth to be always trying to feed the worst of Nilson scum. It was on such a mission that she had found Arlan as a boy. "Be Saschy knowing where her Mum be?"

Deliaja snorted her disgust. "Ruth be not fond of Network soldiers. She be not telling them her name."

"If she be in prison," growled Arlan, "Network be knowing her name without her telling. Be you lying to me?"

"Why be you thinking yourself worthy of my lies? It be you attacking me, all unprovoked."

"I be sorry for hurting you," he said, but he did not repeat his mistake of loosening his hold of her. He was torn now: more than ever desperate to reach Nilson and help Miz Ruth, unwilling to leave Deliaja unguarded, but not eager to abet Deliaja's intent to reach Nilson. He needed Deliaja's knowledge and her friends, but to release her was to aid her cause.

" 'Sorry' be a poor excuse," grunted Deliaja, but she responded to the softening of his tone. She added with a kindlier attitude, "I be not knowing why Network be holding Ruth without naming her. May be Network flaw. May be Ruth's own knack for secret-keeping at work. Ruth be not listed on the prison roster, but there be friends aplenty that be saying she be there."

"Be you planning to help her?" asked Arlan slowly.

Deliaja snatched the opportunity to regain a measure of his trust. "Not until we be sure of her need for help. My kind of help be a good means of rousing suspicion, where now may be none. I be caring about her, too." The portal whined, and both of them jumped nervously. Deliaja recovered first, "Be you thinking that I be using an old woman, the lieutenant governor's own mum, to be planting bombs or bribing guards? I be not even liking her charity work in these bad times. She be taking too many risks for her stubborn reasons, and it be no surprise that trouble be coming of it."

"Saschy be needing to know," whispered Arlan.

"I be not the one to tell her."

"Yah," agreed Arlan unhappily. "That be for me."

Deliaja's bright eyes narrowed. "Be you through squeezing my bones to dust, then? This portal be chancy, at best, and we both be needing to reach Nilson as quick as may be."

"Be you promising no tricks against me, if I be freeing you?"

"I be promising. Be you trusting my word?"

"Yah," said Arlan with a thin smile. "In this case, I be." He released her hands and eased away from her. "Be you hurt?" he asked, almost shyly.

Deliaja stretched her arms tentatively, then shook her head. "You be a strange man, Arlan."

"Why?"

"You be not the first man to beat me, but you be the first to be so sad in the doing of it." It was an expression of her disbelief, pursued by bitter sarcasm. "Be you a son of Nilson?"

Arlan touched her bruised wrist gently, wondering how many beatings had preceded the warping of her. "You be knowing the answer already, Dee."

Her eyes flickered in an instant of doubt, but she shifted their focus pointedly to the two crates. With a grimace, Arlan pushed the crates onto the transfer plate and into the portal. He winced at the shrill whine of transfer. "We be needing you, Arlan," said Deliaja. "Breamas be right. I be good at destroying. That be all my knowing. That be all that men like Vin and Cullen and the rest be knowing. You be different. Nilson be needing you."

Arlan looked away from her smooth, young face, now as sad and earnest as it had been suspicious a moment earlier. He could not suppress an unwelcome vision of her face overlaid onto Tempest's ruined body, bleeding on a sandy floor. "I be needing to talk to Saschy."

"The portal be ready to carry us." When he did not move, she asked, "Why be you hesitant? You be able to come and go without Network's permission."

"The cargo ports be not pleasant to use at best. Of late, they be a misery, working only once in half a dozen tries, and they be slower than sludge to connect."

"Talking to Saschy Firl be not pleasant either."

"You be right enough about that. Saschy be never one to like listening. She certainly be not liking to listen to me."

"You be fond of her?" asked Deliaja.

"I be not even knowing." Arlan looked at Deliaja's frown, and he shrugged self-consciously. "Long ago, I be fond of her. She be a different person then." He moved away from Deliaja, though he kept her within his range of vision. "Why be you running to Nilson now, just as your revolution be turning real?"

"Wharton be only a battle in this war."

"I be not helping you, Dee. I be taking you to someone who be able to force sense into you."

"Who? Some port boy? Breamas be owning the prisons by now."

"He be not owning Network. He be not owning Saschy," answered Arlan grimly.

"No," admitted Deliaja.

Her mind raced with new calculations, but Arlan saw only the deepening of her frown. "These be my terms, Dee: You be giving me your key to this portal and you be going back upstairs, or I be taking you to Saschy. Be you still eager to go to Nilson?"

"I be needed on Nilson, and I still be thinking you be son of Nilson. If you be not changing your mind. . . ." Deliaja shrugged. "Well enough. I be used to worse than Saschy Firl."

Arlan nodded, and he took her arm to lead her onto the transfer plate, gripping her securely in preparation for arrival on Nilson. Before he kicked the activation switch that would hurl them across the infinities, he murmured, "I be a son of Nilson, but I be a son of Network, too."

***

Deliaja blinked, momentarily wondering whether she has misread Arlan first, in trusting him, or now, in doubting him. As the initialization of transfer wrenched the space around her, she steeled herself against more than the intense physical discomfort. She stifled the guilty awareness of how deeply Arlan would hate what she hoped to achieve with his naive complicity. Having been misused so often herself, she knew the bitterness of being thus victimized.

Even as Arlan expressed his intention to take Deliaja to Saschy, Deliaja had hurriedly reevaluated her plans, calculating new options. She knew that Arlan was Ruth Firl's designated emergency contact, equipped thereby with Network-authorized kin-access to the Lieutenant Governor for emergency purposes. Deliaja did not overestimate Arlan's influence with Saschy Firl. Ruth had confided much to Deliaja about the closeness that Arlan and Saschy had once shared and about Saschy's bitter resentment of that common past. But Deliaja would be satisfied to enter the least waiting room of the governor's palace. Network would authorize that token privilege, irrespective of Saschy's predictable disregard for Arlan's request for any personal appointment.

Breamas had persuaded Deliaja that the necessities of vengeance demanded a hardening of emotions against any weakness, such as sympathy or regret. Network had created the misery of Nilson, which was the misery of Deliaja's ephemeral youth. The price must be paid. Deliaja did not matter. Arlan could not matter. Deliaja winced inwardly.

According to Breamas' original plan, it would have been Ruth whose bond with Saschy would place the governor's palace within Breamas' reach. The imprisonment had been an unexpected obstacle, which

Deliaja had intended to bypass via the secondary scheme of setting another, more powerful explosion near the transfer port. Arlan, however, had just restored the first, more satisfying plan to Deliaja's grasp. To have involved Ruth in the execution of her own daughter would have been crueler than using Arlan for similar purpose. In a perverse way, Deliaja felt grateful to the Network soldiers for incarcerating Ruth.

You only need a moment near the governor's palace, murmured the echo of Breamas in Deliaja's mind. *The explosives are the best, the smallest, the most easily implanted that Network can produce. The taking of them from the Network soldiers cost the lives of a dozen of our most dedicated comrades, so we must use them well.*

The guilt about Arlan tickled Deliaja's conscience yet again, but the prospect of at last achieving her vengeance against Ned Racker enabled her to suppress her qualms. Breamas had assured her that the advanced explosives stolen from the soldiers would make the destruction as satisfying as even Deliaja could hope. *It be fitting,* Deliaja told herself grimly, *that Network soldiers be making the revolution real.*

III.

TRANSFORMATIONS

CHAPTER 26

Shattering

The prison scene sprawled in ugliness across Saschy's office. The moldy plaster and oozing ceiling of Filcher's cell obscured the clean lines of her office's polished walls and the cloudy view from her windows. Saschy huddled in her leather chair, so obsessed by the recording that she had ordered Network to insulate her from all but the direst emergency alerts.

Saschy watched the noisy recording repeatedly, trying to decipher the sense of what she saw and heard. The volume rose and fell erratically, stealing many of the individual words, defying even Network's interpretative powers, but the three-sided conversation still impressed Saschy as an exhibit of crossed forces that she could not quite identify. Her inability to understand a scene of such apparent simplicity frustrated her, compounding a dread within her that everything in which she trusted was spiraling out of control.

Played against the center of her office, the ugly prison scene enveloped her, making of her desk an incongruously dignified artifact. The projection lacked the dimensionality that better Network sensors were capable of providing, but it was a sophisticated system by Nilson standards. Saschy could easily imagine herself as a silent participant. It was a role she had fulfilled for much of her life, especially in Racker's company.

She berated herself for the wasted effort, when she had much more urgent matters to attend. The loss of contact with Wharton, though likely due to some commonplace failure of flawed Nilson equipment, might draw attention to the nonstandard transfer portal

equipment at an awkward time. For once, Racker had
not dismissed the matter as quickly as Saschy. Racker
had personally briefed the technical crew with the captain of the Network squadron as witness. She was glad
to see Racker accept a measure of his own responsibilities, even if his motive was no more than his usual concern for his Network image, but she was also piqued to
be excluded. She justified the time that she had squandered on the prison recording on that basis.

Racker knew that Saschy preferred to handle Wharton matters herself, and he usually agreed with her
reasons. Though Racker would not allow her to take
charge in front of a Network audience, she could not
trust him to ask the right questions. This was the same
technical crew that had provided the betas at a fraction
of the usual cost of transfer portals, and Saschy considered herself much better qualified than Racker to negotiate with individuals who were clever as well as
dishonest. Though the betas that connected Nilson and
Wharton did not accord with Network standards, they
did function, and any successful use of applied topology required a level of intelligence and education beyond Racker's capacity—beyond Saschy's, as well, but
at least she knew her limitations.

She should have found an excuse to join Racker.
She had no time for these C-human meddlers and their
alien friend, who was obviously no friend of theirs at
all: liars, all three of them. And how had they fastened
themselves so fixedly into her interest, even persuading her to cooperate with their insidious schemes? This
was a lesser problem, one that would be promptly resolved with the smuggler's execution. The careful
wording of a report to address the transfer port investigation had a much higher priority and deserved the
bulk of her attention.

She replayed the recording of the cell visit for the
sixth time, despite herself. Had the Cuui told his visitors anything more than he had told Network? She
wished that she could hear the Cuui's answer regarding
the name of his contact, if indeed he spoke the name at
all. There were clearly multiple levels of communica-

tion at work among those three. Even when the words
sounded clear to Saschy, the participants obviously
understood more in each other's references than
Saschy could interpret. As an indicator of the darker
aspects of Consortium culture, this recording was quite
probably unsurpassed by anything in Network's previous archives. If she could ensure that Saschy Firl received due credit without acquiring the stigma of being
sympathetic to aliens, she might put the recording to
profitable use.

Saschy stopped the recording abruptly and stared at
the still image of the man, Jase, and the unnatural position of his fingers, spread in enigmatic gesture. In
that frozen moment, the C-human seemed as weirdly
flexible as Filcher Ikthan Cuui. "He is not human," she
murmured to herself, seeking an obvious answer to an
unsatisfactory puzzle. She studied the man in frame after recorded frame, hoping to confirm her theory, but
managed only to convince herself that he appeared
as human as she, except in that extraordinary flexing
of his fingers. "Network," she asked slowly, "have
the port boys returned the C-humans to the spaceport
compound?"

"No." Reactivated by her question, Network urged
her to accept her backlogged messages, "The incidents
of violent attack in the past hour have exceeded statis-
tical norm and are increasing in both frequency and
distribution."

"Let the Council Governor's soldiers deal with the
problems," retorted Saschy, dismissing the trouble as
the inevitable result of Nilsonites colliding with Network soldiers. She did not bother to question the procedural aberration regarding the C-human visitors. She
accepted the reality of the C-human man's persuasive
powers, though she did not understand the method any
better than she understood her own obsession with the
man. "Where are the C-humans?"

"The woman is in the main waiting room downstairs," replied Network evenly. "She has an appointment with Governor Racker."

"Repeat previous statement, please," demanded

Saschy incredulously. Official appointments with Racker were virtually unattainable without months of effort and the expensive cultivation of appropriate personal contacts. An elaborate system of obstacles existed to prevent ordinary Nilson citizens from obtaining direct, deliberate access to any Network official of real influence, and neither Saschy nor Racker ever tolerated an official discussion without such an official appointment. A legion of staff members existed solely to placate the frustrated visitors whose individual status or alliances rated more than the usual, bland Network dismissal.

After Network recited again the same, implausible words, Saschy sputtered, "How did she gain an appointment with Racker?" As soon as she had spoken, Saschy aborted the question with a wave of her hand, ridiculing herself for equating this alien pair with average Nilson citizens. The man, Jase, probably arranged the appointment just as he had arranged all other matters to his liking since his arrival. And if he had not bothered to exert those undefinable skills of persuasion, the woman could have fared easily for herself in this cause. A woman like *that* would need only to place herself once in Racker's sight, and he would tumble all the barriers of ordinary protocol to meet her. Less sophisticated women than this C-human piranha had mastered that trick easily enough. "Where is the man?" asked Saschy, pointing at the image still frozen on her office wall.

"He is approaching this office. He has the fifth appointment on your afternoon schedule."

Saschy straightened in her chair. "Repeat that, please!"

"He is approaching. . . ."

"Stop. I heard you. Is the guard still with him?"

"No. His visitor's pass allows unescorted travel through this quadrant of the city."

"Including the Governor's palace?" scoffed Saschy, though she could not doubt Network's statement. "No C-human is authorized to that level of passage."

"Pass was authorized by port guardsman Mimo, city officer Pringle, government clerk Ladislaw. . . ."

"Stop," sighed Saschy. "What is this man, Network, that everyone he meets bends to his demands?"

"He is a C-human, registered by name, Jasen Margrave."

"Jasen Margrave," she grumbled, pondering the meager value of a name that she assumed was false. Since Network did not acknowledge any legal identities outside its own codes, first-time visitors to Nilson could claim any name they wished, but most travelers provided at least a point-of-origin in addition to family designation. The point-of-origin tended to be a more accurate and more informative statistic. "Based on our scans, is he human or an alien hybrid?"

"Minor anomalous sensor readings are inadequate to contradict his claim of humanity."

Saschy felt relieved by Network's answer: Humanity made him more vulnerable to Network analysis. Saschy grunted, "I'm surprised he tolerated less than the first appointment slot."

"He requested the last slot. The earlier slots conflicted with his appointment at the city prison."

"Of course," she muttered, wryly unsurprised. "He would not want to hurry his visit with Filcher Ikthan Cuui." Saschy found herself examining her taupe skirt with regret for its shabbiness. Image was Racker's expertise, not hers, and she had never pretended to share his aptitude in that area. She did not usually interact with anyone but Nilson natives, who appreciated her lack of pretention. In her rare diplomatic encounters with off-world Network officials, she relied on Racker to establish the outward show, while she supervised all the practical details. She enjoyed sneering at Racker's type of skill, but she was nearly tempted to call him for consultation regarding this C-human's unorthodox visit.

No. She would not give Racker the satisfaction of thinking she respected anything about him. Besides, he would not appreciate an interruption of his own C-human encounter. Saschy pushed herself away from her desk and paced the office, scaling it mentally to the dimensions of Filcher's prison cell. With a commanding gesture to Network, she reversed the recording, separating Jase from the revolting alien creature. She stopped in front of Jase's image. She could see the grainy texture of her office wall through him, for the projection was flawed. "Why are you here?" she whispered.

She turned away from the man's image with an abrupt and graceless motion, colliding with a chair. The woman, Tori, who represented everything Saschy envied, seemed to be smiling in mockery directly at Saschy. "When Racker looks at you," muttered Saschy to Tori's image, "he won't be able to think of anything above his belt." Racker was adept at obtaining what he wanted without making awkward concessions in return, but most of *his* women were professional whores or Nilson adolescents, too overwhelmed by his status to be demanding. Perhaps Racker *did* deserve a warning of what he might be facing today.

"Connect me to Racker," ordered Saschy, tugging pensively at her lower lip. "Tell him it's urgent."

"Acknowledged," agreed Network.

Within the instant, Racker's voice snapped into her office, "What is it, Saschy? Are you tracking these outbursts by Breamas' rabble? I have appointments to keep."

"Watch your step with that woman, Racker. She's more than she seems."

"What woman?" he demanded, but Saschy was accustomed to his innocent pretenses. "What are you talking about?"

"The C-human siren in your waiting room."

The pause made Saschy wonder if he really did not know about the woman who awaited him. The duration of delay was long enough for Racker to request and view a Network snapshot of his waiting room. "She's a C-human?" he asked slowly.

"She's one of the pair that visited Filcher Ikthan Cuui this morning. Her partner has made an appointment with *me*."

"I thought we executed that Consortium scum," murmured Racker, sounding more distracted than irate.

"His execution is set to occur at dusk, the day after tomorrow. It was the earliest timeslot that fit into the prison's waste disposal schedule. The C-humans claim to be his friends."

Racker made a slight, choking noise. Saschy smiled grimly to herself, imagining Racker's current effort to deal with the image on his viewscreen in conjunction with all that Saschy had implied. The possibility that he could feel attracted to any of the alien-lovers would repulse him, but he would be unable to dispute Saschy's Network-documented claims. "You said that a pair of C-humans visited the alien this morning?"

"Yes, Racker," she confirmed patiently. "That woman in your waiting room is one of them. Didn't you ask her to identify herself when she requested the appointment?"

"Why is any C-human wandering freely through the public rooms of the Governor's palace?" countered Racker sharply.

"Ask Network," snapped Saschy, as a chime announced her fourth afternoon appointment, a status meeting regarding the ongoing Network investigation of the Nilson transfer portals. "I need to go. Just watch what you say to *her*." Racker did not even argue.

***

The clouds above Nilson swelled with unspent rain. A distant torrent scratched dark lines beyond the city, where the swampland oozed languorously into a murky sea. Arlan tasted the bitter Nilson air with delight. The sky, thick with foul moisture, opened above him. Free of Wharton's closeness, Arlan breathed exultantly.

"Rain be moving this way," said Deliaja, breaking his moment of rapt relief.

"Yah," he acknowledged tersely, plummeting from his momentary joy to the recognition of time and place. The Wharton cargo portal, programmed to connect only to its Nilson counterpart, had transferred Arlan and Deliaja into the barricaded yard behind the public transfer port building. Customarily, Network and at least three port boys guarded this area. A ragged Network speaker voiced the usual meaningless welcome and instructions for shipment processing, but no port boy stepped forward to confirm identification or purpose. Arlan was unable to feel surprised, but he gripped Deliaja more tightly and demanded, "Be this your doing?"

"Be you thinking Breamas be idle here, while Wharton be fighting alone? The ports be ours. The revolution be real. Five beamers be trained on you, Arlan," answered Deliaja. She sounded almost weary with the declaration of so much success. "If you be letting me walk free, they be knowing you as friend."

"I be not wanting any part of rebel charity." Arlan edged forward, testing Deliaja's claim. Yellow fire scorched a line in front of his feet, and he stopped abruptly.

"Be glad of the charity, before I be regretting it."

Two armed men, wearing soiled uniforms that identified them as Nilson port boys, emerged from the gate. One shouted, "Be you wanting him dead, Dee?"

Arlan dropped his hold on her, knowing himself outmatched. "You be disappointing me, Dee," he told her, then strode past the renegades and through the gate without a pause. They let him go, because Deliaja raised one hand in signal. She closed her eyes for a moment, weighing painful choices, then she pursued Arlan with hasty steps.

"I be not breaking my promise to you, Arlan! Be you wanting me to face Saschy Firl, then I be facing her. May be, I be telling more than she be wanting to hear." She raised her chin proudly. "I be a daughter of Nilson, and I be keeping my word to a Nilson son."

"I be not softening again to your wheedling ways, Dee," he warned, not sure what to believe from Deliaja Sylar. "I be serious about going to the governor's palace, and I be taking you with me if I be able."

"I be giving my word to you, and I be keeping it." Hard lines of determination etched her young face.

There was such bitter sternness in her frown, Arlan reminded himself of all the reasons he had so long avoided a closer friendship with her. He hated her fanaticism, but he could not stop himself from regretting whatever had twisted her. "Be coming with me, then, and be telling your lads to leave us be."

***

Spectacular, thought Racker, assessing his visitor with a connoisseur's appreciative capacity. Having dedicated himself to an in-depth familiarity with the infinite variations of human beauty, he could not look at this elegantly seductive young woman without relishing the contour of an eyebrow arched in ironic humor, the enigmatic curve of lips, the slant of slim legs as she accepted the guest chair, and the tantalizing display of firm, shapely flesh where the travel suit arched away from rose-gold throat and breast. He delighted in her obvious awareness of her own attractions and her overt, shameless use of them to stir him. He enjoyed studying her without coy pretense. Innocence had never excited Racker nearly as much as the intelligent, experienced exploitation of human appetites.

Saschy's cold accusation nagged him: This extraordinary creature—a C-human? It would be the most tragic irony to contemplate those species-bigoted, egomaniacal Calongi looking on this intensely human beauty and seeing only an illness to be scoured from the universe. Their simple method, the gradual reduction of human reproductive capability, was evident to any Network citizen who had dealt with C-humans for any length of time. Racker could not comprehend how any intelligent human could fail to recognize the Calongi's perfidious nature and diabolical intentions. Even Nilson-bred scum like Saschy Firl understood the obvious evils of the Calongi.

His visitor smiled, a subtle but irresistible evocation of physical response from a man of Racker's tastes. He resented her travel suit, a tediously common uniform that he loathed for its non-Network origins, even as he relished contemplation of the sumptuous flesh that filled it. The thought of a woman like *this* being degraded by alien filth enraged Racker, perversely swelling his desire.

"It is kind of you to grant me an appointment on such short notice," said the woman. Her voice reminded Racker of raw silk.

"For the pleasure of looking at you, citizeness, I would grant any appointment." It irked him that he did not recall authorizing the appointment, but his staff members placed so many requests before him that he could hardly be expected to remember them all. "For the greater pleasures that we might share, I would gladly beg."

She laughed prettily, "You are a very direct man, Governor."

Her own directness startled him, but he adjusted, "I react to a woman who knows how to appreciate physical delights."

"So," she smiled, "you have calibrated me already."

"Am I wrong?"

"No." Dark lashes swept demurely low, but Racker experienced a moment's unnerving certainty that she found him contemptible. "You are everything I expected, Governor Racker. We shall work well together."

Her voice held rich promise beyond her simple words, and Racker discarded his brief, ugly impression. "Are you applying for a position in the Nilson government?" he asked her, mildly amused that she might prove to be so ordinary, after all. Ambitious women often approached him via his well-known passions. Few women were clever enough to understand that a personal relationship with Ned Racker guaranteed their ineligibility for any influential office in his administration. Racker, knowing his own weaknesses, protected himself from awkward personal and professional entanglements in that small fashion. There was good reason for his tolerance of Saschy Firl, who had never attracted him or aspired to any personal relationship with him.

"Are you offering?"

"Do you have any qualifications?" he responded.

"I am qualified for a great many things that I think would interest you, Governor."

"I don't doubt it," he replied. "What position interests you at present?"

"I enjoy being close to power."

"That's why you're here, isn't it?"

"I wanted to meet you," she admitted. "You are the reason I came to Nilson."

Saschy's words forced him to probe, where he would ordinarily have no interest, "Where do you live, when you're not granting me the privilege of your company?"

"Is my planet of origin more intriguing to you than my name?"

Racker disliked the evasiveness that lent credence to Saschy's claims. "What is your name?" he asked with a forced smile.

"Tori."

"Where do you live, Tori?"

"Wherever I choose."

"Did you arrive by portal?"

"That is the conventional Network mode of travel, is it not?"

"Nilson's portals are somewhat unusual, which gives me more than the usual amount of control over the destinations and origins of visitors. The advantage of our uniqueness is our exclusive right of access to certain useful worlds. The disadvantage is that our portals are linked to few cities where I might expect to find a woman of your obvious sophistication."

"You flatter me, Governor Racker."

"Network, identify my guest," ordered Racker, proud of his cool exhibit of self-control.

He was prouder still of his ability to restrain a shudder when Network replied, "Victoria Mirelle, C-human, Nilson visitor identification code Ix1736."

"You have been misleading me, C-human."

"You don't like Consortium members?" asked Tori mildly.

"No."

"Does that mean that you're retracting your offer?"

"Why are you here?" he asked. Racker imagined that intimacy with a C-human must qualify as the most debasing form of perversion, next to a similar liaison with an actual member of an alien species. He assured himself that he would never have considered such an experiment with anyone less exceptional than this woman.

"I told you: I wanted to meet you. I heard your speech about Filcher Ikthan Cuui."

"You heard me condemn him, so you rushed to the alien's defense?"

"Not at all. Your speech impressed me."

He raised his brows, emotionally excited, though he told himself that he should doubt her. "Your Calongi masters would disapprove of that sentiment."

"I am well accustomed to Calongi disapproval."

"You are an unusual C-human, Tori."

"I was not raised to be conventional, Governor." She leaned deeper into the chair. "I'd like to hear more of your ideas. Perhaps we can discover a mutually agreeable position, despite our differences."

He moved his chair closer to hers, and he whispered, "Why should I spend my valuable time with a C-human whose purpose for being here is decidedly suspect?"

"The purpose for which I was bred and trained, Governor Racker, is concubinage. It is a family profession for which we are decidedly renowned. We are also extremely selective regarding our patrons." Her smile curled into enigma. "If you wish to learn more about me, tell me more about yourself." Because he enjoyed few things more than self-discussion, Racker complied.

***

Racker's recounting magnified his petty inconveniences of office into major burdens. Tori made the expected sounds of sympathy, despising him increasingly because he so clearly believed that *he* was manipulating *her*. She cooperated with the rules of the ancient game, wrapping her attention around him, but the effort of listening to someone so ignorant was painful. She had never enjoyed this sort of deception, though she admitted her own talent for it. She did not think that Jase fully understood how she plied this aspect of her trade. He had admitted often enough that his personal perspective biased his judgment of her. Simply because she had earned *his* approval without significant exertion, Jase seemed to imagine that she could gain the confidence of other, less civilized men with equal dearth of contrivance or manipulation. She promised herself that she would educate Jase one day regarding her family's uncivilized specialty.

Something flickered beyond Racker's head, breaking Tori's frayed interest in Racker's self-aggrandizements. Near eye-level in the vicinity of the entry door, a lopsided cylinder of air began to ripple as if with intense heat. A cascade of crimson fireflies tumbled out of it, alternately burning hotly and fading into a ghostly swarm. The cylinder blackened and warped into a dizzying distortion of space.

Tori averted her eyes hurriedly, wishing that she had Jase's array of senses to help her define this Network mystery and calculate the magnitude of danger it might present. She measured the distance to the door, wondering if the phenomenon blocked the exit deliberately. She experienced an unnerving conviction that she had badly underestimated Racker and his Network's capacity for scheming.

Racker turned his head, belatedly realizing that he had lost Tori's attention. He did not share Tori's calmly calculating reaction. "Network, explain!" he growled hoarsely. A blare of sirens answered him. He pushed himself out of his chair, overturning it and a small table in his haste to reach the double doors that led to the inner chamber.

By the time Tori reached the doors after him, they were locked securely. She shouted indignantly, "Racker! Unlock the doors!" She saw the whirl of darkness from the corner of her eye. She stared into its vortex, a blur of nothingness that tore all her calm rationality away from her. She felt the floor leave her feet, and she felt space ripping itself from her body. From a dark, dizzying distance, she saw Governor Ned Racker's plush parlor exploded into ghostly scarlet flames. A pulsing black void consumed the view, and the universe bled.

***

Saschy knew that she was betraying her nervousness by her fidgeting, but she could not stop herself. She told herself that she had good cause. This C-human had demonstrated an inexplicable ability to bypass Network protocols and to exert unlikely influence. She kept searching his face and posture for the common indicators of deception, but he did not reveal himself that easily.

She asked dryly, "Please explain to me why I should release a condemned criminal simply because you, a stranger with no evidence or credentials, protest that the criminal is innocent?"

"I request only that Filcher be accorded justice in keeping with your own law." Jase leaned forward, resting his crossed arms upon Saschy's desk. The fabric of the left sleeve was newly scorched, and Saschy wondered what retaliatory mark this capable C-human had left on his opponent. Saschy suspected that the streets of Nilson, always alert to new dangers, would soon be filled with talk of this strange visitor. "I think you share my distaste for injustice, Lieutenant Firl. I think you are too good a lieutenant to indict your Governor by admitting that you agree with me, but I think we can negotiate a compromise. Revoke the order for Filcher's immediate execution. Give me ten days, and I shall give you the truth of what occurred on the night of his arrest. I shall entrust the use of that information to your judgment, if you allow me to take Filcher with me when I leave."

"In ten days, you expect to prove the innocence of a

man that Network has convicted conclusively? You
overtax my credulity."

"I dispute the premise that the conviction was based
on conclusive evidence."

"You have obviously not heard the trial transcripts."

"I have talked to Filcher."

"I have yet to meet a criminal who did not protest
his innocence."

"Ten days, Lieutenant, is surely a small request
when weighed against a man's life, especially when
that man's fate has attracted such universal attention.
Your cooperation would be noticed and respected on a
wider scale than you might suppose."

He is more than he seems, Saschy reiterated to herself, *or he is an extraordinarily talented grifter.* "Mister Margrave...." Saschy paused artfully. "Not
knowing your planet-of-origin, I am unfamiliar with
your culture. How should I address you?"

"Jase is sufficient."

"I am uncomfortable with a usage that implies familiarity in my culture."

He laughed, making Saschy doubt the wisdom of her
effort to manipulate him. She had derived her limited
knowledge of Consortium courtesy from her own observations in dealing with spaceport visitors, and she
was not confident of her conclusions. "Miss Firl," he
said, astonishing her with an approving grin that
seemed entirely uncontrived, "I hope Network appreci-
ates you. You are quite correct: I have been inconsiderate in disregarding your social preferences. Please,
address me as best suits your own cultural comfort. I
have no particular bias in the matter, since the Truth of
a name is inherently contextual."

What is he talking about? she wondered, sensing
that she was missing some clue to the mystery of him.
"Is Jasen Margrave your real name?"

"From the Network perspective, as I understand it,
my legal name is defined solely by my Network registration code. Is my understanding of your laws accurate
in this regard?"

"Network," demanded Saschy, "wasn't a C-human

named Margrave involved in early Network-Consortium negotiations?"

Network answered her evenly, "Jasen Margrave of Escolar drafted the original Network-Consortium trade treaty one hundred and sixty-two Network-standard years ago."

Saschy smiled thinly, pleased with herself for catching him in his lie. "You wear your age uncommonly well, Mister Margrave."

"Thank you," replied Jase.

His coolness impressed Saschy as much as any of his previously demonstrated skills. She knew the hardest men and women of Nilson, and she had dealt successfully with Racker and other important Network schemers, but she had never seen a better controlled display of quiet, persuasive confidence. He exuded sincerity, even confronted by Network's blunt revelation of his name's implausibility. "What can you expect to accomplish in ten days?" asked Saschy. "You do not have any meaningful level of Network access. You do not know Nilson. Citizens of this city do not take kindly to inquisitive strangers."

"I expect to discern Truth, Lieutenant, a purpose for which my perspective as an outsider may give me an advantage. For example, familiarity might cause you to dismiss the threats of an aging revolutionary like Breamas, simply because you remember his previous failures too well. I, however, would judge the danger of such a man purely on the basis of current evidence, a much more accurate set of criteria."

"Where did you hear that name?" snapped Saschy.

"Nilson has an open spaceport, Lieutenant, which implies a considerable amount of open history." Jase shook his head, dismissing the subject. "You don't need a galactic incident regarding Filcher Ikthan Cuui. You have other, more pressing problems to address. Whether I succeed or fail in my endeavor, you will gain by your display of tolerance for alien customs, your sense of justice and your cooperative spirit. Be sure, Lieutenant, that every independent trader in this sector is observing the case of Filcher Ikthan Cuui most attentively. The future status of Nilson—as a profitable trade center, if nothing else—rests on your reply to me."

"What sort of problem could outweigh a matter of the magnitude you describe?" asked Saschy with cold sarcasm.

Jase seemed to take her question more seriously than she had intended. He became a still, taut receptacle of leashed energy, and his peculiarly vivid eyes focused past her. "I am not sure," he answered slowly, "but it distracts your attention. You are anxious to dispose of Filcher simply to reduce the number of outstanding issues on your agenda. Since you are too clever a woman to underestimate the significance of Network executing an alien without strong evidence, I must conclude that your *other* difficulty is extremely severe. Its potential outcome frightens you—more than you have yet recognized consciously—and you are not a woman who fears easily."

Saschy discovered that she was gaping at him and snapped her mouth closed. "If I were to allow you to investigate the Cuui's crime, I would insist that you wear an embedded monitor throughout your stay on Nilson. Network's coverage of Nilson is sporadic, and I do *not* need a galactic incident. If you have your throat cut in some dark alley, I want documented evidence to show that it was an ordinary act of violence and not part of a Network anti-alien conspiracy."

"I appreciate your concern and your cooperation."

"I have made no commitment to you. I *can* make no commitment without Governor Racker's concurrence."

"I don't think that will be a problem."

"You're overly confident. I warned the governor about your *companion*. Governor Racker is not fond of C-humans."

"Tori has a talent for overcoming prejudices."

"It isn't hard to see the nature of her *talent*."

"Superficial judgments can be very misleading." Jase stopped speaking abruptly. His attention transitioned from an emphatic *presence* to an equally intense *absence.* He whispered to himself, "Too late? This cannot be Truth." His face twisted with pain.

"What. . . ?" began Saschy, but she forgot the question within the instant, disoriented without knowing why. She stared at the iridescent sheen now evident on Jase's face, and her suspicions of him solidified into a certainty of danger. She reached for the weapon that she kept on a ledge inside her desk, but her knees insisted on interfering. She could not seem to coordinate her movements for even the simplest of goals.

She could not name the crisis that she felt assaulting her very cells of life, but Saschy did not doubt its reality. She chewed down her panic. In Jase, she expected to see triumph or guilt. Instead, her glare met accusation. She nearly exonerated him in her mind, but he slid to his feet and reached the door even before Network sensors could trigger the alarm sirens. An innocent could not anticipate such events.

He knows what is happening, thought Saschy, her uncooperative hands still struggling to find the weapon that might overcome him. She added to herself in complacent silence, *But he is not quite quick enough,* as Jase tore open the paneled door only to see the steel safety shield that had fallen into place behind it. He pounded once, futilely, on the solid barrier, then whirled as the window sheaths slid securely into place, sealing the room as a vault. The alarms howled.

Jase glared at Saschy with a feral fury. He shouted at her, though his voice seemed to bypass her assaulted ears, "How could you be such fools!"

Though his condemnation reached her past the sirens' din, the ensuing explosion jarred her bones and tissues with a specious sense of silence. The office, secured as it was for emergency, rattled and shifted, hurling Saschy's simple furnishings against the wall. Jase dodged the desk tray nimbly, obviously unaffected by any failure of muscular control such as Saschy suffered. If the heavy desk had not protected her from sliding across the room, she would have felt her own body smashed against the wall like her china vase.

The shrieking of the sirens pierced her, but she

could not cover her ears. Decorative plaster cracked
and curled from the walls, but she could not wipe its
dust from her stinging eyes. The room's cream walls
shuddered and warped. With a great effort of concentration, Saschy squeezed her eyes closed. The rolling
motion of her own body made her nauseated.

Only once before had she experienced such an inward sickening, transporting from the Wharton mine
on a day when the portals were malfunctioning and the
protective light curtain had failed altogether. Though
that misery had lasted only seconds, Saschy had vowed
never to travel to or from Wharton again without
first checking the portal status with Network. In those
terrible seconds, she had not expected to survive, and
she did not know how she could survive that same
writhing feeling now. She could not measure the time
that passed. She could focus on nothing but the contortions deep inside of her.

Strong fingers gripped her arm, digging sharply into
her flesh. Beneath the bruising pain, her deeper misery
receded. Saschy ordered her hands to cover her ears,
and her body responded correctly. She opened her eyes
to see Jase, centimeters away.

He was mouthing words that she could not hear, but
the sense of them seemed to reach inside of her—or
perhaps it was simply her own senses returning: *Deactivate the sirens!*

It should be simple. It should have been done already. Where was the security team, whose first duty
was to restore order in just such an emergency? For
that matter, why did Network shriek at that appalling
pitch, instead of issuing the calm instructions that were
programmed?

Saschy fumbled toward the wall, seeking the
emergency panel. She was grudgingly aware that
only Jase's support enabled her to traverse those few
short steps. The necessary dependence grated even
amid chaos.

She pried free the safety cover and slammed her
hand against the identifier sensor. It was the most
primitive of the security overrides in the building, a

failsafe system that she had personally demanded—despite Racker's preference for more expensive devices. She felt the mechanical click of acknowledgment, and she pressed the silencing code.

The sirens stopped abruptly, leaving an underlying whine that was unpleasant rather than deafening. The building creaked, but the obvious swaying had stopped. "Can you open the door?" asked Jase.

"The emergency team will open this vault when they've prepared a secure evacuation route. Until then, we're safer here."

"No," said Jase, and his insistent voice crawled inside of her against her will. "Waiting here is assuredly not safe." Saschy believed him, though she could not give the reason.

"There is a pneumatic override in the wall beside the door." She started to point, but he fairly dragged her across the room. Without further instruction, he located and activated the trigger beneath the paneling. The metal barricade groaned in protest as its two halves split and shot back inside the shielding walls.

The corridor was a tunnel of rubble, but Saschy scarcely noticed the broken structures and furnishings that littered it. Her focus raced beyond the precariously dangling beams and the carpeted remnants of the upper floor. At the end of the crushed and ruined hallway, black emptiness swirled with flickering ruby lights.

"Where is the Governor's office?" demanded Jase, and his voice sounded hollow.

Saschy directed a shaking finger toward the void at the end of the hall.

CHAPTER 27

Mourning

Katerin had nearly abandoned hope of finding Lady Rhianna, when she spotted the Infortiare's slender figure in the shadow of an oak tree. "Lady Rhianna," hailed Katerin, hurrying forward, "I need to speak to you."

Rhianna said quietly, "You are a stubborn woman, Lady Katerin, to seek me here."

"Quin once told me of your fondness for this part of the castle gardens," replied Katerin impatiently. "It is about Quin that I must speak to you. This world of Nilson has already taken my father from us, Lady Rhianna. How can you allow Quin to return there?" snapped Katerin. She had seldom dared to speak sharply to the perilous Lady of Ixaxis. Her frustration had risen as she searched frantically for the Infortiare, whose exact location none of the Tower servants seemed to know. Finding the Lady walking along a tree-lined garden path, apparently at ease, had not improved Katerin's temper.

"How can I forbid it?" retorted Rhianna calmly, but there was a brittle quality to her voice.

"You are his Infortiare," said Katerin bitterly. "He obeys no one else."

Rhianna leaned against an oak, as if its support were vital to her ability to remain standing. "Understand, Lady Katerin, that I rule Quinzaine only by his accord. I can, if necessary, enforce my will over most Ixaxins. At one time, I held similar authority over your husband, but he has far outgrown that mode of discipline. There *are* limits to the demands he will accept from me. I retain his loyalty by respecting those limits. Would *you* use threats against him?"

"I have nothing with which to threaten," replied Katerin with a grimace. She clenched her arms around herself, for the evening's breezy chill pierced through her shawl.

"You have his love. That gives you more control of him than any skill or rank of mine."

"Dictating sense to Quin is almost impossible when he sets his mind to something."

"That is my point," said Rhianna crisply. Abruptly, she walked away from the younger woman, who could not know the searing conflicts that Rhianna felt in regard to Quin's intended mission. Far better than Katerin, Rhianna understood the nature of the threat, as well as the magnitude of the need. "Be grateful that Quinzaine told you of his intentions before leaving. He has not seen fit to inform me similarly."

Though chastened by the Lady's dry admission, Katerin followed determinedly as Rhianna left the ordered path and delved into a leafy maze. At last, Rhianna paused in a narrow clearing, and Katerin murmured quietly, "I'm sorry that I spoke to you so abruptly. I assumed that you knew of Quin's intention—or gave Quin the order yourself."

"You erred in that assumption."

"Will you speak to him, at least? I'm afraid that I only make him more determined to go, because he wants to confirm the report about my father. I think Quin feels my loss more clearly than he hears my words."

"I daresay he does." Rhianna emitted a brusque laugh, and she raised her slender arms toward the overhanging branches of the mingled trees. Instead of her usual finery, she wore a dress and cloak of rough brown wool, the color of the tree boles, making her resemble an elusive wood sprite, the soul of the forest made visible. "Your loss, Lady Katerin, is a shouting wound that I would heal if I were able." Rhianna turned a burning gaze on Katerin. "That shout is as a whisper to the noise of my Power's shrieking. If you shared your husband's Immortal gifts, you would not be able now to endure my company. Please, take your grief away from here, and leave me to mine."

"Since I do *not* share your wizards' Power, I cannot know the nature of your personal trouble," answered Katerin with the hardness of desperation, "but I know that you alone can dissuade Quin from risking his life on some quixotic whim. If you value all the service he has given to you, then come with me and speak to him now. He plans to leave in the morning."

"Is that what he told you? He misled you, presumably to avoid your further efforts to stop him. He is already gone, Katerin. He left while you searched for me. I felt the patterns shift. I can recognize Quinzaine's Power easily enough."

Katerin shook her head slowly, reluctant to trust the Infortiare's strange sensitivities in this odd mood, but she asked, "Where is he?"

"I do not know. The patterns are unsettled, as am I. Please, let me go." Rhianna added with a passion near despair, "I can help no one now." She turned and ran from Katerin. Just short of reaching a thicket of briars, Rhianna vanished without as much as a ripple of the damp air. Often as Katerin had observed the phenomenon of Power with Quin as instigator, she had never witnessed an escape that seemed more emphatically permanent. Brooding, Katerin threaded her way back to the Infortiare's bleak Tower.

***

Quin found Evjenial alone in the Healers' cottage, seated before a dying fire and staring at its embers. He entered without invitation, having received no reply to his knocking. He felt a slow pulsation of energies surrounding her, but she exuded no clearer sign of life. A woven, undyed blanket wrapped her. Her face was flushed. Quin hastened to her side in concern. Without considering the meaning of his question, he asked, "Jeni, are you ill?"

She answered weakly, "It will pass. It is only the

valley fever. I survived it as a girl. That should give me some immunity." She looked toward him but did not seem to see him. "You should not stay, Quin. I do not know whether wizards are immune."

"Immortals are immune to nearly everything." Quin touched her forehead tentatively, confirming his Power's perception of her dangerously elevated temperature. "Jeni, where is Marrach?"

"Gone. With Andrew Caragen. I don't know."

"Are there other Healers nearby?"

She forced a smile. "They cannot help. With all your marvelous Power, Quin, don't you understand? I am ill with fever because the Mirlai are gone from us. In grief, they left. There is no Healing without the Mirlai."

Quin frowned, but his Power could find no evidence to dispute her claim. "Why did they leave?"

"I told you the only I answer I could feel from them: grief."

"The Mirlai grieved for Marrach?"

"They grieved for Suleifas, who is Rabh Marrach again. They let go of their Chosen symbiont." She seemed to gather herself for the effort of explaining. "I felt it happen. It was agony for them, though I suppose they will recover. They have made such decisions before—the first was when they abandoned the Adraki, their original partners. That was the crime for which the Consortium condemned them. The Mirlai maintain that they could no longer fulfill the Adraki needs, but it was the Adraki who suffered most from the loss. It is always the host that suffers most deeply when the bond is weakened or destroyed. The Mirlai grieve, but they can be relentless. I suppose it is a necessary aspect of their wisdom. They have lived forever with the bitter dichotomy of their tremendous gifts countered by the burden of an inability to Heal more than a small fraction of those who need." She drooped, as if exhausted by her brief speech.

"Where are your herbs for this type of fever, Jeni?"

"In the kitchen. In the blue and white tin on the shelf closest to the stove."

"You brew them in water?"

"Infusion. Yes."

"I'll prepare some for you." Quin tucked the blanket more securely around her shoulders, then hurried into the kitchen to make the tea. He felt a level of helplessness that verged on panic, and it was an unfamiliar sensation. He could not fathom the Mirlai's abandonment of their own Healer. It did not accord with anything he expected of the race that had—in his experience—given freely of their wondrous healing gifts with no expectation of repayment. He could not comprehend how Marrach could have left Siatha with Caragen, whether Jeni referred to a physical meeting or simply to a reconciliation of the two old conspirators. Though Marrach had indicated that there was at least one transfer portal—rarely activated—on Siatha, Quin could not imagine how Marrach could have brought himself to use it for a distant journey. Even with Quin's Power muting the pain, the process of separating Marrach from Siatha and the Mirlai had been nearly unendurable for the Healer.

But if the Mirlai had initiated the release, none of Quin's normal assumptions held. Quin had not known Marrach before the Mirlai, but Quin knew something of the horrors that Marrach had wrought against Katerin. If the Mirlai broke the symbiosis with a Healer, would that Healer revert to his original state? Even if Quin could successfully search the wounded patterns for the minute traces of the entity who was Marrach, would that Marrach be ally or deadliest enemy?

Quin had counted on exploring Marrach's unique knowledge before returning to Nilson. He had intended to question Marrach about Jon Terry, Nilson, Network, Caragen and whatever alien entities might be entwined with the Nilson cataclysm. Quin no longer thought of Nilson in terms of a potential disaster. The shattering of Nilson's stability had surged through the infinities like a tidal wave. Even Ixaxins who had never touched the Taormin, far less learned its lessons of infinite connectivities, had felt the jolt of terrible change.

The tea kettle whistled angrily, recalling Quin to the

troubled present. He scalded himself on the kettle's copper handle before he thought to protect his hand with one of the woven towels that hung beside the stove. He opened the blue and white tin and sniffed at its contents, trying to equate the herbs to any Seriin counterparts. They seemed fragrantly familiar, but he was too poor an herbalist to name the mixture. He shook a careful thimbleful of leaves from the tin, basing the dosage on nearly forgotten boyhood lessons that the old wizardess, Luki, had tried to drill into his absentminded head. Though Quin seldom indulged in futile regrets, he wished that he had paid more attention to Luki when he had the opportunity. He hoped fervently that Jeni would be able to tell him if he had made a toxic error.

Jeni accepted the cup without comment and sipped it listlessly. "Thank you, Quin," she whispered, but she laid the teacup on the table beside her after only one more sip. With a tentative brush of his Power, Quin tried to probe her to heal her personal pattern of energy, but even that slight touch caused her to groan in pain. He felt sluggish anger inside of her, and Quin retreated quickly. This was not the woman he knew.

"Tell me where I may find another Healer, Jeni. Even without Mirlai help, a Healer will be better able than I to help you."

"Neighbors will come. Those whom I have Healed will do what can be done for me."

"I want to help you," said Quin earnestly.

"Stoke the fire, then." As Quin complied, she continued, "The greatest help you could give would be to return my Suleifas to me, to us."

Kneeling before the fire, Quin looked up at her, lit by firelight that danced from her crown of coppery braids. "I shall try to find him, Jeni." He owed her honesty, but he would have lied had he been less certain that she would recognize this particular falsehood. "If he is serving Caragen again, he may meet me as an enemy."

"If he reverts to what he was, you must not hesitate to defend yourself from him," said Jeni with a sternness belied by a glow of tears. "You must be exceptionally cautious with him, if you have any doubt about him all. Caragen's servant would kill without remorse for the sake of any trifling inconvenience."

"I am not afraid of Marrach. I am trying to apologize in advance for what I may need to do to him."

Jeni emitted a choking sound that might have been a laugh. "I knew *that* Rabh Marrach, as you never did, and I cannot give you enough warning against him. The man that served Caragen was a genius of destruction and deception. Without your Power, you would have *no* chance to survive a conflict with him. With your Power, *that* Marrach might well defeat you by treachery. Unless you are absolutely sure that he retains some part of his bond to the Mirlai, do not trust him."

"Larger problems may confront us both."

"If Caragen orders *that* Marrach to kill you, *that* Marrach *will* kill you though a planet be breaking apart beneath his feet."

"I know something of Caragen's methods," Quin reminded her gently.

Bitterness filled her voice. "You defeated him while he still reeled from the shock of Rabh Marrach's desertion. Caragen would destroy a universe to prevent a recurrence of that loss. Nothing could better restore Caragen's certainty of Rabh Marrach than your death at Rabh Marrach's hands." She blinked, and the tears flowed freely. "I do know what I am saying to you, Lord Quinzaine. Bring back my Suleifas, if he still exists. If he is gone, it would be better that you kill the man who wore that name. As Marrach's original Healer, I tell you that if that Healing fails, no second Healing will ever suffice to restore him."

Quin nodded, silenced by her grief. He prodded the fire, recalling the man who had hewn the logs. Jeni's admonitions had shaken Quin's confidence more deeply than he wanted to admit. He had arrived on Siatha with many questions, and he left with many more.

When Quin had gone, Jeni rocked herself in her misery

and whispered a mournful litany, "Bring him back to me, Quin. I shall never be whole again without him. How shall I remain a Healer, if I am emptied of love?" She sipped once more of the tea, now cold. A distant echo of the Mirlai stirred dimly in her awareness, and she cried her frustration at them, "How can you leave us? It was not we, your Chosen people, who asked Suleifas to heal a universe!" The Mirlai did not answer her. The fire crackled loudly, as the highest log split and crashed upon the grate.

CHAPTER 28

Revenging

Nilson's sky seethed with angry clouds, streaked by fire and smoke and the biting scent of a harsh, cold wind. Rain doused the fires, but the fury did not abate. In the shouts and screams that filled the streets, in the contorted faces of the Nilsonites who erupted from dank dens and sewers to rebel against their wretched lives, in the smashing of buildings and every Network artifact, years of stifled pain wrought its vengeance. *Breamas* was the name cried in hope by those who thought they knew their cause and purpose, but the Nilson revolution was a blindly destructive beast.

At the eastern end of a broken palace, a patch of ghostly darkness pulsed. Too ill-defined to be seen easily, much less to be comprehended, the damage birthed by anger began to grow, but inflamed rebels saw only their success against their planet's Governor. Soldiers and government officials, born to other Network worlds, suffered as much from the unexplained silencing of Network's ubiquitous voice as from the mob that celebrated their victory in violence, but they did not correlate a shadowy blotch of darkness with the loss of Network contact.

Amid the rampant frenzy of destruction, a few patches of organized rebellion enacted considered attacks. The Nilsonites who truly believed in Breamas' long cause of independence led the most determined and effective of these assaults against the government district. The rubble of the first explosions of the outer government buildings improved the effectiveness of Nilsonites' guerrilla tactics against better armed Network soldiers. The city closed upon the Network forces, herding them within the government plaza and imprisoning them there. The broken Governor's palace, burdened by a blackened cancer of severely damaged space, became a castle besieged. The only government building that remained outside the siege wall was the main transfer port building, and the rebels held that prize closely, obedient to Breamas' most emphatic orders. When ghost lights burned where the light curtains of public portals should have functioned, willfully ignorant Nilsonites perceived only hated Network mysteries successfully destroyed, and they averted their eyes.

Deliaja escaped Arlan in the shock of the explosion that she had quietly caused at the heart, the east wing of the palace, almost directly beneath Racker's own office. By enabling her to approach her target so closely, Arlan had served her vengeful cause better than she had dared to expect. While Arlan dragged survivors from a collapsed building, Deliaja ran from the governmental center, knowing its fate as prison for any remaining Network loyalists. She felt the bite of guilt on Arlan's behalf, until she regarded the ruination that had replaced Racker's suite. Grim triumph cast all guilt aside. From a certain angle, the void seemed to be a tangible thing, a fitting symbol to her of the force that had beaten Ned Racker. She did not yet realize the scope of disaster that her explosion had triggered. She saw only a glorious achievement of personal vengeance, the utter destruction of a man who had managed to hurt her a little more deeply than the rest, because he had first made her realize the poverty of her life and her people.

She encouraged her comrades as she passed them, exchanging shouts of glee and praise for their determined destruction of all Network traces. None tried to stop her, not even the interlopers who aided the revolution without a trace of comprehension of its reasons. There was a deadly euphoria about her and a ferocious strength of will that deflected any casual attack. Those who might have targeted her intelligently were kept too preoccupied by her fellow fanatics.

In the streets of Nilson, while rain and blood flowed together in the gutters, Deliaja moved freely, unhindered by the riots and purposeless fighting that had exploded with her most deftly targeted bomb. Where Nilsonites fought each other without reason, she paused to redirect their furious energies against targets of Network constructs. Her words sent multitudes racing toward the port and the prison and any other site of Network holding. A group of port boys cursed her as they fell beneath the hammer blows of a Nilson mob, who risked death by the port boys' beamers because of her urging. More Nilsonites than port boys died in that huddle of charred flesh, but Deliaja cheered the victory, and her status rose higher among the Nilson throngs who watched.

She met Breamas in his dingy retreat, where he gloated over each report that came to him. As she proclaimed her triumphs and her plans to complete the rout of Network influence, she did not notice that Breamas observed her with new guardedness. He was an old man, crippled by his contentious schemings, but he was not blind to the new respect that his other captains bestowed on Deliaja. Neither was he blind to the expansion of her ego and ambitions.

Deliberately goading her, he demanded for the third time, "You did remind our followers not to damage any transfer portals?"

She snapped, "The portals be damaged enough without our help, but they be guarded well by our lads."

"We need the portals to reach Wharton."

"I be knowing Wharton needs better than you."

Breamas recognized the criticality of such fire as Deliaja's in finally achieving his revolution. He appreciated her duly. He also watched her, awaiting the inevitable moment when she would become more of a liability than an aid. If he had forced himself to climb the stairs from his shelter to view the darkening blemish above the fallen palace, he would have understood that he had already waited too long.

CHAPTER 29

Smoldering

Arlan stared at the smoldering ruin that had been the larger part of the Governor's palace. Bubbling from the remains of the east wing loomed a rough sphere of lurching darkness, flecked with ruby stars so like the cavern ghosts of Wharton that Arlan had to look repeatedly at the cloudy sky to remind himself of where he stood. Where there had been outer buildings filled with offices and elegant suites of Network luxury, broken ruins shielded an encampment of Network soldiers, as panicked and nearly as disorganized as the remnants of the Governor's staff. A few of the soldiers were trying to penetrate the collapsed buildings in search of survivors. Most of them were guarding the fallen ediface of government from anything that moved from the Nilson streets. Occasional beamer traces skittered across the darkness of the plaza, between the defending soldiers and the grim, invading army of the revolution. Where the rubble of Nilson's cruelest streets began, the armies of Breamas' rebels lurked in waiting, equipped with the motley scavengings of Breamas' long career. Breamas' captains were patient.

Arlan had been near enough to the palace to hear and feel the concussive explosion, though Deliaja had devised an excuse to take them both to the safer streets at the critical time. He did not know the moment when she had escaped him. He had begun to suspect how she had used him only as he stumbled among the collapsed offices, hearing soldiers mutter their speculations of how the terrorists had breached Network security to plant their explosives in the Governor's own palace.

Arlan lifted a stone block to free one of the same

clerks who had treated him so disdainfully earlier in
the day. The grateful clerk did not recognize his rescuer. Arlan had no inclination to offer a reminder. He
seethed with a deep anger, but he felt only pity for the
clerk.

Arlan gazed from the pulsing shadow of darkness,
which spread by hourly centimeters from the tumbled
palace, reaching toward the port building and the
Nilson streets, and he cursed Breamas for the wreckage. Across mounds of rubble, Arlan saw the bright,
pale hair of a woman who resembled Deliaja. Arlan
stumbled toward her, heedless of the dangers from both
sides of the plaza expanse. Arlan shouted at her, "This
nightmare be your glorious revolution? What be you
thinking?"

Instead of a reply from any Nilsonite, Arlan found
his shoulder gripped by a hard, restraining hand.
"Don't stand here in the open, man. Do you want to
draw their fire to us?" The speaker was one of the Network soldiers, a man of ruddy coloring with a white-
streaked beard. Arlan did not resist as the soldier
tugged him back to the shelter of a half-standing wall.
The woman who might have been Deliaja had disappeared back into the shadowy streets. "You're local,
aren't you?"

"I be born of Nilson, if that be your meaning," an-
swered Arlan absently. He needed to reach Deliaja. He
needed to understand Miz Ruth's part in this horror.
He needed to learn if there was truth in anything that
Deliaja had told him, including the claim of Miz
Ruth's imprisonment. Arlan had become certain that
Deliaja had made terrible use of his gullibility, as well
as Miz Ruth's. He simply did not know the extent of
Deliaja's fanatical treachery.

"Do you know the floor plan of the Governor's
palace at all?"

"Why be you asking?" retorted Arlan, though he privately scoffed at the soldier's ignorant expectations.
Who but a Wharton worker would wear shorn hair and
a miner's worksuit? And what contact would a Wharton worker have with the Governor? The fact that

Arlan had actually entered the reception room that very day and once—only once, when Saschy wanted a favor for Miz Ruth—visited Saschy Firl's office in that building was an oddity that Arlan dismissed entirely.

"There's an area of the east wing that still seems to be intact, but we haven't found a way to reach it yet." The soldier added with a descriptive gesture and an incongruous smile, "It's the area next to that bubbling black nightmare. If there is anyone alive in there, we need to reach them before the bubble grows."

For the first time, Arlan stared directly at the swirling darkness and tried to imagine its position relative to what had been the golden-domed governor's palace. He shaded his eyes instinctively, though his hand could not successfully defend his eyes against the troubling view. Until that moment, he had not considered Saschy as a possible survivor. He could barely remember the little he had seen of the building's interior, but he knew that her office window had looked out from the rear of the wing that had been truncated so brutally. "That part, there," murmured Arlan, comparing his memories to the standing office section, "be near to Saschy's office, if it be not the spot itself."

"That's the Governor's suite, the section we want to reach," said the soldier. "Could you draw a map of that area, as it was before the explosion?"

Arlan dropped his hand quickly to his side. "There be others that be better able to help you."

"We haven't found anyone who admits it yet."

"Others be knowing," answered Arlan with dry honesty. "They be not willing."

Arlan's cynical reply did not seem to discourage the bearded soldier. "Are you willing?"

"Yah," sighed Arlan. "I be. If I be able. I be needing to go closer, to be seeing if I be able to recall anything of it. Where be you working to enter?"

"Over here." The bearded soldier led, ducking behind the cover of each available barrier as if dodging terrorists were an utterly natural part of his daily routine. Arlan tried to follow the soldier's example, especially after a terrorist's beam nearly removed his scalp.

Approaching the core of the ruin, heat blasted the two men from charred fragments of the building, still decaying from the explosion's lingering energies. The soldier led Arlan to a mass of glass, fused from bricks that had experienced the most concentrated heat. Arlan stepped a little too close and felt his skin blistering. He retreated quickly to match the soldier's careful distancing.

The soldier informed him with another smile, "The remaining rooms seem to be encased in this stuff. The captain has a crew trying to break through it, but their weapons are just spreading the damage."

"There be nothing I be able to tell you to solve this," said Arlan. Inwardly, he winced, imagining Saschy entombed in this thick, bleak glass. "To break through it by hammer blow be taking months, I be thinking."

"That's what one of my mates said, which is why he set me searching for another way. He worked port duty on this planet once, and he remembered a sewer tunnel access to the palace."

To Arlan, it was clear that the bearded soldier respected his mate more than his captain. From the evidence suggested by the two proposed methods of entry, Arlan felt inclined to concur with the bearded soldier's assessment. "There be wide sewer accesses throughout Nilson," confirmed Arlan pensively, "but they be blocked to the important buildings." Arlan added wanly, "There be always a need to guard against crimes by terrorists and such. To be entering, we be needing to descend within the old perimeter of the building, then be climbing back up in the midst of yon glass palace."

The soldier nodded. "I've found a way to reach the underground level, but we'll have to blast a hole in the ceiling to get inside the building proper. I tried one spot that seemed midway in the wing, thinking it might be a hallway without much blockage, but I ran into such a mess of electrical conduit that I nearly electrocuted myself. That's why I'd like the help of someone who can suggest a more convenient place to enter. I wouldn't like to blow apart an emergency ventilator or waste effort on trying to penetrate somebody's ten-meter cubic diamond sculpture."

Arlan smiled hesitantly at the soldier's hyperbole. "Not even Wharton mines be growing diamond blocks of that size, but I be taking your meaning. May be a good place to climb near the service markings in the sewer walls. That be usual for the sewers that I be knowing best, and Nilson sewers be mostly similar in design." The bearded soldier frowned slightly, as if beginning to debate the qualifications of his local adviser. Arlan recognized the expression of doubt, weighed the chance to escape this unsought, unpleasant task, but instead explained patiently, "I be little familiar with the inside of this building, but I be knowing the sewer routes and methods as well as any Nilson son, and that may be of greater use to you. I be not eager to try this daft entry you be planning, but I be more willing than any other child of Nilson. There may be someone inside that be mattering to me once."

***

"What are you trying to do?" demanded Saschy, her fear surfacing in the guise of impatience.

"I am trying to discern the Truth of what has occurred," answered Jase distractedly. By a painfully slow progression, he had moved toward the gaping black wound where the hallway ended.

Saschy stood, watching without comprehension his odd, methodical movements. She had already searched the remaining accessible offices and discovered collapsed walls, the crushed bodies of three of the Governor's clerical assistants, and no means of escaping this half-dissolved tomb. With neither Network nor the Nilson sky to help her quantify the passage of time, Saschy could only guess that the day had passed into late night. She had not abandoned hope of surviving—she had not attained her position in the Nilson government by lack of perseverance—but she had exhausted all her own ideas for exiting from this fragment of the devastated Governor's palace. She counted on rescue efforts from the outside, refusing to acknowledge the possibility of a city-wide calamity. Tired and frustrated, she had returned her attention to the strange C-human, whose behavior since the explosion had only puzzled her more completely.

He had shown phenomenal capabilities to overcome the initial chaos, which had so overwhelmed Saschy. Having initially impressed her to the point of awe, he had spent the past few hours eroding his standing in her eyes. Once she regained control of her own body and mind, he had virtually ignored her. He had made no offer to help her in the search. He had dismissed her requests for his assistance with an arrogant declaration of the futility of her intentions. Meanwhile, he made his weird, labored journey down the few steps of carpeted hallway to the thing—or nothingness—that made Saschy's nerves feel like burning needles. She could not see that he had accomplished anything. His answer, the same that he had given her repeatedly, did not enlighten her in the least. She would have tried shaking answers from him physically if she could have forced herself to approach the unsettling black fog that closely.

"Have you learned anything at all yet?" she snapped at him.

"Of course."

"Have you learned anything *useful?*"

"Most of what I perceive is terrible in its widespread implications, but I shall need time to assimilate it. Meanwhile, you are interested in a more immediate sort of usefulness." Jase lowered his arms, for the first time relaxing from his prowling gestures, and he walked to Saschy's side with the utmost casualness. "Someone has entered the level below us. They are searching for survivors. When they find none, they will burn an access hole in the ceiling to reach us. I shall tell you which area to avoid when I detect that stage of the process."

Saschy stared at him doubtfully. "If that were true, how could you know?"

"I hear them. I sense them in other ways that I cannot

explain to you without more of a lecture than you feel inclined to tolerate." He sounded sincerely apologetic. "I should have told you sooner and saved you some worrying. You and I have escaped the first stage of this calamity, though that is not necessarily a boon. We must deal with the monster in our midst. The danger is growing as we speak." He glanced toward the lurking darkness, and his expression hardened. "I am not sure about those who were beyond that missing section of the building. Most of what you see is what it appears to be: an emptiness, reflecting nothing, not visible light or heat or any other part of the familiar frequency spectrum. Some of it is not empty, but what I sense of *that* part is contradictory. If you watch long enough, you can see patterns in the appearance of the flecks of light, but the light does not seem to be issued or reflected from any substance."

"The ghost lights," whispered Saschy, recalling Arlan's words, "color the caves with stars."

Jase grabbed her arm suddenly, forcing her to meet his intense eyes. "You already know something about this phenomenon."

"No."

"By all the heavens, tell me what you know or suspect. We do not have the luxury to indulge your anti-Consortium prejudice and your personal suspicions about me. That *phenomenon* is expanding. If we cannot understand it, we shall have no chance of containing it or repairing it."

His plea reached deeply inside of her, forcing itself piercingly past all the self-protective barriers she had cultivated throughout her life. She had never wanted anything more than to give this man the answers that he sought. "I don't know," Saschy told him earnestly. "I was only repeating something that I heard from a mineworker. There have been wild reports about mine ghosts since the opening of Wharton, but they are only stories. It's just . . ." Saschy hesitated. She did not speak this freely even to her mum, but those hypnotic, blazingly blue eyes would not tolerate her restraint. "The description came back to me as you were speaking, and it seemed to fit. The mineworker—he was a friend once—seldom talks to me much these days. He's always had poetic notions."

"What is Wharton?"

"A mine. A planet."

"Where?"

"At the other end of a transfer portal," replied Saschy, unable to give a clearer answer.

Jase breathed deeply, conveying his disapproval without a word. "Wharton is a Network mine under Nilson's jurisdiction?"

"Yes. We discovered it. We opened it. We have the only portals that are configured to reach it."

"Have you heard these 'poetic' stories from anyone outside of the Wharton community?"

"No. I asked Network, but I doubt . . ." Saschy stopped, assailed by her awareness of Network regulations flouted, Network investigations in progress, and a dimly comprehended discourse by the developers of the Wharton portals that attempted to dismiss various "potential" risks associated with their design. The portal developers had wasted their time in trying to convince Racker of the safety of their approach. The economic advantages had already won his confidence. Racker had no better understanding of topological theories than Saschy.

"Tell me," urged Jase.

Even as she answered Jase, she despised her inability to resist his influence. "I saw something in the Nilson streets one night, not long ago. I don't know what I saw, but it made me remember Arlan's words about the ghost lights. It made me start to wonder if we, Racker and I, had damaged something that we did not know enough to protect." Saschy conceded to a C-human the information which she had so diligently defended from the Network Council Governor. "The Wharton portals were not established according to Network standards. For that and other, political, reasons, Network is currently conducting an investigation of Nilson. When we first began large-scale operations on Wharton, we had an excessive number of equipment failures and frequent reports of erratic transfer behavior.

By restricting the access to the portals and limiting the number of daily transfers, we were able to reduce the problems." She added defensively, "We never lost anyone in transfer after establishing the control procedures."

"Until now."

"This cannot be part of *that* problem." Saschy was trying to convince herself. "The portals are on the other side of the plaza."

With a patience that approached condescension, Jase explained, "By their nature, your portals do not obey the traditional perceptions of time and space. In attempting to define a new Truth, you have defined a catastrophe." Jase walked stiffly away from her and faced the seething void.

His cool accusation made Saschy feel every shame, every petty embarrassment and every humbling incident in her life. For the first time in many years, she wanted to cry, but her eyes seemed to have forgotten the technique. Even that release was lost to her.

As she tottered on the precipice of despair, Jase pulled her back to a precarious stability, "Do not try to claim the guilt alone. You have all of Network to share it with you. A large measure belongs to the individual who used a bomb to wreak havoc in the Nilson government."

"Terrorists," grunted Saschy.

"Breamas' zealots," amended Jase.

"What do you know of Breamas?"

"I know that Breamas is a long-neglected Nilson problem. I know that Breamas recruited an uncivilized Cuui named Filcher to help smuggle armaments for him. I know that your Governor was so busy inventing Consortium conspiracies, he neglected the real conspiracy of terror within your own people." Jase lifted his dark head, as if tasting the air. "We should go back into your office. Our rescuers will be coming through the floor momentarily, not far from where you're standing." Saschy could not even think of doubting his claim.

CHAPTER 30

Fleeing

Tori winced at the sting of dust in her green eyes. The wind roared, its tidal voice as angry as the slender, dark-haired woman that it buffeted. The branches of black, denuded trees whipped the pallid sky, adding their misery to hers.

She moved with determination, even as she stumbled through the sparse, winter-gray woodland. She fell repeatedly in her haste but did not stop, anxious to reach a destination that she had never seen. The stony soil, glittering with flecks of crystal, had torn her blue trousers and scraped her knees. Her hands bled, and her clear-polished nails were broken.

When the dull gleam of solid, dirty silver metal peered through the trees, she veered toward it. Even such small evidence of civilization beckoned her irresistibly, confirming the subtle, almost unconscious senses that had drawn her in this direction. She expected little more than a few moments' rest, but the shed, its squat form corrugated with rust, rekindled her hope. A faint, bitter smile curled her lips.

Tori struggled through the briars and brush that guarded the shed's single access. To free stiff hinges, she kicked the door, denting its thin metal. She succeeded in bruising the already-battered sole of her foot, poorly protected by frayed slippers that had been intended for much gentler use. She applied three more kicks before the door yielded, and she tumbled inside the crude shelter.

Tori scanned the room quickly and comprehensively, mentally dividing the room into manageable segments, absorbing and assessing as she had been taught. The sophisticated Consortium technique of observation gave her scant satisfaction. There was nothing to see in the shed but an uneven dirt floor and the partly buried refuse of a prior tenant.

Tori shoved the door closed against the wind, sacrificing daylight's remnant. The dry air had eliminated any stench, but Tori remained as far as possible from the evidence of another being's desperation. She sat cross-legged in the dirt and the darkness, and she whispered a mild imprecation in a language of another world.

The wind had snarled her black hair, its silken fineness a disadvantage on this harsh world. She tried to comb and braid the knotted lengths with her fingers, but her hands drooped into her lap. She had no energy left in her.

She dozed for a time, her nervous dreams filled with images of alien worlds, colored in fire and destruction. Part memory, part fear of future calamities, the dreams gave her a poor rest. Awaking abruptly, she struggled to become alert. She listened for any disturbance above the wind, any reason for sleep to have left her. She could identify nothing, but she did not relax.

With rueful self-mockery, she acknowledged an uncivilized envy of alien resources. She did not equate her limited perceptions with the absolute, Sesserda Truth that a Calongi might observe. She had only the senses of a Soli woman, slightly enhanced by the Calongi adaptation fluid in her veins and by the smattering of lore that she had amassed from living with a Sesserda scholar named Jase Sleide.

From living with Jase, she knew a little more about Sesserda skills and methods than most Soli. From working with Jase, she had landed in her present predicament. *Ambivalence,* she mused, *seems to infest every aspect of our relationship. A man like Ned Racker, whose emotions and ambitions run to extremes, could never understand the uneven friendship that Jase and I share. If they have shared my journey into insanity, Racker is too rigid in his conceits to accept the changes needed to extract himself. Will my almost-alien Jase escape or adapt too well?*

Dizziness curtailed her wry introspection. In the lightless room, colors rolled before her eyes, spilling inside of her from some unsettled otherness. The turbulence fouled her senses, which cried denial.

When the nausea struck her, she welcomed it, because she recognized it and knew that her instincts—whether a gift of Soli nature, a Calongi-like perception imparted by the Consortium's adaptation fluid, or some chance comment from Jase—remained sound. The prior darkness shimmered with distortions of color and light from elsewhere. The portal was here.

Her head pounded blindingly with reaction to the portal's destabilizing effect. Recalling lessons from Jase, Tori focused on the center of pain in her own head and visualized the pain shifting outward from her body. Less practiced than Jase, she could not sustain the necessary concentration long enough to dismantle the pain altogether, but she needed only moments. Stifling pain and queasiness, Tori hurled herself across the dirt floor.

She did not strike the opposite wall, because it no longer faced her. The ground-level dropped, and she fell, sprawling, onto a smooth bed of black sand that spread around her to the horizon. Where the sand ended, the sky glowed red. A single sun peered cautiously from behind a distant hill. The inner pain, the nausea, and the portal were equally gone. Tori climbed slowly to her feet, dusting sand gently from her many scrapes and bruises.

Tori inhaled cautiously of the cold, bitter air. She had received her last dose of adaptation fluid shortly before embarking on the trip to Nilson, but she did not trust her Soli body to adapt at the speed of Network's abominable transfer portals—for that was what she assumed had entrapped her. She credited her survival less to the Consortium's adaptation fluid than to the fact that Network's Soli had designed their portals to serve their own species. The portals were programmed to connect between Soli-tolerant environments.

She had not expected that those portals might blink in and out of existence. Such erratic behavior did not seem consistent with the rigid Network culture that she had observed. Ned Racker, however, had admitted that the portals under his jurisdiction were of nonstandard character. He had boasted of his exclusive ability to control certain access points, expecting to impress Tori, though the banality of his tactic had confirmed Tori's low opinion of him. She had known too many men like Racker, who readily imagined that she represented whatever they desired most. Tori did not trust Racker, but she did not fear that he would destroy her intentionally; she did not attribute her present situation to any deliberate action on his part. Such grasping, ambitious men did not easily relinquish the prizes that they coveted.

Tori did fear for the greater damage that Racker's greed might have caused. Jase had said it speculatively, before either he or Tori had guessed the full extent of Racker's activities: Destabilization of the spatial fabric could threaten even Sesserda Truth.

Tori was not a Sesserda adept, trained to the Inquisitor's arts of recognizing and enabling justice, but the magnitude of the wrongness of Racker's worlds struck her deeply. She could not protect that absolute Calongi Truth that she barely understood, but she could try to reach someone who could help. She longed fervently for Jase, but she would welcome any Consortium member. She would rejoice to find even a citizen of brutal, uncivilized Network, if that citizen would lead her back to the familiarity of her own universe. She would have welcomed Ned Racker.

Tori pushed her tangled hair away from her eyes. Worrying about the destabilized portals—or about Planetary Governor Ned Racker—would not help her immediate predicament, and she was too practical to indulge her anger without channeling its energy into a productive form. She made a slow survey of the empty land around her, trying to locate any sign of the portal's present location. One portal brought her to a world; another portal would carry her forward, if she had the courage and wits to find it. This was the pattern defined by the force that had whipped her from Racker's office, and it had held true for fourteen worlds and at least as many hours. Tori wondered if this journey represented not a threat, but some twisted, manipulative humor of Racker's making. Even the speculation made Tori long to condemn Racker to a very uncivilized and violent end. Jase would disapprove of her anger, but Tori was not in a mood to emulate Sesserda tranquility.

Black sand spread cold, flat, and uninformative beneath a ruddy sky. The sand's fine grains squeaked as Tori moved. She had no beacon to direct her. She had only herself and a confidence that the deeper perceptions did exist for relanine to tap among the fallow, untried resources of the Soli species. Jase was her proof, and she cherished her awareness of his singular accomplishments, even as she gathered her energy from anger that he would have decried.

Tori tried to sense her surroundings as she imagined that Jase would sense them. She lacked his training—and faith—in the Calongi religion of Sesserda. She lacked also the relanine addiction that made him more, and less, than a Soli, but she did not let herself be discouraged from her intentions. By determination and the conscious use of the adaptation fluid in her veins, she coaxed impossibilities from the undeveloped senses of an ordinary Soli woman. Where these portals flickered in and out of existence, there existed subtle signs that she had proven that she could recognize. She selected her direction, and she began her long walk across the cold sand.

***

The familiar had become deadly. The unfamiliar had become enticing and terrible and altogether uncertain. Quin navigated with acute precision, concentrating his Power as formidably as if he faced a deliberate antagonist of his own Powerful kind, rather than an opponent made of emptiness and energies indifferent to his fate. Nothing remained constant. The patterns' threads snapped and snaked into tortuous new contiguities.

The pattern that had been Nilson resembled nothing

that Quin had ever encountered. Discontinuities abounded, reminding Quin of Jon Terry's abstruse explanations of how he isolated the original Immortals of Network-3. Until viewing Nilson in turmoil, Quin had never been entirely able to equate his own experiences to Jon Terry's theoretical descriptions of topological spaces, closed sets, and limit points. Sections of the remaining Nilson pattern appeared dull and dead to the perceptions of Quin's Power, while the rest of it flickered between explosive fury and collapse. Quin skirted the lethal strands that pulsed to the greatest extremes, and the dead strands were unusable. He leaped between tenuous points of stability, recognizing that each instant of his passage increased the damage by another minute amount. At each step, he wondered if enough pattern would endure to enable him to return, even if he could discover a path of retreat. After a time without measure, he realized that he had lost all sight of the goal forward, as well as back.

To become lost was the worst of the dangers that Lady Rhianna had drilled into his head so long ago, before ever she allowed him access to the Taormin. To become lost meant to become eventually entrapped in some pattern's burning strands. To become trapped meant to be indeed Immortal—in a form of hell that only an Ixaxin wizard could begin to comprehend. It had happened to other Ixaxins on rare occasions, according to Lady Rhianna, who had explained punctiliously how much worse was that interminable fate than her husband's form of purgatory. Dreading Kaedric's insubstantial existence, Quin could hardly imagine anything worse, but he did not doubt the Infortiare's statement.

He watched attentively for any recognizable route to a tangible world, no longer caring if he emerged on Nilson or on a desolate moon in the depths of the Consortium, as long as the place could sustain his physical form. The intensity of his concentration had nearly exhausted him. Here, where there was no single measure of time, a journey of this length had meaning only with

respect to his own perspective. Quin felt that he had
traveled without rest for a month or more.

When he finally detected a pattern that seemed to retain some integral stability, it emitted such a faint glow
of energy that Quin could barely maintain his focus on
it. He tracked it, edging closer to it by as direct a path
as he could identify. Its position shifted relative to the
larger pattern, leading Quin to conclude that it was
moving through the patterns, like him. That meant it
was not a world, certainly not a full spatial topology,
but a living being, too dimly visible to house the Power
of a wizard—perhaps a Network citizen who had the
misfortune to enter a transfer portal during a transition
stage of one of these flickering pattern points, perhaps
even Jon Terry. Quin, having considerable trust in his
own good luck, as well as in his Power, had no difficulty in grasping at the latter hope. Tracking an unknown living entity was an unreliable process that
Quin would not ordinarily have attempted, but he
adhered his attention to this individual pattern unre-
lentingly. When he watched it shift again, this time
brightening perceptibly, he did not pause to calculate
the risks. He hurled himself after it bodily.

Quin spat sand from his mouth and shoved himself to his knees. His lungs gulped the cold, bitter air
hungrily. He looked upon black sand, stretching toward distant hills without relief. A red sky blazed in
sunset.

Every new world represented a curiosity to Quin,
and curiosities held a druglike attraction to Quin. However, the most enticing ideas that Quin could imagine
at that moment were eating and sleeping, in that order.
He dug a biscuit from his pocket and nibbled a few of
its precious crumbs, but he did not dare to eat the
whole of it. This world, though evidently compatible
with his physiology, did not look promising from a for-
aging perspective. Neither did it present any obvious,
immediate threats. Quin had convinced himself to curl
up on the sand and take a nap, when he perceived the
being that matched the pattern he had followed here.
With Power to guide his sight, he managed to spot the

distant figure striding toward the hills. Sleeping would have to wait.

For once, Quin experienced no temptation to escape physical exertion by means of Power's convenience. He was not yet ready to venture back into the turmoil that he had just escaped. He attempted to run but found the sand too soft to allow more than a graceless trot. Still, with long, steady strides, he managed gradually to close the distance between him and the object of his pursuit. To Quin's relief, the sun, instead of sinking rapidly, skimmed the horizon, allowing him to continue without resorting to Power for illumination. The exercise increased his wistfulness for a Seriin banquet.

Where the land began to rise into hills, the sand hardened enough to enable Quin to accelerate his chase. When he came close enough to recognize the figure of a woman, he hailed her in the language of Network. He had given no particular thought to her reaction or to any plan beyond the reaching of her. From her startled jump, he realized that he ought to have prepared a more considered approach. The truth would be awkward to explain, and Quin had little desire to relate it to a deservedly suspicious audience. He grinned to achieve his least threatening demeanor and ambled toward her.

When she returned his smile, Quin felt rewarded beyond anything he deserved. Even dusty, bruised and tired, she was a stunningly beautiful woman. When she addressed him in a lilting rendition of Network's language, he thought that Network Basic had never sounded more like a siren song. "Whoever you are, sir, you are a welcome sight. I had begun to think I was alone on this world."

"Do you know what world this is?" asked Quin.

Her smile thinned with disappointment. "No. I gather that you share my ignorance in that regard."

"Entirely, I'm afraid. I had expected to arrive on Nilson, but I seem to have missed a turn."

"Either that, or Nilson is not what it was when I arrived upon it." She offered a Network handshake, which Quin accepted eagerly. Aided by touch, his Power could sense her with greater clarity. By the time he released her hand, he had fixed her pattern firmly in his memory. "My name is Tori," she informed him. "I was on Nilson when something went very wrong, and I found myself elsewhere. Since then, I have been bouncing from world to world with disconcerting frequency."

"I'm called Quin. Where were you headed?"

"Where I felt led to go. I have a sense that I need to keep moving to escape something. I feel like I've been traveling this way for days, but I'm sure my sense of time is badly skewed. I haven't eaten or felt a great need to do so." Tori grimaced. "All of that sounds absurd, but it's the truth."

"It falls a little short of a detailed plan, but it does not sound absurd under the circumstances," replied Quin soberly. "I envy your disinterest in food. I do have a few biscuits, if you reconsider. They're a little dry for this climate."

"I haven't seen any evidence of water here."

"I haven't seen much to recommend this world at all." Quin kicked at the hard-packed sand. "Do you still feel 'led'?"

"I'm not sure," answered Tori warily, and Quin wondered what *she* was hiding. "I don't have much experience at recognizing interplanetary doorways. Do you?"

"Some," admitted Quin with conscious modesty.

"I'm open to reasonable suggestions." Tori added dryly, "My definition of reason is very liberal at the moment."

"I do hope you mean that." The hills had finally swallowed the sun. Quin recognized none of the emerging stars. He did, however, sense a familiarly disturbing shift of the pattern of this place. "I don't think we should stay here any longer. Would you mind shaking my hand again? It will make things easier."

Tori gave him a look of weary distrust. "I don't think holding your hand qualifies as a reasonable request."

Quin laughed at her cynical interpretation, though he had already begun to concentrate his Power elsewhere. "You are a beautiful woman, my lady, but I assure you that I am not trying to take advantage of you. I am doing as *I* am led. I do have some experience in these matters, and I urge you to accept my advice quickly. This world is unstable. By the time I could prove that claim to you, neither of us would be able to discuss it."

Tori wrapped her fingers firmly around his. "Why do I always collect men of mysterious talents?" she muttered, but she lost any awareness of Quin's reply. Quin had carried her with him into a maelstrom of infinities.

Infinities' strands blazed brightly in a radiating web, but a coppery stain had darkened the pattern that Quin would have chosen in accordance with the Taormin's training and his own Power's instincts. Distrusting the stability of the damaged region, he veered slightly, holding Tori firmly within Power's shelter. The strands he chose brightened at his Power's touch, and their underlying texture solidified with insistency. Quin would have retreated, for he could feel the desolate nature of the world that had awakened to him, but the instabilities had thronged at the stirring of the solid world, cutting off other paths. Though his own activation of physical portals seemed destined to spread the damage, there seemed to be no safe route through the infinities alone. He might have risked more if he had not carried a passenger. Instead, he allowed the opened portal to accept them both.

Quin tried to soften their jolting arrival, but the hillside was steep. He and Tori both skidded through several meters of ragged shrubbery, before thudding to rest on a horizontal protrusion of feathery gray stone, which cracked and crumbled disturbingly as they landed. "There's fresh water below us," observed Tori, before Quin had realigned his physical senses. "How are your swimming skills?"

"Adequate, but I'm not sure I want to test them here. There's something alive in that water."

"I saw the ripples," answered Tori, "and I don't know if the water's actually potable, but I can't see any other way off this island. This looks like an old caldera."

Quin cocked his head to look at her, admiring her calm and her quickness of perception. He had only begun to recognize that they occupied a lonely peak submerged amid a deep, blue-black lake mirroring a cloudless sky that was almost the same color. While he excused his slow recovery on the basis of Power's struggles to carry them through a damaged infinity, she deserved equal excuse on the basis of the transfer disorientation that she had unquestionably experienced. "Where do you think we need to go next?" he asked her, though his Power had already identified a cleft of stone not far inland from the lake's nearest edge.

Tori hesitated only briefly before pointing in the same direction that Power had sensed. "There," she answered tersely and clambered to her feet with remarkable grace under the circumstances. "Give me those biscuits of yours." Startled, Quin offered her the most intact members of his crumbled horde. She sealed them into the pockets of her battered travel suit, while Quin watched curiously.

"How do you seal those pockets? They're not even visible now."

She gave him a look that he recognized, from frequent experience, as a derogatory comment on his mental processes, but she replied evenly, "A form of chemical magnetism is incorporated into the fabric during construction. If you have any useful comments to make regarding the lake or its occupants, tell me now. Otherwise, I'm going swimming before sunset makes me even colder."

"The occupants seem to be nothing more than large fish. I think I can discourage them from approaching us too closely. Just don't go too far ahead of me."

She did not question his assertions. "Then don't dawdle." She scrambled over the edge of the rock and down the rest of the slope, splashing into the water and kicking away from the shore. She set out directly with clean overhead strokes that scarcely troubled the water's surface.

Quin called after her, "Don't you know that judicious laziness can be healthy sometimes?" He scanned the rippling water for evidence of increased agitation or any new wakes veering toward Tori. He saw none but grumbled to himself, nonetheless, as he hurried to follow her. He belted his cloak at his waist, already regretting the weight of wet wool that would drag at him.

The water was bitterly cold, but the self-protective instincts of Immortal genealogy did not protest a cautious taste of it, followed by a much more satisfying swallow. The lake's large denizens projected hunger, but Quin was not sure if they had actually recognized the interlopers into their domain. He did not intend to learn. A sting of Power discouraged the nearest from a closer approach. Quin could feel infinity shudder at even so slight a use of active Power, but he repeated the warning four times before the unseen fish lost interest.

Tori swam quickly, and Quin did not manage to catch up with her until she stopped and awaited him at the grassy shore. She sat clenching her knees, shivering, while Quin dragged himself out of the water. Though her dark hair was soaked, her clothing seemed to have shed the water completely. She offered him one of his own biscuits. He accepted the dry lump of dough with gratitude. "I admire your pockets," he informed her solemnly.

With a crisp laugh, she pointed toward a grassy slope that rose into a stand of glowering trees. "That's where I intend to go. Any objections?"

Quin shook his head. "I admire your instincts as well."

"Good." Without further discussion, Tori arose and began the hike toward a goal she could not fully define.

"I do not admire your intolerance for rest," sighed Quin, but he joined her quickly after squeezing excess water from his drenched cloak. "Are you always this driven?"

"Would you prefer to sit and starve, while contemplating the severity of our predicament?"

Quin shrugged. "The path will be quicker, though a little less direct, if we circumvent the center of the wooded area." At her pensive frown, Quin grinned. "You're not the only one with instincts."

"Then lead the way."

The way was not far, though the density of the trees, even at the forest's fringe, made rapid progress difficult. By the time they reached the cleft of stone that drew Quin, his clothing was barely damp, and Tori's hair had dried into amazingly glorious, errant waves. Facing the riven pair of black, glassy slabs, Tori hesitated for the first time since their arrival. "I think we're where we need to be," she said. "Do you have an 'instinct' as to how we proceed from here?"

"Take my hand again," answered Quin, girding his Power to confront the turmoil ahead of them. This time, Tori did not argue.

The infinities burned even darker and more dangerously here. Quin concentrated on finding any single path of bright, healthy fire, but the course was erratic and demanding of all his Power's focus. He maintained his hold on Tori almost unconsciously, and he could not afford to scan his surroundings for any other traces of life. He trod treacherous routes, because there were none of stabler nature, until another world-blaze summoned him. He stumbled forth exhausted into a snowbank. "Swimming in icy water was better than this," he muttered.

"It could be worse," answered Tori with no evidence of sympathy, though her shivering had resumed. "I don't think the next port is far from here."

"That's the worst part of all," groaned Quin, contemplating how bad the next foray between worlds might be. "I am going to become exceedingly tired of this."

"So save your complaints for a better cause."

"You have seriously tyrannical tendencies."

"Stop sounding like my late husband."

"Should I ask how he died or simply offer condolences?"

"Neither, unless you want to share his fate." She began to trudge through the snow. Quin followed in her wake without qualms for allowing her the larger effort of forging the path.

CHAPTER 31

Battling

Marrach observed the fumbling rescue efforts with the tolerant disdain of a practiced cynic. The young captain had achieved a level of frantic desperation, bereft of the Network advice on which he depended, bereft of any local authority, and bereft of any inherent gift of leadership. Contrarily, the rebel captains had impressed Marrach with their competency. Quietly and efficiently, they eliminated any Network soldier who came individually within their reach. Even the inexperienced young squadron commander could have countered a frontal attack, but these stealthy, sporadic killings daunted him entirely.

A more sympathetic part of Marrach could appreciate the young captain's predicament: too inexperienced for his position, quite unaware that he was merely Caragen's chosen means of taunting Marrach into a role of active leadership, adrift from all normal Network ties, assaulted by a local revolution whose leader the uninformed captain could not help but underestimate. . . . The young captain could not be expected to enjoy the failure that Caragen and Breamas had jointly destined for him. The scorched white ruin of Nilson's government beneath its shadow of bedevilment was a besieged island in a troubled stone sea. It compounded the discouragement of all who viewed it.

Almost as keenly as the young captain, Marrach hoped that some senior official of the Nilson government would yet be found. The captain needed to lean on a more confident authority, and Marrach wanted no part of ruling Nilson, even on a temporary basis. Marrach had a more serious mission to tend, and he could not afford to divide his attentions further. Already, he contended with the continuous pain of separation from the Mirlai, as well as the sharply surging pain of the Network implants in his head. His contact with Network had become noisy and intermittent, ebbing in synchronism with each incremental expansion of the swirling spatial catastrophe that clung like a shadowy fungus to the shards of the Governor's palace.

Marrach moved purposefully through the troops and refugees, exerting influence without exercising overt authority beyond his pretended role. A hint, a suggestion, an apparently idle remark could trigger actions that appeared independent and spontaneous. It was a technique of manipulation that Marrach knew intimately and employed with unerring agility. By its use, the captain obeyed Marrach's directive to fortify a former office building as a central command center. Protective resources and repair efforts were concentrated around the infirmary. The bearded soldier, Rust, pursued Marrach's suggestion to search for surviving government officials by creating a subterranean entry. Several soldiers survived rebel forays on the basis of Marrach's remarks regarding the rebels' tactics. A watch was set on the plaza area nearest to the shattered transfer port building, but no effort was made to wrest that damaged prize from Breamas' forces; Marrach had encouraged fear of the newly dubbed "ghost shadow" stretching from the palace toward the port building, because he preferred to leave the portals, for now, in the control of Network-hating rebels rather than Network soldiers who might try to use the portals injudiciously.

Meanwhile, Marrach surveyed the plaza perimeter and analyzed the probability of reaching the spaceport alive, if the spaceport still existed and any ships still remained there. The destabilized topology made the spaceport the best hope of restoring a reliable form of outside contact, since the normal Network methods for both travel and communications depended on topological techniques. Knowing something about the types of ships—and alien owners—that visited Nilson, however, Marrach calculated a high probability that any ships that could escape the Nilson catastrophe had already left.

For the first time in years, Marrach actually wanted to communicate with Caragen, but he had been unable to complete that link—or any other for more than an instant. Marrach seized each opportunity to issue a general distress call on behalf of Nilson, but he doubted that any Network nodes beyond Nilson had received the data, and Nilson's local nodes were woefully inadequate. Network had unquestionably recorded the loss of contact with the planet, but it would be days before Network analysis identified the cause as more than the usual erratic nature of Nilson equipment. Caragen might accelerate that process, or he might have his own reasons to delay or halt any serious investigation. Marrach relied on nothing with respect to Network's Council Governor, except Caragen's adherence to the tenets of his own advantage.

The ghost shadow pulsed and expanded, tearing at Marrach's nerves, though he showed no sign of his internal strife. A *wrongness* about the dark anomaly abraded the raw wounds of separation from the Mirlai, and he stifled the pain only by driving himself deeper into the hard, disciplined persona of the man who had served Caragen. Bleakly, he forced himself to stare into the midst of the swirling darkness. Crimson pinpoints dotted the emptiness, and a few of them had blurred into lines of fire. "The stars bleed," murmured Marrach, torn almost unbearably between Caragen's cold creation and Mirlai's exiled Healer, "and I cannot staunch the flow."

The soft words attracted the notice of a nearby sergeant, stacking collapsed bricks into a defensive barricade. "What was that, soldier?"

"Nothing, sir," replied Marrach crisply. He begrudged the interruption of his thoughts.

"Give me a hand here, soldier."

"Sorry, sir. I'm on a special errand for the captain." Marrach did not await dismissal. He had no cause to fear angry repercussions from any mere sergeant, even if the loss of Network contact had not threatened to dissolve the remaining semblance of military order. At worst, the rankless soldier that he pretended to be would receive special reprieve from a Network Council Chancellor, the uniquely influential title that Caragen had created for Marrach and never revoked. More likely, the rankless soldier would disappear altogether.

As Marrach hurried to complete his survey of the rebel watchposts, he began to prioritize them for destruction, if the need arose. Realizing the nature of his instinctive plotting, he stopped mid-stride and sank cross-legged into a glass hollow that the terrorist's explosion had burned into the plaza cobbles. "I am no longer your creature, Caragen," he whispered, though his voice shook with doubt. He thrust his face into his hands and felt the texture of skin, graft upon graft built upon the travesty of his natural visage by Caragen's orders. "Jeni," he pleaded, "do not give up on me. Do not let the Mirlai give up on me."

A flash of beamer fire lit the plaza, and Marrach's head snapped upright. The scent of burning flesh stung his nostrils. "Survive," he muttered harshly to himself, restating the overriding imperative of a Network agent.

"I am a Healer still," he whispered in reply, a gentler voice emerging from him.

"You cannot be both at once," he hissed. His expression grew so hard and cold that it seemed to transform him into another species, an inhuman species that was ultimately human in the basest sense. "You must focus," insisted Rabh Marrach.

". . . or go mad," sighed the Healer Suleifas, and all the disparate parts of Rabhadur Marrach concurred.

Marrach struggled to his feet. The rain began to fall.

***

Jase watched without comment as Saschy Firl accosted their rescuer with questions. The soldier stoically endured the deluge from the Nilson Lieutenant Governor. Most of the soldier's answers consisted of denials of knowledge and repeated deferrals to the soldier's commanding officer. One clear, definite reply was the soldier's confirmation that Governor Racker was missing.

Pitying the man who had risked his life to rescue such a difficult woman, Jase slipped out of the Lieutenant Governor's office. Jase felt no particular compulsion to await Saschy Firl, who had recovered her own confidence now that she had regained some form of contact with Network and its legions. The soldier was clearly capable, though Jase's nonvisual perceptions made the man younger than the white-streaked beard suggested; the white was owed to injuries rather than age, concluded Jase. Foremost in Jase's personal concerns, ranking even higher than the general calamity and the sensory pain that it was causing him, was the survival of Tori.

He could not accept the likeliest hypothesis: that she had died in the dissolution of Governor Racker's office. The Sesserda disciplinarian inside of him denounced his emotional refusal of a probable Truth. He had not felt so like an ordinary, vulnerable Soli since the accursed accident that had saturated his body with the purest relanine of Calongi lifeblood.

Again, he attempted to study the phenomenon that occupied the space where last he had seen Tori, and again he recognized the futility of his effort. Wherever she was—if she still lived—she was not to be found here. "Blast all of Network to the iciest hell of Uccula," he grunted with impassioned ferocity, "and condemn me likewise for bringing her among these barbaric desecrators of Truth."

"Curses be not much use against yon ghost lights."

Jase whipped his attention toward the speaker, a youngish man with a well-shaped head that had been shaved nearly bald. As a measure of internal conflict, Jase's failure to observe the man earlier weighed ominously large. Any Sesserda master would prescribe an immediate meditative course to restore internal balance, but Jase's distress had progressed beyond willing compliance even if the opportunity had been available. "Why do you refer to the phenomenon as ghost lights?" asked Jase more sharply than he intended. "The overriding effect is uttermost darkness across every frequency I can identify."

"The darkness be nothing but shadow. The lights, when they be showing, be the proof of danger." The speaker shrugged. "We be seeing the spread of them in Wharton mines this past year."

"Are the mines on this planet?" demanded Jase, though he had already heard the answer from Saschy. The realization that this phenomenon had been developing unreported for a year compounded Jase's fury against Network's uncivilized, uncomprehending society.

"Nah. They be governed from here, but they be reached by portal only."

"You work in the mines." *And you hate them.*

"Yah. I be a retriever."

"Arlan?" said Saschy Firl from her office door. She made the name an accusation. "How do you come to be here?"

The depth of Arlan's sigh assured Jase that a complex relationship existed between this improbable pair, and Jase began immediately to analyze potential problems and benefits. Arlan answered mildly, "I be coming to see you, Saschy, about Wharton and about your mum." Arlan glanced at the bearded soldier, who stood behind Saschy and looked impatient to end these pointless discussions and leave the uncertain dangers of this location. "Your mum be in prison, Saschy, by cause of a Network soldier's mistake and her pride. May be as safe a place for her as any—now."

While Saschy gaped, silenced by one shock more than she wanted to endure, the bearded soldier took advantage of the moment to inject his own opinion, "Lieutenant Firl, I think we can find a safer place for you to continue this discussion." He nodded toward the seething darkness without actually looking at it.

Jase murmured, "You offer sound advice, sir."

The soldier grunted but wasted no time in moving to the ragged hole that his weapon had burned through the floor. "The high ceilings in this place make for a bit of a drop. We had a devil of a time scaling brittle furni-

ture to get up here, and I don't recommend reversing
the process. A straight jump would be easier," he said. "I'll
descend first to arrange for a softer landing. There's
plenty of rugs and furnishings to use. Arlan, you
can help lower the Lieutenant Governor and this
gentleman."

"I can manage for myself," retorted Saschy gruffly,
though she showed no inclination to move.

"Yes, ma'am," answered the soldier with a dutiful
tone that hinted of extensive experience with the foolish pride of his superiors in rank. His glance skimmed
toward Jase, then darted away quickly to avoid staring
into the disturbing darkness.

"I think I should be able to cope with the descent. I
welcome your offer to arrange a cushioned landing,"
answered Jase to the soldier's unspoken query. Jase declined to mention the Sesserda training that had taught
him to cope with considerably greater physical obstacles. The soldier was already demonstrating resentful signs of feeling unappreciated, and the present
situation would require considerable effort to sustain
morale even without needless aggravations incurred
by the Lieutenant Governor's prickly temper. Jase
suspected that the tension of Saschy's relationship
with Arlan was worsening the Lieutenant Governor's
tendency toward contrariness. "May I ask your name,
soldier?"

"Rust."

"Thank you for rescuing us, Rust." Jase added, "I
suggest that you go first and Arlan next. I'll follow the
Lieutenant Governor."

Rust growled an agreement, perched himself on the
most stable edge of the hole, and shoved himself forward to drop to the floor below. Even as he thudded to
a landing, Arlan followed, not even looking again at
Saschy. *He knows his negative effect on her,* thought
Jase with increasing respect for the Nilsonite.

"Go, C-human," ordered Saschy. "I want to collect a
few things first."

Jase directed persuasive Sesserda vocal skills at
Saschy, and he forced Truth upon her, "You are in

shock, and you want to hide yourself in your familiar refuge until you feel in control of yourself again, but you cannot remain here. You are needed elsewhere. You *need* to restore order to this world, Lieutenant Firl."

"I am not the Governor," argued Saschy in a hollow tone that sounded more like obstinacy than sincere belief.

Jase sympathized with her fear; he shared it, though it affected him less visibly. Nonetheless, he made his voice brutally harsh, recognizing Saschy's precarious state and the need to jolt her into rational behavior. He disliked manipulating her so extensively, but she carried a lifetime of interior wounds that made gentler, less invasive methods impractical in a crisis situation. "You have no leisure to indulge your injured pride. Governor Racker has not been found. Connections to the rest of Network are inoperative, and local systems are functioning erratically, if at all. You *are* the Governor of Nilson."

From the widening of her eyes, Jase knew that he had successfully reached past her guarded exterior and imposed at least a part of Truth upon her. Ignorance made her vulnerable to the simplest Sesserda tactics. Saschy murmured, "Yes. You're right, of course." Cautiously, she approached the hole in the floor. "I do hate heights."

The confession of her obvious fear made Jase smile in approval. "It's not a great distance, and they've already positioned a substantial pad of rugs to make it easier." Saschy edged hesitantly closer. "Here, this side is more stable." Jase could feel the tension in her. He offered her his hand to lead her, and she stared at it without response. "We all have our own fears, Lieutenant Firl, our own individual weaknesses—and strengths. Heights do not happen to disturb me, but I'd be terrified at the prospect of being Lieutenant Governor of Nilson. You should never be ashamed to admit Truth."

She answered tartly, "Then you shouldn't be lying to me now. I don't believe that anything terrifies you,

C-human." With a scowl, Saschy accepted his guidance in positioning herself for the jump, inhaled deeply to prepare herself, and launched herself bravely into a shadowy mound of torn carpeting.

Jase awaited only her landing before leaping into the ragged opening after her. When Jase rolled lightly to his feet beside her, he replied, "I am terrified by the consequences of what we are witnessing here and now."

Saschy bit her lip and nodded. "So am I, C-human." She straightened her rumpled clothing, glanced at the glassy walls of the burned room, and demanded, "Soldier, find your captain and inform him that the Acting Governor requires his personal report regarding the status of this insurgence and his progress in restoring order."

"We be needing still to exit by the sewer route," offered Arlan mildly, "past the melted steel kitchen, there."

"I've traveled by sewer before," snapped Saschy. "Soldier, go ahead of us and tell your captain to establish my headquarters in the west reception room, until a more suitable accommodation can be prepared. C-human, stop dawdling. Arlan, where is this sewer access?" She began to stride toward the distorted remains of the kitchen, trampling the fused remnants of Racker's prized chandeliers and porcelains.

CHAPTER 32

Calculating

Caragen's fingers thrummed the polished surface of his desk with seething impatience. "Attempt alternate channels again, Network," he insisted with quiet ferocity. "Marrach cannot block all access indefinitely."

After several minutes pulsed by the count of rain-pelted waves beyond Caragen's window, Network informed him, "Link failed."

"Connect me to Ned Racker."

"Link failed. All channels to Nilson are currently inoperative."

"Has every piece of equipment on that pathetic planet failed at once?" hissed Caragen. Possibly, he had underestimated the magnitude of the threat. If a natural disaster had actually occurred, would the losses ripple beyond Nilson? If it was not a natural occurrence, if Marrach had conspired with Jon Terry to steal another world from Network, would Marrach have advertised the fact? There were several members of the Network Council, highly accomplished manipulators, who might have indulged their egos with such a dangerous tactic, but Marrach was not of that ilk. Marrach had always moved quietly.

"Unknown. Analysis is proceeding. Nilson equipment is old, inexpensive, and subject to frequent disruptions of service."

"Service disruptions last for hours, not for days, and it is not Nilson's 'inexpensive' equipment alone that has become unreachable. Nothing about Marrach is inexpensive, and his disruptions of service have never occurred unintentionally. Is he blocking access to all of Nilson as well as to himself, or is he damaged?"

"Unknown. Analysis is proceeding."

"It has been *proceeding* for over three days," growled Caragen, "which diminishes the probability of a successful resolution."

"Probability of accurate resolution, in the absence of further input, is twenty-one percent."

Caragen shoved himself away from his desk and fixed his gaze on the stormy sea. "Are there any accessible ships in the vicinity of Nilson?"

"One ship, registered as a trading vessel of Cuui ownership, is leaving the Nilson solar system at maximum speed."

Caragen could not bring himself to question a Cuui about the status of a Network world, though he hungered to know if the Cuui's speed indicated flight from an unknown disaster. There was not a Network planet near enough to Nilson to allow practical access by a conventional space vessel. Nilson was much too close to Consortium space.

Requesting Consortium assistance was not a viable solution as far as Caragen was concerned. To ask for Calongi help would be worse than consulting a Cuui. However, help could be taken rather than requested. "Network, what is the status of that C-human who sought access to Racker's Cuui prisoner?"

"No departure of Jasen Margrave was registered prior to loss of Nilson contact."

"Notify the Consortium that one of their members, Mister Jasen Margrave, has suffered an accident on Nilson and requires assistance to return to his home world. If Consortium officials request additional information, inform me before replying."

"Acknowledged."

***

Saschy restrained her temper, though the young Network captain had forced her patience past its normal limits. Under the intensely blue gaze of the C-human, who had seen her at her worst and had made sure she knew the humbling scope of his insightful observations, she felt compelled to prove her competence as a leader of Nilson. She knew that Racker would have wasted no time in ridding himself of the C-human's company, but Saschy had concluded that the enigmatic Mister Margrave was too useful an ally to discard in the present circumstances. She certainly could not expect much aid from this helpless captain. "Have you questioned *any* of the rebels yet?"

"Of course," replied the captain with injured dignity. "But we have taken only two alive, and they disclaimed all connection with any organized effort against Network government. They both denied obeying any single leader, and the chaotic form of the ongoing attacks supports the idea of isolated rioters taking advantage of this situation."

"There are always opportunists to be found," snapped Saschy, "but listen to the shouts from the streets! There is a single leader of the terrorists that started this madness, and his name is Breamas. I am interested in what Breamas' followers used to tear a hole in space. If they can tell us how they created that *thing* that's taken the place of Governor Racker's office, then maybe we can *un*create it."

The captain grunted, "The two prisoners died of their wounds shortly after capture."

"Then question the prisoners that filled the city prison before the explosion! Breamas' followers have never been difficult to find."

Jase murmured softly, "I doubt that Breamas' followers expected their bomb to cause such impressive damage."

Saschy turned toward Jase and weighed all the strange abilities that he had evidenced. She knew little about the Consortium, but Consortium justice was legendary even in Network. "You learned more from Filcher Ikthan Cuui in one meeting than Network discovered in months of incarceration. Could you question human prisoners and obtain the truth with equal success?" The Network captain shuffled uncomfortably.

"Yes," agreed Jase after a lengthy pause, "but I'm

not sure that you realize what you're suggesting. Inquisition is not a process to impose on those who have refused to acknowledge Consortium law."

"Does Filcher Ikthan Cuui acknowledge your Consortium law?" she countered.

"Not officially."

"You questioned him anyway."

"Yes. He is at least marginally aware of what Sesserda Truth means."

"We need all the answers we can find, Mister Margrave. I think you would be wise to assist us in that effort—to the best of your abilities." She added cunningly, "Your pretty lady friend is among those we are trying to locate."

"I have not forgotten her," replied Jase crisply.

Saschy chose to interpret his answer as concession. "Captain, arrange an escort to accompany Mister Margrave to the prison and provide him with free access to all of the prisoners. Perhaps Mister Margrave can learn something useful from *one* of them."

The captain protested, "Lieutenant Governor, there are a few thousand rebels between us and the prison. For all we know, the prison has been taken and the prisoners freed."

"The prison is not that easy to take. It has some of the best automated defenses on Nilson, and no terrorist bomb could destroy them without killing the inmates, many of whom are Breamas' followers. It is less than a kilometer from here, Captain. If your well-armed, well-trained soldiers cannot protect one man for a journey of that short distance, then we have additional *serious* problems to address. You are fighting Breamas' ragtag rabble, not a full-fledged, fully equipped army. If you cannot organize a rout of such a pathetic foe, then perhaps you should consider relinquishing your command to someone more capable."

The captain grunted his acknowledgment and departed stiffly. Jase observed quietly, "You should not antagonize your allies, Lieutenant Firl."

"Take your own advice, C-human."

***

"The Network Council Governor has gone to some trouble to send this lie to us," observed Mintaka in the crystalline meditation chamber of her honored Calongi colleague. The light of a golden sky danced in rainbows through the faceted windows. "He begins to recognize the disaster that his greed has wrought."

"Jase-lai understood the difficult nature of the task," replied Ukitan. "He honors Truth."

Mintaka raised a wandlike, iridescent limb from beneath her velvety cloak, and she laid its tip gently against the largest sensor patch on the upper lobe of Ukitan's braincase. It was a gesture of deep empathy. "We asked too much, Ukitan-lai. He is Soli."

Golden cilia above Ukitan's eyes trembled with emotion. "Calongi blood flows in him."

"We asked too much."

"We asked what was necessary. We asked what is necessary."

"We did not tell him all the Truth of what he faced."

"He knew our restraint and accepted our judgment. We could not bias the Inquisition."

"It is hard for you, who taught him."

"It is hard for us. It is less hard for him."

With a myriad of subtle, broken harmonies, Mintaka began to sing of sorrow. She strengthened the melody in a pure, single voice. The crystalline chamber resonated as Ukitan added rich layers that told of honor and sacrifice and millenia of noble history. As evening changed the golden sky to violet, their song became a prayer for the healing of the wound that an ignorant people had inflicted on Sesserda Truth.

CHAPTER 33

Spelunking

The air thinned, or so it seemed to Tori at first. She inhaled a little more deeply, a little more rapidly, as the burning in her veins indicated an imperfect adaptation. Her last inoculation of adaptation fluid should not have been that close to expiration, but she could not calibrate normal doses under the strangeness of these abnormal shifts through space.

Feeling solid ground beneath her feet, she dared to open her eyes, but she found herself in unrelieved darkness. She still clutched the hand of the peculiar young man who had brought her here so abruptly, and she derived some comfort from the tactile sense. The air was warm and only slightly stale. "Do you have any insight as to where we've landed this time?" she asked of her odd companion.

"From the stones poking into my back, I'd say we're in a cave or a natural tunnel," he answered. "Extend your arm toward your left and see if you can feel a wall."

She reached blindly with her left arm and struck a sharp stone slightly above her head. She tugged Quin with her as she sidled along a floor of undulating stone, intermittently pillared, to trace the tapering rocky ceiling down to its meeting with the ground. From there she moved forward cautiously, exploring with her hand, until a curving portion of the low ceiling began to rise, and she pursued it to a standing height. With her fingers dragging lightly against the uneven wall, she began to walk forward, moving with extreme care to negotiate unseen obstacles.

Quin asked her curiously, "Are you feeling 'led'

toward a specific goal, or are you just testing my ability to dodge stalactites?"

She answered with impatience, because her only reason was the certainty that their current location was not acceptable to her, "You brought us here. You tell me where we should be heading."

"I like your choice of direction," replied Quin affably. "I was only wondering if you had something particular in mind."

Thinking of Jase's elegant home on Calong with rare wistfulness, she replied wryly, "What I have in mind is neither practical nor suitable to the moment." Sharp crystals splintered into her fingers, and she muttered a warning to Quin, but he had evidently decided to leave the primitive tactile navigation to her. She might have dismissed him as a lazy, scatterbrained, fairly useless companion-in-crisis, if not for those singular moments that preceded transfer. She finally felt warm enough and safe enough to take the time to ask him, "How do you control the transfer between worlds?"

Quin evaded a direct answer, compensating for dearth of actual explanation with a plethora of rapid chatter. "That place we left was seriously unstable. This isn't ideal, but it's a significant improvement. I've never gone spelunking before, have you? There is a mining colony called Wharton associated closely with the Nilson space, and that may be where we've landed. If so, we should be able to find some more civilized regions if we just keep moving. The atmosphere tastes artificial, don't you think?"

"I am not that familiar with barbaric Network devices for converting a perfectly good environment into something altogether unnatural." It was one of Jase's many arguments regarding uncivilized Network practices, but recent events had elevated it to a newly high status with Tori.

"You're not a Network citizen?" demanded Quin, no longer sounding frivolous or scatterbrained at all. His grip on her hand tightened perceptibly, reminding her of one of Jase's probing techniques.

"No." His question surprised Tori, for Quin had displayed no such pointed curiosity about her until now. She wondered if he shared her sense that this world was sufficiently stable to warrant some redirection of energy away from the task of mere survival. *How easy it would be to imagine Jase here with me,* thought Tori, but she recalled herself immediately from her self-indulgent drifting. This young man was emphatically *not* Jase, and she could not afford to risk the despair that could come from speculation. She did not dare contemplate the possibility that she would not find Jase again.

"If you're not a Network citizen," insisted Quin, "what are you?"

Quin's increased tension and the aura of urgency in his question almost inspired Tori to lie, but imaginings of Jase berated her. She also decided that such a falsehood would be unsustainable. "I am a member of the Consortium who had the misfortune of visiting Nilson at an inopportune time. Do you have an aversion to spelunking in the company of a Consortium member?"

"Not at all," replied Quin earnestly. Excitement had replaced tension in his voice, which only puzzled Tori more completely. Distrust and distaste comprised the typical Network reaction to Consortium members. "In fact, I was only trying to visit Nilson originally in the hope of meeting an alien. I never met a Consortium member before now. What is it like?"

"The Consortium?" asked Tori, grumbling as she stubbed her toe on a protruding wedge of rock. Just as she began to conclude that the tunnel was too uniformly wide and level for an artifact of nature, some unseen obstacle arose to change her opinion.

"The Consortium, living side-by-side with all those different species, giving your allegiance to Calongi government . . . all of it, any of it."

"I didn't think Network citizens took an interest in anything outside of Network."

"I'm not the most conventional of Network citizens."

"Obviously." Tori could think of no reason to refuse to educate him, though his curiosity contradicted every

Network profile that she had encountered. There was
nothing secretive about the general nature of the Consortium. There was certainly nothing more palatable to
discuss as they crept through these interminably dark
corridors, since he seemed as ignorant as she about the
specifics of their situation. "What do you want to hear,
aside from everything?"

She could feel his shrug from the swinging of his
hand. "What does a Calongi look like?"

Thinking of her first personal encounter with a Calongi Inquisitor, Tori answered, "Like the personifica-
tion of doom."

"Did I choose a bad first question?"

"No!" she laughed in self-mockery. "You cannot
understand the Consortium without understanding
something about Calongi. You just chose to ask of
someone who gives bad answers, unless you have a
taste for flippancy." She relented and paraphrased a
formal description from a Prili text, "A Calongi looks
like a very tall, very imposing, darkly cloaked biped
with a smooth, unevenly patterned head that houses an
oversized, multisegmented brain. The 'cloak' and its
sublayers consist of various limbs that the Calongi
grow consciously and tailor to suit their individual
wishes and needs. Their optical organs resemble oversized feline eyes of blue or green or yellow, situated on
mounds atop their heads. The placement and number of
their obvious facial features corresponds fairly closely
to the Soli design. However, they have vastly more
sensory organs than any normal Soli can even identify,
from the blue sensor patches covering their heads to
the golden tendrils on their necks and eye ridges. They
worship Truth."

"You don't like the Calongi."

"I did not mean to be taken literally regarding their
resemblance to 'doom.' "

"I know. That's not what I meant either. I mean that
you dislike them for personal reasons."

"Is it that obvious?" Tori usually managed to keep
her discussions of Calongi emotionless and unrevealing, even to trained observers, but she *was* tired. "It is

hard to like them. It's almost impossible not to respect them, once you've met any of them."

"I'd enjoy meeting one."

"Then you really are unconventional—or simply too naive to know better. I have hardly ever met a Soli who actually enjoys Calongi company. I don't think Calongi are much more fond of us uncivilized Soli on a personal level, but we have a 'proper purpose' in the totality of creation, and the Calongi respect creation unreservedly. That respect is fundamental to their definition of Sesserda Truth. As part of their of endless, compulsive identification of Truth in all its details, they strive to define the proper purpose of every species and every individual. I don't always care for Calongi methods, but I believe in the value of the results."

"What is your 'proper purpose' in the Consortium?"

Tori hesitated before replying, "I facilitate alien relations."

"That sounds like a difficult undertaking."

"The level of difficulty depends on the aliens." As Quin laughed, a sound of sincere merriment, she added, "You're certainly cheerful for a man lost in a potentially endless tunnel on an unknown world with no particularly promising resources for survival."

"It must be your talent for alien relations, my lady. I was feeling uncommonly discouraged, but you've revived my optimism to a spectacular degree. Would you care for the last remains of a biscuit?"

"Not yet, thank you. I haven't recovered from the previous sample, and I'd rather be armed with potable water before testing a second. Does the air smell damp to you?"

"Maybe. I'm not sure. It's been a long time since I studied the arts of wilderness survival, and I never was the best of students."

"I think we're approaching water—or at least some form of moisture." As she spoke, she blinked to confirm the reality of what her eyes were telling her. "Is that a light ahead of us?"

"If not, we're both delusional."

"You said something about a mine called Wharton?" murmured Tori, wishing she could find something about it in her memories, but the Consortium's access to Network data records was not that complete.

"I was just making a guess, but I'm beginning to believe it's where we've really landed." Tori began to move more quickly, as the tunnel acquired rough, but visible contours. She would have shaken free of Quin's hand, but he stopped her. "Wait. There's something wrong in front of us."

"What do you mean?"

In the dim light, she could barely see him shake his head. "I'm not sure yet. I feel something. . . ."

"Like another transfer coming?" demanded Tori, tensing instinctively. She could inquire later about the unconventional aspects of his perceptions.

"No. It's a different type of instability—a thickening rather than a thinning of the patterns."

"What patterns?"

"The patterns of infinity," he answered vaguely, then seemed to shake himself free of a self-imposed entrancement. "I'm sorry. I'm rambling."

"Network and its pointless secrets," muttered Tori, though her explanation of his mysterious behavior did not entire satisfy her.

"I've always loathed secrecy," agreed Quin innocently.

Tori realized that he had slid free of her hand only when he strode several paces ahead of her. He turned into a side corridor that she had not noticed. "Where are you going? The light is coming from the other direction."

"Not every light deserves to be pursued," retorted Quin. "That one could be downright unhealthy. Anyway, this tunnel is smooth. I think it's been tooled."

Because her fingers confirmed his assessment, Tori did not argue, but she began to wonder if he were as ignorant of their location as he pretended. A shared plight encouraged trust that would otherwise be withheld. As danger lost its sense of imminence, Tori's suspicions of him began to expand.

"I think there's a door here," said Quin. "Yes. Here's the lever." The door squeaked as it rose. The light that slid beneath it seemed blindingly bright in contrast to the tunnel, though its origin seemed to be no more than an expiring emergency beacon. A distant hammering was muffled but unmistakably regular and deliberate. "It looks like a utility center."

When Tori's eyes adjusted, she agreed with him. Polished pipes and trusses snarled their pathway, but it was a navigable course. "Network," she demanded, according to the custom she had observed, "is this Wharton?"

"There are no acoustic sensors in here," said Quin, "and no speakers."

"How do you know?" countered Tori.

"Network did not challenge us."

"Does this look like a restricted area?"

"Yes."

"Then why wasn't the door locked?"

"It's an interior door. I'd guess that access is blocked from the populated regions. Fortunately, we're on the inside, and Network usually supplies emergency exits for the benefit of authorized maintenance personnel."

"How do you people live with such rules?"

Quin shrugged and grinned cheerfully. "It's not so bad, when you get accustomed to it."

Get accustomed to it? echoed the suspicious part of Tori's mind. *He's not an ordinary Network citizen, if he's a Network citizen at all. How many other ways has he misled me? Was it truly an accident that swept me away from Nilson, Governor Racker, and Jase?* Tori replied to Quin's broad grin with an equally uncommunicative smile. She let him take the lead as they moved through a maze of tunnels, and she watched him warily.

CHAPTER 34

Allying

For the hundredth time, Katerin prowled through the gardens of the castle of Tul in search of Lady Rhianna. She had even ventured as far as the peak of Tul Mountain, which loomed above the Infortiare's Tower, thinking that Lady Rhianna might have sought a form of emotional refuge at the reputed site of her husband's mortal death. Katerin did not know why the probable loss of her own husband and father should impose a debilitating level of distress on Lady Rhianna, but she had no doubt of the reality of the Infortiare's state. As far as Katerin could determine from reluctant servants, who were always wary of the Infortiare's strange visitors, no one had seen the Infortiare since Katerin's own unsettling encounter over a week ago.

Frustration had compounded grief but risen above fear, as Katerin forced herself to accept the real possibility that she might be trapped in this pseudo-medieval kingdom for the rest of a very lonely life. In a somber mood, she walked closer to the castle than was usual for her, deriving solace from the structured plantings that suited the Seriin monarchs better than the unruly growth that was Rhianna's preference. Avoiding members of the court who strolled in the evening's bright moonlight, Katerin ducked inside an arbor.

An elderly woman's amused voice emerged from the shadow of the arbor's wooden bench. "They are only courtiers, my dear, not dragons, though I admit that they gossip ferociously. Step into the light, my dear. My old eyes are no longer very useful at night."

Feeling trapped, Katerin complied, hoping that her awkward curtsy sufficed to satisfy the old dowager's faulty vision. "I apologize for intruding, my lady," murmured Katerin in her best Seriin.

To Katerin's surprise, the woman declared with a firm confidence, "You are Lady Katerin dura Hamley, Lord Quinzaine's wife."

Katerin had never accustomed herself to the grandiose Seriin titles, but she answered, "Yes, my lady." Katerin struggled to conjure a reciprocal name as facilely as the old woman, but the shadows around the bench were too deep, and the voice no more than dimly familiar. Katerin had met fewer than a dozen noblewomen in Tulea, and nearly all of them made their permanent home in Ixaxis. Quin had taken her to Hamley on a few occasions, but Katerin could not imagine any of that clan recognizing her in the moonlit Tulean garden. Feeling trapped in an awkward conversation, Katerin regretted having strayed so close to the castle proper.

"Calm yourself, my dear. I am not as frightening as that."

"I am sorry, my lady, but your face is in the shadows and I cannot see you clearly. I do not know to whom I am speaking."

"That is quite clear from your manner of addressing me, but it is also quite understandable and entirely forgivable. My proper title is 'Your Majesty,' which is a clumsy thing to say and undoubtedly uncomfortable for you, who are unaccustomed to our pretentious aristocracy. I would be pleased if you would call me Joli, though the stuffier members of my family would be appalled to hear me say it. Hardly anyone calls me by my name any longer."

Realization struck hard at Katerin: This whimsical woman was absolute monarch of this land of Serii, the largest and most influential country of this world. Confinement to Serii would make Katerin subject to whatever law the queen of Serii might decree. Even more nervous than before, Katerin spoke the unfamiliar words stumblingly, "Your Majesty, forgive my unintentional rudeness." While Katerin had long ago recognized the enormous magnitude of the cultural

adjustments that would be required of her to survive in
Serii, the reality had never seemed more dauntingly
immediate than now, here in the chance presence of
Queen Joli in a dusky garden. Just as Quin had never
truly accepted Network citizenship—despite his multitude of official identities—Katerin had never num-
bered herself among the subjects of the Seriin
monarchy. If Quin did not return, Katerin would need
to change her perspective dramatically.

Joli chuckled deeply. "You will wear as many
wrinkles as I do if you make a habit of fretting so visibly. Child, I do not expect you to adhere to courtly
etiquette, unless some tedious public proceeding demands it of us both. Rhianna has told me a great deal
about you, Lady Katerin."

Katerin attempted to form a reply that she imagined
Lady Rhianna might give, since Quin was a self-
proclaimed poor example. "Your Majesty is generous."
Katerin tried to recall any exceptions to the rules about
formal dismissal required before taking leave of a
monarch. There were undoubtedly accepted methods of
departing inoffensively, but Katerin had never studied
such subtleties of courtly behavior.

The queen showed no inclination to end the conversation quickly. "If I were not so decrepit with age, I
would dearly love to visit your world—or should I say
worlds? I am still not quite clear on what your Network
actually comprises. Rhianna explains these things to
me in terms of patterns and Power, and I seldom understand her completely. I have no wizardly Power, of
course, and I have never had the luxury to travel as extensively as I once dreamed. When I do travel, I am so
surrounded by my guards and aides that I feel as if I
were still in my own home." Velvet rustled against silk
as Joli adjusted her cloak. "Rhianna has told me that
you are a scholar of some repute in your own world.
Your specialty, as she described it, seems rather alarming: studying the way people think and react in order to
control their behavior on a widespread basis. It seems
to resemble one of the most detested aspects of Ixaxin
Power."

For the sake of diplomacy, Katerin preferred to avoid a discussion of mathematical psychology with Queen Joli, whose talent for enforcing her personal will was renowned. "My only remaining reputation in Network is that of a fugitive from Network's ruler."

"He sounds like an unpleasant man from what I have heard, but pleasant people rarely last in positions of such power. I have known some exceedingly difficult individuals who made quite competent leaders. Goodness knows, there are enough people who consider me a tyrant."

Unable to think of any polite reply that would not sound obviously forced, Katerin asked the question that remained uppermost in her mind, "Your Majesty, have you seen Lady Rhianna within the past few days?"

"No, child. Since I have not been declared 'near death' in that time, Rhianna has not come to see me." Joli sighed. "I should not be so unkind toward her. Rhianna is the dearest friend I have. I suppose you know that she persuaded me to accept the rule of Serii initially, when I was terribly young and completely intimidated by Lord Venkarel—and by the entire court, for that matter."

"I regret to admit that my knowledge of your country's history is limited."

"Never mind, child. Most Seriins know little more of our history than the names of Tul and Ceallagh, who jointly ended the long tyranny of the Immortal Sorcerer Kings. Though as King Tul's descendant, I should not admit it, I have always thought Celleagh played much the nobler role. How many men of such Power would have given mortal Tul the larger share of governing authority and created for himself the much humbler title and duties of Infortiare?"

Katerin wondered wildly if Seriin citizenship would often require her to navigate meandering conversations with an elderly, absolute monarch in a moonlit garden. "They must both have been extraordinary men, Your Majesty."

"Yes," agreed Joli. "But you inquired quite solemnly

about Rhianna, and I answer with an old woman's ramblings. What is troubling you, Lady Katerin?"

"I can find no one who has seen Lady Rhianna in several days. When I last saw her, she seemed quite unwell."

"Unwell? Rhianna is never ill. She looks like a porcelain doll, but she has the constitution of a plowhorse."

"She was emotionally unwell, Your Majesty, if not physically ill. As you are apparently aware, I do have some knowledge of the workings of the human mind, and Lady Rhianna was in severe distress. She spoke incoherently, and she fled from me into the woods."

"Rhianna has always taken solace from her trees," mused Joli. "I have noticed that she reverts more often to her old, isolated habits when Lord Arineuil goes on one of his extended voyages across the seas, as is presently the case. He is one of the few mortals who shares her confidence and yet remains unintimidated by her. Does your husband share your concern?"

Katerin tried to curtail her frustration at the queen's digressions. To have the attention of the Seriin monarch merited an exertion of patience. "My husband is missing, Your Majesty, as is my father."

"Dear child, no wonder you are fretting." Joli's slight body straightened, and her voice firmed into regality, "You should have come to me sooner, Lady Katerin, but I shall not reprimand you in your personal grief. Do the Ixaxins know of these matters?"

"Ixaxins do not generally confide in me, nor have I had an opportunity to question any of them recently."

"Indeed, that does not surprise me. Wizards do not communicate well outside their chalky island and its school of wizardry, even among themselves. Power breeds rivalry and suspicion by its nature." The bench creaked. "Help me up, child. We need to send messengers immediately both to Ixaxis and to Lady Rhianna's son, Lord Evaric." Katerin felt the queen's fragile hands shake, as Katerin helped her to rise. There was, however, no weakness evident in the queen's bright, insightful eyes as she asked, "Do you know Lord Evaric?"

"I have seen him once, very briefly." *And heard enough from Quin to seek no closer meeting. But the queen is correct: Who would be more likely to know Rhianna's whereabouts?* "Does he not live on Ixaxis?"

"No, my dear! He has a mortal wife, who loathes the place, and she entirely dominates their lifestyle and social contacts. He is an odd man, not comfortable with people as a rule. I suppose he resembles his father in that regard."

"His father, Lord Venkarel," mused Katerin uncomfortably, as the two women began the walk to the castle. Joli leaned heavily on Katerin.

"Lord Venkarel was the oddest man of all the Ixaxins in history, most think, and Ixaxins are all a little strange to us mortals. I have often wondered if Ceallagh was a great deal like him."

The queen's meandering reminiscences suddenly triggered a sense of personal astonishment that pierced through Katerin's deeper concerns. "You imagine Ceallagh to have resembled Lord Venkarel?" Neither Rhianna's impassioned devotion nor the more common fearful and fearsome allusions to Lord Venkarel had ever evoked in Katerin an image of Venkarel as hero. Katerin struggled to link the whispered stories of the previous Infortiare with a man who had won friends, as well as enemies.

"Is it too fanciful to equate Serii's legendary savior with the devil Venkarel? Perhaps. It is true that I have listened often to Rhianna, who remains obsessively devoted to her Kaedric, even after all these years. But I think I have more reason than her prejudice to support my theory. I did know him, after all, though I was just a girl when he left us. Few Seriins realize that Kaedric sacrificed himself knowingly. He entered into battle, fully aware of the price that he would pay."

"Did he have a choice? It was a time of war, was it not?"

"A war of wizards," answered Joli dryly, "more truly than of mortal soldiers, because Kaedric chose to fight the larger battle that few Seriins recognized amid the normal, terrible carnage of mortal war. Kaedric had a heroic soul, but it was so difficult for most of us to see the man beyond the angry Power that all of us dreaded—for good reason, since his Power destroyed the city of Ven before he reached manhood. The abbot who found him in the rubble required exceptional courage, as well as wisdom, to take that deadly boy directly to Ixaxis. Abbot Medwyn was also a hero recognized by few."

Moonlight blanched the frail, velvet-cloaked queen who hobbled beside Katerin on a grassy path. Queen Joli's accounts of history that she had witnessed had seemed aimless at first, but Katerin began to appreciate a purpose in their direction. "Lord Venkarel must have been a formidable man."

"I cannot assess the magnitude of a wizard's skills to know if he had more than a major Power's 'ordinary' share, but there was a strangeness in him, a dangerous quality that even a mortal could not escape seeing. Many Ixaxins cite Kaedric, Lord Venkarel, as a prime example of the dangers of letting Power develop outside the confines of Ixaxin regimen, and he concurred vociferously with that assessment. It was why he nearly removed the head of the ruling Lord of Tyntagel on discovering that the Lady Rhianna, daughter of that noble family, had been hidden from Ixaxis throughout her youth. She was forced to deny her Power even from herself."

"She was not educated on Ixaxis?" asked Katerin, understanding many past conversations via the queen's calm words.

"No, my dear child. Her father would not tolerate an admission of Power in his family. When she came to court, Lord Venkarel trained her secretly, there in the Tower of the Infortiare. I think both of them resented the arrangement at first, but Lord Venkarel would not allow another major Power to grow, like his, too long without proper Ixaxin discipline. He required her to accept the training, and he was not a man to be contradicted easily. Indeed, Lord Venkarel was the most

terrifying man I ever met. You could almost see the
fire of his Power in him, if you could escape the deadly
cold of those ice-blue eyes of his."

Katerin murmured pensively, "Lady Rhianna still
speaks of him as if he were alive."

"She says that his Power survives."

"Do you believe her?"

"I would not contradict the Infortiare in a matter of
Power."

Frowning at her own hypothesis, Katerin speculated,
"If Lord Venkarel, or whatever remained of him, were
lost like Quin and my father, what would be the effect
on Lady Rhianna?"

"I think that it would kill her," answered Joli
promptly, and Katerin realized that the queen had
reached this conclusion before beginning her apparent
ramblings. "I hope that we are wrong, my dear. I do
most fervently hope that we are wrong."

**

Once Queen Joli's bent shoulders assumed the burden of worry, Katerin found herself able to rediscover
hope, though not calm. Katerin spent most of the ensuing days in the queen's bright white-and-gilt personal
suite, answering the queen's questions, and wondering
what her former friends in Network would have
thought to see Katerin's portrayal of a Seriin lady-
in-waiting. The messenger from Ixaxis returned with a
letter that expressed concern and ignorance in equal
parts, but Queen Joli merely remarked on the predictable inability to coax useful information out of
Ixaxins. Katerin continued to hope, but her nerves became as raw as her tear-stained skin.

Katerin continued to hope until Lord Evaric arrived
and issued his matter-of-fact acknowledgement that his
mother was missing—not just from the Infortiare's
Tower but from anywhere in reach of his Power. Too
tall, too thin, too emphatically dark of nature for Katerin's tastes, Lord Evaric resembled an aloof messenger of death as he stood before the queen, his clothing

as black as his hair, his lean shadow extending the length of the white marble floor. Queen Joli had allowed only Katerin to remain with her in the sunny morning room upon the announcement of Lord Evaric's arrival, but the queen had also ordered Katerin to remain at silent attention behind the queen's gilt chair. Obedience came with difficulty, as Katerin restrained herself from voicing the questions that seethed inside of her. Queen Joli might be forthright and amiable in private, but she was entirely a monarch when she performed the functions of her position. On this morning, as hope died, Katerin found the legal pretentions ludicrous and nearly unendurable.

This morning, there was no mistaking Joli's intention to be recognized as queen. A thin crown of silver and emeralds rested on her coiled white hair, and Katerin had never seen such intricate needlework as the embroidery that adorned the queen's garnet brocade gown. Katerin wondered how many Seriin servants had devoted their entire lifetimes to the adorning of a single garment in the royal wardrobe.

"Lady Rhianna told you nothing of her plans?" asked Joli.

Evaric answered with a wryness that many of the queen's courtiers would have denounced as disrespectful, "My mother reports to me even less often than to you, Your Majesty." Even the careless draping of his black cloak displayed an indifference to the usual court protocols.

Queen Joli raised whitened brows, eloquent contrast on her birthmark-reddened face. "You seem unconcerned by the discovery of her absence."

"She has a keener aptitude for self-preservation than anyone else I have ever known." His gaze flickered toward Katerin, appraising without comment, then returned to the queen. Katerin stiffened with resentment of his arrogant dismissal. "Even when my mother chooses to take some phenomenal risk, she remains guarded at a fundamental level. It is a dominant aspect of her Power."

"Do you have any idea of where she may be?"

"I have many ideas, Your Majesty, but I have only a single pertinent *fact* to offer you: I cannot reach her. Since I find myself equally unable to contact my ethereal father, there is some reason to believe that they are together. If they are together, they are content even if they are jointly in danger, for they require nothing and no one but each other." His elusive, misty silver eyes darted once more toward Katerin, but this time they lingered. She had a brief, unwelcome awareness of his coldly burning Power delving inside her, evaluating her. "Lady Katerin's concern is well-founded, however, if her husband has been roaming the infinities according to his usual practice. The patterns beyond the space of our world are reeling."

Katerin opened her mouth to speak, but Queen Joli raised an imperious hand and preceded her, "Explain yourself more clearly, Lord Evaric. You know how I dislike hearing explanations that have meaning only to other wizards."

Evaric shifted his cloak across his shoulder, and Katerin was afforded a glimpse of the hilt and scabbard of a long-knife, troubling in context of his history. "Somewhere, presumably among worlds that Lady Katerin could identify far better than I, a rending has occurred. There was a similar event on this world once, as Your Majesty undoubtedly recalls, and the repair of it was difficult."

"You may speak plainly of it, Lord Evaric," grumbled Joli. "The repair of this world's Rending nearly killed you, and you have devoted the majority of your Power since that time to the effort of maintaining the seal. Certain Ixaxin scholars fret that our world cannot outlive you."

"The repair can last as long as my *Immortal* Power. The Taormin predicted our world's Rending a few thousand years before its occurrence and bred me and my Power specifically for the purpose of repair. I doubt that a similar service has preceded the recent event, which I believe to be far more severe in magnitude than our own trouble." Katerin clenched her thin hands tightly, recalling her father's fascination with the product of his invention, this dark and ominous man who was intrinsic to the stability of his world's topology. "Our Rending made us vulnerable to the dangers of the single space that crossed boundaries with ours. I think that a cataclysm is in progress now that will eventually cross all boundaries, including our own, unless its damage is reversed soon. With increasing frequency over the past few months, I have found myself struggling consciously just to keep our own patterns stable, and that represents a degree of effort that has not been required of me in many years."

Joli twisted one of the multijeweled rings that decorated her mottled hands. "Lady Rhianna is aware of this rending?"

"Considering how my father has embedded himself in the patterns of infinity, she could not help but be aware of the trouble, because he would be inextricably aware of it. Could this rending explain their disappearance? Possibly, though I would not expect either of them to attempt to resolve such a situation without discussing the matter with me—if they had a choice." To Katerin's critical eye, his smile seemed almost cruel. "They have, however, been known to exclude me in the past. They trust no outsider as thoroughly as each other. We Immortals are not a trusting breed."

Too many fears and frustrations, compounded by this hard wizard's disdainful attitude, tore away the last defense of Katerin's frail hope and inflamed her temper. She could no longer pretend to be a submissive Seriin noblewoman, silent at her queen's side. "You Power-mad Immortals take as much pride in your weaknesses as in your strengths. Do any of you ever consider seeking help beyond your narrow ranks? You, Lord Evaric, have recognized a problem for several months, and yet you did not choose to inform my husband, whom you know to be deeply involved in 'roaming the infinities.' Lady Rhianna sent my father to investigate a dangerous matter of which you were acutely conscious, and none of you saw fit to tell him what he might be confronting. That Lady Rhianna has disappeared without a word to you, Lord Evaric, seems only too consistent with the endemic self-centered nature of Ixaxins."

Evaric looked amused, but Queen Joli rebuked Katerin sharply, "You interrupt us, Lady Katerin, and your remarks are discourteous. I realize that you were not raised to appreciate our culture, but you are in my court, and you will please either behave accordingly or depart now."

Katerin replied stiffly, knowing that she deserved censure but too sorely hurt to care, "I would like nothing better than to depart from this entire country, Your Majesty."

There was sympathy in Joli's expression, but her answer was stern, "You must settle for departing from this room, until you have calmed yourself."

Without any attempt at a curtsy or other indulgence of autocratic ego, Katerin strode toward the door as rapidly as her unwieldy Seriin skirts would allow. She struggled with the gold handle of the heavy inlaid door, but haste made her clumsy and slow. To Katerin's surprise, Evaric defended her before she could complete her escape, "Lady Katerin is understandably distraught, Your Majesty, and her accusations are not entirely unjustified. If I may accompany her, perhaps I can allay some of her concerns and better educate myself simultaneously. There is little more that I can tell Your Majesty at this point."

"Go," sighed Joli. "These matters of Power weary me, and I would contemplate for a while alone. Expect a summons from me later, when I am rested."

The quaver of exhaustion in the queen's voice stemmed Katerin's anger and instilled regret. Katerin turned to offer a belated curtsy, but Joli only waved a hand limply in dismissal. Evaric swept to the door and opened it easily. His hard fingers bit into Katerin's arm, and he coaxed her from the room inarguably. When he had closed the door behind them, he took his own turn at giving reprimand, "Queen Joli is not well. Rail at me, if you wish, but do not air your temper needlessly before her. Her health does not fare well under such circumstances." With rapid strides of his long legs, he was virtually dragging Katerin toward the passage that connected the queen's castle to the Infortiare's Tower.

"I know that I behaved badly, and I am sorry for having upset her," answered Katerin, though she disliked apologizing to this austere and aggravating man, who continued to grip her arm with bruising force. "That does not excuse your current bullying of me. You present a poor example of a Seriin gentleman." A serving woman scurried from their path with an expression of alarm.

"I have my own share of brittle temper, Lady Katerin," he retorted, "and I have never been known as a gentle man, much less a gentleman." Nonetheless, he relaxed his hold on her and slowed his rapid pace. He released her altogether in order to unlatch the cumbersome wooden door that led into the Tower's stairwell. Once inside the Tower's stone confines, he leaned against the wall and folded his arms. "If you want my help, tell me what has been happening here. I think you have been a closer witness than I to my mother's recent schemings."

"I thoroughly dislike men who try to intimidate me by physical force," said Katerin coldly. She matched his posture on the opposite side of the stair.

He smiled crookedly, which helped to alleviate his otherwise grim demeanor. "Your point is made—again. Will you accept my apology, Lady Katerin, or would you prefer a duel of honor? I should warn you that I have some experience in fighting duels."

"Quin calls you the deadliest swordmaster in Serii."

"He exaggerates slightly. I have not killed anyone in a swordfight in at least a dozen years."

"Because no one dares to challenge you."

"No one with any sense," agreed Evaric. "Just as I doubt that anyone with any sense would attempt to best you in an argument more than once."

Katerin almost conceded a smile. Her temper had cooled, and she wondered how large a part his Power played in calming her. "When did you last communicate with Lady Rhianna?"

"Half a year ago, at least. I try to maintain regular contact with her, but time seems to disappear more quickly every year."

Katerin nodded, recalling that the Infortiare's saturnine son, despite his youthful appearance, was not much younger than the aged and infirm Queen Joli. "Have you communicated with any Ixaxins in that time?"

"No," he laughed dryly. "Like most Seriins, the knowledgeable wizards of Ixaxis tend to distrust me. They recognize too much of my father in me, especially as the years distort their memories of him."

Memories of the devil Venkarel, thought Katerin, *whom the queen likened to the heroic Ceallagh.* Katerin tried to analyze Evaric by the Network regimens she knew intimately, but he was an elusive subject. She could only resort to her recollections of Quin's occasional comments about the Infortiare's son: alarming in the particulars, but spoken with respect. She had little enough to lose by extending her trust. "Then it seems that I have a great deal to tell you, Lord Evaric."

Meticulously, Katerin began to recount all the potentially relevant events that she had witnessed, directly or indirectly, since Quin developed his unhealthy curiosities following the escape from Geisen University. Evaric sank cross-legged to the slate floor after half an hour. Katerin imitated him immediately, paying little heed to the Seriin notions of propriety as she fumbled impatiently with bulky skirts. Evaric listened attentively and interrupted only twice to request clarification of unfamiliar Network terms. He asked few questions, but they were insightful and formulated with impressive clarity for a Seriin who had no personal experience of Network, its technologies, or its culture. Katerin found herself approving of him much more readily as a student than as a man. He was extraordinarily quick and absolutely unwavering in his concentration. As Katerin's initial antagonism toward him waned, she could almost begin to imagine how his father had managed to captivate the young Lady Rhianna dur Tyntagel.

When Katerin finished her recital, Evaric stared upward at the spiraling staircase in pensive silence for several minutes, his wrists resting lightly on his bent knees. Katerin pondered the faded brand of a sword, seared into the skin of his hand, with an uneasy recollection of the way Quin had emphasized the *deadliness* of Evaric's swordsmanship. Two hours of assessing Evaric by the techniques of her profession had only intensified Katerin's certainty that this was a singularly dangerous man, his father's heir in more than lean physique and night-black hair. She had no difficulty concluding that Evaric would be a lethal enemy—but she had also decided that he could be a priceless ally. She asked him quietly, "What course of action would you recommend, my lord?" Her deliberate use of the Seriin honorific elicited a wry smile from him.

His answer startled her, "A comparison of notes with your Network Council Governor, my lady."

She scoffed, "I hardly think that Caragen would cooperate."

"Your Council Governor Caragen may be ruthless, but he is obviously not a fool. His Network has a gaping, gangrenous wound. Any intelligent ruler knows how to make a temporary alliance of mutual necessity."

"I have nothing that he needs."

Evaric raised his branded fist and began to tally reasons with his long fingers. "You have knowledge that he can obtain nowhere else. You understand Network, and you have a better grasp of wizardry and Power than anyone of comparable background. You know something of your father's intentions in going to this world of *Nilson*. You know your husband's goals and peculiar way of thinking. By my mother's calculated arrangement, you met recently with the man, Marrach, who was once Caragen's most prized asset. My mother obviously considered that meeting important to Marrach's imminent actions, and I think that significance will not be lost on Caragen. If Caragen is reluctant to meet with you, inform him of the facts I have just cited, and he will reconsider."

"He will have me thrown into prison for the rest of my life."

Evaric shook his head emphatically. "No. You are not personally a threat to him. He torments you as a means of sustained attack against Quin and your father, but that has no meaning while Quin and your father are missing. Caragen will neither kill you nor imprison you until he is sure that he no longer can use you to locate and destroy his greater enemies."

"Caragen may have taken one or both of them."

"Quin would not be 'taken' without a fight of Power that would have shaken the infinities, and I have sensed nothing of that sort. If your father has been 'taken,' then he is now dead, which eliminates any potential for Caragen to use you to manipulate your father's actions." Katerin shivered at Evaric's harsh statement, but she could not dispute it. Her father was old by any Network standard, and he would have no will to survive again under Caragen's control. Evaric continued calmly, "There is probably some element of direct antagonism in his actions against you, but vengeance is less important to him than his personal power. While the latter is threatened, you are in no danger from him. Unless the rending is healed, he will lose everything, and if Caragen knew how to heal the rending, it would not still be spreading. He needs your help, and we need his."

Katerin found herself oddly comforted by the inclusiveness of Evaric's final statement, then realized how deftly he had manipulated her emotions. "It is a pity you were not born in Network," she observed. "You would have made a superb mathematical psychologist."

"I am not sure if that is meant as an insult or a compliment, so I shall simply accept it as a theory that neither of us shall ever have an opportunity to prove or to disprove."

"I *could* prove it by teaching you the subject, but you are already much too dangerous for my peace of mind." She sighed into her folded hands, thinking of her husband, equally dangerous beneath his clownish affectations. "Without Quin, I have no way of reaching Network."

"Your husband is not the only Ixaxin who travels to and from Network. We shall find someone to escort you."

"I thought you were at odds with Ixaxis."

"Ixaxis was at odds with my father when they named him as their Infortiare." A broad smile lightened the thin, saturnine face. "Power preserves itself relentlessly, Lady Katerin, and self-preservation demands odd alliances." With feline grace, he leaped to his feet. Again, she tried to duplicate his change of position, but a rose cloud of Seriin silks and stiff underskirts defeated her. Evaric reached out to her while she quietly cursed her status as a Seriin noblewomen. He extended his branded hand to help her rise. "My wife concurs with you about the impracticality of wearing fabric by the acre. Even at court, Lyrial refuses to conform to the habits of the nobility."

"Perhaps she and I can conspire to reform them," replied Katerin wryly.

"Odd alliances indeed."

CHAPTER 35

Regretting

What have we done?

"No," muttered Deliaja, angrily denouncing her own interior voices, "this be no time for weakness." All night, she had listened to reports from Nilson children who served as messengers for the rebels, had conveyed her orders in return, and had watched the results as her companions in revolution scurried through the streets and sewers. The Network soldiers had taken an inevitable toll, but the rebels had fared much better than she had expected. Even Breamas was pleased, except with the rumor that the cargo portals had joined their public counterparts in disarray and were now unable to complete a transfer to Wharton or anywhere else. The rumor remained unproven, as far as Deliaja was concerned, and there was much else to celebrate. After all these years and failures, Breamas had achieved the first stage of his dream. If he gloated a little too pointedly regarding a Network Council Governor who meant nothing to Nilsonites, his captains could forgive him. He had given them more than he had promised.

Deliaja looked out from the cracked window of the high, barren room where she had snatched an hour of sleep. Below her, the roofs of the city issued slim curls of smoke and steam, where tired Nilsonites huddled in the aftermath of euphoria. A ghost shadow of darkness stretched its blurred fingers to the sky above the crushed wing of the governor's palace. Even from across the city, she could see the pulsation of its intangible substance and the flickering lights that crossed it. *But what will be left of Nilson for us to reclaim? What have we done?*

"Stop," she growled at herself. She had heard Arlan condemn her from across the plaza. She could not stop hearing him.

She had not expected Arlan to remain there with the soldiers in their Network bastion. She should have killed him rather than risk having him tell what he knew of Breamas—and of her. She had lied to Breamas, claiming that Arlan had escaped her when the Network soldiers overran the plaza; she could have executed the kill of Arlan at any of a dozen opportunities. Deliaja lied also to herself, claiming that she had spared him only for the practical need to retain Ruth's good will, a commodity of increased value now that Saschy Firl had assumed the role of Governor.

The attack on the Governor's palace had progressed according to Deliaja's plan, and her fellow rebel captains had neutralized the Network soldiers as effectively as they had eliminated or recruited the port boys. The transfer portals, however ineffectual at present, were secure under rebel guard. The spaceport perimeter was controlled by Breamas' loyalists. Though two ships had taken flight since the revolution, Breamas assured his followers that Cuui traders would not attempt to interfere in the revolution's progress, and the Consortium's disdain for internal Network strifes was well known.

The entire undertaking had exceeded Breamas' hopes, though it had horrified several of its most direct instigators. Cullen, if he had been able to transfer out of Wharton, would have lectured Deliaja furiously for abetting Breamas' darkest form of terrorism. Had Cullen known to blame her for Vin's death, the fury would have grown a hundredfold. Even in Wharton, the only restraint to Cullen's anger had been that he, like many others, believed that Breamas had planned all that had occurred. Breamas supported that delusion among all his followers, but Deliaja knew it for the basest of lies. Breamas was as astonished as anyone by the success of his revolution.

To sustain her influence, she had to keep the full truth from Breamas. Control of the voices that reached the old man had come easily during the first hours of success, when the excitement of achievement was new and fresh. However, the triumph had already soured for average Nilsonites, who had lost family and possessions to the general chaos, and even for a few of the Nilson rebels, who had decided that this boiling black monstrosity exceeded their personal thresholds of destructive intentions. Those few were generally Wharton miners of Cullen's ilk, who had tasted enough success in Wharton to value their own lives. Most of the Nilson rebels, recruited from Nilson's most despairing children, had no such incentive to survive, but Deliaja could not eradicate all of the troublemakers without antagonizing the followers that she needed.

The scent of Network blood had drawn every voracious predator from the Nilson sewers. The taste of hope, the possibility that the Network government could be thwarted, had filled Breamas' ranks more effectively in a day than in all the previous years of his violent life. Nilson sons and daughters, who had scoffed at Breamas two days ago, clamored yesterday to take part in his glorious success. Today, the mood of uncertainty had become palpable, but still the name of Breamas was voiced with new respect.

They understand nothing.

Deliaja caressed the polished metal of the weapon that she had taken from the corpse of a Network soldier. The revolution meant more than any latecoming opportunist could comprehend. The revolution meant more than Nilson's long awaited independence. Breamas' revolution would tear the artificial soul from Network in every Nilson holding, and no Network Governor would ever have the power to hurt Deliaja again.

Racker has already paid.

"Not enough," hissed Deliaja, "not while his Saschy be living still." Rescuing Ruth Firl had ascended in priority. The port boys were in as much disarray as the Network soldiers encamped in the battered remnants of Network's government on Nilson. From all reports, the prison had so far defeated the efforts against it, but

Deliaja had not turned her own attentions toward it. Its isolated location near the swamplands at the city's edge, not far from the spaceport, made attacking forces visible and vulnerable, but Deliaja was sure that most of the human guards had abandoned the prison to Network's automated defenses. As a symbol of Network in the mind of Breamas, the prison could be made a focal point of Nilson anger almost as easily as the Governor's palace. Deliaja would offer the released prisoners as a gift to the old man. Breamas would be pleased.

***

"I be going with you," Arlan informed Rust firmly. "I be knowing Nilson better than you, and I be knowing better the places to be avoiding between here and the prison."

Rust only nodded, but he felt heartily glad of the offer. He had been none too pleased to reap this daft assignment: This was a fine time to be taking the Lieutenant Governor's odd friend on a tour of the city, ending at the Nilson prison. For once, Rust concurred with his captain's reluctance to support the endeavor, though Rust disliked being the captain's token sacrifice to the cause. Rust had not detected any particular enthusiasm on the part of the "friend" in question either, despite Jase Margrave's adamance about fulfilling the Lieutenant Governor's orders promptly.

Jase irritated Rust further by questioning Arlan's offer, "You have a fondness for prisons?"

Arlan answered bluntly, "A friend of mine be there, Mister Margrave, and I be not wanting to miss a chance to talk to her. I be not knowing your reasons or Saschy's for this trip of yours, but mine be no secret."

"Your friend is Ruth Firl."

"Yah," agreed Arlan.

Jase studied Arlan in silence, while Rust fidgeted impatiently. At last, Jase slapped the soldier's back amiably, a gesture that Rust did not appreciate or comprehend. "We welcome your guidance, Mister Willowan. Let us waste no more time."

You're the only one wasting time, thought Rust grumpily. Aloud, he asked of both Arlan and Jase, "Can either of you fire a beamer?"

"Yah," answered Arlan, though he sounded reluctant.

"Good," replied Rust. "I'll get you a weapon. We have no shield units that function against physical projectiles, so you'll need the protection." He glanced at Jase. "You?"

"I believe I'm ineligible to accept your generous offer," murmured Jase with a peculiar, twisted smile. "Though I am presently serving Lieutenant Firl in the cause of mutual need, I am not a Network citizen. I would not want you to disobey your Network laws by arming a member of the Consortium."

Rust snarled a string of curses beneath his breath. All he needed in the midst of this insane mission was to play nursemaid to a C-human on a pleasure trip. Arlan Willowan seemed to be a competent man, but he was obviously no soldier, and his allegiances might well be shaky in confronting his fellow Nilsonites on behalf of a C-human. If the captain could not muster the courage to override the Lieutenant Governor's orders, he ought to have assigned more than a single guard to the task. The discipline of this makeshift troop had nearly disintegrated already, and the captain's lack of leadership would soon result in disaster, unless someone began to make intelligent decisions.

Rust toyed with ideas of mutiny and desertion. Since the Geisen mission's ending in enigma and the resultant disbanding of his former corps, Rust's cynicism had begun to mature into a darker dissatisfaction. The Nilson revolutionaries almost earned a measure of sympathy from him, though he would fight them to the death without compunction. That was his sworn duty while Network paid him.

Where is that battered ex-mercenary? wondered Rust, who thought he had glimpsed the soldier roaming the perimeter of the fortified plaza. *I could use the help of a capable man.*

Collecting a weapon for Arlan from a wounded

corporal, Rust inquired about the weathered, unranked soldier. The corporal recalled the man but did not know his current assignment. "If you see him," said Rust to the corporal and to others, "tell him to look out for my return. I have orders from Lieutenant Firl." It could not hurt to have an ally on alert, though Rust doubted that he or his charges would survive to make the return trip. Rust did not trust the raw captain to worry about one expendable soldier among all the rest.

Rust asked Arlan, "Can we reach the prison by those underground passages that you seem to know so well?"

"The sewer passages be blocked beneath the plaza, because the Governor be not a complete fool," replied Arlan.

"We can cross the plaza with the help of distracting firepower from the captain's next foray," said Rust. "What chance do we have past the plaza?"

"Past the plaza, the sewers be more dangerous than the streets. There be better ways to travel—through buildings that be less used by those that be wanting to kill you." He jerked his thumb over his shoulder. "There be an old green tenement that be a good starting point."

Rust gave orders to the C-human, "I want you to run low and keep out of sight as much as possible. If I tell you to jump, obey me without question. My orders are to keep you alive, and that's what I mean to do, if you cooperate."

"At your service, sir," murmured Jase. "But I do have a fairly well-developed talent for detecting trouble, among other things. I am quite willing to listen to your advice, if you're willing to listen to mine." Before Rust could express his disgust with the entire exercise, Jase pointed emphatically, beginning with the ruined palace. "For reasons that are irrelevant at the moment, I have somewhat more than the ordinary share of human senses. Would you like me to tell you the current positions of every soldier in your troop? Behind that wall are five men lifting bodies from the rubble. At the base of that smoky haze are two men, trying to repair a generator. On the opposite side of that smashed tram, a man is cursing Nilson's paucity of such powered vehicles. There are at least thirty rebel soldiers watching the plaza from that hollow shell of a building. Mister Willowan's tenement seems to be empty, though someone is rummaging through a trash heap behind it. In an alley past that smaller structure, half a dozen men are arguing over the palace spoils that they have not yet taken. . . ."

"What are you proving?" demanded Rust, though he had an uneasy conviction that the C-human was speaking with absolute sincerity. Arlan, twice the C-human's size, was staring at Jase with a strange wariness.

"That you should trust my judgment."

Rust hesitated briefly before replying, "Sorry. I have other orders."

Jase did not argue, though his lips thinned to a grim line. "As you wish."

Minutes later, an exchange of blazing energy beams, as bright and cheerfully colored as festive fireworks, crossed the plaza between soldiers and rebels. Bent low, led by Rust, the three men scurried among the drizzle and shadows of such little shelter as the open plaza offered. By the time the flurry of confrontation had settled again into uneasy silence, the men had darted inside Arlan's designated green tenement.

The walls were black with mold and stank of rot, but Arlan pressed forward heedlessly. Aside from the dripping of leaky pipes, no clear sound came from any of the locked rooms that lined the long hallway. If any hidden tenants whispered behind their doors of their fear, only Jase heard. Arlan led the way quickly through the dark maze and down a dark flight of creaking stairs. From a slit between boards, Rust saw a frightened old woman scurry away from the trash heap where she had hidden, and he cast a troubled glance toward Jase, who merely shrugged. Arlan pried open a basement door. From the basement, a narrow passage led to the adjacent building, where another blighted stairway led them upward.

Up and down they traveled, weaving an erratic path away from the besieged plaza. None of them spoke. All of them listened. The dearth of enemies made Rust wonder if his entire squadron had over-estimated the extent of the Nilson revolution, or if three men were simply too insignificant to draw rebel fire. An exhausted silence had replaced the raucous noise of the revolution's first surge of excitement. Those few Nilsonites that they glimpsed ran from them, disappearing behind slammed doors. Much of this part of Nilson had long been abandoned.

After sampling a dozen equally miserable tene-ments, Arlan at last opened a door onto daylight. The gray street looked almost fair by comparison with the wretchedness inside, and the tainted air smelled nearly sweet, though it was the deceptive sweetness of swampwater. "There be no good way but the street for these next blocks," said Arlan. He pointed. "Straight ahead to the trash bin at that far corner, then we be turning left. The prison be at the end of the next row."

Rust studied the dingy apartments and boarded shops that seemed to have been deserted since some prior century. Cracked pavement gaped and oozed with the green-gray swamp that sought to reclaim its old ex-panse. The streets were unnervingly quiet, but Rust only smiled slightly against his private fear of being stalked by unseen foes. "It looks quiet enough, but I'll lead. Keep your weapon ready, Arlan." He glanced at Jase. "You keep alert."

"I always do," answered Jase softly.

The three men filed into the daylight. Rust scanned the empty street constantly. There was nothing to see, no faces at windows, no movement on rooftop. The loudest sound was his own booted footfalls, echoed by Arlan. Jase moved too silently for Rust's ears.

"Be watching the gutters," Arlan reminded them in a whisper, but the advice seemed unnecessary. Not even the trickles of fouled water could seem to pene-trate the clogged drainage system of this desolate neighborhood.

They had nearly reached the corner, when a flash of reflected light caught Rust's eyes. He whirled toward the last building of the block. The boards had been pried from the windows, and broken glass littered the sidewalk and street. Rust relaxed fractionally, recognizing the glint of his own weapon's reflection.

"Look down!" shouted Jase, but Rust heard the warning too late to save himself.

Fire stabbed through thick Network boots, splitting the bones of Rust's ankle and toppling him. With his face at gutter level, he could see the bright, angry eyes of his enemies through the narrow sewer grates. He rolled away from the crimson trace of an old-style disruptor beam and sent his own retort of deadly blue-green energy showering into the depths. He did not see the beam that hit him squarely. Agony exploded in his side.

He heard Arlan, sounding distant, crying bitter protests on his behalf. The disruptive energy burrowed more deeply inside of him. There were many shouts now, and the hiss of beams striking the dark, deceptive stream of sewage and turning it to caustic steam. Rust felt his body rebel against the distortion of its cells. He heard another voice, a familiar voice, calling orders to stay low, but he could not place the speaker. His body began to shake with the commencing of serious nerve damage. He realized that his recently acquired friend, the unranked soldier, owned the voice that had reassured him momentarily, and he regretted that he had never learned the soldier's name or shared his own. He had never wanted to know the names of the men who died before him.

***

The attack occurred so swiftly that Arlan had scarcely recognized it when its dynamics changed abruptly. The crimson beams that had erupted from camouflaged sewer grates became suddenly targeted by a brighter blaze from a rooftop. Arlan dropped behind the trash bin. He saw the bearded soldier lying prone but could not tell whether Rust was injured or simply holding close to the ground defensively. Arlan could not locate Jase.

The rooftop ally's beams pierced unseen doors and twisted through crevices, maneuvering by curves instead of the straight lines that Arlan expected. Familiar only with Nilson weaponry, Arlan knew nothing of the more sophisticated Network instruments of warfare. Few Network soldiers knew the breadth of specialized capability that a well-informed, well-trained user could tap from certain standard issue weapons. Death cries told the effectiveness of the rooftop ally's strikes. Arlan lifted his head slightly. "Stay low!" shouted a voice that Arlan did not recognize.

He recognized the woman's voice that answered with a string of curses. "Dee," groaned Arlan.

Arlan hugged the filthy ground, hating it and hating what Nilson had made of its children. The lopsided battle around him did not matter to him now. Ruth had claimed Deliaja as a friend, and Miz Ruth was undoubtedly Deliaja's current goal. Not even Miz Ruth was free of Nilson's taint. Having abetted Deliaja in destroying the palace, he acknowledged himself as guiltier than Miz Ruth.

Beamers hissed through misty air and musty buildings. Pavement groaned as heated blows cracked it. A strong smell of charred flesh mingled with the sewer stench. *So many be dead,* thought Arlan, wondering if Deliaja was among them. *So many more be dying. Why be we killing each other, Dee?* Arlan did not move. He remembered the face of a boy named Tempest as he awaited his own death.

It was many minutes before Arlan realized that the sounds of conflict had ended. After a lengthy silence, Arlan heard the C-human observe with calm objectivity, "You constitute a remarkable army, sir."

Arlan raised his head to see Jase, dirtied but apparently undamaged, facing a soldier, a disheartening array of dead Nilsonites splayed against walls and gutters, and a single surviving prisoner. The prisoner's hood had fallen from her bleached hair, and a fury close to madness distorted her face. To have found her among the dead could not have caused Arlan more pain than to see her contorted with such insane anger.

Wearily, Arlan holstered his unused weapon and climbed to his feet. "Why, Dee?" he asked.

She saw him clearly, but the anger did not ebb. "It be for Nilson, for Ruth, and for us all," shouted Deliaja, writhing furiously but ineffectively within a binding field. She asked, as she had asked before, "Be you one of *them,* Arlan, or be you a son of Nilson?" A new note of despair riddled her voice.

While Arlan struggled inside himself, torn between loathing and grief, Jase hissed sharply, "Do not try to answer a question that offers only a false choice. She is manipulating you."

Truth, insisted a silent voice in Arlan's head. The C-human touched Arlan's shoulder briefly and tapped an oddly comforting sequence of pressures. An old dream of peaceful golden fields swept cleansingly through Arlan's mind. Arlan nodded, as a weight of uncertainty lifted from him. "Be not hurting her," said Arlan to the strange soldier who had enacted their rescue, but the soldier and Deliaja had both disappeared. Arlan shook his head, unable to account for an apparent lapse of several seconds.

An urgent call from Jase tugged Arlan from his reverie, "I need your help here, Arlan." Jase was kneeling beside Rust, whose body was now racked with convulsions from the disruptive energy that was killing him from within. "What foul weapons your Network has created," sighed Jase.

Wearily recognizing a new cause to grieve, Arlan joined them swiftly. "Disrupters be the worst," agreed Arlan with concern. He had seen few survivors of a disrupter beam's direct hit, but Arlan refused to accept the inevitability of any death until all trace of life failed. "We be only a turn away from the prison. I be able to carry him."

"He won't survive the trip in his present condition."

"I be not leaving him," retorted Arlan in an adament voice.

Jase smiled wanly. "Just hold him still for a moment."

Beset by an overwhelming need to obey the terse

command, Arlan complied, though he had enough mental strength to wonder what made the C-human so difficult to refuse. It required all of Arlan's considerable physical strength to restrain Rust's thrashing even partially. Rust, despite his wounded condition, remained a powerful fighter.

Concentrating on the soldier's unconscious struggles, Arlan did not see Jase select a sharp fragment of a broken window. Arlan did not realize what was occurring until Jase had drive the fragment deeply into his own dark skin. Blood, an iridescent burgundy sparked with gold, seeped from the C-human's wrist. To Arlan's further horror, Jase pried the broken glass from his own body and plunged the bloodied dagger into the raw, seething wound in Rust's side. Rust screamed and arched in agony. "Be you trying to kill him and yourself?" cried Arlan in protest, but he could not free himself of the struggling soldier in order to thwart Jase.

"I'm saving him," croaked Jase. He squeezed together the self-inflicted rent in the flesh of his forearm. Beads of darkly iridescent blood bubbled from the long seam.

Rust gasped and went limp beneath Arlan's restraining pressure. Certain that the soldier had died, Arlan pushed away from him and turned furiously toward Jase. "If death be a 'saving,' then you be a hero," growled Arlan.

Jase nodded, his own face creased with pain. The scar on Jase's arm, sealed by an iridescent band, registered in Arlan's awareness. The scar looked old and faded, but Arlan knew that it had not existed seconds earlier. Jase muttered, "Carry him now." Jase staggered to his feet and began to walk. His movements strengthened with each step.

"What did you do?" whispered Rust in a hollow voice. He had sat upright and was gingerly probing the hole in his uniform jacket, where the gaping wound inflicted by disrupter fire had filled with smooth pink flesh. Only a hint of an iridescent sheen differentiated the newly healed area from its uninjured surroundings.

He tested his ankle cautiously, but his movements were firm.

Arlan stared at the soldier in amazement, then broke into a hesitant grin. "I be doing nothing. I be *seeing* a miracle." Arlan did not understand the method, but he did not require such understanding in his own mind—not at present. He hefted Rust with gentle care and supported the soldier across his back and shoulder, as he had gathered so many Wharton victims.

Rust groaned, "I feel like somebody poured acid inside me."

"May be true," answered Arlan curiously. He regarded Jase's unimpressive form, just ahead of him, with a faint, puzzled smile. "May be more than odd manners to this C-human." An array of hopes that had never before occurred to Arlan spread through him, easing long-carried burdens. His smile faded quickly, however. Not even the C-human could restore Deliaja, who had almost been a friend, or more.

*   *   *

"Where be you taking me?" demanded Deliaja sullenly, as Marrach turned their steps away from the prison that she had expected him to enter. She did not let herself despair completely, though her bitter mind could only envision a destination of torture. From slitted eyes, she evaluated Marrach for any weaknesses in the hope that the binding field would fade before he noticed. Twice her size and strength, experienced at combat, and dispassionate about his work, he would be difficult to escape unless she could find aid, a rare and costly commodity on Nilson. Seeing her as captive, rebels who supported her eagerly in the fire of shared anger would lose their fervor without the incentive of personal reward.

"I am taking you to visit your great leader, Breamas," answered Marrach, startling Deliaja and setting her mind to new calculations. He guided her, nearly dragging her, by a strong grip on her shoulder, near enough to the neck to threaten physical disciplinary tactics beyond the teeth-gritting nerve tears of the binding field. "I have estimated his current dwelling from a variety of Network data, but I am sure that you can lead me to him directly."

Deliaja sniffed contemptuously, "I be not knowing the man."

"Your loyalty is commendable," observed Marrach coldly, "as is your courage, but your ignorance negates the worth of both. Even on this primitively equipped world, you must realize that you will tell me all that I wish to know. If I were not confident of my ability to extract the information from you, I would have let you 'escape' me already, so that I might follow you to him."

"I be not afraid of you or any man," answered Deliaja with a sneer, though the reminder of her ignorance taunted her insidiously. "There be more men than you that be testing how much hurt I be able to take, and there be years of practice for me. I be glad enough to die. Quick be best, sure, but there be *nothing* of life that be not part of a slow death."

Almost, her captor's taut lips quirked into a smile. Almost, Deliaja detected a hint of regret in him. "Your observation is accurate, in its embittered way, but irrelevant. Decades ago, Network identified effective techniques for stimulating critical centers in the human nervous system as a method of targeted behavioral modification. Intensive training and long experience have given me an unsurpassed expertise in applying those techniques to elicit information from reluctant witnesses like yourself." The dry admission produced a flicker of reaction from Deliaja, but she had long practiced hiding her fears, even from herself.

"Information," she spat, "be of no use to you. The revolution be more than anyone be stopping. Our time be already come. Be you blind to the boiling of the sky? Our cause be won!"

Marrach stopped abruptly, dropping Deliaja to the ground. "Are you proud to claim a part in destabilizing a universe?"

"If that universe be Network! Yah, I be proud to

be its executioner. I be proud to be Ned Racker's executioner."

"I always wondered which woman would take vengeance on him," said Marrach. "You instigated the explosion of the Governor's palace."

"I be proud of firing the fuse."

"How blind are the angry. How destructive are those who refuse to think beyond themselves." Marrach slid a thin, metallic rod from the lining of his vest, bent and squeezed it briefly against her throat, imparting a chill that spread and tingled into her bones. "Feel a small sampling of the consequences."

Deliaja maintained control of her fear until the trembling began. It afflicted her fingers first, then spread up her arms, until her shoulders heaved with the force of involuntary muscular contractions. Deep inside her skull, she sensed an icy pinprick that began to grow and spread, until the pain of it forced a gurgled protest from her throat.

Marrach continued blandly, "The most effective persuader drugs have unfortunate side effects, if used for more than an hour's duration, but that is seldom a problem. Once the questioning is complete, we tend to dispose promptly of those on whom we use such techniques." He gripped Deliaja's bleached hair, thwarting the harshest of her tremors, and he leaned toward her. With cold sarcasm, he hissed, "You do not fear death? You are indeed fortunate. That will make the next few minutes much easier for you." She felt her body cease its shuddering, but it did not return to her control. Numbness stiffened her limbs. Marrach traced a line from her ear down her neck and let his fingers pause, resting hard against her throbbing jugular. "I feel little compunction about killing terrorists. I am too intimately familiar with the means and minds of those who can destroy life without remorse." His fingers eased their pressure slightly, as he asked in a quiet voice, "What type of explosive did you use to destroy the governor's palace?"

"Standard mine issue," she answered, though she would willingly have bitten through her tongue rather than reply, if she had been able. "I be not knowing what be in them. They be used for blasting tunnels."

"Lies will not serve."

His fingers squeezed her throat, and icy needles raced through her veins. She screamed, "Breamas be taking them from Network soldiers."

"Breamas lied to you. We carried nothing that exotic," murmured Marrach, but he nodded as if his expectations had been confirmed. "What did you expect to achieve?"

"Racker's death," she growled without regret.

"He was obviously a personal friend of yours," said Marrach dryly. "Is his death all that you expected?"

"Freedom from Network tyrants like him."

"Yes, of course," said Marrach with a trace of impatience. "You expect to fulfill the idealized dream of that vicious, brain-damaged opportunist, Tay Breamas. Did you think you succeeded after you saw the results of the explosion?"

Deliaja muttered, "Nilson success be not measured in Network terms of plenty. May be, Wharton ghost lights be dooming us as well as Racker, but Nilson be dying free."

"Wharton," echoed Marrach, testing the word. "Is that the mine from which you have been liberating most of your explosives?"

"Be Nilson owning any other mine?"

"What are the ghost lights?"

"Trouble in the deep places. None be knowing more." A terrible itching crawled across her back, but she could do nothing to relieve it, just as she could do nothing to curtail her own responses. "Unless Arlan Willowan—that you be helping back there—be knowing more than he be telling. Retrievers be seeing things that be not always in their reports. Arlan be seeing more than most."

"You know him from Wharton?"

"Yah," she whispered.

"Is Breamas still haunting that old storm cellar on Three Crow?"

Deliaja choked, but the word forced itself from her,

"Yah." She felt a tingling in her feet. "If you be know-ing all the answers, why be you questioning me?" The tingling spread, awaking a hope in her that the drug's effect might have begun to weaken. Her hope did not go far, however, for Marrach slung her inelegantly over his shoulder and began to stride in the direction of Breamas' retreat.

After several silent blocks, he dropped her uncere-moniously into a mound of trash and tatters. "You have earned no mercy, citizeness, but you have made one valid point: Ned Racker's government is currently de-funct. Since Nilsonites have now developed a taste for Network blood, antagonizing Breamas' assets at this belated juncture can only undermine Nilson's limited potential for recovery. I assume that Breamas would prefer that I avoid damaging one of his prize captains permanently."

"You be not caring about Nilson."

"Master Breamas and I developed an alliance of mu-tual benefit long before you were born, citizeness. When you tell him that Chancellor Marrach wishes to speak to him, he will be eager to meet with me."

The binding field shimmered briefly as Marrach ex-tinguished it. Expecting a killing beam in the back, Deliaja made no movement beyond a stretching of cramped limbs. Except for the bruising of her shins when she struck the ground, she felt nearly as hale as normal. She tested the freedom cautiously, "What busi-ness be Breamas having with an unranked Network grunt like you?"

In a voice suddenly gruff and altered past recogni-tion, Marrach answered, "Be you believing only what a bit of uniform braid and cloth be telling you, even now? I be no more a Network soldier than you be the Governor of Nilson." Deliaja jerked away from him, nearly as shocked by his flawless transition into Nilson dialect as by the most chilling of his previous words and deeds. If he was a son of Nilson, all of her argu-ments against him changed. She stopped herself short of flight, remembering caution and the lack of protec-tive cover in the stark alleyway. Marrach laughed at her, "If you be thinking I be planning to kill you by effort-wasting treachery, you be a fool. If you be thinking that I be needing to follow you to Breamas, when I be already learning all I be wanting from you, you be calling me a fool, as I be *not*. I be asking you only to carry news to me of Breamas. Be you quick about it. As I be reckoning, Breamas be no more than a minute's distance from here."

Deliaja glared at him across her tattooed shoulder, bared by the tearing of her sleeve. Marrach holstered his weapon and spread his arms wide. Deliaja turned and sprinted the length of the alley. Breathing hard, she angled into the first side street that she reached, and she continued to run without looking back. "Chancellor," she whispered to herself when at last she achieved her goal, a building that she considered to be a reasonably defensible sanctuary. "What manner of title be that?"

She plowed through doors that opened in front of her, whistling the shrill tune that identified her. Though she was well known to all the rebels, a hefty guard stopped her near the cellar stairs. "What be wrong with you, Dee? Where be the others? Be the Network soldiers coming?"

"There be worse than soldiers after me. Let me be passing, Skar, or it be the worst for all of us. I be needing to see Breamas—now." Though Skar was much the stronger, the suddenness of Deliaja's jab caught him unaware. She pushed free of him and skidded down the stairs, sliding against the snaking metal rail to keep from tumbling headlong.

It was a cold room, mildewed from the accumulation of rain that trickled into the walls. The two tall lamps were veiled in blue. The rug, patterned in chaos of black and green, smelled of old smoke and rotted summer. The shrunken old man called Breamas occupied the one upholstered chair, a tattered monstrosity made of reptile skin and bone.

"Calm yourself, Deliaja," murmured Breamas in a voice as clinging as pitch. "I take it that the prison rescue did not go well."

She did not take the time to answer him. "There be a man coming here that be calling himself Chancellor Marrach. He be claiming to be known to you."

"Marrach," sighed Breamas, and his eyes blazed. His shriveled lips stretched with satisfaction. He half rose to his feet, then settled back into the recesses of scaled leather. From his throat issued a dry rasp of laughter. "Why do you shout as if in fear, Dee? You should be shouting with delight."

"He be of Network."

"Ignorant girl, you do not fathom the glorious truth of what you say. Marrach is more truly Network than man. We have won, Dee. We have won at last." Deliaja backed away from the figure seated in the shadows. "Bring him here immediately!"

"She has already complied," murmured Marrach, as he descended the stairs unhurriedly.

The old man froze but for a flaring of nostrils, like a great cat sniffing out its prey. "I had heard that you died, Rabh," he said with a trace of a vicious smile, garnering a troubled stare from Deliaja.

"Like you, Tay, I am a difficult man to kill." Marrach ambled into the room and surveyed its smoky recesses critically. "You have not squandered your fee on personal comforts."

"I have used your parting gifts judiciously—and effectively." Breamas leaned forward into the light that painted him unkindly with wrinkled shadows. "Such largesse does not come often to an old revolutionary, whose cause is viewed by many as ancient history."

"I have encountered some of the *effects* of your recent work. Impressive."

"I do hope that my soldiers did not inconvenience you, Council Chancellor."

"The inconvenience was chiefly theirs. I was compelled to eliminate a number of them."

"You always were a superior combatant. My poor rebels could hardly have anticipated an opponent such as yourself."

Marrach bowed slightly, acknowledging the compliment and returning it, "Their tactical skills, though somewhat naive, show promise. You have chosen some talented captains." Marrach extended his bow toward Deliaja, who remained stiffly wary.

"Talent and desperation," said Breamas, "make a formidable team. How is the Council Governor?"

"As manipulative as ever."

With one emaciated hand, Breamas gestured toward the braided rug. "Please, Chancellor, sit and tell me how I may serve you."

Marrach remained standing, but he answered, "We have a shared problem, you and I."

"As of old," sighed Breamas with complacency.

"The immediate problem is somewhat more troublesome than an injudicious planetary Governor. The obstreperous forces of nature have decided to join your rebellion against Network, but they may prove to be treacherous allies."

"An army of limited means cannot afford to discriminate."

Marrach clucked, "Breamas, old ally, you need not defend your strategies to me. I commend your resourcefulness." Deliaja's eyes narrowed suspiciously, but she said nothing. "However," continued Marrach sadly, "this particular disruption of nature has now served its purpose for you and become a liability. I propose to solve your problem for you—with your concurrence, of course."

"Do expand upon this intriguing subject."

"I have some reason to believe that the solution to the problem is linked to the Wharton mines, over which you have some control, I believe."

"They are mine," replied Breamas. "Their largess should comfort me in my retirement." His smug declaration irked Deliaja. *She* had fought for Wharton. She had claimed Wharton for the revolution. She had won Nilson from Network. She had sacrificed everything for this old man, who sounded more like a gloating Ned Racker than Nilson's liberator.

"Tay, old friend, you have overreached yourself again. After all these years, your weakness remains the same." Deliaja stared at the floor, reining her fury at

Marrach's bland insults because Breamas had annoyed her almost equally. "Provide me with the information that I need regarding Wharton, without restraint of access or treachery. Grant me the freedom of the port building that your people hold, and I shall do my best to restore the Nilson/Wharton portal connections to their former reliability. If those portals are not stabilized soon, your spoils of war will be spoiled indeed. You have awaited this victory too long to be satisfied with a ruined world."

"Forgive my distrust, Rabh, but having freed Wharton at some cost, I would prefer to keep that enclave free of resurgent Network tyranny." At last, Deliaja felt a measure of her usual confidence in Breamas' wisdom, though she disliked his display of familiarity with her recent tormentor. "If I provided access for you, the direct servant of Andrew Caragen, I fear that all of my followers' great sacrifices would soon prove to have been in vain."

At the naming of the Network Council Governor, Deliaja restrained herself no longer, "Who be this man, Breamas?"

Marrach spoke as if Deliaja were not present, "You have conquered nothing substantive as yet, Tay." He approached Breamas more closely than the old man generally tolerated, but Breamas did not censure him. "I am willing to guarantee Network forgiveness for both Nilson and Wharton, if you but assist me in this small, mutually necessary matter."

Breamas smiled. "How satisfying it must be to be in a position to make such a guarantee. I would enjoy meeting with Caragen to express my admiration."

"You be not treating with this man, Breamas!" protested Deliaja. "He be a Network soldier."

Again, Marrach ignored her. "You and Caragen have some attributes in common, Tay, but he would not care for your taste in accommodations." Marrach gestured broadly at the sorry room. "Have we an agreement?"

"Could I ever refuse you, Rabh?" asked Breamas. His expression remained cold in its pleasure, but eagerness creaked in his aged voice. "Yes, we have an agreement, if my personal pardon is a part of it."

"But of course, Tay. You served Caragen long and well. You merit a comfortable retirement."

The old man's face crinkled with satisfaction. "Deliaja will introduce you to our humble army, so that you will be recognized as an ally. She will escort you to the port building, where you will doubtless find answers of interest to you. Our people there will be glad to see reinforcements." At last, Breamas gave the furious woman his attention, and he said placatingly, "You must trust me, Dee. Chancellor Marrach is an ally of long acquaintance."

Deliaja bristled at the condescending tone of the one man to whom she had given her respect, but she said nothing. There was madness in the old man's eyes. She had seen its like before and knew the futility of arguing with it. To recognize it in Breamas shocked her, as did his calm acceptance of Marrach's words: *served Caragen*. All of her doubts raged in her mind, undefended now by the certainty of Breamas' cause that had sustained her.

Marrach apologized with a shade of mockery, "I regret that circumstances forced me to treat the lady unkindly. I do not expect her to forgive me quickly."

"She will assist you, nonetheless," said Breamas with cold insistence. "Will you not, Dee?"

"Yah," she grunted, "if that be your order." With her back straight and stiff, she stalked up the narrow stairway. Marrach nodded a silent farewell to Breamas, before following her. He watched her with a pensive distrust. The man who ascended the stairs in Deliaja's wake was entirely the product of Caragen's lethal design, except for a single knot of terrible pain deep inside of him.

CHAPTER 36

Raveling

The emptiness ached inside of her. She had mourned him more than once. She had worn the shades of a widow's grief for most of her life. She had thought she knew what it meant to lose him, who was so integrally a part of her.

The trees remained serene. She felt their stolid presence and loved them, but they did not comfort her. Their long, slow lives approached the Immortals' scheme of time, but they lacked the brightness of the instant. Their lives were long-burning embers, where he was a blue-hot star. Their thrashing twigs raised welts upon her skin, but the sensation lacked the strength to reach her. Her Power needed his to be complete, and her Power could no longer find him.

She would be a child again, befriended only by the trees that did not know to fear her. She had lived many years without him. She had grown to womanhood without knowing anything more of him than superstitious whispers and her father's condemnations. She had been without him; she would be without him; she would be without anyone or anything.

Alone in the wild fringes of the Mountains of Mindar, straying ever further from the boarders of Tulea, Rhianna fled from herself as she had long ago fled from her father's keep. She could not remember duty. She could remember little amid the agony of the present. Wraithlike, she wove between the stone-hard world that had created her and the patterns that her Power touched. She sought Kaedric in both material and immaterial frameworks of existence and met nothingness. She wept to be without him, knowing that his loss of her would cost him more than tears.

Her Power drove her. Her Power ruled her. Ixaxis named it crime: to yield control to the Power that, unchecked by reason, would inevitably destroy. Without him, the tenuous reins of Ixaxin discipline snapped into limp strands of memory, and her remaining memories were all of him.

He still existed; she clung to that fragile hope. She believed, because her own Power continued to exist, despite the imbalance that his absence had caused. She had found him once in a wilderness of Serii, Power drawn to Power, though neither of them had understood at first. Until the Taormin drew them into its patterns and taught them, they could not know that the Taormin had bred them to be each other's complement of Power, the stabilizing force that would reach fulfillment in their son.

With the recollection of the Taormin's intricate, fiery patterns came the reaching into it. The woman who was Rhianna vanished from a rocky mountainside in Serii and stepped fully into the realms of her Power. She merged her broken self with the pattern that was closest to *his,* the pattern of the Taormin, a time-distorted evolution of a Network device, wrapped in a silken shroud and locked in the Infortiare's Tower. Jon Terry had built rudimentary intelligence into the Taormin, the prototype of all Network topological controllers, to enable it to preserve the stability of its intersecting spaces. Not even Jon Terry had understood how effectively he had created, and none of his Network imitators had ever recognized the criticality of that particular design for the controller's intelligence. Network duplicated his design meticulously for the connecting of a thousand worlds. Designers of the Nilson controller stripped the design to achieve their concept of a more efficient minimum.

That is the error, realized the Power that was Rhianna. *That is the antecedent of the instability.* Entwined with the Taormin, the explanation seemed utterly clear and simple to her. It was also without

meaning, because the understanding reached her
through the Taormin's impersonal filter of reality. The
Taormin's minimal self-awareness existed to preserve
itself and the topologies that it touched. It did not know
how to care.

Akin to the Taormin's cold imperative to survive,
the Power of a wizardess demanded the restoration of
its own stability, even at the cost of its mortal host.
Without remembrance of emotion, Power sought its
completing half implacably and indefatigably. It
sought and it analyzed, and when the Taormin's realm
did not answer the need, it moved outside the patterns
of its formation. It studied and it sifted, and it moved
by deliberate, calculated increments across the infinities that it identified as Network nodes by some shade
of commonality with the Taormin's design. To Network, *he* had taken the Taormin's creator. To regain
him, her Power would willingly dissect the entirety of
connected Network space.

The instability, the roiling of spatial interstices that
ought to have comprised an orderly sequence of patterns, seared its presence on her Power's consciousness. She had witnessed nothing like it since the
Rending of her own integral world, and that Rending
had been a much cleaner, more localized phenomenon.
At that time of Rending, she had known little of the
mechanisms of the patterns. Beyond Power's instinctive recognition of personal safety, she had not known
what to observe. The Sorcerer Kings, those long-lived
genetic catastrophes who refashioned Network-3, had
excised any such technical understanding from the
world they conquered. Until she discovered Jon Terry,
who had isolated the first Immortals' cancerous invasion and recognized the ensuing restoration of connectivity, she had never imagined the extent of Power's
potential. At the time of her world's Rending, she
would never have dared to touch the instability that
confronted her now. Ignorant, she would never have
survived it.

Entire and sane, Rhianna would have recoiled from
the deadliness and the certainty of loss, but her bereft

Power immersed itself without compunction. She felt *him,* where traces of his precise control spread a sparse, fragile lacework of order upon a universe of chaos. So widely dispersed, his Power could not retain awareness of identity, but each fragment knew its mate in hers. When a lost, helpless entity chanced to stir between them, they jointly hurled the distraction back to its own pattern, barely recognizing it as a man. The threads of two sundered Powers abandoned their remnants of individuality, leaped across infinities, and coiled inextricably. Blazing far brighter than its parts, a single complex pattern emerged with strands strong enough to bind the void that abutted it.

In a deep Wharton cavern, incoherent light sparkled into new clarity. A seething tear in the space of Nilson contracted and spat a planet's Governor from its maw, only to abandon him in a spiderweb of infinity. Satisfied by its own perceived completion, the pattern of intertwined Power did not try to achieve more.

CHAPTER 37

Questioning

The prison had neither improved nor deteriorated since Jase and Tori had visited Filcher Ikthan Cuui, but Jase had not felt Tori's absence so sharply until he entered the dank building without her. The Network barriers remained the same, evidently unaffected by the blight that had overtaken the government district. The gate guard, whose job was rendered immaterial by Network's automated vigilance, accepted the soldier's access code indifferently and gave Jase the same look of bored resignation. Without Tori's acrid comments to inspire contradiction, Jase found himself much more critical of the dreary trappings of Network justice.

Jase could imagine how delightedly Tori would chaff him for that bit of counter-Sesserda hypocrisy. Jase could not muster any respect for either the prisoners or their captors; he could not view any of them as civilized beings. The vile look and smell of the stained corridors spoke badly of the Nilson officials, but the cells, which the long-term incarcerated prisoners were equipped to keep clean, showed a bestial filth. Jase kicked a chip of plaster into a crack in the concrete floor, but there was no one present who knew him well enough to recognize the depth of frustration that the small gesture signified.

The soldier, Rust, clearly exhausted by his nearly mortal wound and its unconventional repair, stopped at the junction of two main corridors, where a dilapidated Network terminal offered to guide them to the requested cell. The voice of the terminal had acquired a stilted languor that Jase attributed to loss of contact with its larger self. Arlan silently provided the soldier with a supporting arm. Rust entered a manual code into the terminal, but he stared at the monitor without comment.

"Where would you like me to begin?" asked Jase of his battered military escort, and he managed to sound utterly at peace with himself and the events around him.

"I'd like you to begin by telling me what you did to me," muttered Rust without raising his eyes from Network's hypnotic display of prisoner's names and crimes.

Of course you would, thought Jase, feeling uncommonly burdened by his inability to alleviate the soldier's concerns. *But I cannot explain to you the gifts and dangers of the pure relanine that is Calongi lifeblood, because your ancestors refused Consortium membership, and you cannot even imagine changing your personal allegiance.* Both Rust and Arlan had watched Jase with a changed form of suspicion since the nearly fatal rebel attack: a suspicion of the unknown instead of the more ordinary Network suspicion of any C-human's motives. To Jase, their emotions were naively transparent. Rust feared; Arlan admired; neither man wanted to accept his own reaction. "You might consider it a form of inoculation," answered Jase, imagining Tori's comments on his equivocation and his own retort to her. The blood of a relanine addict was, after all, conceptually similar to the weaker form of relanine used in adaptation fluid, with which every Consortium traveler was inoculated prior to entering an otherwise inimicable environment.

With a troubled expression, Rust peered at Jase, clearly struggling for words that were beyond his reach, "I feel . . . strange. Drained, but aware."

"The sensation will pass in a few days." . . . *when the relanine has adapted you into the man you will become.* "Lieutenant Firl did not identify any particular prisoner that she wished to have questioned." *Because she sent me here only from general desperation, augmented by an inability to deal with the wrongful imprisonment of her own mother.* "Have you any suggestions?"

Arlan interrupted before Rust could speak, "What be your method of questioning, Mister Margrave? Be it causing any hurt?"

"There is no hurt involved. I shall simply ask questions and observe." Because the answer did not seem to satisfy either Arlan or the soldier, Jase added, "The skill lies in the process of observing. The Calongi have spent millennia developing and refining techniques for discerning Truth." Observing Arlan's conflicted emotions, Jase asked quietly, "Did you have someone in mind?"

"Yah," admitted Arlan.

"Ruth Firl?" asked Jase, assessing Arlan's deep layers of concern curiously. From a Network citizen, especially an uneducated Nilsonite like Arlan, the shades of intelligent awareness and selfless interest were unexpected.

"She be knowing the rebels, but she be a good lady, not deserving to be here."

"You want me to confirm that she is what you believe her to be."

Arlan hesitated. "May be. Yah. That be my wanting." He scratched at his head. "How be you knowing this? You be not knowing me that well."

"I told you: by observing." *Yes,* concluded Jase, *this man is worthy of respect. I must not judge Nilson—or Network—solely by its obvious ills and errors.*

Rust asked with an incongruous smile, "Are all C-humans like you? Able to 'inoculate' and 'observe' the way you do?"

The soldier smiles to hide his fear, but both of these Network men are willing to learn, even here amid the most wretched evidence of their corrupt, misguided society. While they progress, how can I despair and call myself the more civilized? I do not know that Tori is lost to me, and I must not lose sight of hope. If she is lost, I must remember that my own work is not ended.

"The Consortium would be far less productive if we all possessed identical gifts." The words of Sesserda

Truth heartened Jase, though his own voice sounded small to him in the echoing corridors. "Other Soli, like the diverse members of any other species, are as unlike me as they are unlike you. Everyone has a unique set of gifts. Applying those gifts to their proper purpose enhances the whole of creation. Misuse or lack of use of such gifts damages us all." Jase scanned the two men, dividing his attention equally between Rust and Arlan. "It is easy to blame circumstances for our personal fears."

Rust squirmed away from Arlan's supporting arm. To Jase, the soldier's reaction shouted boldly: Curiosity did not equate with a willingness to tolerate Consortium preaching. The soldier desperately wanted this duty ended. He wanted to rejoin his squadron, little as he enjoyed its current, awkward position, because he dreaded all imagined alternatives. The transforming force of relanine, dimly sensed but misunderstood, terrified him. This C-human was altogether too strange for the tastes of a battle-weary soldier. "Network, direct us to Ruth Firl," he ordered crisply.

Network replied with mechanical coldness, "Coordinates 7E."

Rust headed immediately in the direction indicated. Arlan said, too quietly to reach the soldier, "May be more than me that be needing to hear Miz Ruth. May be why Saschy be sending you here."

"That seems likely," agreed Jase.

"Miz Ruth be knowing Breamas, and he may be knowing why Wharton ghost lights be burning now in the Governor's palace. I be willing to help in finding him." Arlan hesitated before adding, "I be knowing something of where to find him, but I be not knowing how to reach him alive without invitation. He be well guarded. May be Miz Ruth trusted by him."

"Your confidence honors me," answered Jase, bowing slightly. "I shall do my best to justify it."

"Yah. I be thinking you will." Arlan glanced from a cracked Network sensor panel to Rust, now far down the sterile corridor. "The woman that be leading the attack against us, Dee Sylar, be knowing more than Miz Ruth. Be she still alive?"

"As far as I know." *More layers, more conflicts.* "Our rescuer took her with him. After watching the man demolish an army, I did not feel qualified to argue with him. Did I err?"

"I be thinking you better equipped to judge than me."

Surprise made Jase doubt his own perceptions. He had not intended to recruit a disciple. "Do you want my true judgment?"

"Yah. If you be willing to give it."

"Our rescuer intended the woman no harm. She would have killed him—or any of us—given the opportunity. If he had not taken her captive, she would have tried to kill us, and we would have been forced to kill her." Arlan nodded faintly, his mouth tight. Jase's second assessment of Arlan confirmed the signs that would have been cause for elation in another part of the galaxy. Jase's immediate reaction was dismay that circumstances would make Arlan's incipient interest in the deeper Truths almost impossible to sustain. A broken discipleship could lead to a bitterness and disillusionment worse than ignorance.

As Arlan fell into step behind Jase, the Sesserda scholar pondered his options frantically. On any Consortium world, the answer would have been the easy formula known to every Sesserda adherent: Teach, encourage, and refer the novice to a Sesserda school. Few Soli studied Sesserda seriously, knowing that Soli physical limitations made true mastery nearly impossible, but there were several respected schools that specialized in teaching the basics of Sesserda philosophy to Soli and other, similarly limited species. Jase himself had once been such a student, and only an appalling accident had made him into something much more rare. To discover a disciple was generally a great and wondrous delight for any Sesserda adept. For the first time, however, Jase could understand the full sorrow-joy of which Calongi sang on discovering such disciples among a species like the Soli. What

Sesserda wisdom could Jase possibly impart to an adult Nilsonite that would not lead to grief and frustration?

Engrossed in his own dilemma, Jase realized with a start that they had reached cell 7E, and the gray woman hugging Arlan with painful desperation was Ruth Firl. Rust had remained outside the cell, evidently unwilling to witness any more demonstrations of strange Consortium skills. Arlan was trying to reassure Ruth, whose eyes were red from weeping, that this questioning would accelerate her release. Jase set aside his personal concerns as he gathered his energies and focused his perceptions for a limited Inquisition.

Fear. Pain. Wounds of soul and body that had never healed. This was a badly broken woman, but she had a powerful courage to sustain her. Jase could sense a strong similarity to the daughter who had taken such a different life path.

Ruth and Saschy Firl also shared a strong sense of conscious guilt, albeit for different reasons. "What is *your* hope for the revolution, Ruth Firl?" asked Jase with the solemn, insistent voice of Sesserda persuasion.

"Hope?" asked Ruth, looking at Jase for the first time. She frowned at him, as if something about his face or form disturbed her. "There is no hope in Nilson's streets. That is what must change."

"Terrorism feeds despair, not hope."

"We are not terrorists," answered Ruth proudly.

With a pained voice, Arlan protested, "You be not one of them, Miz Ruth, but terrorists they be. Dee Sylar be lying to us both. Breamas be the same trouble brewer that he be for decades past."

Jase had only to motion slightly, and Arlan fell silent. Though Arlan had clearly understated his own involvement in the palace disaster, Jase considered briefly, sadly, that Arlan would be an admirable candidate for elementary Sesserda schooling—if he were a Consortium member. "Do you know what has occurred at the Governor's palace?"

Ruth clutched at her chest. "Is Saschy hurt?"

"She was well when we left her." Ruth glanced at

Arlan, who nodded in concurrence. The old woman's shoulders drooped in relief. "Why did you abet a plan that might easily have caused your daughter's death?" Ruth shook her grayed head but did not answer. "You value the cause of Breamas' revolution above the life of your child."

"Revolution is not a cause," she explained with an expression of deepest grief. Her mouth remained tight, but she raised her face proudly toward Jase. "Revolution is only a method of achieving freedom from Network tyranny—freedom to live, freedom to *hope*."

"Freedom to die," retorted Jase harshly, though he felt her desperation and ached to offer sympathy. "Freedom to watch your world being consumed by a spatial anomaly catalyzed by your unwise, overly zealous companions in rebellion. You have erred in your judgment, Ruth Firl. Your daughter has chosen the better path."

"She has forgotten Nilson," muttered Ruth, though she stared at Arlan, questioning him with her faded eyes.

Jase nodded his permission, and Arlan explained, "Alongside the palace now, there be something dark, something empty. It be deadly, like a shadow of the ghost lights in the deep places of Wharton, as I be telling you. Dee be guilty of the explosion, but it be causing more than she be capable of planning."

"Do you meet with Breamas directly, or is Dee Sylar your link to him?" asked Jase, testing the name that seemed to signify much more than Breamas to Arlan.

Ruth did not want to reply, but Arlan coaxed her, "You be needed to answer him, Miz Ruth."

"Why?" she countered with bitter laughter. "I have nothing to lose that I value."

"Miz Ruth, please. I be valuing you. I be needing you. You be all the family I be knowing."

Ruth touched his shorn head gently. "Dee is my contact. I have only heard Breamas speak in the gatherings, which have become rare since the rebellion turned serious, a year ago or more. I met Dee at the last such meeting. She sought me later."

"What is your role in the rebel organization?"

"I have spied on my own daughter," admitted Ruth with great weariness. Arlan shook his head almost imperceptibly, but he placed his large hand on Ruth's back to comfort her. "Saschy tells me little, but I sometimes know when she has important shipments coming or important meetings to attend."

"How do you contact Dee, when you have information to give?"

Ruth smiled, lifting years from her tired face. "I have a Network terminal, old but operational. It is the most precious gift that my husband left to me, except for Saschy. He never told me how he obtained it."

Arlan murmured for Jase's benefit, "Soldiers be telling me that Network communication be not functioning properly now, not on Nilson, not since the ghost shadow be appearing beside the palace."

He is wasted here indeed, thought Jase, appreciating Arlan's perceptive comment and weighing the political impossibilities of discussing Consortium membership with Arlan. "Do you have any other method of contacting the rebel organization, Miz Ruth?"

"I know other sympathizers, who have other means of contact."

"Could you help me meet with this man, Breamas?"

Ruth opened her mouth but fashioned no words. She leaned against Arlan, and he accepted her unspoken plea to answer for her. "You be asking more than Miz Ruth be able to promise you."

"I do not demand her promise. I simply state Truth, as I discern it. Breamas is a critical factor in the events unfolding on Nilson. Ergo, communication with Breamas is desirable. Can you supply a link to him, Arlan?"

Startled, Arlan answered forcefully, "Nah!"

"Then you understand my request of this well-informed lady." Jase directed his voice and skills of persuasion toward Ruth. "I shall arrange your release from this place. In the wake of revolution, it hardly remains effective as a prison, but I shall make the proper legal gestures. I am convinced that your incarceration is due to a mistaken view of Truth, and I shall take the necessary measures to correct that error. Because you love Nilson, you will work with me to repair her."

"There be other prisoners here that may be greater help to you," said Arlan, but he had no confidence in his own proffering.

"I have assessed the roll. I have not yet completed my inquiries. There is at least one additional prisoner whom I intend to question before our departure. I begin to perceive that we have limited time, however, and your own recommendation of Miz Ruth has satisfied me."

"You be a persuasive man, C-human, but be you able to persuade Network to be doing your bidding?"

"I need only persuade those who issue the commands that Network enforces." Jase added, "And I am a Soli, Arlan Willowan, like you. My Consortium membership does not alter my species. 'C-human' is a term without Truth. My name is Jase Sleide—or Jase Margrave if you prefer the Network version." Arlan listened attentively, pleasing Jase. "Miz Ruth, do you know a man named Filcher Ikthan Cuui?"

"Isn't that an alien name?" she asked with puzzlement.

"Filcher belongs to the Cuui species."

"I don't know any aliens," she replied, as if offended by the possibility.

"You know me," said Jase wryly, "at least to a limited extent." Her frown wavered at Arlan's reassuring nod. "However, you obviously have not had the pleasure of making Filcher's acquaintance." He turned to Arlan. "Miz Ruth will need your assistance to process her release. I shall complete my questioning while you negotiate the maze of Network procedures."

"I? I be not able to free her."

"Our soldier friend has sufficient authority with Network in this regard, thanks to the orders of Miz Ruth's daughter. I shall ensure that he understands what we require."

"He be fearing you already."

"At present, yes. I think he will . . . adapt."

Arlan asked no more questions, and Jase approved

his quiet confidence. Rust, predictably, grumbled against the release of a prisoner, but he did not argue seriously. He presented only one troubling comment: "I hope the old woman can save us from another attack when we go back into the streets. She can hardly walk, and I'm not in the best condition to move quickly."

Jase shared the soldier's hope, as well as his concern, but did not admit any such doubts. He coaxed the soldier to escort both Arlan and Ruth to the processing room, one of those foolish pretensions of Nilson bureaucracy, after obtaining what he had sought all along: permission to speak privately to Filcher Ikthan Cuui. The corridor echoed hollowly as Jase traversed its length alone. The metal cell doors, their polished surfaces corroded by age and the excessive Nilson dampness, threw Jase's light footfalls back at him. He hardly trusted Network to open Filcher's cell to him, as the soldier had commanded, but Network fulfilled its duty without hesitation or complaint. An intrepid prisoner might well have taken the opportunity to escape, seeing an unguarded entry and a single visitor, but Filcher was either too indolent or too wary of the skills of a Sesserda adept. The Cuui raised his red-rimmed eyes.

"You have taken some pains to conceal vital aspects of Truth from me, Filcher Ikthan Cuui," said Jase with the cold authority of a trained Inquisitor, beginning his pursuit in earnest. "It is time to make amends."

Filcher growled, "I am unjustly accused."

"You are unjustly accused of being employed by the Consortium, and I tolerated your lie temporarily on behalf of the Consortium's tenuous accord with Network. The convenience of that accord is outweighed by the prospect of a larger calamity that now threatens us all. You shall tell me precisely whom you serve, your mission in coming here, the status of that mission, your contacts and *any* information you have gathered about this place and these people. You shall tell me, Filcher, everything: willingly or unwillingly, irrespective of the excellent subliminal programming that you have undergone." Jase seated himself next to Filcher on the

squalid cot. The red-rimmed eyes squinted into burning
slits. "You err," answered Jase to Filcher's unspoken
retort. "The severity of the situation gives me all the
Sesserda jurisdiction that I require to enact any judgment I might make against you. However, the subject
of this Inquisition is not you but the society known
as Network. You are a witness for the prosecution,
Filcher. Make the best of the opportunity."

***

Arlan paced the floor of the prison's stark, white
processing room, deeply frustrated with Miz Ruth for
the first time in his life. "How can you be defending
Dee, after all that I be telling you?" Rust merely
watched the two Nilsonites in moody silence, his body
still in shock.

"Network has exploited our resources, encouraged
the violence surrounding our spaceport simply as an insult to the Consortium, and denied us education as well
as every other right of Network citizenship. Arlan,
revolution cannot be as pure and noble as we wish to
imagine, but this revolution is necessary."

"You be not seeing the monstrosity that be growing
from the palace."

Jase spoke from the doorway, "She will see it soon.
She is accompanying us back to where her daughter is
attempting to maintain a government on this regrettable world." Lines of weariness creased his eyes.

"I did as you asked," grumbled Rust, "but Network
refuses to release her."

"No longer," replied Jase tersely.

"Miz Ruth be no longer a prisoner here?" asked Arlan. His awe of Jase acquired another layer of cause.

"I persuaded the commandant to release her to us."

"Do you work for my daughter?" asked Ruth, curiously eying the slight, oddly attired stranger.

"She sent me here," replied Jase obliquely. Arlan
did not augment the answer.

"Saschy wants to see me?" asked Ruth, a hesitant
hopefulness brightening her sad expression. She tucked

a stray white curl beneath her cap and straightened her sweater.

"Your daughter needs to see you urgently. She needs," sighed Jase, "to understand what she has abetted." As Ruth moved to rise, Arlan offered his hand in help, but Ruth smiled and stood unaided. Hope, even slight, made the old woman younger.

Rust muttered, "Crossing this city was hard for us to survive. It's not a stroll for a crippled old woman."

"I be able to carry her," said Arlan staunchly.

Miz Ruth's crisp laughter drowned his words, and Arlan stared at her in surprise for the merriment of her. "Young man, Nilson is my home, and the people whom you fear are my friends. You will find a walk through Nilson's streets is much safer in my company, even if I slow your progress. Sir," she said, turning to Jase, "if you will allow an old woman to guide you, I can ensure that we reach my daughter safely."

"I welcome your guidance and your wisdom," answered Jase with a faint bow, "more than you imagine." His fingers wove a Sesserda honor sign that no one else in the room understood, but Ruth followed Arlan out of the room with a proud, light step, almost unhampered by her limp. Rust shook his head in bewilderment.

CHAPTER 38

Doubting

The caves looked almost civilized here, their walls smoothed with white plaster, arched light tubes brightening them to a semblance of flickering daylight, albeit of a gloomy Nilson-like hue. The floors were tiled in a glassy, mottled gray that might have resulted from heat or chemical fusing of the natural stone, but the result was not unattractive. The corridors, presumably obeying some measure of nature's original plan for Wharton, twisted and sloped more erratically than most Network constructs. Once Tori had convinced herself that this was indeed the Wharton mine that Quin claimed it to be, whether by her strange companion's design or by less discernable fortune, Tori found the tunnel city's unexpected curves, climbs and crannies a refreshing assurance that even Network tolerated some limitations to its control.

Tori had allowed Quin to guide her, distrusting his motives but respecting his perceptions. Together, they had approached a group of a dozen men, who were sorting laboriously through wagonloads of clay and gravel, only to turn away from the noisy group when Quin decided that something about the men warranted avoidance. Quin had similarly shunned other groups, heard but never seen, and individuals, glimpsed but quickly dodged. He declined to confess his criteria beyond such unsatisfying statements as, "They're trawling for treasure. I think they'd give a poor welcome." Knowing something about the unpleasant Nilson culture, Tori was inclined to share Quin's reluctance to greet strangers freely.

That Quin was hiding something of serious

consequence, Tori had ceased to doubt. Quin had become increasingly evasive and hesitant to speak at all, except for frivolous absurdities. Tori had an uncomfortable suspicion that if she took her eyes away from Quin for more than a microspan, he would vanish altogether. She would not have minded losing an acquaintance of such brief, unsettling duration, if she had not felt that he was somehow critical to her ability to understand what had occurred—and to use that understanding to reunite with Jase.

She almost refused to accompany Quin when he finally decided that one stray caver was acceptable as a source of information. She acquiesced only after deciding that the dust-drenched caver, little more than a boy, was too gawky and uncertain to present a threat even to her alone. When the boy's eyes widened on seeing her, and he began to fumble awkwardly with his helmet, she nearly laughed at the comforting familiarity of the reaction. Despite the struggle to communicate verbally, Tori's smile coaxed the boy, but her attention never left the clownishly grinning young man who had accompanied her from another world, another space. For more than her merely personal concerns, she wished that she had Jase beside her. She even wished—for an instant—that any of the Calongi masters was present to observe and offer judgment on what this odd man called Quin was hiding.

The thickness of the boy's Nilsonite dialect almost defied her comprehension: "What cause be bringing you here deepside?" he asked her.

"I'm just a lost lady looking for home or a transfer portal," she replied. The boy seemed as troubled to hear her accent as she had been to endure his. Though the tunnel's lighting seemed uniform, and Quin had retreated only a pace away from her, a shadow cloaked him. The boy showed no sign of noticing Quin at all, but his eyes had narrowed in assessing Tori.

"Portals be above the commerce levels. Nearest lift be a mile past cavern yon." He jerked his elbow in the direction of a widening in the tunnel. "May be portal down time still. Power be back only an hour past."

"I'd appreciate your guidance to them anyway, if it's not too much trouble for you."

He nodded at first but seemed to reconsider. "I be a retriever, miz. I be getting a signal summons hereabout. Be you sending? Why be you here? These be old tunnels to an outworked mine."

"I don't seem to know how I arrived here, but I am certainly glad that you found me."

Her reply brought a hunted look to the boy's dark eyes. "Be you seeing the ghost lights, then?"

Quin answered smoothly, "Yes. We saw the ghost lights. Have you seen them often near here?"

Startled to observe Quin's presence, the boy jumped nervously. "Yah. Often since Vin be caught in the gold shaft, week past. Oftener since the power breakage. Not just here. You be not of Wharton. How be you here?"

Tori said, "We were on Nilson. We'd like to return there, if you wouldn't mind helping us a little longer. Was it this way to the lifts?" She began to move in the direction that the boy had indicated.

"Yah," he admitted, but he followed her with obvious suspicion. "Be you those portal investigators that Network be telling us be coming?"

Again, Quin spoke, "What do you know about the investigation?"

"Only what all be knowing," replied the boy defensively. "Network be announcing the investigation just after old Vin's last troublemaking. Network be asking all portal users to declare any unusual transfer effects."

"Has Network made any announcements about the investigation in the last two days?" asked Quin.

"Nah," he countered with a sneer that troubled Tori. "No announcements at all. Network be not talking to us now. May be more failures than you be knowing."

"Has anyone used the portals in the past two days?"

The boy's intention to deceive was clear, though Tori wished she could discern the cause. "I be not knowing. I be new to Wharton. I be having nil to do with transfer portals."

"I'm not accusing you—or anyone—of anything!"

laughed Quin, and he was again the image of harmless, cheerful curiosity. The light seemed to grow clearer around him, and the openness of his expression made suspicions about him seem absurd.

The boy relaxed visibly, apparently satisfied with the success of his deception. He even returned a hesitant echo of Quin's broad smile. Tori, however, having some experience with the Truth-seeking tactics of Sesserda scholars, found the boy's reaction and Quin's shifting persona equally clear indicators of conscious deceit. She did not condemn Quin's deceit in itself; indeed, she supported it to some measure by encouraging the boy to believe Quin's implicit lie. The boy now seemed certain that Tori and Quin were Network officials, performing an investigation of transfer portal malfunctions, and the boy imagined that he had outwitted them and gained their confidence. The result was an attitude of deference, tinged with cynical contempt and amusement at the commonplace ignorance of Important Persons. He led them now with a brisk professionalism, no longer hesitant or shy.

They climbed two levels by a narrow ladder and emerged from rough caverns and utility passages to a city. Bright, broken signs of shops and services, even a partially constructed tram, gave better resemblance to a civilized community than the dilapidated streets of Nilson, but they were shattered. Despite the evidence of recent violence, if these polished Wharton corridors had been less lifeless, Tori might have felt relief that she had returned to the universe she knew. If she had not observed a change, a heightened wariness, in Quin's swinging walk, she would not have turned to see the troop of tense miners that had gathered silently behind them. One man shouted, and a dozen more miners dropped from the ceiling traps, encircling Tori and Quin. Their erstwhile guide grinned wickedly as he aligned himself with his comrades. Tori returned the smile as if she were unaware of any threatening intentions. She did not look at Quin, now immobile at her side.

"Network spies," growled a sallow, pinched-face man. His bristle of a mustache arched angrily.

Tori laughed with merry brightness, though her nerves stung. "You mistake me for a Network spy?" she drawled. The hard expressions of the miners refused to yield to charm. She could have conquered any one or two or three of these angry men, but they were too many, each man anxious to remain stern and determined before his comrades. The circle of men began to close upon their prisoners. In desperation, Tori began to turn toward the boy who had served as guide, for she thought she had affected him before his suspicions hardened.

"Do not move," whispered an urgent voice that had no obvious source.

Unsure of whether the sharp order represented a threat or a warning, Tori obeyed. All of the blazing lights, corridor panels and garish shop signs and miners' helmets, flickered in synchroneity, and all became dark, except for a smattering of ruby fireflies. Amid the sudden howls of outrage—and of fear—Tori felt hard fingers clench her arm and pull at her.

"Come quickly," hissed the voice, now clearly Quin's. Tori did not hesitate. The certain dangers of the miners negated, for the moment, any of her nebulous concerns about Quin. As he tugged her out of the imprisoning circle, shoving past miners who could not distinguish ally from enemy in the darkness, she wondered if he were indeed a Network spy, as the miners seemed to believe. The theory provided her no revelation of his motives. "Through here," he urged after they had run a lengthy, blind race. They passed through a sliding door into a brightly lit hallway of silver metal, striped with white enamel doors, evenly spaced like close living quarters.

A shout behind them, as the light flooded their backs like a beacon, was not distant enough for Tori's comfort. Quin did not hesitate in choosing a door, which looked like all its neighbors but led into another hallway. He dragged Tori with him as surely as if he knew from long experience every twisting hall and crooked stair or ladder.

"A stranger here," she muttered, doubting Quin but obeying his lead, for she had no better hope.

"Yes," he retorted, though she had not made a question of her cynical observation. Pursuit clattered loudly, then softly, distorted by echoing lengths and turns of polished tunnels. "But there is a portal not far ahead of us, and I feel its energy. If we can reach it, I hope to find a stable pattern, or at least a stable strand to follow. I do not dare to transfer us from here." He added with a worried grunt, "The infinities are crumbling around us."

Tori did not think that he expected her to understand him, but he clearly knew more about their circumstances than he had yet acknowledged. He was chattering from nervousness, she thought, not quite entrusting her with truth but granting her a measure of respect in common plight. "Crumbling walls are bad enough," she answered, jumping aside as sharp chips of the polished walls scattered with a heated hiss. A blemish of the underlying stone glowed red. She ducked, just as a second fiery beam scorched the same wall. Quin pulled her through another door. "We can't outrun beamer fire much longer," she said, as they climbed a narrow ladder to a black stone landing. She joined Quin on the landing. The ladder continued upward to a barred metal hatch, sealed with a padlock. There was no other route to take, except to return the way they had come. "It doesn't look like we can run any farther this way."

"I can absorb the beams, if they don't destabilize the patterns completely before we can transfer. We're close, I think."

"Close to being caught," gulped Tori, as distinct voices rushed into the room below them. She yelped as fire brushed the landing's edge. Quin extended his hand, and his outstretched palm first engulfed the beam, then turned it. Cries sounded below, then the silence returned like a pall.

"The fools don't know what they're feeding," grunted Quin. As Tori stared at him, certain now that he was a Network spy equipped with Network devices beyond her comprehension, Quin turned his gaze intently toward the metal hatch in the ceiling. The padlock burst into flame. Its pieces tumbled past the ladder into the darkness many levels down. The hatch fell open, and Quin nodded at Tori. She did not dare to argue with him. Reluctantly, she clambered up the ladder, half expecting attack from her companion, who had transitioned in her opinion from odd to seriously alarming.

Quin joined her quickly in a yellow-and-white checkerboard room that seemed incongruously frivolous for this darksome cave warren. It was a large room with a silvered rectangular pad consuming much of the floor space. Several hatches, much wider than the floor access that Quin had opened, were equally well sealed. The necks of massive lading cranes extended from two checkered walls. A few dim windows opened from a ceiling dome of unfinished stone, high above the floor. Towers of stacked crates leaned against each other precariously. The air shivered visibly above the rectangular pad, but the distortion was too painful to observe for long.

"A transfer portal?" speculated Tori.

"Intended for cargo only," answered Quin. "That's why there's no light curtain. Try not to focus on the ripples of space, unless you want to make yourself thoroughly dizzy." Quin frowned. "Someone is here, other than the oblivious guards outside the door," he whispered, though Tori could detect no other presence but theirs, now that pursuit had grown still. "Power," he added, a glaze of remoteness clouding his eyes. "Lords, this cannot be."

"What's wrong?" demanded Tori, though little seemed to be right.

"Take my hand, and close your eyes. Walk forward with me." Quin did not wait for her to obey. He did not merely pull her by hand but by the force of Power.

She did not seal away the vision quickly enough. The floor receded abruptly. The cavern warped into streams of white cloud, shadowed in gray, shadows

painted not by absence of light but by their own abstract, nervous mists and mountains of feathery dew. A
universe turned, whirled its stars and wept with tears of
red and wrenching pain. Tori tasted the salt of her own
tears, though the terrible grief and hurt both existed beyond her mind's capacity to reason. She would have
cried aloud the sorrow that beset her, but her throat
grew tight with her distress. She could not protest the
injury; it was not hers to own or to dispute.

Then air surged back into her starved lungs, and the
world became solid again beneath her. She stepped
through a smoldering curtain of light. Before her was a
view of sky, gray with clouds of rain and not of terror.
Above her head, a broken dome rose white, held aloft
by cracked pillars instead of solid walls. The floor was
made of chipped white tile. The scents were sour but
familiar.

"Ten minutes to curfew," announced a tinny voice.
"All Nilson visitors wishing to leave the port at this
time, please depart now."

Tori looked around her at the port building. She had
arrived without Quin, but two tattered Nilsonites were
strolling toward her in patrol fashion. They were, as
yet, unaware of her presence. She remained motionless
in front of the portal, and they passed her by unseen,
for they kept their eyes averted determinedly from the
turbulence behind her. Nervously observing the cause
of their aversion, she raced out of the building and
down the sprawling stairs into the Nilson streets. She
clung to the evening shadows and tried to derive direction from inadequate recollection of the Nilson city's
maps. A crash, a cry, and the hiss of beamer fire turned
her head toward the gilded dome of the Governor's
palace. Fire leaped between the palace and port building behind her. She frowned to see the writhing darkness that hid the palace's eastern wing and climbed
now into the sky, but that was where she had left Jase.
That was where she must search. She refused to doubt
that she would find him.

CHAPTER 39

Bartering

"You are sure that you can place me accurately?" asked Katerin for the third time. She turned away from the Tower window and the ruddy sun setting beyond Ixaxis. "You have never been to Network, have you?"

"You know that I have not," replied Evaric evenly, "and I assure you again that I can." He quirked one dark brow at her. Lazily draped across an armchair in his mother's office, he seemed less concerned by the effort that he proposed to undertake for her than by his private game of tossing a wicked knife and catching it midair. It was his apparent indifference that had spurred Katerin's worries. Even Quin, who had more experience with topological transfer than any other Ixaxin, never took the success of the process entirely for granted. "After you arrive, you will be on your own, so I do hope that you have selected your destination carefully. I have no intention of accompanying you, even to confirm your safe arrival. I do not dare to travel that far. If you dislike my terms, remain here."

"Do you regret your offer to transfer me back to Network?" Katerin tried vainly to decipher Evaric's twisted smile. All of her skill at psychological analysis availed her little with this enigmatic son of two Infortiares. She wondered for the hundredth time how closely Evaric resembled his infamous father.

"I will regret the offer, if you ask me one more time whether I can achieve it. Please make your decision, Lady Katerin. I am not a particularly patient man."

There was no one else willing to help her. Ixaxins who had made the journey to Network had refused. She had no choice to make. She heaved a deep sigh and nodded. "Whenever you are ready, Lord Evaric."

"You may prefer to close your eyes."

Once more, she glanced at the sunset. Even if the transfer succeeded, she might not survive to see another day end. She swallowed and closed her eyes.

Fire engulfed her. Red and gold and spiraling blue, the flames that filled her mind were cold but deadly. She sensed herself immersed in space and time, rushing to a distant point that burned, minute but distinct, upon a fiery plain. Katerin had never experienced such a consciousness of perilous travel in all her journeys with Quin's protective aid or Network's portals. Evaric did not shield her from awareness of the dangers that he negotiated or the danger that he represented. His was a lethal form of Power, and he made no pretense of gentleness in this formless place that comprised his most vivid reality. His directness gratified Katerin, despite the associated discomfort, because in here there were no barriers of culture and pride to pierce, and she recognized his attitude as respect.

She had no chance to thank him. Evaric delivered Katerin efficiently and retreated from her as immediately as he had promised. She emerged from a Network portal and inhaled the hot wind of Rendl. She strode to the nearest Network terminal and confirmed that the apartment Quin had rented for them remained registered in their names. Network had not exposed Quin's falsified identities. Katerin verified the date twice, mentally accounting for the discrepancies between Seriin and Rendl calendars. Evaric had delivered better than he had promised.

Belief came slowly, though Katerin knew the history of Network-3, closed by her father, then time-shifted and reopened by the same saturnine man that she had left in the Infortiare's Tower. Awareness that Evaric had just moved *her* through time—however minimally—provided her with a moment's queasiness. Evaric had eradicated the hours of her indecision, as well as the futile requests for help from other wizards. For a moment, she wished that she had thought to ask him for a more significant boon of time, but she abandoned the regret hurriedly. With even her limited knowledge of applied topology, she knew the instabilities that any temporal manipulation must impart. Either Evaric had acted from his own strange instincts, heedless of adverse effects, or the instabilities that Quin had reported were more widespread than he had admitted. For all Evaric's menacing air, he did not strike her as a man who destroyed by carelessness. She added one more uncomfortable fact to the list that she would offer to Network's Council Governor.

She took the tram to the apartment that still held the telltale bits and pieces of her transitory personal life with Quin: a hairbrush, a coffee pot, a sketchpad with a few of her carefully innocuous drawings of local scenery. She had bought and abandoned such personal accoutrements too often to feel attached to these, but they imposed on her a wistfulness, nonetheless, because she had returned to them without Quin. Determined to act before she could change her mind, she seated herself and demanded of Network, "Establish contact with Council Governor Andrew Caragen."

"That contact point is restricted, Kate," remonstrated Network gently.

She gripped the arms of her chair but proceeded determinedly. "My identity code as Kate Welor is forged, Network. Perform a comprehensive identity scan of me now and compare the results with your data files on Dr. Katerin Merel. Inform the Council Governor that I need to speak to him in regard to my father, Dr. Jonathan Terry."

Receiving no reply at all from Network, Katerin knew that she had triggered a massive analysis program. She could easily envision the storm of Network communications crossing between worlds and universes in response to her identity, as confirmed by local Network sensors, self-repaired by now from Quin's daily meddling to deflect and distort their standard readings. Her father's name alone had probably activated several thousand alerts.

"How delightful to hear from you, Dr. Merel,"

drawled Caragen's distinctive, cold voice after no more than ten minutes. Katerin could not suppress a shudder.

"Do not trouble yourself with false pleasantries, Council Governor. I presume that you have already reported my presence to your favorite local militia, and I'd like to state my purpose before they arrive. My husband encountered a serious disturbance in the connected space that constitutes our universe. Due to the severity of the potential problem, my father chose to investigate personally. Both my husband and my father have now disappeared, and I am convinced that the topological 'problem' exceeded both their expectations and their individual capabilities. The combined resources of Network may not suffice to resolve this instability that Quin discovered. Because I believe that the alternative will be cataclysmic for us all, I am here to contribute my help in the form of all the relevant data that my husband and my father bequeathed to me."

"Your offer is generous, Dr. Merel, but implausible. Why should I expect anything but treachery from you, who have proven your disloyalty to Network at every opportunity?"

"Your accusation is as meaningless as it is absurd," retorted Katerin crisply. "I have never represented any personal threat to you. You have made use of me only as leverage, first as a reserve asset to wield against my father, more recently as a means of manipulating my husband. You do not need me now, Council Governor, because there is no longer even the slightest possibility of using me against either of the men who have valued me in their own ways. Both have left me, and I find myself quite unable to care what you do to me."

"You tell a pitiful story, Dr. Merel," observed Caragen without evidence of emotion.

"You may as well pity yourself. It is the fabric of your empire that has rotted from misuse. Your fall has made me alone again. That is why I have ceased to hide from you. You no longer matter."

"Where did they go?" asked Caragen, almost as if he were a normal citizen conversing in a normal manner.

"To Nilson," answered Katerin, betraying nothing, hoping dimly that this man, this deadly enemy, would recognize advantage of a cooperative truce, as facilely as Evaric had predicted. Katerin knew the methods of the manipulator as a student of that science, but Caragen was the master of the craft.

"A troublesome little world, Nilson. I prefer to entrust its turmoils to my Council Chancellor, Rabhadur Marrach."

"He no longer works for you," replied Katerin, but she recognized the success of Caragen's well-aimed barb. Her nerves frayed a little more, threatening her self-control.

"You err, Dr. Merel. Marrach remains, as always, my most loyal and capable servant. He serves me now—on Nilson, as it happens."

"You still need my help. He has not succeeded for you this time." She could hear the pounding of booted feet approaching the apartment building. The soldiers did not trouble to hide their coming. She spoke hurriedly, "I can give you information that you will obtain nowhere else. I can give you victory over every enemy who has ever defeated you. I can give you control of the Immortal wizards of Network-3." The soldiers burst through the door with their weapons raised.

"Keep her alive," said Caragen, "and bring her to me."

IV.

TRUTH

CHAPTER 40

Reunion

The ballroom that Racker had never used made an odd headquarters for a Network government, but Saschy did not notice the indignities that would have horrified Racker. The ugly emergency beacons of the Network squadron dangled from the crystal chandeliers, painting the gilt and glitter room with a callous glare that amplified the opulent tawdriness. Desks had been dragged from abandoned offices, scratching the synthetic wood floor. The flotsom of disaster, along with assorted objects that Saschy had identified as potentially valuable, leaned haphazardly against the mirrored walls. Saschy had set every government official she could find to work on tasks that ranged from cataloging survivors' names to searching for a means of restoring Network functionality. Some of the officials, unused to such work, had grumbled, but many had begun to find enthusiasm in their joint efforts. One man, an innovative hobbyist, had managed to restore limited, local operation to a Network terminal. His success had pleased Saschy, though the limitations of local Nilson databases lessened the achievement's real worth.

Saschy hated the cacophony of the besieged officials' voices, of scattered warfare and of damaged palace wings creaking toward collapse. She hated the incomprehensible phenomenon that grew like a noisome sewer fungus from the east wing, spreading now to darken the sky above the transfer port building. She hated the loneliness that mounted with each order that she issued in a convincing display of confidence.

Even the young captain of the Network soldiers had yielded responsibility to her, after she berated him for his inept handling of the rebel attacks. She did not doubt that her censure of him was justified, but she had no idea of what to do with the result. She issued commands to junior officers as if she had an overall strategy for defeating the siege, which she lacked. The rebels still escaped serious damage, while eroding her army's limited resources. Only the black horror stretching across the plaza achieved any retreat by Breamas' captains, and that hardly constituted a victory. Saschy's own people shunned that region equally. Saschy commanded occasional beamer blasts toward the rebels who held the ports, but she did not try to order anyone to cross the darkened ground to reach the port building. Much as she coveted that goal, she knew that such an order would result in mutiny.

Saschy's temper, always brittle, had become a terror to those who approached her. The result served her well by weeding out reports and complaints that did not truly require her attention, but she did not know how long she could retain control. Network could not help her, unless contact spontaneously restored itself, but Saschy had lost hope of that event. She even found herself regretting the absence of Racker with his aptitude for pleasant, albeit shallow, talk. Racker did know how to charm an audience.

When Jase entered the ballroom under escort of the bearded soldier, Saschy felt relief surge through her. The C-human's persuasive talents exceeded any of Racker's wiles. When Saschy's Mum appeared with Arlan, following closely behind Jase, her disciplined exterior nearly crumbled. Mum was limping heavily, her age apparent in her pained steps, but the pangs of memory—of childhood hunger, fear, and pain assuaged by Mum's gentle strength—returned as if freshly learned. Even Arlan, so long a guilty burden, seemed a welcome sight.

Saschy did not await the odd foursome but hurried to meet them. For the first time in many years, she hugged her Mum voluntarily, and she smiled at Arlan. As Mum shed tears and Arlan returned a hesitant smile, Jase said quietly, "The siege is collapsing. The city is almost silent, for the people have retreated to their homes. Breamas' followers are as alarmed as any of us by the phenomenon that their revolution has unleashed. You can regain control of Nilson if you speak rationally to your people, seek no vengeance, and ask to meet with Breamas for the purpose of solving the larger problem that you share."

"Meet with the terrorist who caused this disaster?" snapped Saschy, her momentary relief evaporating. "C-human, you are naive." Ruth stiffened, and Saschy withdrew from her, remembering their breach. "Breamas is an old fool. His followers will abandon him as soon as they realize that he cannot keep his promises to them."

"Breamas may be a figurehead, but he is not as helpless as you imagine," retorted Jase. "Along with some dangerously capable Nilsonites, he has acquired the support of a renegade Cuui sect known as the Halaad, who advocate anarchy as a means of improving their own trade in illicit military merchandise. The Halaad manufacture nothing, but they excel at acquisition. They supplied Breamas with the majority of his current arsenal, as well as with the explosives that brought down this building's east wing. Your Governor's accusations against Filcher Ikthan Cuui were not as far from Truth as many of us hoped."

"The Cuui admitted this to you?"

"Yes." Jase added with a grimace, "Reluctantly."

Arlan said slowly, "Be believing this man, Saschy." He patted Ruth's bowed shoulders. "He be more than we be understanding."

Saschy had reached the same conclusion hours ago, but Arlan's confirmation surprised her. It gave her the courage to ask of Jase, "What are you?"

"A man who loves Truth."

"Consortium truth?"

"Truth does not differ between Network and Consortium. Truth is the constant among all people, all places and all time. Only the perception of Truth is variable."

A soldier, wet with rain, hurled himself through the

door so abruptly that he collided with Rust. "Watch yourself, soldier," growled Rust, displaying edgier behavior with every insight into the C-human's alien ideas.

"What is the problem?" demanded Saschy, glad to turn her attention away from Jase, whose words and actions seemed to exert such disproportionate effects.

"Lieutenant Firl, a woman has surrendered to us. We discovered her near the edge of the ghost shadow. She is not a Nilsonite, but she has an odd accent. She says she knows the Governor. She insists on seeing you."

"I have no time for social visits," snapped Saschy.

Jase had enveloped the soldier with a sharply focused stare. "You find the woman unusually attractive," observed Jase intensely.

The comment embarrassed the startled soldier, but he answered quickly, "Yes, sir."

In a softly musical voice that was nearly hypnotic, Jase continued, "She has hair like black velvet, eyes as bitingly clear as rain and as vivid as new spring moss, and a smile that could tear your heart in half."

"Yes, sir," answered the acutely puzzled soldier.

"Take me to her," ordered Jase in a whisper that was inescapable.

"I need your assistance here, C-human," countered Saschy, though she knew she could not prevent Jase's departure. She tried to disregard a sharp twinge of envy. It was not hard to deduce the woman's identity, or to recognize the C-human's besotted state, the most ordinary—and most irritating—reaction that Saschy had observed in him.

"I shall return, Lieutenant," replied Jase, but he forcefully ushered the bewildered soldier ahead of him and out the door.

Saschy sighed in resignation, "Mum, you need rest. I have a cot in the small salon—first room on your right as you go down this hallway. Arlan, take her there, please."

"Yah," agreed Arlan, but he gave Saschy a sad, knowing look. "That man be more far removed from you than you be from me, and that be too far even for dreaming."

Ruth chided, "Arlan, don't talk so."

"It be only truth."

Brittle as Wharton crystal, Saschy whirled away from her only family to return to her frantic work. She snapped at an aide, "Have that useless Network captain brought to me. Tell him that he can redeem himself by delivering an invitation to Breamas."

***

"I'm sure you'll get your audience with the Lieutenant Governor," a young soldier assured Tori. She smiled at him encouragingly, though she wished he would take his annoying chatter elsewhere than on the bench beside her. She was tired and nervous, and she was in no mood to fend off unwanted attentions. "We haven't found too many visitors, especially under the ghost shadow. Not even the rabble troubles us much on that side now. We've seen them fleeing the port building, a few at a time. We expect to regain control of the ports soon, and then we can put an end to this rebellion."

Tori nodded vaguely. She had hardly heard the soldier. She had demanded an audience with the Governor primarily as a tactic in promoting respect from the soldiers, when first she decided that surrender was her best option for reaching the Governor's palace. She had no interest in seeing Racker again, much less his Lieutenant, except for the purpose of extracting information about Jase. Through the fractured window of the occupied office building, Tori watched the sky boil and wondered if Jase had survived, if he, too, had been swept from this horrid place, and if he could possibly have shared her peculiar fortune in encountering an odd escort capable of making the return journey.

She thought fatigue had propelled her imagination too far when Jase's voice first reached her, "Thank you for keeping her out of trouble, soldier. I'll tend her now." Without visible effort, Jase lifted the soldier from the bench and set him on his feet. The soldier, a burly youth, stared at the slightly built man who had evicted him and usurped his place so adroitly. The rare display of the strength that evolved from Sesserda training and relanine-saturated musculature impressed even Tori, who knew the physiological origins.

She flung her arms around Jase in her own indulgence of uncharacteristic behavior. She expected him to execute his customary adept retreat or, at best, endure her emotional display with Sesserda tolerance for her stressed state. Instead, he squeezed her to him tightly, and she laughed with joy to realize that he had feared to lose her. "I'll never believe in your Sesserda detachment again, Jase. You missed me."

"Like a familiar thorn in my side," he retorted, but his sensitive fingers traced the lines of her face hungrily. "I thought you abandoned me and ran off with your handsome Network Governor."

"Racker's not here?" she asked, though she cared about nothing except the man in front of her. Relanine's aura tingled across her exposed skin, and she knew that assessment of her own health and relanine levels comprised part of Jase's ethereal contact with the skin of her face and throat, but neither the complexity of his motives nor the hazards of contamination weighed heavily in her immediate concerns.

"He disappeared along with his entire office suite, following the explosion that birthed that nightmare." Jase raised one finger from its searching caress of her shoulder and pointed toward the seething cloud of darkness. "I thought you were with him."

"I was with him," whispered Tori, digging her hands into Jase's back, as if to affix herself to him firmly enough to prevent any future parting. Relanine's gingery scent, despite its ominous potential, had never seemed more precious to her. "I was with Racker, then I was elsewhere: lost on a world entirely different from this, another world after that, and another and another."

"That explains why you've nearly depleted the contents of your last adaptation inoculation," he murmured.

"Then you had better hold me close enough and long enough to replenish my supply, and please don't bother to remind me that contact with you is too addictive a method for frequent application."

"Too addictive for both of us. Too dangerous for you. But present circumstances qualify as extenuating."

"I promise not to be too greedy." She wanted nothing more of the moment than to feel him as a Soli man who valued her, but she needed also the reassurance of his confident Sesserda observation and reasoning, for all its Calongi origins. "Jase, what has happened here? What happened to me?"

"I don't know, Tori." His smoothly deft Sesserda voice had acquired an edge that seemed almost frantic to Tori, who knew him so well. "I need to learn what you've experienced. I need to tell you what I've observed. You cannot imagine how much I have wanted to discuss this catastrophe with someone who could understand." Concealing lenses, intended to be replaced daily, submitted to relanine's permeation, asserting itself in the intensity of his emotions. His eyes began to blaze with the iridescence of the relanine that filled him. Jase glanced at the nearby soldiers who witnessed the reunion of the two C-humans with prurient curiosity. The nearest soldier, the same youth who had tried to entertain Tori, recoiled from the strangeness of iridescent eyes.

"Can you find us a more private place to talk?" murmured Tori in the softest of whispers. Jase traced a sign of affirmation on her wrist. In a united, fluid movement, Jase and Tori arose and ducked hurriedly past the soldiers.

CHAPTER 41

Anger

Quin moved more cautiously through the planes of Power than in even his earliest journeys, when the Taormin taught him the potential of his gifts. Then, he had feared only for his own life, subject to the dangers of his ignorance. Now, he had good cause to dread for the universe around him. Every fiery strand of his reality's fabric shivered and flickered on the verge of dark extinction or inconceivable change. Nothing seemed stable now, except for that momentary flare of brilliance that he had seen by Power's deepest vision. Quin had witnessed it too briefly to be sure of his initial conclusion, and he had not dared investigate without risking Tori's life, but he was determined to find it again.

The faint glow of a living being snatched at his awareness. In hope, he rushed to meet the creature caught in webs of crimson fire. Disappointment stopped him. The life pulsed too dimly for wizard kind, too erratically for the disciplined pattern of Jon Terry. Frustrated by the additional delay, Quin freed the hapless mortal from the snare of Power and carried the feeble energy back to the place where Quin had left Tori. Because the being was so damaged, Quin stepped with him into the mortal world of Nilson's port building.

The man tumbled from the portal and lay panting with exaggerated distress. "You are not badly damaged," Quin assured him. "This is the planet-city Nilson."

"I know where I am," grumbled the man. "What have you done to me?"

"Saved your ungrateful little life," retorted Quin amiably. "Can you walk?"

"No," he choked. "Network, status!" Network did not reply.

"The portal malfunctions seem to have damaged your Network terminals." Unsure of whether the man's struggles to rise were due to real injuries or to self-pity, Quin offered his hand to speed the process. "Here, let me help you."

At Quin's touch, the man jerked away in panic. His fear, at least, was real. "Network, I want this person arrested immediately for attacking the Governor of Nilson."

Quin rolled his eyes. Because he had to acknowledge that entrapment in the infinities merited some lingering distress, he did not leave immediately, as he wished. He said only, "You are a most unimpressive Network Governor. I wonder what old Caragen finds useful about you." Racker snarled. Quin shrugged. "Nilson's contact with the rest of Network is currently inoperative, but as Planetary Governor, you should be able to find your way back home." Quin added softly, as his Power observed the distortion of infinities that churned the space nearby, "Home may not be as comfortable as you might wish, but I cannot solve that problem without leaving you. Good luck, Governor." Quin turned to reenter the portal.

"You cannot leave!" shouted Racker. "I am the Governor of Nilson!"

Quin paused, sensing the consequences of Racker's prideful protest. Echoing from damaged tile, the shout brought two of Breamas' rebel guards from behind the rubble of damaged lockers. Recognition transformed their lazy patrol into a resurgence of rebellious goals. Loudly, they proclaimed their discovery of the hated Governor to their fellows and began to close the distance at a run. Racker tried to stand and fell. He redirected his panic to the latest threat, and he pleaded with Quin, "You cannot leave me here alone. Those men will kill me."

"You probably deserve it," answered Quin, but he felt the fear and fury that drove the approaching rebels and suspected that the Governor was right about their intentions. The instability of the neighborhood made Quin hesitate to act, until beamer fire erupted from the rebels' weapons. Racker shrieked.

Quin's Power reacted instinctively, deflecting the energy beams and hurling each back to its source. Both rebels collapsed where they stood, their skin seared black. Lightning, triggered by the flare of Power, crackled across the sky and vanished into the ghost shadow. Behind Quin, the portal's light curtain radiated ribbons of scarlet and gold, rippling and fanning toward the ceiling. The ribbons' tips darkened to mahogany, then black. A burning darkness rushed along the ribbons, swallowing the light curtain and enfolding the portal in a trembling cloud of jet and ruby fire. Above the Governor's palace, the black ghost shadow leaped to swallow new lightning.

Racker gaped at Quin, until the distortion of the portal space forced him to turn his eyes toward the floor. The Governor did not stop his nervous whining. "What have you done? What kind of weapon did you fire? No weapon of that magnitude should be transferred without my authorization. What have you done to the portal?"

"Will you stop prattling?" said Quin irritably. The portal pulsed insanely with the effects of Quin's incautious use of Power, causing even Quin to wince from the tortured sight. "This thing is on the verge of implosion."

Racker did not obey the plea for silence, but Quin ignored him. Tentatively, Quin extended a probe of Power to evaluate the damage. He recoiled from a burning fury intense enough to confuse his nervous system and torment his skin. He nearly tripped over Racker. Blisters spouted on Quin's wrists. Stinging fire slit his sleeves. Quin focused his Power and tried to patch together a semblance of temporary stability.

Racker screamed in new terror, but Quin barely heard him. Distantly, Quin sensed a dozen or more rebels storming into the building, summoned to urgent action by the lightning and driven by a knowing leader. Again, Racker struggled to rise and escape, but his legs collapsed beneath him. Quin touched infinity, and the tatters of the light curtain dripped fire.

The first rebel soldiers paused by their fallen comrades and cried their anger, heightened by their fear, as they hurtled toward Racker and Quin. Those twenty rebellious Nilsonites sufficed to make Racker cringe and imagine an invading army of thousands against him. A shrill roar of hatred stopped them. Deliaja had recognized their prey, and she no longer cared about Nilson, Breamas, or the Network Council Chancellor who had forced her—for his own enigmatic motives—to converge a squadron on the port building.

"Leave be! That one be my death enemy," she growled, shoving past rebels who were nearly as fanatical as she in their hatred of Network. Respecting her claim to the most personal, most severe brand of Nilson vengeance, they yielded to her.

Quin tied severed strands of infinity into knots that he knew could not hold for long. His body shook from the strains, but only Marrach, standing slightly isolated from the rebel ranks, took note of him. Deliaja's followers, kindred souls in vengeful fury, watched only Deliaja's movements, and she stared only at the cowering Governor. Racker shrank from Deliaja's shadow, his handsome face squinting with the effort of elusive recognition.

"Be you not remembering me, Racker?" snapped Deliaja. She stowed her beamer in her belt and drew her knife instead. A dark infinity pulsed behind her, but she did not even pause to fear it or to notice the curly-haired man who fought it in lonely battle. She squatted to wave the knife before Racker's horrified eyes. He did not know her, but he recognized madness intent on death. Marrach recognized the same grim phantom, but the brutal instincts that belonged to Caragen's agent detached him from such personal concern; the Healer's soul battled for its fading life inside him. "Be you still fond of pain, Ned? Or be you still fonder of inflicting than receiving? You be still a coward, that be clear."

"You mistake me, citizeness," protested Racker,

attempting a voice of reason but achieving only a pathetic squeak.

"It be you that be mistaken." Deliaja scowled, while her hard eyes poured tears. "Dee Sylar, Ned. Be you remembering now?"

"Dee!" exclaimed Racker, as if hailing his dearest friend. He reached toward her with an open hand.

"Be you false even now?" she asked raggedly. "You be not remembering."

"But of course I remember. I have missed you, Dee. I've wanted to find you again." His fingers almost touched hers, where she gripped the knife's hilt. As she watched him, bitterness twisted her young face into the mask of a crone. "I always loved your smile, Dee. Smile for me?"

"Liar," she howled. In a quick, clean strike, she drove the knife's blade through his hand, pinning it to the floor. Racker screamed, and his blood spurted across the white floor. With his undamaged hand, he tried to extract the blade, but she gripped the knife with both fists and twisted it. He struck her across the eyes, and his ring of office gouged her pale flesh, but she did not flinch. "You be good at talking of love and longing, Ned," she cried, "but you be not even knowing who I be. So be it, Ned, for that *love* of you, I be bringing you a gift of ghost lights to feed on your fouled soul." She jerked her head toward the monstrous void behind her. Racker's attention flickered unwillingly toward that horror. Deliaja tore her blade free and raised it to strike again.

The moment the blade came free, Racker reacted with all his remaining energy, and he tried to crawl away from her. But injury, fear and the snares of infinity had weakened him, and Deliaja was strong with vengeful certainty. She pinned his leg with her second blow, and she dragged the knife through his flesh. Racker made a weak effort to kick her, but his own blood made him slide away from his target. Deliaja mocked him, "What be wrong, Ned? Be you not a man without your clever Network tools about you? I be not even binding you first. That be your evil trick, not mine." She raised her bloodied knife again.

Long, hard fingers squeezed her wrist until it cracked, pried the knife from her and snatched the beamer from her waist. Deliaja spun to her feet, the hatred in her eyes turned against the man who dared to interfere in her long-planned vengeance. "Order your vengeance-mad followers out of this building now, Dee," said Marrach sharply. "This blood sport serves neither Breamas nor Nilson." He grabbed her, lifting her from the floor, and forced her to face the light curtain. Seething portal and shimmering curtain had merged and expanded to engulf Quin with slivering crimson light and troubled darkness. "Foolish, ignorant woman, you are too blinded by your hatred to see disaster approach behind you. Get out of here." Marrach pushed her urgently toward the other rebels and repeated his warning, "All of you, get away from this building before it collapses around us!"

Several members of the rebel force were already leaping down the stairs of the port building. Only one rebel, a slant-eyed man suited in thick layers of green and black canvas, showed some small concern for Deliaja, "Dee, if he be your death enemy, be killing him now. It be trouble to stay here. Be you coming?"

The floor shuddered, as if in reply, and the pillars creaked. Thin sheets of plaster sealant glided lazily from the ceiling, unleashing a hail of dust. The prosaic irritant broke the trance of horror and shared vengeance-lust that had held the remaining rebels, and they ran. The slant-eyed man joined them after Deliaja turned her back on him. She stared at Marrach with loathing. Racker howled in pain.

Marrach spoke in a clear, penetrating voice, attempting to reach Quin above Power's distraction and Racker's noise. "Quin, you are tearing apart this building. Finish your work quickly, or finish it elsewhere."

Quin did not move or speak. Crimson fire writhed around him, dancing upon his skin and clothing. Marrach stepped toward him cautiously, but fire snaked toward him, and he stopped short of its reach. Sparks erupted from a chunk of plaster that tumbled into the portal's range, and the plaster blackened before it struck the floor beside Quin. Wizards' Power preserved itself, even at the expense of its physical host. Power would not hesitate to destroy Marrach if he attempted to remove Quin bodily from the danger.

Deliaja cared nothing for Quin or the ghost lights swirling around him, except as they distracted Marrach. She waited for Marrach to forget her. She glared a violent promise at Racker. He could not escape her now. She would finish with him leisurely. She was shaking with all of her anger against Racker and his kind, against Stonebreaker, others who had used her, and others who had hurt her mother during all those terrified nights of huddling in closets and corners. She looked into the darkness pulsing from a shattered portal and saw nothing more than the weight of helpless fear that she had carried all her life.

Deliaja did not intend to live out the day, but she expected to complete her vengeance first. She had succeeded well for Breamas, giving him Wharton and Nilson both. She could not realize that she had fought only inferior enemies and conquered nothing, for she did not recognize her terrible, intangible ally. She could not judge a man who had executed so many of the schemes of Network's Council Governor. She could not match the calculating mind that had survived so many wars, assassins, and subterfuge.

Even on the rim of cataclysm, Rabhadur Marrach could not forget a nearby enemy. He had awaited Deliaja's attack since leaving Breamas. Peripherally judging the shadows, Marrach saw Deliaja launch herself at his back. He dodged her nimbly, striking her with unthinking force. Before he could take hold of her, she skidded across the bloodied floor past Quin and into the fire of Power and infinity. All visible manifestations of that fire disappeared with Deliaja.

Marrach could not know whether Power had hurled her into hell or to a kindlier world. He watched as Quin sank to his knees before the cold metal framework of a dead portal. Marrach stepped forward slowly. He touched Quin first with the tip of Deliaja's knife to see if lightning sprouted from the wizard's body. When the only result was a mist of plaster dust, Marrach dropped the knife and raised Quin by both arms. In a shaken voice, he said, "Friend wizard, you are hard on the architecture."

Quin blinked at Marrach sightlessly for several seconds before awareness returned the life to storm-gray eyes. "Friend," sighed Quin, smiling weakly, "I have stitched only the tiniest patch on the rent fabric of this space. It will not hold, even with that wretched woman's life energy to sate its hunger for stability. You gave her a terrible death for little gain."

"Tell me later," said Marrach, and half carried Quin away from the portal.

"I need a medic," wailed Racker, trailing into a moan. "You cannot leave me here. I need help!"

When Quin hesitated, Marrach said, "I'll return for him. We need to get you out of here first. Governors are much more plentiful than wizards on this world." Quin nodded. Racker's panicked plaint pursued them to the stairs beneath the seething sky.

"Let me rest a moment, Marrach." Quin seated himself on the lowest step with slow care. The soft drizzle spattered his cloak. "The building will not collapse for several hours. Network buildings have enough structural redundancies to survive a lot of abuse, even from Power's backlash. Go rescue that wretched man who calls himself Governor. Then come back and tell me what you are doing here at all."

"Like you, I am here because the stars bleed," answered Marrach obliquely. Quin slanted him a curious stare and wondered if Marrach himself knew what the odd reply meant. It was a semi-mystical description that Quin would not have expected to hear from either Rabhadur Marrach or Healer Suleifas, but its very peculiarity comforted Quin. The icy grip of Jeni's warnings melted as Quin realized that he would never, could never have acted upon those warnings against a friend, even at risk of life.

"I thought I came here in search of Jon Terry. You haven't seen him, have you?"

"No. He arrived, was injured, and was hospitalized in one of the worst of the local infirmaries. He was then removed from that hospital. I haven't been able to determine if he was transferred or buried. I've been a little preoccupied." For an instant, an overwhelming sense of Marrach's buried pain assaulted Quin, but then it was gone as if it had never existed. The acute contrast troubled Quin as much as the harsh awareness of anguish suppressed. The weathered man in the muddy uniform continued crisply, "Watch for attack from any direction. You *are* sitting in the middle of a revolution."

Quin grunted, "I am not too tired to defend myself from a few scared soldiers, who are too busy watching a disrupted sky to notice one wayward traveler. Look at them scurrying like rabbits over there. They have not even noticed us yet."

"Think kindly toward them. They will soon provide our refuge."

"Then stop dawdling before this rain freezes me." Marrach complied.

***

A furor echoed from the hallway that approached the ballroom, and Saschy looked up from a hand-scrawled report with a frown on her face. Her first thought was that Breamas had finally responded to the invitation that she had regretted upon its issuance, but the messenger who approached her was not the benighted young captain. The messenger saluted her, and she waved at him impatient to speak. "Lieutenant Firl," he announced uneasily, "we have located the Governor."

"You found Racker?"

"Yes, ma'am. He is in the infirmary."

"Badly hurt?"

"Yes, ma'am, but he's expected to recover."

The answer raised Saschy's spirits more than she

would ever have anticipated. The realization that she might actually *like* Racker, even in a limited sense, amused her. "Where was he found?"

"One of the soldiers found him and took him to the medics."

"Where is this soldier?"

"I'm not sure, ma'am."

"Who received his report?"

The messenger, clearly unprepared for a barrage of questions, hesitated. "Perhaps the senior medic. I'm not sure, ma'am."

Useless, thought Saschy. She thrust the report that she had been reviewing at an aide, and she informed the bewildered woman, "I shall be at the infirmary." As she strode across the ballroom, sending the messenger scurrying out of her way, Saschy issued a rapid spate of orders for completion of the myriad mundane organizational tasks at which she excelled. She turned for a moment at the door and pointed at the alarmed messenger, "You find that C-human, Jase Margrave, and tell him to meet me in the infirmary *now!*"

CHAPTER 42

Endurance

The private infirmary that had served the minor needs of government officials had never been put to such extensive use, but it was well equipped to handle more workload than had ever previously been demanded of it. Even deprived of its connection to the rest of Network, the infirmary's diagnostic equipment and procedural implements functioned capably. The clean, spacious facility had delighted the military medics, who had gladly assumed those normally automated functions that the break with Network left untended.

Sedated and partially hidden by the beginning formation of the medical cocoon, Racker's well shaped features achieved an appearance of helpless innocence that stirred something maternal in Saschy. Though she muttered a curse against him even as she stood at his bedside, her anger directed itself against Breamas and his fanatical followers. The C-human said quietly, "We don't need more anger, Lieutenant Firl. Anger catalyzed this situation into the crisis that it has become."

She had not heard Jase approach, and his words startled her. Without looking at him, she retorted, "Look at this man and his injuries, and tell me how we can possibly hope to negotiate peace with the people who would cause this brutality. This is Nilson, C-human, not some coddled Consortium world, where Calongi can impose their false peace because Consortium members have no initiative to rule themselves."

"Uncivilized behavior occurs everywhere. The difference between civilized and uncivilized societies lies in the reaction. A civilized society condemns improper behavior and thereby evolves to higher behavioral standards. An uncivilized society accepts uncivilized behavior as natural and thereby encourages greater violations."

"You are quick to preach, but your only suggestion for restoring peace was to negotiate with the terrorist, Breamas. He does not seem to be interested. What do you recommend that I try next, C-human?"

"I could go to him," sighed Jase. He jerked his head toward the door, where two men had just entered. One was a soldier, stained and muddied; the other was a curly-haired young man wrapped in a preposterously antiquated gray cloak. "Who are they?" demanded Jase in a strangely hollow voice.

Saschy turned to see whose appearance had so upset the unflappable C-human. Because one of the medics signaled to Saschy, she answered, "The tall soldier is the man who found Racker. I don't know about the shorter man, but I intend to learn. You and I will resume our discussion shortly." She looked at Jase, to ensure that he had heard her, and she stepped back in astonishment from the iridescent eyes that blazed back at her.

"As you say, Lieutenant, we shall resume our discussion later." Jase glided toward the door, pausing for only an instant to exchange penetrating stares with each of the two newcomers. Both the soldier and his companion watched Jase's retreat with wary frowns.

When Saschy reached the men, the rankless soldier disregarded all normal protocol and asked her bluntly, "Why is a C-human here?"

The curly-haired man murmured in a tone of wonder, "That was a member of the Consortium?"

Conscious of the C-human's disproportionate impact on *her*, Saschy could not muster her usual indignation toward anyone who treated her, the Lieutenant Governor of Nilson, so casually. She did not censure them; neither did she answer them. "You are the man who found Governor Racker?"

To her surprise, it was the curly-haired youth who replied, "Yes. I encountered him during transfer." With a sudden broad grin, he extended a red and blistered hand to Saschy and announced, "My name is Quin. You are Lieutenant Firl?"

His injuries were too obvious, his impertinence too cheerful to incur more than a flicker of disapproval from Saschy. She answered, "Yes, I am Lieutenant Firl. You found Governor Racker while transferring here from off-world?"

"Yes. Was I unclear? I am sorry. Incoherence is a bad habit of mine. How is the Governor doing? He was in bad shape when I left him, but so was I, for that matter. Travel conditions have become a bit rough in these parts. Is that him in the medical cocoon? Those things terrify me, the way they cut a person off from all sense or sensing, but I suppose that sort of temporary almost-death is preferable to the permanent alternative. I always wonder what would happen if someone were cocooned and then forgotten. Would that person be considered alive, because of the potential to live again, or dead because of the actual dearth of any evidence of life?"

The soldier quelled the spurt of chatter, "Enough, Quin. Lieutenant Firl is not a woman to be befuddled by clownish pretense. Lieutenant, the three of us need to have a private talk."

Where Quin's prattle seemed merely annoying, the soldier's hard command roused all of Saschy's offended dignity. "You are out of line, soldier."

"No, Lieutenant. I am simply out of uniform." To Saschy's fury, he grabbed her wrist, but her reaction chilled when he pressed an identity key into her palm.

The key was an expensive device that Saschy had seen only in the possession of rare, high-ranking Network visitors—like Andrew Caragen. Her palm prickled briefly, as the key transmitted its message directly into the nerve centers of Saschy's brain, "Council Chancellor Rabhadur Marrach . . ." it began, then proceeded with a recital of ranks and titles that turned Saschy's face ashen. Even on brutal Nilson, the name of Caragen's agent was generally whispered in terror.

How much more can I endure? wondered Saschy, wishing that Mum—or Arlan—had remained. Saschy returned the key in silence. She allowed herself to be led through the halls of the battered Governor's palace by the man who was every knowledgeable Network official's greatest nightmare.

***

The room had been designed as an office for some lesser official of Nilson's government. A few personal touches still adorned it: a tiny painting of a child, a preserved flower from some distant world, a leather desk set from an earlier era. The phenomenon that even the most pragmatic soldiers now called 'ghost shadow' touched the ground a few meters from the office window. The tenant of the office, currently compiling lists for Saschy Firl, would have been horrified to know that C-humans had usurped her domain, if she had dared to come close enough to the bleak ghost shadow to discover them.

Jase paced the floor with strides of such intensely suppressed energy that Tori remarked, "Are you preparing to launch into orbit without benefit of ship?"

"I wish I could adequately describe to you the nature of what I sensed," answered Jase.

Confronted by his rare distress, Tori laid aside her own disquiet. She folded her legs beneath her on the singularly uncomfortable couch, and she leaned forward to listen to him without her usual cynical commentary. She suspected that he would have preferred an audience of Calongi masters or even lesser Sesserda adepts, but she was the nearest available approximation. She felt slightly smug to be needed, for once, by him. "Try to make me understand, Jase."

"There are no sufficient words," he explained earnestly, "even in the Calongi tongue, for this is a sense outside the ninety-six that define Sesserda Truth. This man, this being that I perceived, is not simply composed of energy—that would make him fundamentally similar to a hundred well-defined Consortium species. He is essentially a Soli male, but his senses, his essence of life, seem to spread across uncountably infinite dimensions. What I perceived of him was present both here and elsewhere. For all I could tell, he occupied an infinite extent of time, as well."

Tori sighed, "I wish that I could tell you that I understand, but you are being even less coherent than usual."

Revealing the magnitude of his distress, Jase actually sat beside her and took her hands in his. He had touched her more extensively since their recent reunion than in all the span preceding it, and she relished the result, even as she worried about the cause. She told herself that he had simply become more of a Soli while embedded in a Soli environment, according to his usual facile skill of adaptation, but she knew that a darker need was driving him to a state perilously near desperation. Warmth pulsed through her palms and fingertips, penetrating more deeply by relanine's inexorable hunger to be absorbed.

Though Tori could not interpret the intended meaning of each shifting pressure, she knew that Jase was speaking to her as truly by hands as by voice. He was trying to make her understand by all the arts he knew. "Tori, I have no coherent words in any language for what I have observed, because what I have observed is not within Sesserda Truth as I have learned to understand it. I am not a Calongi. Even saturated with the purest relanine of Calongi lifeblood, I have the most rudimentary skills of perception beside theirs, and I am the least of Sesserda scholars, but I have *no* doubt of the wrongness of what has been done here. By whatever means, for whatever reasons or by whatever accidents, Network has created something outside of Truth."

"Something outside of your definition of Truth," amended Tori, trying desperately to comprehend his words according to the subtle fashion of Sesserda shaded meanings.

"Something that cannot exist unless Sesserda Truth is redefined," he whispered, and his desperation to be understood by her was at least as deep as her desire to understand. He struggled to speak in terms that Consortium Basic could encompass with clarity, "To defy the natural law that underlies Truth with a device such as a Network transfer portal is *wrong,* but it impacts only those who enact the wrong. To create a life-form based on that distortion of reality is much more than an individual or an individual society's crime. It shifts the soul of the universe."

"Jase," she whispered desperately, "you are making no sense to me."

"I know." He squeezed her hands once before releasing them, and she had to stop herself from reaching to reclaim contact. "I am making little sense even to myself. I have probably lost my reason to relanine poisoning, at last."

"Nonsense," she argued, but then demanded with a sudden sense of panic, "Is it beginning again?"

"Possibly," replied Jase with a nonchalant shrug that did not deceive Tori. "When my senses begin to go awry, it becomes difficult to distinguish between the effects of external chaos and internal, misbehaving relanine."

"You squeezed my hands. . . ."

". . . and you felt no surge of relanine burning through your skin," he finished for her calmly. "I am not so far gone yet that I can't control it. I've only weakened to the point of yielding to the temptation of touching you." One dark brow tilted in wry self-disparagement.

Not possible, she shouted to herself, refusing to accept that she might lose him, having just regained him. To speak calmly required all of the odd discipline that Tiva disorder enabled in her, "Even my own inoculation has reacted unconventionally to the stress of recent events, making my senses behave strangely. You cannot be short of relanine yet, Jase. It has been no more than a quarter span since your implant was last recharged."

"I have observed too many impossibilities lately to deny one more, but that is not my greatest concern at the moment. . . ."

She interrupted, "We may both be simply experiencing

the unaccustomed effects of adapting from the biochemical rigors of Calong to our natural Soli environment."

He answered her patiently, "We cannot be sure. When Truth itself is ailing, who can be sure of anything?"

"Jase," she pleaded and leaned against him, "how can you ponder Sesserda philosophy on the brink of disaster?"

"Either it is all one wrongness, infecting all of Truth, or it is all a skewing of my own perceptions. I am not experiencing the normal signs of relanine sickness—only an intermittent disorientation that may be the result of these abnormal phenomena around us. The explosion that separated us, the cloud of darkness, this man who is not what he seems. . . ."

"Those are not relanine delusions, unless I am affected also."

"We are both entitled to self-doubts."

"You're humoring me, Jase. You never humor me about anything of consequence. I know what *I* have endured since we arrived here, but what has happened to *you* that has you so badly rattled?" None of the recent horrors had frightened her more completely than his strange nervousness.

"Tori, my dear, I honestly do not know the answer. I do know that there is nothing to gain by worrying about the possibility of relanine sickness compounding our other problems. We have no way of reaching a pure relanine source in the near future. And we have much larger concerns. Sesserda Truth is of infinitely more consequence than any one man."

"Not to me," argued Tori. "I'm too selfish and uncivilized. I care more about you than about Sesserda or Nilson or anything or anyone."

"Tori, stop. . . ."

"We have my store of adaptation fluid on the ship. It might slow the sickness. We can take that ship and leave this tortured world."

"Even if we could reach the spaceport across that war zone out there, our small ship would not survive the energy distortions that are rippling through this world's upper atmosphere. The effects of that ghost shadow extend far beyond the visible range. Aside from that little problem, you know that adaptation fluid has virtually no impact on me. The substance that I need becomes toxic to non-Calongi if stored outside of double-vaulted Calongi bio-vials or a living Calongi. You do remember how I became addicted to relanine originally?"

"In one of your most foolish heroic fits, you entered the wrong vault in the company of a madman, but you did survive that contamination."

"I defied the trillion-to-one odds." Jase gave her a lopsided smile. "Maybe we need similar fortune now. Maybe I'm just hungry for your sympathy in my abject state of misery and befuddlement. You are hardly ever this nice to me."

Tori slid her hand onto his knee. "I'd be much nicer, much more often, if you let me."

"It is not wise to be that nice to a relanine addict."

"Wisdom is your department."

"That's why I have to be wise for us both."

Tori sniffed, masking the depth of her concern with light mockery, "If you really are descending into relanine withdrawal, you're in no condition to make such judgments."

Jase sighed, "My skin would have seared you like acid if I were near the delirium stage."

"Then you had better enjoy my sympathy while the opportunity lasts." In a whisper, she added, "I do not know what else to offer you, Jase. I am not a Sesserda scholar. I have only the most limited comprehension of Sesserda Truth under the best of circumstances."

"You offer what I need most right now: a balancing of spirit that is mandatory for clear judgment," answered Jase solemnly. "You *are* wise, my dear Tori, and you have always been more practical than I, but even sympathy must be expressed with caution."

Shared need trembled in the meeting of their fingers, the tight enfolding of their hands, the bowing together of heads that dared draw no closer than to breathe of each other's hair and skin. Even acute Sesserda perceptions failed to note the opening of the door or the woman who observed and understood only a fraction of what she saw. Saschy withdrew silently, nurturing a resentful mood that she did not attempt to justify or explain.

***

"That office is already occupied," said Saschy with a coldness that inspired Quin to mime an exaggerated shiver. For very different reasons, Saschy and Marrach both glared at him in disapproval.

Quin pretended to be oblivious. "By the C-human?" he asked.

"By the two C-humans," replied Saschy, opening the door to the next office and sighing her relief at finding it empty.

"The woman is from the Consortium also?" asked Quin with convincing innocence, as if he had not recognized Tori immediately. "Does she have those same, strange eyes? I never saw anything like it before. I didn't know the C-humans differed from us physically. What causes that effect?"

"I can't explain the effect," replied Saschy, trying to sound dismissive, though she was as curious as Quin for her own reasons. "Perhaps it's cosmetic. Mister Margrave seemed to have fairly ordinary blue eyes earlier."

Marrach claimed the chair facing the window and fixed his gaze on the fingers of darkness piercing the clouds. He murmured, "Iridescence of the optical tissue is usually an indicator of relanine poisoning, relanine being the major component of Calongi blood. Mister Margrave's ability to survive in such an advanced state of toxicity suggests that he is a relanine addict of extreme dependency. What do you know about Mister Margrave, Lieutenant?"

"Very little," answered Saschy, staring incredulously at Marrach. To be lectured by a legend, on the subject of a C-human who had obsessed her since first meeting, was almost beyond her ability to assimilate. "He requested an audience with an imprisoned Cuui smuggler named Filcher." She forced herself to speak with the cool discipline expected of a Network Lieutenant Governor. "Do we not have more important matters to discuss, Council Chancellor?"

Marrach said crisply, "No. Mister Margrave's presence at this time and place is an improbability. I distrust improbabilities, until I can explain them in a more probable fashion. I particularly distrust improbabilities that attract Caragen's notice."

Quin leaned against the desk and asked quietly, "Caragen told you about this C-human?" Saschy looked from one man to the other with a humbling certainty that she had stepped into matters far beyond the petty politics of Nilson. Her one brief meeting with Caragen had convinced her that she wanted no closer experience of his realm of schemes, but that realm had managed somehow to engulf her. She remained silent, thinking how much Racker would relish this opportunity.

"Caragen informed me of the C-human's arrival and interest in Filcher Ikthan Cuui." Marrach furled and unfurled his left hand, staring at each digit. "I did not pursue the topic extensively, since I determined that Caragen was using it primarily to bait me. Network did inform me that this Mister Margrave is a probable relative of his namesake, who negotiated several major Consortium/Network trade agreements. That analysis indicates that he belongs to a family of significant status in the Consortium—not a likely associate of a minor Cuui smuggler. His free use of the Margrave name suggests that he wanted us to make the connection, but his purpose remains unclear."

"Maybe we should ask Mister Margrave," suggested Quin.

"Maybe you should not be present at that meeting. Remember my warnings to you."

"About encountering Calongi."

"A high-ranking, unofficial Soli visitor may present an equal threat. I am not sure what to conclude about the signs of relanine addiction, but the possibilities trouble me. Little is known about relanine outside of the Consortium, except that its diluted version has 'useful' properties for interplanetary travel, whereas it is an extremely dangerous substance in its pure form. Relanine is one reason that injuring a Calongi is such a hazardous occupation for the uninformed."

"Do you think Mister Margrave was sent here to investigate the topological instability?" asked Quin, tugging at a curl that tickled his neck.

"I think a correlation is highly probable."

Quin grinned at Saschy, though she suspected that he regretted her presence. He swept his ridiculous cloak tightly around him. "I know you distrust the Consortium, Marrach, but we are not in a position to scorn anyone's assistance. That shadowy blemish on the infinities has trapped us here with only the resources of this sorry world to aid us. You are ready to fly into pieces from the pain of your separation. Caragen, even if he would help us, is beyond our reach. Short of breaking into every medical cocoon on the planet, at risk of killing all the occupants on a desperate chance, we haven't a hope of locating Jon Terry to ask his advice. If you are expecting me to cure this instability by myself, I must disappoint you." Quin glanced warily at Saschy, but he continued, "You should know, Marrach, that I think the Infortiare already attempted the approach of applying sheer, directed Power. I sensed her, Marrach, in the process of coming here. I think I sensed Lord Venkarel as well, but I could not reach either of them. You saw what happened at the portal. I am not sure that I could achieve even that much a second time. The damage continues to spread. I doubt that I could return here if I managed to escape."

To Saschy's surprise, Marrach turned his deep gaze on her. "What is your opinion, Lieutenant? Do you trust Mister Margrave? You seem to have given him considerable freedom."

"He is a very persuasive man who has some useful insights," she answered, not knowing how else to explain her own behavior in his regard. Thinking of his female counterpart and the scene in the next office, Saschy added bitterly, "I would not say that I trust him. In fact, I am gravely suspicious of his motives."

After a protracted silence, Quin asked, "What do you recommend, Marrach?"

"I wish I knew. Old Breamas seems to have won a very hollow sort of victory."

Saschy was rarely intimidated, but the notorious Rabh Marrach and his odd companion had made her feel sharply aware of her lowly Nilson origins. She could not help but wonder if they allowed her to remain simply from contempt of her. Saschy said hesitantly, "I tried to summon Breamas here for peace negotiations, on Mister Margrave's recommendation."

"That is the recommendation I would expect from a Consortium diplomat," responded Marrach. "It is a necessary opening for diplomatic discussion, presuming that this planet remains intact long enough to worry about who has won the revolution. Breamas, however, is too proud and too crippled to leave his den. If any of us survive, we will need to negotiate with him in his own territory, and it will not be easy. The woman who was his ablest captain is probably dead and certainly lost to us."

"Mister Margrave claims," persisted Saschy, "that this revolution was backed by a Cuui organization known as Halaad, of which Filcher is a member."

"The Halaad's presence would explain certain aspects of Breamas' recent success," mused Marrach, giving Saschy a thoughtful look that further unnerved her.

Quin asked, "You know of this organization?"

"The Halaad and I have crossed paths on occasion. They are a small sect but they are well-equipped for their size. Their participation could explain the magnitude and narrow focus of the palace explosion. I had wondered how Breamas managed to get hold of such a sophisticated bomb. The rest of his weaponry is standard black market dross."

"I think that we need to talk to Mister Margrave,"

said Quin, "more than we need to protect me from his notice. There seems to be little reason to hide me from anyone at this point." He offered Saschy an elaborate bow.

Saschy could restrain herself no longer. With pent frustration, she demanded, "Who are you, and why are you hiding at all?"

"Forgive my rudeness, dear lady," replied Quin with a Seriin courtier's airy formality. "I am Lord Quinzaine dur Hamley, wizard in the service of the Infortiare of Ixaxis. You, my lady, have made the most profound mess of your world and all its connectivities. Please call me Quin."

Saschy experienced a pronounced longing for her Mum.

CHAPTER 43

Storms

The silver sea thrashed in silence, a stormy vision beyond clear glass. Watching it, Katerin could not persuade herself that a real ocean sprawled in front of her. It might have been a Network construct, all illusion. Andrew Caragen could easily afford to pay the exorbitant cost of perfection.

"I am pleased that you enjoy the view, Dr. Merel," murmured Caragen from his desk.

"What more do you want of me?" asked Katerin, refusing to face his parchment face and ponderous body again. Aided by Network and her own invasive algorithms, Caragen had questioned her for hours. The old man showed no sign of fatigue. Despite the steady contention of strong wills, the fierce arguments, and the mutual exercises of manipulative techniques more sophisticated than anything imagined by most Network citizens, the ordeal that exhausted Katerin seemed to have energized Caragen. She was not sure that she had lost the battle, but she knew that Caragen had gained a far greater share of pleasure from the experience.

"What have you given me?" he countered. "Analytical insights that you programmed into Network years ago? I want to understand the *Power* of these Ixaxins, not their psychology."

"I have told you my father's assessment: In the process of breeding an extended lifespan, the Network-3 geneticists gave the 'Immortals' the ability to manipulate energy as you or I might move a physical object. 'Wizardry' is simply the name that the Immortals' descendants give to the science of their own skills, and they excel at it, because they have honed it for ten millennia." With a sigh, precisely calculated to convey disdain for a poor listener, she repeated the words that were the price of Caragen's cooperation, "From their contact with Network-3's original transfer port controller, which they call the Taormin, the most Powerful of them have learned to apply their unique abilities to move through topologies, as well as conventional space. These few now share much of the functionality of the transfer port controllers, augmented by their human intellect and perceptions. Their greatest weakness is their natural contentiousness among themselves, resulting from an overriding instinct for self-preservation even at the expense of the species. This weakness, which they attempt to control by imposing rigorous disciplines from earliest childhood, is possibly a by-product of their exceptionally long individual lifespans."

Mockingly, Caragen brought his manicured hands together in three slow claps. "You are a superbly talented scholar, Dr. Merel, as I would expect given your own genetic antecedents."

"I have upheld my part of our bargain, Council Governor," said Katerin coldly. She met his eyes by their reflection in the window. She repeated to herself the analysis that sustained her: *He is nothing but a lonely old man, who has narrowed all of his remaining life pleasures into the machinations that made him powerful. Nothing I have told him can give him anything more tangible than an extra illusion of control.* "Do you still doubt the existence of the topological catastrophe that I have described, a calamity terrible enough to engulf my father as well as my husband?"

Caragen leaned forward and folded his hands on his desk. "Dr. Merel, I have never doubted your desperate sincerity. You are not the first to bring this news about Nilson's little problem to me."

"The problem is not limited to Nilson!" snapped Katerin. "Network, extrapolate damage resulting from the uncontrolled destabilization and partial extraction of a single connected set from the Network topology."

Caragen said quietly, "Network, answer her."

The smoothly simulated voice replied, "Extrapolated damage: Reconfiguration of all topologically connected space. Random, uncontrolled transfers with eventual fracturing of original entities. Extinction of conventional life forms in the parent universe and its connectivities."

Caragen added with a sardonic smile, "Network categorizes the Network-3 Immortals as unconventional life-forms. You and I, however, are regrettably conventional in this regard."

"You already ran this analysis." Katerin revised her own analysis of Caragen: *He is lonely, yes, but also frightened. We have that in common.*

"Of course," answered Caragen. "Rabh Marrach, whom you remember so painfully, alerted me to the Nilson danger some time ago. I assigned him to lead the investigation, since he is the most capable agent who ever entered my employment. So you see, Dr. Merel, I have indeed given this problem my highest priority."

"What has your agent discovered?" asked Katerin tensely. *Lonely, frightened—and bereaved: Marrach was always Caragen's most prized possession.*

"To be honest, Dr. Merel, I do not know. All contact with Nilson has been lost."

"What are you doing to regain contact?"

"Network and several legions of applied topologists have been working on that issue since its occurrence. They have not yet identified a solution. It is a pity that you, rather than your father, elected to come to me. His expertise might have been of use. Even one of your superstitious wizards might have been of some small value to me, but I suppose that your husband's failure proves the limitations of that approach."

Katerin ignored the barbs, though they struck her sorely. She did not trust herself to indulge any emotion during this improbably equable turn of conversation with her bitterest enemy. She had begun to believe that Caragen's desire to discuss this problem with another human being matched her own, but she did not know how long Caragen's indulgent mood would last.

"Don't you have any ships capable of reaching Nilson by conventional means? Nilson does occupy this physical universe."

"The only ships that make conventional journeys to Nilson belong to alien civilizations. Nilson's proximity to Consortium territory is why Nilson has the only Network spaceport open to alien travelers. The Cuui find it a convenient trading post."

Katerin forced herself to ignore what she knew to be deliberate Network conditioning, and she asked, "Have you requested Consortium assistance?" The Network heresy made her deeply uncomfortable.

"I sent word to them. The Calongi have not chosen to respond."

"There are several independent Cuui organizations . . . ," began Katerin.

"Really, Dr. Merel, you will exhaust my patience if you deteriorate into such nonsense. The Cuui are not a heroic species. If any of Nilson's troubles are readily detectable from space or spaceport, I doubt that there is a Cuui vessel remaining on or near Nilson. If the arrogant Calongi are too frightened to take advantage of this unprecedented opportunity to gloat at Network weakness, I am certain that no Cuui will hurry to our rescue."

"The Consortium will be affected equally," murmured Katerin, considering that enormous ramification for the first time. She feared the Consortium, but its age and immensity made any damage to it seem impossible. "You must contact them again. You must tell them everything that has occurred and everything that is projected to occur." Knowing Caragen's methods, she finished dryly, "This time, you must tell them the truth."

"The Calongi dispute the existence of topological transfer, Dr. Merel," explained Caragen with exaggerated care. "How can we possibly explain to them the phenomenon that stymied even your learned father, the foremost applied topologist of our history? If experienced Network researchers fail to find a solution, how could a willfully ignorant species succeed?"

"We must try something, and I have heard no better suggestions from you. We cannot simply wait and hope for a miraculous revelation to strike some Network theorist, who might eventually condescend to see his grand idea put to practical use."

The rasp of Caragen's dry laughter grated on Katerin's ears. "You did inherit your father's technical arrogance, didn't you? He used to argue with me during his presentations to the Council, even when he was seeking research funding from me. I always admired his fearless professional integrity."

"If you had not already exhausted all of your own ideas, you would not be wasting your precious time listening to me."

"You underestimate your importance to me, my dear. I have always had tender feelings toward your family."

"When you weren't trying to exterminate us."

"Every worthwhile relationship has its ups and downs." Caragen's fingers barely twitched, but Katerin recognized the indication of a change in mood or course of thought: a hopeful sign or a dangerous omen, she did not know. "Network, Dr. Merel would like to communicate with the Consortium. I authorize the access." He smiled slyly. "Dr. Merel, the opportunity to prove your point is now yours."

CHAPTER 44

Understanding

"It's worsening, isn't it, Jase?" asked Tori with concern.

"Something is," he murmured, then leaned away from her. The remoteness indicative of concentrated Sesserda perceptions cloaked him. "There are so many conflicting senses, even within my limited range. No wonder the Calongi chose me as their delegate. . . . Proximity to this chaos would tear them apart spiritually."

"They expected this disaster?" demanded Tori, indignation overtaking concern.

"Of course," answered Jase in the matter-of-fact, superior manner that so irritated Tori. Recognizing her reaction, he elaborated gently, "With the acuteness of the Calongi bond to Sesserda Truth, they could not help but feel a change of this magnitude. They undoubtedly knew that something here was desperately wrong, though they could not judge Truth properly without a process of Inquisition. Since this is not a Consortium world, official Inquisition was out of the question, even if it were otherwise feasible. You and I were selected as the compromise."

"The Calongi elected you as Network's Inquisitor?"

"In a purely unofficial sense."

"Did you know about this when we left?"

"Certainly not. Such knowledge would have biased the judgment."

"What good is an Inquisitor's judgment of Truth, when the universe is disintegrating around us?"

"Is that what you think is happening?"

"Don't you?"

"I haven't made my judgment yet. Why do *you* perceive such enormity of catastrophe, Tori?"

"Look at you, trembling," she said, her concern for him rising again to the forefront. "It is relanine sickness, isn't it?"

He did not let her touch his hand to still its shaking, which only amplified her fears. "First, answer me, Tori," he commanded with stern Sesserda force.

She recognized the technique but did not protest its use, because she understood his urgency. "I saw the disintegration when Quin brought me here. I saw it while we transferred out of the caverns."

"You have never used a Network transfer portal under normal circumstances of operation. You have no valid basis for comparison."

"I can't give name to as many senses as you, Jase, but I am certain of what I perceived. Perhaps it's a dormant Soli sense that the transfer process activates. Maybe I experienced a lesser version of the *wrongness* that you perceive."

After shaking his head for several seconds, Jase said abruptly, "Describe Quin to me."

"Quin?" echoed Tori, startled by the shift in direction. "He's about your height. A little stockier. Light complexion. Light brown, curly hair. Gray eyes. Prone to chatter. Incorrigibly cheerful, even when he's complaining."

"With eccentric taste in clothes," finished Jase, as Tori nodded, "exemplified by a rather anachronistic cloak. You just described the infirmary visitor who turned all my perceptions of Truth upside down." Jase's words began to race, "I think that whatever you sensed in transfer came from him, originating in *his* sensory array. He projects energies, like a number of other species, but across a much broader spectrum."

"An ordinary Soli like me can only detect his projections during transfer?"

"Probably because during transfer, he's projecting at a much higher power level. At rest, he might be indetectable by either of us. In the infirmary, he may have been exercising some form of projection, not realizing or not caring that I could detect him." Jase grimaced. "Maybe he was trying to evaluate *me.* He seems to have extraordinarily fine control of his energy usage."

"He looks and acts like a Soli. Could he be synthetic?"

"No, he is a living being. A Soli derivative, I'd guess. Deliberate or accidental, isolated or representative of an entire subspecies, I don't know." Jase sat stiffly upright an instant before the knock sounded on the door. "We may soon learn." With a flickering gesture of his hand, he signaled Tori to assume the lead role.

Tori nodded and brushed her fingers against his sleeve to give herself courage. Despite her battered attire, Tori donned the smile that had made her ancestress famous, and it was the captivating image of that Mirelle who opened the door. Before Saschy Firl could speak, Tori took the woman by the hand and pulled her warmly into the room. "How delightful to see you again, Lieutenant Firl. Sorry, I have such limited hospitality to offer you, but do, please, accept a chair. I'm afraid there aren't enough chairs for us and your two escorts, but the rug is quite comfortable. Hello, Quin. Did you come to apologize for abandoning me so unceremoniously at the port?"

"I am glad you arrived here safely," answered Quin. He grinned sheepishly at Marrach and at Saschy. "I found Tori before I found Governor Racker. She was in better shape."

"Evidently," said Marrach.

"Mister Margrave," said Saschy, snatching her hand away from Tori with awkward force, "these men are Network Council Chancellor Rabhadur Marrach and *Lord* Quinzaine dur Hamley." Her tone and expression made clear her distaste for Quin's antiquated title. "They wish to know who you really *are* and what brought you to Nilson at this eventful time."

After a quick glance at Marrach, Jase watched Quin fixedly. He replied to Saschy with a strained precision that made her wince, "Jasen Margrave was the name my parents gave me. The Consortium sent me here to investigate the serious charges brought against Filcher

Ikthan Cuui by Governor Racker. I have already told you the results of my investigation. Filcher is an agent of the Halaad."

Marrach moved to the chair that Tori had offered to Saschy. He turned it to face Jase directly. "You are a member of a prestigious family, Mister Margrave."

Jase smiled but did not remove his attention from Quin. "You have your own share of notoriety, Chancellor, even in the Consortium. I was not aware, however, that Network still recognized titles of nobility. I am not familiar with the line of Hamley, Lord Quinzaine. If I may inquire, what is your planet-of-origin?"

"My planet-of-origin is most commonly known as Network-3," replied Quin.

Quin and Jase smiled at each other as amiably as two staunch old friends, but Jase grew noticeably paler. Tori was sure that he was suppressing a fit of shuddering only by the most rigid Sesserda self-control. "Stop it, Quin," she ordered, stirring Saschy's disapproval, Marrach's studied interest and Quin's solemn curiosity. "Stop whatever you're doing to him, before you kill him."

"I'll be fine, Tori," said Jase with only the faintest quaver in his voice. "Lord Quinzaine is just trying to assess me. It's a fair exchange, since I'm doing much the same to him."

"*Your* assessment doesn't damage its object," snapped Tori.

"That's not what you say when I assess you."

"I did not intend . . . ," began Quin.

Marrach interrupted, "I think we should begin again. Quin, restrain your Power for the moment, since it seems to distress our Consortium visitors. Mister Margrave, whatever techniques you are using to dissect us, please try to keep them within the bounds of diplomatic standards, as negotiated by your own ancestor. Miss . . ." He gestured toward Tori.

". . . Tori Mirelle," she said.

"Miss Mirelle, please rest assured that we mean no harm to your companion or to you. We are here in search of a solution to a problem that affects all of us.

Lieutenant Firl, kindly stop edging toward the door. You are included in this gathering because you are the Acting Governor of Nilson and presumably know more than the rest of us about the events that have brought us to this point. Your administrative minions can certainly function without you for an hour or two. Indeed, I think that you should begin the discussion. How long have you known about Nilson's portal instabilities?"

"I don't know anything about them," replied Saschy with the gruff defensiveness of a threatened child of Nilson.

Jase injected quietly, "If I may make a suggestion, Chancellor, a promise of immunity might aid Lieutenant Firl's memory."

"Of course," said Marrach with a cynical drawl. "I guarantee you immunity from any Network repercussions that might result from admissions made here, Lieutenant, though I doubt that any action from me will be required in that regard. I think we all have reasons to keep these discussions confidential."

"Answer truthfully, Lieutenant," ordered Jase. Though his voice lacked its customary smooth timbre, its Sesserda forcefulness still directed its quiet impact.

Saschy looked at him helplessly. "The Network portals did not comply with Network standards," answered Saschy with bitter reluctance. She wanted to hate Jase for inflicting this painful fit of honesty on her, especially in such deadly company, but she could only envy Tori on that and many other counts. "Racker and I both knew what we were buying, but we could not afford to open the Wharton mines as quickly as the people of this city demanded. Breamas had accelerated his war of terrorism again. We needed to quiet the anger. We chose to make compromises. Nilson is a poor world. The mines offered hope, for a little while. We bought standard cargo portals first, but the public portals were too costly. Every day of delay gave strength to men like Breamas, who claimed that the delays were just Network's way of taking Wharton's wealth away from the people who discovered it. You can't understand our desperation—Nilson's desperation—unless you've lived in Nilson's streets."

"I have lived here, Lieutenant," said Marrach, causing Saschy to blink in disbelief. "I appreciate the predicament. I am interested in the results."

She had said too much to stop now, and the confession had actually begun to ease her conscious burdens, though she wondered how much of her reaction was owed to the insistent, eerie stare of iridescent eyes. "At first, the problems were isolated to Wharton. We thought we could maintain the portals with regular repairs." Saschy shrugged helplessly. "We succeeded, until Breamas's terrorists resumed their activities."

"This pitiful revolution only accelerated the process that had already begun," said Quin, shaking his head.

"It's a peculiar revolution," mused Tori. "Listen to its silence."

"We Nilsonites have strong survival instincts," said Saschy. "We know when to retreat." She looked at Jase, though it took all of her courage to face him, and it required a humbling of all her pride to continue, "Let *me* retreat to something I know how to do. I am of no use here. I am only a daughter of Nilson, a little more fortunate than most, because my Mum is a particularly wise and foresighted woman. You have your beautiful lady. You don't need me."

Marrach replied with a weary scowl, "Go when you please, Lieutenant. I have no more questions for you."

Jase said gently, "You undervalue yourself, Miss Firl, and have elevated me far beyond what I deserve." Saschy shook her head, as she backed out of the room. She smiled slightly, cherishing relief and a crumb of praise, as she strode back to the people and the work she knew to be part of her own proper place and purpose.

***

"Poor, overwhelmed woman," signed Tori as soon as the door closed behind Saschy. "She's torn apart inside."

Jase walked toward the door as if he might follow Saschy, but he stopped just short of it. "She will heal," he said, then became silent and still in the full enactment of Sesserda concentration. He turned abruptly and asked, "When were you Chosen by the Mirlai, Chancellor?"

Both Quin and Marrach looked at Jase in astonishment. Tori watched him with alarm. She thought she saw him tremble. "Jase," she began.

He gestured a curt, emphatic sign to wait. "That is why you scowl at Lieutenant Firl—because she needs much healing, and you cannot help her. You cannot help because you are here for another reason," continued Jase intensely, as if explaining a trivial concept to an uncomprehending audience, though Tori was sure that his conclusions were forming only as he spoke. Expressive hands waved Sesserda signs of Truth and wonder. "You know more about what has occurred here than anyone. You have known longer than anyone. Have you forgotten why you came here? Has your personal torment blinded you to the Truth?"

"We are not Sesserda adepts, Jase," murmured Tori, going to his side quickly, for his shudders had become clearly visible. She reached for him with caution, fearing the acidic substance that relanine sickness could make of his skin. When she touched his hand without pain, she also felt the fragility of his control. Terrified, she took tighter hold of him to keep him from collapsing. "What are you talking about?"

He did not reject her support or pretend a lack of need. "Healers, Tori. The Mirlai are the Healers. That is their proper purpose. That has always been their purpose."

"I thought that was the purpose of the Vidilati," answered Tori, trying to still the tremors that now drove Jase to his knees. She cast an accusing glance at Quin, but he shook his head in innocent, astonished protest. He stepped forward to offer help, but he retreated immediately from Tori's glare.

Jase persisted, "The Vidilati gift is in repairing the mechanics of living bodies. They attempt the broader

healings only because of the Mirlai sundering." Jase
breathed laboriously, nodding toward the growing
void beyond the window. "This is an injury to the
whole of Truth. It must be Healed by those who are
best qualified."

"What are *you*, Mister Margrave?" demanded Marrach, but his own voice was shaken.

Jase's formal answer twisted through Tori with
painful memories and dread of his present purpose, but
she clung to him stubbornly. "I am a Sesserda adept,
the designated Inquisitor for the crime of this injury,
and I have discerned Truth and reached judgment." It
was to Tori that he turned, explaining at an excited
pace that showed no evidence of his physical weakening. "It is entirely clear to me at last, Tori. The Calongi
had no need to perceive this trouble for themselves.
They were warned of it. You and I were sent here in
answer to a Mirlai request for justice." Tori opened her
mouth to speak, but Jase silenced her again, this time
with a faint touch that made her pity the room's other
occupants. She knew the ruthlessly manipulative methods of Inquisition.

"The Mirlai are exiles," said Marrach slowly.

"The request of a Level I people is never rejected,"
countered Jase, turning his intense gaze upon Marrach,
"even when that people live in self-imposed exile in a
society where the Calongi are unwelcome." His laughter held a rueful note. "Ukitan-lai told me that the task
would be larger than I imagined, but I did not understand how large until now." Gently, he released himself from Tori's hold and rose unsteadily to his feet. He
faced Marrach, though he seemed to speak into the air
above Marrach's head. In the weighty tone reserved for
an Inquisitor's official judgment, Jase declared, "The
Mirlai were condemned by formal Inquisition centuries
ago for the wrong that they inflicted on their Adraki
symbionts. The Mirlai sentence was left incomplete,
because the Mirlai departed from Consortium space.
By my authority as a Sesserda adept, I now decree their
proper penance to you, their Chosen Healer: They must

heal this wound. By this deed, their atonement will be complete."

"This deed would destroy them," said Quin, staring at Jase in fascination.

"If they were unwilling to confront that possibility," retorted Jase, "they would not have sent the two of you here to prepare the way for them. You *still* do not understand? Even you, their Chosen?" His words conveyed the terrible certainty, strength and calm of Sesserda at its purest. "It is the nature of the Mirlai gift that they require a symbiont, akin to the ill or injured being, to carry and to convert their Healing energies into an active form. I do not know what species you represent, Quin Hamley, but the Mirlai have obviously decided that you are as nearly kin to this injured entity as any being they can find. And you, Chancellor Marrach, are just as obviously the host who has enabled them to come here at this critical time." With a trace of compassion, Jase added, "You could not sense their presence inside you, because it was necessary for them to prepare themselves by a time of dormancy. They must have selected you for your ability to survive the agony of such a journey, deprived of their support. Your knowledge of their presence would have forced them to remain active, because your pain would have called upon them, despite even your phenomenal strength of endurance and self-denial, before the proper time. The sacrifices would have been for nothing."

Marrach retreated one step and stopped. For one moment, his expression conveyed more pain than Tori had ever imagined a face could hold, but he gasped with wonder, "The proper time has come." To Tori, it seemed that a veil of golden light flowed over him, clothing the hard, battered warrior in peace. He breathed heavily, as if he had just fought clear of a arduous ordeal, but for the first time, Tori saw him smile warmly. "They accept your judgment," answered the Healer who was also Marrach. The lines of cynicism cleared from his face, and Healer's serenity softened his shadowed eyes. He laid his hand on Quin's shoulder. Quin returned him a curiously wary look. "Continue what you began, Lord Quinzaine, but not alone this time." He looked at Jase. "We shall try to spare you, but I cannot promise to leave you untouched. Relanine entwines you with Truth."

Jase grimaced. "I am tougher than I look."

Tori protested automatically, though she knew the futility of it by the set of Jase's expression, "Jase, at least let us move away from this room."

"Moving away from this planet would not preserve me from the pain, and I'd rather endure it here than in the middle of a revolution." He seated himself on the couch beside her. "Just hold onto me and let me focus on you instead of on them. I don't think I'll be a danger to you, because this process is more likely to nullify relanine than activate its volatile tendencies."

"I can think of ways I'd rather earn your complete attention," she grumbled, but she clung to him protectively, as the two of them watched the brightly flickering Mirlai extend their golden veil over Quin as well as Marrach. Because Power's flaring tore through Jase like a blade of fire, neither Tori nor Jase saw the men and the Mirlai vanish.

***

On burning planes, strands of infinity writhed but could not evade the golden mist that seared each break and smoothed each knot. Life and not-life merged and shared a common, terrible knowing. For each healed strand, a fleck of gold was lost to keep the newly made bond intact. The loss of each fleck, each Mirlai life, tore through the Mirlai whole with a grief beyond healing, but the Mirlai continued, knowing the cost. They carried their hosts and were carried, and none knew one element of the symbiotic entity from another in the whole.

As they weakened from too much grief, they gathered new hosts, and strength again surged through them. Some hosts fed the whole in a quick, bright surge that faded quickly, unable to survive the ordeal of grief: A part of the whole knew that one such host had

lived as an angry woman known as Deliaja. The whole
mourned her loss.

Some hosts were stronger. Power gave them more
than mortal life. They knew this place, and the whole
learned. The healing continued.

It would not be the same. There would be scars. But
it would be whole. It would be well.

***

"What is it, Arlan?" asked Ruth. "What are you
watching?" She struggled to lift her head enough to see
the window.

"Don't try to rise, Mum," said Saschy with concern.
"You heard the medic. You're too weak. You need to
rest."

"Ghost lights and ghost shadow," answered Arlan,
"be ended, Miz Ruth. The darkness be gone." A broad
smile of joy spread across his face. "Saschy, the darkness be gone."

Saschy released her mother's fragile hands and
joined Arlan at the window. "Yes, Arlan," replied
Saschy with an answering smile of awe, "Our Nilson
be well."

CHAPTER 45

Change

Tori awoke when Jase touched her hair. A thin line of sunlight crossed her and the couch's worn fabric. She blinked at its brightness in her eyes and sat upright to escape the direct glare.

"Sunrise is the kindliest hour on Nilson," said Jase with a crooked grin. "It's the only time the sun seems willing to dominate the clouds."

"Some people enjoy the rain," muttered Tori, "especially when they are allowed to sleep through it."

"I know it's early, and you were awake most of the night watching over me, but I didn't want to leave without telling you."

"I should hope not!" Tentatively, she rested the back of her hand against his jawline. Relanine announced itself with no more than the customary faint tingle. "No more symptoms?" she asked.

"Not since that abomination shrank back into itself and disappeared from my senses."

"Have the healers returned?"

"No." Jase combed his fingers through his unruly dark hair, and he frowned. "I think that they will not return to Nilson."

"Do you think they survived?"

"Not unchanged." Jase shrugged. "None of us survive such an event unchanged."

"I don't feel particularly different," sighed Tori. "I still don't understand half of what you say."

"You understand that there is more to understand," said Jase, his smile returning. "That is wisdom." He took hold of her by both hands and tugged her to her feet. "Come along, partner. We have some alien relations to heal. This world still needs a great deal of help."

"Your ardent admirer, the Lieutenant Governor, would prefer to work with you alone," said Tori tartly.

"Tori, my dear, if you give her one iota of encouragement in that direction, I shall feel compelled to take drastic steps in retaliation."

"I thought you liked her."

"I do. But she understands a *lot* less than half of what I tell her, and she doesn't handle frustration as well as you."

"You're just afraid of my retaliation if you became enamored with someone whose civilization rank is even lower than mine."

"I think you're beginning to understand me too well."

***

The ship, like its owner, wore its power confidently. Pale gold of walls and furnishings conveyed a subtle opulence. Katerin felt awkward, seated at the oblong table where Network's ruling Council often met. Caragen ignored her. Since arriving in the room, he had spoken only to Network.

Network opened the doors in silence to admit the visitors. Despite all her Network study and Network-aided conditioning to prepare her for this moment, Katerin gasped softly at her first sight of the aliens. She could not mistake the Calongi, his imposing head brushing the lintel, his dark, living cloak rustling against the floor. The other alien bore an almost comical resemblance to a wizened old gnome from a childhood fable, but Katerin felt no impulse to laugh.

"I am Nara of Calong," announce the Calongi with a voice that seemed to spill forth melodies purer than any instrument had ever produced. "This is Don Tatakaqua of Escolar. Council Governor, I am pleased to see that your good health persists." The Calongi's bow resembled the graceful bending of a strong, young tree. "Dr. Merel, your disquiet is unwarranted and disruptive. Please, calm your spirit. Don Tatakaqua, please be seated. You will be more comfortable and therefore more productive." Without comment, the Escolari seated himself across from Katerin.

While Katerin concluded that the Calongi were at least as arrogant as their reputation, Caragen said simply, "You come late, Nara-lai. Contact with Nilson was restored an hour ago. Network reports that no lasting damage has occurred."

"I come at the proper time," replied Nara. "Your invitation came too early."

"We have resolved matters without your assistance."

"We were assisting you before you knew of your problem's existence. You still remain unaware of the extent of the damage you have wrought." With an iridescent flickering, a handlike appendage emerged from the Calongi's cloak and drew a complex gesture in the air. "We come here now to prevent future such incidents. We dislike interfering in the affairs of nonmembers, but you have interfered in ours and left us no alternative."

"Indeed," responded Caragen dryly.

"Your people are ignorant. You are ignorant. Don Tatakaqua is a superb educator of ignorant people, such as yourselves. Beginning the education of your people in the fundamentals of Truth is his proper purpose. Dr. Merel's expertise in the methods of Network education will assist his fulfillment of purpose. We were pleased to receive her request for our aid. It indicates a primitive form of wisdom, on which our teachings can build."

"The magnitude of Calongi arrogance never fails to impress me," answered Caragen.

"Shrewdness does not imply wisdom."

"Are insults indicative of wisdom?"

"Yes. If they are used to educate wisely."

Caragen dismissed the Calongi's statement with a weary shake of his head. "This meeting serves no purpose, Nara-lai. I regret that you made your lengthy journey for nothing."

"I am here at Dr. Merel's request, not yours, Council Governor. Speak your concerns, please, Dr. Merel."

Caragen waved a languid hand in permission, though Katerin did not think the Calongi would have tolerated resistance. She gathered her courage to address the formidable being who could intimidate Network's Council Governor. "I have a husband and a father who both went to Nilson to tend to this *problem*, which you claim to have solved for us. Though contact with Nilson is restored, I have been unable to obtain any word of the fate of those who matter most to me—those whom I trust. It is difficult for me to feel confident of the problem's solution, when I have heard no mention of the method of resolution. Network has given me no adequate explanation. Can you do better?"

As Caragen smiled faintly, Katerin realized that she had pleased him.

Nara answered, "The Mirlai have healed the injury. It is their atonement, the proper resolution of the Inquisition against them."

"They accompanied Marrach," whispered Caragen.

"He was their Chosen host in this undertaking. He was not alone in the final healing."

"Is Marrach still alive?" asked Caragen with a rigidity that betrayed deep emotion, even to Katerin. The Calongi's cloak rippled.

"I have received no report of his death, but that aspect of Truth is not known to me." Nara turned his great emerald eyes toward Katerin. "For answers to your personal concerns, I would recommend that you contact our honored member, Jase-lai, who can give you whatever Truth is perceptible from Nilson. He is known to the Nilson governors as Jasen Margrave. He is currently abiding on that world to assist in resolving some difficulties between the Network government and the Nilson populace. I recommend strongly, Council Governor, that you accept his advice. Jase-lai is a most honored Sesserda adept."

"Have you any other advice to give me?" demanded Caragen tartly.

"None that you are ready to hear at this time.

Don Tatakaqua will remain with you to increase your receptivity."

"I am not fond of lengthy visits," retorted Caragen.

A whistling like wind in a forest made Katerin shiver as if she had been physically threatened. From Caragen's sudden increase in pallor, she concluded that the threat was real, though not aimed at her. Nara said with a softness that yet held an undeniable power, "Your influence has waned badly, Council Governor. You need external assistance to maintain control of your Council and your entire society, and you are acutely aware of that fact. We offer our help, because Network needs you to maintain stability at this critical time in its history. You are a convenience to us, for now. We are your only hope." A lighter melody trickled forth from Nara. "Don Tatakaqua, teach well."

"You honor me, Nara-lai," replied the Escolari solemnly. "I shall endeavor to be worthy."

With a return to the stern, irresistible voice of Sesserda command, Nara spoke again to Caragen. "Your enmity with Dr. Merel and her associates must likewise end. Your fate is too tightly bound with hers and theirs. You cannot survive without them, or without us. This is Truth." The Calongi turned with extraordinary grace and drifted toward the door. Network allowed him to pass unimpeded.

"Network," said Caragen with pointed distaste, "prepare accommodations for Don Tatakaqua. He will be staying with us for an indefinite time. Arrange for Dr. Merel's transfer to Rendl, where I believe she remains employed." He waved both hands, dismissing Katerin and Tatakaqua equally.

Tatakaqua arose first. "I appreciate your hospitality, Council Governor." He showed no dismay at Caragen's sour glare but turned to Katerin. "I look forward to communicating with you, Dr. Merel, about the application of your methods to achievement of my proper purpose."

Katerin nodded and smiled weakly. She glanced at Caragen. His parchment face was pinched and weary, but he said with his customary authority, "Network, drop all charges against Dr. Merel and restore her Network privileges." He added with a throaty sound that resembled a harsh chuckle, "Do the same for her parents and her impossible husband, if any of them still live. Make it clear to Quin Hamley, however, that this tolerance will be retracted if he enacts even one prank against me. Leave me, Dr. Merel. I am fatigued." Katerin followed the Escolari from the room, too unsure of what she had witnessed to feel her burden's lifting.

***

The sky above the Healers' cottage burned hot and clear. Jeni stretched her arms, too long chilled and shadowed, to the sun. The health pulsed through her, fresh as the herb scents from the garden. She felt the Mirlai and knew their gladness—and their grief.

They were fewer now. She felt each of the losses, though she could neither count the survivors nor identify any individual among them. Because Jeni had known anger too well, she grieved especially for an embittered young woman named Deliaja, who had not lived to recognize her own healing.

"You made a proper healing, Dee, and earned your own," said Jeni to a ring of yellow blossoms, wreathed like a lion's mane.

"She was well Chosen," murmured the Healer Suleifas, wrapping his arms around his wife.

"As were you, my dear."

***

Katerin applied balm liberally to combat Rendl's parched wind. She had accepted her termination from the university with quiet satisfaction. It spared her the need to resign.

She had nearly completed the packing of the apartment's scanty contents. "If my husband returns," she informed Network for the fifteenth time, "tell him immediately that I have resumed my old position at Harberg University." She sighed as she sealed the last packing crate. Network had been unable—or unwilling, by Caragen's decree—to give her any information about Quin or her father. Without Quin, she had no means of contacting Serii and the Ixaxins. She had learned nothing more than the C-human, Jasen Margrave, had told her in his message, describing the events that led to the healing and advising her to be patient with the Change in Truth. Following receipt of that unsatisfying message, she had even asked Network to contact Rabh Marrach for her, but she had received no reply. Network could not even tell her if Rabh Marrach still lived.

She performed the final check on the apartment, searching for any overlooked items, though the apartment had never contained any objects of great value to her. Network had already confirmed the thoroughness of her packing. She knew that she was searching only to satisfy an inner desire to confirm what she believed she had already lost.

When she reentered the living room and first saw the cloaked man silhouetted against the window, her heart surged with hope for an instant, but he was clearly too tall for Quin. He turned, and she recognized Evaric with a sense of shock that he should be here. "Lady Katerin," he said with a formal bow, incongruous in a dismal Network apartment, "will you trust me to facilitate one more journey for you?"

"I thought you could not leave Serii."

"When the infinities themselves are rearranged, my lady, few assumptions remain constant." He extended to her his hand, which wore the odd, sword-shaped discoloration, and asked again, "Will you come?"

"Network, lock the apartment." She accepted the callused hand of the swordsman-wizard, blinked against a sudden golden brightness, and reopened her eyes in the Infortiare's twilit study.

"Thank you, Evaric," said the Infortiare, still and frail-seeming in the brown velvet depths of a heavy chair. Evaric squeezed Katerin's hand slightly before releasing it and making his silent exit from the room.

Katerin fell to her knees in front of the Infortiare's chair. "Lady Rhianna, what has happened to Quin?"

The Infortiare reached forward to rest her hand on Katerin's head. Warmth surged from the delicate flesh, wrapping Katerin in sheltering Power. "He is well, Katerin, but he is changed. We are all changed." Rhianna leaned forward into the light, and Katerin saw that the Infortiare's golden hair had turned brightly silver above the still-young face. "Some changes will pass. Some will remain. We do not yet know the final shape of the result."

Be patient with the Change of Truth, echoed the words of an alien stranger in Katerin's mind. "Where is he?" asked Katerin.

"Hamley."

"Not Ixaxis?" asked Katerin slowly, sensing a significance yet unspoken.

"Not Ixaxis. For the moment, the presence of major Power causes him pain."

"He *is* a major Power."

Rhianna sighed, "We are not sure what form his gifts will take when he recovers his strength. At present, however, he appears to be unable to exercise his Power or to tolerate its use in his vicinity. We cannot perform the normal tests for Power without harming him, but by all the lesser signs, he is as mortal as you."

"We are no longer different?" murmured Katerin with wonder. Unconsciously, she started to smile, until the warmth from Rhianna's hand deepened noticeably.

"No, my dear. He is still very different from you. Only the nature of the difference has changed. He may regain his Power. We do not know. We do know that he cannot now travel topologically by his gifts, by any other wizard's gifts, or by the devices of Network. He may eventually recover. Until that time, he cannot leave this world, this world that you abhor."

Katerin met the clear gray eyes that were the strongest visible sign of the Infortiare's kinship to Quin. "Will you send me to Hamley, Lady Rhianna?"

"I could send you to Cuira, where you could join a train for the rest of the journey, a few days' travel if the weather remains fair. Cuira seems to be far enough removed from Hamley to allow the use of major Power without hurt to Quin. I would ask you to consider well, however, what you will do upon your arrival."

"He will need me more now than ever before," answered Katerin.

"Only if you can make the choice to remain with him. If you cannot make that choice, it would be better that you not go to him at all. His memory is confused now, and he will grieve for you less if you do not stir his recollections."

"He is my husband," answered Katerin, but understanding was beginning to grow. Her eyes blurred with tears.

"Katerin, I do not believe that you could ever find contentment as the coddled, ineffectual wife of a lesser lord of Serii. Because I think Quin will reach the same conclusion, I do not believe that Quin will allow you to stay with him."

"The decision is mine."

"With or without the Power of a wizard, Quin is a singularly stubborn young man. If he wants you to leave him, he is quite capable of irritating you into departure. That is a talent of his that is entirely distinct from any skill taught on Ixaxis, and he has honed it since birth."

Katerin twisted her lips into a sardonic smile. She had witnessed—and experienced—Quin's talent for being selectively annoying. "I understand, Lady Rhianna, and I appreciate your advice, but I must still go to him. Will you send me?"

With a sigh, Rhianna nodded. "In a few days, Evaric will take you to Cuira and make further travel arrangements for you from there. Queen Joli must first send word to Cuira to prepare your entourage. A Seriin noblewoman is expected to travel with suitable escorts."

The moment of surprise passed quickly. "Yes," said Katerin with stiff acceptance. "Of course."

"If you wish to arrange your Network affairs first, Evaric can assist you in that journey as well."

Katerin swallowed her pain. "Lady Rhianna, have you learned anything about my father's fate?"

"No. I have notified your mother. You may wish to visit her also in the next few days."

"Yes. Thank you."

"Evaric is downstairs, awaiting you in the rose salon."

Katerin trudged from the room, as slowly as a joint-stiffened old woman. When she was gone, Rhianna rested her face in her hands. The last sliver of sunlight struck the milky pendant that hung from her neck.

"She will not return from Network," said the dark voice that only Rhianna heard.

"I know, dear Kaedric. I know." Her hand met his. For them, the meeting was real.

***

In the central hall of the ancestral manor of the lords of Hamley, Lord Quinzaine suddenly lifted his giggling nephew off of his shoulders and set the boy on his feet. Not hearing the boy's protests, Quin frowned, walked to window and stared at the night sky, filled with stars. He closed his eyes in grief.

CHAPTER 46

Truth

Two scholars of disparate species walked in a garden and observed the golden waning of the day, mirrored in the water of the fountain. "Even mountains move in their own time," observed Jase, continuing a conversation long interrupted.

"All creations evolve," answered Ukitan, honored Sesserda master.

"Truth is more constant than the mountains."

"Truth is the only constant," agreed Ukitan solemnly. He touched the fountain's water, and it turned to fiery orange. "But not even Calongi perceptions of Sesserda Truth are imperishable. We, too, are creations, Jase-lai. We, too, evolve." Ukitan began to sing in his multilayered voice. Jase smiled, touched the water and joined his voice to the Calongi's evening song in praise of Truth.

***

Arlan helped the man to rise. The invalid had only awakened days ago, and he was still weak. There were so many casualties of the revolution.

The connection to Wharton had been restored, but Arlan had declined to return. Miz Ruth needed him here. Others like her, weakened or injured, needed him. That was what the strange C-human, Jase, had advised him before departing—to stay and work on Nilson, to fulfill his own proper purpose. Somehow, by Jase's intervention, one more miracle materialized: the offer of a good, well-paid job, such as Nilsonites like Arlan never anticipated receiving. Arlan had remained at work in the infirmary after the soldiers and their medics left.

Only one soldier had remained: The man known as Rust had resigned from his military service. He had taken a battered old apartment with Arlan. He did not explain his reasons, but Arlan understood. Jase had also spoken privately to Rust.

The invalid grunted with the strain of using muscles nearly atrophied. Network had no record of the man's admission. Many of the local Network records from the time of darkness had been lost or corrupted. As badly injured men like this invalid began to awaken from the medical cocoons, the cost of the revolution became increasingly apparent. So many were hurt, maimed, or killed. Miz Ruth still insisted that the cost was well worthwhile. Breamas had accepted a nominal role as adviser to Saschy, who had received notice of her appointment as Planetary Governor from Council Governor Caragen himself. Breamas received a pension and an apartment, and his followers either scattered in confusion or accepted the hope that Saschy now offered in Breamas' name. Racker, healed of his injuries, had departed from Nilson and was not missed.

There were already changes—to Nilson's advantage. The semicriminal port boys of Racker's reign had largely disappeared in the wake of near catastrophe, and men like Rust had replaced them. There would be more improvements in time. Arlan had faith in these hopes, because Jase had promised them. Aside from simple trust in the C-human's word, Arlan had observed that an influx of new wealth, as indicated by the improved pay for port boys and Arlan's own salary, had followed each of Jase's specific promises.

The invalid groaned, and Arlan shifted his hands to give support. The invalid was not a young man. It was remarkable that he had recovered so well. No one knew how long he had been in the cocoon. No one knew his name. He was not from Nilson.

"Be you taking a few more steps," urged Arlan. "Then we be finding you some breakfast."

"I am hungry," admitted the man with a rueful grimace. "Network nutritional injections do little to satisfy the instincts of the stomach. How long was I cocooned?"

"We be not knowing that or anything else about you," answered Arlan. "We be having some trouble while you be sleeping." At the old man's frown, Arlan added hurriedly, "But it be well now—like you."

"I am far from well, young man," grumbled the invalid.

"Soon, you be feeling better. My name be Arlan."

"Jon," replied the man, conceding a weak smile. "This is Nilson, isn't it?"

"Yah. This be Nilson."